PRAISE FOR

HOUSE OF EARTH AND BLOOD

"A master class in world-building adventure. Don't miss it."
—#1 *New York Times* bestselling author Charlaine Harris

"*House of Earth and Blood* is a game changer! A must read. Sarah J. Maas has set the new standard with this book."
—#1 *New York Times* bestselling author J. R. Ward

"Tender, funny, . . . hot, and satisfying."
—#1 *New York Times* bestselling author Laurell K. Hamilton

"A dizzying, suspenseful whirl that surprises at every turn." —*Entertainment Weekly*

"All of the fantastic elements, colorful characters, steamy romance, and action-packed plot Maas' readers look for. The mystery element presents a stunning twist, and the emotional depth of Bryce's relationships . . . is incredibly moving. Fans will eagerly await the next installment." —*Booklist,* starred review

"[An] electrifying series launch. . . . A richly imagined tale spiced with snarky humor and smoldering romance." —*Publishers Weekly*

"Rich and sensuous, a dark urban fantasy with mythic overtones. Perfect for readers looking for both dramatic and romantic tension, it will make you hold your breath and leave your heart pounding." —*BookPage*

PRAISE FOR
THE COURT OF THORNS AND ROSES SERIES

A COURT OF THORNS AND ROSES

"Simply dazzles." —*Booklist*, starred review

"Passionate, violent, sexy and daring. . . .
A true page-turner." —*USA Today*

"Suspense, romance, intrigue and action.
This is not a book to be missed!" —HuffPost

"Vicious and intoxicating. . . . A dazzling world, complex characters and sizzling romance." —*RT Book Reviews*, Top Pick

"A sexy, action-packed fairytale." —Bustle

A COURT OF MIST AND FURY

"Fiercely romantic, irresistibly sexy and hypnotically magical.
A veritable feast for the senses." —*USA Today*

"Hits the spot for fans of dark, lush, sexy fantasy." —*Kirkus Reviews*

"An immersive, satisfying read." —*Publishers Weekly*

"Darkly sexy and thrilling." —Bustle

A COURT OF WINGS AND RUIN

"Fast-paced and explosively action-packed." —*Booklist*

"The plot manages to seduce you with its alluring characters, irresistible world and never-ending action, leaving you craving more." —*RT Book Reviews*

CRESCENT CITY

HOUSE of EARTH and BLOOD

Books by Sarah J. Maas

The Throne of Glass series

The Assassin's Blade
Throne of Glass
Crown of Midnight
Heir of Fire
Queen of Shadows
Empire of Storms
Tower of Dawn
Kingdom of Ash
•
The Throne of Glass Coloring Book

The Court of Thorns and Roses series

A Court of Thorns and Roses
A Court of Mist and Fury
A Court of Wings and Ruin
A Court of Frost and Starlight
A Court of Silver Flames
•
A Court of Thorns and Roses Coloring Book

The Crescent City series

House of Earth and Blood
House of Sky and Breath
House of Flame and Shadow

CRESCENT CITY

HOUSE of EARTH and BLOOD

SARAH J. MAAS

BLOOMSBURY PUBLISHING
NEW YORK • LONDON • OXFORD • NEW DELHI • SYDNEY

BLOOMSBURY PUBLISHING
Bloomsbury Publishing Inc.
1385 Broadway, New York, NY 10018, USA
29 Earlsfort Terrace, Dublin 2, Ireland

BLOOMSBURY, BLOOMSBURY PUBLISHING, and the
Diana logo are trademarks of Bloomsbury Publishing Plc

First published in the United States 2020
This paperback edition published 2021

Map by Virginia Allyn
Interior art by Carlos Quevedo

ISBN: PB: 978-1-63557-702-0

The Library of Congress has cataloged the hardcover edition as follows:
Names: Maas, Sarah J., author.
Title: House of earth and blood : a Crescent City novel / Sarah J. Maas.
Description: New York : Bloomsbury Publishing, 2020. | Series: Crescent City
Summary: Half-Fae, half-human Bryce Quinlan and Fallen angel Hunt Athalar team up to catch a killer and end a demonic reign of terror.
Identifiers: LCCN 2019050990 (print) • LCCN 2019050991 (e-book)
ISBN 978-1-63557-404-3 (hardback) • ISBN 978-1-63557-405-0 (e-book)
Subjects: GSAFD: Fantasy fiction.
Classification: LCC PS3613.A175 H68 2020 (print) | LCC PS3613.A175 (e-book) |
DDC 813/.6—dc23
LC record available at https://lccn.loc.gov/2019050990

18 20 19

Typeset by Westchester Publishing Services
Printed and bound in the U.S.A.

For Taran—
The brightest star in my sky

Lunathion

Crescent City

The Angels' Gate

Central Business District

The Meat Market

The Merchants' Gate

Western Road

Istros River

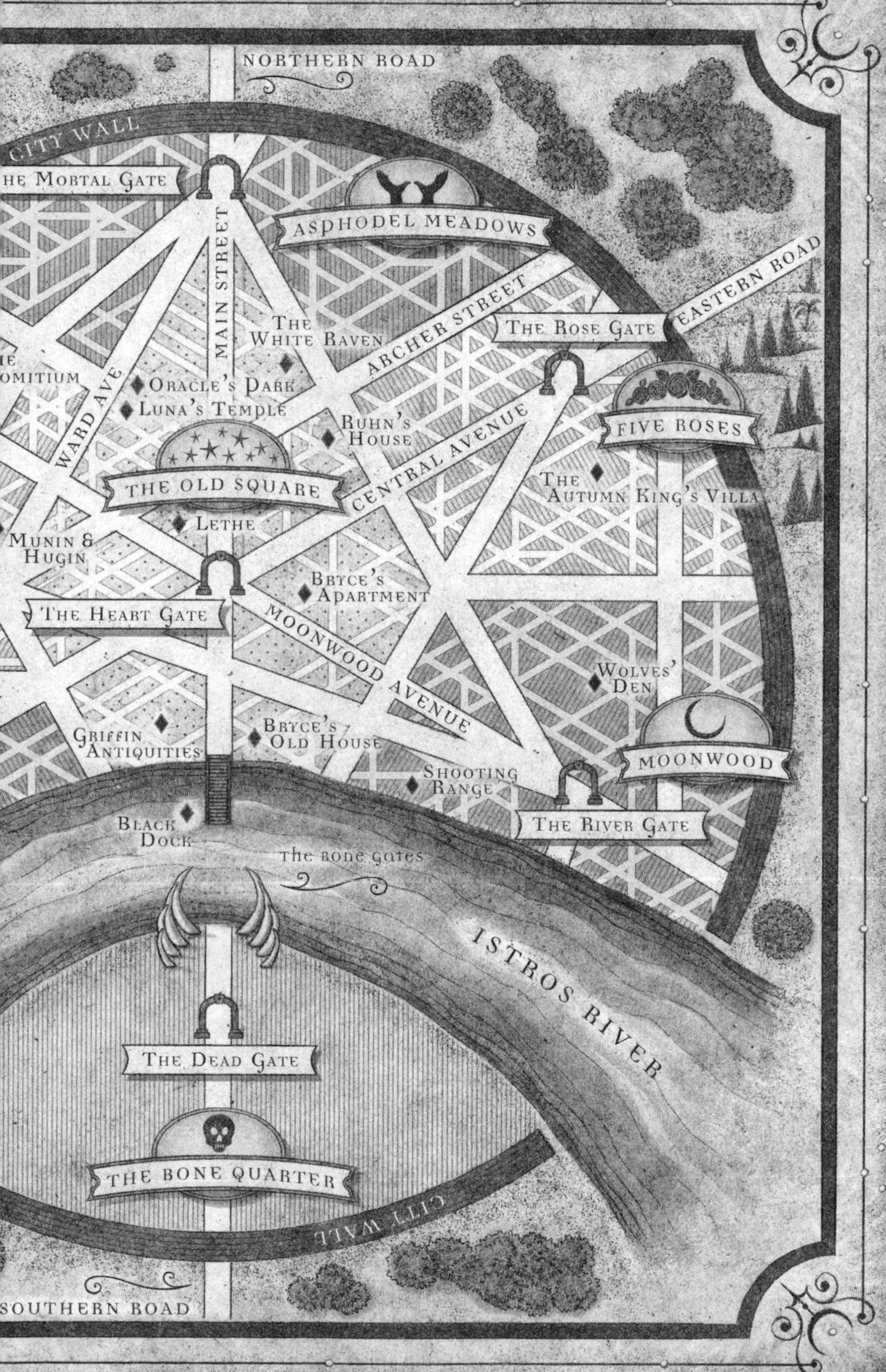

NORTHERN ROAD
CITY WALL
HE MORTAL GATE
ASPHODEL MEADOWS
MAIN STREET
THE WHITE RAVEN
ARCHER STREET
THE ROSE GATE
EASTERN ROAD
OMITIUM
WARD AVE
ORACLE'S PARK
LUNA'S TEMPLE
RUHN'S HOUSE
FIVE ROSES
CENTRAL AVENUE
THE OLD SQUARE
THE AUTUMN KING'S VILLA
LETHE
MUNIN & HUGIN
BRYCE'S APARTMENT
THE HEART GATE
MOONWOOD AVENUE
WOLVES' DEN
GRIFFIN ANTIQUITIES
BRYCE'S OLD HOUSE
MOONWOOD
SHOOTING RANGE
BLACK DOCK
THE RIVER GATE
THE BONE GATES
ISTROS RIVER
THE DEAD GATE
THE BONE QUARTER
CITY WALL
SOUTHERN ROAD

THE FOUR HOUSES OF MIDGARD

As decreed in 33 V.E. by the Imperial Senate in the Eternal City

HOUSE OF EARTH AND BLOOD

Shifters, humans, witches, ordinary animals, and many others to whom Cthona calls, as well as some chosen by Luna

HOUSE OF SKY AND BREATH

Malakim (angels), Fae, elementals, sprites,* and those who are blessed by Solas, along with some favored by Luna

HOUSE OF MANY WATERS

River-spirits, mer, water beasts, nymphs, kelpies, nøkks, and others watched over by Ogenas

HOUSE OF FLAME AND SHADOW

Daemonaki, Reapers, wraiths, vampyrs, draki, dragons, necromancers, and many wicked and unnamed things that even Urd herself cannot see

**Sprites were kicked out of their House as a result of their participation in the Fall, and are now considered Lowers, though many of them refuse to accept this.*

PART I
THE HOLLOW

1

There was a wolf at the gallery door.

Which meant it must be Thursday, which meant Bryce had to be *really* gods-damned tired if she relied on Danika's comings and goings to figure out what day it was.

The heavy metal door to Griffin Antiquities thudded with the impact of the wolf's fist—a fist that Bryce knew ended in metallic-purple painted nails in dire need of a manicure. A heartbeat later, a female voice barked, half-muffled through the steel, "Open the Hel up, B. It's hot as shit out here!"

Seated at the desk in the modest gallery showroom, Bryce smirked and pulled up the front door's video feed. Tucking a strand of her wine-red hair behind a pointed ear, she asked into the intercom, "Why are you covered in dirt? You look like you've been rootling through the garbage."

"What the fuck does *rootling* mean?" Danika hopped from foot to foot, sweat gleaming on her brow. She wiped at it with a filthy hand, smearing the black liquid splattered there.

"You'd know if you ever picked up a book, Danika." Glad for the break in what had been a morning of tedious research, Bryce smiled as she rose from the desk. With no exterior windows, the gallery's extensive surveillance equipment served as her only warning of who stood beyond its thick walls. Even with her sharp half-Fae hearing, she couldn't make out much beyond the iron door save for the occasional banging fist. The building's unadorned sandstone walls belied the latest tech and grade A spellwork that kept it operational and preserved many of the books in the archives below.

As if merely thinking about the level beneath Bryce's high heels had summoned her, a little voice asked from behind the six-inch-thick archives door to her left, "Is that Danika?"

"Yes, Lehabah." Bryce wrapped her hand around the front door's handle. The enchantments on it hummed against her palm, slithering like smoke over her freckled golden skin. She gritted her teeth and withstood it, still unused to the sensation even after a year of working at the gallery.

From the other side of the deceptively simple metal door to the archives, Lehabah warned, "Jesiba doesn't like her in here."

"*You* don't like her in here," Bryce amended, her amber eyes narrowing toward the archives door and the tiny fire sprite she knew was hovering just on the other side, eavesdropping as she always did whenever someone stood out front. "Go back to work."

Lehabah didn't answer, presumably drifting back downstairs to guard the books below. Rolling her eyes, Bryce yanked open the front door, getting a face full of heat so dry it threatened to suck the life from her. And summer had only just begun.

Danika didn't just look like she'd been rootling through the garbage. She smelled like it, too.

Wisps of her silvery blond hair—normally a straight, silken sheet—curled from her tight, long braid, the streaks of amethyst, sapphire, and rose splattered with some dark, oily substance that reeked of metal and ammonia.

"Took you long enough," Danika groused, and swaggered into the gallery, the sword strapped at her back bobbing with each step. Her braid had become tangled in its worn leather hilt, and as she stopped before the desk, Bryce took the liberty of prying the plait free.

She'd barely untangled it before Danika's slim fingers were unbuckling the straps that kept the sword sheathed across her worn leather motorcycle jacket. "I need to dump this here for a few hours," she said, pulling the sword off her back and aiming for the supply closet hidden behind a wooden panel across the showroom.

Bryce leaned against the lip of the desk and crossed her arms, fingers brushing against the stretchy black fabric of her skintight dress. "Your gym bag's already stinking up the place. Jesiba's due back later this afternoon—she'll throw your shit in the dumpster again if it's still here."

It was the mildest Hel Jesiba Roga could unleash if provoked.

A four-hundred-year-old enchantress who'd been born a witch and defected, Jesiba had joined the House of Flame and Shadow and now answered only to the Under-King himself. Flame and Shadow suited her well—she possessed an arsenal of spells to rival any sorcerer or necromancer in the darkest of the Houses. She'd been known to change people into animals when irritated enough. Bryce had never dared ask if the small animals in the dozen tanks and terrariums had always been animals.

And Bryce tried never to irritate her. Not that there were any safe sides when the Vanir were involved. Even the least powerful of the Vanir—a group that covered every being on Midgard aside from humans and ordinary animals—could be deadly.

"I'll get it later," Danika promised, pushing on the hidden panel to spring it open. Bryce had warned her three times now that the showroom supply closet wasn't her personal locker. Yet Danika always countered that the gallery, located in the heart of the Old Square, was more centrally located than the wolves' Den over in Moonwood. And that was that.

The supply closet opened, and Danika waved a hand in front of her face. "*My* gym bag's stinking up the place?" With a black boot, she toed the sagging duffel that held Bryce's dance gear, currently wedged between the mop and bucket. "When the fuck did you last wash those clothes?"

Bryce wrinkled her nose at the reek of old shoes and sweaty clothing that wafted out. Right—she'd forgotten to bring home the leotard and tights to wash after a lunchtime class two days ago. Mostly thanks to Danika sending her a video of a heap of mirthroot on their kitchen counter, music already blasting from the beat-up boom box by the windows, along with a command to hurry home quick. Bryce had obeyed. They'd smoked enough that there was a good chance Bryce had still been high yesterday morning when she'd stumbled into work.

There was really no other explanation for why it had taken ten minutes to type out a two-sentence email that day. Letter by letter.

"Never mind that," Bryce said. "I have a bone to pick with you."

Danika rearranged the crap in the closet to make space for her own. "I told you I was sorry I ate your leftover noodles. I'll buy you more tonight."

"It's not that, dumbass, though again: fuck you. That was my lunch for today." Danika chuckled. "This tattoo hurts like Hel," Bryce complained. "I can't even lean against my chair."

Danika countered in a singsong voice, "The artist warned you it'd be sore for a few days."

"I was so drunk I spelled my name wrong on the waiver. I'd hardly say I was in a good place to understand what 'sore for a few days' meant." Danika, who'd gotten a matching tattoo of the text now scrolling down Bryce's back, had already healed. One of the benefits to being a full-blooded Vanir: swift recovery time compared to humans—or a half-human like Bryce.

Danika shoved her sword into the mess of the closet. "I promise I'll help you ice your sore back tonight. Just let me take a shower and I'll be out of here in ten."

It wasn't unusual for her friend to pop into the gallery, especially on Thursdays, when her morning patrol ended just a few blocks away, but she'd never used the full bathroom in the archives downstairs. Bryce motioned to the dirt and grease. "What *is* that on you?"

Danika scowled, the angular planes of her face scrunching. "I had to break up a fight between a satyr and a nightstalker." She bared her white teeth at the black substance crusting her hands. "Guess which one spewed its *juices* onto me."

Bryce snorted and gestured to the archives door. "Shower's yours. There are some clean clothes in the bottom drawer of the desk down there."

Danika's filthy fingers began pulling the handle of the archives door. Her jaw tightened, the older tattoo on her neck—the horned, grinning wolf that served as the sigil for the Pack of Devils—rippling with tension.

Not from the effort, Bryce realized as she noted Danika's stiff back. Bryce glanced to the supply closet, which Danika had not bothered to shut. The sword, famed both in this city and far beyond it, leaned against the push broom and mop, its ancient leather scabbard nearly obscured by the full container of gasoline used to fuel the electric generator out back.

Bryce had always wondered why Jesiba bothered with an old-fashioned generator—until the citywide firstlight outage last week. When the power had failed, only the generator had kept the mechanical locks in place during the looting that followed, when creeps had rushed in from the Meat Market, bombarding the gallery's front door with counterspells to break through the enchantments.

But—Danika ditching the sword in the office. Danika needing to take a shower. Her stiff back.

Bryce asked, "You've got a meeting with the City Heads?"

In the five years since they'd met as freshmen at Crescent City University, Bryce could count on one hand the number of times Danika had been called in for a meeting with the seven people important enough to merit a shower and change of clothes. Even while delivering reports to Danika's grandfather, the Prime of the Valbaran wolves, and to Sabine, her mother, Danika usually wore that leather jacket, jeans, and whatever vintage band T-shirt wasn't dirty.

Of course, it pissed off Sabine to no end, but *everything* about Danika—and Bryce—pissed off the Alpha of the Scythe Moon Pack, chief among the shifter units in the city's Auxiliary.

It didn't matter that Sabine was the Prime Apparent of the Valbaran wolves and had been her aging father's heir for centuries, or that Danika was officially second in line to the title. Not when whispers had swirled for years that Danika should be tapped to be the Prime Apparent, bypassing her mother. Not when the old wolf had given his granddaughter their family's heirloom sword after centuries of promising it to Sabine only upon his death. The blade had called to Danika on her eighteenth birthday like a howl on a moonlit night, the Prime had said to explain his unexpected decision.

Sabine had never forgotten that humiliation. Especially when Danika carried the blade nearly everywhere—especially in front of her mother.

Danika paused in the gaping archway, atop the green carpeted steps that led down to the archives beneath the gallery—where the true treasure in this place lay, guarded by Lehabah day and night. It was the real reason why Danika, who'd been a history major at CCU, liked to drop by so often, just to browse the ancient art and books, despite Bryce's teasing about her reading habits.

Danika turned, her caramel eyes shuttered. "Philip Briggs is being released today."

Bryce started. "*What?*"

"They're letting him go on some gods-damned technicality. Someone fucked up the paperwork. We're getting the full update in the meeting." She clenched her slim jaw, the glow from the first-lights in the glass sconces along the stairwell bouncing off her dirty hair. "It's so fucked up."

Bryce's stomach churned. The human rebellion remained confined to the northern reaches of Pangera, the sprawling territory across the Haldren Sea, but Philip Briggs had done his best to bring it over to Valbara. "You and the pack busted him right in his little rebel bomb lab, though."

Danika tapped her booted foot on the green carpet. "Bureaucratic fucking nonsense."

"He was going to blow up a *club*. You literally found his blueprints for blowing up the White Raven." As one of the most popular nightclubs in the city, the loss of life would have been catastrophic. Briggs's previous bombings had been smaller, but no less deadly, all designed to trigger a war between the humans and Vanir to match the one raging in Pangera's colder climes. Briggs made no secret of his goal: a global conflict that would cost the lives of millions on either side. Lives that were expendable if it meant a possibility for humans to overthrow those who oppressed them—the magically gifted and long-lived Vanir and, above them, the Asteri, who ruled the planet Midgard from the Eternal City in Pangera.

But Danika and the Pack of Devils had stopped the plot. She'd busted Briggs and his top supporters, all part of the Keres rebels, and spared innocents from their brand of fanaticism.

As one of the most elite shifter units in Crescent City's Auxiliary, the Pack of Devils patrolled the Old Square, making sure drunken, handsy tourists didn't become drunken, dead tourists when they approached the wrong person. Making sure the bars and cafés and music halls and shops stayed safe from whatever lowlife had crawled into town that day. And making sure people like Briggs were in prison.

The 33rd Imperial Legion claimed to do the same, but the angels who made up the fabled ranks of the Governor's personal army just glowered and promised Hel if challenged.

"Believe me," Danika said, stomping down the stairs, "I'm going to make it perfectly fucking clear in this meeting that Briggs's release is unacceptable."

She would. Even if Danika had to snarl in Micah Domitus's face, she'd get her point across. There weren't many who'd dare piss off the Archangel of Crescent City, but Danika wouldn't hesitate. And given that all seven Heads of the City would be at this meeting, the odds of that happening were high. Things tended to escalate swiftly when they were in one room. There was little love lost between the six lower Heads in Crescent City, the metropolis formally known as Lunathion. Each Head controlled a specific part of the city: the Prime of the wolves in Moonwood, the Fae Autumn King in Five Roses, the Under-King in the Bone Quarter, the Viper Queen in the Meat Market, the Oracle in the Old Square, and the River Queen—who very rarely made an appearance—representing the House of Many Waters and her Blue Court far beneath the Istros River's turquoise surface. She seldom deigned to leave it.

The humans in Asphodel Meadows had no Head. No seat at the table. Philip Briggs had found more than a few sympathizers because of it.

But Micah, Head of the Central Business District, ruled over them all. Beyond his city titles, he was Archangel of Valbara. Ruler of this entire fucking territory, and answerable only to the six Asteri in the Eternal City, the capital and beating heart of Pangera. Of the entire planet of Midgard. If anyone could keep Briggs in prison, it would be him.

Danika reached the bottom of the stairs, so far below that she was cut off from sight by the slope of the ceiling. Bryce lingered in the archway, listening as Danika said, "Hey, Syrinx." A little yip of delight from the thirty-pound chimera rose up the stairs.

Jesiba had purchased the Lower creature two months ago, to Bryce's delight. *He is not a pet,* Jesiba had warned her. *He's an expensive, rare creature bought for the sole purpose of assisting Lehabah in guarding these books. Do not interfere with his duties.*

Bryce had so far failed to inform Jesiba that Syrinx was more interested in eating, sleeping, and getting belly rubs than monitoring the precious books. No matter that her boss might see that at any point, should she bother to check the dozens of camera feeds in the library.

Danika drawled, the smirk audible in her voice, "What's got your panties in a twist, Lehabah?"

The fire sprite grumbled, "I don't wear panties. Or clothes. They don't pair well when you're made of flame, Danika."

Danika snickered. Before Bryce could decide whether to go downstairs to referee the match between the fire sprite and the wolf, the phone on the desk began ringing. She had a good idea who it would be.

Heels sinking into the plush carpeting, Bryce reached the phone before it went to audiomail, sparing herself a five-minute lecture. "Hi, Jesiba."

A beautiful, lilting female voice answered, "Please tell Danika Fendyr that if she continues to use the supply closet as her own personal locker, I *will* turn her into a lizard."

2

By the time Danika emerged on the gallery's showroom floor, Bryce had endured a mildly threatening reprimand from Jesiba about her ineptitude, one email from a fussy client demanding Bryce expedite the paperwork on the ancient urn she'd bought so she could show it off to her equally fussy friends at her cocktail party on Monday, and two messages from members of Danika's pack inquiring about whether their Alpha was about to kill someone over Briggs's release.

Nathalie, Danika's Third, had gotten straight to the point: *Has she lost her shit about Briggs yet?*

Connor Holstrom, Danika's Second, took a little more care with what he sent out into the ether. There was always a chance of a leak. *Have you spoken to Danika?* was all he'd asked.

Bryce was writing back to Connor—*Yes. I've got it covered*—when a gray wolf the size of a small horse pushed the iron archives door shut with a paw, claws clicking on the metal.

"You hated my clothes that much?" Bryce asked, rising from her seat. Only Danika's caramel eyes remained the same in this form—and only those eyes softened the pure menace and grace the wolf radiated with each step toward the desk.

"I've got them on, don't worry." Long, sharp fangs flashed with each word. Danika cocked her fuzzy ears, taking in the computer that had been shut down, the purse Bryce had set on the desk. "You're coming out with me?"

"I've got to do some sleuthing for Jesiba." Bryce grabbed the ring of keys that opened doors into various parts of her life. "She's been hounding me about finding Luna's Horn again. As if I haven't been trying to find it nonstop for the last week."

Danika glanced to one of the visible cameras in the showroom, mounted behind a decapitated statue of a dancing faun dating back ten thousand years. Her bushy tail swished once. "Why does she even want it?"

Bryce shrugged. "I haven't had the balls to ask."

Danika stalked to the front door, careful not to let her claws snag a single thread in the carpet. "I doubt she's going to return it to the temple out of the goodness of her heart."

"I have a feeling Jesiba would leverage its return to her advantage," Bryce said. They strode onto the quiet street a block off the Istros, the midday sun baking the cobblestones, Danika a solid wall of fur and muscle between Bryce and the curb.

The theft of the sacred horn during the power outage had been the biggest news story out of the disaster: looters had used the cover of darkness to break into Luna's Temple and swipe the ancient Fae relic from its resting place atop the lap of the massive, enthroned deity.

The Archangel Micah himself had offered a hefty reward for any information regarding its return and promised that the sacrilegious bastard who'd stolen it would be brought to justice.

Also known as public crucifixion.

Bryce always made a point of not going near the square in the CBD, where they were usually held. On certain days, depending on the wind and heat, the smell of blood and rotting flesh could carry for blocks.

Bryce fell into step beside Danika as the massive wolf scanned the street, nostrils sniffing for any hint of a threat. Bryce, as half-Fae, could scent people in greater detail than the average human. She'd entertained her parents endlessly as a kid by describing the scents of everyone in their little mountain town, Nidaros—humans possessed no such way to interpret the world. But her abilities had nothing on her friend's.

As Danika scented the street, her tail wagged once—and not from happiness.

"Chill," Bryce said. "You'll make your case to the Heads, then they'll figure it out."

Danika's ears flattened. "It's all fucked, B. All of it."

Bryce frowned. "You really mean to tell me that any of the Heads want a rebel like Briggs at large? They'll find some technicality and throw his ass right back in jail." She added, because Danika still wouldn't look at her, "There's no way the 33rd's not monitoring his every breath. Briggs so much as blinks wrong and he'll see what kind of pain angels can rain down on us all. Hel, the Governor might even send the Umbra Mortis after him." Micah's personal assassin, with the rare gift of lightning in his veins, could eliminate almost any threat.

Danika snarled, teeth gleaming. "I can handle Briggs myself."

"I know you can. Everyone knows you can, Danika."

Danika surveyed the street ahead, glancing past a poster of the six enthroned Asteri tacked up on a wall—with an empty throne to honor their fallen sister—but loosed a breath.

She would always have burdens and expectations to shoulder that Bryce would never have to endure, and Bryce was thankful as Hel for that privilege. When Bryce fucked up, Jesiba usually griped for a few minutes and that was that. When Danika fucked up, it was blasted on news reports and across the interweb.

Sabine made sure of it.

Bryce and Sabine had hated each other from the moment the Alpha had sneered at her only child's improper, half-breed roommate that first day at CCU. And Bryce had loved Danika from the moment her new roommate had offered her a hand in greeting anyway, and then said Sabine was just pissy because she'd been hoping for a muscle-bound vampyr to drool over.

Danika rarely let the opinions of others—especially Sabine—eat away at her swagger and joy, yet on rough days like this . . . Bryce lifted a hand and ran it down Danika's muscled ribs, a comforting, sweeping stroke.

"Do you think Briggs will come after you or the pack?" Bryce asked, her stomach twisting. Danika hadn't busted Briggs alone—he had a score to settle with all of them.

Danika's snout wrinkled. "I don't know."

The words echoed between them. In hand-to-hand combat, Briggs would never survive against Danika. But one of those bombs would change everything. If Danika had made the Drop into immortality, she'd probably survive. But since she hadn't—since she was the only one of the Pack of Devils who hadn't yet done it . . . Bryce's mouth turned dry.

"Be careful," Bryce said quietly.

"I will," Danika said, her warm eyes still full of shadows. But then she tossed her head, as if shaking it free of water—the movement purely canine. Bryce often marveled at this, that Danika could clear away her fears, or at least bury them, enough to move onward. Indeed, Danika changed the subject. "Your brother will be at the meeting today."

Half brother. Bryce didn't bother to correct her. *Half brother and full-Fae prick*. "And?"

"Just thought I'd warn you that I'll be seeing him." The wolf's face softened slightly. "He's going to ask me how you're doing."

"Tell Ruhn I'm busy doing important shit and to go to Hel."

Danika huffed a laugh. "Where, exactly, are you doing this sleuthing for the Horn?"

"The temple," Bryce said with a sigh. "Honestly, I've been looking into this thing for days on end, and can't figure out anything. No suspects, no murmurings at the Meat Market about it being for sale, no motive for who'd even bother with it. It's famous enough that whoever's got it has it wrapped up *tight*." She frowned at the clear sky. "I almost wonder if the power outage was tied to it—if someone shut down the city's grid to steal it in the chaos. There are about twenty people in this city capable of being that crafty, and half of them possess the resources to pull it off."

Danika's tail twitched. "If they're able to do something like that, I'd suggest staying away. Lead Jesiba around a bit, make her think you're looking for it, and then let it drop. Either the Horn will show up by then, or she'll move on to her next stupid quest."

Bryce admitted, "I just . . . It'd be good to find the Horn. For my own career." Whatever the Hel that would be. A year of working at the gallery hadn't sparked anything beyond disgust at the obscene amounts of money that rich people squandered on old-ass shit.

Danika's eyes flickered. "Yeah, I know."

Bryce zipped a tiny golden pendant—a knot of three entwined circles—along the delicate chain around her neck.

Danika went on patrol armed with claws, a sword, and guns, but Bryce's daily armor consisted solely of this: an Archesian amulet barely the size of her thumbnail, gifted by Jesiba on the first day of work.

A hazmat suit in a necklace, Danika had marveled when Bryce had shown off the amulet's considerable protections against the influence of various magical objects. Archesian amulets didn't come cheap, but Bryce didn't bother to delude herself into thinking her boss's gift was given out of anything but self-interest. It would have been an insurance nightmare if Bryce didn't have one.

Danika nodded to the necklace. "Don't take that off. Especially if you're looking into shit like the Horn." Even though the Horn's mighty powers had long been dead—if it had been stolen by someone powerful, she'd need every magical defense against them.

"Yeah, yeah," Bryce said, though Danika was right. She'd never taken the necklace off since getting it. If Jesiba ever kicked her to the curb, she knew she'd have to find some way to make sure the necklace came with her. Danika had said as much several times, unable to stop that Alpha wolf's instinct to protect at all costs. It was part of why Bryce loved her—and why her chest tightened in that moment with that same love and gratitude.

Bryce's phone buzzed in her purse, and she fished it out. Danika peered over, noted who was calling, and wagged her tail, ears perking up.

"Do not say a word about Briggs," Bryce warned, and accepted the call. "Hi, Mom."

"Hey, sweetie." Ember Quinlan's clear voice filled her ear, drawing a smile from Bryce even with three hundred miles between them. "I wanted to double-check that next weekend is still okay to visit."

"Hi, Mommy!" Danika barked toward the phone.

Ember laughed. Ember had always been *Mom* to Danika, even from their first meeting. And Ember, who had never borne any children beyond Bryce, had been more than glad to find herself with a second—equally willful and troublesome—daughter. "Danika's with you?"

Bryce rolled her eyes and held out the phone to her friend. Between one step and the next, Danika shifted in a flash of light, the massive wolf shrinking into the lithe humanoid form.

Snatching the phone from Bryce, Danika pinned it between her ear and shoulder as she adjusted the white silk blouse Bryce had loaned her, tucking it into her stained jeans. She'd managed to wipe a good amount of the nightstalker gunk off both the pants and leather jacket, but the T-shirt had apparently been a lost cause. Danika said into the phone, "Bryce and I are taking a walk."

With Bryce's arched ears, she could hear her mother perfectly as she said, "Where?"

Ember Quinlan made overprotectiveness a competitive sport.

Moving here, to Lunathion, had been a test of wills. Ember had only relented when she'd learned who Bryce's freshman-year roommate was—and then gave Danika a lecture on how to make sure Bryce stayed safe. Randall, Bryce's stepfather, had mercifully cut his wife off after thirty minutes.

Bryce knows how to defend herself, Randall had reminded Ember. *We saw to that. And Bryce will keep up her training while she's here, won't she?*

Bryce certainly had. She'd hit up the gun range just a few days ago, going through the motions Randall—her true father, as far as she was concerned—had taught her since childhood: assembling a gun, taking aim at a target, controlling her breathing.

Most days, she found guns to be brutal killing machines, and felt grateful that they were highly regulated by the Republic. But given that she had little more to defend herself beyond speed and a few well-placed maneuvers, she'd learned that for a human, a gun could mean the difference between life and slaughter.

Danika fibbed, "We're just heading to one of the hawker stalls in the Old Square—we wanted some lamb kofta."

Before Ember could continue the interrogation, Danika added, "Hey, B must have forgotten to tell you that we're actually heading down to Kalaxos next weekend—Ithan's got a sunball game there, and we're all going to cheer him on."

A half-truth. The game was happening, but there had been no discussion of going to watch Connor's younger brother, CCU's star player. This afternoon, the Pack of Devils was actually heading over to the CCU arena to cheer for Ithan, but Bryce and Danika hadn't bothered to attend an away game since sophomore year, when Danika had been sleeping with one of the defensemen.

"That's too bad," Ember said. Bryce could practically hear the frown in her mother's tone. "We were really looking forward to it."

Burning Solas, this woman was a master of the guilt trip. Bryce cringed and snatched back the phone. "So were we, but let's reschedule for next month."

"But that's so long from now—"

"Shit, a client's coming down the street," Bryce lied. "I gotta go."

"Bryce Adelaide Quinlan—"

"Bye, Mom."

"Bye, Mom!" Danika echoed, just as Bryce hung up.

Bryce sighed toward the sky, ignoring the angels soaring and flapping past, their shadows dancing over the sun-washed streets. "Message incoming in three, two . . ."

Her phone buzzed.

Ember had written, *If I didn't know better, I'd think you were avoiding us, Bryce. Your father will be very hurt.*

Danika let out a whistle. "Oh, she's good."

Bryce groaned. "I'm not letting them come to the city if Briggs is running free."

Danika's smile faded. "I know. We'll keep pushing them off until it's sorted out." Thank Cthona for Danika—she always had a plan for everything.

Bryce slid her phone into her purse, leaving her mother's message unanswered.

When they reached the Gate at the heart of the Old Square, its quartz archway as clear as a frozen pond, the sun was just hitting its upper edge, refracting and casting small rainbows against one of the buildings flanking it. On Summer Solstice, when the sun lined up perfectly with the Gate, it filled the entire square with rainbows, so many that it was like walking inside a diamond.

Tourists milled about, a line of them snaking across the square itself, all waiting for the chance at a photo with the twenty-foot-high landmark.

One of seven in this city, all carved from enormous blocks of quartz hewn from the Laconian Mountains to the north, the Old Square Gate was often called the Heart Gate, thanks to its location in the dead center of Lunathion, with the other six Gates located equidistant from it, each one opening onto a road out of the walled city.

"They should make a special access lane for residents to cross the square," Bryce muttered as they edged around tourists and hawkers.

"And give tourists fines for slow walking," Danika muttered back, but flashed a lupine grin at a young human couple that recognized her, gawked, and began snapping photos.

"I wonder what they'd think if they knew that nightstalker's special sauce is all over you," Bryce murmured.

Danika elbowed her. "Asshole." She threw a friendly wave to the tourists and continued on.

On the other side of the Heart Gate, amid a small army of vendors selling food and touristy crap, a second line of people waited to access the golden block sticking out of its southern side. "We'll have to cut through them to get across," Bryce said, scowling at the tourists idling in the wilting heat.

But Danika halted, her angular face turned to the Gate and the plaque. "Let's make a wish."

"I'm not waiting in that line." Usually, they just shouted their wishes drunkenly into the ether late at night when they were staggering home from the White Raven and the square was empty. Bryce checked the time on her phone. "Don't you have to get over to the Comitium?" The Governor's five-towered stronghold was at least a fifteen-minute walk away.

"I've got time," Danika said, and grabbed Bryce's hand, tugging her through the crowds and toward the real tourist draw of the Gate.

Jutting out of the quartz about four feet off the ground lay the dial pad: a solid-gold block embedded with seven different gems, each for a different quarter of the city, the insignia of each district etched beneath it.

Emerald and a rose for Five Roses. Opal and a pair of wings for the CBD. Ruby and a heart for the Old Square. Sapphire and an oak tree for Moonwood. Amethyst and a human hand for Asphodel Meadows. Tiger's-eye and a serpent for the Meat Market. And onyx—so black it gobbled the light—and a set of skull and crossbones for the Bone Quarter.

Beneath the arc of stones and etched emblems, a small, round disk rose up slightly, its metal worn down by countless hands and paws and fins and any other manner of limb.

A sign beside it read: *Touch at your own risk. Do not use between sundown and sunrise. Violators will be fined.*

The people in line, waiting for access to the disk, seemed to have no problem with the risks.

A pair of giggling teenage male shifters—some kind of feline from their scents—goaded each other forward, elbowing and taunting, daring the other to touch the disk.

"Pathetic," Danika said, striding past the line, the ropes, and a bored-looking city guard—a young Fae female—to the very front. She fished a badge from inside her leather coat and flashed it at the guard, who stiffened as she realized who'd cut the line. She didn't even look at the golden emblem of the crescent moon bow with an arrow nocked through it before stepping back.

"Official Aux business," Danika declared with an unnervingly straight face. "It'll just be a minute."

Bryce stifled her laughter, well aware of the glares fixed on their backs from the line.

Danika drawled to the teenage boys, "If you're not going to do it, then clear off."

They whirled toward her, and went white as death.

Danika smiled, showing nearly all her teeth. It wasn't a pleasant sight.

"Holy shit," whispered one of them.

Bryce hid her smile as well. It never got old—the awe. Mostly because she knew Danika had earned it. Every damned day, Danika earned the awe that bloomed across the faces of strangers when they spotted her corn-silk hair and that neck tattoo. And the fear that made the lowlifes in this city think twice before fucking with her and the Pack of Devils.

Except for Philip Briggs. Bryce sent a prayer to Ogenas's blue depths that the sea goddess would whisper her wisdom to Briggs to keep his distance from Danika if he ever really did walk free.

The boys stepped aside, and it only took a few milliseconds for them to notice Bryce, too. The awe on their faces turned to blatant interest.

Bryce snorted. *Keep dreaming.*

One of them stammered, turning his attention from Bryce to Danika, "My—my history teacher said the Gates were originally communication devices."

"I bet you get all the ladies with those stellar factoids," Danika said without looking back at them, unimpressed and uninterested.

Message received, they slunk back to the line. Bryce smirked and stepped up to her friend's side, peering down at the dial pad.

The teenager was right, though. The seven Gates of this city, each set along a ley line running through Lunathion, had been designed as a quick way for the guards in the districts to speak to each other centuries ago. When someone merely placed a hand against the golden disk in the center of the pad and spoke, the wielder's voice would travel to the other Gates, a gem lighting up with the district from which the voice originated.

Of course, it required a drop of magic to do so—literally sucked it like a vampyr from the veins of the person who touched the pad, a tickling *zap* of power, gone forever.

Bryce raised her eyes to the bronze plaque above her head. The quartz Gates were memorials, though she didn't know for which conflict or war. But each bore the same plaque: *The power shall always belong to those who give their lives to the city.*

Considering it was a statement that could be construed as being in opposition to the Asteri's rule, Bryce was always surprised that they allowed the Gates to continue to stand. But after becoming obsolete with the advent of phones, the Gates had found a second life when kids and tourists began using them, having their friends go to the other Gates in the city so they could whisper dirty words or marvel at the sheer novelty of such an antiquated method of communication. Not surprisingly, come weekends, drunk assholes—a category to which Bryce and Danika firmly belonged—became such a pain in the ass with their shouting through the Gates that the city had instituted hours of operation.

And then dumb superstition grew, claiming the Gate could make wishes come true, and that to give over a droplet of your power was to make an offering to the five gods.

It was bullshit, Bryce knew—but if it made Danika not dread Briggs's release so much, well, it was worth it.

"What are you going to wish for?" Bryce asked when Danika stared down at the disk, the gems dark above it.

The emerald for FiRo lit up, a young female voice coming through to shriek, "*Titties!*"

People laughed around them, the sound like water trickling over stone, and Bryce chuckled.

But Danika's face had gone solemn. "I've got too many things to wish for," she said. Before Bryce could ask, Danika shrugged. "But I think I'll wish for Ithan to win his sunball game tonight."

With that, she set her palm onto the disk. Bryce watched as her friend let out a shiver and quietly laughed, stepping back. Her caramel eyes shone. "Your turn."

"You know I have barely any magic worth taking, but okay," Bryce said, not to be outdone, even by an Alpha wolf. From the moment Bryce walked into her dorm room freshman year, they'd done everything together. Just the two of them, as it always would be.

They even planned to make the Drop together—to freeze into immortality at the same breath, with members of the Pack of Devils Anchoring them.

Technically, it wasn't true immortality—the Vanir did age and die, either of natural causes or other methods, but the aging process was so slowed after the Drop that, depending on one's species, it could take centuries to show a wrinkle. The Fae could last a thousand years, the shifters and witches usually five centuries, the angels somewhere between. Full humans did not make the Drop, as they bore no magic. And compared to humans, with their ordinary life spans and slow healing, the Vanir *were* essentially immortal—some species bore children who didn't even enter maturity until they were in their eighties. And most were very, very hard to kill.

But Bryce had rarely thought about where she'd fall on that spectrum—whether her half-Fae heritage would grant her a hundred years or a thousand. It didn't matter, so long as Danika was there for all of it. Starting with the Drop. They'd take the deadly plunge into their matured power together, encounter whatever lay at the bottom of their souls, and then race back up to life before the lack of oxygen rendered them brain-dead. Or just plain dead.

Yet while Bryce would inherit barely enough power to do cool party tricks, Danika was expected to claim a sea of power that would put her ranking far past Sabine's—likely equal to that of Fae royalty, maybe even beyond the Autumn King himself.

It was unheard of, for a shifter to have that sort of power, yet all the standard childhood tests had confirmed it: once Danika Dropped, she'd become a considerable power among the wolves, the likes of which had not been seen since the elder days across the sea.

Danika wouldn't just become the Prime of the Crescent City

wolves. No, she had the potential to be the Alpha of *all* wolves. On the fucking planet.

Danika never seemed to give two shits about it. Didn't plan for her future based on it.

Twenty-seven was the ideal age to make the Drop, they'd decided together, after years of mercilessly judging the various immortals who marked their lives by centuries and millennia. Right before any permanent lines or wrinkles or gray hairs. They merely said to anyone who inquired, *What's the point of being immortal badasses if we have sagging tits?*

Vain assholes, Fury had hissed when they'd explained it the first time.

Fury, who had made the Drop at age twenty-one, hadn't chosen the age for herself. It'd just happened, or had been forced upon her—they didn't know for sure. Fury's attendance at CCU had only been a front for a mission; most of her time was spent doing *truly* fucked-up things for disgusting amounts of money over in Pangera. She made it a point never to give details.

Assassin, Danika claimed. Even sweet Juniper, the faun who occupied the fourth side of their little friendship-square, admitted the odds were that Fury was a merc. Whether Fury was occasionally employed by the Asteri and their puppet Imperial Senate was up for debate, too. But none of them really cared—not when Fury always had their back when they needed it. And even when they didn't.

Bryce's hand hovered over the golden disk. Danika's gaze was a cool weight on her.

"Come on, B, don't be a wimp."

Bryce sighed, and set her hand on the pad. "I wish Danika would get a manicure. Her nails look like shit."

Lightning zapped through her, a slight vacuuming around her belly button, and then Danika was laughing, shoving her. "You fucking *dick*."

Bryce slung an arm around Danika's shoulders. "You deserved it."

Danika thanked the security guard, who beamed at the attention, and ignored the tourists still snapping photos. They didn't speak until they reached the northern edge of the square—where Danika would head toward the angel-filled skies and towers of the CBD, to the sprawling Comitium complex in its heart, and Bryce toward Luna's Temple, three blocks up.

Danika jerked her chin toward the streets behind Bryce. "I'll see you at home, all right?"

"Be careful." Bryce blew out a breath, trying to shake her unease.

"I know how to look out for myself, B," Danika said, but love shone in her eyes—gratitude that crushed Bryce's chest—merely for the fact that someone cared whether she lived or died.

Sabine was a piece of shit. Had never whispered or hinted who Danika's father might be—so Danika had grown up with absolutely no one except her grandfather, who was too old and withdrawn to spare Danika from her mother's cruelty.

Bryce inclined her head toward the CBD. "Good luck. Don't piss off too many people."

"You know I will," Danika said with a grin that didn't meet her eyes.

3

The Pack of Devils was already at her apartment by the time Bryce got home from work.

It had been impossible to miss the roaring laughter that met her before she'd even cleared the second-floor stairwell landing—as well as the canine yips of amusement. Both had continued as she ascended the remaining level of the walk-up apartment building, during which time Bryce grumbled to herself about her plans for a quiet evening on the couch being ruined.

Chanting a string of curses that would make her mother proud, Bryce unlocked the blue-painted iron door to the apartment, bracing for the onslaught of lupine bossiness, arrogance, and general nosiness in all matters of her life. And that was just Danika.

Danika's pack made each of those things an art form. Mostly because they claimed Bryce as one of their own, even if she didn't bear the tattoo of their sigil down the side of her neck.

Sometimes she felt bad for Danika's future mate, whoever that would be. The poor bastard wouldn't know what hit him when he bound himself to her. Unless he was wolf-kind himself—though Danika had about as much interest in sleeping with a wolf as Bryce did.

That is to say, not a gods-damned shred.

Giving the door a good shove with her shoulder—its warped edges got stuck more often than not, mostly thanks to the romping of the hellions currently spread across the several sagging couches and armchairs—Bryce sighed as she found six pairs of eyes fixed on her. And six grins.

"How was the game?" she asked no one in particular, chucking her keys into the lopsided ceramic bowl Danika had half-assed during a fluff pottery course in college. She'd heard nothing from Danika regarding the Briggs meeting beyond a general *I'll tell you at home*.

It couldn't have been that bad, if Danika made it to the sunball game. She'd even sent Bryce a photo of the whole pack in front of the field, with Ithan a small, helmeted figure in the background.

A message from the star player himself had popped up later: *Next time, you better be with them, Quinlan.*

She'd written back, *Did baby pup miss me?*

You know it, Ithan had answered.

"We won," Connor drawled from where he lounged on *her* favorite spot on the couch, his gray CCU sunball T-shirt rumpled enough to reveal the cut of muscle and golden skin.

"Ithan scored the winning goal," Bronson said, still wearing a blue-and-silver jersey with *Holstrom* on the back.

Connor's little brother, Ithan, held an unofficial membership in the Pack of Devils. Ithan also happened to be Bryce's second-favorite person after Danika. Their message chain was an endless stream of snark and teasing, swapped photos, and good-natured grousing about Connor's bossiness.

"Again?" Bryce asked, kicking off her four-inch, pearl-white heels. "Can't Ithan share some of the glory with the other boys?" Normally, Ithan would have been sitting right on that couch beside his brother, forcing Bryce to wedge herself between them while they watched whatever TV show was on, but on game nights, he usually opted to party with his teammates.

A half smile tugged at a corner of Connor's mouth as Bryce held his stare for longer than most people considered wise. His five packmates, two still in wolf form with bushy tails swishing, wisely kept their mouths and maws shut.

It was common knowledge that Connor would have been Alpha of the Pack of Devils if Danika weren't around. But Connor didn't resent it. His ambitions didn't run that way. Unlike Sabine's.

Bryce nudged her backup dance bag over on the coatrack to make room for her purse, and asked the wolves, "What are you watching tonight?" Whatever it was, she'd already decided to curl up with a romance novel in her room. With the door shut.

Nathalie, flipping through celebrity gossip magazines on the couch, didn't lift her head as she answered, "Some new legal procedural about a pack of lions taking on an evil Fae corporation."

"Sounds like a real award winner," Bryce said. Bronson grunted his disapproval. The massive male's tastes skewed more toward art house flicks and documentaries. Unsurprisingly, he was never allowed to select the entertainment for Pack Night.

Connor ran a calloused finger down the rolled arm of the couch. "You're home late."

"I have a job," Bryce said. "You might want to get one. Stop being a leech on my couch."

This wasn't exactly fair. As Danika's Second, Connor acted as her enforcer. To keep this city safe, he'd killed, tortured, maimed, and then gone back out and done it again before the moon had even set.

He never complained about it. None of them did.

What's the point in bitching, Danika had said when Bryce asked how she endured the brutality, *when there's no choice in joining the Auxiliary?* The predator-born shifters were destined for certain Aux packs before they were even born.

Bryce tried not to glance at the horned wolf tattooed on the side of Connor's neck—proof of that predestined lifetime of service. Of his eternal loyalty to Danika, the Pack of Devils, and the Aux.

Connor just looked Bryce over with that half smile. It set her teeth to grinding. "Danika's in the kitchen. Eating half the pizza before we can get a bite."

"*I am not!*" was the muffled reply.

Connor's smile grew.

Bryce's breathing turned a shade uneven at that smile, the wicked light in his eyes.

The rest of the pack remained dutifully focused on the television screen, pretending to watch the nightly news.

Swallowing, Bryce asked him, "Anything I should know?" Translation: *Was the Briggs meeting a disaster?*

Connor knew what she meant. He always did. He jerked his head to the kitchen. "You'll see."

Translation: *Not great.*

Bryce winced, and managed to tear her gaze away from him so she could pad into the galley kitchen. She felt Connor's stare on her every step of the way.

And maybe she swished her hips. Only a tiny bit.

Danika was indeed shoveling a slice down her throat, her eyes wide in warning for Bryce to keep her mouth shut. Bryce noted the unspoken plea, and merely nodded.

A half-empty bottle of beer dripped condensation onto the white plastic counter Danika leaned against, her borrowed silk shirt damp with sweat around the collar. Her braid drooped over her slim shoulder, the few colorful streaks unusually muted. Even her pale skin, usually flushed with color and health, seemed ashen.

Granted, the crappy kitchen lighting—two meager recessed orbs of firstlight—wasn't exactly favorable to anyone, but . . . Beer. Food. The pack keeping their distance. And that hollow weariness in her friend's eyes—yeah, some shit had gone down in that meeting.

Bryce tugged open the fridge, grabbing a beer for herself. The pack all had different preferences, and were prone to coming over whenever they felt like it, so the fridge was crammed with bottles and cans and what she could have sworn was a jug of . . . mead? Must be Bronson's.

Bryce grabbed one of Nathalie's favorites—a cloudy, milky-tasting beer, heavy on the hops—and twisted off the top. "Briggs?"

"Officially released. Micah, the Autumn King, and the Oracle pored over every law and bylaw and still couldn't find a way around that loophole. Ruhn even had Declan run some of his fancy tech searches and found nothing. Sabine ordered the Scythe Moon Pack to watch Briggs tonight, along with some of the 33rd." The packs had mandatory nights off once a week, and this was the Pack of Devils'—no negotiating. Otherwise, Bryce knew Danika would be out there, watching Briggs's every move.

"So you're all in agreement," Bryce said. "At least that's good."

"Yeah, until Briggs blows something or someone up." Danika shook her head with disgust. "It's fucking bullshit."

Bryce studied her friend carefully. The tension around her mouth, her sweaty neck. "What's wrong?"

"Nothing's wrong."

The words were spoken too quickly to be believable. "Something's been eating at you. Shit like this thing with Briggs is big, but you always bounce back." Bryce narrowed her eyes. "What aren't you telling me?"

Danika's eyes gleamed. "Nothing." She swigged from her beer.

There was only one other answer. "I take it Sabine was in rare form this afternoon."

Danika just tore into her pizza.

Bryce swallowed two mouthfuls of beer, watching Danika blankly consider the teal cabinets above the counter, the paint chipping at the edges.

Her friend chewed slowly, then said around a mouthful of bread and cheese, "Sabine cornered me after the meeting. Right in the hall outside Micah's office. So everyone could hear her tell me that two CCU research students got killed near Luna's Temple last week during the blackout. My shift. My section. My fault."

Bryce winced. "It took a *week* to hear about this?"

"Apparently."

"Who killed them?"

Crescent City University students were *always* out in the Old Square, always causing trouble. Even as alums Bryce and Danika often bemoaned the fact that there wasn't a sky-high electric fence penning CCU students into their corner of the city. Just to keep them from puking and pissing all over the Old Square every Friday night to Sunday morning.

Danika drank again. "No clue who did it." A shiver, her caramel eyes darkening. "Even with their scents marking them as human, it took twenty minutes to identify who they were. They were ripped to shreds and partially eaten."

Bryce tried not to imagine it. "Motive?"

Danika's throat bobbed. "No idea, either. But Sabine told me in front of everyone exactly what she thought of such a public butchering happening on my watch."

Bryce asked, "What'd the Prime say about it?"

"Nothing," Danika said. "The old man fell asleep during the meeting, and Sabine didn't bother to wake him before cornering me." It would be soon now, everyone said—only a matter of a year or two until the current Prime of the wolves, nearly four hundred years old, had his Sailing across the Istros to the Bone Quarter for his final sleep. There was no way the black boat would tip for him during the final rite—no way his soul would be deemed unworthy and given to the river. He'd be welcomed into the Under-King's realm, granted access to its mist-veiled shores . . . and then Sabine's reign would begin.

Gods spare them all.

"It's not your fault, you know," Bryce said, flipping open the cardboard lids of the two closest pizza boxes. Sausage, pepperoni, and meatball in one. The other held cured meats and stinky cheeses—Bronson's choice, no doubt.

"I know," Danika muttered, draining the last of her beer, clunking the bottle in the sink, and rooting around in the fridge for another. Every muscle in her lean body seemed taut—on a hair trigger. She slammed the fridge shut and leaned against it. Danika didn't meet Bryce's eyes as she breathed, "I was three blocks away that night. *Three*. And I didn't hear or see or smell them being shredded."

Bryce became aware of the silence from the other room. Keen hearing in both human and wolf form meant endless, *entitled* eavesdropping.

They could finish this conversation later.

Bryce flipped open the rest of the pizza boxes, surveying the culinary landscape. "Shouldn't you put them out of their misery and let them get a bite before you demolish the rest?"

She'd had the pleasure of witnessing Danika eat three large pies in one sitting. In this sort of mood, Danika might very well break her record and hit four.

"Please let us eat," begged Bronson's deep, rumbling voice from the other room.

Danika swigged from her beer. "Come get it, mongrels."

The wolves rushed in.

In the frenzy, Bryce was nearly flattened against the back wall of the kitchen, the monthly calendar pinned to it crumpling behind her.

Damn it—she loved that calendar: *Hottest Bachelors of Crescent City: Clothing-Optional Edition*. This month had the most gorgeous daemonaki she'd ever seen, his propped leg on a stool the only thing keeping *everything* from being shown. She smoothed out the new wrinkles in all the tan skin and muscles, the curling horns, and then turned to scowl at the wolves.

A step away, Danika stood among her pack like a stone in a river. She smirked at Bryce. "Any update on your hunt for the Horn?"

"No."

"Jesiba must be thrilled."

Bryce grimaced. "Overjoyed." She'd seen Jesiba for all of two minutes this afternoon before the sorceress threatened to turn Bryce into a donkey, and then vanished in a chauffeured sedan to the gods knew where. Maybe off on some errand for the Under-King and the dark House he ruled.

Danika grinned. "Don't you have that date with what's-his-face tonight?"

The question clanged through Bryce. "Shit. *Shit*. Yes." She winced at the kitchen clock. "In an hour."

Connor, taking an entire pizza box for himself, stiffened. He'd made his thoughts on Bryce's rich-ass boyfriend clear since the first date two months ago. Just as Bryce had made it perfectly clear she did not give a fuck about Connor's opinion regarding her love life.

Bryce took in his muscled back as Connor stalked out, rolling his broad shoulders. Danika frowned. She never missed a fucking thing.

"I need to get dressed," Bryce said, scowling. "And his name is Reid, and you know it."

A wolfish smile. "Reid's a stupid fucking name," Danika said.

"One, *I* think it's a hot name. And two, *Reid* is hot." Gods help her, Reid Redner was hot as Hel. Though the sex was . . . fine. Standard. She'd gotten off, but she'd really had to work for it. And not in the way she sometimes *liked* to work for it. More in the sense of *Slow down, Put that here, Can we switch positions?* But she'd slept with him only twice. And she told herself that it could take time to find the right rhythm with a partner. Even if . . .

Danika just said it. "If he grabs his phone to check his messages before his dick's barely out of you again, please have the self-respect to kick his balls across the room and come home to me."

"Fucking Hel, Danika!" Bryce hissed. "Say it a little gods-damn louder."

The wolves had gone silent. Even their munching had stopped. Then resumed just a decibel too loudly.

"At least he's got a good job," Bryce said to Danika, who crossed her slender arms—arms that hid tremendous, ferocious strength—and gave her a look. A look that said, *Yeah, one that Reid's daddy gave him.* Bryce added, "And at least he's not some psychotic alphahole who will demand a three-day sex marathon and then call me his mate, lock me in his house, and never let me out again." Which was why Reid—human, okay-at-sex Reid—was perfect.

"You could use a three-day sex marathon," Danika quipped.

"You're to blame for this, you know."

Danika waved a hand. "Yeah, yeah. My first and last mistake: setting you two up."

Danika knew Reid casually through the part-time security work she did for his father's business—a massive human-owned magitech company in the Central Business District. Danika claimed that the work was too boring to bother explaining, but paid well enough that she couldn't say no. And more than that—it was a job she *chose*. Not the life she'd been shoved into. So between her patrols and obligations with the Aux, Danika was often at the towering skyscraper in the CBD—pretending she had a shot at a normal life. It was unheard of for any Aux member to have a secondary job—for an Alpha, especially—but Danika made it work.

It didn't hurt that everyone wanted a piece of Redner Industries these days. Even Micah Domitus was a major investor in its cutting-edge experiments. It was nothing out of the ordinary, when the Governor invested in everything from tech to vineyards to schools, but since Micah was on Sabine's eternal shit list, pissing off her mother by working for a human company he supported was likely even better for Danika than the sense of free will and generous pay.

Danika and Reid had been in the same presentation one afternoon months ago—exactly when Bryce had been single and complaining constantly about it. Danika had given Bryce's number to Reid in a last-ditch effort to preserve her sanity.

Bryce smoothed a hand over her dress. "I need to change. Save me a slice."

"Aren't you going out for dinner?"

Bryce cringed. "Yeah. To one of those frilly spots—where they give you salmon mousse on a cracker and call it a meal."

Danika shuddered. "Definitely fill up before, then."

"A slice," Bryce said, pointing at Danika. "Remember my slice." She eyed the one remaining box and padded out of the kitchen.

The Pack of Devils were now all in human form—save for Zelda—pizza boxes balanced on knees or spread on the worn blue rug. Bronson was indeed swigging from the ceramic jug of mead, his brown eyes fixed on the nightly news broadcast. The news about Briggs's release—along with grainy footage of the human male being escorted out of the jail complex in a white jumpsuit—began blasting. Whoever held the remote quickly changed the channel to a documentary on the Black River delta.

Nathalie gave Bryce a shit-eating grin as she strode for her bedroom door at the opposite end of the living room. Oh, Bryce wouldn't live down that little tidbit about Reid's performance in the bedroom anytime soon. Especially when Nathalie was sure to make it a reflection on Bryce's skills.

"Don't even start," Bryce warned her. Nathalie clamped her lips together, like she could hardly keep the howl of wicked amusement contained. Her sleek black hair seemed to quiver with the effort of holding in her laughter, her onyx eyes near-glowing.

Bryce pointedly ignored Connor's heavy golden stare as he tracked her across the space.

Wolves. Gods-damned wolves shoving their noses into her business.

There would never be any mistaking them for humans, though their forms were nearly identical. Too tall, too muscled, too still. Even the way they tore into their pizzas, each movement deliberate and graceful, was a silent reminder of what they could do to anyone who crossed them.

Bryce walked over Zach's sprawled, long legs, and carefully avoided stepping on Zelda's snow-white tail, where she lay on the floor beside her brother. The twin white wolves, both slender and dark-haired in human form, were utterly terrifying when they shifted. *The Ghosts*—the whispered nickname followed them everywhere.

So, yeah. Bryce tried really hard not to step on Zelda's fluffy tail.

Thorne, at least, threw Bryce a sympathetic smile from where he sat in the half-rotted leather armchair near the television, his CCU sunball hat turned backward. He was the only other person in the apartment who understood how meddlesome the pack could be. And who cared as much about Danika's moods. About Sabine's ruthlessness.

It was a long shot for an Omega like Thorne to ever be noticed by an Alpha like Danika. Not that Thorne had ever so much as hinted at it to any of them. But Bryce saw it—the gravitational pull that seemed to happen whenever Danika and Thorne were in a room together, like they were two stars orbiting each other.

Mercifully, Bryce reached her bedroom without any comments

regarding her sort-of boyfriend's prowess, and shut the door behind her firmly enough to tell them all to fuck off.

She made it three steps toward her sagging green dresser before laughter barked through the apartment. It was silenced a moment later by a vicious, not-quite-human snarl. Deep and rumbling and utterly lethal.

Not Danika's snarl, which was like death incarnate, soft and husky and cold. This was Connor's. Full of heat and temper and feeling.

Bryce showered off the dust and grime that seemed to coat her whenever she made the fifteen-block walk between the apartment and the slim sandstone building that Griffin Antiquities occupied.

A few carefully placed pins erased the end-of-day limpness that usually plagued her heavy sheet of wine-red hair, and she hastily applied a fresh coat of mascara to bring some life back into her amber eyes. From shower to sliding on her black stiletto heels, it was a grand total of twenty minutes.

Proof, she realized, of how little she really cared about this date. She spent a gods-damned *hour* on her hair and makeup every morning. Not counting the thirty-minute shower to get herself gleaming, shaved, and moisturized. But twenty minutes? For dinner at the Pearl and Rose?

Yeah, Danika had a point. And Bryce knew the bitch was watching the clock, and would probably ask if the short prep time was reflective of how long, exactly, Reid could keep it going.

Bryce glared in the direction of the wolves beyond the door of her cozy bedroom before surveying the quiet haven around her. Every wall was bedecked in posters of legendary performances at the Crescent City Ballet. Once, she'd imagined herself up there among the lithe Vanir, exploding across the stage in turn after turn, or making audiences weep with an agonizing death scene. Once, she'd imagined there might be a spot for a half-human female on that stage.

Even being told, over and over, that she had the *wrong body type* hadn't stopped her from loving to dance. Hadn't stopped that heady rush seeing a dance performed live, or her taking amateur classes after work, or her following CCB's dancers the way Connor, Ithan, and Thorne followed sports teams. Nothing could ever stop her from craving that soaring sensation she found when she was dancing, whether in class or at a club or even on the gods-damned street.

Juniper, at least, hadn't been deterred. Had decided that she was in it for the long haul, that a faun *would* defy the odds and grace a stage built for Fae and nymphs and sylphs—and leave them all in her dust. She'd done it, too.

Bryce loosed a long sigh. Time to go. It was a twenty-minute walk to the Pearl and Rose, and in these heels, it'd take her twenty-five. No point in getting a taxi during the chaos and congestion of Thursday night in the Old Square when the car would just *sit* there.

She stabbed pearl studs into her ears, hoping half-heartedly that they'd add some class to what might be considered a somewhat scandalous dress. But she was twenty-three, and she might as well enjoy her generously curved figure. She gave her gold-dusted legs a little smile as she twisted in front of the full-length mirror propped against the wall to admire the slope of her ass in the skintight gray dress, the hint of text from that still-sore new tattoo peeking over the plunging back, before she stepped into the living room again.

Danika let out a wicked laugh that rumbled over the nature show the wolves were watching. "I bet fifty silver marks the bouncers don't let you through the doors looking like that."

Bryce flipped off her friend as the pack chuckled. "I'm sorry if I make you feel self-conscious about your bony ass, Danika."

Thorne barked a laugh. "At least Danika makes up for it with her winning personality."

Bryce smirked at the handsome Omega. "That must explain why I have a date and she hasn't been on one in . . . what's it now? Three years?"

Thorne winked, his blue eyes sliding toward Danika's scowling face. "Must be why."

Danika slouched in her chair and propped her bare feet on the coffee table. Each toenail was painted a different color. "It's only been two years," she muttered. "Assholes."

Bryce patted Danika's silken head as she passed. Danika nipped at her fingers, teeth flashing.

Bryce chuckled, entering the narrow kitchen. She pawed through the upper cabinets, glass rattling as she searched for the—

Ah. The gin.

She knocked back a shot. Then another.

"Rough night ahead?" Connor asked from where he leaned against the kitchen doorway, arms crossed over his muscular chest.

A drop of gin had landed on her chin. Bryce narrowly avoided wiping the sin-red lipstick off her mouth with the back of her wrist and instead opted for patting it away with a leftover napkin from the pizza place. Like a proper person.

That color should be called Blow Job Red, Danika had said the first time Bryce had worn it. *Because that's all any male will think about when you wear it.* Indeed, Connor's eyes had dipped right to her lips. So Bryce said as nonchalantly as she could, "You know I like to enjoy my Thursday nights. Why not kick it off early?"

She balanced on her toes as she put the gin back in the upper cupboard, the hem of her dress rising precariously high. Connor studied the ceiling as if it were immensely interesting, his gaze only snapping to hers as she settled on her feet again. In the other room, someone turned the volume on the television up to an apartment-rattling level.

Thank you, Danika.

Even wolf hearing couldn't sort through that cacophony to eavesdrop.

Connor's sensuous mouth twitched upward, but he remained in the doorway.

Bryce swallowed, wondering how gross it would be to chase away the burn of the gin with the beer she'd left warming on the counter.

Connor said, "Look. We've known each other a while . . ."

"Is this a rehearsed speech?"

He straightened, color staining his cheeks. The Second in the Pack of Devils, the most feared and lethal of all the Auxiliary units, was *blushing*. "No."

"That sounded like a rehearsed introduction to me."

"Can you let me ask you out, or do I need to get into a fight with you about my phrasing first?"

She snorted, but her guts twisted. "I don't date wolves."

Connor threw her a cocky grin. "Make an exception."

"No." But she smiled slightly.

Connor merely said with the unwavering arrogance that only an immortal predator could achieve, "You want me. I want you. It's been that way for a while, and playing with these human males hasn't done a damn thing to make you forget that, has it?"

No, it hadn't. But she said, her voice mercifully calm despite her thundering heart, "Connor, I'm not going out with you. Danika is bossy enough. I don't need another wolf, especially a *male* wolf, trying to run my life. I don't need any more Vanir shoving into my business."

His golden eyes dimmed. "I'm not your father."

He didn't mean Randall.

She shoved off the counter, marching toward him. And the apartment door beyond. She was going to be late. "That has nothing to do with this—with you. My answer is no."

Connor didn't move, and she halted mere inches away. Even in heels, even though she fell on the taller side of average height, he towered over her. Dominated the entire space just by breathing.

Like any alphahole would. Like what her Fae father had done to nineteen-year-old Ember Quinlan, when he'd pursued her, seduced her, tried to keep her, and gone so far into possessive territory that the moment Ember had realized she was carrying his child—carrying *Bryce*—she ran before he could scent it and lock her up in his villa in FiRo until she grew too old to interest him.

Which was something Bryce didn't let herself consider. Not after the blood tests had been done and she'd walked out of the medwitch's office knowing that she'd taken after her Fae father in more ways than the red hair and pointed ears.

She would have to bury her mother one day, bury Randall, too. Which was utterly expected, if you were a human. But the fact that she'd go on living for a few more centuries, with only photos and videos to remind her of their voices and faces, made her stomach twist.

She should have had a third shot of gin.

Connor remained unmoving in the doorway. "One date won't send me into a territorial hissy fit. It doesn't even have to be a date. Just . . . pizza," he finished, glancing at the stacked boxes.

"You and I go out plenty." They did—on nights when Danika was called in to meet with Sabine or the other Aux commanders, he often brought over food, or he met up with her at one of the many restaurants lining the apartment's lively block. "If it's not a date, then how is it different?"

"It'd be a trial run. For a date," Connor said through his teeth.

She lifted a brow. "A date to decide if I want to date you?"

"You're impossible." He pushed off the doorjamb. "See you later."

Smiling to herself, she trailed him out of the kitchen, cringing at the monstrously loud television the wolves were all watching very, *very* intently.

Even Danika knew there were limits to how far she could push Connor without serious consequences.

For a heartbeat, Bryce debated grabbing the Second by the shoulder and explaining that he'd be better off finding a nice, sweet wolf who wanted to have a litter of pups, and that he didn't really want someone who was ten kinds of fucked-up, still liked to party until she was no better than a puking-in-an-alley CCU student, and wasn't entirely sure if she *could* love someone, not when Danika was all she really needed anyway.

But she didn't grab Connor, and by the time Bryce scooped her keys from the bowl beside the door, he'd slumped onto the couch—again, in *her* spot—and was staring pointedly at the screen. "Bye," she said to no one in particular.

Danika met her gaze from across the room, her eyes still wary but faintly amused. She winked. "Light it up, bitch."

"Light it up, asshole," Bryce replied, the farewell sliding off her tongue with the ease of years of usage.

But it was Danika's added "Love you" as Bryce slipped out into the grimy hallway that made her hesitate with her hand on the knob.

It'd taken Danika a few years to say those words, and she still used them sparingly. Danika had initially hated it when Bryce said them to her—even when Bryce explained that she'd spent most of her life saying it, just in case it *was* the last time. In case she wouldn't get to say goodbye to the people who mattered most. And it had taken one of their more fucked-up adventures—a trashed motorcycle, and literally having guns pointed at their heads—to get Danika to utter the words, but at least she now said them. Sometimes.

Forget Briggs's release. Sabine must have really done a number on Danika.

Bryce's heels clacked on the worn tile floor as she headed for the stairs at the end of the hall. Maybe she should cancel on Reid. She could grab some buckets of ice cream from the corner market and cuddle in bed with Danika while they watched their favorite absurd comedies.

Maybe she'd call up Fury and see if she could pay a little visit to Sabine.

But—she'd never ask that of Fury. Fury kept her professional shit out of their lives, and they knew better than to ask too many questions. Only Juniper could get away with it.

Honestly, it made no sense that any of them were friends: the future Alpha of all wolves, an assassin for high-paying clients waging war across the sea, a stunningly talented dancer and the only faun *ever* to grace the stage of the Crescent City Ballet, and . . . her.

Bryce Quinlan. Assistant to a sorceress. Would-be, *wrong-body-type* dancer. Chronic dater of preening, breakable human men who had no idea what to do with her. Let alone what to do with Danika, if they ever got far enough into the dating crucible.

Bryce clomped down the stairs, scowling at one of the orbs of firstlight that cast the crumbling gray-blue paint in flickering relief. The landlord went as cheap as possible on the firstlight, likely siphoning it off the grid rather than paying the city for it like everyone else.

Everything in this apartment building was a piece of shit, to be honest.

Danika could afford better. Bryce certainly couldn't. And Danika knew her well enough not to even suggest that she alone pay for one of the high-rise, glossy apartments by the river's edge or in the CBD. So after graduation, they'd only looked at places Bryce could swing with her paycheck—this particular shithole being the least miserable of them.

Sometimes, Bryce wished she'd accepted her monstrous father's money—wished she hadn't decided to develop some semblance of morals at the exact moment the creep had offered her mountains of gold marks in exchange for her eternal silence about him. At least then she'd currently be lounging by some sky-high pool deck, ogling oiled-up angels as they swaggered past, and not avoiding the letch of a janitor who leered at her chest anytime she had to complain about the trash chute being blocked yet again.

The glass door at the bottom of the stairwell led onto the night-darkened street, already packed with tourists, revelers, and bleary-eyed residents trying to squeeze their way home through the rowdy crowds after a long, hot summer day. A draki male clad in a suit and tie rushed past, messenger bag bobbing at his hip as he wove his way around a family of some sort of equine shifters—perhaps horses, judging by their scents full of open skies and green fields—all so busy snapping photos of everything that they remained oblivious to anyone trying to get somewhere.

At the corner, a pair of bored malakim clad in the black armor of the 33rd kept their wings tucked in tight to their powerful bodies, no doubt to avoid any harried commuter or drunk idiot touching them. Touch an angel's wings without permission and you'd be lucky to lose just a hand.

Firmly shutting the glass door behind her, Bryce soaked in the tangle of sensations that was this ancient, vibrant city: the dry summer heat that threatened to bake her very bones; the honk of car horns slicing through the steady hiss and dribble of music leaking from the revel halls; the wind off the Istros River, three blocks away, rustling the swaying palms and cypresses; the hint of brine from the nearby turquoise sea; the seductive, night-soft smell of the crawling jasmine wrapped around the iron park fence nearby; the tang of puke and piss and stale beer; the beckoning, smoky spices crusting the slow-roasting lamb at the vendor's cart on the corner . . . It all hit her in one awakening kiss.

Trying not to snap her ankles on the cobblestones, Bryce breathed in the nightly offering of Crescent City, drank it deep, and vanished down the teeming street.

4

The Pearl and Rose was everything Bryce hated about this city.

But at least Danika now owed her fifty silver marks.

The bouncers had let her stride past them, up the three steps, and through the open bronze-plated doors of the restaurant.

But even fifty silver marks wouldn't put so much as a dent in paying for this meal. No, this would be firmly in the *gold* zone.

Reid could certainly afford it. Given the size of his bank account, he likely wouldn't even glance at the check before handing over his black card.

Seated at a table in the heart of the gilded dining room, under the crystal chandeliers dangling from the intricately painted ceiling, Bryce went through two glasses of water and half a bottle of wine while she waited.

Twenty minutes in, her phone buzzed in her black silk clutch. If Reid was canceling on her, she'd kill him. There was no fucking way she could afford to pay for the wine—not without having to give up dance classes for the next month. Two months, actually.

But the messages weren't from Reid, and Bryce read them three times before chucking her phone back in her purse and pouring another glass of very, very expensive wine.

Reid was rich *and* he was late. He owed her.

Especially since the upper echelons of Crescent City were entertaining themselves by sneering at her dress, the skin on display, the Fae ears but clearly human body.

Half-breed—she could nearly hear the hateful term as they thought it. They considered her a lowly worker at best. Prey and dumpster fodder at worst.

Bryce took out her phone and read the messages a fourth time. Connor had written, *You know I'm shit with talking. But what I wanted to say—before you tried to get into a fight with me instead, by the way—was that I think it's worth it. You and me. Giving us a shot.*

He'd added: *I'm crazy about you. I don't want anyone else. I haven't for a long while. One date. If it doesn't work, then we'll deal with it. But just give me a chance. Please.*

Bryce was still staring at the messages, her head spinning from all that gods-damned wine, when Reid finally appeared. Forty-five minutes late.

"Sorry, babe," he said, leaning in to kiss her cheek before sliding onto his chair. His charcoal-gray suit remained immaculate, his golden skin glowing above the collar of his white shirt. Not one dark brown hair on his head was out of place.

Reid had the easy manners of someone brought up with money, education, and no doors locked to his desires. The Redners were one of the few human families who had risen into Vanir high society—and dressed for the part. Reid was meticulous about his appearance, down to the very last detail. Every tie he wore, she'd learned, was selected to bring out the green in his hazel eyes. His suits were always impeccably cut to his toned body. She might have called him vain, had she not put such consideration into her own outfits. Had she not known that Reid worked with a personal trainer for the exact reason that she kept dancing—beyond her love for it—making sure her body was primed for when its strength might be needed to escape any would-be predator hunting the streets.

Since the day the Vanir had crawled through the Northern Rift and overtaken Midgard eons ago, an event historians called the Crossing, running was the best option if a Vanir decided to make a meal of you. That is, if you didn't have a gun or bombs or any of the horrid things people like Philip Briggs had developed to kill even a long-lived, quick-healing creature.

She often wondered about it: what it had been like before this planet had found itself occupied by creatures from so many different worlds, all of them far more advanced and *civilized* than this one, when it was just humans and ordinary animals. Even their calendar system hearkened to the Crossing, and the time before and after it: H.E. and V.E.—*Human Era* and *Vanir Era*.

Reid lifted his dark brows at the mostly empty bottle of wine. "Nice choice."

Forty-five minutes. Without a call or a message to tell her he'd be late.

Bryce gritted her teeth. "Something came up at work?"

Reid shrugged, scanning the restaurant for high-ranking officials to hobnob with. As the son of a man who had his name displayed in twenty-foot letters on three buildings in the CBD, people usually lined up to chat with him. "Some of the malakim are restless about developments in the Pangeran conflict. They needed reassurance their investments were still sound. The call ran long."

The Pangeran conflict—the fighting Briggs so badly wanted to bring to this territory. The wine that had gone to her head eddied into an oily pool in her gut. "The angels think the war might spread here?"

Spying no one of interest in the restaurant, Reid flipped open his leather-bound menu. "No. The Asteri wouldn't let that happen."

"The Asteri let it happen over there."

His lips twitched downward. "It's a complicated issue, Bryce."

Conversation over. She let him go back to studying the menu.

Reports of the territory across the Haldren Sea were grim: the human resistance was prepared to wipe themselves out rather than submit to the Asteri and their "elected" Senate's rule. For forty years now, the war had raged in the vast Pangeran territory, wrecking cities, creeping toward the stormy sea. Should the conflict cross it, Crescent City, sitting on Valbara's southeastern coast—midway up a peninsula called the Hand for the shape of the arid, mountainous land that jutted out—would be one of the first places in its path.

Fury refused to talk about what she saw over there. What she did over there. What side she fought for. Most Vanir did not find a challenge to more than fifteen thousand years of their reign amusing.

Most humans did not find fifteen thousand years of near-slavery, of being prey and food and whores, to be all that amusing, either. Never mind that in recent centuries, the Imperial Senate had granted humans more rights—with the Asteri's approval, of course. The fact remained that anyone who stepped out of line was thrown right back to where they'd started: literal slaves to the Republic.

The slaves, at least, existed mostly in Pangera. A few lived in Crescent City, namely among the warrior-angels in the 33rd, the Governor's personal legion, marked by the *SPQM* slave tattoo on their wrists. But they blended in, for the most part.

Crescent City, for all that its wealthiest were grade A assholes, was still a melting pot. One of the rare places where being a human didn't necessarily mean a lifetime of menial labor. Though it didn't entitle you to much else.

A dark-haired, blue-eyed Fae female caught Bryce's cursory glance around the room, her boy toy across the table marking her as some sort of noble.

Bryce had never decided whom she hated more: the winged malakim or the Fae. The Fae, probably, whose considerable magic and grace made them think they were allowed to do what they pleased, with anyone they pleased. A trait shared by many members of the House of Sky and Breath: the swaggering angels, the lofty sylphs, and the simmering elementals.

House of Shitheads and Bastards, Danika always called them. Though her own allegiance to the House of Earth and Blood might have shaded her opinion a bit—especially when the shifters and Fae were forever at odds.

Born of two Houses, Bryce had been forced to yield her allegiance to the House of Earth and Blood as part of accepting the civitas rank her father had gotten her. It had been the price paid for accepting the coveted citizen status: he'd petition for full citizenship, but she would have to claim Sky and Breath as her House.

She'd resented it, resented the bastard for making her choose, but even her mother had seen that the benefits outweighed the costs.

Not that there were many advantages or protections for humans within the House of Earth and Blood, either. Certainly not for the young man seated with the Fae female.

Beautiful, blond, no more than twenty, he was likely a tenth of his Fae companion's age. The tanned skin of his wrists held no hint of the four-lettered slave tattoo. So he had to be with her through his own free will, then—or desire for whatever she offered: sex, money, influence. It was a fool's bargain, though. She'd use him until she was bored, or he grew too old, and then dump his ass at the curb, still craving those Fae riches.

Bryce inclined her head to the noblewoman, who bared her too-white teeth at the insolence. The Fae female was beautiful—but most of the Fae were.

She found Reid watching, a frown on his handsome face. He shook his head—at *her*—and resumed reading the menu.

Bryce sipped her wine. Signaled the waiter to bring over another bottle.

I'm crazy about you.

Connor wouldn't tolerate the sneering, the whispering. Neither would Danika. Bryce had witnessed *both* of them rip into the stupid assholes who'd hissed slurs at her, or who mistook her for one of the many half-Vanir females who scraped a living in the Meat Market by selling their bodies.

Most of those women didn't get the chance to complete the Drop—either because they didn't make it to the threshold of maturity or because they got the short end of the stick with a mortal life span. There were predators, both born and trained, who used the Meat Market as a personal hunting ground.

Bryce's phone buzzed, right as the waiter finally made his way over, fresh bottle of wine in hand. Reid frowned again, his disapproval heavy enough that she refrained from reading the message until she'd ordered her beef-with-cheese-foam sandwich.

Danika had written, *Dump the limp-dicked bastard and put Connor out of his misery. A date with him won't kill you. He's been waiting years, Bryce. Years. Give me something to smile about tonight.*

Bryce cringed as she shoved her phone back into her bag. She looked up to find Reid on his own phone, thumbs flying, his chiseled features illuminated by the dim screen. Their invention five decades ago had occurred right in Redner Industries' famed tech lab, and vaulted the company into unprecedented fortune. A new era of linking the world, everyone claimed. Bryce thought they just gave people an excuse not to make eye contact. Or be bad dates.

"Reid," she said. He just held up a finger.

Bryce tapped a red nail on the base of her wineglass. She kept her nails long—and took a daily elixir to keep them strong. Not as effective as talons or claws, but they could do some damage. At least enough to potentially get away from an assailant.

"Reid," she said again. He kept typing, and looked up only when the first course appeared.

It was indeed a salmon mousse. Over a crisp of bread, and encaged in some latticework of curling green plants. Small ferns, perhaps. She swallowed her laugh.

"Go ahead and dig in," Reid said distantly, typing again. "Don't wait for me."

"One bite and I'll be done," she muttered, lifting her fork but wondering how the Hel to eat the thing. No one around them used their fingers, but . . . The Fae female sneered again.

Bryce set down the fork. Folded her napkin into a neat square before she rose. "I'm going."

"All right," Reid said, eyes fixed on his screen. He clearly thought she was going to the bathroom. She could feel the eyes of a well-dressed angel at the next table travel up her expanse of bare leg, then heard the chair groan as he leaned back to admire the view of her ass.

Exactly why she kept her nails strong.

But she said to Reid, "No—I'm leaving. Thank you for dinner."

That made him look up. "What? Bryce, sit down. Eat."

As if his being late, being on the phone, weren't part of this. As if she were just something he needed to feed before he fucked. She said clearly, "This isn't working out."

His mouth tightened. "Excuse me?"

She doubted he'd ever been dumped. She said with a sweet smile, "Bye, Reid. Good luck with work."

"Bryce."

But she had enough gods-damned self-respect not to let him explain, not to accept sex that was merely okay basically in exchange for meals at restaurants she could never afford, and a man who had indeed rolled off her and gotten right back on that phone. So she swiped the bottle of wine and stepped away from the table, but not toward the exit.

She went up to the sneering Fae female and her human plaything and said in a cool voice that would have made even Danika back away, "Like what you see?"

The female gave her a sweeping glance, from Bryce's heels to her red hair to the bottle of wine dangling from her fingers. The Fae female shrugged, setting the black stones in her long dress sparkling. "I'll pay a gold mark to watch you two." She inclined her head to the human at her table.

He offered Bryce a smile, his vacant face suggesting he was soaring high on some drug.

Bryce smirked at the female. "I didn't know Fae females had gotten so cheap. Word on the street used to be that you'd pay us gold by the armful to pretend you're not lifeless as Reapers between the sheets."

The female's tan face went white. Glossy, flesh-shredding nails snagged on the tablecloth. The man across from her didn't so much as flinch.

Bryce put a hand on the man's shoulder—in comfort or to piss off the female, she wasn't sure. She squeezed lightly, again inclining her head toward the female, and strode out.

She swigged from the bottle of wine and flipped off the preening hostess on her way through the bronze doors. Then snatched a handful of matchbooks from the bowl atop the stand, too.

Reid's breathless apologies to the noble drifted behind her as Bryce stepped onto the hot, dry street.

Well, shit. It was nine o'clock, she was decently dressed, and if she went back to that apartment, she'd pace around until Danika bit her head off. And the wolves would shove their noses into her business, which she didn't want to discuss with them *at all*.

Which left one option. Her favorite option, fortunately.

Fury picked up on the first ring. "What."

"Are you on this side of the Haldren or the wrong one?"

"I'm in Five Roses." The flat, cool voice was laced with a hint of amusement—practically outright laughter, coming from Fury. "But I'm not watching television with the pups."

"Who the Hel would want to do that?"

A pause on the line. Bryce leaned against the pale stone exterior of the Pearl and Rose. "I thought you had a date with what's-his-face."

"You and Danika are the worst, you know that?"

She practically heard Fury's wicked smile through the line. "I'll meet you at the Raven in thirty minutes. I need to finish up a job."

"Go easy on the poor bastard."

"That's not what I was paid to do."

The line went dead. Bryce swore and prayed Fury wouldn't reek of blood when she got to their preferred club. She dialed another number.

Juniper was breathless when she picked up on the fifth ring, right before it went to audiomail. She must have been in the studio, practicing after-hours. As she always did. As Bryce loved to do whenever she had a spare moment herself. To dance and dance and dance, the world fading into nothing but music and breath and sweat. "Oh, you dumped him, didn't you?"

"Did motherfucking Danika send a message to *everyone*?"

"No," the sweet, lovely faun replied, "but you've been on your date for only an hour. Since the recap calls usually happen the morning after . . ."

"We're going to the Raven," Bryce snapped. "Be there in thirty." She hung up before Juniper's quicksilver laugh set her cursing.

Oh, she'd find a way to punish Danika for telling them. Even though she knew it'd been meant as a warning, to prepare them for any picking up the pieces, if necessary. Just as Bryce had checked in with Connor regarding Danika's state earlier that evening.

The White Raven was only a five-minute walk away, right in the heart of the Old Square. Which left Bryce with enough time to either really, truly get into trouble, or face what she'd been avoiding for an hour now.

She opted for trouble.

Lots of trouble, enough to empty out the seven hard-earned gold marks in her purse as she handed them over to a grinning draki female, who slipped everything Bryce asked for into her waiting palm. The female had tried to sell her on some new party drug—*Synth will make you feel like a god*, she said—but the thirty gold marks for a single dose had been well above Bryce's pay grade.

She was still left with five minutes. Standing across from the White Raven, the club still teeming with revelers despite Briggs's failed plan to blast it apart, Bryce pulled out her phone and opened the thread with Connor. She'd bet all the money she'd just blown on mirthroot that he was checking his phone every two seconds.

Cars crawled past, the bass of their sound systems thumping over the cobblestones and cypresses, windows down to reveal passengers eager to start their Thursday: drinking; smoking; singing along to the music; messaging friends, dealers, whoever might get them into one of the dozen clubs that lined Archer Street. Queues already snaked from the doors, including the Raven's. Vanir peered up in anticipation at the white marble facade, well-dressed pilgrims waiting at the gates of a temple.

The Raven was just that: a temple. Or it had been. A building now encased the ruins, but the dance floor remained the original, ancient stones of some long-forgotten god's temple, and the carved stone pillars throughout still stood from that time. To dance inside was to worship that nameless god, hinted at in the age-worn carvings of satyrs and fauns drinking and dancing and fucking amid grapevines. A temple to pleasure—that's what it had once been. And what it had become again.

A cluster of young mountain-lion shifters prowled past, a few twisting back to growl in invitation. Bryce ignored them and sidled over to an alcove at the left of the Raven's service doors. She leaned against the slick stone, tucked the wine into the crook of her arm, braced a foot on the wall behind her as she bobbed her head to the music pouring out of a nearby car, and finally typed: *Pizza. Saturday night at six. If you're late, it's over.*

Instantly, Connor began typing in reply. Then the bubble paused. Then started again.

Then finally, the message came.

I'll never keep you waiting.

She rolled her eyes and wrote, *Don't make promises you can't keep.*

More typing, deleting, typing. Then, *You mean it—about the pizza?*

Do I look like I'm joking, Connor?

You looked delicious when you left the apartment.

Heat curled in her, and she bit her lip. Charming, arrogant bastard. *Tell Danika I'm going to the Raven with Juniper and Fury. I'll see you in two days.*

Done. What about what's-his-face?

REID is officially dumped.

Good. I was getting worried I'd have to kill him.

Her gut churned.

He quickly added, *Kidding, Bryce. I won't go alphahole on you, I promise.*

Before she could answer, her phone buzzed again.

Danika, this time. *HOW DARE YOU GO TO THE RAVEN WITHOUT ME. TRAITOR.*

Bryce snorted. *Enjoy Pack Night, loser.*

DO NOT HAVE FUN WITHOUT ME. I FORBID YOU.

She knew that as much as it killed Danika to stay in, she wouldn't leave the pack. Not on the one night they all had together, the night they used to keep the bonds between them strong. Not after this shitstorm of a day. And especially not while Briggs was on the loose, with a reason to get back at the whole Pack of Devils.

That loyalty was why they loved Danika, why they fought so fiercely for her, went to the mat for her again and again when Sabine publicly wondered if her daughter was worthy of the responsibilities and status as second in line. The power hierarchy among the wolves of Crescent City was dictated by dominance alone—but the three-generation lineage that made up the Prime of the wolves, Prime Apparent, and whatever Danika was (the Apparent Prime Apparent?) was a rarity. Powerful, ancient bloodlines was the usual explanation.

Danika had spent countless hours looking into the history of the dominant shifter packs in other cities—why lions had come to rule in Hilene, why tigers oversaw Korinth, why falcons reigned in Oia. Whether the dominance that determined the Prime Alpha status passed through families or skipped around. Non-predatory shifters could head up a city's Aux, but it was rare. Honestly, most of it bored Bryce to tears. And if Danika had ever learned why the Fendyr family claimed such a large share of the dominance pie, she'd never told Bryce.

Bryce wrote back to Connor, *Good luck handling Danika.*

He simply replied, *She's telling me the same about you.*

Bryce was about to put her phone away when the screen flashed again. Connor had added, *You won't regret this. I've had a long while to figure out all the ways I'm going to spoil you. All the fun we're going to have.*

Stalker. But she smiled.

Go enjoy yourself. I'll see you in a few days. Message me when you're home safe.

She reread the conversation twice because she really was an absolute fucking loser, and was debating asking Connor to skip waiting and just meet her *now*, when something cool and metal pressed against her throat.

"And you're dead," crooned a female voice.

Bryce yelped, trying to calm the heart that had gone from stupid-giddy to stupid-scared in the span of one beat.

"Don't fucking *do* that," she hissed at Fury as the female lowered the knife from Bryce's throat and sheathed it across her back.

"Don't be a walking target," Fury said coolly, her long onyx hair tied high in a ponytail that brought out the sharp lines of her light brown face. She scanned the line into the Raven, her deep-set chestnut eyes marking everything and promising death to anyone who crossed her. But beneath that . . . mercifully, the black leather leggings, skintight velvet top, and ass-kicking boots did *not* smell of blood. Fury gave Bryce a once-over. "You barely put on any makeup. That little human should have taken one look at you and known you were about to dump his ass."

"He was too busy on his phone to notice."

Fury glanced pointedly at Bryce's own phone, still clenched in a death grip in her hand. "Danika's going to nail your balls to the wall when I tell her I caught you distracted like that."

"It's her own damn fault," Bryce snapped.

A sharp smile was her only response. Bryce knew Fury was Vanir, but she had no idea what kind. No idea what House Fury belonged to, either. Asking wasn't polite, and Fury, aside from her preternatural speed, grace, and reflexes, had never revealed another form, nor any inkling of magic beyond the most basic.

But she was a civitas. A full citizen, which meant she had to be something they deemed worthy. Given her skill set, the House of Flame and Shadow was the likeliest place for her—even if Fury was certainly not a daemonaki, vampyr, or even a wraith. Definitely not a witch-turned-sorceress like Jesiba, either. Or a necromancer, since her gifts seemed to be taking life, not illegally bringing it back.

"Where's the leggy one?" Fury asked, taking the wine bottle from Bryce and swigging as she scanned the teeming clubs and bars along Archer Street.

"Hel if I know," Bryce said. She winked at Fury and held up the plastic bag of mirthroot, jostling the twelve rolled black cigarettes. "I got us some goodies."

Fury's grin was a flash of red lips and straight white teeth. She reached into the back pocket of her leggings and held up a small bag of white powder that glittered with a fiery iridescence in the glow of the streetlamp. "So did I."

Bryce squinted at the powder. "Is that what the dealer just tried to sell me?"

Fury went still. "What'd she say it was?"

"Some new party drug—gives you a godlike high, I don't know. Super expensive."

Fury frowned. "Synth? Stay away from it. That's some bad shit."

"All right." She trusted Fury enough to heed the warning. Bryce peered at the powder Fury still held in her hand. "I can't take anything that makes me hallucinate for days, please. I have work tomorrow." When she had to at least pretend she had some idea how to find that gods-damned Horn.

Fury tucked the bag into her black bra. She swigged from the wine again before passing it back to Bryce. "Jesiba won't be able to scent it on you, don't worry."

Bryce linked elbows with the slender assassin. "Then let's go make our ancestors roll over in their graves."

5

Going on a date with Connor in a few days didn't mean she had to behave.

So within the inner sanctum of the White Raven, Bryce savored every delight it offered.

Fury knew the owner, Riso, either through work or whatever the Hel she did in her personal life, and as such, they never had to wait in line. The flamboyant butterfly shifter always left a booth open for them.

None of the smiling, colorfully dressed waiters who brought over their drinks so much as blinked at the lines of glittering white powder Fury arranged with a sweep of her hand or the plumes of smoke that rippled from Bryce's parted lips as she tipped her head back to the domed, mirrored ceiling and laughed.

Juniper had a studio class at dawn, so she abstained from the powder and smoke and booze. But it didn't stop her from sneaking away for a good twenty minutes with a broad-chested Fae male who took in the dark brown skin, the exquisite face and curling black hair, the long legs that ended in delicate hooves, and practically begged on his knees for the faun to touch him.

Bryce reduced herself into the pulsing beat of the music, to the euphoria glittering through her blood faster than an angel diving out of the sky, to the sweat sliding down her body as she writhed on the ancient dance floor. She would barely be able to walk tomorrow, would have half a brain, but holy shit—*more, more, more.*

Laughing, she swooped over the low-lying table in their private booth between two half-crumbling pillars; laughing, she arched away, a red nail releasing its hold on one nostril as she sagged against the dark leather bench; laughing, she knocked back water and elderberry wine and stumbled again into the dancing throng.

Life was good. Life was fucking *good*, and she couldn't godsdamn wait to make the Drop with Danika and do this until the earth crumbled into dust.

She found Juniper dancing amid a pack of sylph females celebrating a friend's successful Drop. Their silvery heads were adorned with circlets of neon glow sticks chock-full of their friend's designated allotment of her own firstlight, which she'd generated when she successfully completed the Drop. Juniper had managed to swipe a glow-stick halo for herself, and her hair shone with blue light as she extended her hands to Bryce, their fingers linking as they danced.

Bryce's blood pulsed in time to the music, as if she had been crafted just for this: the moment when she *became* the notes and rhythm and the bass, when she became song given form. Juniper's glittering eyes told Bryce that she understood, had always understood the particular freedom and joy and unleashing that came from dancing. Like their bodies were so full of sound they could barely contain it, could barely stand it, and only *dance* could express it, ease it, honor it.

Males and females gathered to watch, their lust coating Bryce's skin like sweat. Juniper's every movement matched hers without so much as a lick of hesitation, as if they were question and answer, sun and moon.

Quiet, pretty Juniper Andromeda—the exhibitionist. Even dancing in the sacred, ancient heart of the Raven, she was sweet and mild, but she shone.

Or maybe that was all the lightseeker Bryce had ingested up her nose.

Her hair clung to her sweaty neck, her feet were utterly numb thanks to the steep angle of her heels, her throat was ravaged from screaming along to the songs that blasted through the club.

She managed to shoot a few messages to Danika—and one video, because she could barely read any of what was coming in anyway.

She'd be so royally fucked if she showed up at work tomorrow unable to *read*.

Time slowed and bled. Here, dancing among the pillars and upon the timeworn stones of the temple that had been reborn, no time existed at all.

Maybe she'd live here.

Quit her job at the gallery and live in the club. They could hire her to dance in one of the steel cages dangling from the glass ceiling high above the temple ruins that made up the dance floor. They certainly wouldn't spew bullshit about a *wrong body type*. No, they'd pay her to do what she loved, what made her come alive like nothing else.

It seemed like a reasonable enough plan, Bryce thought as she stumbled down her own street later with no recollection of leaving the Raven, saying goodbye to her friends, or of how the Hel she'd even gotten here. Taxi? She'd blown all her marks on the drugs. Unless someone had paid . . .

Whatever. She'd think about it tomorrow. If she could even sleep. She wanted to stay awake, to dance for-gods-damn-*ever*. Only . . . oh, her feet fucking *hurt*. And they were near-black and *sticky*—

Bryce paused outside her building door and groaned as she unstrapped her heels and gathered them in a hand. A code. Her building had a code to get in.

Bryce contemplated the keypad as if it'd open a pair of eyes and tell her. Some buildings did that.

Shit. Shiiit. She pulled out her phone, the glaring screen light burning her eyes. Squinting, she could make out a few dozen message alerts. They blurred, her eyes trying and failing to focus enough to read one single coherent letter. Even if she somehow managed to call Danika, her friend would rip her head off.

The screech of the building buzzer would piss off Danika even more. Bryce cringed, hopping from foot to foot.

What was the code? The code, the code, the cooooode . . .

Oh, there it was. Tucked into a back pocket of her mind.

She cheerfully punched in the numbers, then heard the buzz as the lock opened with a faint, tinny sound.

She scowled at the reek of the stairwell. That gods-damned janitor. She'd kick his ass. Impale him with these useless, cheap stilettos that had wrecked her feet—

Bryce set a bare foot on the stairs and winced. This was going to hurt. Walking-on-glass hurt.

She let her heels clunk to the tile floor, whispering a fervent promise to find them tomorrow, and gripped the black-painted metal banister with both hands. Maybe she could straddle the banister and scoot herself up the stairs.

Gods, it stunk. What did the people in this building *eat*? Or, for that matter, *who* did they eat? Hopefully not wasted, stupid-high, half-Fae females who couldn't manage to walk up the stairs.

If Fury had laced the lightseeker with something else, she'd fucking *kill* her.

Snorting at the idea of even attempting to kill the infamous Fury Axtar, Bryce hauled herself up the stairs, step by step.

She debated sleeping on the second-level landing, but the stench was overwhelming.

Maybe she'd get lucky and Connor would still be at the apartment. And then she'd *really* get lucky.

Gods, she wanted good sex. No-holds-barred, scream-your-lungs-out sex. Break-the-bed sex. She knew Connor would be like that. More than that. It'd go far beyond the physical with him. It might honestly melt whatever was left of her mind after tonight.

It was why she'd been a coward, why she'd avoided thinking about it from the moment he'd leaned in her doorway five years ago, having come to say hi to Danika and meet her new roommate, and they'd just . . . stared at each other.

Having Connor living four doors down freshman year had been

the worst sort of temptation. But Danika had given the order to stay away until Bryce approached *him*, and even though they hadn't yet formed the Pack of Devils, Connor obeyed. It seemed Danika had lifted the order tonight.

Lovely, wicked Danika. Bryce smiled as she half crawled onto the third-floor landing, found her balance, and dug her keys out of her purse—which she'd managed to hold on to by some miracle. She took a few swaying steps down the hall they shared with one other apartment.

Oh, Danika was going to be so pissed. *So* pissed that Bryce had not only had fun without her, but that she'd gotten so wasted she couldn't remember how to read. Or the code to the building.

The flickering firstlight stung her eyes enough that she again squinted them to near-darkness and staggered down the hall. She should shower, if she could remember how to operate the handles. Wash off her filthy, numb feet.

Especially after she stepped in a cold puddle beneath some dripping ceiling pipe. She shuddered, bracing a hand on the wall, but kept staggering ahead.

Fuck. Too many drugs. Even her Fae blood couldn't clear them out fast enough.

But there was her door. Keys. Right—she had them in her hand already.

There were six. Which one was hers? One opened the gallery; one opened the various tanks and cages in the archives; one opened Syrinx's crate; one was to the chain on her scooter; one was *to* her scooter . . . and one was to the door. This door.

The brass keys tinkled and swayed, shining in the firstlights, then blending with the painted metal of the hall. They slipped out of her slackening fingers, clanking on the tile.

"Fuuuuuuck." The word was a long exhale.

Bracing a hand on the doorframe to keep from falling clean on her ass, Bryce stooped to pick up the keys.

Something cool and wet met her fingertips.

Bryce closed her eyes, willing the world to stop spinning. When she opened them, she focused on the tile before the door.

Red. And the smell—it wasn't the reek of before.

It was blood.

And the apartment door was already open.

The lock had been mangled, the handle wrenched off completely.

Iron—the door was *iron*, and enchanted with the best spells money could buy to keep out any unwanted guests, attackers, or magic. Those spells were the one thing Bryce had ever allowed Danika to purchase on her behalf. She hadn't wanted to know how much they'd cost, not when it was likely double her parents' annual salary.

But the door now looked like a crumpled piece of paper.

Blinking furiously, Bryce straightened. Fuck the drugs in her system—fuck Fury. She'd promised no hallucinations.

Bryce was *never* drinking or polluting her body with those drugs *ever again*. She'd tell Danika first thing tomorrow. No more. No. More.

She rubbed her eyes, mascara smearing on her fingertips. On her blood-soaked fingertips—

The blood remained. The mangled door, too.

"Danika?" she croaked. If the attacker was still inside . . . "Danika?"

That bloody hand—her own hand—pushed the half-crumpled door open farther.

Blackness greeted her.

The coppery tang of blood, and that festering odor, slammed into her.

Her entire body seized, every muscle going on alert, every instinct screaming to *run, run, run*—

But her Fae eyes adjusted to the dark, revealing the apartment.

What was left of it.

What was left of them.

Help—she needed to get *help*, but—

She staggered into the trashed apartment.

"Danika?" The word was a raw, broken sound.

The wolves had fought. There wasn't a piece of furniture that was intact, that wasn't shredded and splintered.

There wasn't a body intact, either. Piles and clumps were all that remained.

"DanikaDanikaDanika—"

She needed to call someone, needed to scream for help, needed to get Fury, or her brother, her father, needed Sabine—

Bryce's bedroom door was destroyed, the threshold painted in blood. The ballet posters hung in ribbons. And on the bed . . .

She knew in her bones it was not a hallucination, what lay on that bed, knew in her bones that what bled out inside her chest was her heart.

Danika lay there. In pieces.

And at the foot of the bed, littering the torn carpet in even smaller pieces, as if he'd gone down defending Danika . . . she knew that was Connor.

Knew the heap just to the right of the bed, closest to Danika . . . That was Thorne.

Bryce stared. And stared.

Perhaps time stopped. Perhaps she was dead. She couldn't feel her body.

A clanging, echoing *thunk* sounded from outside. Not from the apartment, but the hall.

She moved. The apartment warped, shrinking and expanding as if it were breathing, the floors rising with each inhale, but she managed to move.

The small kitchen table lay in fragments. Her blood-slick, shaking fingers wrapped around one of its wooden legs, silently lifting it over her shoulder. She peered into the hall.

It took a few blinks to clear her contracting vision. The gods-damned drugs—

The trash chute hatch lay open. Blood that smelled of wolf coated the rusty metal door, and prints that did not belong to a human stained the tile floor, aiming toward the stairs.

It was real. She blinked, over and over, swaying against the door—

Real. Which meant—

From far away, she saw herself launch into the hallway.

Saw herself slam into the opposite wall and rebound off it, then scramble into a sprint toward the stairwell.

Whatever had killed them must have heard her coming and hidden inside the trash chute, waiting for the chance to leap out at her or slink away unnoticed—

Bryce hit the stairs, a glowing white haze creeping over her vision. It blazed through every inhibition, disregarded every warning bell.

The glass door at the bottom of the stairs was already shattered. People screamed outside.

Bryce leapt from the top of the landing.

Her knees popped and buckled as she cleared the stairs, her bare feet shredding on the glass littering the lobby floor. Then they ripped open more as she hurtled through the door and into the street, scanning—

People were gasping to the right. Others were screaming. Cars had halted, drivers and passengers all staring toward a narrow alley between the building and its neighbor.

Their faces blurred and stretched, twisting their horror into something grotesque, something strange and primordial and—

This was no hallucination.

Bryce sprinted across the street, following the screams, the *reek*—

Her breath tore apart her lungs as she hurtled along the alley, dodging piles of trash. Whatever she was chasing had gotten only a brief head start.

Where was it, where was it?

Every logical thought was a ribbon floating above her head. She read them, as if following a stock ticker mounted on a building's side in the CBD.

One glimpse, even if she couldn't kill it. One glimpse, just to ID it, for Danika—

Bryce cleared the alley, careening onto bustling Central Avenue, the street full of fleeing people and honking cars. She leapt over their hoods, scaling them one after another, every movement as smooth as one of her dance steps. *Leap, twirl, arch*—her body did not fail her. Not as she followed the creature's rotting stench to another alley. Another and another.

They were almost at the Istros. A snarl and roar rent the air ahead. It had come from another connected alley, more of a dead-end alcove between two brick buildings.

She hefted the table leg, wishing she'd grabbed Danika's sword instead, wondering if Danika had even had time to unsheathe it—

No. The sword was in the gallery, where Danika had ignored Jesiba's warning and left it in the supply closet. Bryce launched herself around the alley's corner.

Blood everywhere. *Everywhere.*

And the thing halfway down the alley . . . not Vanir. Not one she'd encountered before.

A demon? Some feral thing with smooth, near-translucent gray skin. It crawled on four long, spindly limbs, but looked vaguely humanoid. And it was feasting on someone else.

On—on a malakh.

Blood covered the angel's face, soaking his hair and veiling the swollen, battered features beneath. His white wings were splayed and snapped, his powerful body arced in agony as the beast ripped at his chest with a maw of clear, crystalline fangs that easily dug through skin and bone—

She did not think, did not feel.

She moved, fast like Randall had taught her, brutal like he'd made her learn to be.

She slammed the table leg into the creature's head so hard that bone and wood cracked.

It was thrown off the angel and whirled, its back legs twisting beneath it while its front legs—*arms*—gouged lines in the cobblestones.

The creature had no eyes. Only smooth planes of bone above deep slits—its nose.

And the blood that leaked from its temple . . . it was clear, not red.

Bryce panted, the malakh male groaning some wordless plea as the creature sniffed at her.

She blinked and blinked, willing the lightseeker and mirthroot out of her system, willing the image ahead to stop blurring—

The creature lunged. Not for her—but the angel. Right back to the chest and heart it was trying to get to. The more considerable prey.

Bryce launched forward, table leg swinging again. The reverberations against bone bit into her palm. The creature roared, blindly surging at her.

She dodged, but its sharp, clear fangs ripped her thigh clean open as she twisted away.

She screamed, losing her balance, and swung upward as it leapt again, this time for her throat.

Wood smashed those clear teeth. The demon shrieked, so loudly that her Fae ears nearly ruptured, and she dared all of one blink—

Claws scraped, hissing sounded, and then it was gone.

It was just clearing the lip of the brick building the malakh lay slumped against. She could track it from the streets, could keep it in sight long enough for the Aux or 33rd to come—

Bryce had dared one step when the angel groaned again. His hand was against his chest, pushing weakly. Not hard enough to stop the death-bite from gushing blood. Even with his fast healing, even if he'd made the Drop, the injuries were substantial enough to be fatal.

Someone screamed in a nearby street as the creature jumped between buildings.

Go, go, *go*.

The angel's face was so battered it was barely more than a slab of swollen flesh.

The table leg clattered into a puddle of the angel's blood as she dove for him, biting down her scream at the burning gash in her thigh. Someone had poured *acid* onto her skin, her bones.

Unbearable, impenetrable darkness swept through her, blanketing everything within.

But she shoved her hand against the angel's wound, not allowing herself to feel the wet, torn flesh, the jagged bone of his cleaved sternum. The creature had been eating its way into his heart—

"Phone," she panted. "Do you have a phone?"

The angel's white wing was so shredded it was mostly red splinters. But it shifted slightly to reveal the pocket of his black jeans. The square lump in them.

How she managed to pull out the phone with one hand was beyond her. Time was still snagging, speeding and stopping. Pain lanced through her leg with every breath.

But she gripped the sleek black device in her wrecked hands, her red nails almost snapping with the force as she punched in the emergency number.

A male voice answered on the first ring. "Crescent City Rescue—"

"Help." Her voice broke. *"Help."*

A pause. "Miss, I need you to specify where you are, what the situation is."

"Old Square. River—off the river, near Cygnet Street . . ." But that was where she lived. She was blocks away from that. Didn't know the cross streets. "Please—please help."

The angel's blood soaked her lap. Her knees were bleeding, scraped raw.

And Danika was

And Danika was

And Danika was

"Miss, I need you to tell me where you are—we can have wolves on the scene in a minute."

She sobbed then, and the angel's limp fingers brushed against her torn knee. As if in comfort.

"Phone," she managed, interrupting the responder. "His phone—track it, track us. Find us."

"Miss, are you—"

"Track this phone number."

"Miss, I need a moment to—"

She pulled up the main screen of the phone, clicking through pages in a haze until she found the number herself. *"112 03 0577."*

"Miss, the records are—"

"112 03 0577!" she screamed into the phone. Over and over. *"112 03 0577!"*

It was all she could remember. That stupid number.

"Miss—holy gods." The line crackled. "They're coming," the responder breathed.

He tried to inquire about the injuries on the male, but she dropped the angel's phone as the drugs pulled her back, yanked her down, and she swayed. The alley warped and rippled.

The angel's gaze met hers, so full of agony she thought it was what her soul must look like.

His blood poured out between her fingers. It did not stop.

6

The half-Fae female looked like Hel.

No, not Hel, Isaiah Tiberian realized as he studied her through the one-way mirror in the legion's holding center. She looked like death.

Looked like the soldiers he'd seen crawl off the blood-drenched battlefields of Pangera.

She sat at the metal table in the center of the interrogation room, staring at nothing. Just as she had done for hours now.

A far cry from the screaming, thrashing female Isaiah and his unit had found in the Old Square alley, her gray dress ripped, her left thigh gushing enough blood that he wondered if she'd faint. She'd been half-wild, either from the sheer terror of what had occurred, the grief sinking in, or the drugs that had been coursing through her system.

Likely a combination of all three. And considering that she was not only a source of information regarding the attack, but also currently a danger to herself, Isaiah had made the call to bring her into the sterile, subterranean processing center a few blocks from the Comitium. A witness, he'd made damn sure the records stated. Not a suspect.

He blew out a long breath, resisting the urge to rest his forehead against the observation window. Only the incessant hum of the firstlights overhead filled the space.

The first bit of quiet he'd had in hours. He had little doubt it would end soon.

As if the thought had tempted Urd herself, a rough male voice spoke from the door behind him. "She's still not talking?"

It took all two centuries of Isaiah's training on and off the battlefield to avoid flinching at that voice. To turn slowly toward the angel he knew would be leaning against the doorway, wearing his usual black battle-suit—an angel who reason and history reminded him was an ally, though every instinct roared the opposite.

Predator. Killer. Monster.

Hunt Athalar's angular dark eyes, however, remained fixed on the window. On Bryce Quinlan. Not one gray feather on his wings rustled. Ever since their first days in the 17th Legion in southern Pangera, Isaiah had tried to ignore the fact that Hunt seemed to exist within a permanent ripple of stillness. It was the bated silence before a thunderclap, like the entire land held its breath when he was near.

Given what he'd seen Hunt do to his enemies and chosen targets, it came as no surprise.

Hunt's stare slid toward him.

Right. He'd been asked a question. Isaiah shifted his white wings. "She hasn't said a word since she was brought in."

Hunt again regarded the female through the window. "Has the order come down yet to move her to another room?"

Isaiah knew exactly what sort of room Hunt referred to. Rooms designed to get people to talk. Even witnesses.

Isaiah straightened his black silk tie and offered up a halfhearted plea to the five gods that his charcoal business suit wouldn't be stained with blood by sunrise. "Not yet."

Hunt nodded once, his golden-brown face betraying nothing.

Isaiah scanned the angel, since Hunt sure as Hel wasn't going to volunteer anything without being prompted. No sign of the skull-faced helmet that had earned Hunt a nickname whispered down every corridor and street in Crescent City: the Umbra Mortis.

The Shadow of Death.

Unable to decide whether to be relieved or worried at the absence of Hunt's infamous helmet, Isaiah wordlessly handed Micah's personal assassin a thin file.

He made sure his dark brown fingers didn't touch Hunt's gloved ones. Not when blood still coated the leather, its scent creeping through the room. He recognized the angelic scent in that blood, so the other scent had to be Bryce Quinlan's.

Isaiah jerked his chin to the white-tiled interrogation room. "Bryce Quinlan, twenty-three years old, half-Fae, half-human. Blood test from ten years ago confirmed she'll have an immortal life span. Power rating near-negligible. Hasn't made the Drop yet. Listed as a full civitas. Found in the alley with one of our own, trying to keep his heart from falling out with her bare hands."

The words sounded so damn clinical. But he knew Hunt was well versed in the details. They both were. They'd been in that alley, after all. And they knew that even here, in the secure observation room, they'd be fools to risk saying anything delicate aloud.

It had taken both of them to get Bryce to her feet, only for her to collapse against Isaiah—not from grief but from pain.

Hunt had realized it first: her thigh had been shredded open.

She'd still been nearly feral, had thrashed as they guided her back to the ground, Isaiah calling for a medwitch as the blood gushed out of her thigh. An artery had been hit. It was a godsdamn miracle she wasn't dead before they arrived.

Hunt had cursed up a storm as he knelt before her, and she'd bucked, nearly kicking him in the balls. But then he'd pulled off his helmet. Looked her right in the eye.

And told her to calm the fuck down.

She'd fallen completely silent. Just stared at Hunt, blank and hollow. She didn't so much as flinch with each punch of the staple gun Hunt had pulled from the small medkit built into his battlesuit. She just stared and stared and stared at the Umbra Mortis.

Yet Hunt hadn't lingered after he'd stapled her leg shut—he'd launched into the night to do what he did best: find their enemies and obliterate them.

As if noticing the blood on his gloves, Hunt swore and peeled them off, dumping them into the metal trash can by the door.

Then the male leafed through Quinlan's thin file, his shoulder-length black hair slipping over his unreadable face.

"Seems like she's your standard spoiled party girl," he said, turning the pages. A corner of Hunt's mouth curved upward, anything but amused. "And what a surprise: she's Danika Fendyr's roommate. The Party Princess herself."

No one but the 33rd used that term—because no one else in Lunathion, not even the Fae royals, would have dared. But Isaiah motioned to keep reading. Hunt had left the alley before he'd learned the entire scope of this disaster.

Hunt kept reading. His brows rose. "Holy fucking Urd."

Isaiah waited for it.

Hunt's dark eyes widened. "Danika Fendyr is dead?" He read further. "Along with the entire Pack of Devils." He shook his head and repeated, "Holy fucking Urd."

Isaiah took back the file. "It is totally and completely fucked, my friend."

Hunt's jaw clenched. "I didn't find any trace of the demon that did this."

"I know." At Hunt's questioning glance, Isaiah clarified, "If you had, you'd be holding a severed head in your hands right now and not a file."

Isaiah had been there—on many occasions—when Hunt had done just that, returning triumphant from a demon-hunting mission he'd been ordered to go on by whatever Archangel currently held their reins.

Hunt's mouth twitched slightly, as if remembering the last time he'd presented a kill in such a manner, but he crossed his powerful arms. Isaiah ignored the inherent dominance in the position. There was a pecking order among them, the five-warrior team who made up the triarii—the most elite of all the Imperial Legion units. Micah's little cabal.

Though Micah had appointed Isaiah the Commander of the 33rd, he'd never formally declared him its leader. But Isaiah had always assumed he stood right at the top, the unspoken finest soldier of the triarii, despite his fancy suit and tie.

Where Hunt fell, however . . . no one had really decided in the two years since he'd arrived from Pangera. Isaiah wasn't entirely sure he really wanted to know, either.

Tracking down and eliminating any demons who crept through cracks in the Northern Rift or entered this world through an illegal summoning was his official role, and one well suited to Hunt's particular skill set. The gods knew how many of them he'd tracked down over the centuries, starting from that very first Pangeran unit they'd been in together—the 17th—dedicated to sending the creatures into the afterlife.

But the work Hunt did in the shadows for the Archangels—for Micah, currently—that was what had earned him his nickname. Hunt answered directly to Micah, and the rest of them stayed out of his way.

"Naomi just arrested Philip Briggs for the murders," Isaiah said, naming the captain of the 33rd's infantry. "Briggs got out of jail today—and Danika and the Pack of Devils were the ones who busted him in the first place." That the honor hadn't gone to the 33rd had irked Isaiah to no end. At least Naomi had been the one to apprehend him tonight. "How the fuck a human like Briggs could summon a demon that powerful, I don't know."

"I suppose we'll find out soon enough," Hunt said darkly.

Yeah, they fucking would. "Briggs has to be ten kinds of stupid to have been released only to go for a kill that big." The leader of the Keres rebels—an offshoot of the larger rebellion movement, the Ophion—hadn't seemed dumb, though. Just a fanatic hell-bent on starting a conflict to mirror the war raging across the sea.

"Or maybe Briggs acted on the sole chance of freedom he had before we found an excuse to bring him back into custody," Hunt countered. "He knew his time was limited and wanted to make sure he got one up on the Vanir first."

Isaiah shook his head. "What a mess." Understatement of the century.

Hunt blew out a breath. "Has the press gotten wind of anything?"

"Not yet," Isaiah said. "And I got the order a few minutes ago that we're to keep it quiet—even if it'll be all over the news tomorrow morning."

Hunt's eyes gleamed. "I've got no one to tell."

Indeed, Hunt and the concept of *friends* didn't mesh well. Even among the triarii, even after being here for two years, Hunt still kept to himself. Still worked relentlessly toward one thing: freedom. Or rather, the slim chance of it.

Isaiah sighed. "How soon until Sabine gets here?"

Hunt checked his phone. "Sabine's on her way downstairs right—" The door blew open. Hunt's eyes flickered. "Now."

Sabine looked barely older than Bryce Quinlan, with her fine-boned face and long, silvery blond hair, but there was only an immortal's rage in her blue eyes. "Where is that half-breed whore—" She simmered as she spotted Bryce through the window. "I'll fucking *kill* her—"

Isaiah extended a white wing to block the Prime Apparent's path back out the door and into the interrogation room, a few steps to its left.

Hunt fell into a casual stance on her other side. Lightning danced along his knuckles.

A mild showing of the power Isaiah had witnessed being unleashed upon their enemies: lightning, capable of bringing down a building.

Whether ordinary angel or Archangel, the power was always some variation of the same: rain, storms, the occasional tornado—Isaiah himself could summon wind capable of keeping a charging enemy at bay, but none in living memory possessed Hunt's ability to harness lightning to his will. Or the depth of power to make it truly destructive. It had been Hunt's salvation and destruction.

Isaiah let one of his cold breezes sift through Sabine's corn-silk hair, over to Hunt.

They'd always worked well together—Micah had known it when he put Hunt with Isaiah two years ago, despite the entwined thorns tattooed across both their brows. Most of Hunt's mark was hidden by his dark hair, but there was no concealing the thin black band on his forehead.

Isaiah could barely remember what his friend had looked like before those Pangeran witches had branded him, working their infernal spells into the ink itself so they might never let his crimes be forgotten, so the witch-magic bound the majority of his power.

The halo, they called it—a mockery of the divine auras early humans had once portrayed angels as possessing.

There was no hiding it on Isaiah's brow, either, the tattoo on it the same as on Hunt's, and on the brows of the nearly two thousand rebel angels who had been such idealistic, brave fools two centuries ago.

The Asteri had created the angels to be their perfect soldiers and loyal servants. The angels, gifted with such power, had relished their role in the world. Until Shahar, the Archangel they'd once called the Daystar. Until Hunt and the others who'd flown in Shahar's elite 18th Legion.

Their rebellion had failed—only for the humans to begin their own forty years ago. A different cause, a different group and species of fighters, but the sentiment was essentially the same: the Republic was the enemy, the rigid hierarchies utter bullshit.

When the human rebels had started their war, one of the idiots should have asked the Fallen angels how their rebellion had failed, long before those humans were even born. Isaiah certainly could have given them some pointers on what not to do. And enlightened them about the consequences.

For there was also no hiding the second tattoo, stamped on their right wrists: *SPQM*.

It adorned every flag and letterhead of the Republic—the four letters encircled with seven stars—and adorned the wrist of every being owned by it. Even if Isaiah chopped off his arm, the limb that regrew would bear the mark. Such was the power of the witch-ink.

A fate worse than death: to become an eternal servant to those they'd sought to overthrow.

Deciding to spare Sabine from Hunt's way of dealing with things, Isaiah asked mildly, "I understand you are grieving, but do you have reason, Sabine, to want Bryce dead?"

Sabine snarled, pointing at Bryce, "She took the sword. That wannabe wolf took Danika's sword. I know she did, it's not at the apartment—and it's *mine*."

Isaiah had seen those details: that the heirloom of the Fendyr family was missing. But there was no sign of Bryce Quinlan possessing it. "What does the sword have to do with your daughter's death?"

Rage and grief warred in that feral face. Sabine shook her head, ignoring his question, and said, "Danika couldn't stay out of trouble. She could never keep her mouth *shut* and know when to be quiet around her enemies. And look what became of her. That stupid little bitch in there is still breathing, and Danika is *not*." Her voice nearly cracked. "Danika should have known better."

Hunt asked a shade more gently, "Known better about what?"

"All of it," Sabine snapped, and again shook her head, clearing her grief away. "Starting with that slut of a roommate." She whirled on Isaiah, the portrait of wrath. "Tell me *everything*."

Hunt said coolly, "He doesn't have to tell you shit, Fendyr."

As Commander of the 33rd Imperial Legion, Isaiah held an equal rank to Sabine: they both sat on the same governing councils, both answered to males of power within their own ranks and their own Houses.

Sabine's canines lengthened as she surveyed Hunt. "Did I fucking speak to you, Athalar?"

Hunt's eyes glittered. But Isaiah pulled out his phone, typing as he cut in calmly, "We're still getting the reports in. Viktoria is coming to talk to Miss Quinlan right now."

"I'll talk to her," Sabine seethed. Her fingers curled, as if ready to rip out Hunt's throat. Hunt gave her a sharp smile that told her to just try, the lightning around his knuckles twining up his wrist.

And fortunately for Isaiah, the interrogation room's door opened and a dark-haired woman in an immaculately tailored navy suit walked in.

They were a front, those suits that he and Viktoria wore. A sort of armor, yes, but also a last attempt to pretend that they were even remotely normal.

It was no wonder Hunt never bothered with them.

As Viktoria made her graceful approach, Bryce gave no acknowledgment of the stunning female who usually made people of *all* Houses do a double take.

But Bryce had been that way for hours now. Blood still stained the white bandage around her bare thigh. Viktoria sniffed delicately, her pale green eyes narrowing beneath the halo's dark tattoo on her brow. The wraith had been one of the few non-malakim who had rebelled with them two centuries ago. She'd been given to Micah soon afterward, and her punishment had gone beyond the brow tattoo and slave markings. Not nearly as brutal as what Isaiah and Hunt had endured in the Asteri's dungeons, and then in various Archangels' dungeons for years afterward, but its own form of torment that lasted even when their own had stopped.

Viktoria said, "Miss Quinlan."

She didn't respond.

The wraith dragged over a steel chair from the wall and set it on the other side of the table. Pulling a file from her jacket, Viktoria crossed her long legs as she perched on the seat.

"Can you tell me who is responsible for the bloodshed tonight?"

Not even a hitch of breath. Sabine growled softly.

The wraith folded her alabaster hands in her lap, the unnatural elegance the only sign of the ancient power that rippled beneath the calm surface.

Vik had no body of her own. Though she'd fought in the 18th, Isaiah had learned her history only when he'd arrived here ten years ago. How Viktoria had acquired this particular body, who it had once belonged to, he didn't ask. She hadn't told him. Wraiths wore bodies the way some people owned cars. Vainer wraiths switched them often, usually at the first sign of aging, but Viktoria had held on to this one for longer than usual, liking its build and movement, she'd said.

Now she held on to it because she had no choice. It had been Micah's punishment for her rebellion: to trap her within this body. Forever. No more changing, no more trading up for something newer and sleeker. For two hundred years, Vik had been contained, forced to weather the slow erosion of the body, now plainly visible: the thin lines starting to carve themselves around her eyes, the crease now etched in her forehead above the tattoo's twining band of thorns.

"Quinlan's gone into shock," Hunt observed, monitoring Bryce's every breath. "She's not going to talk."

Isaiah was inclined to agree, until Viktoria opened the file, scanned a piece of paper, and said, "I, for one, believe that you are not in full control of your body or actions right now."

And then she read a shopping list of a cocktail of drugs and alcohol that would stop a human's heart dead. Stop a lesser Vanir's heart, too, for that matter.

Hunt swore again. "Is there anything she didn't snort or smoke tonight?"

Sabine bristled. "Half-breed trash—"

Isaiah threw Hunt a look. All that was needed to convey the request.

Never an order—he'd never dared to order Hunt around. Not when the male possessed a hair-trigger temper that had left entire imperial fighting units in smoldering cinders. Even with the spells of the halo binding that lightning to a tenth of its full strength, Hunt's skills as a warrior made up for it.

But Hunt's chin dipped, his only sign that he'd agreed to Isaiah's request. "You'll need to complete some paperwork upstairs, Sabine." Hunt blew out a breath, as if reminding himself that Sabine was a mother who had lost her only child tonight, and added, "If you want time to yourself, you can take it, but you need to sign—"

"Fuck signing things and fuck time to myself. Crucify the bitch if you have to, but get her to give a statement." Sabine spat on the tiles at Hunt's booted feet.

Ether coated Isaiah's tongue as Hunt gave her the cool stare that served as his only warning to opponents on a battlefield. None had ever survived what happened next.

Sabine seemed to remember that, and wisely stormed into the hall. She flexed her hand as she did, four razor-sharp claws appearing, and slashed them through the metal door.

Hunt smiled at her disappearing figure. A target marked. Not today, not even tomorrow, but at one point in the future . . .

And people claimed the shifters got along better with the angels than the Fae.

Viktoria was saying gently to Bryce, "We have video footage from the White Raven, confirming your whereabouts. We have footage of you walking home."

Cameras covered all of Lunathion, with unparalleled visual and audio coverage, but Bryce's apartment building was old, and the mandatory monitors in the hallways hadn't been repaired in decades. The landlord would be getting a visit tonight for the code violations that had fucked this entire investigation. One tiny sliver of audio was all the building cameras had managed to catch—just the audio. It held nothing beyond what they already knew. The phones of the Pack of Devils had all been destroyed in the attack. Not one message had gone out.

"What we don't have footage of, Bryce," Viktoria went on, "is what happened in that apartment. Can you tell me?"

Slowly, as if she drifted back into her battered body, Bryce turned her amber eyes to Viktoria.

"Where's her family?" Hunt asked roughly.

"Human mother lives with the stepfather in one of the mountain towns up north—both peregrini," Isaiah said. "The sire wasn't registered or refused to acknowledge paternity. Fae, obviously. And likely one with some standing, since he bothered to get her civitas status."

Most of the offspring born to human mothers took their peregrini rank. And though Bryce had something of the Fae's elegant beauty, her face marked her as human—the gold-dusted skin, the smattering of freckles over her nose and high cheekbones, the full mouth. Even if the silken flow of red hair and arched ears were pure Fae.

"Have the human parents been notified?"

Isaiah dragged a hand over his tight brown curls. He'd been awoken by his phone's shrill ringing at two in the morning, hurtled from the barracks a minute after that, and was now starting to feel the effects of a sleepless night. Dawn was likely not far off. "Her mother was hysterical. She asked over and over if we knew why they'd attacked the apartment, or if it was Philip Briggs. She saw on the news that he'd been released on a technicality and was certain he did this. I have a patrol from the 31st flying out right now; the parents will be airborne within the hour."

Viktoria's voice slid through the intercom as she continued her interview. "Can you describe the creature that attacked your friends?"

But Quinlan was gone again, her eyes vacant.

They had fuzzy footage thanks to the street cameras, but the demon had moved faster than the wind and had known to keep out of lens range. They hadn't been able to ID it yet—even Hunt's extensive knowledge hadn't helped. All they had of it was a vague, grayish blur no slowdown could clarify. And Bryce Quinlan, charging barefoot through the city streets.

"That girl isn't ready to give a statement," Hunt said. "This is a waste of our time."

But Isaiah asked him, "Why does Sabine hate Bryce so much—why imply she's to blame for all this?" When Hunt didn't answer, Isaiah jerked his chin toward two files on the edge of the desk. "Look at Quinlan's. Only one standing crime before this—for public indecency during a Summer Solstice parade. She got a little frisky against a wall and was caught in the act. Holding cell overnight, paid the fine the next day, did community service for a month to get it wiped off any permanent record." Isaiah could have sworn a ghost of a smile appeared on Hunt's mouth.

But Isaiah tapped a calloused finger on the impressively thick stack beside it. "This is part *one* of Danika Fendyr's file. Of seven. Starts with petty theft when she was ten, continues until she reached her majority five years ago. Then it goes eerily quiet. If you ask me, Bryce was the one who was led down a road of ruination—and then maybe led Danika out of hers."

"Not far enough to keep from snorting enough lightseeker to kill a horse," Hunt said. "I'm assuming she didn't party alone. Were there any other friends with her tonight?"

"Two others. Juniper Andromeda, a faun who's a soloist at the City Ballet, and . . ." Isaiah flipped open the case file and muttered a prayer. "Fury Axtar."

Hunt swore softly at the mercenary's name.

Fury Axtar was licensed to kill in half a dozen countries. Including this one.

Hunt asked, "Fury was with Quinlan tonight?"

They'd crossed paths with the merc enough to know to stay the Hel away. Micah had even ordered Hunt to kill her. Twice.

But she had too many high-powered allies. Some, it was whispered, on the Imperial Senate. So both times, Micah had decided that the fallout over the Umbra Mortis turning Fury Axtar into veritable toast would be more trouble than it was worth.

"Yes," Isaiah said. "Fury was with her at the club."

Hunt frowned. But Viktoria leaned in to speak to Bryce once more.

"We're trying to find who did this. Can you give us the information we need?"

Only a shell sat before the wraith.

Viktoria said, in that luxurious purr that usually had people eating out of her palm, "I want to help you. I want to find who did this. And punish them."

Viktoria reached into her pocket, pulled out her phone, and set it faceup on the table. Instantly, its digital feed appeared on the small screen in the room with Isaiah and Hunt. They glanced between the wraith and the screen as a series of messages opened.

"We downloaded the data from your phone. Can you walk me through these?"

Glassy eyes tracked a small screen that rose from a hidden compartment in the linoleum floor. It displayed the same messages Isaiah and Hunt now read.

The first one, sent from Bryce, read, *TV nights are for waggle-tailed pups. Come play with the big bitches.*

And then a short, dark video, shaking as someone roared with laughter while Bryce flipped off the camera, leaned over a line of white powder—lightseeker—and sniffed it right up her freckled nose. She was laughing, so bright and alive that the woman in the room before them looked like a gutted corpse, and she shrieked into the camera, "LIGHT IT UP, DANIKAAAAA!"

Danika's written reply was precisely what Isaiah expected from the Prime Apparent of the wolves, whom he'd seen only from a distance at formal events and who had seemed poised to start trouble wherever she went: *I FUCKING HATE YOU. STOP DOING LIGHTSEEKER WITHOUT ME. ASSHOLE.*

Party Princess, indeed.

Bryce had written back twenty minutes later, *I just hooked up with someone in the bathroom. Don't tell Connor.*

Hunt shook his head.

But Bryce sat there as Viktoria read the messages aloud, the wraith stone-faced.

Danika wrote back, *Was it good?!!?*

Only good enough to take the edge off.

"This isn't relevant," Hunt murmured. "Pull in Viktoria."

"We have our orders."

"Fuck the orders. That woman is about to break, and not in a good way."

Then Bryce stopped responding to Danika.

But Danika kept messaging. One after another. Over the next two hours.

The show's over. Where are you assholes?

Why aren't you picking up your phone? I'm calling Fury.

Where the FUCK is Fury?

Juniper never brings her phone, so I'm not even gonna bother with her. Where are you?!!!

Should I come to the club? The pack's leaving in ten. Stop fucking strangers in the bathroom, because Connor's coming with me.

BRYYYYCE. When you look at your phone, I hope the 1,000 alerts piss you off.

Thorne is telling me to stop messaging you. I told him to mind his own fucking business.

Connor says to grow the Hel up and stop doing shady-ass drugs, because only losers do that shit. He wasn't happy when I said I'm not sure I can let you date a holier-than-thou priss.

Okay, we're leaving in five. See you soon, cocksucker. Light it up.

Bryce stared at the screen unblinkingly, her torn face sickly pale in the light of the monitor.

"The building's cameras are mostly broken, but the one in the hall was still able to record some audio, though its video footage was down," Viktoria said calmly. "Shall I play it?"

No response. So Viktoria played it.

Muffled snarling and screaming filled the speakers—quiet enough that it was clear the hall camera had picked up only the loudest noises coming from the apartment. And then someone was roaring—a feral wolf's roar. "*Please, please—*"

The words were cut off. But the hall camera's audio wasn't.

Danika Fendyr screamed. Something tumbled and crashed in the background—as if she'd been thrown into furniture. And the hall camera kept recording.

The screaming went on, and on, and on. Interrupted only by the camera's fritzed system. The muffled grunts and growls were wet and vicious, and Danika was begging, sobbing as she pleaded for mercy, wept and screamed for it to stop—

"Turn it off," Hunt ordered, stalking from the room. "Turn it off *now*." He was out so fast Isaiah couldn't stop him, instantly crossing the space to the door beside theirs and flinging it open before Isaiah had cleared the room.

But there was Danika, audio crackling in and out, the sound of her voice still pleading for mercy coming from the speakers in the ceiling. Danika, being devoured and shredded.

The silence from the murderer was as chilling as Danika's sobbing screams.

Viktoria twisted toward the door as Hunt barreled in, his face dark with fury, wings spreading. The Shadow of Death unleashed.

Isaiah tasted ether. Lightning writhed at Hunt's fingertips.

Danika's unending, half-muffled screams filled the room.

Isaiah stepped into the chamber in time to see Bryce explode.

He summoned a wall of wind around himself and Vik, Hunt no doubt doing the same, as Bryce shot out of her chair and flipped the table. It soared over Viktoria's head and slammed into the observation window.

A feral growl filled the room as she grabbed the chair she'd been sitting on, hurling it against the wall, so hard its metal frame dented and crumpled.

She vomited all over the floor. If his power hadn't been around Viktoria, it would have showered her absurdly expensive bespoke heels.

The audio finally cut off when the hall camera went on the fritz again—and stayed that way.

Bryce panted, staring at her mess. Then fell to her knees in it.

She puked again. And again. And then curled over her knees, her silky hair falling into the vomit as she rocked herself in the stunned silence.

She was half-Fae, assessed at a power level barely on the grid. What she'd just done to the table and chair . . . Pure, physical rage. Even the most aloof of the Fae couldn't halt an eruption of primal wrath when it overtook them.

Unfazed, Hunt approached her, his gray wings high to avoid dragging through the vomit.

"Hey." Hunt knelt at Bryce's side. He reached for her shoulder, but lowered his hand. How many people ever saw the hands of the Umbra Mortis reach for them with no hint of violence?

Hunt nodded toward the destroyed table and chair. "Impressive."

Bryce bowed farther over herself, her tan fingers near-white as they dug into her back hard enough to bruise. Her voice was a broken rasp. "I want to go home."

Hunt's dark eyes flickered. But he said nothing more.

Viktoria, frowning at the mess, slipped away to find someone to clean it.

Isaiah said, "You can't go home, I'm afraid. It's an active crime scene." And it was so wrecked that even if they scrubbed it with bleach, no Vanir would be able to walk in and not scent the slaughter. "It's not safe for you to return until we've found who did this. And why they did it."

Then Bryce breathed, "Does S-Sabine—"

"Yes," Isaiah said gently. "Everyone who was in Danika's life has been notified."

The entire world would know in a few hours.

Still kneeling beside her, Hunt said roughly, "We can move you to a room with a cot and a bathroom. Get you some clothes."

Her dress was so torn that most of her skin was on display, a rip along the waist revealing the hint of a dark tattoo down her back. He'd seen whores in the Meat Market wearing more modest clothes.

The phone in Isaiah's pocket buzzed. Naomi. The voice of the captain of the 33rd's infantry was strained when Isaiah answered. "Let the girl go. Right now. Get her out of this building, and for all our sakes, do *not* put anyone on her tail. Especially Hunt."

"Why? The Governor gave us the opposite order."

"I got a phone call," Naomi said. "From Ruhn fucking Danaan. He's livid that we didn't notify Sky and Breath about bringing in the girl. Says it falls under the Fae's jurisdiction and whatever the fuck else. So screw what the Governor wants—he'll thank us later for avoiding this enormous fucking headache. Let the girl go *now*. She can come back in with a Fae escort, if that's what those assholes want."

Hunt, having heard the entire conversation, studied Bryce Quinlan with a predator's unflinching assessment. As one of the triarii, Naomi Boreas answered only to Micah and owed them no explanation, but to disregard his direct order in favor of the Fae . . . Naomi added, "Do it, Isaiah." Then she hung up.

Despite Bryce's pointed Fae ears, her glazed eyes registered no sign that she'd heard.

Isaiah pocketed his phone. "You're free to go."

She uncurled on surprisingly steady legs, despite the bandage on one of them. Yet blood and dirt caked her bare feet. Enough of the former that Hunt said, "We've got a medwitch on-site."

But Bryce ignored him and limped out, through the open door and into the hall.

His eyes fixed on the doorway as the scuffle-hop of her steps faded.

For a long minute, neither of them spoke. Then Hunt blew out a breath and rose. "What room is Naomi putting Briggs in?"

Isaiah didn't get the chance to answer before footsteps sounded down the hall, approaching fast. Definitely not Bryce's.

Even in one of the most secure places in this city, Isaiah and Hunt positioned their hands within easy reach of their weapons, the former crossing his arms so that he might draw the gun hidden beneath his suit jacket, the latter letting his hand dangle at his thigh, inches from the black-hilted knife sheathed there. Lightning again writhed at Hunt's fingers.

A dark-haired Fae male burst through the interrogation room door. Even with a silver hoop through his lower lip, even with one side of his long raven-black hair buzzed, even with the sleeves of tattoos beneath the leather jacket, there was no disguising the heritage the strikingly handsome face broadcasted.

Ruhn Danaan, Crown Prince of the Valbaran Fae. Son of the Autumn King and the current possessor of the Starsword, fabled dark blade of the ancient Starborn Fae. Proof of the prince's Chosen One status among the Fae—whatever the Hel that meant.

That sword was currently strapped across Ruhn's back, its black hilt devouring the glaring firstlights. Isaiah had once heard someone say the sword was made from iridium mined from a meteorite, forged in another world—before the Fae had come through the Northern Rift.

Danaan's blue eyes simmered like the heart of a flame—though Ruhn himself bore no such magic. Fire magic was common among the Valbaran Fae, wielded by the Autumn King himself. But rumor claimed Ruhn's magic was more like those of his kin who ruled the sacred Fae isle of Avallen across the sea: power to summon shadows or mist that could not only veil the physical world, but the mind as well. Perhaps even telepathy.

Ruhn glanced at the vomit, scenting the female who'd just left. "Where the fuck is she?"

Hunt went still at the cold command in the prince's voice.

"Bryce Quinlan has been released," Isaiah said. "We sent her upstairs a few minutes ago."

Ruhn had to have taken a side entrance if he'd missed her, and they hadn't been warned by the front desk of his arrival. Perhaps he'd used that magic of his to worm through the shadows.

The prince turned toward the doorway, but Hunt said, "What's it to you?"

Ruhn bristled. "She's my cousin, asshole. We take care of our own."

A distant cousin, since the Autumn King had no siblings, but apparently the prince knew Bryce well enough to intervene.

Hunt threw Ruhn a grin. "Where were you tonight?"

"Fuck you, Athalar." Ruhn bared his teeth. "I suppose you heard that Danika and I got into it over Briggs at the Head meeting. What a lead. Good job." Each word came out more clipped than the last. "If I wanted to kill Danika, I wouldn't summon a fucking demon to do it. Where the fuck is Briggs? I want to talk to him."

"He's incoming." Hunt was still smiling. That lightning still danced at his knuckles. "And you don't get the first shot at him." Then he added, "Daddy's clout and cash only get you so far, Prince."

It made no difference that Ruhn headed up the Fae division of the Aux, and was as well trained as any of their elite fighters. Or that the sword on his back wasn't merely decorative.

It didn't matter to Hunt. Not where royals and rigid hierarchies were concerned.

Ruhn said, "Keep talking, Athalar. Let's see where it gets you."

Hunt smirked. "I'm shaking."

Isaiah cleared his throat. Burning Solas, the last thing he needed tonight was a brawl between one of his triarii and a prince of the Fae. He said to Ruhn, "Can you tell us if Miss Quinlan's behavior before the murder tonight was unusual or—"

"The Raven's owner told me she was drunk and had snorted a pile of lightseeker," Ruhn snapped. "But you'll find Bryce with that kind of shit in her system at least one night a week."

"Why does she do it at all?" Isaiah asked.

Ruhn crossed his arms. "She does what she wants. She always has." There was enough bitterness there to suggest history—bad history.

Hunt drawled, "Just how close are you two?"

"If you're asking whether I'm fucking her," Ruhn seethed, "the answer, asshole, is no. She's family."

"Distant family," Hunt pointed out. "I heard the Fae like to keep their bloodline undiluted."

Ruhn held his stare. And as Hunt smiled again, ether filled the room, the promise of a storm skittering over Isaiah's skin.

Wondering if he'd be dumb enough to get between them when Ruhn attempted to bash in Hunt's teeth and Hunt turned the prince into a pile of smoldering bones, Isaiah said quickly, "We're just trying to do our job, Prince."

"If you assholes had kept an eye on Briggs like you were supposed to, maybe this wouldn't have happened at all."

Hunt's gray wings flared slightly—a malakh's usual stance when preparing for a physical fight. And those dark eyes . . . They were the eyes of the feared warrior, the Fallen angel. The one who had smashed apart the battlefields he'd been ordered to fight on. The one who killed on an Archangel's whim, and did it so well they called him the Shadow of Death.

"Careful," Hunt said.

"Stay the fuck away from Bryce," Ruhn snarled before striding back through the door, presumably after his cousin. At least Bryce would have an escort.

Hunt flipped off the empty doorway. After a moment, he murmured, "The tracking device in the water Quinlan drank when she got here. What's the time frame on it?"

"Three days," Isaiah replied.

Hunt studied the knife sheathed at his thigh. "Danika Fendyr was one of the strongest Vanir in the city, even without making the Drop. She begged like a human by the end."

Sabine would never recover from the shame.

"I don't know of a demon that kills like that," Hunt mused. "Or disappears that easily. I couldn't find a trace. It's like it vanished back to Hel."

Isaiah said, "If Briggs is behind it, we'll learn what the demon is soon enough."

If Briggs talked at all. He certainly hadn't when he'd been busted in his bomb lab, despite the best efforts of the 33rd's interrogators and the Aux.

Isaiah added, "I'll have every available patrol quietly looking out for other young packs in the Auxiliary. If it winds up not being related to Briggs, then it could be the start of a pattern."

Hunt asked darkly, "If we find the demon?"

Isaiah shrugged. "Then make sure it's not a problem anymore, Hunt."

Hunt's eyes sharpened into lethal focus. "And Bryce Quinlan—after the three days are up?"

Isaiah frowned at the table, the crumpled chair. "If she's smart, she'll lie low and not attract the attention of any other powerful immortals for the rest of her life."

7

The black steps ringing the foggy shore of the Bone Quarter bit into Bryce's knees as she knelt before the towering ivory gates.

The Istros spread like a gray mirror behind her, silent in the predawn light.

As quiet and still as she had gone, hollowed out and drifting.

Mist curled around her, veiling all but the obsidian steps she knelt on and the carved bone gates looming overhead. The rotting black boat at her back was her only companion, its moldy, ancient rope draped over the steps in lieu of a mooring. She'd paid the fee—the boat would linger here until she was done. Until she had said what she needed to say.

The living realm remained a world away, the spires and skyscrapers of the city hidden by that swirling mist, its car horns and array of voices rendered mute. She'd left behind any mortal possessions. They would have no value here, among the Reapers and the dead.

She'd been glad to leave them—especially her phone, so full of anger and hatred.

Ithan's latest audiomail had come only an hour ago, stirring her from the unsleeping stupor in which she'd spent the past six nights, staring at the dark ceiling of the hotel room she was sharing with her mother. Ignoring every call and message.

Ithan's words had lingered, though, when she'd slipped into the hotel bathroom to listen.

Don't come to the Sailing tomorrow. You're not welcome there.

She'd listened to it over and over, the first words to echo in her silent head.

Her mother hadn't woken from the bed beside hers when Bryce had exited the hotel room on Fae-soft feet, taking the service elevator and leaving through the unwatched alley door. She hadn't left that room for six days, just sat staring vacantly at the floral hotel wallpaper. And now, with the seventh dawning . . . Only for this would she leave. Would she remember how to move her body, how to speak.

Danika's Sailing would commence at dawn, and the Sailings for the rest of the pack would follow. Bryce would not be there to witness them. Even without the wolves banning her from it, she couldn't have endured it. To see the black boat pushed from the dock, all that was left of Danika with it, her soul to be judged either worthy or unworthy of entering the sacred isle across the river.

There was only silence here. Silence and mist.

Was this death? Silence and fog?

Bryce ran her tongue over her dry, chapped lips. She did not remember the last time she'd drunk anything. Had a meal. Only her mother coaxing her to take a sip of water.

A light had gone out inside her. A light had been extinguished.

She might as well have been staring inside herself: Darkness. Silence. Mist.

Bryce lifted her head, peering up toward the carved bone gates, hewn from the ribs of a long-dead leviathan who'd prowled the deep seas of the north. The mist swirled tighter, the temperature dropping. Announcing the arrival of something ancient and terrible.

Bryce remained kneeling. Bowed her head.

She was not welcome at the Sailing. So she had come here to say goodbye. To give Danika this one last thing.

The creature that dwelt in the mist emerged, and even the river at her back trembled.

Bryce opened her eyes. And slowly lifted her gaze.

PART II
THE TRENCH

8

TWENTY-TWO MONTHS LATER

Bryce Quinlan stumbled from the White Raven's bathroom, a lion shifter nuzzling her neck, his broad hands grabbing at her waist.

It was easily the best sex she'd had in three months. Maybe longer than that. Maybe she'd keep him for a while.

Maybe she should learn his name first. Not that it mattered. Her meeting was at the VIP bar across the club in . . . well, shit. Right now.

The beat of the music pounded against her bones, echoing off the carved pillars, an incessant summons that Bryce ignored, denied. Just as she had every day for the past two years.

"Let's dance." The golden-haired lion's words rumbled against her ear as he gripped her hand to drag her toward the teeming throng on the ancient stones of the dance floor.

She planted her feet as firmly as her four-inch stilettos would allow. "No, thanks. I've got a business meeting." Not a lie, though she would have turned him down regardless.

The corner of the lion's lip twitched as he surveyed her short-as-sin black dress, the bare legs she'd had wrapped around his waist moments ago. Urd spare her, his cheekbones were unreal. So were those golden eyes, now narrowing in amusement. "You go to business meetings looking like that?"

She did when her boss's clients insisted on meeting in a neutral space like the Raven, fearful of whatever monitoring or spells Jesiba had at the gallery.

Bryce never would have come here—had so rarely come back here at all—on her own. She'd been sipping sparkling water at the *normal* bar within the club, not the VIP one she was supposed to be sitting at on the mezzanine, when the lion approached her with that easy smile and those broad shoulders. She'd been in such need of a distraction from the tension building in her with each moment in here that she'd barely finished her glass before she'd dragged him into the bathroom. He'd been all too happy to oblige her.

Bryce said to the lion, "Thanks for the ride." *Whatever your name is.*

It took him a blink to realize she was serious about the business meeting. Red crept over his tanned cheeks. Then he blurted, "I can't pay you."

It was her turn to blink. Then she tipped her head back and laughed.

Just perfect: he thought she was one of the whores in Riso's employ. *Sacred* prostitution, Riso had once explained—since the club lay on the ruins of a temple to pleasure, it was his duty to continue its traditions.

"Consider it on the house," she crooned, patting him on the cheek before she turned toward the glowing golden bar on the glass mezzanine hovering over the cavernous space.

She didn't let herself look toward the booth tucked between two age-worn pillars. Didn't let herself see who might now be occupying it. Not Juniper, who was too busy these days for more than the occasional brunch, and certainly not Fury, who didn't bother to take her calls, or answer messages, or even visit this city.

Bryce rolled her shoulders, shoving the thoughts away.

The jaguar shifters standing guard atop the illuminated golden staircase that linked the VIP mezzanine with the converted temple pulled aside their black velvet rope to let her pass.

Twenty glass stools flanked the solid gold bar, and only a third of them were occupied. Vanir of every House sat in them. No humans, though.

Except for her, if she even counted.

Her client was already seated at the far end of the bar, his dark suit tight over his bulky frame, long black hair slicked back to reveal a sharp-boned face and inky eyes.

Bryce rattled off his details to herself as she sauntered up to him, praying he wasn't the sort to mark that she was technically two minutes late.

Maximus Tertian: two-hundred-year-old vampyr; unwed and unmated; son of Lord Cedrian, richest of the Pangeran vamps and the most monstrous, if rumor was to be believed. Known for filling bathtubs with the blood of human maidens in his frosty mountain keep, bathing in their youth—

Not helpful. Bryce plastered on a smile and claimed the stool beside his, ordering a sparkling water from the bartender. "Mr. Tertian," she said by way of greeting, extending her hand.

The vampyr's smile was so smooth she knew ten thousand pairs of underwear had likely dropped at the sight of it over the centuries. "Miss Quinlan," he purred, taking her hand and brushing a kiss to the back of it. His lips lingered just long enough that she suppressed the urge to yank her fingers back. "A pleasure to meet you in the flesh." His eyes dipped toward her neck, then the cleavage exposed by her dress. "Your employer might have a gallery full of art, but you are the true masterpiece."

Oh please.

Bryce ducked her head, making herself smile. "You say that to all the girls."

"Only the mouthwatering ones."

An offer for how this night could end, if she wanted: being sucked and fucked. She didn't bother to inform him she'd already had that particular need scratched, minus the sucking. She liked her blood where it was, thank you very much.

She reached into her purse, pulling out a narrow leather folio—an exact replica of what the Raven used to hand out steep bills to its most exclusive patrons. "Your drink's on me." She slid the folio toward him with a smile.

Maximus peered at the ownership papers for the five-thousand-year-old onyx bust of a long-dead vampyr lord. The deal had been a triumph for Bryce after weeks of sending out feelers to potential buyers, taunting them with the chance to buy a rare artifact before any of their rivals. She'd had her eye on Maximus, and during their endless phone calls and messages, she'd played him well, drawing upon his hatred for other vampyr lords, his fragile ego, his unbearable arrogance.

It was an effort now to suppress her smile as Maximus—*never Max*—nodded while he read. Giving him the illusion of privacy, Bryce pivoted on the stool to peer at the teeming club below.

A cluster of young females adorned in firstlight glow-stick halos danced together near a pillar, laughing and singing and passing a bottle of sparkling wine among them.

Bryce's chest tightened. She'd once planned to have her Drop party at the Raven. Had planned to be as obnoxious as those females down there, partying with her friends from the moment she emerged from the Ascent until she either passed out or was kicked to the curb.

The party, honestly, was what she'd wanted to focus on. What most people tried to focus on. Rather than the sheer terror of the Drop ritual itself.

But it was a necessary rite. Because the firstlight grid's power was generated by the pure, undiluted light each Vanir emitted while making the Drop. And it was only during the Drop that the flash of firstlight appeared—raw, unfiltered magic. It could heal and destroy and do everything in between.

Captured and bottled, the first glow was always used for healing, then the rest of it was handed over to the energy plants to fuel their lights and cars and machines and tech; some of it was used for spells, and some was reserved for whatever shady shit the Republic wanted.

The "donation" of the firstlight by each citizen was a key element of the Drop ritual, part of why it was always done in a government center: a sterile room, where the light from the person making the Drop was gobbled up during the transition into immortality and true power. All tracked by the Eleusian system, able to monitor every moment of it through vibrations in the world's magic. Indeed, family members sometimes watched the feeds in an adjacent room.

The Drop was the easy part: falling into one's power. But once the bottom was reached, one's mortal body expired. And then the clock began counting down.

Mere minutes were allowed for the race back up to life—before the brain shut down permanently from lack of oxygen. Six minutes to start barreling down a psychic runway along the bottom of one's power, a single desperate shot at launching skyward toward life. The alternative to successfully making that leap: tumbling into an endless black pit and awaiting death. The alternative to getting enough momentum on that runway: tumbling into an endless black pit and awaiting death.

Which was why someone else had to act as an Anchor: a beacon, a lifeline, a bungee cord that would snap their companion back up to life once they leapt off the runway. To make the Drop alone was to die—to reach the bottom of one's power, to have one's heart stop beating upon hitting that nadir. No one knew if the soul continued living down there, lost forever, or if it died along with the body left in life.

It was why Anchors were usually family—parents or siblings—or trusted friends. Someone who wouldn't leave you stranded. Or a government employee who had a legal obligation not to do so. Some claimed those six minutes were called the Search—that during that time, you faced the very depths of your soul. But beyond that, there was no hope of survival.

It was only upon making the Ascent and reaching that threshold back to life, brimming with new power, that immortality was attained, the aging process slowed to a glacial drip and the body rendered near-indestructible as it was bathed in all that ensuing firstlight, so bright it could blind the naked eye. And at the end of it, when the Drop Center's sleek energy panels had siphoned off that firstlight, all any of them were left with to mark the occasion was a mere pinprick of that light in a bottle. A pretty souvenir.

These days, with Drop parties like the one below all the rage, the newly immortal often used their allotment of their own firstlight to make party favors to hand out to their friends. Bryce had planned for glow sticks and key chains that said *Kiss My Sparkly Ass!* Danika had just wanted shot glasses.

Bryce tucked away that old ache in her chest as Maximus shut the folio with a snap, his reading done. A matching folio appeared in his hand, then he nudged it across the shining gold surface of the bar.

Bryce glanced at the check within—for a mind-boggling sum that he handed over as if passing her an empty gum wrapper—and smiled again. Even as some small part of her cringed at the tiny fact that she wouldn't receive any part of her commission on the piece. On any art in Jesiba's gallery. That money went elsewhere.

"A pleasure doing business with you, Mr. Tertian."

There. Done. Time to go home and climb into bed and snuggle with Syrinx. The best form of celebrating she could think of these days.

But a pale, strong hand landed on the folio. "Going so soon?" Maximus's smile grew again. "It'd be a shame for a pretty thing like you to leave when I was about to order a bottle of Serat." The sparkling wine from the south of Valbara started at roughly a hundred gold marks a bottle. And apparently made pricks like him believe they were entitled to female company.

Bryce gave him a wink, trying to pull the folio with the check toward her awaiting purse. "I think you'd be the one feeling sorry if a pretty thing like me left, Mr. Tertian."

His hand remained on the folio. "For what I paid your boss, I'd think some perks came with this deal."

Well, it had to be a record: being mistaken for a whore twice within ten minutes. She had no disdain for the world's oldest profession, only respect and sometimes pity, but being mistaken for one of them had led to more unfortunate incidents than she liked. Yet Bryce managed to say calmly, "I'm afraid I have another meeting."

Maximus's hand slipped to her wrist, gripping hard enough to demonstrate that he could snap every bone inside it with barely a thought.

She refused to allow her scent to shift as her stomach hollowed out. She had dealt with his kind and worse. "Take your hand off me, please."

She added the last word because she owed it to Jesiba to at least sound polite—just once.

But Maximus surveyed her body with all the male, immortal entitlement in the world. "Some like their prey to play hard to get." He smiled up at her again. "I happen to be one of them. I'll make it good for you, you know."

She met his stare, hating that some small part of her wanted to recoil. That it recognized him as a predator and her as his prey and she'd be lucky to even get the chance to run before she was eaten whole. "No, thank you."

The VIP mezzanine went quiet, the ripple of silence a sure sign that some bigger, badder predator had prowled in. Good.

Maybe it'd distract the vampyr long enough for her to snatch her wrist back. And that check. Jesiba would flay her alive if she left without it.

Indeed, Maximus's gaze drifted over her shoulder to whoever had entered. His hand tightened on Bryce's. Just hard enough that Bryce looked.

A dark-haired Fae male stalked up to the other end of the bar. Looking right at her.

She tried not to groan. And not the way she'd groaned with that lion shifter.

The Fae male kept looking at her as Maximus's upper lip pulled back from his teeth, revealing the elongated canines he so badly wanted to sink into her. Maximus snarled in warning. "You are mine." The words were so guttural she could barely understand him.

Bryce sighed through her nose as the Fae male took a seat at the bar, murmuring his drink order to the silver-haired sylph behind it. "That's my cousin," Bryce said. "Relax."

The vampyr blinked. "What?"

His surprise cost him: his grip loosened, and Bryce stashed the folio with the check in her purse as she stepped back. At least her Fae heritage was good for moving quickly when necessary. Walking away, Bryce purred over a shoulder, "Just so you know—I don't do possessive and aggressive."

Maximus snarled again, but he'd seen who her "cousin" was. He didn't dare follow.

Even when the world thought they were only distantly related, one didn't fuck with the relatives of Ruhn Danaan.

If they had known Ruhn was her brother—well, technically her half brother—no male would ever go near her. But thankfully, the world thought he was her cousin, and she was glad to keep it that way. Not just because of who their sire was and the secrecy that she'd long ago sworn to maintain. Not just because Ruhn was the legitimate child, the fucking Chosen One, and she was . . . not.

Ruhn was already sipping from his whiskey, his striking blue eyes fixed on Maximus. Promising death.

She was half-tempted to let Ruhn send Maximus scurrying back to his daddy's castle of horrors, but she'd worked so hard on the deal, had tricked the asshole into paying nearly a third more than the bust was worth. All it would take was one phone call from Maximus to his banker and that check in her purse would be dead on arrival.

So Bryce went up to Ruhn, drawing his attention from the vampyr at last.

Her brother's black T-shirt and dark jeans were tight enough to show off the muscles Fae went to pieces over, and that plenty of people on the VIP level were now ogling. The tattooed sleeves on his golden-skinned arms, however, were colorful and beautiful enough to piss off their father. Along with the line of rings in one arched ear, and the straight black hair that flowed to his waist save for one shaved side. All painting a glaring billboard that said *Fuck You, Dad!*

But Ruhn was still a Fae male. Still fifty years older than her. Still a domineering dick whenever she ran into him or his friends. Which was whenever she couldn't avoid it.

"Well, well, well," Bryce said, nodding her thanks to the

bartender as another sparkling water appeared before her. She took a swig, swishing the bubbles to rinse away the lingering taste of lion and alphahole. "Look who decided to stop frequenting poseur rock clubs and start hanging with the cool kids. Seems like the Chosen One's finally getting hip."

"I always forget how annoying you are," Ruhn said by way of greeting. "And not that it's any of your business, but I'm not here to party."

Bryce surveyed her brother. No sign of the Starsword tonight—and, glancing at him, beyond the telltale physical heritage of the Starborn line, little declared that he'd been anointed by Luna or genetics to usher their people to greater heights. But it had been years since they'd really spoken. Maybe Ruhn had crawled back into the fold. It'd be a shame, considering the shit that had gone down to pull him out of it in the first place.

Bryce asked, "Is there a reason why you're here, other than to ruin my night?"

Ruhn snorted. "Still happy playing slutty secretary, I see."

Spoiled prick. For a few glittering years, they'd been best friends, a dynamic duo against Motherfucker Number One—aka the Fae male who'd sired them—but that was ancient history. Ruhn had seen to that.

She frowned at the packed club below, scanning the crowd for any sign of the two friends who trailed Ruhn everywhere, both pains in her ass. "How'd you get in here, anyway?" Even a Fae Prince had to wait in line at the Raven. Bryce had once delighted in watching preening Fae assholes be turned away at the doors.

"Riso's my buddy," Ruhn said. "He and I play poker on Tuesday nights."

Of course Ruhn had somehow managed to befriend the club's owner. A rare breed of butterfly shifter, what Riso lacked in size he made up for with sheer personality, always laughing, always flitting about the club and dancing above the crowd. Feeding off its merriment as if it were nectar. He was picky about his close circle, though—he liked to cultivate *interesting* groups of people to entertain him. Bryce and Danika had never made the cut, but odds were that Fury was in that poker group. Too bad Fury didn't answer her calls for Bryce to even ask about it.

Ruhn bared his teeth at Maximus as the glowering vamp headed toward the golden steps. "Riso called me a few minutes ago and said you were here. With that fucking creep."

"Excuse me?" Her voice sharpened. It had nothing to do with the fact that she highly doubted the diplomatic club owner had used those terms. Riso was more the type to say, *She's with someone who might cause the dancing to cease*. Which would have been Riso's idea of Hel.

Ruhn said, "Riso can't risk tossing Tertian to the curb—he implied the prick was being handsy and you needed backup." A purely predatory gleam entered her brother's eyes. "Don't you know what Tertian's father *does*?"

She grinned, and knew it didn't reach her eyes. None of her smiles did these days. "I do," she said sweetly.

Ruhn shook his head in disgust. Bryce leaned forward to grab her drink, each movement controlled—if only to keep from taking the water and throwing it in his face.

"Shouldn't you be home?" Ruhn asked. "It's a weekday. You've got *work* in six hours."

"Thanks, Mom," she said. But getting home and taking off her bra did sound fantastic. She'd been up before dawn again, sweat-soaked and breathless, and the day hadn't improved from there. Maybe she'd be exhausted enough tonight to actually sleep.

But when Ruhn made no move to leave, Bryce sighed. "Let's hear it, then."

There had to be another reason why Ruhn had bothered to come—there always was, considering who had sired them.

Ruhn sipped from his drink. "The Autumn King wants you to lie low. The Summit meeting is in just over a month, and he wants any loose cannons tied down."

"What does the Summit meeting have to do with me?" They occurred every ten years, a gathering of Valbara's ruling powers to debate whatever issues or policies the Asteri ordered them to deal with. Each territory in the Republic held its own Summit meeting on a rotating schedule, so that one occurred in the world each year—and Bryce had paid attention to exactly zero of them.

"The Autumn King wants everyone associated with the Fae on their best behavior—rumor says the Asteri are sending over some of their favored commanders, and he wants us all looking like good, obedient subjects. Honestly, I don't fucking care, Bryce. I was just ordered to tell you to not . . . get into trouble until the meeting's over."

"You mean, don't do anything embarrassing."

"Basically," he said, drinking again. "And look: beyond that, shit always gets intense around the Summit meetings, so be careful, okay? People come out of the woodwork to make their agendas known. Be on your guard."

"I didn't know Daddy bothered to care about my safety." He never had before.

"He doesn't," Ruhn said, lips thinning, the silver hoop through the bottom one shifting with the movement. "But I'll make him care about it."

She considered the rage in his blue eyes—it wasn't directed at her. Ruhn hadn't yet fallen in line, then. Hadn't bought into his Chosen One greatness. She took another sip of water. "Since when does he listen to you?"

"Bryce. Just stay out of trouble—on all fronts. For whatever reason, this Summit is important to him. He's been on edge about it—beyond the whole everyone-needing-to-behave-themselves bullcrap." He sighed. "I haven't seen him this riled since two years ago . . ."

The words trailed off as he caught himself. But she got his meaning. Since two years ago. Since Danika. And Connor.

The glass in her hands cracked.

"Easy," Ruhn murmured. "Easy."

She couldn't stop clutching the glass, couldn't get her body to back down from the primal fury that surged up, up—

The heavy crystal glass exploded in her hands, water spraying across the golden bar. The bartender whirled, but kept away. No one along the bar dared look for more than a breath—not at the Crown Prince of the Valbaran Fae.

Ruhn gripped Bryce's face with a hand. *"Take a fucking breath."*

That horrible, useless Fae side of her obeyed the dominance in his command, her body falling back on instincts that had been bred into her, despite her best attempts to ignore them.

Bryce sucked in a breath, then another. Gasping, shuddering sounds.

But with each breath, the blinding wrath receded. Eddied away.

Ruhn held her gaze until she stopped snarling, until she could see clearly. Then he slowly released her face—and took a deep breath of his own. "Fuck, Bryce."

She stood on wobbling legs and adjusted the strap of her purse over her shoulder, making sure Maximus's outrageous check was still inside. "Message received. I'll lie low and act my classiest until the Summit."

Ruhn scowled and slid off the stool with familiar Fae grace. "Let me walk you home."

"I don't need you to." Besides, no one went to her apartment. Which wasn't technically even *her* apartment, but that was beside the point. Only her mom and Randall, and occasionally Juniper if she ever left the dance studio, but no one else was allowed inside. It was her sanctuary, and she didn't want Fae scents anywhere near it.

But Ruhn ignored her refusal and scanned the bar. "Where's your coat?"

She clenched her jaw. "I didn't bring one."

"It's barely spring."

She stomped past him, wishing she'd worn boots instead of stilettos. "Then it's a good thing I have my alcohol sweater on, isn't it?" A lie. She hadn't touched a drink in nearly two years.

Ruhn didn't know that, though. Nor did anyone else.

He trailed her. "You're hilarious. Glad all those tuition dollars went to something."

She strode down the stairs. "At least I went to college and didn't sit at home on a pile of Daddy's cash, playing video games with my dickbag friends."

Ruhn growled, but Bryce was already halfway down the

staircase to the dance floor. Moments later, she was elbowing her way through the crowds between the pillars, then breezing down the few steps into the glass-enclosed courtyard—still flanked on two sides by the temple's original stone walls—and toward the enormous iron doors. She didn't wait to see if Ruhn still trailed before she slipped out, waving at the half-wolf, half-daemonaki bouncers, who returned the gesture.

They were good guys—years ago, on rougher nights, they had always made sure Bryce got into a taxi. And that the driver knew exactly what would happen if she didn't get home in one piece.

She made it a block before she sensed Ruhn catching up, a storm of temper behind her. Not close enough for someone to know they were together, but near enough for her senses to be full of his scent, his annoyance.

At least it kept any would-be predators from approaching her.

When Bryce reached the glass-and-marble lobby of her building, Marrin, the ursine shifter behind the front desk, buzzed her through the double doors with a friendly wave. Pausing with a hand on the glass doors, she glanced over a shoulder to where Ruhn leaned against a black-painted lamppost. He lifted a hand in farewell—a mockery of one.

She flipped him off and walked into her building. A quick hello to Marrin, an elevator ride up to the penthouse, five levels above, and the small cream-colored hallway appeared. She sighed, heels sinking into the plush cobalt runner that flowed between her apartment and the one across the hall, and opened her purse. She found her keys by the glow of the firstlight orb in the bowl atop the blackwood table against the wall, its radiance gilding the white orchid drooping over it.

Bryce unlocked her door, first by key, then by the finger pad beside the knob. The heavy locks and spells hissed as they faded away, and she stepped into her dark apartment. The scent of lilac oil from her diffuser caressed her as Syrinx yowled his greeting and demanded to be immediately released from his crate. But Bryce leaned back against the door.

She hated knowing that Ruhn still lurked on the street below, the Crown Fucking Prince of Possessive and Aggressive Alphaholes, staring at the massive floor-to-ceiling wall of windows across the great room before her, waiting for the lights to come on.

His banging on the door in three minutes would be inevitable if she refused to turn on the lights. Marrin wouldn't be stupid enough to stop him. Not Ruhn Danaan. There had never been a door shut for him, not once in his entire life.

But she wasn't in the mood for that battle. Not tonight.

Bryce flicked on the panel of lights beside the door, illuminating the pale wood floors, the white plush furniture, the matching white walls. All of it as pristine as the day she'd moved in, almost two years ago—all of it far above her pay grade.

All of it paid for by Danika. By that stupid fucking will.

Syrinx grumbled, his cage rattling. Another possessive and aggressive alphahole. But a small, fuzzy one, at least.

With a sigh, Bryce kicked off her heels, unhooked her bra at last, and went to let the little beast out of his cage.

9

Please."

The male's whimper was barely discernible with the blood filling his mouth, his nostrils. But he still tried again. "Please."

Hunt Athalar's sword dripped blood onto the soaked carpet of the dingy apartment in the Meadows. Splatters of it coated the visor of his helmet, speckling his line of vision as he surveyed the lone male standing.

Kneeling, technically.

The male's friends littered the living room floor, one of them still spurting blood from what was now his stump of a neck. His severed head lay on the sagging sofa, gaping face rolled into the age-flattened cushions.

"I'll tell you everything," the male pleaded, sobbing as he pressed his hand against the gash on his shoulder. "They didn't tell you all of it, but I can."

The male's terror filled the room, overpowering the scent of blood, its reek as bad as stale piss in an alley.

Hunt's gloved hand tightened on his blade. The male noted it and began shaking, a stain paler than blood leaking across his pants. "I'll tell you more," the man tried again.

Hunt braced his feet, rooting his strength into the floor, and slashed his blade.

The male's innards spilled onto the carpet with a wet slap. Still the male kept screaming.

So Hunt kept working.

Hunt made it to the Comitium barracks without anyone seeing him.

At this hour, the city at least appeared asleep. The five buildings that made up the Comitium's complex did, too. But the cameras throughout the 33rd Legion's barracks—the second of the Comitium's spire-capped towers—saw everything. Heard everything.

The white-tiled halls were dim, no hint of the hustle that would fill them come dawn.

The helmet's visor cast everything into stark relief, its audio receptors picking up sounds from behind the shut bedroom doors lining either side of hallway: low-level sentries playing some video game, doing their best to keep their voices down as they cursed at each other; a female sentry talking on the phone; two angels fucking each other's brains out; and several snorers.

Hunt passed his own door, instead aiming for the shared bathroom in the center of the long hallway, accessible only through the common room. Any hope for an unnoticed return vanished at the sight of the golden light leaking from beneath the shut door and the sound of voices beyond it.

Too tired, too filthy, Hunt didn't bother to say hello as he entered the common room, prowling past the scattering of couches and chairs toward the bathroom.

Naomi was sprawled on the worn green couch before the TV, her black wings spread. Viktoria lounged in the armchair next to her, watching the day's sports highlights, and on the other end of the couch sat Justinian, still in his black legionary armor.

Their conversation stalled as Hunt entered.

"Hey," Naomi said, her inky braid draping over her shoulder. She wore her usual black—the triarii's usual black—though there was no trace of her wicked weapons or their holsters.

Viktoria seemed content to let Hunt pass without greeting. It was why he liked the wraith more than nearly anyone else in

Micah Domitus's inner circle of warriors, had liked her since those early days in the 18th, when she'd been one of the few non-angel Vanir to join their cause. Vik never pushed when Hunt didn't want to be bothered. But Justinian—

The angel sniffed, scenting the blood on Hunt's clothes, his weapons. How many different people it belonged to. Justinian blew out a whistle. "You are one sick fuck, you know that?"

Hunt continued toward the bathroom door. His lightning didn't so much as hiss inside him.

Justinian went on, "A gun would have been a Hel of a lot cleaner."

"Micah didn't want a gun for this," Hunt said, his voice hollow even to his ears. It had been that way for centuries now; but tonight, these kills he'd made, what they'd done to earn the wrath of the Archangel . . . "They didn't deserve a gun," he amended. Or the swift bolt of his lightning.

"I don't want to know," Naomi grumbled, punching up the volume of the TV. She pointed with the remote at Justinian, the youngest in the triarii. "And neither do you, so shut it."

No, they really didn't want to know.

Naomi—the only one of the triarii who was not Fallen—said to Hunt, "Isaiah told me that Micah wants you two playing investigators tomorrow for some shit in the Old Square. Isaiah will call you after breakfast with the details."

The words barely registered. Isaiah. Tomorrow. Old Square.

Justinian snorted. "Good luck, man." He swigged from his beer. "I hate the Old Square—it's all university brats and tourist creeps." Naomi and Viktoria grunted their agreement.

Hunt didn't ask why they were up, or where Isaiah was, given that he couldn't deliver the message. The angel was likely with whatever handsome male he was currently dating.

As Commander of the 33rd, acquired by Micah to shore up Crescent City's defenses, Isaiah had enjoyed every second here since he'd arrived more than a decade ago. In four years, Hunt hadn't seen the city's appeal beyond it being a cleaner, more organized version of any Pangeran metropolis, with streets in clean lines rather than meandering curves that often doubled back on themselves, as if in no hurry to get anywhere.

But at least it wasn't Ravilis. And at least it was Micah ruling over it, not Sandriel.

Sandriel—the Archangel and Governor of the northwestern quadrant of Pangera, and Hunt's former owner before Micah had traded with her, desiring to have Hunt clear Crescent City of any enemies. Sandriel—his dead lover's twin sister.

The formal papers declared that Hunt's duties would be to track down and dispatch any loose demons. But considering that those sorts of disasters happened only once or twice a year, it was glaringly obvious why he'd really been brought over. He'd done most of the assassinating for Sandriel, the Archangel who bore the same face as his beloved, for the fifty-three years she'd possessed him.

A rare occurrence, for both siblings to bear an Archangel's title and power. A good omen, people had believed. Until Shahar—until Hunt, leading her forces—had rebelled against everything the angels stood for. And betrayed her sister in the process.

Sandriel had been the third of his owners after the defeat at Mount Hermon, and had been arrogant enough to believe that despite the two Archangels before her who had failed to do so, she might be the one to break him. First in her horror show of a dungeon. Then in her blood-soaked arena in the heart of Ravilis, pitting him against warriors who never stood a chance. Then by commanding him to do what he did best: slipping into a room and ending lives. One after another after another, year after year, decade after decade.

Sandriel certainly had motivation to break him. During that too-short battle at Hermon, it was her forces that Hunt had decimated, his lightning that turned soldier after soldier into charred husks before they could draw their swords. Sandriel had been Shahar's prime target, and Hunt had been ordered to take her out. By whatever means necessary.

And Shahar had good reason to go after her sister. Their parents had both been Archangels, whose titles had passed to their daughters after an assassin had somehow managed to rip them to shreds.

He'd never forget Shahar's theory: that Sandriel had killed their parents and framed the assassin. That she'd done it for herself and her sister, so they might rule without *interference*. There had never been proof to pin it on Sandriel, but Shahar believed it to her dying day.

Shahar, the Daystar, had rebelled against her fellow Archangels and the Asteri because of it. She'd wanted a world free of rigid hierarchies, yes—would have brought their rebellion right to the crystal palace of the Asteri if it had been successful. But she'd also wanted to make her sister pay. So Hunt had been unleashed.

Fools. They had all been fools.

It made no difference if he'd admitted his folly. Sandriel believed he'd lured her twin into the rebellion, that *he* had turned Shahar against her. That somehow, when sister had drawn blade against sister, so nearly identical in face and build and fighting technique that it was like watching someone battle their reflection, it was *his fucking fault* that it had ended with one of them dead.

At least Micah had offered him the chance to redeem himself. To prove his utter loyalty and submission to the Archangels, to the empire, and then one day get the halo removed. Decades from now, possibly centuries, but considering that the oldest angels lived to be nearly eight hundred . . . maybe he'd earn back his freedom in time to be old. He could potentially die free.

Micah had offered Hunt the bargain from his first day in Crescent City four years ago: a kill for every life he'd taken that bloody day on Mount Hermon. Every angel he'd slaughtered during that doomed battle, he was to pay back. In the form of more death. *A death for a death*, Micah had said. *When you've fulfilled the debt, Athalar, we'll discuss removing that tattoo on your brow.*

Hunt had never known the tally—how many he'd killed that day. But Micah, who'd been on that battlefield, who'd watched while Shahar fell at her twin sister's hand, had the list. They'd had to pay out commissions for all the legionaries. Hunt had been about to ask how they'd been able to determine which killing blows had been made by his blade and not someone else's, when he'd seen the number.

Two thousand two hundred and seventeen.

It was impossible for him to have personally killed that many in one battle. Yes, his lightning had been unleashed; yes, he'd blasted apart entire units, but that many?

He'd gaped. *You were Shahar's general*, Micah said. *You commanded the 18th. So you will atone, Athalar, not only for the lives you took, but those your traitorous legion took as well.* At Hunt's silence, Micah had added, *This is not some impossible task. Some of my missions will count for more than one life. Behave, obey, and you will be able to reach this number.*

For four years now, he had behaved. He had obeyed. And tonight had put him at a grand total of eighty-fucking-two.

It was the best he could hope for. All he worked for. No other Archangel had ever offered him the chance. It was why he'd done everything Micah had ordered him to do tonight. Why every thought felt distant, his body pulled from him, his head full of a dull roaring.

Micah was an Archangel. A Governor appointed by the Asteri. He was a king among angels, and law unto himself, especially in Valbara—so far from the seven hills of the Eternal City. If he deemed someone a threat or in need of justice, then there would be no investigation, no trial.

Just his command. Usually to Hunt.

It would arrive in the form of a file in his barracks mailbox, the imperial crest on its front. No mention of his name. Just *SPQM*, and the seven stars surrounding the letters.

The file contained all he needed: names, dates, crimes, and a timeline for Hunt to do what he did best. Plus any requests from Micah regarding the method employed.

Tonight it had been simple enough—no guns. Hunt understood the unwritten words: make them suffer. So he had.

"There's a beer with your name on it when you come out," Viktoria said, her eyes meeting Hunt's even with the helmet on. Nothing but a casual, cool invitation.

Hunt continued into the bathroom, the firstlights fluttering to life as he shouldered his way through the door and approached one of the shower stalls. He cranked the water to full heat before stalking back to the row of pedestal sinks.

In the mirror above one, the being who stared back was as bad as a Reaper. Worse.

Blood splattered the helmet, right over the painted silver skull's face. It gleamed faintly on the intricate leather scales of his battle-suit, on his black gloves, on the twin swords peeking above his shoulders. Flecks of it even stained his gray wings.

Hunt peeled off the helmet and braced his hands on the sink.

In the harsh bathroom firstlights, his light brown skin was pallid under the black band of thorns across his brow. The tattoo, he'd learned to live with. But he shrank from the look in his dark eyes. Glazed. Empty. Like staring into Hel.

Orion, his mother had named him. Hunter. He doubted she would have done so, would have so lovingly called him Hunt instead, if she'd known what he'd become.

Hunt glanced to where his gloves had left red stains on the porcelain sink.

Tugging off the gloves with brutal efficiency, Hunt prowled to the shower stall, where the water had reached near-scalding temperatures. He removed his weapons, then his battle-suit, leaving more streaks of blood on the tiles.

Hunt stepped under the spray, and submitted himself to its relentless burning.

10

It was barely ten in the morning, and Tuesday was already fucked.

Keeping a smile pasted on her face, Bryce lingered by her ironwood desk in the showroom of the gallery while a Fae couple browsed.

The elegant plucking of violins trickled through the hidden speakers in the two-level, wood-paneled space, the opening movement of a symphony that she'd switched on as soon as the intercom had buzzed. Given the couple's attire—a pleated tan skirt and white silk blouse for the female, a gray suit for the male—she'd doubted they'd appreciate the thumping bass of her morning workout mix.

But they'd been browsing the art for ten minutes now, which was enough time for her to politely inquire, "Are you here for anything in particular, or just to browse?"

The blond Fae male, older-looking for one of his kind, waved a dismissive hand, leading his companion toward the nearest display: a partial marble relief from the ruins of Morrah, salvaged from a wrecked temple. The piece was about the size of a coffee table, with a rearing hippocamp filling most of it. The half-horse, half-fish creatures had once dwelled in the cerulean waters of the Rhagan Sea in Pangera, until ancient wars had destroyed them.

"Browsing," the male replied coldly, his hand coming to rest on his companion's slender back as they studied the waves carved in strikingly precise detail.

Bryce summoned another smile. "Take your time. I'm at your disposal."

The female nodded her thanks, but the male sneered his dismissal. His companion frowned deeply at him.

The silence in the small gallery turned palpable.

Bryce had gleaned from the moment they'd walked through the door that the male was here to impress the female, either by buying something outrageously expensive or pretending he could. Perhaps this was an arranged pairing, testing out the waters before committing to anything further.

Had Bryce been full-blooded Fae, had her father claimed her as his offspring, she might have been subjected to such things. Ruhn, especially with his Starborn status, would one day have to submit to an arranged marriage, when a young female deemed suitable to continue the precious royal bloodline came along.

Ruhn might sire a few children before then, but they wouldn't be acknowledged as royalty unless their father chose that path. Unless they were *worthy* of it.

The Fae couple passed the mosaic from the courtyard of the once-great palace in Altium, then studied the intricate jade puzzle box that had belonged to a princess in a forgotten northern land.

Jesiba did most of the art acquisitions, which was why she was away so often, but Bryce herself had tracked down and purchased a good number of the pieces. And then resold them at a steep profit.

The couple had reached a set of fertility statues from Setmek when the front door buzzed.

Bryce glanced toward the clock on her desk. The afternoon client appointment wasn't for another three hours. To have multiple browsers in the gallery was an oddity given the notoriously steep price tags of the art in here, but—maybe she'd get lucky and sell something today.

"Excuse me," Bryce murmured, ducking around the massive desk and pulling up the outside camera feed on the computer. She'd barely clicked the icon when the buzzer rang again.

Bryce beheld who was standing on the sidewalk and froze.

Tuesday was indeed fucked.

No windows lined the sandstone facade of the slender two-story building a block off the Istros River. Only a bronze plaque to the right of the heavy iron door revealed to Hunt Athalar that it was a business of any sort.

Griffin Antiquities had been etched there in archaic, bold lettering, the words adorned with a set of glaring owl eyes beneath them, as if daring any shoppers to enter. An intercom with a matching bronze button lay beneath.

Isaiah, in his usual suit and tie, had been staring at the buzzer for long enough that Hunt finally drawled, "There aren't any enchantments on it, you know." Despite the identity of its owner.

Isaiah shot him a look, straightening his tie. "I should have had a second cup of coffee," he muttered before stabbing a finger onto the metal button. A faint buzzing sounded through the door.

No one answered.

Hunt scanned the building exterior for a hidden camera. Not a gleam or hint. The nearest one, in fact, was mounted on the chrome door of the bomb shelter halfway down the block.

Hunt scanned the sandstone facade again. There was no way Jesiba Roga wouldn't have cameras covering every inch, both outside and within.

Hunt unleashed a crackle of his power, small tongues of lightning tasting for energy fields.

Nearly invisible in the sunny morning, the lightning bounced off a skintight enchantment coating the stone, the mortar, the door. A cold, clever spell that seemed to laugh softly at any attempt to enter.

Hunt murmured, "Roga isn't screwing around, is she?"

Isaiah pushed the buzzer again, harder than necessary. They had their orders—ones that were pressing enough that even Isaiah, regardless of the lack of coffee, was on a short fuse.

Though it could also have been due to the fact that Isaiah had been out until four in the morning. Hunt hadn't asked about it, though. Had only heard Naomi and Justinian gossiping in the common room, wondering if this new boyfriend meant Isaiah was finally moving on.

Hunt hadn't bothered to tell them there was no fucking way. Not when Isaiah obeyed Micah only because of the generous weekly salary that Micah gave them all, when the law declared that slaves weren't owed a paycheck. The money Isaiah amassed would buy someone else's freedom. Just as the shit Hunt did for Micah went toward earning his own.

Isaiah rang the buzzer a third time. "Maybe she's not in."

"She's here," Hunt said. The scent of her still lingered on the sidewalk, lilac and nutmeg and something he couldn't quite place—like the gleam of the first stars at nightfall.

And indeed, a moment later, a silky female voice that definitely did not belong to the gallery's owner crackled through the intercom. "I didn't order a pizza."

Despite himself, despite the mental clock ticking away, Hunt choked on a laugh.

Isaiah rustled his white wings, plastering on a charming smile, and said into the intercom, "We're from the 33rd Legion. We're here to see Bryce Quinlan."

The voice sharpened. "I'm with clients. Come back later."

Hunt was pretty sure that "come back later" meant "go fuck yourselves."

Isaiah's charming smile strained. "This is a matter of some urgency, Miss Quinlan."

A low hum. "I'm sorry, but you'll have to make an appointment. How about . . . three weeks? I've got the twenty-eighth of April free. I'll pencil you in for noon."

Well, she had balls, Hunt would give her that much.

Isaiah widened his stance. Typical legion fighting position, beaten into them from their earliest days as grunts. "We need to talk right now, I'm afraid."

No answer came. Like she'd just walked away from the intercom.

Hunt's snarl sent the poor faun walking behind them bolting down the street, his delicate hooves clopping on the cobblestones. "She's a spoiled party girl. What did you expect?"

"She's not stupid, Hunt," Isaiah countered.

"Everything I've seen and heard suggests otherwise." What he'd seen when he skimmed her file two years ago, combined with what he'd read this morning and the pictures he'd gone through, all painted a portrait that told him precisely how this meeting would go. Too bad for her it was about to get a Hel of a lot more serious.

Hunt jerked his chin toward the door. "Let's see if a client's even in there." He stalked back across the street, where he leaned against a parked blue car. Some drunken reveler had used its hood as a canvas to spray-paint an unnecessarily detailed, massive cock—with wings. A mockery of the 33rd's logo of a winged sword, he realized. Or merely the logo stripped down to its true meaning.

Isaiah noted it as well and chuckled, following Hunt's lead and leaning against the car.

A minute passed. Hunt didn't move an inch. Didn't take his gaze away from the iron door. He had better things to do with this day than play games with a brat, but orders were orders. After five minutes, a sleek black sedan rolled up and the iron door opened.

The Fae driver of the car, which was worth more than most human families saw in a lifetime, got out. He was around the other side of the vehicle in a heartbeat, opening the back passenger door. Two Fae paraded out of the gallery, a male and a female. The pretty female's every breath radiated the easy confidence gained from a lifetime of wealth and privilege.

Around her slim neck lay a strand of diamonds, each as large as Hunt's fingernail. Worth as much as the car—more. The male climbed into the sedan, face tight as he slammed the door before his driver could do it for him. The well-heeled female just rushed down the street, phone already to her ear, grousing to whoever was on the line about *No more blind dates, for Urd's sake*.

Hunt's attention returned to the gallery door, where a curvy, red-haired woman stood.

Only when the car rounded the corner did Bryce slide her eyes toward them.

She angled her head, her silken sheet of hair sliding over the shoulder of her white skintight dress, and smiled brightly. Waved. The delicate gold amulet around her tan neck glinted.

Hunt pushed off the parked car and stalked toward her, his gray wings flaring wide.

A flick of Bryce's amber eyes took in Hunt from his tattoo to his ass-kicking boot tips. Her smile grew. "See you in three weeks," she said cheerfully, and slammed the door shut.

Hunt cleared the street in a matter of steps. A car screeched to a stop, but the driver wasn't stupid enough to blast the horn. Not when lightning wreathed Hunt's fist as he pounded it into the intercom button. "Don't waste my fucking time, Quinlan."

Isaiah let the near-frantic driver pass before coming up behind Hunt, his brown eyes narrowing. But Bryce replied sweetly, "My boss doesn't like legionaries in her place. Sorry."

Hunt slammed his fist into the iron door. That same blow had smashed cars, shattered walls, and splintered bones. And that was without the aid of the storm in his veins. The iron didn't so much as shudder; his lightning skittered off it.

To Hel with threats, then. He'd go for the jugular, as deep and sure as any of his physical kills. So Hunt said into the intercom, "We're here about a murder."

Isaiah winced, scanning the street and skies for anyone who might have heard.

Hunt crossed his arms as the silence spread.

Then the iron door hissed and clicked, and inched open.

Bull's-fucking-eye.

It took Hunt a heartbeat to adjust from the sunlight to the dimmer interior, and he used that first step into the gallery to note every angle and exit and detail.

Plush pine-green carpets went wall to wood-paneled wall in the two-story showroom. Alcoves with soft-lit art displays dotted the edges of the room: chunks of ancient frescoes, paintings, and statues of Vanir so strange and rare even Hunt didn't know their names.

Bryce Quinlan leaned against the large ironwood desk in the center of the space, her snow-white dress clinging to every generous curve and dip.

Hunt smiled slowly, showing all his teeth.

He waited for it: the realization of who he was. Waited for her to shrink back, to fumble for the panic button or gun or whatever the fuck she thought might save her from the likes of him.

But maybe she was stupid, after all, because her answering smile was saccharine in the extreme. Her red-tinted nails idly tapped on the pristine wood surface. "You have fifteen minutes."

Hunt didn't tell her that this meeting would likely take a good deal longer than that.

Isaiah turned to shut the door, but Hunt knew it was already locked. Just as he knew, thanks to legion intel gathered over the years, that the small wood door behind the desk led upstairs to Jesiba Roga's office—where a floor-to-ceiling internal window overlooked the showroom they stood in—and the simple iron door to their right led down into another full level, stocked with things that legionaries weren't supposed to find. The enchantments on those two doors were probably even more intense than those outside.

Isaiah loosed one of his long-suffering sighs. "A murder occurred on the outskirts of the Meat Market last night. We believe you knew the victim."

Hunt marked every reaction that flitted across her face as she maintained her perch on the edge of the desk: the slight widening of her eyes, the pause in those tapping nails, the sole blink that suggested she had a short list of possible victims and none of the options were good.

"Who?" was all she said, her voice steady. Wisps of smoke from the conical diffuser beside the computer drifted past her, carrying the bright, clean scent of peppermint. Of course she was one of those aromatherapy zealots, conned into handing over her marks for the promise of feeling happier, or being better in bed, or growing another half a brain to match the half she already had.

"Maximus Tertian," Isaiah told her. "We have reports that you had a meeting with him in the VIP mezzanine of the White Raven two hours before his death."

Hunt could have sworn Bryce's shoulders sagged slightly. She said, "Maximus Tertian is dead." They nodded. She angled her head. "Who did it?"

"That's what we're trying to figure out," Isaiah said neutrally.

Hunt had heard of Tertian—a creep of a vamp who couldn't take no for an answer, and whose rich, sadistic father had taught him well. And shielded him from any fallout from his hideous behavior. If Hunt was being honest, Midgard was better off without him. Except for the headache they'd now have to endure when Tertian's father got word that his favored son had been killed . . . Today's meeting would be just the start.

Isaiah went on, "You might have been one of the last people to see him alive. Can you walk us through your encounter with him? No detail is too small."

Bryce glanced between them. "Is this your way of feeling out whether I killed him?"

Hunt smiled slightly. "You don't seem too cut up that Tertian's dead."

Those amber eyes slid to him, annoyance lighting them.

He'd admit it: males would do a lot of fucked-up things for someone who looked like that.

He'd done precisely those sort of things for Shahar once. Now he bore the halo tattooed across his brow and the slave tattoo on his wrist because of it. His chest tightened.

Bryce said, "I'm sure someone's already said that Maximus and I parted on unfriendly terms. We met to finish up a deal for the gallery, and when it was done, he thought he was entitled to some . . . personal time with me."

Hunt understood her perfectly. It lined up with everything he'd heard regarding Tertian and his father. It also offered a good amount of motive.

Bryce went on, "I don't know where he went after the Raven. If he was killed on the outskirts of the Meat Market, I'd assume he was heading there to purchase what he wanted to take from me." Cold, sharp words.

Isaiah's expression grew stony. "Was his behavior last night different from how he acted during previous meetings?"

"We only interacted over emails and the phone, but I'd say no. Last night was our first face-to-face, and he acted exactly as his past behavior would indicate."

Hunt asked, "Why not meet here? Why the Raven?"

"He got off on the thrill of acting like our deal was secretive. He claimed he didn't trust that my boss wasn't recording the meeting, but he really just wanted people to notice him—to see him doing deals. I had to slide him the paperwork in a bill folio, and he swapped it with one of his own, that sort of thing." She met Hunt's stare. "How did he die?"

The question was blunt, and she didn't smile or blink. A girl used to being answered, obeyed, heeded. Her parents weren't wealthy—or so her file said—yet her apartment fifteen blocks away suggested outrageous wealth. Either from this job or some shady shit that had escaped even the legion's watchful eyes.

Isaiah sighed. "Those details are classified."

She shook her head. "I can't help you. Tertian and I did the deal, he got handsy, and he left."

Every bit of the camera footage and eyewitness reports from the Raven confirmed that. But that wasn't why they were here. What they'd been sent over to do.

Isaiah said, "And when did Prince Ruhn Danaan show up?"

"If you know everything, why bother asking me?" She didn't wait for them to answer before she said, "You know, you two never told me your names."

Hunt couldn't read her expression, her relaxed body language. They hadn't initiated contact since that night in the legion's holding center—and neither of them had introduced themselves then. Had she even registered their faces in that drug-induced haze?

Isaiah adjusted his pristine white wings. "I'm Isaiah Tiberian, Commander of the 33rd Imperial Legion. This is Hunt Athalar, my—"

Isaiah tripped up, as if realizing that it had been a damn long time since they'd had to introduce themselves with any sort of rank attached. So Hunt did Isaiah a favor and finished with, "His Second."

If Isaiah was surprised to hear it, that calm, pretty-boy face didn't let on. Isaiah was, technically, his superior in the triarii and in the 33rd as a whole, even if the shit Hunt did for Micah made him directly answerable to the Governor.

Isaiah had never pulled rank, though. As if he remembered those days before the Fall, and who'd been in charge then.

As if it fucking mattered now.

No, all that mattered about that shit was that Isaiah had killed at least three dozen Imperial Legionaries that day on Mount Hermon. And Hunt now bore the burden of paying back each one of those lives to the Republic. To fulfill Micah's bargain.

Bryce's eyes flicked to their brows—the tattoos there. Hunt braced for the sneering remark, for any of the bullshit comments people still liked to make about the Fallen Legion and their failed rebellion. But she only said, "So, what—you two investigate crimes on the side? I thought that was Auxiliary territory. Don't you have better things to do in the 33rd than play buddy cop?"

Isaiah, apparently not amused that there was one person in this city who didn't fall at his feet, said a tad stiffly, "Do you have people who can verify your whereabouts after you left the White Raven?"

Bryce held Isaiah's gaze. Then flicked her eyes to Hunt. And he still couldn't read her mask of boredom as she pushed off the desk and took a few deliberate steps toward them before crossing her arms.

"Just my doorman . . . and Ruhn Danaan, but you already knew that."

How anyone could walk in heels that high was beyond him. How anyone could breathe in a dress that tight was also a mystery. It was long enough that it covered the area on her thigh where the scar from that night two years ago would be—that is, if she hadn't paid some medwitch to erase it. For someone who clearly took pains to dress nicely, he had little doubt she'd gotten it removed immediately.

Party girls didn't like scars messing with how they looked in a swimsuit.

Isaiah's white wings shifted. "Would you call Ruhn Danaan a friend?"

Bryce shrugged. "He's a distant cousin."

But apparently invested enough to have charged into the interrogation room two years ago. And shown up at the VIP bar last night. If he was that protective of Quinlan, that might be one Hel of a motive, too. Even if Ruhn and his father would make the interrogation a nightmare.

Bryce smiled sharply, as if she remembered that fact, too. "Have fun talking to him."

Hunt clenched his jaw, but she strode for the front door, hips swishing like she knew precisely how spectacular her ass was.

"Just a moment, Miss Quinlan," Isaiah said. The commander's voice was calm, but take-no-shit.

Hunt hid his smile. Seeing Isaiah angry was always a good show. So long as you weren't on the receiving end.

Quinlan hadn't realized that yet as she glanced over a shoulder. "Yes?"

Hunt eyed her as Isaiah at last voiced their true reason for this little visit. "We weren't just sent here to ask you about your whereabouts."

She gestured to the gallery. "You want to buy something pretty for the Governor?"

Hunt's mouth twitched upward. "Funny you should mention him. He's on his way here right now."

A slow blink. Again, no sign or scent of fear. "Why?"

"Micah just told us to get information from you about last night, and then make sure you were available and have you get your boss on the line." Given how infrequently Hunt was asked to help out on investigations, he'd been shocked as Hel to get the order. But considering that he and Isaiah had been there that night in the alley, he supposed that made them the top choices to head this sort of thing up.

"Micah is coming here." Her throat bobbed once.

"He'll be here in ten minutes," Isaiah said. He nodded toward her phone. "I suggest you call your boss, Miss Quinlan."

Her breathing turned slightly shallow. "Why?"

Hunt dropped the bomb at last. "Because Maximus Tertian's injuries were identical to the ones inflicted upon Danika Fendyr and the Pack of Devils." Pulped and dismembered.

Her eyes shuttered. "But—Philip Briggs killed them. He summoned that demon to kill them. And he's in prison." Her voice sharpened. "He's been in prison for *two years*."

In a place worse than prison, but that was beside the point.

"We know," Hunt said, keeping his face devoid of any reaction.

"He can't have killed Tertian. How could he possibly summon the demon from jail?" Bryce said. "He . . ." She swallowed, catching herself. Realizing, perhaps, why Micah was coming. Several people she'd known had been killed, all within hours of interacting with her. "You think Briggs didn't do it. Didn't kill Danika and her pack."

"We don't know that for sure," Isaiah cut in. "But the specific details of how they all died never leaked, so we have good reason to believe this wasn't a copycat murder."

Bryce asked flatly, "Have you met with Sabine?"

Hunt said, "Have *you*?"

"We do our best to stay out of each other's way."

It was perhaps the only smart thing Bryce Quinlan had ever decided to do. Hunt remembered Sabine's venom as she'd glared through the window at Bryce in the observation room two years ago, and he had no doubt Sabine was just waiting for enough time to pass for Quinlan's unfortunate and untimely death to be considered nothing more than a fluke.

Bryce walked back to her desk, giving them a wide berth. To her credit, her gait remained unhurried and solid. She picked up the phone without so much as looking at them.

"We'll wait outside," Isaiah offered. Hunt opened his mouth to object, but Isaiah shot him a warning look.

Fine. He and Quinlan could spar later.

Phone held in a white-knuckled grip, Bryce listened to the other end ring. Twice. Then—

"Morning, Bryce."

Bryce's heartbeat pounded in her arms, her legs, her stomach. "Two legionaries are here." She swallowed. "The Commander of the 33rd and . . ." She blew out a breath. "The Umbra Mortis."

She'd recognized Isaiah Tiberian—he graced the nightly news and gossip columns often enough that there would never be any mistaking the 33rd's beautiful Commander.

And she'd recognized Hunt Athalar, too, though he was never on television. Everyone knew who Hunt Athalar was. She'd heard of him even while growing up in Nidaros, when Randall would talk about his battles in Pangera and whispered when he mentioned Hunt. The Umbra Mortis. The Shadow of Death.

Then, the angel hadn't worked for Micah Domitus and his legion, but for the Archangel Sandriel—he'd flown in her 45th Legion. Demon-hunting, rumor claimed his job was. And worse.

Jesiba hissed, "Why?"

Bryce clutched the phone. "Maximus Tertian was murdered last night."

"Burning *Solas*—"

"The same way as Danika and the pack."

Bryce shut out every hazy image, breathing in the bright, calming scent of the peppermint vapors rippling from the diffuser on her desk. She'd bought the stupid plastic cone two months after Danika had been killed, figuring it couldn't hurt to try some aromatherapy during the long, quiet hours of the day, when her thoughts swarmed and descended, eating her up from the inside out. By the end of the week, she'd bought three more and placed them throughout her house.

Bryce breathed, "It seems like Philip Briggs might not have killed Danika."

For two years, part of her had clung to it—that in the days following the murder, they'd found enough evidence to convict Briggs, who'd wanted Danika dead for busting his rebel bomb ring. Briggs had denied it, but it had added up: He'd been caught purchasing black summoning salts in the weeks before his initial arrest, apparently to fuel some sort of new, horrible weapon.

That Danika had then been murdered by a Pit-level demon—which would have required the deadly black salt to summon it into this world—couldn't have been a coincidence. It seemed quite clear that Briggs had been released, gotten his hands on the black salt, summoned the demon, and set it loose upon Danika and the Pack of Devils. It had attacked the 33rd soldier who'd been patrolling the alleyway, and when its work was done, it had been sent back to Hel by Briggs. Though he'd never confessed to it, or what the breed even was, the fact remained that the demon hadn't been seen again in two years. Since Briggs had been locked up. Case closed.

For two years, Bryce had clung to those facts. That even though her world had fallen apart, the person responsible was behind bars. Forever. Deserving of every horror his jailors inflicted on him.

Jesiba let out a long, long breath. "Did the angels accuse you of anything?"

"No." Not quite. "The Governor is coming here."

Another pause. "To interrogate you?"

"I hope not." She liked her body parts where they were. "He wants to talk to you, too."

"Does Tertian's father know he's dead?"

"I don't know."

"I need to make some phone calls," Jesiba said, more to herself. "Before the Governor comes." Bryce understood her meaning well enough: So Maximus's father didn't show up at the gallery, demanding answers. Blaming Bryce for his death. It'd be a mess.

Bryce wiped her sweaty palms on her thighs. "The Governor will be here soon."

Faint tapping sounded on the iron archives door before Lehabah whispered, "BB? Are you all right?"

Bryce put a hand over the mouthpiece of her phone. "Go back to your post, Lele."

"Were those two angels?"

Bryce ground her teeth. "Yes. Go downstairs. Keep Syrinx quiet."

Lehabah let out a sigh, audible through six inches of iron. But the fire sprite didn't speak further, suggesting she'd either returned to the archives beneath the gallery or was still eavesdropping. Bryce didn't care, as long as she and the chimera stayed quiet.

Jesiba was asking, "When does Micah get there?"

"Eight minutes."

Jesiba considered. "All right." Bryce tried not to gape at the fact that she didn't push for more time—especially with a client's death in the balance.

But even Jesiba knew not to screw around with an Archangel. Or maybe she'd finally found a scrap of empathy where Danika's murder was concerned. She sure as Hel hadn't demonstrated it when she'd ordered Bryce to get back to work or be turned into a pig two weeks after Danika's death.

Jesiba said, "I don't need to tell you to make sure everything is on lockdown."

"I'll double-check." But she'd made sure before the angels had even set foot in the gallery.

"Then you know what to do, Quinlan," Jesiba said, the sound of rustling sheets or clothes filling the background. Two male voices grumbled in protest. Then the line went dead.

Blowing out a breath, Bryce launched into motion.

11

The Archangel rang the buzzer precisely seven minutes later.

Calming her panting, Bryce scanned the gallery for the tenth time, confirming that all was in place, the art dust-free, any contraband stored below—

Her legs felt spindly, the old ache in her thigh clawing at the bone, but her hands remained steady as she reached the front door and hauled it open.

The Archangel was gorgeous. Horrifically, indecently gorgeous.

Hunt Athalar and Isaiah Tiberian stood behind him—almost as good-looking; the latter giving her another bland smile he obviously believed was charming. The former . . . Hunt's dark eyes missed nothing.

Bryce lowered her head to the Governor, stepping back, her stupid heels wobbling on the carpet. "Welcome, Your Grace. Please come in."

Micah Domitus's brown eyes devoured her. His power pressed against her skin, ripped the air from the room, her lungs. Filled the space with midnight storms, sex and death entwined.

"I assume your employer will be joining us through the vidscreen," the Archangel said, stepping in from the glaringly bright street.

Fucking Hel, his *voice*—silk and steel and ancient stone. He could probably make someone come by merely whispering filthy things in their ear.

Even without that voice, it would have been impossible to forget what Micah was, what the Governor radiated with every breath, every blink. There were currently ten Archangels who ruled the various territories of the Republic, all bearing the title of Governor—all answering only to the Asteri. An ordinary angel's magic might level a building if they were considered powerful. An Archangel's power could level an entire metropolis. There was no predicting where the extra strength that separated Archangel from angel came from—sometimes, it was passed on, usually upon the careful breeding orders of the Asteri. Other times, it popped up in unremarkable bloodlines.

She didn't know much about Micah's history—had never paid attention during history class, too busy drooling over the unfairly perfect face currently before her to listen to her teacher's droning.

"Miss Roga is waiting for our call," she managed to say, and tried not to breathe too loudly as the Governor of Valbara swept past. One of his pristine white feathers brushed her bare collarbone. She might have shuddered—were it not for the two angels behind him.

Isaiah just gave her a nod as he trailed Micah toward the chairs before the desk.

Hunt Athalar, however, lingered. Holding her gaze—before he glanced at her collarbone. As if the feather had left a mark. The tattoo of thorns across his forehead seemed to turn darker.

And just like that, that scent of sex rippling off the Archangel turned to rot.

The Asteri and the Archangels could have easily found another way to hobble the power of the Fallen, yet they'd enslaved them with the witch spells woven into magical tattoos stamped onto their foreheads like fucked-up crowns. And the tattoos on their wrists: *SPQM*.

Senatus Populusque Midgard.

The Midgard Senate and People. Total fucking bullshit. As if the Senate was anything but a puppet ruling body. As if the Asteri weren't their emperors and empresses, ruling over everything and everyone for eternity, their rotted souls regenerating from one form to the next.

Bryce shoved the thought from her mind as she shut the iron door behind Hunt, just barely missing his gray feathers. His black eyes flashed with warning.

She gave him a smile to convey everything she didn't dare say aloud regarding her feelings about this ambush. *I've faced worse than you, Umbra Mortis. Glower and snarl all you like.*

Hunt blinked, the only sign of his surprise, but Bryce was already turning toward her desk, trying not to limp as pain speared through her leg. She'd dragged up a third chair from the library, which had aggravated her leg further.

She didn't dare rub at the thick, curving scar across her upper thigh, hidden under her white dress. "Can I get you anything, Your Grace? Coffee? Tea? Something stronger?" She'd already laid out bottled sparkling water on the small tables between the chairs.

The Archangel had claimed the middle seat, and as she smiled politely at him, the weight of his gaze pressed on her like a silken blanket. "I'm fine." Bryce looked to Hunt and Isaiah, who slid into their chairs. "They're fine, too," Micah said.

Very well, then. She strode around the desk, sliding her hand beneath its ledge to push a brass button and sending up a prayer to merciful Cthona that her voice remained calm, even as her mind kept circling back to the same thought, over and over: *Briggs didn't kill Danika, Briggs didn't kill Danika, Briggs didn't kill Danika—*

The wood panel in the wall behind her split open, revealing a large screen. As it flickered to life, she picked up the desk phone and dialed.

Briggs had been a monster who had planned to hurt people, and he deserved to be in jail, but—he'd been wrongly accused of the murder.

Danika's killer was still out there.

Jesiba answered on the first ring. "Is the screen ready?"

"Whenever you are." Bryce typed the codes into her computer, trying to ignore the Governor staring at her like she was a steak and he was . . . something that ate steak. Raw. And moaning. "I'm dialing you in," she declared.

Jesiba Roga appeared on the screen an instant later—and they both hung up their phones.

Behind the sorceress, the hotel suite was decorated in Pangeran splendor: paneled white walls with gilded molding, plush cream carpets and pale pink silk drapes, a four-poster oak bed big enough for her and the two males Bryce had heard when she called before.

Jesiba played as hard as she worked while over on the massive territory, seeking out more art for the gallery, either through visiting various archaeological digs or courting high-powered clients who already possessed them.

Despite having less than ten minutes, and despite using most of that time to make some very important calls, Jesiba's flowing navy dress was immaculate, revealing tantalizing glimpses of a lush female body adorned with freshwater pearls at her ears and throat. Her cropped ash-blond hair glowed in the golden firstlight lamps—cut shorter on the sides, longer on the top. Effortlessly chic and casual. Her face . . .

Her face was both young and wise, bedroom-soft yet foreboding. Her pale gray eyes gleamed with glittering magic, alluring and deadly.

Bryce had never dared ask why Jesiba had defected from the witches centuries ago. Why she'd aligned herself with the House of Flame and Shadow and its leader, the Under-King—and what she did for him. She called herself a sorceress now. Never a witch.

"Morning, Micah," Jesiba said mildly. A pleasant, disarming voice compared to that of other members of Flame and Shadow—the hoarse rasp of Reapers, or the silken tones of vampyrs.

"Jesiba," Micah purred.

Jesiba gave him a slight smile, as if she'd heard that purr a thousand different times, from a thousand different males. "Pleased as I am to see your handsome face, I'd like to know why you called this meeting. Unless the Danika thing was an excuse to talk to sweet Bryce."

The Danika thing. Bryce kept her face neutral, even as she felt

Hunt watching her carefully. As if he could hear her heart thundering, scent the sweat now coating her palms.

But Bryce gave him a bored look in return.

Micah leaned back in his chair, crossing his long legs, and said without so much as glancing at Bryce, "Tempting as your assistant is, we have important matters to discuss."

She ignored the outright entitlement, the timbre of that sensual voice. *Tempting*—as if she were a piece of dessert on a platter. She was used to it, but . . . these gods-damned Vanir males.

Jesiba waved with ethereal grace to continue, silver nails sparkling in the hotel's lamplight.

Micah said smoothly, "I believe my triarii informed Miss Quinlan of the murder last night. One that was an exact match for the deaths of Danika Fendyr and the Pack of Devils two years ago."

Bryce kept herself still, unfeeling. She took a subtle inhale of the soothing peppermint wisps from the infuser a few inches away.

Micah went on, "What they did not mention was the other connection."

The two angels flanking the Governor stiffened almost imperceptibly. This was clearly the first they were hearing of this as well.

"Oh?" Jesiba said. "And do I have to pay for this information?"

Vast, cold power crackled in the gallery, but the Archangel's face remained unreadable. "I am sharing this information so we might combine resources."

Jesiba arched a blond brow with preternatural smoothness. "To do what?"

Micah said, "For Bryce Quinlan to find the true murderer behind this, of course."

12

Bryce had gone still as death—so unmoving that Hunt wondered if she knew it was a solid tell. Not about her own nerves, but about her heritage. Only the Fae could go that still.

Her boss, the young-faced sorceress, sighed. "Is your 33rd so incompetent these days that you truly need my assistant's help?" Her lovely voice hardly softened her question. "Though I suppose I already have my answer, if you falsely convicted Philip Briggs."

Hunt didn't dare grin at her outright challenge. Few people could get away with speaking to Micah Domitus, let alone any Archangel, like that.

He considered the four-hundred-year-old sorceress on the screen. He'd heard the rumors: that Jesiba answered to the Under-King, that she could transform people into common animals if they provoked her, that she'd once been a witch who'd left her clan for reasons still unknown. Most likely bad ones, if she'd wound up a member of the House of Flame and Shadow.

Bryce breathed, "I don't know anything about this. Or who wanted to kill Tertian."

Jesiba sharpened her gaze. "Regardless, you are *my* assistant. You don't work for the 33rd."

Micah's mouth tightened. Hunt braced himself. "I invited you to this meeting, Jesiba, as a courtesy." His brown eyes narrowed with distaste. "It does indeed appear that Philip Briggs was wrongly convicted. But the fact remains that Danika Fendyr and the Pack of Devils apprehended him in his laboratory, with undeniable evidence regarding his intention to bomb innocents at the White Raven nightclub. And though he was initially released due to a loophole, in the past two years, enough evidence has been found for his earlier crimes that he has been convicted of them, too. As such, he will remain behind bars and serve out the sentence for those earlier crimes as leader of the now-inactive Keres sect, and his participation in the larger human rebellion."

Quinlan seemed to sag with relief.

But then Micah went on, "However, this means a dangerous murderer remains loose in this city, able to summon a lethal demon—for sport or revenge, we do not know. I will admit that my 33rd and the Auxiliary have exhausted their resources. But the Summit is in just over a month. There are individuals attending who will see these murders as proof that I am not in control of my city, let alone this territory, and seek to use it against me."

Of course it wasn't about catching a deadly killer. No, this was pure PR.

Even with the Summit so far off, Hunt and the other triarii had been prepping for weeks now, getting the units in the 33rd ready for the pomp and bullshit that surrounded the gathering of Valbaran powers every ten years. Leaders from across the territory would attend, airing their grievances, with maybe a few guest appearances from the ruling assholes across the Haldren.

Hunt hadn't yet attended one in Valbara, but he'd been through plenty of other Summits in Pangera, with rulers who all pretended they had some semblance of free will. The Summit meetings usually amounted to a week of powerful Vanir arguing until the overseeing Archangel laid down the law. He had little doubt Micah would be any different. Isaiah had experienced one already, and had warned him that the Archangel liked to flex his military might at the Summits—liked to have the 33rd in marching and flying formation, decked out in imperial regalia.

Hunt's golden breastplate was already being cleaned. The thought of donning the formal armor, the seven stars of the Asteri's crest displayed across his heart, made him want to puke.

Jesiba examined her silver nails. "Anything exciting happening at the Summit this time?"

Micah seemed to weigh Jesiba's casual expression as he said, "The new witch-queen will be formally recognized."

Jesiba didn't let one speck of emotion show. "I heard of Hecuba's passing," the sorceress said. No tinge of grief or satisfaction. Just fact.

But Quinlan tensed, as if she'd shout at them to get back to the murder. Micah added, "And the Asteri are sending Sandriel to deliver a report from the Senate regarding the rebel conflict."

Every thought eddied out of Hunt's head. Even the usually unflappable Isaiah went rigid.

Sandriel was coming *here*.

Micah was saying, "Sandriel will arrive at the Comitium next week, and at the Asteri's request, she will be my guest until the Summit."

A month. That fucking monster would be in this city for a month.

Jesiba angled her head with unnerving grace. She might not have been a Reaper, but she sure as shit moved like one. "What does my assistant have to offer in finding the murderer?"

Hunt shoved it down—the roaring, the trembling, the stillness. Shoved it down and down and down until it was just another wave in the black, roiling pit inside himself. Forced himself to concentrate on the conversation. And not on the psychopath on her way to this city.

Micah's stare settled on Bryce, who had turned so pale her freckles were like splattered blood across the bridge of her nose. "Miss Quinlan is, thus far, the only person alive to have witnessed the demon the murderer summoned."

Bryce had the nerve to ask, "What about the angel in the alley?"

Micah's face remained unchanged. "He had no memories of the attack. It was an ambush." Before Bryce could push, he went on, "Considering the delicate nature of this investigation, I am now willing to look outside the box, as they say, for assistance in solving these murders before they become a true problem."

Meaning, the Archangel needed to look good in front of the powers that be. In front of Sandriel, who would report it all to the Asteri and their puppet Senate.

A murderer on the loose, capable of summoning a demon that could kill Vanir as easily as humans? Oh, it'd be precisely the sort of shit Sandriel would delight in telling the Asteri. Especially if it cost Micah his position. And if she gained it for herself. What was the northwestern quadrant of Pangera compared to *all* of Valbara? And Micah losing everything meant his slaves—Hunt, Isaiah, Justinian, and so many others—went to whoever inherited his Governor's title.

Sandriel would never honor Micah's bargain with Hunt.

Micah turned to Hunt, a cruel tilt to his lips. "You can guess, Athalar, who Sandriel will be bringing with her." Hunt went rigid. "Pollux would be all too happy to report his findings as well."

Hunt fought to master his breathing, to keep his face neutral.

Pollux Antonius, Sandriel's triarii commander—the Malleus, they called him. The Hammer. As cruel and merciless as Sandriel. And an absolute motherfucking asshole.

Jesiba cleared her throat. "And you still don't know what kind of demon it was?" She leaned back in her chair, a frown on her full mouth.

"No," Micah said through his teeth.

It was true. Even Hunt hadn't been able to identify it, and he'd had the distinct pleasure of killing more demons than he could count. They came in endless breeds and levels of intelligence, ranging from the beasts that resembled feline-canine hybrids to the humanoid, shape-shifting princes who ruled over Hel's seven territories, each one darker than the last: the Hollow, the Trench, the Canyon, the Ravine, the Chasm, the Abyss, and the worst of them all—the Pit.

Even without a specific identification, though, given its speed and what it had done, the demon fit with something belonging to the Pit, perhaps a pet of the Star-Eater himself. Only in the depths of the Pit could something like that evolve—a creature who had never seen light, never needed it.

It didn't matter, Hunt supposed. Whether the demon was accustomed to light or not, his particular skills could still turn it into chunks of sizzling meat. A quick flash of light and a demon would either turn tail or writhe in pain.

Quinlan's voice cut through the storm in Hunt's head. "You said that there was another connection between the murders then and the one now. Beyond the . . . style."

Micah looked at her. To her credit, Quinlan didn't lower her eyes. "Maximus Tertian and Danika Fendyr were friends."

Bryce's brows twitched toward each other. "Danika didn't know Tertian."

Micah sighed toward the wood-paneled ceiling high above. "I suspect there might have been a good deal about which she didn't inform you."

"I would have known if she was friends with Maximus Tertian," Quinlan ground out.

Micah's power murmured through the room. "Careful, Miss Quinlan."

No one took that kind of tone with an Archangel, at least not anyone with nearly zero power in their veins. It was enough to get Hunt to set aside Sandriel's visit and focus on the conversation.

Micah went on, "There is also the fact that *you* knew both Danika and Maximus Tertian. That you were at the White Raven nightclub on each of the nights the murders happened. The similarity is enough to be . . . of interest."

Jesiba straightened. "Are you saying that Bryce is a suspect?"

"Not yet," Micah said coldly. "But anything is possible."

Quinlan's fingers curled into fists, her knuckles going white as she no doubt tried to restrain herself from spitting at the Archangel. She opted to change the subject instead. "What about investigating the others in the Pack of Devils? None of them might have been a target?"

"It has already been looked into and dismissed. Danika remains our focus."

Bryce asked tightly, "You honestly think I can find anything, when the Aux and 33rd couldn't? Why not get the Asteri to send over someone like the Hind?"

The question rippled through the room. Surely Quinlan wasn't dumb enough to wish for that. Jesiba threw a warning look at her assistant.

Micah, unfazed by the mention of Lidia Cervos, the Republic's most notorious spy-hunter—and breaker—replied, "As I said, I do not wish for knowledge of these . . . events to pass beyond the walls of my city."

Hunt heard what Micah left unspoken: despite being part of Sandriel's triarii, the deer shifter known as the Hind reported directly to the Asteri and was known to be Pollux's lover.

The Hammer and the Hind—the smasher of battlefields and the destroyer of the Republic's enemies. Hunt had seen the Hind a few times in Sandriel's stronghold and always walked away unnerved by her unreadable golden eyes. Lidia was as beautiful as she was ruthless in her pursuit of rebel spies. A perfect match for Pollux. The only one who might have suited Pollux more than the Hind was the Harpy, but Hunt tried not to think about the second in command of Sandriel's triarii when he could avoid it.

Hunt smothered his rising dread. Micah was saying, "Crime statistics suggest that it's likely Danika knew her killer." Another pointed silence that left Quinlan bristling. "And despite the things she might not have told you, you remain the person who knew Danika Fendyr better than anyone. I believe you can provide unparalleled insight."

Jesiba leaned toward the screen in her plush hotel room, all grace and restrained power. "All right, Governor. Let's say you commandeer Bryce to look into this. I'd like compensation."

Micah smiled, a sharp, thrilling thing that Hunt had witnessed only before the Archangel blasted someone into wind-torn smithereens. "Regardless of your allegiance to the Under-King, and the protection you believe it affords you, you remain a citizen of the Republic."

And you will answer to me, he didn't need to add.

Jesiba said simply, "I'd think you'd be well versed in the bylaws, Governor. Section Fifty-Seven: If a government official requires the services of an outside contractor, they are to pay—"

"Fine. You will send your invoice to me." Micah's wings rustled, the only sign of his impatience. But his voice was kind, at least, as he turned to Quinlan. "I am out of options, and shall soon be out of time. If there is someone who might retrace Danika's steps in her final days and discover who murdered her, it would be you. You are the only tie between the victims." She just gaped. "I believe your position here at the gallery also grants you access to individuals who might not be willing to talk to the 33rd or Auxiliary. Isaiah Tiberian will report to me on any progress you make, and keep a keen eye on this investigation." His brown eyes appraised Hunt, as if he could read every line of tension on his body, the panic seeping through his veins at the news of Sandriel's arrival. "Hunt Athalar is experienced in hunting demons. He shall be on protection duty, guarding you during your search for the person behind this."

Bryce's eyes narrowed, but Hunt didn't dare say a word. To blink his displeasure—and relief.

At least he would have an excuse not to be at the Comitium while Sandriel and Pollux were around. But to be a glorified babysitter, to not be able to work toward earning back his *debts* . . .

"Very well," Jesiba said. Her gaze slid to her assistant. "Bryce?"

Bryce said quietly, her amber eyes full of cold fire, "I'll find them." She met the Archangel's gaze. "And then I want you to wipe them off the fucking planet."

Yeah, Quinlan had balls. She was stupid and brash, but at least she had nerve. The combination, however, would likely see her dead before she completed the Drop.

Micah smiled, as if realizing that, too. "What is done with the murderer will be up to our justice system." Mild, bureaucratic nonsense, even as the Archangel's power thundered through the room, as if promising Quinlan he'd do exactly as she wished.

Bryce muttered, "Fine."

Jesiba Roga frowned at her assistant, noting that her face still burned with that cold fire. "Do try not to die, Bryce. I'd hate to endure the inconvenience of training someone new." The feed cut off.

Bryce stood in those absurd shoes. Walking around the desk, she swept the silky curtain of red hair over a shoulder, the slightly curled ends almost brushing the generous curve of her ass.

Micah stood, eyes sliding down Bryce as if he, too, noted that particular detail, but said to none of them in particular, "We're done here."

Bryce's dress was so tight that Hunt could see the muscles in her thighs strain as she hauled open the iron door for the Archangel. A faint wince passed over her face—then vanished.

Hunt reached her as the Archangel and his Commander paused outside. She only gave Hunt a winning, bland smile and began closing the door on him before he could step onto the dusty street. He wedged a foot between the door and jamb, and the enchantments zinged and snapped against his skin as they tried to align around him. Her amber eyes flared. "*What.*"

Hunt gave her a sharp grin. "Make a list of suspects today. Anyone who might have wanted Danika and her pack dead." If Danika knew her murderer, odds were that Bryce probably did, too. "And make a list of Danika's locations and activities during the last few days of her life."

Bryce only smiled again, as if she hadn't heard a damn word he said. But then she hit some button beside the door that had the enchantments *burning* like acid—

Hunt jumped back, his lightning flaring, defending against an enemy that was not there.

The door shut. She purred through the intercom, "I'll call you. Don't bother me until then."

Urd fucking spare him.

13

Atop the roof of the gallery a moment later, Isaiah silent at his side, Hunt watched the late morning sunlight gild Micah's pristine white wings and set the strands of gold in his hair to near-glowing as the Archangel inspected the walled city sprawled around them.

Hunt instead surveyed the flat roof, broken up only by equipment and the doorway to the gallery below.

Micah's wings shifted, his only warning that he was about to speak. "Time is not our ally."

Hunt just said, "Do you really think Quinlan can find whoever is behind this?" He let the question convey the extent of his own faith in her.

Micah angled his head. An ancient, lethal predator sizing up prey. "I think this is a matter that requires us to use every weapon in our arsenal, no matter how unorthodox." He sighed as he looked out at the city again.

Lunathion had been built as a model of the ancient coastal cities around the Rhagan Sea, a near-exact replica that included its sandstone walls, the arid climate, the olive groves and little farms that lined distant hills beyond the city borders to the north, even the great temple to a patron goddess in the very center. But unlike those cities, this one had been allowed to adapt: streets lay in an orderly grid, not a tangle; and modern buildings jutted up like lances in the heart of the CBD, far surpassing the strict height codes of Pangera.

Micah had been responsible for it—for seeing this city as a tribute to the old model, but also a place for the future to thrive. He'd even embraced using the name Crescent City over Lunathion.

A male of progress. Of tolerance, they said.

Hunt often wondered what it would feel like to rip out his throat.

He'd contemplated it so many times he'd lost count. Had contemplated blasting a bolt of his lightning into that beautiful face, that perfect mask for the brutal, demanding bastard inside.

Maybe it was unfair. Micah had been born into his power, had never known a life as anything but one of the major forces on this planet. A near-god who was unused to having his authority questioned and would put down any threats to it.

A rebellion led by a fellow Archangel and three thousand warriors had been just that. Even though nearly all of his triarii was now made up of the Fallen. Offering them a second chance, apparently. Hunt couldn't fathom why he'd bother being that merciful.

Micah said, "Sabine is certainly already putting her people on this case and will be visiting my office to tell me precisely what she thinks of the fuckup with Briggs." An icy glance between them. "I want *us* to find the murderer, not the wolves."

Hunt said coolly, "Dead or alive?"

"Alive, preferably. But dead is better than letting the person run free."

Hunt dared ask, "And will this investigation count toward my quota? It could take months."

Isaiah tensed. But Micah's mouth curled upward. For a long moment, he said nothing. Hunt didn't so much as blink.

Then Micah said, "How about this incentive, Athalar: you solve this case quickly—you solve it before the Summit, and I'll lower your debts to ten."

The very wind seemed to halt.

"Ten," Hunt managed to say, "more assignments?"

It was outrageous. Micah had no reason to offer him anything. Not when his word was all that was needed for Hunt to obey.

"Ten more assignments," Micah said, as if he hadn't dropped a fucking bomb into the middle of Hunt's life.

It could be a fool's bargain. Micah might draw out those ten assignments over decades, but . . . Burning fucking Solas.

The Archangel added, "You tell no one about this, Athalar." That he didn't bother to also warn Isaiah suggested enough about how much he trusted his commander.

Hunt said, as calmly as he could, "All right."

Micah's stare turned merciless, though. He scanned Hunt from head to toe. Then the gallery beneath their booted feet. The assistant within it. Micah growled, "Keep your dick in your pants and your hands to yourself. Or you'll find yourself without either for a long while."

Hunt would regrow both, of course. Any immortal who made the Drop could regrow just about anything if they weren't beheaded or severely mutilated, with arteries bleeding out, but . . . the recovery would be painful. Slow. And being dickless, even for a few months, wasn't high up on Hunt's to-do list.

Fucking around with a half-human assistant was the least of his priorities, anyway, with freedom potentially ten kills away.

Isaiah nodded for both of them. "We'll keep it professional."

Micah twisted toward the CBD, assessing the river breeze, his pristine wings twitching. He said to Isaiah, "Be in my office in an hour."

Isaiah bowed at the waist to the Archangel, a Pangeran gesture that made Hunt's hackles rise. He'd been forced to do that, at the risk of having his feathers pulled out, burned off, sliced apart. Those initial decades after the Fall had not been kind.

The wings he knew were mounted to the wall in the Asteri throne room were proof.

But Isaiah had always known how to play the game, how to stomach their protocols and hierarchies. How to dress like them, dine and fuck like them. He'd Fallen and risen back to the rank of commander because of it. It wouldn't surprise anyone if Micah recommended that Isaiah's halo be removed at the next Governors' Council with the Asteri after the Winter Solstice.

No assassinating, butchering, or torturing required.

Micah didn't so much as glance at them before he shot into the skies. Within seconds he'd become a white speck in the sea of blue.

Isaiah blew out a breath, frowning toward the spires atop the five towers of the Comitium, a glass-and-steel crown rising from the heart of the CBD.

"You think there's a catch?" Hunt asked his friend.

"He doesn't scheme like that." Like Sandriel and most of the other Archangels. "He means what he says. He's got to be desperate, if he wants to give you that kind of motivation."

"He owns me. His word is my command."

"With Sandriel coming, maybe he realized it'd be advantageous if you were inclined to be . . . loyal."

"Again: slave."

"Then I don't fucking know, Hunt. Maybe he was just feeling generous." Isaiah shook his head again. "Don't question the hand Urd dealt you."

Hunt blew out a breath. "I know." Odds were, the truth was a combination of those things.

Isaiah arched a brow. "You think you can find whoever is behind this?"

"I don't have a choice." Not with this new bargain on the table. He tasted the dry wind, half listening to its rasping song through the sacred cypresses lining the street below—the thousands of them in this city planted in honor of its patron goddess.

"You'll find them," Isaiah said. "I know you will."

"If I can stop thinking about Sandriel's visit." Hunt blew out a breath, dragging his hands through his hair. "I can't believe she's coming *here*. With that piece of shit Pollux."

Isaiah said carefully, "Tell me you realize that Micah threw you *another* big fucking bone just now in stationing you to protect Quinlan instead of keeping you around the Comitium with Sandriel there."

Hunt knew that, knew Micah was well aware of how Hunt felt about Sandriel and Pollux, but rolled his eyes. "Whatever. Trumpet all you want about how fantastic Micah is, but remember that the bastard is welcoming her with open arms."

"The Asteri ordered her to come for the Summit," Isaiah countered. "It's standard for them to send one of the Archangels as their emissary to these meetings. Governor Ephraim came to the last one here. Micah welcomed him, too."

Hunt said, "The fact remains that she'll be here for a whole month. In that fucking complex." He pointed to the five buildings of the Comitium. "Lunathion isn't her scene. There's nothing to amuse her here."

With most of the Fallen either scattered to the four winds or dead, Sandriel enjoyed nothing better than strolling through her castle dungeons, crammed full of human rebels, and selecting one, two, or three at a time. The arena at the heart of her city was just for the pleasure of destroying these prisoners in various ways. Battles to the death, public torture, unleashing Lowers and basic animals against them . . . There was no end to her creativity. Hunt had seen and endured it all.

With the conflict currently surging, those dungeons were sure to be packed. Sandriel and Pollux must have been enjoying the Hel out of the pain that flowed from that arena.

The thought made Hunt stiffen. "Pollux will be a fucking menace in this city." The Hammer was well known for his favorite activities: slaughter and torture.

"Pollux will be dealt with. Micah knows what he's like—what he does. The Asteri might have ordered him to welcome Sandriel, but he isn't going to let her give Pollux free rein." Isaiah paused, eyes going distant as he seemed to weigh something internally. "But I can make you unavailable while Sandriel visits—permanently."

Hunt lifted an eyebrow. "If you're referring to Micah's promise to make me dickless, I'll pass."

Isaiah laughed quietly. "Micah gave you an order to investigate with Quinlan. Orders that will make you very, very busy. Especially if he wants Bryce protected."

Hunt threw him a half grin. "So busy that I won't have time to be around the Comitium."

"So busy that you'll be staying on the roof across from Quinlan's building to monitor her."

"I've slept in worse conditions." So had Isaiah. "And it'd be an easy cover for keeping an eye on Quinlan for more than protection."

Isaiah frowned. "You honestly mark her as a suspect?"

"I'm not ruling it out," Hunt said, shrugging. "Micah didn't clear her, either. So until she proves otherwise, she's not off *my* list." He wondered who the Hel might make it onto Quinlan's list of suspects. When Isaiah only nodded, Hunt asked, "You're not going to tell Micah I'm watching her around the clock?"

"If he notices that you're not sleeping at the barracks, I'll tell him. But until then, what he doesn't know won't hurt him."

"Thanks." It wasn't a word in Hunt's normal vocabulary, not to anyone with wings, but he meant it. Isaiah had always been the best of them—the best of the Fallen, and all the legionaries Hunt had ever served with. Isaiah should have been in the Asterian Guard, with those skills and those pristine white wings, but like Hunt, Isaiah had come from the gutter. Only the highborn would do for the Asteri's elite private legion. Even if it meant passing over good soldiers like Isaiah.

Hunt, with his gray wings and common blood, despite his lightning, had never even been in the running. Being asked to join Shahar's elite 18th had been privilege enough. He'd loved her almost instantly for seeing his worth—and Isaiah's. All of the 18th had been like that: soldiers she'd selected not for their status, but their skills. Their true value.

Isaiah gestured toward the CBD and the Comitium within it. "Grab your gear from the barracks. I need to make a stop before I meet with Micah." At Hunt's blink, Isaiah winced. "I owe Prince Ruhn a visit to confirm Quinlan's alibi."

It was the last fucking thing Hunt wanted to do, and the last fucking thing he knew Isaiah wanted to do, but protocols were protocols. "You want me to go with you?" Hunt offered. It was the least he could offer.

The corner of Isaiah's mouth lifted. "Considering that you broke Danaan's nose the last time you were in a room together, I'm going to say no."

Wise move. Hunt drawled, "He deserved it."

Micah, mercifully, had found the entire event—the Incident, as Naomi called it—amusing. It wasn't every day that the Fae had their asses handed to them, so even the Governor had discreetly gloated over the altercation at the Spring Equinox celebrations the previous year. He'd given Hunt a whole week off for it. *A suspension*, Micah had claimed—but that suspension had come with an especially padded paycheck. And three less deaths to atone for.

Isaiah said, "I'll call you later to check in."

"Good luck."

Isaiah threw him a weary, worn smile—the only hint of the grind of all these years with those two tattoos—and went to track down Ruhn Danaan, the Crown Prince of the Fae.

Bryce paced the showroom once, hissed at the pain in her leg, and kicked off her heels hard enough that one slammed into the wall, setting an ancient vase shuddering.

A cool voice asked behind her, "When you nail Hunt Athalar's balls to the wall, will you do me a favor and take a picture?"

She glared at the vidscreen that had come on again—and the sorceress still sitting there. "You really want to get mixed up in this, boss?"

Jesiba leaned back in her gilded chair, a queen at ease. "Good old-fashioned revenge doesn't hold any appeal?"

"I have no idea who wanted Danika and the pack dead. None." It had made sense when it seemed like Briggs had summoned the demon to do it: he'd been released that day, Danika was on edge and upset about it, and then she had died. But if it wasn't Briggs, and with Maximus Tertian killed . . . She didn't know where to start.

But she'd do it. Find whoever had done this. A small part of it was just to make Micah Domitus eat his words hinting that she might be *of interest* in this case, but . . . She ground her teeth. She'd find whoever had done this and make them regret ever being born.

Bryce walked over to the desk, stifling the limp. She perched on the edge. "The Governor must be desperate." And insane, if he was asking for her help.

"I don't care about the Governor's agenda," Jesiba said. "Play vengeful detective all you want, Bryce, but do remember that you have a job. Client meetings will not take a back seat."

"I know." Bryce chewed on the inside of her cheek. "If whoever is behind this is strong enough to summon a demon like that to do their dirty work, I'll likely wind up dead, too." Very likely, given that she hadn't decided if or when to make the Drop yet.

Those gray glittering eyes roved over her face. "Then keep Athalar close."

Bryce bristled. As if she were some little female in need of a big, strong warrior to guard her.

Even if it *was* partially true. Mostly true.

Totally and definitely true, if that demon was being summoned again.

But—make a list of suspects, indeed. And the other task he'd given her, to make a list of Danika's last locations . . . Her body tightened at the thought.

She might accept Athalar's protection, but she didn't need to make it easy for the swaggering asshole.

Jesiba's phone rang. The female glanced at the screen. "It's Tertian's father." She threw Bryce a warning glare. "If I start losing money because you're off playing detective with the Umbra Mortis, I'll turn you into a turtle." She lifted the phone to her ear and the feed ended.

Bryce blew out a long breath before she hit the button to close the screen into the wall.

The silence of the gallery twined around her, gnawing at her bones.

Lehabah for once, seemed to not be eavesdropping. No tapping on the iron door filled the thrumming silence. Not a whisper of the tiny, incurably nosy fire sprite.

Bryce braced her arm on the cool surface of the desk, cupping her forehead in her hand.

Danika had never mentioned knowing Tertian. They'd never even spoken of him—not once. And that was all she had to go on?

Without Briggs as the summoner-killer, the murder didn't make sense. Why had the demon chosen their apartment, when it was three stories up and located in a supposedly monitored building? It had to be intentional. Danika and the others, Tertian included, must have been targeted, with Bryce's connection to the latter a sick coincidence.

Bryce toyed with the amulet on the end of her golden chain, zipping it back and forth.

Later. She'd think it over tonight, because—she glanced at the clock. Shit.

She had another client coming in forty-five minutes, which meant she should get through the tsunami of paperwork for the Svadgard wood carving purchased yesterday.

Or maybe she should work on that job application she'd kept in a secret, deceptively named file on her computer: *Paper Vendor Spreadsheets*.

Jesiba, who left her in charge of everything from restocking toilet paper to ordering printer paper, would never open the file. She'd never see that among the actual documents Bryce had thrown in there, there was one folder—*March Office Supply Invoices*—that didn't contain a spreadsheet. It held a cover letter, a résumé, and half-completed applications for positions at about ten different places.

Some were long shots. *Crescent City Art Museum Associate Curator.* As if she'd ever get that job, when she had neither an art nor a history degree. And when most museums believed places like Griffin Antiquities should be illegal.

Other positions—*Personal Assistant to Miss Fancypants Lawyer*—would be more of the same. Different setting and boss, but same old bullshit.

But they were a way out. Yeah, she'd have to find some kind of arrangement with Jesiba regarding her debts, and avoid finding out if just mentioning she wanted to leave would get her turned into some slithering animal, but dicking around with the applications, endlessly tweaking her résumé—it made her feel better, at least. Some days.

But if Danika's murderer had resurfaced, if being in this dead-end job could help . . . Those résumés were a waste of time.

Her phone's dark screen barely reflected the lights high, high above.

Sighing again, Bryce punched in her security code, and opened the message thread.

You won't regret this. I've had a long while to figure out all the ways I'm going to spoil you. All the fun we're going to have.

She could have recited Connor's messages from memory, but it hurt more to see them. Hurt enough to feel through every part of her body, the dark remnants of her soul. So she always looked.

Go enjoy yourself. I'll see you in a few days.

The white screen burned her eyes. *Message me when you're home safe.*

She shut that window. And didn't dare open up her audiomail. She usually had to be in one of her monthly emotional death-spirals to do that. To hear Danika's laughing voice again.

Bryce loosed a long breath, then another, then another.

She'd find the person behind this. For Danika, for the Pack of Devils, she'd do it. Do anything.

She opened up her phone again and began typing out a group message to Juniper and Fury. Not that Fury ever replied—no, the thread was a two-way conversation between Bryce and June. She'd written out half of her message: *Philip Briggs didn't kill Danika. The murders are starting again and I'm—* when she deleted it. Micah had given an order to keep this quiet, and if her phone was hacked . . . She wouldn't jeopardize being taken off the case.

Fury had to know about it already. That her so-called *friend* hadn't contacted her . . . Bryce shoved the thought away. She'd tell Juniper face-to-face. If Micah was right and there was somehow a connection between Bryce and how the victims were chosen, she couldn't risk leaving Juniper unaware. Wouldn't lose anyone else.

Bryce glanced at the sealed iron door. Rubbed the deep ache in her leg once before standing.

Silence walked beside her during the entire trip downstairs.

14

Ruhn Danaan stood before the towering oak doors to his father's study and took a bracing, cooling breath.

It had nothing to do with the thirty-block run he'd made from his unofficial office above a dive bar in the Old Square over to his father's sprawling marble villa in the heart of FiRo. Ruhn let out a breath and knocked.

He knew better than to barge in.

"Enter." The cold male voice leached through the doors, through Ruhn. But he shoved aside any indication of his thundering heart and slid into the room, shutting the door behind him.

The Autumn King's personal study was larger than most single-family houses. Bookshelves rose two stories on every wall, crammed with tomes and artifacts both old and new, magic and ordinary. A golden balcony bisected the rectangular space, accessible by either of the spiral staircases at the front and back, and heavy black velvet curtains currently blocked the morning light from the tall windows overlooking the interior courtyard of the villa.

The orrery in the far back of the space drew Ruhn's eye: a working model of their seven planets, moons, and sun. Made from solid gold. Ruhn had been mesmerized by it as a boy, back when he'd been stupid enough to believe his father actually gave a shit about him, spending hours in here watching the male make whatever observations and calculations he jotted down in his black leather notebooks. He'd asked only once about what his father was looking for, exactly.

Patterns was all his father said.

The Autumn King sat at one of the four massive worktables, each littered with books and an array of glass and metal devices. Experiments for whatever the fuck his father did with those *patterns*. Ruhn passed one of the tables, where iridescent liquid bubbled within a glass orb set over a burner—the flame likely of his father's making—puffs of violet smoke curling from it.

"Should I be wearing a hazmat suit?" Ruhn asked, aiming for the worktable where his father peered through a foot-long prism ensconced in some delicate silver contraption.

"State your business, Prince," his father said shortly, an amber eye fixed to the viewing apparatus atop the prism.

Ruhn refrained from commenting about how the taxpaying people of this city would feel if they knew how one of their seven Heads spent his days. The six lower Heads were all appointed by Micah, not elected by any democratic process. There were councils within councils, designed to give people the illusion of control, but the main order of things was simple: The Governor ruled, and the City Heads led their own districts under him. Beyond that, the 33rd Legion answered only to the Governor, while the Aux obeyed the City Heads, divided into units based upon districts and species. It grew murkier from there. The wolves claimed the shifter packs were the commanders of the Aux—but the Fae insisted that this distinction belonged to them, instead. It made dividing—*claiming*—responsibilities difficult.

Ruhn had been heading up the Fae division of the Aux for fifteen years now. His father had given the command, and he had obeyed. He had little choice. Good thing he'd trained his entire life to be a lethal, efficient killer.

Not that it brought him any particular joy.

"Some major shit is going down," Ruhn said, halting on the other side of the table. "I just got a visit from Isaiah Tiberian. Maximus Tertian was murdered last night—in exactly the same way that Danika and her pack were killed."

His father adjusted some dial on the prism device. "I received the report earlier this morning. It appears Philip Briggs wasn't the murderer."

Ruhn stiffened. "You were going to tell me when?"

His father glanced up from the prism device. "Am I beholden to you, Prince?"

The bastard certainly wasn't, his title aside. Though they were close in depth of power, the fact remained that Ruhn, despite his Starborn status and possession of the Starsword, would always have just a little less than his father. He'd never decided, after he'd gone through his Ordeal and made the Drop fifty years ago, whether it was a relief or a curse to have come up short on the power ranking. On the one hand, had he surpassed his father, the playing field would have tipped in his favor. On the other, it would have established him firmly as a rival.

Having seen what his father did to rivals, it was better to not be on that list.

"This information is vital. I already put out a call to Flynn and Declan to amp up patrols in FiRo. We'll have every street watched."

"Then it does not appear that I needed to tell you, does it?"

His father was nearing five hundred years old, had worn the golden crown of the Autumn King for most of that time, and had been an asshole for all of it. And he still showed no signs of aging—not as the Fae did, with their gradual fading into death, like a shirt washed too many times.

So it'd be another few centuries of this. Playing prince. Having to knock on a door and wait for permission to enter. Having to kneel and obey.

Ruhn was one of about a dozen Fae Princes across the whole planet Midgard—and had met most of the others over the decades. But he stood apart as the only Starborn among them. Among all the Fae.

Like Ruhn, the other princes served under preening, vain kings stationed in the various territories as Heads of city districts or swaths of wilderness. Some of them had been waiting for their thrones for centuries, counting down each decade as if it were mere months.

It disgusted him. Always had. Along with the fact that everything he had was bankrolled by the bastard before him: the office above the dive bar, the villa in FiRo adorned with priceless antiques that his father had gifted him upon winning the Starsword during his Ordeal. Ruhn never stayed at the villa, instead choosing to live in a house he shared with his two best friends near the Old Square.

Also purchased with his father's money.

Officially, the money came from the "salary" Ruhn received for heading up the Fae Auxiliary patrols. But his father's signature authorized that weekly check.

The Autumn King lifted the prism device. "Did the Commander of the 33rd say anything of note?"

The meeting had been one step short of a disaster.

First, Tiberian had grilled him about Bryce's whereabouts last night, until Ruhn was about one breath away from beating the shit out of the angel, Commander of the 33rd or no. Then Tiberian had the balls to ask about *Ruhn's* whereabouts.

Ruhn had refrained from informing the commander that pummeling Maximus Tertian for grabbing Bryce's hand had been tempting.

She'd have bitten his head off for it. And she'd been able to handle herself, sparing Ruhn the political nightmare of setting off a blood feud between their two Houses. Not just between Sky and Breath and Flame and Shadow, but between the Danaans and the Tertians. And thus every Fae and vampyr living in Valbara and Pangera. The Fae didn't fuck around with their blood feuds. Neither did the vamps.

"No," Ruhn said. "Though Maximus Tertian died a few hours after having a business meeting with Bryce."

His father set down the prism, his lip curling. "I told you to warn that girl to stay *quiet*."

That girl. Bryce was always *that girl*, or *the girl*, to their father.

Ruhn hadn't heard the male speak her name in twelve years. Not since her first and last visit to this villa.

Everything had changed after that visit. Bryce had come here for the first time, a coltish thirteen-year-old ready to finally meet her father and his people. To meet Ruhn, who had been intrigued at the prospect of finding he had a half sister after more than sixty years of being an only child.

The Autumn King had insisted that the visit be discreet—not saying the obvious: *until the Oracle whispers of your future*. What had gone down had been an unmitigated disaster not only for Bryce, but for Ruhn as well. His chest still ached when he remembered her leaving the villa in tears of rage, refusing to look back over her shoulder even once. His father's treatment of Bryce had opened Ruhn's eyes to the Autumn King's true nature . . . and the cold Fae male before him had never forgotten this fact.

Ruhn had visited Bryce frequently at her parents' place over the next three years. She'd been a bright spot—the brightest spot, if he felt like being honest. Until that stupid, shameful fight between them that had left things in such shambles that Bryce still hated his guts. He didn't blame her—not with the words he'd said, that he'd immediately regretted as soon as they'd burst from him.

Now Ruhn said, "*Bryce's* meeting with Maximus preceded my warning to behave. I arrived right as she was wrapping up." When he'd gotten that call from Riso Sergatto, the butterfly shifter's laughing voice unusually grave, he'd sprinted over to the White Raven, not giving himself time to second-guess the wisdom of it. "I'm her alibi, according to Tiberian—I told him that I walked her home, and stayed there until well after Tertian's time of death."

His father's face revealed nothing. "And yet it still does not seem very flattering that the girl was at the club on both nights, and interacted with the victims hours before."

Ruhn said tightly, "Bryce had nothing to do with the murders. Despite the alibi shit, the Governor must believe it, too, because Tiberian swore Bryce is being guarded by the 33rd."

It might have been admirable that they bothered to do so, had all the angels not been arrogant assholes. Luckily, the most arrogant of those assholes hadn't been the one to pay Ruhn this particular visit.

"That girl has always possessed a spectacular talent for being where she shouldn't."

Ruhn controlled the anger thrumming through him, his shadow magic seeking to veil him, shield him from sight. Another reason his father resented him: beyond his Starborn gifts, the bulk of his magic skewed toward his mother's kin—the Fae who ruled Avallen, the mist-shrouded isle in the north. The sacred heart of Faedom. His father would have burned Avallen into ashes if he could. That Ruhn did not possess his father's flames, the flames of most of the Valbaran Fae, that he instead possessed Avallen abilities—more than Ruhn ever let on—to summon and walk through shadows, had been an unforgivable insult.

Silence rippled between father and son, interrupted only by the ticking metal of the orrery at the other end of the room as the planets inched around their orbit.

His father picked up the prism, holding it up to the firstlights twinkling in one of the three crystal chandeliers.

Ruhn said tightly, "Tiberian said the Governor wants these murders kept quiet, but I'd like your permission to warn my mother." Every word grated. *I'd like your permission.*

His father waved a hand. "Permission granted. She'll heed the warning."

Just as Ruhn's mother had obeyed everyone her entire life.

She'd listen and lie low, and no doubt gladly accept the extra guards sent to her villa, down the block from his own, until this shit was sorted out. Maybe he'd even stay with her tonight.

She wasn't queen—wasn't even a consort or mate. No, his sweet, kind mother had been selected for one purpose: breeding. The Autumn King had decided, after a few centuries of ruling, that he wanted an heir. As the daughter of a prominent noble house that had defected from Avallen's court, she'd done her duty gladly, grateful for the eternal privilege it offered. In all of Ruhn's seventy-five years of life, he'd never heard her speak one ill word about his father. About the life she'd been conscripted to.

Even when Ember and his father had their secret, disastrous relationship, his mother had not been jealous. There had been so many other females before her, and after her. Yet none had been formally chosen, not as she was, to continue the royal bloodline. And when Bryce had come along, the few times his mother had met her, she'd been kind. Doting, even.

Ruhn couldn't tell if he admired his mother for never questioning the gilded cage she lived in. If something was wrong with *him* for resenting it.

He might never understand his mother, yet it didn't stop his fierce pride that he took after her bloodline, that his shadow-walking set him apart from the asshole in front of him, a constant, welcome reminder that he didn't *have* to turn into a domineering prick. Even if most of his mother's kin in Avallen were little better. His cousins especially.

"Perhaps you should call her," Ruhn said, "give the warning yourself. She'd appreciate your concern."

"I'm otherwise engaged," his father said calmly. It had always astonished Ruhn: how cold his father was, when those flames burned in his veins. "You may inform her yourself. And you will refrain from telling me how to manage my relationship with your mother."

"You don't have a relationship. You bred her like a mare and sent her out to pasture."

Cinders sparked through the room. "You benefited quite well from that *breeding*, Starborn."

Ruhn didn't dare voice the words that tried to spring from his mouth. *Even as my stupid fucking* title *brought you further influence in the empire and among your fellow kings, it still chafed, didn't it? That your son, not you, retrieved the Starsword from the Cave of Princes in Avallen's dark heart. That your son, not you, stood among the long-dead Starborn Princes asleep in their sarcophagi and was deemed worthy to pull the sword from its sheath. How many times did you try to draw the sword when you were young? How much research did you do in this very study to find ways to wield it without being chosen?*

His father curled a finger toward him. "I have need of your *gift*."

"Why?" His Starborn abilities were little more than a sparkle of starlight in his palm. His shadow talents were the more interesting gift. Even the temperature monitors on the high-tech cameras in this city couldn't detect him when he shadow-walked.

His father held up the prism. "Direct a beam of your starlight through this." Not waiting for an answer, his father again put an eye to the metal viewing contraption atop the prism.

It ordinarily took Ruhn a good amount of concentration to summon his starlight, and it usually left him with a headache for hours afterward, but . . . He was intrigued enough to try.

Setting his index finger onto the crystal of the prism, Ruhn closed his eyes and focused upon his breathing. Let the clicking metal of the orrery guide him down, down, down into the black pit within himself, past the churning well of his shadows, to the little hollow beneath them. There, curled upon itself like some hibernating creature, lay the single seed of iridescent light.

He gently cupped it with a mental palm, stirring it awake as he carefully brought it upward, as if he were carrying water in his hands. Up through himself, the power shimmering with anticipation, warm and lovely and just about the only part of himself he liked.

Ruhn opened his eyes to find the starlight dancing at his fingertip, refracting through the prism.

His father adjusted a few dials on the device, jotting down notes with his other hand.

The starlight seed became slippery, disintegrating into the air around them.

"Just another moment," the king ordered.

Ruhn gritted his teeth, as if it'd somehow keep the starlight from dissolving.

Another click of the device, and another jotted note in an ancient, rigid hand. The Old Language of the Fae—his father recorded everything in the half-forgotten language their people had used when they had first come to Midgard through the Northern Rift.

The starlight shivered, flared, and faded into nothing. The

Autumn King grunted in annoyance, but Ruhn barely heard it over his pounding head.

He'd mastered himself enough to pay attention as his father finished his notes. "What are you even doing with that thing?"

"Studying how light moves through the world. How it can be shaped."

"Don't we have scientists over at CCU doing this shit?"

"Their interests are not the same as mine." His father surveyed him. And then said, without a hint of warning, "It is time to consider females for an appropriate marriage."

Ruhn blinked. "For you?"

"Don't play stupid." His father shut his notebook and leaned back in his chair. "You owe it to our bloodline to produce an heir—and to expand our alliances. The Oracle decreed you would be a fair and just king. This is the first step in that direction."

All Fae, male and female, made a visit to the city's Oracle at age thirteen as one of the two Great Rites to enter adulthood: first the Oracle, and then the Ordeal—a few years or decades later.

Ruhn's stomach churned at the memory of that first Rite, far worse than his harrowing Ordeal in so many ways. "I'm not getting married."

"Marriage is a political contract. Sire an heir, then go back to fucking whomever you please."

Ruhn snarled. "I am *not* getting married. Certainly not in an arranged marriage."

"You will do as you are told."

"You're not fucking married."

"I did not need the alliance."

"But now we do?"

"There is a war raging overseas, in case you weren't aware. It worsens by the day, and it may very well spread here. I do not plan to enter it without insurance."

Pulse hammering, Ruhn stared at his father. He was completely serious.

Ruhn managed to say, "You plan to make me marry so we have solid allies in the war? Aren't we the Asteri's allies?"

"We are. But war is a liminal time. Power rankings can easily be reshuffled. We must demonstrate how vital and influential we are."

Ruhn considered the words. "You're talking about a marriage to someone not of the Fae." His father had to be worried, to even consider something so rare.

"Queen Hecuba died last month. Her daughter, Hypaxia, has been crowned the new witch-queen of Valbara."

Ruhn had seen the news reports. Hypaxia Enador was young, no more than twenty-six. No photos of her existed, as her mother had kept her cloistered in her mountain fortress.

His father went on, "Her reign will be officially recognized by the Asteri at the Summit next month. I will tie her to the Fae soon after that."

"You're forgetting that Hypaxia will have a say in this. She might very well laugh you off."

"My spies tell me she will heed her mother's old friendship with us—and will be skittish enough as a new ruler to accept the friendly hand we offer."

Ruhn had the distinct feeling of being led into a web, the Autumn King drawing him ever closer to its heart. "I'm not marrying her."

"You are the Crown Prince of the Valbaran Fae. You do not have a choice." His father's cold face became so like Bryce's that Ruhn turned away, unable to stomach it. It was a miracle no one had figured out their secret yet. "Luna's Horn remains at large."

Ruhn twisted back to his father. "So? What does one have to do with the other?"

"I want you to find it."

Ruhn glanced to the notebooks, the prism. "It went missing two years ago."

"And I now have an interest in locating it. The Horn belonged to the Fae first. Public interest in retrieving it has waned; now is the right time to attain it."

His father tapped a finger on the table. Something had riled him. Ruhn considered what he'd seen on his father's schedule this morning when he'd done his cursory scan of it as commander of the Fae Auxiliary. Meetings with preening Fae nobility, a workout with his private guard, and— "The meeting with Micah went well this morning, I take it."

His father's silence confirmed his suspicions. The Autumn King pinned him with his amber eyes, weighing Ruhn's stance, his expression, all of it. Ruhn knew he'd always come up short, but his father said, "Micah wished to discuss shoring up our city's defenses should the conflict overseas spread here. He made it clear the Fae are . . . not as they once were."

Ruhn stiffened. "The Fae Aux units are in just as good shape as the wolves are."

"It is not about our strength of arms, but rather our strength as a people." His father's voice dripped with disgust. "The Fae have long been fading—our magic wanes with each generation, like watered-down wine." He frowned at Ruhn. "The first Starborn Prince could blind an enemy with a flash of his starlight. You can barely summon a sparkle for an instant."

Ruhn clenched his jaw. "The Governor pushed your buttons. So what?"

"He insulted our strength." His father's hair simmered with fire, as if the strands had gone molten. "He said we gave up the Horn in the first place, then let it be lost two years ago."

"It was stolen from Luna's Temple. We didn't fucking *lose* it." Ruhn barely knew anything about the object, hadn't even cared when it went missing two years ago.

"We let a sacred artifact of our people be used as a cheap tourist attraction," his father snapped. "And I want *you* to find it again." So his father could rub it in Micah's face.

Petty, brittle male. That's all his father was.

"The Horn has no power," Ruhn reminded him.

"It is a symbol—and symbols will always wield power of their own." His father's hair burned brighter.

Ruhn suppressed his urge to cringe, his body tensing with the memory of how the king's burning hand had felt wrapped around his arm, sizzling through his flesh. No shadows had ever been able to hide him from it. "Find the Horn, Ruhn. If war comes to these shores, our people will need it in more ways than one."

His father's amber eyes blazed. There was more the male wasn't telling him.

Ruhn could think of only one other thing to cause this much aggravation: Micah again suggesting that Ruhn replace his father as City Head of FiRo. Whispers had swirled for years, and Ruhn had no doubt the Archangel was smart enough to know how much it'd anger the Autumn King. With the Summit nearing, Micah knew pissing off the Fae King with a reference to his fading power was a good way to ensure the Fae Aux was up to snuff before it, regardless of any war.

Ruhn tucked that information aside. "Why don't *you* look for the Horn?"

His father loosed a breath through his long, thin nose, and the fire in him banked to embers. The king nodded toward Ruhn's hand, where the starlight had been. "I have been looking. For two years." Ruhn blinked, but his father went on, "The Horn was originally the possession of Pelias, the first Starborn Prince. You may find that like calls to like—merely researching it could reveal things to you that were hidden from others."

Ruhn hardly bothered to read anything these days beyond the news and the Aux reports. The prospect of poring over ancient tomes just in case something jumped out at him while a murderer ran loose . . . "We'll get into a lot of trouble with the Governor if we take the Horn for ourselves."

"Then keep it quiet, Prince." His father opened his notebook again. Conversation over.

Yeah, this was nothing more than political ego-stroking. Micah had taunted his father, insulted his strength—and now his father would show him precisely where the Fae stood.

Ruhn ground his teeth. He needed a drink. A strong fucking drink.

His head roiled as he headed for the door, the pain from summoning the starlight eddying with every word thrown at him.

I told you to warn that girl to stay quiet.

Find the Horn.

Like calls to like.

An appropriate marriage.

Produce an heir.

You owe it to our bloodline.

Ruhn slammed the door behind him. Only when he'd gotten halfway down the hall did he laugh, a harsh, rasping sound. At least the asshole still didn't know that he'd lied about what the Oracle had told him all those decades ago.

With every step out of his father's villa, Ruhn could once more hear the Oracle's unearthly whispering, reading the smoke while he'd trembled in her dim marble chamber:

The royal bloodline shall end with you, Prince.

15

Syrinx pawed at the window, his scrunched-up face smooshed against the glass. He'd been hissing incessantly for the past ten minutes, and Bryce, more than ready to settle into the plush cushions of the L-shaped couch and watch her favorite Tuesday night reality show, finally twisted to see what all the fuss was about.

Slightly bigger than a terrier, the chimera huffed and pawed at the floor-to-ceiling glass, the setting sun gilding his wiry golden coat. The long tail, tufted with dark fur at the end like a lion's, waved back and forth. His folded little ears were flat to his round, fuzzy head, his wrinkles of fat and the longer hair at his neck—not quite a mane—were vibrating with his growling, and his too-big paws, which ended in birdlike talons, were now—

"*Stop that!* You're scratching the glass!"

Syrinx looked over a rounded, muscled shoulder, his squished face more dog than anything, and narrowed his dark eyes. Bryce glared right back.

The rest of her day had been long and weird and exhausting, especially after she'd gotten a message from Juniper, saying Fury had alerted her about Briggs's innocence and the new murder, and warning Bryce to be careful. She doubted either friend knew of her involvement in finding the murderer, or of the angel who'd been assigned to work with her, but it had stung—just a bit. That Fury hadn't bothered to contact her personally. That even June had done it over messaging and not face-to-face.

Bryce had a feeling tomorrow would be just as draining—if not worse. So throwing in a battle of wills with a thirty-pound chimera wasn't her definition of a much-needed unwinding.

"You just got a walk," she reminded Syrinx. "*And* an extra helping of dinner."

Syrinx gave a *hmmph* and scratched the window again.

"*Bad!*" she hissed. Half-heartedly, sure, but she *tried* to sound authoritative.

Where the little beast was concerned, dominance was a quality they both pretended she had.

Groaning, Bryce hauled herself from the nest of cushions and padded across wood and carpet to the window. On the street below, cars inched past, a few late commuters trudged home, and some dinner patrons strolled arm-in-arm to one of the fine restaurants along the river at the end of the block. Above them, the setting sun smeared the sky red and gold and pink, the palm trees and cypresses swayed in the balmy spring breeze, and . . . And that was a winged male sitting on the opposite roof. Staring right at her.

She knew those gray wings, and the dark, shoulder-length hair, and the cut of those broad shoulders.

Protection duty, Micah had said.

Bullshit. She had a strong feeling the Governor still didn't trust her, alibi or no.

Bryce gave Hunt Athalar a dazzling smile and slashed the heavy curtains shut.

Syrinx yowled as he was caught in them, reversing his stout little body out of the folds. His tail lashed from side to side, and she braced her hands on her hips. "You were *enjoying* the sight?"

Syrinx showed all his pointy teeth as he let out another yowl, trotted to the couch, and threw himself onto the warmed cushions where she'd been sitting. The portrait of despair.

A moment later, her phone buzzed on the coffee table. Right as her show began.

She didn't know the number, but she wasn't at all surprised when she picked up, plopping down onto the cushions, and Hunt growled, "Open the curtains. I want to watch the show."

She propped both bare feet on the table. "I didn't know angels deigned to watch trash TV."

"I'd rather watch the sunball game that's on right now, but I'll take what I can get."

The idea of the Umbra Mortis watching a dating competition was laughable enough that Bryce hit pause on the live show. At least she could now speed through commercials. "What are you doing on that roof, Athalar?"

"What I was ordered to do."

Gods spare her. "Protecting me doesn't entitle you to invade my privacy." She could admit to the wisdom in letting him guard her, but she didn't have to yield all sense of boundaries.

"Other people would disagree." She opened her mouth, but he cut her off. "I've got my orders. I can't disobey them."

Her stomach tightened. No, Hunt Athalar certainly could not disobey his orders.

No slave could, whether Vanir or human. So she instead asked, "And how, exactly, did you get this number?"

"It's in your file."

She tapped her foot on the table. "Did you pay Prince Ruhn a visit?" She would have handed over a gold mark to watch her brother go head-to-head with Micah's personal assassin.

Hunt grunted, "Isaiah did." She smiled. "It was standard protocol."

"So even after your boss tasked me with finding this murderer, you felt the need to look into whether my alibi checked out?"

"I didn't write the fucking rules, Quinlan."

"Hmm."

"Open the curtains."

"No, thank you."

"Or you could invite me in and make my job easier."

"Definitely no."

"Why?"

"Because you can do your job just as well from that roof."

Hunt's chuckle skittered along her bones. "We've been ordered to get to the bottom of these murders. So I hate to tell you this, sweetheart, but we're about to get real up close and personal."

The way he said *sweetheart*—full of demeaning, condescending swagger—made her grind her teeth.

Bryce rose, padding to the floor-to-ceiling window under Syrinx's careful watch, and tugged the curtains back enough to see the angel standing on the opposite roof, phone to his ear, gray wings slightly flared, as if balancing against the wind. "I'm sure you get off on the whole protector-of-damsels thing, but *I* was asked to head this case. You're the backup."

Even from across the street, she could see him roll his eyes. "Can we skip this pecking-order bullshit?"

Syrinx nudged at her calves, then shoved his face past her legs to peer at the angel.

"What *is* that pet of yours?"

"He's a chimera."

"Looks expensive."

"He was."

"Your apartment looks pretty damn expensive, too. That sorceress must pay you well."

"She does." Truth and lie.

His wings flared. "You have my number now. Call it if something goes wrong, or feels wrong, or if you need anything."

"Like a pizza?"

She clearly saw the middle finger Hunt lifted above his head. Shadow of Death, indeed.

Bryce purred, "You *would* make a good delivery boy with those wings." Angels in Lunathion never stooped to such work, though. Ever.

"Keep the damn curtains open, Quinlan." He hung up.

She just gave him a mocking wave. And shut the curtains entirely.

Her phone buzzed with a message just as she plopped down again.

Do you have enchantments guarding your apartment?

She rolled her eyes, typing back, *Do I look stupid?*

Hunt fired back, *Some shit is going down in this city and you've been gifted with grade A protection against it—yet you're busting my balls about boundaries. I think that's answer enough regarding your intelligence.*

Her thumbs flew over the screen as she scowled and wrote, *Kindly fly the fuck off.*

She hit send before she could debate the wisdom of saying that to the Umbra Mortis.

He didn't reply. With a smug smile, she picked up her remote.

A *thud* against the window had her leaping out of her skin, sending Syrinx scrambling in a mad dash toward the curtains, yowling his fuzzy head off.

She stormed around the couch, whipping the curtains back, wondering what the fuck he'd thrown at her window—

The Fallen angel hovered right there. Glaring at her.

She refused to back away, even as her heart thundered. Refused to do anything but shove open the window, the wind off his mighty wings stirring her hair. "*What?*"

His dark eyes didn't so much as blink. Striking—that was the only word Bryce could think of to describe his handsome face, full of powerful lines and sharp cheekbones. "You can make this investigation easy, or you can make it hard."

"I don't—"

"Spare me." Hunt's dark hair shifted in the wind. The rustle and beat of his wings overpowered the traffic below—and the humans and Vanir now gawking up at him. "You don't appreciate being watched, or coddled, or whatever." He crossed his muscled arms. "Neither of us gets a say in this arrangement. So rather than waste your breath arguing about boundaries, why don't you make that list of suspects and Danika's movements?"

"Why don't you stop telling me what I should be doing with my time?"

She could have sworn she tasted ether as he growled, "I'm going to be straight with you."

"Goody."

His nostrils flared. "I will do whatever the Hel it takes to solve this case. Even if it means tying you to a fucking chair until you write those lists."

She smirked. "Bondage. Nice."

Hunt's eyes darkened. "Do. Not. Fuck. With. Me."

"Yeah, yeah, you're the Umbra Mortis."

His teeth flashed. "I don't care what you call me, Quinlan, so long as you do what you're told."

Fucking alphahole.

"Immortality is a long time to have a giant stick up your ass." Bryce put her hands on her hips. Never mind that she was completely undermined by Syrinx dancing at her feet, prancing in place.

Dragging his stare away from her, the angel surveyed her pet with raised brows. Syrinx's tail waved and bobbed. Hunt snorted, as if despite himself. "You're a smart beastie, aren't you?" He threw a scornful glance to Bryce. "Smarter than your owner, it seems."

Make that the King of Alphaholes.

But Syrinx preened. And Bryce had the stupid, overwhelming urge to hide Syrinx from Hunt, from anyone, from anything. He was *hers*, and no one else's, and she didn't particularly like the thought of anyone coming into their little bubble—

Hunt's stare lifted to her own again. "Do you own any weapons?" The purely male gleam in his eye told her that he assumed she didn't.

"Bother me again," she said sweetly, just before she shut the window in his face, "and you'll find out."

Hunt wondered how much trouble he'd get in if he chucked Bryce Quinlan into the Istros.

After the morning he'd had, any punishment from Micah or being turned into a pig by Jesiba Roga was starting to seem well worth it.

Leaning against a lamppost, his face coated with the misting rain that drifted through the city, Hunt clenched his jaw hard enough to hurt. At this hour, commuters packed the narrow streets of the Old Square—some heading to jobs in the countless shops and galleries, others aiming for the spires of the CBD, half a mile westward. All of them, however, noted his wings, his face, and gave him a wide berth.

Hunt ignored them and glanced at the clock on his phone. Eight fifteen.

He'd waited long enough to make the call. He dialed the number and held the phone to his ear, listening to it ring once, twice—

"Please tell me Bryce is alive," said Isaiah, his voice breathless in a way that told Hunt he was either at the barracks gym or enjoying his boyfriend's company.

"For the moment."

A machine beeped, like Isaiah was dialing down the speed of a treadmill. "Do I want to know why I'm getting a call this soon?" A pause. "Why are you on Samson Street?"

Though Isaiah probably tracked his location through the beacon on Hunt's phone, Hunt still scowled toward the nearest visible camera. There were likely ones hidden in the cypresses and palm trees flanking the sidewalks, too, or disguised as sprinkler heads popping from the soggy grass of the flower beds, or built into the iron lampposts like the one he leaned against.

Someone was always watching. In this entire fucking city, territory, and world, someone was always watching, the cameras so bespelled and warded that they were bombproof. Even if this city turned to rubble under the lethal magic of the Asterian Guard's brimstone missiles, the cameras would keep recording.

"Are you aware," Hunt said, his voice a low rasp as a bevy of quails snaked across the street—some tiny shifter family, no doubt—"that chimeras are able to pick locks, open doors, and jump between two places as if they were walking from one room to another?"

"No . . . ?" Isaiah said, panting.

Apparently, Quinlan wasn't, either, if she bothered to have a crate for her beast. Though maybe the damn thing was more to give the chimera a designated comfort space, like people did with their dogs. Since there was no way he would stay contained without a whole host of enchantments.

The Lowers, the class of Vanir to which the chimera belonged, had all sorts of interesting, small powers like that. It was part of why they demanded such high prices on the market. And why, even millennia later, the Senate and Asteri had shot down any attempts to change the laws that branded them as property to be traded. The Lowers were too dangerous, they'd claimed—unable to understand the laws, with powers that could be disruptive if left unchecked by the various spells and magic-infused tattoos that held them.

And too lucrative, especially for the ruling powers whose families profited from their trade.

So they remained Lowers.

Hunt tucked his wings in one at a time. Water beaded off the gray feathers like clear jewels. "This is already a nightmare."

Isaiah coughed. "You watched Quinlan for one night."

"Ten hours, to be exact. Right until her pet chimera just *appeared* next to me at dawn, bit me in the ass for looking like I was dozing off, and then vanished again—right back into the apartment. Just as Quinlan came out of her bedroom and opened the curtains to see me grabbing my own ass like a fucking idiot. Do you *know* how sharp a chimera's teeth are?"

"No." Hunt could have sworn he heard a smile in Isaiah's voice.

"When I flew over to explain, she blasted her music and ignored me like a fucking brat." With enough enchantments around her apartment to keep out a host of angels, Hunt hadn't even tried to get in through a window, since he'd tested them all overnight. So he'd been forced to glower through the glass—returning to the roof only after she'd emerged from her bedroom in nothing but a black sports bra and thong. Her smirk at his backtracking wings had been nothing short of feline. "I didn't see her again until she went for a run. She flipped me off as she left."

"So you went to Samson Street to brood? What's the emergency?"

"The emergency, asshole, is that I might kill her before we find the real murderer." He had too much riding on this case.

"You're just pissed she's not cowering or fawning."

"Like I fucking want anyone to *fawn*—"

"Where's Quinlan now?"

"Getting her nails done."

Isaiah's pause sounded a Hel of a lot like he was about to burst out laughing. "Hence your presence on Samson Street before nine."

"Gazing through the window of a *nail salon* like a gods-damned stalker."

The fact that Quinlan wasn't gunning for the murderer grated as much as her behavior. And Hunt couldn't help being suspicious. He didn't know how or why she might have killed Danika, her pack, and Tertian, but she'd been connected to all of them. Had gone to the same place on the nights they'd been murdered. She knew something—or had done something.

"I'm hanging up now." The bastard was smiling. Hunt knew it. "You've faced down enemy armies, survived Sandriel's arena, gone toe-to-toe with Archangels." Isaiah chuckled. "Surely a party girl isn't as difficult as all that." The line cut off.

Hunt ground his teeth. Through the glass window of the salon, he could perfectly make out Bryce seated at one of the marble workstations, hands outstretched to a pretty reddish-gold-scaled draki female who was putting yet *another* coat of polish on her nails. How many did she *need*?

At this hour, only a few other patrons were seated inside, nails or talons or claws in the process of being filed and painted and whatever the Hel they did to them in there. But all of them kept glancing through the window. To him.

He'd already earned a glare from the teal-haired falcon shifter at the welcome counter, but she hadn't dared come out to ask him to stop making her clients nervous and leave.

Bryce sat there, wholly ignoring him. Chatting and laughing with the female doing her nails.

It had taken Hunt a matter of moments to launch into the skies when Bryce had left her apartment. He'd trailed overhead, well aware of the morning commuters who would film him if he landed beside her in the middle of the street and wrapped his hands around her throat.

Her run took her fifteen blocks away, apparently. She had barely broken a sweat by the time she jogged up to the nail salon, her skin-tight athletic clothes damp with the misting rain, and threw him a look that warned him to stay outside.

That had been an hour ago. A full hour of drills and files and scissors being applied to her nails in a way that would make the Hind herself cringe. Pure torture.

Five minutes. Quinlan had five more fucking minutes, then he'd drag her out. Micah must have lost his mind—that was the only explanation for asking her to help, especially if she prioritized her *nails* over solving her friends' murder.

He didn't know why it came as a surprise. After all he'd seen, everyone he'd met and endured, this sort of shit should have ceased to bother him long ago.

Someone with Quinlan's looks would become accustomed to the doors that face and body of hers opened without so much as a squeak of protest. Being half-human had some disadvantages, yes—a lot of them, if he was being honest about the state of the world. But she'd done well. Really fucking well, if that apartment was any indication.

The draki female set aside the bottle and flicked her claw-tipped fingers over Bryce's nails. Magic sparked, Bryce's ponytail shifting as if a dry wind had blown by.

Like that of the Valbaran Fae, draki magic skewed toward flame and wind. In the northern climes of Pangera, though, he'd met draki and Fae whose power could summon water, rain, mist—element-based magic. But even among the reclusive draki and the Fae, no one bore lightning. He knew, because he'd looked—desperate in his youth for anyone who might teach him how to control it. He'd had to teach himself in the end.

Bryce examined her nails, and smiled. And then hugged the female. Fucking *hugged* her. Like she was some sort of gods-damned war hero for the job she'd done.

Hunt was surprised his teeth weren't ground to stumps by the time she headed for the door, waving goodbye to the smiling falcon shifter at the front desk, who handed her a clear umbrella, presumably to borrow against the rain.

The glass door opened, and Bryce's eyes at last met Hunt's.

"Are you fucking *kidding* me?" The words exploded out of him.

She popped open the umbrella, nearly taking out his eye. "Did you have something better to do with your time?"

"You made me wait in the rain."

"You're a big, tough male. I think you can handle a little water."

Hunt fell into step beside her. "I told you to make those two lists. Not go to a motherfucking beauty salon."

She paused at an intersection, waiting for the bumper-to-bumper cars to crawl past, and straightened to her full height. Not anywhere close to his, but she somehow managed to look down her nose at him while still looking *up* at him. "If you're so good at investigating, why don't you look into it and spare me the effort?"

"You were given an order by the Governor." The words sounded ridiculous even to him. She crossed the street, and he followed. "And I'd think you'd be personally motivated to figure out who's behind this."

"Don't assume anything about my motivations." She dodged around a puddle of either rain or piss. In the Old Square, it was impossible to tell.

He refrained from pushing her into that puddle. "Do you have a problem with me?"

"I don't really care about you enough to have a problem with you."

"Likewise."

Her eyes really did glow then, as if a distant fire simmered within. She surveyed him, sizing up every inch and somehow—some-fucking-how—making him feel about three inches tall.

He said nothing until they turned down her street at last. He growled, "You need to make the list of suspects and the list of Danika's last week of activities."

She examined her nails, now painted in some sort of color

gradient that went from pink to periwinkle tips. Like the sky at twilight. "No one likes a nag, Athalar."

They reached the arched glass entry of her apartment building—structured like a fish's fin, he'd realized last night—and the doors slid open. Ponytail swishing, she said cheerfully, "Bye."

Hunt drawled, "People might see you dicking around like this, Quinlan, and think you were trying to hinder an official investigation." If he couldn't bully her into working on this case, maybe he could scare her into it.

Especially with the truth: She wasn't off the hook. Not even close.

Her eyes flared again, and damn if it wasn't satisfying. So Hunt just added, mouth curving into a half smile, "Better hurry. You wouldn't want to be late for work."

Going to the nail salon had been worth it on so many levels, but perhaps the biggest benefit had been pissing off Athalar.

"I don't see why you can't let the angel in," moped Lehabah, perched atop an old pillar candle. "He's so handsome."

In the bowels of the gallery library, client paperwork spread on the table before her, Bryce cast a sidelong glare at the female-shaped flame. "Do *not* drip wax on these documents, Lele."

The fire sprite grumbled, and plopped her ass on the candle's wick anyway. Wax dribbled down the sides, her tangle of yellow hair floating above her head—as if she were indeed a flame given a plump female shape. "He's just sitting on the roof in the dreary weather. Let him rest on the couch down here. Syrinx says the angel can brush his coat if he needs something to do."

Bryce sighed at the painted ceiling—the night sky rendered in loving care. The giant gold chandelier that hung down the center of the space was fashioned after an exploding sun, with all the other dangling lights in perfect alignment of the seven planets. "The angel," she said, frowning toward Syrinx's slumbering form on the green velvet couch, "is not allowed in here."

Lehabah let out a sad little noise. "One day, the boss will trade my services to some lecherous old creep, and you'll regret ever denying me anything."

"One day, that lecherous old creep will actually make you do your job and guard his books, and you'll regret spending all these hours of relative freedom moping."

Wax sizzled on the table. Bryce whipped her head up.

Lehabah was sprawled belly-down on the candle, an idle hand hanging off the side. Dangerously near the documents Bryce had spent the past three hours poring over.

"Do *not*."

Lehabah rotated her arm so that the tattoo inked amid the simmering flesh was visible. It had been stamped on her arm within moments of her birth, Lehabah had said. *SPQM*. It was inked on the flesh of every sprite—fire or water or earth, it didn't matter. Punishment for joining the angels' rebellion two hundred years ago, when the sprites had dared protest their status as peregrini. As Lowers. The Asteri had gone even further than their enslavement and torture of the angels. They'd decreed after the rebellion that every sprite—not only the ones who'd joined Shahar and her legion—would be enslaved, and cast from the House of Sky and Breath. All of their descendants would be wanderers and slaves, too. Forever.

It was one of the more spectacularly fucked episodes of the Republic's history.

Lehabah sighed. "Buy my freedom from Jesiba. Then I can go live at your apartment and keep your baths and all your food warm."

She could do far more than that, Bryce knew. Technically, Lehabah's magic outranked Bryce's own. But most non-humans could claim the same. And even while it was greater than Bryce's, Lehabah's power was still an ember compared to the Fae's flames. Her father's flames.

Bryce set down the client's purchase papers. "It's not that easy, Lele."

"Syrinx told me you're lonely. I could cheer you up."

In answer, the chimera rolled onto his back, tongue dangling from his mouth, and snored.

"One, my building doesn't allow fire sprites. *Or* water sprites. It's an insurance nightmare. Two, it's not as simple as asking Jesiba. She might very well get rid of you *because* I ask."

Lehabah cupped her round chin in her hand and dripped another freckle of wax dangerously close to the paperwork. "She gave you Syrie."

Cthona give her patience. "She *let* me *buy* Syr*inx* because my life was fucked up, and I lost it when she got bored with him and tried to sell him off."

The fire sprite said quietly, "Because Danika died."

Bryce closed her eyes for a second, then said, "Yeah."

"You shouldn't curse so much, BB."

"Then you really won't like the angel."

"He led my people into battle—*and* he's a member of my House. I deserve to meet him."

"Last I checked, that battle went rather poorly, and the fire sprites were kicked out of Sky and Breath thanks to it."

Lehabah sat up, legs crossed. "Membership in the Houses is not something a government can decree. Our expulsion was in name only."

It was true. But Bryce still said, "What the Asteri and their Senate say goes."

Lehabah had been guardian of the gallery's library for decades. Logic insisted that ordering a fire sprite to watch over a library was a poor idea, but when a third of the books in the place would like nothing more than to escape, kill someone, or eat them—in varying orders—having a living flame keeping them in line was worth any risk. Even the endless chatter, it seemed.

Something thumped on the mezzanine. As if a book had dived off the shelf of its own accord.

Lehabah hissed toward it, turning a deep blue. Paper and leather whispered as the errant book found its place once again.

Bryce smiled, and then the office phone rang. One glance at the screen had her reaching for the phone and hissing at the sprite, "Back on your perch *now*."

Lehabah had just reached the glass dome where she maintained her fiery vigil over the library's wandering books when Bryce answered. "Afternoon, boss."

"Any progress?"

"Still investigating. How's Pangera?"

Jesiba didn't bother answering, instead saying, "I've got a client coming in at two o'clock. Be ready. And stop letting Lehabah prattle. She has a job to do." The line went dead.

Bryce rose from the desk where she'd been working all morning. The oak panels of the library beneath the gallery looked old, but they were wired with the latest tech and best enchantments money could buy. Not to mention, there was a killer sound system that she often put to good use when Jesiba was on the other side of the Haldren.

Not that she danced down here—not anymore. Nowadays, the music was mostly to keep the thrumming of the firstlights from driving her insane. Or for drowning out Lehabah's monologues.

Bookshelves lined every wall, interrupted only by a dozen or so small tanks and terrariums, occupied by all manner of small common animals: lizards and snakes and turtles and various rodents. Bryce often wondered if they were all people who'd pissed off Jesiba. None showed any sign of awareness, which was even more horrifying if it was true. They'd not only been turned into animals, but had also forgotten they were something else entirely.

Naturally, Lehabah had named all of them, each one more ridiculous than the last. *Nutmeg* and *Ginger* were the names of the geckos in the tank closest to Bryce. Sisters, Lehabah claimed. *Miss Poppy* was the name of the black-and-white snake on the mezzanine.

Lehabah never named anything in the biggest tank, though. The massive one that occupied an entire wall of the library, and whose glass expanse revealed a watery gloom. Mercifully, the tank was currently empty.

Last year, Bryce lobbied on Lehabah's behalf for a few iris eels to brighten the murky blue with their shimmering rainbow light. Jesiba had said no, and instead bought a pet kelpie that had humped the glass with all the finesse of a wasted college guy.

Bryce had made sure that motherfucker was given to a client as a gift *really* quickly.

Bryce braced herself for the work before her. Not the paperwork or the client—but what she had to do tonight. Gods fucking help her when Athalar got wind of it.

But the thought of his face when he realized what she had planned . . . Yeah, it'd be satisfying.

If she survived.

16

The mirthroot Ruhn had smoked ten minutes ago with Flynn might have been more potent than his friend had let on.

Lying on his bed, specially shaped Fae headphones over his arched ears, Ruhn closed his eyes and let the thumping bass and sizzling, soaring synthesizer of the music send him drifting.

His booted foot tapped in time to the steady beat, the drumming fingers he'd interlaced over his stomach echoing each flutter of notes high, high above. Every breath pulled him further back from consciousness, as if his very mind had been yanked a good few feet away from where it normally rested like a captain at the helm of a ship.

Heavy relaxation melted him, bone and blood morphing to liquid gold. Each note sent it rippling through him. Every stressor and sharp word and aggravation leaked from him, slithered off the bed like a snake.

He flipped off those feelings as they slid away. He was well aware that he'd taken the hits of Flynn's mirthroot thanks to the hours he'd spent brooding over his father's bullshit orders.

His father could go to Hel.

The mirthroot wrapped soft, sweet arms around his mind and dragged him into its shimmering pool.

Ruhn let himself drown in it, too mellow to do anything but let the music wash over him, his body sinking into the mattress, until he was falling through shadows and starlight. The strings of the song hovered overhead, golden threads that glittered with sound. Was he still moving his body? His eyelids were too heavy to lift to check.

A scent like lilac and nutmeg filled the room. Female, Fae . . .

If one of the females partying downstairs had shown herself into his room, thinking she'd get a nice, sweaty ride with a Prince of the Fae, she'd be sorely disappointed. He was in no shape for fucking right now. At least not any fucking that would be worthwhile.

His eyelids were so incredibly heavy. He should open them. Where the Hel were the controls to his body? Even his shadows had drifted away, too far to summon.

The scent grew stronger. He knew that scent. Knew it as well as—

Ruhn jerked upward, eyes flying open to find his sister standing at the foot of his bed.

Bryce's mouth was moving, whiskey-colored eyes full of dry amusement, but he couldn't hear a word she said, not a word—

Oh. Right. The headphones. Blasting music.

Blinking furiously, gritting his teeth against the drug trying to haul him back down, down, down, Ruhn removed the headphones and hit pause on his phone. "What?"

Bryce leaned against his chipped wood dresser. At least she was in normal clothes for once. Even if the jeans were painted on and the cream-colored sweater left little to the imagination. "I said, you'll blow out your eardrums listening to music that loud."

Ruhn's head spun as he narrowed his eyes at her, blinking at the halo of starlight that danced around her head, at her feet. He blinked again, pushing past the auras clouding his vision, and it was gone. Another blink, and it was there.

Bryce snorted. "You're not hallucinating. I'm standing here."

His mouth was a thousand miles away, but he managed to ask, "Who let you in?" Declan and Flynn were downstairs, along with half a dozen of their top Fae warriors. A few of them people he didn't want within a block of his sister.

Bryce ignored his question, frowning toward the corner of his room. Toward the pile of unwashed laundry and the Starsword he'd chucked atop it. The sword glimmered with starlight, too. He could have sworn the damn thing was singing. Ruhn shook his head, as if it'd clear out his ears, as Bryce said, "I need to talk to you."

The last time Bryce had been in this room, she'd been sixteen and he'd spent hours beforehand cleaning it—and the whole house. Every bong and bottle of liquor, every pair of female underwear that had never been returned to its owner, every trace and scent of sex and drugs and all the stupid shit they did here had been hidden.

And she'd stood right there, during that last visit. Stood there as they screamed at each other.

Then and now blurred, Bryce's form shrinking and expanding, her adult face blending into teenage softness, the light in her amber eyes warming and cooling, his vision surrounding the scene glinting with starlight, starlight, starlight.

"Fucking Hel," Bryce muttered, and aimed for the door. "You're pathetic."

He managed to say, "Where are you going?"

"To get you water." She flung the door open. "I can't talk to you like this."

It occurred to him then that this had to be important if she was not only here, but eager to get him to focus. And that there might still be a chance he was hallucinating, but he wasn't going to let her venture into the warren of sin unaccompanied.

On legs that felt ten miles long, feet that weighed a thousand pounds, he staggered after her. The dim hallway hid most of the various stains on the white paint—all thanks to the various parties he and his friends had thrown in fifty years of being roommates. Well, they'd had this house for twenty years—and had only moved because their first one had literally started to fall apart. This house might not last another two years, if he was being honest.

Bryce was halfway down the curving grand staircase, the firstlights of the crystal chandelier bouncing off her red hair in that shimmering halo. How had he not noticed the chandelier was hanging askew? Must be from when Declan had leapt off the stair railing onto it, swinging around and swigging from his bottle of whiskey. He'd fallen off a moment later, too drunk to hold on.

If the Autumn King knew the shit they did in this house, there was no way he or any other City Head would allow them to lead the Fae Aux division. No way Micah would ever tap him to take his father's place on that council.

But getting wasted was for off-nights only. Never when on duty or on call.

Bryce hit the worn oak floor of the first level, edging around the beer pong table occupying most of the foyer. A few cups littered its stained plywood surface, painted by Flynn with what they'd all deemed was high-class art: an enormous Fae male head devouring an angel whole, only frayed wings visible through the snapped-shut teeth. It seemed to ripple with movement as Ruhn cleared the stairs. He could have sworn the painting winked at him.

Yeah, water. He needed water.

Bryce showed herself through the living room, where the music blasted so loud it made Ruhn's teeth rattle in his skull.

He entered in time to see Bryce striding past the pool table in the rear of the long, cavernous space. A few Aux warriors stood around it, females with them, deep in a game.

Tristan Flynn, son of Lord Hawthorne, presided over it from a nearby armchair, a pretty dryad on his lap. The glazed light in his brown eyes mirrored Ruhn's own. Flynn gave Bryce a crooked grin as she approached. All it usually took was one look and females crawled into Tristan Flynn's lap just like the tree nymph, or—if the look was more of a glower—any enemies outright bolted.

Charming as all Hel and lethal as fuck. It should have been the Flynn family motto.

Bryce didn't stop as she passed him, unfazed by his classic Fae beauty and considerable muscles, but demanded over her shoulder, "What the fuck did you give him?"

Flynn leaned forward, prying his short chestnut hair free from the dryad's long fingers. "How do you know it was me?"

Bryce walked toward the kitchen at the back of the room, accessible through an archway. "Because you look high off your ass, too."

Declan called from the sectional couch at the other end of the living room, a laptop on his knee and a *very* interested draki male half-sprawled over him, running clawed fingers through Dec's dark red hair, "Hey, Bryce. To what do we owe the pleasure?"

Bryce jerked her thumb back at Ruhn. "Checking on the Chosen One. How's your fancy tech crap going, Dec?"

Declan Emmet didn't usually appreciate anyone belittling the lucrative career he'd built on a foundation of hacking into Republic websites and then charging them ungodly amounts of money to reveal their critical weaknesses, but he grinned. "Still raking in the marks."

"Nice," Bryce said, continuing into the kitchen and out of sight.

Some of the Aux warriors were staring toward the kitchen now, blatant interest in their eyes. Flynn growled softly, "She's off-limits, assholes."

That was all it took. Not even a snapping vine of Flynn's earth magic, rare among the fire-prone Valbaran Fae. The others immediately returned their attention to the pool game. Ruhn threw his friend a grateful look and followed Bryce—

But she was already back in the doorway, water bottle in hand. "Your fridge is worse than mine," she said, shoving the bottle toward him and entering the living room again. Ruhn sipped as the stereo system in the back thumped the opening notes of a song, guitars wailing, and she angled her head, listening, weighing.

Fae impulse—to be drawn to music, and to love it. Perhaps the one side of her heritage she didn't mind. He remembered her showing him her dance routines as a young teenager. She'd always looked so unbelievably happy. He'd never had the chance to ask why she stopped.

Ruhn sighed, forcing himself to *focus*, and said to Bryce, "Why are you here?"

She stopped near the sectional. "I told you: I need to talk to you."

Ruhn kept his face blank. He couldn't remember the last time she'd bothered finding him.

"Why would your cousin need an excuse to chat with us?" Flynn asked, murmuring something in the dryad's delicate ear that had her heading for the cluster of her three friends at the pool table, her narrow hips swishing in a reminder of what he'd miss if he waited too long. Flynn drawled, "She knows we're the most charming males in town."

Neither of his friends ever guessed the truth—or at least voiced any suspicions. Bryce tossed her hair over a shoulder as Flynn rose from his armchair. "I have better things to do—"

"Than hang out with Fae losers," Flynn finished for her, heading to the built-in bar against the far wall. "Yeah, yeah. You've said so a hundred times now. But look at that: here you are, hanging with us in our humble abode."

Despite his carefree demeanor, Flynn would one day inherit his father's title: Lord Hawthorne. Which meant that for the past several decades, Flynn had done everything he could to forget that little fact—and the centuries of responsibilities it would entail. He poured himself a drink, then a second one that he handed to Bryce. "Drink up, honeycakes."

Ruhn rolled his eyes. But—it was nearly midnight, and she was at their house, on one of the rougher streets in the Old Square, with a murderer on the loose. Ruhn hissed, "You were given an order to *lie low*—"

She waved a hand, not touching the whiskey in her other. "My imperial escort is outside. Scaring everyone away, don't worry."

Both his friends went still. The draki male took that as an invitation to drift away, aiming for the billiards game behind them as Declan twisted to look at her. Ruhn just said, "Who."

A little smile. Bryce asked, swirling the whiskey in its glass, "Is this house really befitting of the Chosen One?"

Flynn's mouth twitched. Ruhn shot him a warning glare, just daring him to bring up the Starborn shit right now. Outside of his father's villa and court, all that had gotten Ruhn was a lifetime of teasing from his friends.

Ruhn ground out, "Let's hear it, Bryce." Odds were, she'd come here just to piss him off.

She didn't respond immediately, though. No, Bryce traced a circle on a cushion, utterly unfazed by the three Fae warriors watching her every breath. Tristan and Declan had been Ruhn's best friends for as long as he could remember, and always had his back, no questions asked. That they were highly trained and efficient warriors was beside the point, though they'd saved each other's asses more times than Ruhn could count. Going through their Ordeals together had only cemented that bond.

The Ordeal itself varied depending on the person: for some, it might be as simple as overcoming an illness or a bit of personal strife. For others, it might be slaying a wyrm or a demon. The greater the Fae, the greater the Ordeal.

Ruhn had been learning to wield his shadows from his hateful cousins in Avallen, his two friends with him, when they'd all gone through their Ordeal, nearly dying in the process. It had culminated in Ruhn entering the mist-shrouded Cave of Princes, and emerging with the Starsword—and saving them all.

And when he'd made the Drop weeks later, it had been Flynn, fresh from his own Drop, who'd Anchored him.

Declan asked, his deep voice rumbling over the music and chatter, "What's going on?"

For a second, Bryce's swagger faltered. She glanced at them: their casual clothes, the places where she knew their guns were hidden even in their own home, their black boots and the knives tucked inside them. Bryce's eyes met Ruhn's.

"I know what that look means," Flynn groaned. "It means you don't want us to hear."

Bryce didn't take her eyes away from Ruhn as she said, "Yep."

Declan slammed his laptop shut. "You're really gonna go all mysterious and shit?"

She looked between Declan and Flynn, who had been inseparable since birth. "You two dickbags have the biggest mouths in town."

Flynn winked. "I thought you liked my mouth."

"Keep dreaming, lordling." Bryce smirked.

Declan chuckled, earning a sharp elbow from Flynn and the glass of whiskey from Bryce.

Ruhn swigged from his water, willing his head to clear further.

"Enough of this crap," he bit out. All that mirthroot threatened to turn on him as he pulled Bryce toward his bedroom again.

When they arrived, he took up a spot by the bed. "Well?"

Bryce leaned against the door, the wood peppered with holes from all the knives he'd chucked at it for idle target practice. "I need you to tell me if you've heard anything about what the Viper Queen's been up to."

This could not be good. "Why?"

"Because I need to talk to her."

"Are you fucking *nuts*?"

Again, that annoying-ass smile. "Maximus Tertian was killed on her turf. Did the Aux get any intel about her movements that night?"

"Your boss put you up to this?" It reeked of Roga.

"Maybe. Do you know anything?" She angled her head again, that silky sheet of hair—the same as their father's—shifting with the movement.

"Yes. Tertian's murder was . . . the same as Danika's and the pack's."

Any trace of a smile faded from her face. "Philip Briggs didn't do it. I want to know what the Viper Queen was up to that night. If the Aux has any knowledge of her movements."

Ruhn shook his head. "Why are you involved in this?"

"Because I was asked to look into it."

"Don't fuck with this case. Tell your boss to lay off. This is a matter for the Governor."

"And the Governor commandeered me to look for the murderer. He thinks I'm the link between them."

Great. Absolutely fantastic. Isaiah Tiberian had failed to mention that little fact. "You spoke to the Governor."

"Just answer my question. Does the Aux know anything about the Viper Queen's whereabouts on the night of Tertian's death?"

Ruhn blew out a breath. "No. I've heard that she pulled her people from the streets. Something spooked her. But that's all I know. And even if I knew the Viper Queen's alibis, I wouldn't tell you. Stay the fuck out of this. I'll call the Governor to tell him you're done being his personal investigator."

That icy look—their father's look—passed over her face. The sort of look that told him there was a wild, wicked storm raging beneath that cold exterior. And the power and thrill for both father and daughter lay not in sheer force, but in the control over the self, over those impulses.

The outside world saw his sister as reckless, unchecked—but he knew she'd been the master of her fate since before he'd met her. Bryce was just one of those people who, once she'd set her sights on what she wanted, didn't let anything get in her way. If she wanted to sleep around, she did it. If she wanted to party for three days straight, she did it. If she wanted to catch Danika's murderer . . .

"I am going to find the person behind this," she said with quiet fury. "If you try to interfere with it, I will make your life a living Hel."

"The demon that murderer is using is *lethal*." He'd seen the crime scene photos. The thought that Bryce had been saved by mere minutes, by sheer drunken stupidity, still twisted him up. Ruhn continued before she could answer. "The Autumn King *told* you to lie low until the Summit—this is the fucking opposite, Bryce."

"Well, it's now part of my job. Jesiba signed off on it. I can't very well refuse, can I?"

No. *No one* could say no to that sorceress.

He slid his hands into the back pockets of his jeans. "She ever tell you anything about Luna's Horn?"

Bryce's brows lifted at the shift in subject, but considering Jesiba Roga's field of work, she'd be the one to ask.

"She had me look for it two years ago," Bryce said warily. "But it was a dead end. Why?"

"Never mind." He eyed the small gold amulet around his sister's neck. At least Jesiba gave her that much protection. Expensive protection, too—and powerful. Archesian amulets didn't come cheap, not when there were only a few in the world. He nodded to it. "Don't take that off."

Bryce rolled her eyes. "Does everyone in this city think I'm dumb?"

"I mean it. Beyond the shit you do for work, if you're looking for someone strong enough to summon a demon like that, don't take that necklace off." At least he could remind her to be smart.

She just opened the door. "If you hear anything about the Viper Queen, call me."

Ruhn stiffened, his heart thundering. "Do *not* provoke her."

"Bye, Ruhn."

He was desperate enough that he said, "I'll go with you to—"

"*Bye.*" Then she was down the stairs, waving in that annoying-as-fuck way at Declan and Flynn, before swaggering out the front door.

His friends threw inquisitive looks to where Ruhn stood on the second-floor landing. Declan's whiskey was still raised to his lips.

Ruhn counted to ten, if only to keep from snapping the nearest object in half, and then vaulted over the railing, landing so hard that the scuffed oak planks shuddered.

He felt, more than saw, his friends fall into place behind him, hands within easy reach of their hidden weapons, drinks discarded as they read the fury on his face. Ruhn stormed through the front door and out into the brisk night.

Just in time to see Bryce strut across the street. To Hunt fucking Athalar.

"What the actual Hel," Declan breathed, halting beside Ruhn on the porch.

The Umbra Mortis looked pissed, his arms crossed and wings flaring slightly, but Bryce just breezed past him without so much as a glance. Causing Athalar to *slowly* turn, arms slackening at his sides, as if such a thing had never happened in his long, miserable life.

And wasn't that enough to put Ruhn in a killing sort of mood.

Ruhn cleared the porch and front lawn and stepped into the street, holding out a hand to the car that skidded to a screeching halt. His hand hit the hood, fingers curving. Metal dented beneath it.

The driver, wisely, didn't scream.

Ruhn strode between two parked sedans, Declan and Flynn close behind, just as Hunt turned to see what the fuss was about.

Understanding flashed in Hunt's eyes, quickly replaced by a half smile. "Prince."

"What the fuck are you doing here?"

Hunt jerked his chin toward Bryce, already disappearing down the street. "Protection duty."

"Like Hel you're watching her." Isaiah Tiberian had failed to mention *this*, too.

A shrug. "Not my call." The halo across his brow seemed to darken as he sized up Declan and Flynn. Athalar's mouth twitched upward, onyx eyes glinting with an unspoken challenge.

Flynn's gathering power had the earth beneath the pavement rumbling. Hunt's shit-eating grin only spread.

Ruhn said, "Tell the Governor to put someone else on the case."

Hunt's grin sharpened. "Not an option. Not when it plays to my expertise."

Ruhn bristled at the arrogance. Sure, Athalar was one of the best demon-hunters out there, but fuck, he'd even take Tiberian on this case over the Umbra Mortis.

A year ago, the Commander of the 33rd hadn't been dumb enough to get between them when Ruhn had launched himself at Athalar, having had enough of his snide remarks at the fancy-ass Spring Equinox party Micah threw every March. He'd broken a few of Athalar's ribs, but the asshole had gotten in a punch that had left Ruhn's nose shattered and gushing blood all over the marble floors of the Comitium's penthouse ballroom. Neither of them had been pissed enough to unleash their power in the middle of a crowded room, but fists had done just fine.

Ruhn calculated how much trouble he'd be in if he punched the Governor's personal assassin again. Maybe it'd be enough to get Hypaxia Enador to refuse to consider marrying him.

Ruhn demanded, "Did you figure out what kind of demon did it?"

"Something that eats little princes for breakfast," Hunt crooned.

Ruhn bared his teeth. "Blow me, Athalar."

Lightning danced over the angel's fingers. "Must be easy to run your mouth when you're bankrolled by your father." Hunt pointed to the white house. "He buy that for you, too?"

Ruhn's shadows rose to meet the lightning wreathing Athalar's fists, setting the parked cars behind him shuddering. He'd learned from his cousins in Avallen how to make the shadows solidify—how to wield them as whips and shields and pure torment. Physical and mental.

But mixing magic and drugs was never a good idea. Fists it would have to be, then. And all it would take was one swing, right into Athalar's face—

Declan growled, "This isn't the time or place."

No, it wasn't. Even Athalar seemed to remember the gawking people, the upraised phones recording everything. And the red-haired female nearing the end of the block. Hunt smirked. "Bye, assholes." He followed Bryce, lightning skittering over the pavement in his wake.

Ruhn growled at the angel's back, "Do not fucking let her go to the Viper Queen."

Athalar glanced over a shoulder, his gray wings tucking in. His blink told Ruhn that he hadn't been aware of Bryce's agenda. A shiver of satisfaction ran through Ruhn. But Athalar continued down the street, people pressing themselves against buildings to give him a wide berth. The warrior's focus remained on Bryce's exposed neck.

Flynn shook his head like a wet dog. "I literally can't tell if I'm hallucinating right now."

"I wish I were," Ruhn muttered. He'd need to smoke another mountain of mirthroot to mellow the Hel out again. But if Hunt Athalar was watching Bryce . . . He'd heard enough rumors to know what Hunt could do to an opponent. That he, in addition to being a prime bastard, was relentless, single-minded, and utterly brutal when it came to eliminating threats.

Hunt had to obey the order to protect her. No matter what.

Ruhn studied them as they walked away. Bryce would speed up; Hunt would match her pace. She'd drop back; he'd do the same. She'd edge him to the right, right, right—off the curb and into oncoming traffic; he'd narrowly avoid a swerving car and step back onto the sidewalk.

Ruhn was half-tempted to trail them, just to watch the battle of wills.

"I need a drink," Declan muttered. Flynn agreed and the two of them headed back toward the house, leaving Ruhn alone on the street.

Could it really be a coincidence that the murders were starting again at the same time his father had given the order to find an object that had gone missing a week before Danika's death?

It felt . . . odd. Like Urd was whispering, nudging them all.

Ruhn planned to find out why. Starting with finding that Horn.

17

Bryce had just succeeded in nudging Hunt into oncoming traffic when he asked, "Do I get an explanation for why I've had to trail you like a dog all night?"

Bryce shoved her hand into the pocket of her jeans and pulled out a piece of paper. Then silently handed it to Hunt.

His brow furrowed. "What's this?"

"My list of suspects," she said, letting him glance at the names before she snatched it away.

"When did you make this?"

She said sweetly, "Last night. On the couch."

A muscle ticked in his jaw. "And you were going to tell me when?"

"After you'd spent a whole day assuming I was a dumb, vapid female more interested in getting my nails done than solving this case."

"You *did* get your nails done."

She waved her pretty ombre fingernails in his face. He looked half-inclined to bite them. "Do you know what *else* I did last night?" His silence was delightful. "I looked up Maximus Tertian some more. Because despite what the Governor says, there was no fucking way Danika knew him. And you know what? I was right. And you know how I know I'm right?"

"Cthona fucking save me," Hunt muttered.

"Because I looked up his profile on Spark."

"The dating site?"

"The dating site. Turns out even creepy vamps are looking for love, deep down. And it showed that he was in a relationship. Which apparently did nothing to stop him from hitting on me, but that's beside the point. So I did some *more* digging. And found his girlfriend."

"Fuck."

"Aren't there people at the 33rd who should be doing this shit?" When he refused to answer, she grinned. "Guess where Tertian's girlfriend works."

Hunt's eyes simmered. He said through his teeth, "At the nail salon on Samson."

"And guess who did my nails and got to chatting about the terrible loss of her rich-ass boyfriend?"

He ran his hands through his hair, looking so disbelieving that she chuckled. He snarled, "Stop with the fucking questions and just tell me, Quinlan."

She examined her gorgeous new nails. "Tertian's girlfriend didn't know anything about who might have wanted to murder him. She said the 33rd did vaguely question her, but that was it. So I told her that I'd lost someone, too." It was an effort to keep her voice steady as the memory of that bloody apartment flashed. "She asked me who, I told her, and she looked so shocked that I asked if Tertian was friends with Danika. She told me no. She said she would have known if Maximus was, because Danika was famous enough that he'd have been bragging about it. The closest to Danika she or Tertian got was through two degrees of separation—through the Viper Queen. Whose nails she does on Sundays."

"Danika knew the Viper Queen?"

Bryce held up the list. "Danika's job in the Aux made her a friend and enemy to a lot of people. The Viper Queen was one of them."

Hunt paled. "You honestly think the Viper Queen killed Danika?"

"Tertian was found dead just over her borders. Ruhn said she pulled her people in last night. And no one knows what kind of powers she has. She could have summoned that demon."

"That is a big fucking accusation to make."

"Which is why we need to feel her out. This is the only clue we have to go on."

Hunt shook his head. "All right. I can buy the possibility. But we need to go through the right channels to contact her. It could be days or weeks before she deigns to meet with us. Longer, if she gets a whiff that we're onto her."

With someone like the Viper Queen, even the law was flexible.

Bryce scoffed. "Don't be such a stickler for the rules."

"The rules are there to keep us alive. We follow them, or we don't go after her at all."

She waved a hand. "Fine."

A muscle ticked in his jaw again. "And what about Ruhn? You just dragged your cousin into our business."

"My cousin," she said tightly, "will be unable to resist the urge to inform his father that a member of the Fae race has been commandeered for an imperial investigation. How he reacts, who he contacts, might be worth noting."

"What—you think the Autumn King could have done this?"

"No. But Ruhn was given an order to warn me to keep out of trouble the night of Maximus's murder—maybe the old bastard knew something, too. I'd suggest telling your people to watch him. See what he does and where he goes."

"Gods," Hunt breathed, striding past gawking pedestrians. "You want me to just put a tail on the Autumn King like it's not a violation of about ten different laws?"

"Micah said to do whatever was necessary."

"The Autumn King has free rein to kill anyone found stalking him like that."

"Then you better tell your spies to keep themselves hidden."

Hunt snapped his wings. "Don't play games again. If you know something, tell me."

"I was going to tell you everything when I finished up at the nail salon this morning." She put her hands on her hips. "But then you bit my head off."

"Whatever, Quinlan. Don't do it again. You *tell me* before you make a move."

"I'm getting real bored with you giving me orders and forbidding me to do things."

"Whatever," he said again. She rolled her eyes, but they'd reached her building. Neither bothered to say goodbye before Hunt leapt into the skies, aiming for the adjacent roof, a phone already at his ear.

Bryce rode the elevator up to her floor, mulling everything over in the silence. She'd meant what she said to Hunt—she didn't think her father was behind Danika's and the pack's deaths. She had little doubt he'd killed others, though. And would do anything to keep his crown.

The Autumn King was a courtesy title in addition to her father's role as a City Head—as for all the seven Fae Kings. No kingdom was truly their own. Even Avallen, the green isle ruled by the Stag King, still bowed to the Republic.

The Fae had coexisted with the Republic since its founding, answerable to its laws, but ultimately left to govern themselves and retain their ancient titles of kings and princes and the like. Still respected by all—and feared. Not as much as the angels, with their destructive, hideous storm-and-sky powers, but they could inflict pain if they wished. Choke the air from your lungs or freeze you or burn you from the inside out. Solas knew Ruhn and his two friends could raise Hel when provoked.

But she wasn't looking to raise Hel tonight. She was looking to quietly slip into its Midgard equivalent.

Which was precisely why she waited thirty minutes before tucking a knife into her black leather ankle boots, and placed something that packed a bigger punch into the back of her dark jeans, hidden beneath her leather jacket. She kept the lights and television on, the curtains partially closed—just enough to block Hunt's view of her front door as she left.

Sneaking out the rear stairwell of her building to the small alley where her scooter was chained, Bryce took a swift, bracing breath before fitting on her helmet.

Traffic wasn't moving as she unchained the ivory Firebright 3500 scooter from the alley lamppost and waddled it onto the cobblestones. She waited for other scooters, pedicabs, and motorcycles to zip past, then launched into the flow, the world stark through the visor of her helmet.

Her mother still complained about the scooter, begging her to use a car until after the Drop, but Randall had always insisted Bryce was fine. Of course, she never told them of the various *incidents* on this scooter, but . . . her mother had a mortal life span. Bryce didn't need to shave off any more years than necessary.

Bryce cruised down one of the city's main arteries, losing herself in the rhythm of weaving between cars and swerving around pedestrians. The world was a blur of golden light and deep shadows, neon glaring above, all of it accented by pops and flittering shimmers of street magic. Even the little bridges she crossed, spanning the countless tributaries to the Istros, were strung with sparkling lights that danced on the dim, drifting water below.

High above Main Street, a silvery sheen filled the night sky, limning the drifting clouds where the malakim partied and dined. Only a flare of red interrupted the pale glow, courtesy of Redner Industries' massive sign atop their skyscraper in the heart of the district.

Few people walked the streets of the CBD at this hour, and Bryce made sure to get through its canyons of high-rises as swiftly as possible. She knew she'd entered the Meat Market not by any street or marker, but by the shift in the darkness.

No lights stained the skies above the low brick buildings crammed together. And here the shadows became permanent, tucked into alleys and under cars, the streetlamps mostly shattered and never repaired.

Bryce pulled down a cramped street where a few dented delivery trucks were in the process of unloading boxes of spiky green fruit and crates of crustacean-looking creatures that seemed far too aware of their captivity and oncoming demise via boiling pots of water in one of the food stalls.

Bryce tried not to meet their googly black eyes pleading with her through the wooden bars as she parked a few feet away from a nondescript warehouse, removed her helmet, and waited.

Vendors and shoppers alike eyed her to glean if she was selling or for sale. In the warrens below, carved deep into Midgard's womb, lay three different levels just for flesh. Mostly human; mostly living, though she'd heard of some places that specialized in certain tastes. Every fetish could be bought; no taboo was too foul. Half-breeds were prized: they could heal faster and better than full-humans. A smarter long-term investment. And occasional Vanir were enslaved and bound with so many enchantments that they had no hope of escape. Only the wealthiest could afford to purchase a few hours with them.

Bryce checked the time on her scooter's dash clock. Crossing her arms, she leaned against the black leather seat.

The Umbra Mortis slammed to the ground, cracking the cobblestones in a rippling circle.

Hunt's eyes practically glowed as he said, in full view of those cowering along the street, "*I am going to kill you.*"

18

Hunt stormed toward Bryce, stepping over the cobblestones fragmented from his landing. He'd detected her lilac-and-nutmeg scent on the wind the moment she'd stepped outside the back door of her building, and when he'd discovered where, precisely, she was driving on that scooter . . .

Bryce had the nerve to push back the sleeve of her leather jacket, frown at her bare wrist as if she were reading a gods-damned watch, and say, "You're two minutes late."

He was going to throttle her. Someone should have done it a long fucking time ago.

Bryce smiled in a way that said she'd like to see him try, and sauntered toward him, scooter and helmet left behind.

Unbelievable. Un-fucking-believable.

Hunt growled, "There's no way that scooter is there when we get back."

Bryce batted her eyelashes, fluffing out her helmet hair. "Good thing you've made such a big entrance. No one would dare touch it now. Not with the Umbra Mortis as my wrathful companion."

Indeed, people shrank from his gaze, some stepping behind the stacked crates as Bryce aimed for one of the open doors into the labyrinth of subterraneanly interconnected warehouses that made up the blocks of the district.

Even Micah didn't station legionaries here. The Meat Market had its own laws and methods of enforcing them.

Hunt ground out, "I told you that there are protocols to follow if we want to stand a chance of contacting the Viper Queen—"

"I'm not here to contact the Viper Queen."

"What?" The Viper Queen had ruled the Meat Market for longer than anyone could remember. Hunt made a point—all the angels, whether civilians or legionaries, made a point—of staying the fuck away from the serpentine shifter, whose snake form, rumor claimed, was a true horror to behold. Before Bryce could answer, Hunt said, "I'm growing tired of this bullshit, Quinlan."

She bared her teeth. "I'm sorry," she seethed, "if your fragile ego can't handle that *I know what I'm fucking doing*."

Hunt opened and closed his mouth. Fine, he'd misjudged her earlier today, but she hadn't exactly given him any hint of being remotely interested in this investigation. Or that she wasn't trying to hinder it.

Bryce continued through the open doors to the warehouse without saying another word.

Being in the 33rd—or any legion—was as good as putting a target on your back, and Hunt checked that his weapons were in place in the cleverly constructed sheaths along his suit as he followed her.

The reek of bodies and smoke coated his face like oil. Hunt tucked in his wings tightly.

Whatever fear he'd instilled in people on the streets was of no consequence inside the market, packed with ramshackle stalls and vendors and food stands, smoke drifting throughout, the tang of blood and spark of magic acrid in his nostrils. And above it all, against the far wall of the enormous space, was a towering mosaic, the tiles taken from an ancient temple in Pangera, restored and re-created here in loving detail, despite its gruesome depiction: cloaked and hooded death, the skeleton's face grinning out from the cowl, a scythe in one hand and an hourglass in the other. Above its head, words had been crafted in the Republic's most ancient language:

Memento Mori.

Remember that you will die. It was meant to be an invitation for merriment, to seize each moment as if it were one's last, as if tomorrow were not guaranteed, even for slow-aging Vanir. *Remember that you will die, and enjoy each pleasure the world has to offer. Remember that you will die, and none of this illegal shit will matter anyway. Remember that you will die, so who cares how many people suffer from your actions?*

Bryce swept past it, her swaying hair shining like the heart of a ruby. The lights illuminated the worn black leather of her jacket, bringing into stark relief the painted words along the back in feminine, colorful script. It was instinct to translate—also from the ancient language, as if Urd herself had chosen this moment to lay the two ancient phrases before him.

Through love, all is possible.

Such a pretty phrase was a fucking joke in a place like this. Glimmering eyes that tracked Quinlan from the stalls and shadows quickly looked away when they noticed him at her side.

It was an effort not to haul her out of this shithole. Even though he wanted this case solved, having only ten beautiful kills standing between him and freedom, coming here was a colossal risk. What was the use of his freedom if he was left in a dumpster behind one of these warehouses?

Maybe that was what she wanted. To lure him here—use the Meat Market itself to kill him. It seemed unlikely, but he kept one eye on her.

Bryce knew her way around. Knew a few of the vendors, from the nods they exchanged. Hunt marked each one: a metalworker specializing in intricate little mechanisms; a fruit vendor with exotic produce for sale; an owl-faced female who had a spread of scrolls and books bound in materials that were everything but cow leather.

"The metalworker helps me identify if an artifact is a fake," Bryce said under her breath as they wound through the steam and smoke of a food pit. How she'd noticed his observing, he had no idea. "And the fruit lady gets shipments of durian in the early spring and fall—Syrinx's favorite food. Stinks up the whole house, but he goes nuts for it." She edged around a garbage pail near-overflowing with discarded plates and bones and soiled napkins before ascending a rickety set of stairs to the mezzanine flanking either side of the warehouse floor, doors stationed every few feet.

"The books?" Hunt couldn't help asking. She seemed to be counting doors, rather than looking at the numbers. There *were* no numbers, he realized.

"The books," Bryce said, "are a story for another time." She paused outside a pea-green door, chipped and deeply gouged in spots. Hunt sniffed, trying to detect what lay beyond. Nothing, as far as he could detect. He subtly braced himself, keeping his hands within range of his weapons.

Bryce opened the door, not bothering to knock, revealing flickering candles and—brine. Salt. Smoke and something that dried out his eyes.

Bryce stalked down the cramped hallway to the open, rotting sitting room beyond. Scowling, he shut the door and followed, wings tucked in to keep from brushing the oily, crumbling walls. If Quinlan died, Micah's offer would be off the table.

White and ivory candles guttered as Bryce walked onto the worn green carpet, and Hunt held in his cringe. A sagging, ripped couch was shoved against a wall, a filthy leather armchair with half its stuffing bursting from it sat against the other, and around the room, on tables and stacks of books and half-broken chairs, were jars and bowls and cups full of salt.

White salt, black salt, gray salt—in grains of every size: from near-powder to flakes to great, rough hunks of it. Salts for protection against darker powers. Against demons. Many Vanir built their houses with slabs of salt at the cornerstones. Rumor claimed that the entire base of the Asteri's crystal palace was a slab of salt. That it had been built atop a natural deposit.

Fucking Hel. He'd never seen such an assortment. As Bryce peered down the darkened hall to the left, where the shadows yielded three doors, Hunt hissed, "Please tell me—"

"Just keep your snarling and eye rolling to yourself," she snapped at him, and called into the gloom, "I'm here to buy, not collect."

One of the doors cracked open, and a pale-skinned, dark-haired satyr hobbled toward them, his furred legs hidden by trousers. His pageboy hat must have hid little, curling horns. The clopping of the hooves gave him away.

The male barely came up to Bryce's chest, his shrunken, twisted body half the size of the bulls that Hunt had witnessed tearing people into shreds on battlefields. And that he had faced himself in Sandriel's arena. The male's slitted pupils, knobbed at either side like a goat's, expanded.

Fear—and not at Hunt's presence, he realized with a jolt.

Bryce dipped her fingers into a lead bowl of pink salt, plucking up a few pieces and letting them drop into the dish with faint, hollow cracks. "I need the obsidian."

The satyr shifted, hooves clopping faintly, rubbing his hairy, pale neck. "Don't deal in that."

She smiled slightly. "Oh?" She went over to another bowl, stirring the powder-fine black salt in there. "Grade A, whole-rock obsidian salt. Seven pounds, seven ounces. Now."

The male's throat bobbed. "It's illegal."

"Are you quoting the motto of the Meat Market, or trying to tell me that you somehow *don't* have precisely what I need?"

Hunt scanned the room. White salt for purification; pink for protection; gray for spellwork; red for . . . he forgot what the Hel red was for. But obsidian . . . Shit.

Hunt fell back on centuries of training to keep the shock off his face. Black salts were used for summoning demons directly—bypassing the Northern Rift entirely—or for various dark spellwork. A salt that went beyond black, a salt like the *obsidian* . . . It could summon something big.

Hel was severed from them by time and space, but still accessible through the twin sealed portals at the north and south poles—the Northern Rift and the Southern Rift, respectively. Or by idiots who tried to summon demons through salts of varying powers.

A lot of fucked-up shit, Hunt had always thought. The benefit of using salts, at least, was that only one demon could be summoned at a time. Though if things went badly, the summoner could wind up dead. And a demon could wind up stuck in Midgard, hungry.

It was why the creeps existed in their world at all: most had been hunted after those long-ago wars between realms, but every so often, demons got loose. Reproduced, usually by force.

The result of those horrible unions: the daemonaki. Most walking the streets were diluted, weaker incarnations and hybrids of the purebred demons in Hel. Many were pariahs, through no fault of their own beyond genetics, and they usually worked hard to integrate into the Republic. But the lowest-level purebred demon fresh out of Hel could bring an entire city to a standstill as it went on a rampage. And for centuries now, Hunt had been tasked with tracking them down.

This satyr had to be a big-time dealer then, if he peddled obsidian salt.

Bryce took a step toward the satyr. The male retreated. Her amber eyes gleamed with feral amusement, no doubt from her Fae side. A far cry from the party girl getting her nails done.

Hunt tensed. She couldn't be that foolish, could she? To show him that she knew how to and could easily acquire the same type of salt that had probably been used to summon the demon that killed Tertian and Danika? Another tally scratched itself into the Suspect column in his mind.

Bryce shrugged with one shoulder. "I could call your queen. See what she makes of it."

"You—you don't have the rank to summon *her*."

"No," Bryce said, "I don't. But I bet if I go down to the main floor and start screaming for the Viper Queen, she'll drag herself out of that fighting pit to see what the fuss is about."

Burning Solas, she was serious, wasn't she?

Sweat beaded the satyr's brow. "Obsidian's too dangerous. I can't in good conscience sell it."

Bryce crooned, "Did you say that when you sold it to Philip Briggs for his bombs?"

Hunt stilled, and the male went a sickly white. He glanced to Hunt, noting the tattoo across his brow, the armor he wore. "I don't know what you're talking about. I—I was cleared by the investigators. I never sold Briggs anything."

"I'm sure he paid you in cash to hide the money trail," Bryce said. She yawned. "Look, I'm tired and hungry, and I don't feel like playing this game. Name your price so I can be on my way."

Those goatlike eyes snapped to hers. "Fifty thousand gold marks."

Bryce smiled as Hunt held in his curse. "Do you know my boss paid fifty thousand to watch a pack of Helhounds rip apart a satyr? Said it was the best minute of her miserable life."

"Forty-five."

"Don't waste my time with nonsense offers."

"I won't go below thirty. Not for that much obsidian."

"Ten." Ten thousand gold marks was still outrageous. But summoning salts were extraordinarily valuable. How many demons had he hunted because of them? How many dismembered bodies had he seen from summonings gone wrong? Or right, if it was a targeted attack?

Bryce held up her phone. "In five minutes, I'm expected to call Jesiba, and say that the obsidian salt is in my possession. In six minutes, if I do *not* make that phone call, someone will knock on that door. And it will not be someone for me."

Hunt honestly couldn't tell if Quinlan was bluffing. She likely wouldn't have told him—could have gotten that order from her boss while he was sitting on the roof. If Jesiba Roga was dealing with whatever shit the obsidian implied, either for her own uses or on behalf of the Under-King . . . Maybe Bryce hadn't committed the murder, but rather abetted it.

"Four minutes," Bryce said.

Sweat slid down the satyr's temple and into his thick beard. Silence.

Despite his suspicions, Hunt had the creeping feeling that this assignment was either going to be a fuck-ton of fun or a nightmare. If it got him to his end goal, he didn't care one way or another.

Bryce perched on the rotting arm of the chair and began typing into her phone, no more than a bored young woman avoiding social interaction.

The satyr whirled toward Hunt. "You're the Umbra Mortis." He swallowed audibly. "You're one of the triarii. You protect us—you serve the Governor."

Before Hunt could reply, Bryce lifted her phone to show him a photo of two fat, roly-poly puppies. "Look what my cousin just adopted," she told him. "That one is Osirys, and the one on the right is Set." She lowered the phone before he could come up with a response, thumbs flying.

But she glanced at Hunt from under her thick lashes. *Play along, please*, she seemed to say.

So Hunt said, "Cute dogs."

The satyr let out a small whine of distress. Bryce lifted her head, curtain of red hair limned with silver in her screen's light. "I thought you'd be running to get the salt by now. Maybe you should, considering you've got"—a glance at the phone, fingers flying—"oh. Ninety seconds."

She opened what looked like a message thread and began typing.

The satyr whispered, "T-twenty thousand."

She held up a finger. "I'm writing back to my cousin. Give me two seconds." The satyr was trembling enough that Hunt almost felt bad. Almost, until—

"Ten, ten, damn you! Ten!"

Bryce smiled. "No need to shout," she purred, pressing a button that had her phone ringing.

"Yes?" The sorceress picked up after the first ring.

"Call off your dogs."

A breathy, feminine laugh. "Done."

Bryce lowered the phone. "Well?"

The satyr rushed to the back, hooves thumping on the worn floors, and procured a wrapped bundle a moment later. It reeked of mold and dirt. Bryce lifted a brow. "Put it in a bag."

"I don't have a—" Bryce gave him a look. The satyr found one. A stained, reusable grocery bag, but better than holding the slab in public.

Bryce weighed the salt in her hands. "It's two ounces over."

"It's seven and seven! Just what you asked for! It's all cut to sevens."

Seven—the holy number. Or unholy, depending on who was worshipping. Seven Asteri, seven hills in their Eternal City, seven neighborhoods and seven Gates in Crescent City; seven planets, and seven circles in Hel, with seven princes who ruled them, each darker than the last.

Bryce inclined her head. "If I measure it and it's not—"

"It is!" the satyr cried. "Dark Hel, it is!"

Bryce tapped some buttons on her phone. "Ten grand, transferred right to you."

Hunt kept at her back as she strode out, the satyr half-seething, half-trembling behind them.

She opened the door, grinning to herself, and Hunt was about to start demanding answers when she halted. When he also beheld who stood outside.

The tall, moon-skinned woman was dressed in a gold jumpsuit, emerald hoop earrings hanging lower than her chin-length black bob. Her full lips were painted in purple so dark it was nearly black, and her remarkable green eyes . . . Hunt knew her by the eyes alone.

Humanoid in every aspect, but for them. Green entirely, marbled with veins of jade and gold. Interrupted only by a slitted pupil now razor-thin in the warehouse lights. A snake's eyes.

Or a Viper Queen's.

19

Bryce shouldered the canvas bag, surveying the Viper Queen. "Nice outfit."

The serpentine shifter smiled, revealing bright white teeth—and canines that were slightly too elongated. And slightly too thin. "Nice bodyguard."

Bryce shrugged as those snake's eyes dragged over every inch of Hunt. "Nothing going on upstairs, but everything happening where it counts."

Hunt stiffened. But the female's purple lips curved upward. "I've never heard Hunt Athalar described that way, but I'm sure the general appreciates it."

At the near-forgotten title, Hunt's jaw tightened. Yes, the Viper Queen had likely been alive during the Fall. Would have known Hunt not as one of the 33rd's triarii or the Shadow of Death, but as General Hunt Athalar, High Commander of all the Archangel Shahar's legions.

And Bryce had strung him along for two days. She glanced over a shoulder, finding Hunt assessing the Viper Queen and the four Fae males flanking her. Defectors from her father's court—trained assassins in not just weapons, but the queen's specialty: venoms and poisons.

None of them deigned to acknowledge her.

The Viper Queen tilted her head to the side, the razor-sharp bob shifting like black silk. On the ground below, patrons milled about, unaware that their ruler had graced them with her presence. "Looks like you were doing some shopping."

Bryce gave a half shrug. "Bargain hunting is a hobby. Your realm is the best place for it."

"I thought your boss paid you too well for you to stoop to cutting costs. And using salts."

Bryce forced herself to smile, to keep her heartbeat steady, knowing full well the female could pick up on it. Could taste fear. Could likely taste what variety of salt, exactly, sat in the bag dangling from her shoulder. "Just because I make money doesn't mean I have to get ripped off."

The Viper Queen glanced between her and Hunt. "I heard you two have been spotted around town together."

Hunt growled, "It's classified."

The Viper Queen arched a well-groomed black eyebrow, the small beauty mark just beneath the outer corner of her eye shifting with the movement. Her gold-painted nails glinted as she reached a hand into the pocket of her jumpsuit, fishing out a lighter encrusted with rubies forming the shape of a striking asp. A cigarette appeared between her purple lips a moment later, and they watched in silence, her guards monitoring every breath they made, as she lit up and inhaled deeply. Smoke rippled from those dark lips as she said, "Shit's getting interesting these days."

Bryce pivoted toward the exit. "Yep. Let's go, Hunt."

One of the guards stepped in front of her, six and a half feet of Fae grace and muscle.

Bryce stopped short, Hunt nearly slamming into her—his growl likely his first and last warning to the male. But the guard merely gazed at his queen, vacant and beholden. Likely addicted to the venom she secreted and doled out to her inner circle.

Bryce looked over her shoulder at the Viper Queen, still leaning against the rail, still smoking that cigarette. "It's a good time for business," the queen observed, "when key players converge for the Summit. So many ruling-class elites, all with their own . . . interests."

Hunt was close enough to Bryce's back that she could feel the tremor that ran through his powerful body, could have sworn lightning tingled over her spine. But he said nothing.

The Viper Queen merely extended a hand to the walkway behind her, gold nails flashing in the light. "My office, if you will."

"No," Hunt said. "We're going."

Bryce stepped closer to the Viper Queen. "Lead the way, Majesty."

She did. Hunt was bristling at her side, but Bryce kept her eyes on the swaying, glossy bob of the female ahead of them. Her guards kept a few feet behind—far enough away that Hunt deemed it safe to mutter, "This is a terrible idea."

"You were bitching this morning that I wasn't doing anything of value," Bryce muttered back as they trailed the Viper Queen through an archway and down a back set of stairs. From below, roaring and cheers rose to meet them. "And now that I am doing something, you're bitching about it, too?" She snorted. "Get your shit together, Athalar."

His jaw tightened again. But he glanced at her bag, the block of salt weighing it down. "You bought the salt because you knew it'd attract her attention."

"You told me that it'd take weeks to get a meeting with her. I decided to bypass all the bullshit." She tapped the bag, the salt thumping hollowly beneath her hand.

"Cthona's tits," he muttered, shaking his head. They exited the stairwell a level down, the walls solid concrete. Behind them, the roar of the fighting pit echoed down the corridor. But the Viper Queen glided ahead, passing rusty metal doors. Until she opened an unmarked one and swept in without so much as looking back. Bryce couldn't help her smug smile.

"Don't look so fucking satisfied," Hunt hissed. "We might not even walk out of this place alive." True. "I'll ask the questions."

"No."

They glowered at each other, and Bryce could have sworn

lightning forked across his eyes. But they'd reached the door, which opened into—

She'd been expecting the plush opulence of Griffin Antiquities hidden behind that door: gilded mirrors and velvet divans and silk drapes and a carved oak desk as old as this city.

Not this . . . mess. It was barely better than the stockroom of a dive bar. A dented metal desk occupied most of the cramped space, a scratched purple chair behind it—tufts of stuffing poking out of the upper corner, and the pale green paint peeled off the wall in half a dozen spots. Not to mention the water stain gracing the ceiling, made worse by the thrumming fluorescent firstlights. Against one wall stood an open shelving unit filled with everything from files to crates of liquor to discarded guns; on the opposite, stacked cardboard boxes rose above her head.

One glance at Hunt and Bryce knew he was thinking the same: the Viper Queen, mistress of the underworld, feared poisons expert and ruler of the Meat Market, claimed this hovel as an office?

The female slid into the chair, interlacing her fingers atop the mess of papers strewn across the desk. A computer that was about twenty years out of date sat like a fat rock before her, a little statue of Luna poised atop it, the goddess's bow aimed at the shifter's face.

One of her guards shut the door, prompting Hunt's hand to slide toward his hip, but Bryce had already taken a seat in one of the cheap aluminum chairs.

"Not as fancy as your boss's place," the Viper Queen said, reading the disbelief on Bryce's face, "but it does the trick."

Bryce didn't bother agreeing that the space was far from anything befitting a serpentine shifter whose snake form was a moon-white cobra with scales that gleamed like opals—and whose power was rumored to be . . . different. Something *extra* that mixed with her venom, something strange and old.

Hunt took a seat beside her, twisting the chair frontward to accommodate his wings. Roaring from the fighting pit rumbled through the concrete floor beneath their feet.

The Viper Queen lit another cigarette. "You're here to ask about Danika Fendyr."

Bryce kept her face neutral. To his credit, Athalar did, too.

Hunt said carefully, "We're trying to get a clearer picture of everything."

Her remarkable eyes narrowed with pleasure. "If that's what you want to claim, then sure." Smoke rippled from her lips. "I'll spare you the bullshit, though. Danika was a threat to me, and in more ways than perhaps you know. But she was smart. Our relationship was a working one." Another inhale. "I'm sure Athalar can back me up on this," she drawled, earning a warning glare from him, "but to get shit done, sometimes the Aux and 33rd have to work with those of us who dwell in the shadows."

Hunt said, "And Maximus Tertian? He was killed on the outskirts of your territory."

"Maximus Tertian was a spoiled little bitch, but I would never be stupid enough to pick a fight with his father like that. I'd only stand to gain a headache."

"Who killed him?" Bryce asked. "I heard you pulled in your people. You know something."

"Just a precaution." She flicked her tongue over her bottom teeth. "Us serps can taste when shit is about to go down. Like a charge in the air. I can taste it now—all over this city."

Hunt's lightning grumbled in the room. "You didn't think to warn anyone?"

"I warned my people. As long as trouble doesn't pass through my district, I don't care what goes on in the rest of Lunathion."

Hunt said, "Real noble of you."

Bryce asked again, "Who do you think killed Tertian?"

She shrugged. "Honestly? It's the Meat Market. Shit happens. He was probably coming here for drugs, and this is the price he paid."

"What kind of drugs?" Bryce asked, but Hunt said, "Toxicology report says there were no drugs in his system."

"Then I can't help you," the shifter said. "Your guess is as good as mine." Bryce didn't bother to ask about camera footage, not when the 33rd would have already combed through it.

The Viper Queen pulled something from a drawer and chucked

it on the desk. A flash drive. "My alibis from the night Tertian was killed and from the days before and during Danika and her pack's murders."

Bryce didn't touch the tiny metal drive, no bigger than a lipstick tube.

The Viper Queen's lips curved again. "I was at the spa the night of Tertian's murder. And as for Danika and the Pack of Devils, one of my associates threw a Drop party for his daughter that night. Turned into three days of . . . well, you'll see."

"This drive contains footage of you at a three-day orgy?" Hunt demanded.

"Let me know if it gets you hot and bothered, Athalar." The Viper Queen took another hit of the cigarette. Her green eyes drifted toward his lap. "I hear you're one Hel of a ride when you pause the brooding long enough."

Oh please. Hunt's teeth flashed as he bared them in a silent snarl, so Bryce said, "Orgy and Hunt's bedroom prowess aside, you've got a salt vendor in this market." She tapped the bag balanced on her knees.

The Viper Queen tore her eyes from a still-snarling Hunt and said sharply to Bryce, "I don't use what I sell. Though I don't think you live by that rule over at your fancy gallery." She winked. "You ever get sick of crawling for that sorceress, come find me. I have a stable of clients who'd crawl for you. And pay to do it."

Hunt's hand was warm on her shoulder. "She's not for sale."

Bryce leaned out of his grip, throwing him a warning glare.

The Viper Queen said, "Everyone, General, is for sale. You just have to figure out the asking price." Smoke flared from her nostrils, a dragon huffing flames. "Give me a day or two, Athalar, and I'll figure out yours."

Hunt's smile was a thing of deadly beauty. "Maybe I've figured out yours already."

The Viper Queen smiled. "I certainly hope so." She stubbed out the cigarette and met Bryce's stare. "Here's a pro tip for your little investigation." Bryce stiffened at the cool mockery. "Look toward where it hurts the most. That's always where the answers are."

"Thanks for the advice," Bryce gritted out.

The shifter merely snapped her gold-tipped fingers. The office door opened, those venom-addicted Fae males peering in. "They're done," the Viper Queen said, turning on her antique of a computer. "Make sure they get outside." *And don't go poking about.*

Bryce shouldered the block of salt as Hunt snatched up the flash drive, pocketing it.

The guard was smart enough to step away as Hunt nudged Bryce through the door. Bryce made it three steps before the Viper Queen said, "Don't underestimate the obsidian salt, Quinlan. It can bring over the very worst of Hel."

A chill snaked down her spine. But Bryce merely lifted a hand in an over-the-shoulder wave as she entered the hall. "Well, at least I'll be entertained, won't I?"

They left the Meat Market in one piece, thank the five fucking gods—especially Urd herself. Hunt wasn't entirely sure how they'd managed to walk away from the Viper Queen without their guts pumped full of poisoned bullets, but . . . He frowned at the red-haired woman now inspecting her white scooter for damage. Even the helmet had been left untouched.

Hunt said, "I believe her." No way in Hel was he watching the video on that flash drive. He'd be sending it right over to Viktoria. "I don't think she had anything to do with this."

Quinlan and Roga, however . . . He hadn't yet crossed them off his mental list.

Bryce tucked the helmet into the crook of her arm. "I agree."

"So that brings us back to square one." He suppressed the urge to pace, picturing his kill count still in the thousands.

"No," Bryce countered. "It doesn't." She fastened the bag of salt into the small compartment on the back of her scooter. "She said to look where it hurts most for answers."

"She was just spewing some bullshit to mess with us."

"Probably," Bryce said, fitting the helmet over her head before flicking up the visor to reveal those amber eyes. "But maybe she was unintentionally right. Tomorrow . . ." Her eyes shuttered. "I've got to do some thinking tomorrow. At the gallery, or else Jesiba will throw a fit."

He was intrigued enough that he said, "You think you have a lead?"

"Not yet. A general direction, though. It's better than nothing."

He jerked his chin toward the compartment of her scooter. "What's the obsidian salt for?" She had to have another purpose for it. Even if he prayed she wasn't dumb enough to use it.

Bryce just said blandly, "Seasoning my burgers."

Fine. He'd walked into that. "How'd you afford the salt, anyway?" He doubted she had ten grand just sitting around in her bank account.

Bryce zipped up her leather jacket. "I put it on Jesiba's account. She spends more money on beauty products in a month, so I doubt she'll notice."

Hunt had no idea how to even respond to any of that, so he gritted his teeth and surveyed her atop her ride. "You know, even a scooter is a dumb fucking thing to drive before making the Drop."

"Thanks, Mom."

"You should take the bus."

She just let out a barking laugh, and zoomed off into the night.

20

Look toward where it hurts the most.

Bryce had refrained from telling Athalar how accurate the Viper Queen's tip had been. She'd already given him her list of suspects—but he hadn't asked about the other demand he'd made.

So that's what she'd decided to do: compile a list of every one of Danika's movements from the week before her death. But the moment she'd finished opening up the gallery for the day, the moment she'd come down to the library to make the list . . . Nausea had hit her.

She turned on her laptop instead, and began combing through her emails with Maximus Tertian, dating back six weeks. Perhaps she'd find some sort of connection there—or at least a hint of his plans for that night.

Yet with each professional, bland email she reread, the memories from Danika's last days clawed at the welded-shut door of her mind. Like looming specters, they hissed and whispered, and she tried to ignore them, tried to focus on Tertian's emails, but—

Lehabah looked over from where she'd sprawled on the tiny fainting couch Bryce had given her years ago—courtesy of a dollhouse from her childhood—watching her favorite Vanir drama on her tablet. Her glass dome sat behind her atop a stack of books, the plumes of a purple orchid arching over it. "You could let the angel down here and work together on whatever is causing you such difficulty."

Bryce rolled her eyes. "Your fascination with Athalar is taking on stalkerish levels."

Lehabah sighed. "Do you know what Hunt Athalar *looks* like?"

"Considering that he's living on the roof across from my apartment, I'd say yes."

Lehabah hit pause on her show, leaning her head against the backrest of her little fainting couch. "He's *dreamy*."

"Yeah, just ask him." Bryce clicked out of the email she'd been reading—one of about a hundred between her and Tertian, and the first where he'd been mildly flirty with her.

"Hunt's handsome enough to be on this show." Lehabah pointed with a dainty toe toward the tablet propped before her.

"Unfortunately, I don't think the size differences between you and Athalar would work in the bedroom. You're barely big enough to wrap your arms around his dick."

Smoke swirled around Lehabah at her puff of embarrassment, and the sprite waved her little hands to clear it away. "BB!"

Bryce chuckled, then she gestured to the tablet. "I'm not the one who's bingeing a show that's basically porn with a plot. What's it called again? *Fangs and Bangs*?"

Lehabah turned purple. "It's not called that and you know it! And it's *artistic*. They make *love*. They don't . . ." She choked.

"Fuck?" Bryce suggested dryly.

"Exactly," Lehabah said with a prim nod.

Bryce laughed, letting it chase away the swarming ghosts of the past, and the sprite, despite her prudishness, joined her. Bryce said, "I doubt Hunt Athalar is the *making love* type."

Lehabah hid her face behind her hands, humming with mortification.

Just to torture her a bit more, Bryce added, "He's the type to bend you over a desk and—"

The phone rang.

She glanced at the ceiling, wondering if Athalar had somehow heard, but—no. It was worse.

"Hi, Jesiba," she said, motioning Lehabah back to her guardian's perch in case the sorceress was monitoring through the library's cameras.

"Bryce. Glad to see Lehabah is hard at work."

Lehabah quickly shut down the tablet and did her best to look alert. Bryce said, "It was her midmorning break. She's entitled to one."

Lehabah threw her a grateful glance that cut right to the bone.

Jesiba just began rattling off commands.

Thirty minutes later, at the desk in the gallery showroom, Bryce stared toward the shut front door. The ticking of the clock filled the space, a steady reminder of each second lost. Each second that Danika and the pack's killer roamed the streets while she sat in here, checking bullshit paperwork.

Unacceptable. Yet the thought of prying open the door to those memories . . .

She knew she'd regret it. Knew it was probably ten kinds of stupid. But she dialed the number before she could second-guess it.

"What's wrong." Hunt's voice was already sharp, full of storms.

"Why do you assume something's wrong?"

"Because you've never called me before, Quinlan."

This was stupid—really fucking stupid. She cleared her throat to make up some excuse about ordering food for lunch, but he said, "You found something?"

For Danika, for the Pack of Devils, she could do this. Would do this. Pride had no place here. "I need you to . . . help me with something."

"With what?" But before his words finished sounding, a fist banged on the door. She knew it was him without pulling up the camera feed.

She opened the door, getting a face full of wings and rain-kissed cedar. Hunt asked wryly, "Are you going to give me shit about coming in or can we spare ourselves that song and dance?"

"Just get inside." Bryce left Hunt in the doorway and walked to her desk, where she hauled open the bottom drawer to yank out a reusable bottle. She drank straight from it.

Hunt shut the door after himself. "A little early to be drinking, isn't it?"

She didn't bother to correct him, just took another sip and slid into her chair.

He eyed her. "You gonna tell me what this is about?"

A polite but insistent *thump-thump-thump* came from the iron door down to the library. Hunt's wings snapped shut as he turned his head toward the heavy metal slab.

Another *tap-tap-tap* filled the showroom atrium. "BB," Lehabah said mournfully through the door. "BB, are you all right?"

Bryce rolled her eyes. Cthona spare her.

Hunt asked too casually, "Who is that?"

A third little *knock-knock-knock*. "BB? BB, please say you're all right."

"I'm fine," Bryce called. "Go back downstairs and do your job."

"I want to see you with my own eyes," Lehabah said, sounding for all the world like a concerned aunt. "I can't focus on my work until then."

Hunt's brows twitched toward each other—even as his lips tugged outward.

Bryce said to him, "One, hyperbole is an art form for her."

"Oh, BB, you can be so terribly cruel—"

"*Two*, very few people are allowed downstairs, so if you report to Micah about it, we're done."

"I promise," Hunt said warily. "Though Micah can make me talk if he insists."

"Then don't give him a reason to be curious about it." She set the bottle on her desk, and found her legs were surprisingly sturdy. Hunt still towered over her. The horrible twining thorns tattooed across his brow seemed to suck the light from the room.

But Hunt rubbed his jaw. "A lot of the stuff down there is contraband, isn't it."

"Surely you've realized *most* of the shit in here is contraband. Some of these books and scrolls are the last known copies in existence." She pursed her lips, then added quietly, "A lot of people suffered and died to preserve what's in the library downstairs."

More than that, she wouldn't say. She hadn't been able to read most of the books, since they were in long-dead languages or in codes so clever only highly trained linguists or historians might decipher them, but she'd finally learned last year what most of them were. Knew the Asteri and the Senate would order them destroyed. Had destroyed all other copies. There were normal books in there, too, which Jesiba acquired mostly for her own uses—possibly even for the Under-King. But the ones that Lehabah guarded . . . those were the ones people would kill for. Had killed for.

Hunt nodded. "I won't breathe a word."

She assessed him for a moment, then turned to the iron door. "Consider this your birthday present, Lele," she muttered through the metal.

The iron door opened on a sigh, revealing the pine-green carpeted staircase that led straight down into the library. Hunt almost crashed into her as Lehabah floated up between them, her fire shining bright, and purred, "Hello."

The angel examined the fire sprite hovering a foot away from his face. She was no longer than Bryce's hand, her flaming hair twirling above her head.

"Well, aren't you beautiful," Hunt said, his voice low and soft in a way that made every instinct in Bryce sit up straight.

Lehabah flared as she wrapped her plump arms around herself and ducked her head.

Bryce shook off the effects of Hunt's voice. "Stop pretending to be shy."

Lehabah cut her a simmering glare, but Hunt lifted a finger for her to perch on. "Shall we?"

Lehabah shone ruby red, but floated over to his scarred finger and sat, smiling at him beneath her lashes. "He is very nice, BB," Lehabah observed as Bryce walked down the stairs, the sun-chandelier blinking to life again. "I don't see why you complain so much about him."

Bryce scowled over her shoulder. But Lehabah was making

mooncalf eyes at the angel, who gave Bryce a wry smile as he trailed her into the library's heart.

Bryce looked ahead quickly.

Maybe Lehabah had a point about Athalar's looks.

Bryce was aware of every step downward, every rustle of Hunt's wings mere steps behind her. Every bit of air that he filled with his breath, his power, his will.

Other than Jesiba, Syrinx, and Lehabah, only Danika had been down here with her before.

Syrinx stirred enough from his nap to see that they had a guest—and his little lion's tail whacked against the velvet sofa. "Syrie says you can brush him now," Lehabah told Hunt.

"Hunt is busy," Bryce said, heading for the table where she'd left the book open.

"Syrie talks, does he?"

"According to her, he does," Bryce muttered, scanning the table for—right, she'd put the list on Lehabah's table. She aimed for it, heels sinking deep into the carpet.

"There must be thousands of books in here," Hunt said, surveying the towering shelves.

"Oh yes," Lehabah said. "But half of this is also Jesiba's private collection. Some of the books date all the way back to—"

"*Ahem*," Bryce said.

Lehabah stuck out her tongue and said in a conspiratorial whisper to Hunt, "BB is cranky because she hasn't been able to make her list."

"I'm cranky because I'm hungry and you've been a pain in my ass all morning."

Lehabah floated off Hunt's finger to rush to her table, where she plopped on her doll's couch and said to the angel, who looked torn between wincing and laughing, "BB pretends to be mean, but she's a softie. She bought Syrie because Jesiba was going to gift him to a warlord client in the Farkaan mountains—"

"*Lehabah—*"

"It's true."

Hunt examined the various tanks throughout the room and the assortment of reptiles within them, then the empty waters of the massive aquarium. "I thought he was some designer pet."

"Oh, he is," Lehabah said. "Syrinx was stolen from his mother as a cub, then traded for ten years around the world, then Jesiba bought him to be her pet, then *Bryce* bought him—his freedom, I mean. She even had proof of his freedom certified. No one can ever buy him again." She pointed to the chimera. "You can't see it with him lying down like that, but he's got the freed brand on his front right paw. The official *C* and everything."

Hunt twisted from the gloomy water to look Bryce over.

She crossed her arms. "What? You did the assuming."

His eyes flickered. Whatever the fuck that meant.

She tried not to look at his own wrist, though—the *SPQM* stamped there. She wondered if he was resisting the same urge; if he was contemplating whether he'd ever get that *C* one day.

But then Lehabah said to Hunt, "How much do *you* cost to buy, Athie?"

Bryce cut in, "Lele, that's rude. And don't call him Athie."

She sent up a puff of smoke. "He and I are of the same House, and are both slaves. My great-grandmother fought in his 18th Legion during their rebellion. I am allowed to ask."

Hunt's face wholly shuttered at the mention of the rebellion, but he approached the couch, let Syrinx sniff his fingers, then scratched the beast behind his velvety ears. Syrinx let out a low growl of pleasure, his lion's tail going limp.

Bryce tried to block out the squeezing sensation in her chest at the sight of it.

Hunt's wings rustled. "I was sold to Micah for eighty-five million gold marks."

Bryce's heel snagged on the carpet as she reached Lehabah's little station and grabbed the tablet. Lehabah again floated over to the angel. "I cost ninety thousand gold marks," Lehabah confided. "Syrie was two hundred thirty-three thousand gold marks."

Hunt's eyes snapped to Bryce. "You paid that?"

Bryce sat at the worktable and pointed to the empty chair beside hers. Hunt followed obediently, for once. "I got a fifteen percent employee discount. And we came to an arrangement."

Let that be that.

Until Lehabah declared, "Jesiba takes some out of each paycheck." Bryce growled, reining in the instinct to smother the sprite with a pillow. "BB will be paying it off until she's three hundred. Unless she doesn't make the Drop. Then she'll die first."

Hunt dropped into his seat, his wing brushing her arm. Softer than velvet, smoother than silk. He snapped it in tight at the touch, as if he couldn't bear the contact. "Why?"

Bryce said, "Because that warlord wanted to hurt and break him until he was a fighting beast, and Syrinx is my friend, and I was sick of losing friends."

"I thought you were loaded."

"Nope." She finished the word on a popping noise.

Hunt's brow furrowed. "But your apartment—"

"The apartment is Danika's." Bryce couldn't meet his gaze. "She bought it as an investment. Had its ownership written in our names. I didn't even know it existed until after she died. And I would have just sold it, but it had top-notch security, and grade A enchantments—"

"I get it," he said again, and she shrank from the kindness in his eyes. The pity.

Danika had died, and she was alone, and—Bryce couldn't breathe.

She'd refused to go to therapy. Her mother had set up appointment after appointment for the first year, and Bryce had bailed on all of them. She'd bought herself an aromatherapy diffuser, had read up on breathing techniques, and that had been that.

She knew she should have gone. Therapy helped so many people—saved so many lives. Juniper had been seeing a therapist since she was a teenager and would tell anyone who would listen about how vital and brilliant it was.

But Bryce hadn't shown up—not because she didn't believe it

would work. No, she knew it would work, and help, and probably make her feel better. Or at least give her the tools to try to do so.

That was precisely why she hadn't gone.

From the way Hunt was staring at her, she wondered if he knew it—realized why she blew out a long breath.

Look toward where it hurts the most.

Fucker. The Viper Queen could go to Hel with her pro tips.

She turned on Lehabah's electronic tablet. The screen revealed a vampyr and wolf tangled in each other, groaning, naked—

Bryce laughed. "You stopped watching in the middle of *this* to come bother me, Lele?"

The air in the room lightened, as if Bryce's sorrow had cracked at the sight of the wolf pounding into the moaning vampyr female.

Lehabah burned ruby. "I wanted to meet Athie," she muttered, slinking back to her couch.

Hunt, as if despite himself, chuckled. "You watch *Fangs and Bangs*?"

Lehabah shot upright. "That is *not* what it's called! Did you tell him to say that, Bryce?"

Bryce bit her lip to keep from laughing and grabbed her laptop instead, bringing up her emails with Tertian on the screen. "No, I didn't."

Hunt raised a brow, with that wary amusement.

"I'm taking a nap with Syrie," Lehabah declared to no one in particular. Almost as soon as she said it, something heavy thumped on the mezzanine.

Hunt's hand went to his side, presumably for the gun there, but Lehabah hissed toward the railing, "*Do not interrupt my nap.*"

A heavy slithering filled the library, followed by a thump and rustle. It didn't come from Miss Poppy's tank.

Lehabah said to Hunt, "Don't let the books sweet-talk you into taking them home."

He threw her a half smile. "You're doing a fine job ensuring that doesn't happen."

Lehabah beamed, curling along Syrinx's side. He purred with

delight at her warmth. "They'll do anything to get out of here: sneak into your bag, the pocket of your coat, even flop up the stairs. They're desperate to get into the world again." She flowed toward the distant shelves behind them, where a book had landed on the steps. "*Bad!*" she seethed.

Hunt's hand slid within easy reach of the knife at his thigh as the book, as if carried by invisible hands, drifted up the steps, floated to the shelf, and found its place again, humming once with golden light—as if in annoyance.

Lehabah cast a warning simmer toward it, then wrapped Syrinx's tail around herself like a fur shawl.

Bryce shook her head, but a sidelong glance told her that Hunt was now staring at her. Not in the way that males tended to stare at her. He said, "What's up with all the little critters?"

"They're Jesiba's former lovers and rivals," Lehabah whispered from her fur-blanket.

Hunt's wings rustled. "I'd heard the rumors."

"I've never seen her transform anyone into an animal," Bryce said, "but I try to stay on her good side. I'd really prefer not to be turned into a pig if Jesiba gets pissed at me for fucking up a deal."

Hunt's lips twitched upward, as if caught between amusement and horror.

Lehabah opened her mouth, presumably to tell Hunt all the names she'd given the creatures in the library, but Bryce cut her off, saying to Hunt, "I called you because I started to make that list of all of Danika's movements during her final days." She patted the page she'd started writing on.

"Yeah?" His dark eyes remained on her face.

Bryce cleared her throat and admitted, "It's, um, hard. To make myself remember. I thought . . . maybe you could ask me some questions. Help get the . . . memories flowing."

"Ah. Okay." Silence rippled again as she waited for him to remind her that time wasn't on their side, that he had a fucking job to do and she shouldn't be such a wimp, blah blah.

But Hunt surveyed the books; the tanks; the door to the bathroom at the back of the space; the lights high above, disguised like the stars painted across the ceiling. And then, rather than ask her about Danika, he said, "Did you study antiquities at school?"

"I took a few classes, yeah. I liked learning about old crap. I was a classical literature major." She added, "I learned the Old Language of the Fae when I was a kid." She'd taught herself out of a sudden interest in learning more about her heritage. When she'd gone to her father's house a year later—for the first time in her life—she'd hoped to use it to impress him. After everything went to shit, she'd refused to learn another language. Childish, but she didn't care.

Though knowing the most ancient of the Fae languages had been helpful for this job, at least. For the few Fae antiquities that weren't hoarded in their glittering troves.

Hunt again surveyed the space. "How'd you get this job?"

"After I graduated, I couldn't get a job anywhere. The museums didn't want me because I didn't have enough experience, and the other art galleries in town were run by creeps who thought I was . . . appetizing." His eyes darkened, and she made herself ignore the rage she beheld there on her behalf. "But my friend Fury . . ." Hunt stiffened slightly at the name—he clearly knew her reputation. "Well, she and Jesiba worked together in Pangera at some point. And when Jesiba mentioned that she needed a new assistant, Fury basically shoved my résumé down her throat." Bryce snorted at the memory. "Jesiba offered me the job because she didn't want an uptight priss. The work is too dirty, customers too shady. She needed someone with social skills as well as a little background in ancient art. And that was that."

Hunt considered, then asked, "What's your deal with Fury Axtar?"

"She's in Pangera. Doing what Fury does best." It wasn't really an answer.

"Axtar ever tell you what she gets up to over there?"

"No. And I like it to stay that way. My dad told me enough stories about what it's like. I don't enjoy imagining what Fury sees and deals with." Blood and mud and death, science versus magic, machines versus Vanir, bombs of chemicals and firstlight, bullets and fangs.

Randall's own service had been mandatory, a condition of life for any non-Lower in the peregrini class: all humans had to serve in the military for three years. Randall had never said it, but she'd always known the years on the front had left deep scars beyond those visible on him. Being forced to kill your own kind was no small task. But the Asteri's threat remained: Should any refuse, their lives would be forfeit. And then the lives of their families. Any survivors would be slaves, their wrists forever inked with the same letters that marred Hunt's skin.

"There's no chance Danika's murderer might have been connected to—"

"No." Bryce growled. She and Fury might be totally fucked up right now, but she knew that. "Fury's enemies weren't Danika's enemies. Once Briggs was behind bars, she bailed." Bryce hadn't seen her since.

Searching for anything to change the topic, Bryce asked, "How old are you?"

"Two hundred thirty-three."

She did the math, frowning. "You were that young when you rebelled? And already commanded a legion?" The angels' failed rebellion had been two hundred years ago; he'd have been incredibly young—by Vanir standards—to have led it.

"My gifts made me invaluable to people." He held up a hand, lightning writhing around his fingers. "Too good at killing." She grunted her agreement. Hunt eyed her. "You ever killed before?"

"Yes."

Surprise lit his eyes. But she didn't want to go into it—what had happened with Danika senior year that had left them both in the hospital, her arm shattered, and a stolen motorcycle little more than scrap.

Lehabah cut in from across the library, "BB, stop being cryptic! I've wanted to know for years, Athie, but she never tells me anything good—"

"Leave it, Lehabah." The memories of that trip pelted her. Danika's smiling face in the hospital bed beside hers. How Thorne carried Danika up the stairs of their dorm when they got home, despite her protests. How the pack had fussed over them for a week, Nathalie and Zelda kicking the males out one night so they could have a girls-only moviefest. But none of it had compared to what had changed between her and Danika on that trip. The final barrier that had fallen, the truth laid bare.

I love you, Bryce. I'm so sorry.

Close your eyes, Danika.

A hole tore open in her chest, gaping and howling.

Lehabah was still grousing. But Hunt was watching Bryce's face. He asked, "What's one happy memory you have with Danika from the last week of her life?"

Her blood pounded through her entire body. "I—I have a lot of them from that week."

"Pick one, and we'll start with that."

"Is this how you get witnesses to talk?"

He leaned back in his seat, wings adjusting around its low back. "It's how you and I are going to make this list."

She weighed his stare, his solid, thrumming presence. She swallowed. "The tattoo on my back—she and I got it done that week. We got stupid drunk one night, and I was so out of it I didn't even know what the fuck she put on my back until I'd gotten over my hangover."

His lips twitched. "I hope it was something good, at least."

Her chest ached, but she smiled. "It was."

Hunt sat forward and tapped the paper. "Write it down."

She did. He asked, "What'd Danika do during that day before you got the tattoo?"

The question was calm, but he weighed her every movement. As if he were reading something, assessing something that she couldn't see.

Eager to avoid that too-aware look, Bryce picked up the pen, and began writing, one memory after another. Kept writing her recollections of Danika's whereabouts that week: that silly wish on the Old Square Gate, the pizza she and Danika had devoured while standing at the counter of the shop, swigging from bottles of beer and talking shit; the hair salon where Bryce flipped through gossip magazines while Danika had gotten her purple, blue, and pink streaks touched up; the grocery store two blocks down where she and Thorne had found Danika stuffing her face with a bag of chips she hadn't yet paid for and teased her for hours afterward; the CCU sunball arena where she and Danika had ogled the hot players on Ithan's team during practice and called dibs on them . . . She kept writing and writing, until the walls pressed in again.

Her knee bounced relentlessly beneath the table. "I think we can stop there for today."

Hunt opened his mouth, glancing to the list—but her phone buzzed.

Thanking Urd for the well-timed intervention, Bryce glanced at the message on the screen and scowled. The expression was apparently intriguing enough that Hunt peered over her shoulder.

Ruhn had written, *Meet me at Luna's Temple in thirty minutes.*

Hunt asked, "Think it's got to do with last night?"

Bryce didn't answer as she typed back, *Why?*

Ruhn replied. *Because it's one of the few places in this city without cameras.*

"Interesting," she murmured. "You think I should give him a heads-up that you're coming?"

Hunt's grin was pure wickedness. "Hel no."

Bryce couldn't keep herself from grinning back.

21

Ruhn Danaan leaned against one of the marble pillars of the inner sanctum of Luna's Temple and waited for his sister to arrive. Tourists drifted past, snapping photos, none marking his presence, thanks to the shadow veil he'd pulled around himself.

The chamber was long, its ceiling lofty. It had to be, to accommodate the statue enthroned at the back.

Thirty feet high, Luna sat in a carved golden throne, the goddess lovingly rendered in shimmering moonstone. A silver tiara of a full moon held by two crescent ones graced her upswept curling hair. At her sandaled feet lay twin wolves, their baleful eyes daring any pilgrim to come closer. Across the back of her throne, a bow of solid gold had been slung, its quiver full of silver arrows. The pleats of her thigh-length robe draped across her lap, veiling the slim fingers resting there.

Both wolves and Fae claimed Luna as their patron goddess—had gone to war over whom she favored in millennia long past. And while the wolves' connection to her had been carved into the statue with stunning detail, the nod to the Fae had been missing for two years. Maybe the Autumn King had a point about restoring the Fae to glory. Not in the haughty, sneering way his father intended, but . . . the lack of Fae heritage on the statue raked down Ruhn's nerves.

Footsteps scuffed in the courtyard beyond the sanctum doors, followed by excited whispers and the click of cameras.

"The courtyard itself is modeled after the one in the Eternal City," a female voice was saying as a new flock of tourists entered the temple, trailing their guide like ducklings.

And at the rear of the group—a wine-red head of hair.

And a too-recognizable pair of gray wings.

Ruhn gritted his teeth, keeping hidden in the shadows. At least she'd shown up.

The tour group stopped in the center of the inner sanctum, the guide speaking loudly as everyone spread out, cameras flashing like Athalar's lightning in the gloom. "And here it is, folks: the statue of Luna herself. Lunathion's patron goddess was crafted from a single block of marble hewn from the famed Caliprian Quarries by the Melanthos River up north. This temple was the first thing built upon the city's founding five hundred years ago; the location of this city was selected precisely because of the way the Istros River bends through the land. Can anyone tell me what shape the river makes?"

"A crescent!" someone called out, the words echoing off the marble pillars, wending through the curling smoke from the bowl of incense laid between the wolves at the goddess's feet.

Ruhn saw Bryce and Hunt scan the sanctum for him, and he let the shadows peel back long enough for them to spy his location. Bryce's face revealed nothing. Athalar just grinned.

Fan-fucking-tastic.

With all the tourists focused on their guide, no one noticed the unusual pair crossing the space. Ruhn kept the shadows at bay until Bryce and Hunt reached him—and then willed them to encompass them as well.

Hunt just said, "Fancy trick."

Bryce said nothing. Ruhn tried not to remember how delighted she'd once been whenever he'd demonstrated how his shadows and starlight worked—both halves of his power working as one.

Ruhn said to her, "I asked you to come. Not him."

Bryce linked her arm through Athalar's, the portrait they painted laughable: Bryce in her fancy work dress and heels, the angel in his black battle-suit. "We're joined at the hip now, unfortunately for you. Best, best friends."

"The best," Hunt echoed, his grin unfading.

Luna shoot him dead. This would not end well.

Bryce nodded to the tour group still trailing their leader through the temple. "This place might not have any cameras, but they do."

"They're focused on their guide," Ruhn said. "And the noise they're making will mask any conversation we have." The shadows could only hide him from sight, not sound.

Through thin ripples in the shadows, they could make out a young couple edging around the statue, so busy snapping photos they didn't note the denser bit of darkness in the far corner. But Ruhn fell silent, and Bryce and Athalar followed suit.

As they waited for the couple to pass, the tour guide went on, "We'll dive more into the architectural wonders of the inner sanctum in a minute, but let's direct our attention to the statue. The quiver, of course, is real gold, the arrows pure silver with tips of diamond."

Someone let out an appreciative whistle. "Indeed," the tour guide agreed. "They were donated by the Archangel Micah, who is a patron and investor in various charities, foundations, and innovative companies." The tour guide went on, "Unfortunately, two years ago, the third of Luna's treasures was stolen from this temple. Can anyone tell me what it was?"

"The Horn," someone said. "It was all over the news."

"It was a terrible theft. An artifact that cannot be replaced easily."

The couple moved on, and Ruhn uncrossed his arms.

Hunt said, "All right, Danaan. Get to the point. Why'd you ask Bryce to come?"

Ruhn gestured to where the tourists were snapping photos of the goddess's hand. Specifically, the fingers that now curled around air, where a cracked ivory hunting horn had once lain.

"Because I was tasked by the Autumn King to find Luna's Horn."

Athalar angled his head, but Bryce snorted. "Is that why you asked about it last night?"

They were interrupted again by the tour guide saying, as she moved toward the rear of the room, "If you'll follow me, we've been granted special permission to see the chamber where the stag sacrifices are prepared to be burned in Luna's honor." Through the murky shadows, Bryce could make out a small door opening in the wall.

When they'd filtered out, Hunt asked, eyes narrowing, "What is the Horn, exactly?"

"A bunch of fairy-tale bullcrap," Bryce muttered. "You really dragged me here for this? To what—help you impress your daddy?"

Growling, Ruhn pulled out his phone, making sure the shadows held around them, and brought up the photos he'd snapped in the Fae Archives last night.

But he didn't share them, not before he said to Athalar, "Luna's Horn was a weapon wielded by Pelias, the first Starborn Prince, during the First Wars. The Fae forged it in their home world, named it for the goddess in their new one, and used it to battle the demon hordes once they made the Crossing. Pelias wielded the Horn until he died." Ruhn put a hand on his chest. "My ancestor—whose power flows in my veins. I don't know how it worked, how Pelias used it with his magic, but the Horn became enough of a nuisance for the demon princes that they did everything they could to retrieve it from him."

Ruhn held out his phone, the picture of the illuminated manuscript glaringly bright in the thick shadows. The illustration of the carved horn lifted to the lips of a helmeted Fae male was as pristine as it had been when inked millennia ago. Above the figure gleamed an eight-pointed star, the emblem of the Starborn.

Bryce went wholly still. The stillness of the Fae, like a stag halting in a wood.

Ruhn went on, "The Star-Eater himself bred a new horror just to hunt the Horn, using some blood he managed to spill from Prince Pelias on a battlefield and his own terrible essence. A beast twisted out of the collision of light and darkness." Ruhn swiped on his phone, and the next illustration appeared. The reason he'd had her come here—had taken this gamble.

Bryce recoiled at the grotesque, pale body, the clear teeth bared in a roar.

"You recognize it," Ruhn said softly.

Bryce shook herself, as if to bring herself back to reality, and rubbed her thigh absently. "That's the demon I found attacking the angel in the alley on that night."

Hunt gave her a sharp look. "The one that attacked you, too?"

Bryce gave a small, affirmative nod. "What is it?"

"It dwells in the darkest depths of the Pit," Ruhn answered. "So lightless that the Star-Eater named it the kristallos, for its clear blood and teeth."

Athalar said, "I've never heard of it."

Bryce contemplated the drawing. "It . . . There was never a mention of a fucking *demon* in the research I did on the Horn." She met his gaze. "No one put this together two years ago?"

"I think it's *taken* two years to put it together," Ruhn said carefully. "This volume was deep in the Fae Archives, with the stuff that's not allowed to be scanned. None of your research would have ever pulled it up. The entire damn thing was in the Old Language of the Fae." And had taken him most of the night to translate. Throwing in the lingering fog of the mirthroot hadn't helped.

Bryce's brow furrowed. "But the Horn was broken—it basically became a dud, right?"

"Right," Ruhn said. "During the final battle of the First Wars, Prince Pelias and the Prince of the Pit faced each other. The two of them fought for like three fucking days, until the Star-Eater struck the fatal blow. But not before Pelias was able to summon all the Horn's strength, and banished the Prince of the Pit, his brethren, and their armies back to Hel. He sealed the Northern Rift forever—so only small cracks in it or summonings with salt can bring them over now."

Athalar frowned. "So you mean to tell me this deadly artifact, which the Prince of the Pit *literally* bred a new demon species to hunt, was just sitting here? In this temple? And *no one* from this world or Hel tried to take it until that blackout? Why?"

Bryce met Hunt's disbelieving stare. "The Horn cracked in two when Pelias sealed the Northern Rift. Its power was broken. The Fae and Asteri tried for years to renew it through magic and spells and all that crap, but no luck. It was given a place of honor in the Asteri Archives, but when they established Lunathion a few millennia later, they had it dedicated to the temple here."

Ruhn shook his head. "That the Fae allowed for the artifact to be given over suggests they'd dismissed its worth—that even my father might have forgotten its importance." Until it was stolen—and he'd gotten it into his head that it would be a rallying symbol of power during a possible war.

Bryce added, "I thought it was just a replica until Jesiba made me start looking for it." She turned to Ruhn. "So you think someone has been summoning this demon to hunt for the Horn? But why, when it no longer has any power? And how does it explain any of the deaths? You think the victims somehow . . . had contact with the Horn, and it brought the kristallos right to them?" She went on before either of them could answer, "And why the two-year gap?"

Hunt mused, "Maybe the murderer waited until things calmed down enough to resume searching."

"Your guess is as good as mine," Ruhn admitted. "It doesn't seem like coincidence that the Horn went missing right before this demon showed up, though, and for the murders to be starting again—"

"Could mean someone is hunting for the Horn once more," Bryce finished, frowning.

Hunt said, "The kristallos's presence in Lunathion suggests the Horn is still inside the city walls."

Bryce pinned Ruhn with a look. "Why does the Autumn King suddenly want it?"

Ruhn chose his words carefully. "Call it pride. He wants it returned to the Fae. And wants me to find it quietly."

Athalar asked him, "But why ask *you* to look for the Horn?"

The shadows veiling them rippled. "Because Prince Pelias's Starborn power was woven into the Horn itself. And it's in my blood.

My father thinks I might have some sort of preternatural gift to find it." He admitted, "When I was browsing the archives last night, this book . . . jumped out at me."

"Literally?" Bryce asked, brows high.

Ruhn said, "It just felt like it . . . shimmered. I don't fucking know. All I know is I was down there for hours, and then I sensed the book, and when I saw that illustration of the Horn . . . There it was. The crap I translated confirmed it."

"So the kristallos can track the Horn," Bryce said, eyes glittering. "But so can *you*."

Athalar's mouth curled in a crooked grin, catching Bryce's drift. "We find the demon, we find who's behind this. And if we have the Horn . . ."

Ruhn grimaced. "The kristallos will come to us."

Bryce glanced to the empty-handed statue behind them. "Better get cracking, Ruhn."

Hunt leaned against the entry pillars atop the steps leading into Luna's Temple, his phone at his ear. He'd left Quinlan inside with her cousin, needing to make this phone call before they could sort out logistics. He would have made the call right there, but the moment he'd pulled up his contacts list, he'd earned a snipe from Bryce about mobile phones in sacred spaces.

Cthona spare him. Declining to tell her to fuck off, he'd decided to spare them a public scene and stalked out through the cypress-lined courtyard and to the front steps.

Five temple acolytes emerged from the sprawling villa behind the temple itself, bearing brooms and hoses to clean the temple steps and the flagstones beyond it for their midday washing.

Unnecessary, he wanted to tell the young females. With the misting rain yet again gracing the city, the hoses were superfluous.

Teeth gritted, he listened to the phone ring and ring. "Pick the fuck up," he muttered.

A dark-skinned temple acolyte—black-haired, white-robed, and no more than twelve—gaped at him as she walked past, clutching a broom to her chest. He nearly winced, realizing the portrait of wrath he now presented, and checked his expression.

The Fae girl still kept back, the golden crescent moon dangling from a delicate chain across her brow glinting in the gray light. A waxing moon—until she became a full-fledged priestess upon reaching maturity, when she would trade the crescent for the full circle of Luna. And whenever her immortal body began to age and fade, her cycle vanishing with it, she would again trade the charm, this time for a waning crescent.

The priestesses all had their own reasons for offering themselves to Luna. For forsaking their lives beyond the temple grounds and embracing the goddess's eternal maidenhood. Just as Luna had no mate or lover, so they would live.

Hunt had always thought celibacy seemed like a bore. Until Shahar had ruined him for anyone else.

Hunt offered the shrinking acolyte his best attempt at a smile. To his surprise, the Fae girl offered a small one back. The girl had courage.

Justinian Gelos answered on the sixth ring. "How's babysitting?"

Hunt straightened. "Don't sound so amused."

Justinian huffed a laugh. "You sure Micah's not punishing you?"

Hunt had considered the question a great deal in the past two days. Across the empty street, the palm trees dotting the rain-soft grasses of the Oracle's Park shone in the gray light, the domed onyx building of the Oracle's Temple veiled in the mists that had rolled in over the river.

Even at midday, the Oracle's Park was near-empty, save for the hunched, slumbering forms of the desperate Vanir and humans who wandered the paths and gardens, waiting for their turn to enter the incense-filled hallways.

And if the answers they sought weren't what they'd hoped . . . Well, the white-stoned temple on whose steps Hunt now stood could offer some solace.

Hunt glanced over his shoulder to the dim temple interior just visible through the towering bronze doors. In the firstlight from a row of shimmering braziers, he could just barely make out the gleam of red hair in the quiet gloom of the inner sanctum, shining like molten metal as Bryce talked animatedly with Ruhn.

"No," Hunt said at last. "I don't think this assignment was punishment. He was out of options and knew I'd cause more trouble if he stationed me on guard duty around Sandriel." And Pollux.

He didn't mention the bargain he'd struck with Micah. Not when Justinian bore the halo as well and Micah had never shown much interest in him beyond his popularity with the grunt troops of the 33rd. If there was any sort of deal to earn his freedom, Justinian had never said a word.

Justinian blew out a breath. "Yeah—shit's getting intense around here right now. People are on edge and she hasn't even arrived yet. You're better off where you are."

A glassy-eyed Fae male stumbled past the steps of the temple, got a good look at who was barring entry into the temple itself—and aimed for the street, staggering toward the Oracle's Park and the domed building in its heart. Another lost soul looking for answers in smoke and whispers.

"I'm not so sure of that," Hunt said. "I need you to look up something for me—an old-school demon. The kristallos. Just search through the databases and see if anything pops up." He'd have asked Vik, but she was already busy going through the alibi footage from the Viper Queen.

"I'll get on it," Justinian said. "I'll message over any results." He added, "Good luck."

"I'll need it," Hunt admitted. In a hundred fucking ways.

Justinian added slyly, "Though it doesn't hurt that your *partner* is easy on the eyes."

"I gotta go."

"No one gets a medal for suffering the most, you know," Justinian pushed, his voice slipping into uncharacteristic seriousness. "It's been two centuries since Shahar died, Hunt."

"Whatever." He didn't want to have this conversation. Not with Justinian or anyone.

"It's admirable that you're still holding out for her, but let's be realistic about—"

Hunt hung up. Debated throwing his phone against a pillar.

He had to call Isaiah and Micah about the Horn. Fuck. When it had gone missing two years ago, top inspectors from the 33rd and the Aux had combed this temple. They'd found nothing. And since no cameras were allowed within the temple walls, there had been no hint of who might have taken it. It had been nothing more than a stupid prank, everyone had claimed.

Everyone except for the Autumn King, it seemed.

Hunt hadn't paid much attention to the theft of the Horn, and sure as fuck hadn't listened during history lessons as a boy about the First Wars. And after Danika's and the Pack of Devils' murders, they'd had bigger things to worry about.

He couldn't tell what was worse: the Horn possibly being a vital piece of this case, or the fact that he'd now have to work alongside Ruhn Danaan to find it.

22

Bryce waited until Hunt's muscled back and beautiful wings had disappeared through the inner sanctum's gates before she whirled on Ruhn. "Did the Autumn King do it?"

Ruhn's blue eyes glimmered in his shadow-nest or whatever the fuck he called it. "No. He's a monster in so many ways, but he wouldn't kill Danika."

She'd come to that conclusion the other night, but she asked, "How can you be so sure? You have no idea what the Hel his long-term agenda is."

Ruhn crossed his arms. "Why ask me to hunt for the Horn if he's summoning the kristallos?"

"Two trackers are better than one?" Her heart thundered.

"He's not behind this. He's just trying to take advantage of the situation—to restore the Fae to their former glory. You know how he likes to delude himself with that kind of crap."

Bryce trailed her fingers through the wall of shadows, the darkness running over her skin like mist. "Does he know you came to meet with me?"

"No."

She held her brother's stare. "Why . . ." She struggled for words. "Why bother?"

"Because I want to help you. Because this shit puts the entire city at risk."

"How very Chosen One of you."

Silence stretched between them, so taut it trembled. She blurted, "Just because we're working together doesn't mean anything changes between us. You'll find the Horn, and I'll find who's behind this. End of story."

"Fine," Ruhn said, his eyes cold. "I wouldn't expect you to consider listening to me anyway."

"Why would I listen to you?" she seethed. "I'm just a *half-breed slut*, right?"

Ruhn stiffened, a flush flaring. "You know it was a dumb fight and I didn't *mean* that—"

"Yes, you fucking did," she spat, and turned on her heel. "You might dress like you're a punk rebelling against Daddy's rules, but deep down, you're no better than the rest of the Fae shitheads who kiss your Chosen One ass."

Ruhn snarled, but Bryce didn't wait before shoving through the shadows, blinking at the flood of light that greeted her, and aiming for where Hunt had paused at the doors.

"Let's go," she said. She didn't care what he'd overheard.

Hunt lingered in place, his black eyes flickering as he gazed toward the shadowed back of the room, where her so-called cousin was again veiled in darkness. But the angel thankfully said nothing as he fell into step beside her, and she said nothing more to him.

Bryce practically ran back to the gallery. In part to start researching the Horn again, but also thanks to the flurry of messages from Jesiba, demanding to know where she was, whether she still wanted her job, and whether she'd prefer to be turned into a rat or a pigeon. And then an order to get back *now* to greet a client.

Five minutes after Bryce got there, Jesiba's client—a raging asshole of a leopard shifter who believed he was entitled to put his paws all over her ass—prowled in and purchased a small statue of Solas and Cthona, portrayed as a sun with male features burying his face in a pair of mountain-shaped breasts. The holy image was known simply as the Embrace. Her mother even wore its simplified symbol—a circle nestled atop two triangles—as a silver pendant. But Bryce had always found the Embrace cheesy and cliché in every incarnation. Thirty minutes and two blatant rejections to his slimy come-ons later, Bryce was mercifully alone again.

But in the hours she looked, the gallery's databases for Luna's Horn revealed nothing beyond what she already knew, and what her brother had claimed that morning. Even Lehabah, gossip queen extraordinaire, didn't know anything about the Horn.

With Ruhn heading back to the Fae Archives to see if any more information appealed to his Starborn sensibilities, she supposed she'd have to wait for an update.

Hunt had gone to take watch on the roof, apparently needing to make calls to his boss—or whatever Micah pretended he was—and Isaiah regarding the Horn. He hadn't tried to come back down to the library, as if sensing she needed space.

Look toward where it hurts the most. That's always where the answers are.

Bryce found herself staring down at the half-finished list she'd started that morning.

She might not be able to find much on the Horn itself, but maybe she could figure out how the Hel Danika factored into all of it.

Hands shaking, she made herself finish the list of Danika's locations—as far as she knew.

By the time the sun was near setting, and Syrinx was ready to be walked home, Bryce would have traded what was left of her soul to a Reaper just for the quiet comfort of her bed. It had been a long fucking day, full of information she needed to process, and a list that she'd left in her desk drawer.

It must have been a long day for Athalar, too, because he trailed her and Syrinx from the skies without saying a word to her.

She was in bed by eight, and didn't even remember falling asleep.

23

The next morning, Bryce was sitting at the reception desk in the gallery's showroom, staring at her list of Danika's last locations, when her phone rang.

"The deal with the leopard went through," she said to Jesiba by way of greeting. The paperwork had been finalized an hour ago.

"I need you to go up into my office and send me a file from my computer."

Bryce rolled her eyes, refraining from snipping, *You're welcome*, and asked, "You don't have access to it?"

"I made sure this one wasn't on the network."

Nostrils flaring, Bryce rose, her leg throbbing slightly, and walked to the small door in the wall adjacent to the desk. A hand on the metal panel beside it had the enchantments unlocking, the door swinging open to reveal the tight, carpeted staircase upward.

"When I want things done, Bryce, you're to do them. No questions."

"Yes, Jesiba," Bryce muttered, climbing the stairs. Dodging the reaching hands of the leopard shifter yesterday had twinged something in her bad leg.

"Would you like to be a worm, Bryce?" Jesiba purred, voice sliding into something eerily close to a Reaper's rasp. At least Jesiba wasn't one of them—even if Bryce knew the sorceress often dealt with them in the House of Flame and Shadow. Thank the gods none had ever shown up at the gallery, though. "Would you like to be a dung beetle or a centipede?"

"I'd prefer to be a dragonfly." Bryce entered the small, plush office upstairs. One wall was a pane of glass that overlooked the gallery floor a level below, the material utterly soundproof.

"Be careful what you ask of me," Jesiba went on. "You'd find that smart mouth of yours shut up fairly quickly if I transform you. You wouldn't have any voice at all."

Bryce calculated the time difference between Lunathion and the western shores of Pangera and realized Jesiba had probably just come back from dinner. "That Pangeran red wine is heady stuff, isn't it?" She was almost to the wooden desk when the firstlights flicked on. A rack of them illuminated the dismantled gun hanging on the wall behind the desk, the Godslayer Rifle gleaming as fresh as it had the day it'd been forged. She could have sworn a faint whine radiated from the gold and steel—like the legendary, lethal gun was still ringing after a shot.

It unnerved her that it was in here, despite the fact that Jesiba had split it into four pieces, mounted like a work of art behind her desk. Four pieces that could still be easily assembled, but it put her clients at ease, even while it reminded them that she was in charge.

Bryce knew the sorceress never told them about the six-inch engraved golden bullet in the safe beside the painting on the right wall. Jesiba had shown it to her just once, letting her read the words etched onto the bullet: *Memento Mori*.

The same words that appeared in the mosaic in the Meat Market.

It'd seemed melodramatic, but some part of her had marveled at it—at the bullet and at the rifle, so rare only a few existed in Midgard.

Bryce powered up Jesiba's computer, letting the female rattle off instructions before sending the file. Bryce was halfway down the stairs again when she asked her boss, "Have you heard anything new about Luna's Horn?"

A long, contemplative pause. "Does it have to do with this investigation of yours?"

"Maybe."

Jesiba's low, cold voice was an embodiment of the House she served. "I haven't heard anything." Then she hung up. Bryce gritted her teeth as she headed back to her desk on the showroom floor.

Lehabah interrupted her by whispering through the iron door, "Can I see Athie now?"

"No, Lele."

He'd kept his distance this morning, too. Good.

Look toward where it hurts the most.

She had her list of Danika's locations. Unfortunately, she knew what she had to do next. What she'd woken up this morning dreading. Her phone rang in her clenched hand, and Bryce steeled herself for Jesiba calling to bitch that she'd fucked up the file, but it was Hunt.

"Yeah?" she asked by way of greeting.

"There's been another murder." His voice was tight—cold.

She nearly dropped the phone. "Who—"

"I'm still getting the details. But it was about ten blocks from here—near the Gate in the Old Square."

Her heart beat so fast she could scarcely draw breath to say, "Any witnesses?"

"No. But let's go over there."

Her hands shook. "I'm busy," she lied.

Hunt paused. "I'm not fucking around, Quinlan."

No. No, she couldn't do it, endure it, see it again—

Bryce forced herself to breathe, practically inhaling the peppermint vapors from the diffuser. "There's a client coming—"

He banged on the gallery door, sealing her fate. "We're leaving."

Bryce's entire body was taut to the point of near-trembling as she and Hunt approached the magi-screens blocking the alley a few blocks away from the Old Square Gate.

She tried to breathe through it, tried all the techniques she'd read and heard about regarding reining in her dread, that sickening plunging feeling in her stomach. None of them worked.

Angels and Fae and shifters milled about the alley, some on radios or phones.

"A jogger found the remains," Hunt said as people parted to let him pass. "They think it happened sometime last night." He added carefully, "The 33rd's still working on getting an ID, but from the clothes, it looks like an acolyte from Luna's Temple. Isaiah is already asking the temple priestesses who might be missing."

All sounds turned into a blaring drone. She didn't entirely remember the walk over.

Hunt edged around the magi-screen blocking the crime scene from view, took one look at what lay there, and swore. He whirled toward her, as if realizing what he was dragging her back into, but too late.

Blood had splashed across the bricks of the building, pooled on the cracked stones of the alley floor, splattered on the sides of the dumpster. And beside that dumpster, as if someone had chucked them out of a bucket, sat clumps of red pulp. A torn robe lay beside the carnage.

The droning turned into a roar. Her body pulled farther away.

Danika howling with laughter, Connor winking at her, Bronson and Zach and Zelda and Nathalie and Thorne all in hysterics—

Then nothing but red pulp. All of them, all they had been, all she had been with them, became nothing more than piles of red pulp.

Gone, gone, gone—

A hand gripped her shoulder. But not Athalar's. No, Hunt remained where he was, face now hard as stone.

She flinched as Ruhn said at her ear, "You don't need to see this."

This was another murder. Another body. Another year.

A medwitch even knelt before the body, a wand buzzing with firstlight in her hands, trying to piece the corpse—the *girl*—back together.

Ruhn tugged her away, toward the screen and open air beyond—

The movement shook her loose. Snapped the droning in her ears.

She yanked her body free from his grip, not caring if anyone else saw, not caring that he, as head of the Fae Aux units, had the right to be here. "Don't fucking touch me."

Ruhn's mouth tightened. But he looked over her shoulder to Hunt. "You're an asshole."

Hunt's eyes glittered. "I warned her on the walk over what she'd see." He added a touch ruefully, "I didn't realize what a mess it'd be." He had warned her, hadn't he? She'd drifted so far away that she'd barely listened to Hunt on the walk. As dazed as if she'd snorted a heap of lightseeker. Hunt added, "She's a grown woman. She doesn't need you deciding what she can handle." He nodded toward the alley exit. "Shouldn't you be researching? We'll call you if you're needed, princeling."

"Fuck you," Ruhn shot back, shadows twining through his hair. Others were noticing now. "You don't think it's more than a coincidence that an acolyte was killed right after we went to the temple?"

Their words didn't register. None of it registered.

Bryce turned from the alley, the swarming investigators. Ruhn said, "Bryce—"

"Leave me alone," she said quietly, and kept walking. She shouldn't have let Athalar bully her into coming, shouldn't have seen this, shouldn't have had to remember.

Once, she might have gone right to the dance studio. Would have danced and moved until the world made sense again. It had always been her haven, her way of puzzling out the world. She'd gone to the studio whenever she'd had a shit day.

It had been two years since she'd set foot in one. She'd thrown out all her dance clothes and shoes. Her bags. The one at the apartment had all been splattered with blood anyway—Danika's, Connor's, and Thorne's on the clothes in the bedroom, and Zelda's and Bronson's on her secondary bag, which had been left hanging beside the door. Blood patterns just like—

A rain-kissed scent brushed her nose as Hunt fell into step beside her. And there he was. Another memory from that night.

"Hey," Hunt said.

Hey, he'd said to her, so long ago. She'd been a wreck, a ghost, and then he'd been there, kneeling beside her, those dark eyes unreadable as he'd said, *Hey*.

She hadn't told him—that she remembered that night in the interrogation room. She sure as Hel didn't feel like telling him now.

If she had to talk to someone, she'd explode. If she had to do *anything* right now, she'd sink into one of those primal Fae wraths and—

The haze started to creep over her vision, her muscles seizing painfully, her fingertips curled as if imagining shredding into someone—

"Walk it off," Hunt murmured.

"Leave me alone, Athalar." She wouldn't look at him. Couldn't stand him or her brother or *anyone*. If the acolyte's murder *had* been because of their presence at the temple, either as a warning or because the girl might have seen something related to the Horn, if they'd accidentally brought her death about . . . Her legs kept moving, swifter and swifter. Hunt didn't falter for a beat.

She wouldn't cry. Wouldn't dissolve into a hyperventilating mess on the street corner. Wouldn't scream or puke or—

After another block, Hunt said roughly, "I was there that night."

She kept walking, her heels eating up the pavement.

Hunt asked, "How did you survive the kristallos?"

He'd no doubt been looking at the body just now and wondering this. How did she, a pathetic half-breed, survive when full-blooded Vanir hadn't?

"I didn't survive," she mumbled, crossing a street and edging around a car idling in the intersection. "It got away."

"But the kristallos pinned Micah, ripped open his chest—"

She nearly tripped over the curb, and whipped around to gape at him. "That was Micah?"

24

She had saved Micah Domitus that night.

Not some random legionary, but the gods-damned Archangel himself. No wonder the emergency responder had launched into action when he traced the phone number.

The knowledge rippled through her, warping and clearing some of the fog around her memories. "I saved the Governor in the alley."

Hunt just gave her a slow, wincing nod.

Her voice sharpened. "Why was it a secret?"

Hunt waited until a flock of tourists had passed before saying, "For his sake. If word got out that the Governor had his ass handed to him, it wouldn't have looked good."

"Especially when he was saved by a half-breed?"

"No one in our group *ever* used that term—you know that, right? But yes. We did consider how it'd look if a twenty-three-year-old human-Fae female who hadn't made the Drop had saved the Archangel when he couldn't save himself."

Her blood roared in her ears. "Why not tell *me*, though? I looked in all the hospitals, just to see if he'd made it." More than that, actually. She'd demanded answers about how the warrior was recovering, but she'd been put on hold or ignored or asked to leave.

"I know," Hunt said, scanning her face. "It was deemed wiser to keep it a secret. Especially when your phone got hacked right after—"

"So I was just going to live in ignorance forever—"

"Did you want a medal or something? A parade?"

She halted so quickly that Hunt had to splay his wings to pause, too. "*Go fuck yourself.* What I wanted . . ." She tried to stop the sharp, jagged breaths that blinded her, built and built under her skin—"What I wanted," she hissed, resuming her walk as he just stared at her, "was to know that *something* I did made a difference that night. I assumed you'd dumped him in the Istros—some legionary grunt not worth the honor of a Sailing."

Hunt shook his head. "Look, I know it was shitty. And I'm sorry, okay? I'm sorry for all of it, Quinlan. I'm sorry we didn't tell you, and I'm sorry you're on my suspect list, and I'm sorry—"

"I'm on your *what*?" she spat. Red washed over her vision as she bared her teeth. "After all of *this*," she seethed, "you think I am a *fucking suspect*?" She screamed the last words, only pure will keeping her from leaping on him and shredding his face off.

Hunt held up his hands. "That—fuck, Bryce. That didn't come out right. Look—I had to consider every angle, every possibility, but I know now . . . Solas, when I saw your face in that alley, I realized it couldn't ever have been you, and—"

"Get *the fuck* out of my sight."

He watched her, assessing, then spread his wings. She refused to back up a step, teeth still bared. The wind off his wings stirred her hair, throwing his cedar-and-rain scent into her face as he leapt into the skies.

Look toward where it hurts the most.

Fuck the Viper Queen. Fuck *everything*.

Bryce launched into a run—a steady, swift run, despite the flimsy flats she'd switched into at the gallery. A run not toward anything or from anything, but just . . . movement. The pounding of her feet on pavement, the heaving of her breath.

Bryce ran and ran, until sounds returned and the haze receded and she could escape the screaming labyrinth of her mind. It wasn't dancing, but it would do.

* * *

Bryce ran until her body screamed to stop. Ran until her phone buzzed and she wondered if Urd herself had extended a golden hand. The phone call was swift, breathless.

Minutes later, Bryce slowed to a walk as she approached the White Raven. And then stopped entirely before the alcove tucked into the wall just beside its service doors. Sweat ran down her neck, into her dress, soaking the green fabric as she again pulled out her phone.

But she didn't call Hunt. He hadn't interrupted her, but she knew he was overhead.

A few drops of rain splattered the pavement. She hoped it poured on Athalar all night.

Her fingers hesitated on the screen, and she sighed, knowing she shouldn't.

But she did. Standing there in that same alcove where she'd exchanged some of her final messages with Danika, she pulled up the thread. It burned her eyes.

She scrolled upward, past all those final, happy words and teasing. To the photo Danika had sent that afternoon of herself and the pack at the sunball game, decked out in CCU gear. In the background, Bryce could make out the players on the field—Ithan's powerful form among them.

But her gaze drifted to Danika's face. That broad smile she'd known as well as her own.

I love you, Bryce. The worn memory of that mid-May day during their senior year tugged at her, sucked her in.

The hot road bit into Bryce's knees through her torn jeans, her scraped hands trembling as she kept them interlocked behind her head, where she'd been ordered to hold them. The pain in her arm sliced like a knife. Broken. The males had made her put her hands up anyway.

The stolen motorcycle was no more than scrap metal on the dusty highway, the unmarked semitruck pulled over twenty feet away left idle. The rifle had been thrown into the olive grove beyond the mountain road, wrenched from Bryce's hands in the accident that had led them here. The accident Danika had shielded her from, wrapping her body around Bryce's. Danika had taken the shredding of the asphalt for them both.

Ten feet away, hands also behind her head, Danika bled from so many places her clothes were soaked with it. How had it come to this? How had things gone so terribly wrong?

"Where are those fucking *bullets?" the male from the truck shrieked to his cronies, his empty gun—that blessedly, unexpectedly empty gun—clenched in his hand.*

Danika's caramel eyes were wide, searching, as they remained on Bryce's face. Sorrow and pain and fear and regret—all of it was written there.

"I love you, Bryce." Tears rolled down Danika's face. "And I'm sorry."

She had never said those words before. Ever. Bryce had teased her for the past three years about it, but Danika had refused to say them.

Motion caught Bryce's attention to their left. Bullets had been found in the truck's cab. But her gaze remained on Danika. On that beautiful, fierce face.

She let go, like a key turning in a lock. The first rays of the sun over the horizon.

And Bryce whispered, as those bullets came closer to that awaiting gun and the monstrous male who wielded it, "Close your eyes, Danika."

Bryce blinked, the shimmering memory replaced by the photo still glaring from her screen. Of Danika and the Pack of Devils years later—so happy and young and alive.

Mere hours from their true end.

The skies opened, and wings rustled above, reminding her of Athalar's hovering presence. But she didn't bother to look as she strode into the club.

25

Hunt knew he'd fucked up. And he was in deep shit with Micah—*if* Micah found out that he'd revealed the truth about that night.

He doubted Quinlan had made that call—either to the sorceress or to Micah's office—and he'd make sure she didn't. Maybe he'd bribe her with a new pair of shoes or some purse or whatever the fuck might be enticing enough to keep her mouth shut. One fuckup, one misstep, and he had few illusions about how Micah would react.

He let Quinlan run through the city, trailing her from the Old Square into the dark wasteland of Asphodel Meadows, then into the CBD, and back to the Old Square again.

Hunt flew above her, listening to the symphony of honking cars, thumping bass, and the brisk April wind whispering through the palms and cypresses. Witches on brooms soared down the streets, some close enough to touch the roofs of the cars they passed. So different from the angels, Hunt included, who always kept above the buildings when flying. As if the witches wanted to be a part of the bustle the angels defined themselves by avoiding.

While he'd trailed Quinlan, Justinian had called with the information on the kristallos, which amounted to a whole lot of nothing. A few myths that matched with what they already knew. Vik had called five minutes after that: the Viper Queen's alibis checked out.

Then Isaiah had called, confirming that the victim in the alley was indeed a missing acolyte. He knew Danaan's suspicions were right: it couldn't be coincidence that they'd been at the temple yesterday, talking about the Horn and the demon that had slaughtered Danika and the Pack of Devils, and now one of its acolytes had died at the kristallos's claws.

A Fae girl. Barely more than a child. Acid burned through his stomach at the thought.

He shouldn't have brought Quinlan to the murder scene. Shouldn't have pushed her into going, so blinded by his damn need to get this investigation solved quickly that he hadn't thought twice about her hesitation.

He hadn't realized until he'd seen her look at the pulped body, until her face had gone white as death, that her quiet wasn't calm at all. It was shock. Trauma. Horror. And he'd shoved her into it.

He'd fucked up, and Ruhn had been right to call him on that, but—shit.

He'd taken one look at Quinlan's ashen face and known she hadn't been behind these murders, or even remotely involved. And he was a giant fucking asshole for even entertaining the idea. For even *telling* her she'd been on his list.

He rubbed his face. He wished Shahar were here, soaring beside him. She'd always let him talk out various strategies or issues during the five years he'd been with her 18th, always listened, and asked questions. Challenged him in a way no one else had.

By the time an hour had passed and the rain had begun, Hunt had planned a whole speech. He doubted Quinlan wanted to hear it, or would admit what she'd felt today, but he owed her an apology. He'd lost so many essential parts of himself over these centuries of enslavement and war, but he liked to think he hadn't lost his basic decency. At least not yet.

After completing those two thousand–plus kills he still had to make if he failed to solve this case, however, he couldn't imagine he'd have even that left. Whether the person he'd be at that point would deserve freedom, he didn't know. Didn't want to think about it.

But then Bryce got a phone call—got one, didn't make one,

thank fuck—and didn't break her stride to answer it. Too high up to hear, he could only watch as she'd shifted directions again and aimed—he realized ten minutes later—for Archer Street.

Just as the rain increased, she'd paused outside the White Raven and spent a few minutes on her phone. But despite his eagle-sharp eyesight, he couldn't make out what she was doing on it. So he'd watched from the adjacent roof, and must have checked his own phone a dozen times in those five minutes like a pathetic fucking loser, hoping she'd message him.

And right when the rain turned to a downpour, she put her phone away, walked past the bouncers with a little wave, and vanished into the White Raven without so much as a look upward.

Hunt landed, sending Vanir and humans skittering down the sidewalk. And the half-wolf, half-daemonaki bouncer had the nerve to actually hold out a hand. "Line's to the right," the male to his left rumbled.

"I'm with Bryce," he said.

The other bouncer said, "Tough shit. Line's on the right."

The line, despite the early hour, was already down the block. "I'm here on legion business," Hunt said, fishing for his badge, wherever the fuck he'd put it—

The door cracked open, and a stunning Fae waitress peeked out. "Riso says he's in, Crucius."

The bouncer who'd first spoken just held Hunt's stare.

Hunt smirked. "Some other time." Then he followed the female inside.

The scent of sex and booze and sweat that hit him had every instinct rising with dizzying speed as they crossed the glass-framed courtyard and ascended the steps. The half-crumbled pillars were uplit by purple lights.

He'd never set foot in the club—always made Isaiah or one of the others do it. Mostly because he knew it was no better than the palaces and country villas of the Pangeran Archangels, where feasts turned to orgies that lasted for days. All while people starved mere steps from those villas—humans and Vanir alike rooting through garbage piles for anything to fill their children's bellies. He knew his temper and triggers well enough to stay the fuck away.

Some people whispered as he walked by. He just kept his eyes on Bryce, who was already in a booth between two carved pillars, sipping at a glass of something clear—either vodka or gin. With all the scents in here, he couldn't make it out.

Her eyes lifted to him from the rim of her glass as she sipped. "How'd *you* get in?"

"It's a public place, isn't it?"

She said nothing. Hunt sighed, and was about to sit down to make that apology when he scented jasmine and vanilla, and—

"Excuse me, sir—oh. Um. Erm." He found himself looking at a lovely faun, dressed in a white tank top and skirt short enough to show off her long, striped legs and delicate hooves. Her gently arcing horns were nearly hidden in curly hair that was pulled back into a coiled bun, her brown skin dusted with gold that flickered in the club lights. Gods, she was beautiful.

Juniper Andromeda: Bryce's friend in the ballet. He'd read her file, too. The dancer glanced between Hunt and Quinlan. "I—I hope I'm not interrupting anything—"

"He was just leaving," Bryce said, draining her glass.

He finally slid into the booth. "I was just arriving." He extended a hand to the faun. "It's nice to meet you. I'm Hunt."

"I know who you are," the faun said, her voice husky.

Juniper's grip was light but solid. Bryce refilled her glass from a decanter of clear liquid and drank deep. Juniper asked her, "Did you order food? Rehearsal just let out and I'm *starving*." Though the faun was thin, she was leanly muscled, strong as Hel beneath that graceful exterior.

Bryce held up her drink. "I'm having a liquid dinner."

Juniper frowned. But she asked Hunt, "You want food?"

"Hel yes."

"You can order whatever you want—they'll get it for you." She raised a hand, signaling a waitress. "I'll have a veggie burger, no cheese, with a side of fries, vegetable oil only to cook them, and two pieces of pizza—plant-based cheese on it, please." She bit her lip, then explained to Hunt, "I don't eat animal products."

As a faun, meat and dairy were abhorrent. Milk was only for nursing babies.

"Got it," he said. "You mind if I do?" He'd fought alongside fauns over the centuries. Some hadn't been able to stand the sight of meat. Some hadn't cared. It was always worth asking.

Juniper blinked, but shook her head.

He offered the waitress a smile as he said, "I'll have . . . a bone-in rib eye and roasted green beans." What the Hel. He glanced at Bryce, who was guzzling her booze like it was a protein shake.

She hadn't eaten dinner yet, and even though he'd been distracted this morning when she'd emerged from her bedroom in nothing but a lacy hot-pink bra and matching underwear, he'd noted through the living room window that she'd also forgone breakfast, and since she hadn't brought lunch with her or ordered in, he was willing to bet she hadn't eaten that, either.

So Hunt said, "She'll have lamb kofta with rice, roasted chickpeas, and pickles on the side. Thanks." He'd watched her go for lunch a few times now, and had scented precisely what was inside her takeaway bags. Bryce opened her mouth, but the waitress was already gone. Juniper surveyed them nervously. Like she knew precisely what Bryce was about to—

"Are you going to cut my food, too?"

"What?"

"Just because you're some big, tough asshole doesn't mean you get the right to decide when I should eat—or when *I'm* not taking care of my body. I'm the one who lives in it, *I* know when I fucking want to eat. So keep your possessive and aggressive bullshit to yourself."

Juniper's swallow was audible over the music. "Long day at work, Bryce?"

Bryce reached for her drink again. But Hunt moved faster, his hand wrapping around her wrist and pinning it to the table before she could guzzle down more booze.

"Get your fucking hand off me," she snarled.

Hunt threw her a half smile. "Don't be such a cliché." Her eyes simmered. "You have a rough day and you come to drown yourself in vodka?" He snorted, letting go of her wrist and grabbing her glass. He lifted it to his lips, holding her stare over the rim as he said, "At least tell me you have good taste in—" He sniffed the liquor. Tasted it. "This is water."

Her fingers curled into fists on the table. "I don't drink."

Juniper said, "I invited Bryce tonight. It's been a while since we've seen each other, and I have to meet some of the company members here later, so—"

"Why don't you drink?" Hunt asked Bryce.

"You're the Umbra Mortis. I'm sure you can figure it out." Bryce scooted out of the booth, forcing Juniper to get up. "Though considering you thought I killed my best friend, maybe you can't." Hunt bristled, but Bryce just declared, "I'm going to the bathroom." Then she walked right into the throng on the ancient dance floor, the crowd swallowing her as she wove her way toward a distant door between two pillars at the back of the space.

Juniper's face was tight. "I'll go with her."

Then she was gone, moving swift and light, two males gaping as she passed. Juniper ignored them. She caught up to Bryce midway across the dance floor, halting her with a hand on her arm. Juniper smiled—bright as the lights around them—and began speaking, gesturing to the booth, the club. Bryce's face remained cold as stone. Colder.

Males approached, saw that expression, and didn't venture closer.

"Well, if she's pissed at you, it'll make me look better," drawled a male voice beside him.

Hunt didn't bother to look pleasant. "Tell me you've found something."

The Crown Prince of the Valbaran Fae leaned against the edge of the booth, his strikingly blue eyes lingering on his cousin. He'd no doubt used those shadows of his to creep up without Hunt's notice. "Negative. I got a call from the Raven's owner that she was here. She was in bad enough shape when she left the crime scene that I wanted to make sure she was all right."

Hunt couldn't argue with that. So he said nothing.

Ruhn nodded toward where the females stood motionless in the middle of a sea of dancers. "She used to dance, you know. If she'd been able, she would have gone into the ballet like Juniper."

He hadn't known—not really. Those facts had been blips on her file. "Why'd she drop it?"

"You'll have to ask her. But she stopped dancing completely after Danika died."

"And drinking, it seems." Hunt glanced toward her discarded glass of water.

Ruhn followed his line of sight. If he was surprised, the prince didn't let on.

Hunt took a sip of Bryce's water and shook his head. Not a party girl at all—just content to let the world believe the worst of her.

Including him. Hunt rolled his shoulders, wings moving with him, as he watched her on the dance floor. Yeah, he'd fucked up. Royally.

Bryce looked toward the booth and when she saw her cousin there . . . There were trenches of Hel warmer than the look she gave Ruhn.

Juniper tracked her gaze.

Bryce took all of one step toward the booth before the club exploded.

26

One minute, Athalar and Ruhn were talking. One minute, Bryce was about to go rip into both of them for their alphahole protectiveness, smothering her even from afar. One minute, she was just trying not to drown in the weight that had yanked her under that too-familiar black surface. No amount of running could free her from it, buy her a sip of air.

The next, her ears hollowed out, the ground ripped from beneath her, the ceiling rained down, people screamed, blood sprayed, fear scented the air, and she was twisting, lunging for Juniper—

Shrill, incessant ringing filled her head.

The world had been tipped on its side.

Or maybe that was because she lay sprawled on the wrecked floor, debris and shrapnel and *body parts* around her.

But Bryce kept down, stayed arched over Juniper, who might have been screaming—

That shrill ringing wouldn't stop. It drowned out every other sound. Coppery slickness in her mouth—blood. Plaster coated her skin.

"Get up." Hunt's voice cut through the ringing, the screaming,

the shrieking, and his strong hands wrapped around her shoulders. She thrashed against him, reaching for Juniper—

But Ruhn was already there, blood running from his temple as he helped her friend stand—

Bryce looked over every inch of Juniper: plaster and dust and someone else's green blood, but not a scratch, not a scratch, not a scratch—

Bryce swayed back into Hunt, who gripped her shoulders. "We need to get out—*now*," the angel was saying to Ruhn, ordering her brother like a foot soldier. "There could be more."

Juniper pushed out of Ruhn's grip and screamed at Bryce, "*Are you out of your mind?*"

Her ears—her ears wouldn't stop ringing, and maybe her brain was leaking because she couldn't talk, couldn't seem to remember how to use her limbs—

Juniper swung. Bryce didn't feel the impact on her cheek. Juniper sobbed as if her body would break apart. "*I made the Drop, Bryce! Two years ago! You haven't! Have you completely lost it?*"

A warm, strong arm slid across her abdomen, holding her upright. Hunt said, his mouth near her ear, "Juniper, she's shell-shocked. Give it a rest."

Juniper snapped at him, "*Stay out of this!*" But people were wailing, screaming, and debris was still raining down. Pillars lay like fallen trees around them. June seemed to notice, to realize—

Her body, gods, her body wouldn't work—

Hunt didn't object when Ruhn gave them an address nearby and told them to go wait for him there. It was closer than her apartment, but frankly, Hunt wasn't entirely sure Bryce would let him in—and if she went into shock and he couldn't get past those enchantments . . . Well, Micah would spike his head to the front gates of the Comitium if she died on his watch.

He might very well do that just for not sensing that the attack was about to happen.

Quinlan didn't seem to notice he was carrying her. She was heavier than she looked—her tan skin covered more muscle than he'd thought.

Hunt found the familiar white-columned house a few blocks away; the key Ruhn had given him opened a green-painted door. The cavernous foyer was laced with two male scents other than the prince's. A flick of the light switch revealed a grand staircase that looked like it'd been through a war zone, scuffed oak floors, and a crystal chandelier hanging precariously.

Beneath it: a beer pong table painted with remarkable skill—portraying a gigantic Fae male swallowing an angel whole.

Ignoring that particular *fuck you* to his kind, Hunt aimed for the living room to the left of the entry. A stained sectional lay against the far wall of the long room, and Hunt set Bryce down there as he hurried for the equally worn wet bar midway down the far wall. Water—she needed some water.

There hadn't been an attack in the city for years now—since Briggs. He'd felt the bomb's power as it rippled through the club, shredding the former temple and its inhabitants apart. He'd leave it to the investigators to see what exactly it was, but—

Even his lightning hadn't been fast enough to stop it, not that it would have been any protection against a bomb, not in an ambush like that. He'd destroyed enough on battlefields to know how to intercept them with his power, how to match death with death, but this hadn't been some long-range missile fired from a tank.

It had been planted somewhere in the club, and detonated at a predetermined moment. There were a handful of people who might be capable of such a thing, and at the top of Hunt's list . . . there was Philip Briggs again. Or his followers, at least—Briggs himself was still imprisoned at the Adrestia Prison. He'd think on it later, when his head wasn't still spinning, and his lightning wasn't still a crackle in his blood, hungry for an enemy to obliterate.

Hunt turned his attention to the woman who sat on the couch, staring at nothing.

Bryce's green dress was wrecked, her skin was covered in plaster and someone else's blood, her face pale—save for the red mark on her cheek.

Hunt grabbed an ice pack from the freezer under the bar counter and a dish towel to wrap it in. He set the glass of water on the stained wood coffee table, then handed her the ice. "She slugged you pretty damn good."

Those amber eyes lifted slowly to him. Dried blood crusted inside her ears.

A moment's searching in the sorry-looking kitchen and bathroom cabinet revealed more towels and a first aid kit.

He knelt on the worn gray carpet before her, tucking his wings in tight to keep them from tangling with the beer cans that littered the coffee table.

She kept staring at nothing as he cleaned out her bloody ears.

He didn't have med-magic like a witch, but he knew enough battlefield healing to assess her arched ears. The Fae hearing would have made that explosion horrific—the human bloodline then slowing down the healing process. Mercifully, he found no signs of continued bleeding or damage.

He started on the left ear. And when he'd finished, he noticed her knees were scraped raw, with shards of stone embedded in them.

"Juniper stands a shot of being promoted to principal," Bryce rasped at last. "The first faun ever. The summer season starts soon—she's an understudy for the main roles in two of the ballets. A soloist in all five of them. This season is crucial. If she got injured, it could interfere."

"She made the Drop. She would have bounced back quickly." He pulled a pair of tweezers from the kit.

"Still."

She hissed as he carefully pried out some shards of metal and stone from her knee. She'd hit the ground hard. Even with the club exploding, he'd seen her move.

She'd thrown herself right over Juniper, shielding her from the blast.

"This will sting," he told her, frowning at the bottle of healing solution. Fancy, high-priced stuff. Surprising that it was even here, given that the prince and his roommates had all made the Drop. "But it'll keep it from scarring."

She shrugged, studying the massive, dark television screen over his shoulder.

Hunt doused her leg with the solution, and she jerked. He gripped her calf hard enough to keep her down, even as she cursed. "I warned you."

She pushed a breath out between clenched teeth. The hem of her already short dress had ridden up with her movements, and Hunt told himself he looked only to assess if there were other injuries, but—

The thick, angry scar cut across an otherwise sleek, unnervingly perfect thigh.

Hunt stilled. She'd never gotten it healed.

And every limp he'd sometimes caught her making from the corner of his eye . . . Not from her dumb fucking shoes. But from this. From *him*. From his clumsy battlefield instincts to staple her up like a soldier.

"When males are kneeling between my legs, Athalar," she said, "they're not usually grimacing."

"What?" But her words registered, just at the moment he realized his hand still gripped her calf, the silky skin beneath brushing against the calluses on his palms. Just as he realized that he was indeed kneeling between her thighs, and had leaned closer to her lap to see that scar.

Hunt reeled back, unable to help the heat rising to his face. He removed his hand from her leg. "Sorry," he ground out.

Any amusement faded from her eyes as she said, "Who do you think did it—the club?"

The heat of her soft skin still stained his palm. "No idea."

"Could it have anything to do with us looking into this case?" Guilt already dampened her eyes, and he knew the body of the acolyte flashed through her mind.

He shook his head. "Probably not. If someone wanted to stop us, a bullet in the head's a lot more precise than blowing up a club.

It could easily have been some rival of the club's owner. Or the remaining Keres members looking to start more shit in this city."

Bryce asked, "You think we'll have war here?"

"Some humans want us to. Some Vanir want us to. To get rid of the humans, they say."

"They've destroyed parts of Pangera with the war there," she mumbled. "I've seen the footage." She looked at him, letting her unspoken question hang. *How bad was it?*

Hunt just said, "Magic and machines. Never a good mix."

The words rippled between them. "I want to go home," she breathed. He peeled off his jacket and settled it around her shoulders. It nearly devoured her. "I want to shower all this off." She gestured at the blood on her bare skin.

"Okay." But the front door in the foyer opened. One set of booted feet.

Hunt had his gun out, hidden against his thigh as he turned, when Ruhn walked in, shadows in his wake. "You're not going to like this," the prince said.

She wanted to go home. Wanted to call Juniper. Wanted to call her mom and Randall just to hear their voices. Wanted to call Fury and learn what she knew, even if Fury wouldn't pick up or answer her messages. Wanted to call Jesiba and *make her* find out what had happened. But she mostly just wanted to *go home and shower.*

Ruhn, stone-faced and blood-splattered, halted in the archway.

Hunt slid the handgun back into its holster at his thigh before sitting on the couch beside her.

Ruhn went to the wet bar and filled a glass of water from the sink. Every movement was stiff, shadows whispering around him. But the prince exhaled and the shadows, the tension, vanished.

Hunt spared her from demanding that Ruhn elaborate. "I'm assuming this has to do with whoever bombed the club?"

Ruhn nodded and tossed back a gulp of water. "All signs point to the human rebels." Bryce's blood chilled. She and Hunt swapped glances. Their discussion moments ago hadn't been far from the mark. "The bomb was smuggled into the club through some new exploding liquid hidden in a delivery of wine. They left the calling card on the crate—their own logo."

Hunt cut in. "Any potential connection to Philip Briggs?"

Ruhn said, "Briggs is still behind bars." A polite way of describing the punishment the rebel leader now endured at Vanir hands in Adrestia Prison.

"The rest of his Keres group isn't," Bryce croaked. "Danika was the one who made the raid on Briggs in the first place. Even if he didn't kill her, he's still doing time for his rebel crimes. He could have instructed his followers to carry out this bombing."

Ruhn frowned. "I thought they'd disbanded—joined other factions or returned to Pangera. But here's the part you're not going to like. Next to the logo on the crate was a branded image. My team and your team thought it was a warped *C* for Crescent City, but I looked at the footage of the storage area before the bomb went off. It's hard to make out, but it could also be depicting a curved horn."

"What does the Horn have to do with the human rebellion?" Bryce asked. Then her mouth dried out. "Wait. Do you think that Horn image was a message to *us*? To warn us away from looking for the Horn? As if that acolyte wasn't enough?"

Hunt mused, "It can't just be coincidence that the club was bombed when we were there. Or that one of the images on the crate seems like it could be the Horn, when we're knee-deep in a search for it. Before Danika busted him, Briggs planned to blow up the Raven. The Keres sect has been inactive since he went to prison, but . . ."

"They could be coming back," Bryce insisted. "Looking to pick up where Briggs left off, or somehow getting directions from him even now."

Hunt looked somber. "Or it was one of Briggs's followers all along—the planned bombing, Danika's murder, *this* bombing . . . Briggs might not be guilty, but maybe he knows who is. He could be protecting someone." He pulled out his phone. "We need to talk to him."

Ruhn said, "Are you fucking nuts?"

Hunt ignored him and dialed a number, rising to his feet. "He's in Adrestia Prison, so the request might take a few days," he said to Bryce.

"Fine." She blocked out the thought of what, exactly, this meeting would be like. Danika had been unnerved by Briggs's fanaticism toward the human cause, and had rarely wanted to talk about him. Busting him and his Keres group—an offshoot of the main Ophion rebellion—had been a triumph, a legitimization of the Pack of Devils. It still hadn't been enough to win Sabine's approval.

Hunt tucked the phone to his ear. "Hey, Isaiah. Yeah, I'm all right." He stepped into the foyer, and Bryce watched him go.

Ruhn said quietly, "The Autumn King knows I've involved you in looking for the Horn."

She lifted heavy eyes to her brother. "How pissed is he?"

Ruhn's grim smile wasn't comforting. "He warned me of the *poison* you'd spew in my ear."

"I should take that as a compliment, I suppose."

Ruhn didn't smile this time. "He wants to know what you'll do with the Horn if it's found."

"Use it as my new drinking mug on game day."

Hunt gave a snort of laughter as he entered the room, call over. Ruhn just said, "He was serious."

"I'll give it back to the temple," Bryce said. "Not to him."

Ruhn looked at both of them as Hunt again sat on the couch. "My father said that since I have now involved you in something so dangerous, Bryce, you need a guard to . . . remain with you at all times. Live with you. I volunteered."

Every part of her battered body ached. "Over my dead fucking corpse."

Hunt crossed his arms. "Why does your king care if Quinlan lives or dies?"

Ruhn's eyes grew cold. "I asked him the same. He said that she falls under his jurisdiction, as half-Fae, and he doesn't want to have to clean up any messy situations. *The girl is a liability*, he said." Bryce could hear the cruel tones in every word Ruhn mimicked. Could see her father's face as he spoke them. She often imagined how it'd feel to beat in that perfect face with her fists. To give him a scar like the one her mother bore along her cheekbone—small and slender, no longer than a fingernail, but a reminder of the blow he'd given her when his hideous rage drove him too far.

The blow that had sent Ember Quinlan running—pregnant with Bryce.

Creep. Old, hateful creep.

"So he's just concerned about the PR nightmare of Quinlan's death before the Summit," Hunt said roughly, disgust tightening his face.

"Don't look so shocked," Ruhn said, then added to Bryce, "I'm only the messenger. Consider whether it's wise to pick this as your big battle with him."

No chance in Hel was she letting *Ruhn* into her apartment to order her around. Especially with those friends of his. It was bad enough she had to work with him on this case.

Gods, her head was pounding. "Fine," she said, simmering. "He said I needed a guard—not you specifically, right?" At Ruhn's tense silence, Bryce went on, "That's what I thought. Athalar stays with me instead. Order fulfilled. Happy?"

"He won't like that."

Bryce smiled smugly, even as her blood simmered. "He didn't say who the guard had to be. The bastard should have been more precise with his wording."

Even Ruhn couldn't argue against that.

If Athalar was shocked at Bryce's choice of roommates, he didn't let on.

Ruhn watched the angel glance between them—carefully.

Fuck. Had Athalar finally started putting it together—that they were more entwined than cousins should be, that Ruhn's father *shouldn't* be taking such an interest in her?

Bryce seethed at Ruhn, "Did you put your father up to this?"

"No," Ruhn said. His father had cornered him about the temple visit right as he left the ruined club. Honestly, given how pissed the male had been, it was a miracle Ruhn wasn't dead in a gutter. "He's got a network of spies that even I don't know about."

Bryce scowled, but it morphed into a wince as she got off the couch, Athalar keeping a hand within easy reach of her elbow, should she need it.

Ruhn's phone buzzed, and he pulled it from his pocket long enough to read the message on the screen. And the others that began flying in.

Declan had written in the group chain with Flynn, *What the fuck happened?*

Flynn replied, *I'm at the club. Sabine sent Amelie Ravenscroft to head the Aux packs hauling away debris and helping the wounded. Amelie said she saw you leave, Ruhn. You all right?*

Ruhn answered, just so they wouldn't call. *I'm fine. I'll meet you at the club soon.* He squeezed the phone in his fist as Bryce made her way toward the front door and the Helscape beyond. Blue and red sirens blared, casting their light on the oak floors of the foyer.

But his sister paused before reaching for the handle, twisting to ask him, "Why were you at the Raven earlier?"

And here it was. If he mentioned the call Riso had made to him, that Ruhn had been keeping tabs on her, he'd get his head bitten off. So Ruhn half lied, "I want to check out your boss's library."

Hunt paused, a step behind Bryce. It was impressive, really, to watch both of them plaster confused expressions on their faces.

"What library?" she asked, the portrait of innocence.

Ruhn could have sworn Athalar was trying not to smile. But he said tightly, "The one everyone says is beneath the gallery."

"First I've heard of it," Hunt said with a shrug.

"Fuck off, Athalar." Ruhn's jaw ached from clenching it so hard.

Bryce said, "Look, I get that you want in on our little cool kids' club, but there's a strict membership-vetting process."

Yeah, Athalar was trying really hard not to smile.

Ruhn growled, "I want to look at the books there. See if anything about the Horn jumps out." She paused at the tone in his voice, the bit of dominance Ruhn threw into it. He wasn't above pulling rank. Not where this was concerned.

Though Athalar was glaring daggers at him, Ruhn said to his sister, "I've been through the Fae Archives twice, and . . ." He shook his head. "I just kept thinking about the gallery. So maybe there's something there."

"I searched it," she said. "There's nothing about the Horn beyond vague mentions."

Ruhn gave her a half smile. "So you admit there's a library."

Bryce frowned at him. He knew that contemplative look. "What."

Bryce flipped her hair over a dirty, torn shoulder. "I'll make a bargain with you: you can come hunt for the Horn at the gallery, and I'll help in whatever way I can. If—" Athalar whipped his head to her, the outrage on his face almost delightful. Bryce went on, nodding to the phone in Ruhn's hand, "*If* you put Declan at my disposal."

"I'll have to tell him about this case, then. And what he knows, Flynn will learn two seconds later."

"Fine. Go ahead and fill them in. But tell Dec I need intel about Danika's last movements."

"I don't know where he can get that," Ruhn admitted.

"The Den would have it," Hunt said, eyeing Bryce with something like admiration. "Tell Emmet to hack the Den archives."

So Ruhn nodded. "Fine. I'll ask him later."

Bryce gave him that smile that didn't meet her eyes. "Then come by the gallery tomorrow."

Ruhn had to give himself a moment to master his shock at how easy it had been to get access. Then he said, "Be careful out there."

If she and Athalar were right and it *was* some Keres rebels acting on Briggs's request or in his honor . . . the political mess would be a nightmare. And if he hadn't been wrong about that *C* actually being an image of the Horn, if this bombing and the acolyte's murder were targeted warnings to them regarding their search for it . . . then the threat to all of them had just become a Hel of a lot deadlier.

Bryce said sweetly before continuing on, "Tell your daddy we say hello—and that he can go fuck himself."

Ruhn gritted his teeth again, earning another grin from Athalar. Winged asshole.

The two of them strode through the door, and Ruhn's phone rang a heartbeat after that.

"Yeah," he said.

Ruhn could have sworn he could hear his father tense before the male drawled, "Is that how you speak to your king?"

Ruhn didn't bother replying. His father said, "Since you couldn't stop yourself from revealing my business, I wish to make one thing clear regarding the Horn." Ruhn braced himself. "I don't want the angels getting it."

"Fine." If Ruhn had anything to say about it, *no one* would get the Horn. It would go straight back to the temple, with a permanent Fae guard.

"Keep an eye on that girl."

"Both eyes."

"I mean it, boy."

"So do I." He let his father hear the growl of sincerity in his voice.

His father went on, "You, as Crown Prince, revealed the secrets of your king to the girl and Athalar. I have every right to punish you for this, you know."

Go ahead, he wanted to say. *Go ahead and do it. Do me a favor and take my title while you're at it. The royal bloodline ends with me anyway.*

Ruhn had puked after hearing it the first time when he was thirteen, sent to the Oracle for a glimpse of his future, like all Fae. The ritual had once been to foretell marriages and alliances. Today, it was more to get a feel for a child's career and whether they'd amount to anything. For Ruhn—and for Bryce, years later—it had been a disaster.

Ruhn had begged the Oracle to tell him whether she meant he'd die before he could sire a child, or if she meant he was infertile. She only repeated her words. *The royal bloodline shall end with you, Prince.*

He'd been too much of a coward to tell his king what he'd learned. So he'd fed his father a lie, unable to bear the male's disappointment and rage. *The Oracle said I would be a fair and just king.*

His father had been disappointed, but only that the fake prophecy hadn't been mightier.

So, yeah. If his father wanted to strip him of his title, he'd be doing him a favor. Or even unwittingly fulfilling that prophecy at last.

Ruhn had truly worried about its meaning once—the day he'd learned he had a little sister. He'd thought it might foretell an untimely death for her. But his fears had been assuaged by the fact that she was not and would never be formally recognized as part of the royal bloodline. To his relief, she'd never questioned why, in those early years when they were still close, Ruhn hadn't lobbied their father to publicly accept her.

The Autumn King continued, "Unfortunately, the punishment you deserve would render you unable to look for the Horn."

Ruhn's shadows drifted around him. "I'll take a rain check, then."

His father snarled, but Ruhn hung up.

27

The streets were packed with Vanir streaming from the still-chaotic White Raven, all looking for answers about what the Hel had happened. Various legionaries, Fae, and Aux pack members had erected a barricade around the site, a thrumming, opaque magic wall, but the crowds still converged.

Hunt glanced to where Bryce walked beside him, silent, glassy-eyed. Barefoot, he realized.

How long had she been barefoot? She must have lost her shoes in the explosion.

He debated offering to carry her again, or suggesting that he fly them to her apartment, but she held her arms so tightly around herself that he had a feeling one word would send her into a rage-spiral with no bottom.

The look she gave Ruhn before walking out . . . It made Hunt glad she wasn't an acid-spitting viper. The male's face would have *melted*.

Gods help them when the prince arrived at the gallery tomorrow.

Bryce's doorman leapt out of his seat as they walked into the pristine lobby, asking if she was all right, if she'd been in the club. She mumbled that she was fine, and the ursine shifter surveyed Hunt with a predator's focus. Noticing that look, she waved a hand at him, punching the elevator button, and introduced them. *Hunt, this is Marrin; Marrin, this is Hunt; he's staying with me for the foreseeable future, unfortunately.* Then she was padding into the elevator, where she had to lean against the chrome rail along the back, as if she were about to collapse—

Hunt squeezed in as the doors were closing. The box was too small, too tight with his wings, and he kept them close as they shot up to the penthouse—

Bryce's head sagged, her shoulders curving inward—

Hunt blurted, "Why won't you make the Drop?"

The elevator doors opened and she slumped against them before she entered the elegant cream-and-cobalt hallway. But she halted at her apartment door. Then turned to him.

"My keys were in my purse."

Her purse was now in the ruin of the club.

"Does the doorman have a spare?"

She grunted her confirmation, eyeing the elevator as if it were a mountain to climb.

Marrin busted Hunt's balls for a good minute, checking that Bryce was alive in the hallway, asking into the hall vidcom if she approved—to which he got a thumbs-up.

When Hunt returned, he found her sitting against her door, legs up and spread enough to show a pair of hot-pink underwear. Thankfully, the hall cameras couldn't see at that angle, but he had no doubt the shifter monitored them as Hunt helped her to her feet and handed her the spare keys.

She slowly slid in the key, then put her palm to the bespelled finger pad beside the door.

"I was waiting," she murmured as the locks clicked open and the dim apartment lights flickered on. "We were supposed to make the Drop together. We picked two years from now."

He knew who she meant. The reason why she no longer drank, or danced, or really seemed to live her life. The reason why she must keep that scar on her pretty, sleek thigh. Ogenas and all her sacred Mysteries knew that Hunt had punished himself for a damn long while after the colossal failure that had been the Battle of Mount Hermon. Even while he'd been tortured in the Asteri's dungeons, he'd punished himself, flaying his own soul in a way no imperial interrogator ever could.

So maybe it was a stupid question, but he asked as they entered the apartment, "Why bother waiting now?"

Hunt stepped inside and got a good look at the place Quinlan called home. The open-concept apartment had looked nice from outside the windows, but inside . . .

Either she or Danika had decorated it without sparing any expense: a white deep-cushioned couch lay in the right third of the great room, set before a reclaimed wood coffee table and the massive television atop a carved oak console. A fogged-glass dining table with white leather chairs took up the left third of the space, and the center third of it went to the kitchen—white cabinets, chrome appliances, and white marble counters. All of it impeccably clean, soft, and welcoming.

Hunt took it in, standing like a piece of baggage by the kitchen island while Bryce padded down a pale oak hallway to release Syrinx from where he yowled from his crate.

She was halfway down the hallway when she said without looking back, "Without Danika . . . We were supposed to make the Drop together," she said again. "Connor and Thorne were going to Anchor us."

The choice of Anchor during the Drop was pivotal—and a deeply personal choice. But Hunt shoved aside the thoughts of the sour-faced government employee he'd been appointed, since he sure as fuck hadn't had any family or friends left to Anchor him. Not when his mother had died only days before.

Syrinx flung himself through the apartment, claws clicking on the light wood floors, yipping as he leapt upon Hunt, licking his hands. Each one of Bryce's returning steps dragged on her way to the kitchen counter.

The silence pressed on him enough that he asked, "Were you and Danika lovers?"

He'd been told two years ago that they weren't, but friends didn't mourn each other the way Bryce seemed to have so thoroughly shut down every part of herself. The way he had for Shahar.

The patter of kibble hitting tin filled the apartment before Bryce plunked down the bowl, and Syrinx, abandoning Hunt, half threw himself inside it as he gobbled it down.

Hunt turned in place as Bryce padded around the other end of the kitchen island, flinging open the enormous metal fridge to examine its meager contents. "No," she said, her voice flat and cold. "Danika and I weren't like that." Her grip on the fridge's handle tightened, her knuckles going white. "Connor and I—Connor Holstrom, I mean. He and I . . ." She trailed off. "It was complicated. When Danika died, when they all died . . . a light went out in me."

He remembered the details about her and the elder of the Holstrom brothers. Ithan hadn't been there that night, either—and was now Second in Amelie Ravenscroft's pack. A sorry replacement for what the Pack of Devils had once been. This city had also lost something that night.

Hunt opened his mouth to tell Quinlan he understood. Not just the complicated relationship thing, but the loss. To wake up one morning surrounded by friends and his lover—and then to end the day with all of them dead. He understood how it gnawed on bones and blood and the very soul of a person. How nothing could ever make it right.

How cutting out the alcohol and the drugs, how refusing to do the thing she loved most—the dancing—still couldn't make it right. But the words stalled in his throat. He hadn't felt like talking about it two hundred years ago, and sure as Hel didn't feel like talking about it now.

A landline phone somewhere in the house began ringing, and a pleasant female voice trilled, *Call from . . . Home.*

Bryce closed her eyes, as if rallying herself, then padded down the darkened hallway that led to her bedroom. A moment later, she said with a cheerfulness that should have earned her an award for Best Fucking Actor in Midgard, "Hey, Mom." A mattress groaned. "No, I wasn't there. My phone fell in the toilet at work—yep, totally dead. I'll get a new one tomorrow. Yeah, I'm fine. June wasn't there, either. We're all good." A pause. "I know—it was just a long day at work." Another pause. "Look, I've got company." A rough laugh.

"Not that kind. Don't get your hopes up. I'm serious. Yes, I let him into my house willingly. Please don't call the front desk. His name? I'm not telling you." Just the slightest hesitation. "*Mom.* I will call you tomorrow. I'm not telling him hello. Bye—*bye*, Mom. Love you."

Syrinx had finished his food and was staring expectantly at Hunt—silently pleading for more, that lion's tail waggling. "*No*," he hissed at the beast just as Bryce walked back into the main room.

"Oh," she said, as if she'd forgotten he was there. "I'm going to take a shower. Guest room is yours. Use whatever you need."

"I'll swing by the Comitium tomorrow to get more clothes." Bryce just nodded like her head weighed a thousand pounds. "Why'd you lie?" He'd let her decide which one she wanted to explain.

She paused, Syrinx trotting ahead down the hall to her bedroom. "My mom would only worry and come visit. I don't want her around if things are getting bad. And I didn't tell her who you were because that would lead to questions, too. It's easier this way."

Easier to not let herself enjoy life, easier to keep everyone at arm's length.

The mark on her cheek from Juniper's slap had barely faded. Easier to throw herself on top of a friend as a bomb exploded, rather than risk losing them.

She said quietly, "I need to find who did this, Hunt."

He met her raw, aching stare. "I know."

"No," she said hoarsely. "You don't. I don't care what Micah's motives are—if I don't find this fucking person, it is going to *eat me alive*." Not the murderer or the demon, but the pain and grief that he was only starting to realize dwelled inside her. "I need to find who did this."

"We will," he promised.

"How can you know that?" She shook her head.

"Because we don't have another choice. *I* don't have another choice." At her confused look, Hunt blew out a breath and said, "Micah offered me a deal."

Her eyes turned wary. "What sort of deal?"

Hunt clenched his jaw. She'd offered up a piece of herself, so he could do the same. Especially if they were now gods-damned roommates. "When I first came here, Micah offered me a bargain: if I could make up for every life the 18th took that day on Mount Hermon, I'd get my freedom back. All two thousand two hundred and seventeen lives." He steeled himself, willing her to hear what he couldn't quite say.

She chewed on her lip. "I'm assuming that *make up* means . . ."

"Yes," he ground out. "It means doing what I'm good at. A death for a death."

"Micah has more than two thousand people for you to assassinate?"

Hunt let out a harsh laugh. "Micah is a Governor of an entire territory, and he will live for at least another two hundred years. He'll probably have double that number of people on his shit list before he's done." Horror crept into her eyes, and he scrambled for a way to get rid of it, unsure why. "It comes with the job. His job, and mine." He ran a hand through his hair. "Look, it's awful, but he offered me a way out, at least. And when the killings started again, he offered me a different bargain: find the murderer before the Summit meeting, and he'd reduce the debts I owe to ten."

He waited for her judgment, her disgust with him and Micah. But she angled her head. "That's why you've been a bullish pain in the ass."

"Yes," he said tightly. "Micah ordered me not to say anything, though. So if you breathe one word about it—"

"His offer will be rescinded."

Hunt nodded, scanning her battered face. She said nothing more. After a heartbeat, he demanded, "Well?"

"Well, what?" She again began walking toward her bedroom.

"Well, aren't you going to say that I'm a self-serving piece of shit?"

She paused again, a faint ray of light entering her eyes. "Why bother, Athalar, when you just said it for me?"

He couldn't help it then. Even though she was bloodied and covered in debris, he looked her over. Every inch and curve. Tried not to think about the hot-pink underwear beneath that tight green dress. But he said, "I'm sorry I thought you were a suspect. And more than that, I'm sorry I judged you. I thought you were just a party girl, and I acted like an asshole."

"There's nothing wrong with being a party girl. I don't get why the world thinks there is." But she considered his words. "It's easier for me—when people assume the worst about what I am. It lets me see who they really are."

"So you're saying you think I'm really an asshole?" A corner of his mouth curled up.

But her eyes were dead serious. "I've met and dealt with a lot of assholes, Hunt. You're not one of them."

"You weren't singing that tune earlier."

She just aimed for her room once more. So Hunt asked, "Want me to get food?"

Again, she paused. She looked like she was about to say no, but then rasped, "Cheeseburger—with cheese fries. And a chocolate milkshake."

Hunt smiled. "You got it."

The elegant guest room on the other side of the kitchen was spacious, decorated in shades of gray and cream accented with pale rose and cornflower blue. The bed was big enough for Hunt's wings, thankfully—definitely bought with Vanir in mind—and a few photos in expensive-looking frames were propped next to a lopsided, chipped ceramic blue bowl, all adorning a chest of drawers to the right of the door.

He'd gotten them both burgers and fries, and Bryce had torn into hers with a ferocity that Hunt had seen only among lions gathered around a fresh kill. He'd tossed the whining Syrinx a few fries under the white glass table, since she sure as shit wasn't sharing anything.

Exhaustion had set in so thoroughly that neither of them spoke, and once she'd finished slurping down the milkshake, she'd merely gathered up the trash, dumped it into the bin, and headed to her room. Leaving Hunt to enter his.

A mortal scent lingered that he assumed was courtesy of her parents, and as Hunt opened the drawers, he found some of them full of clothes—light sweaters, socks, pants, athletic-looking gear . . . He was snooping. Granted, it was part of the job description, but it was still snooping.

He shut the drawers and studied the framed photos.

Ember Quinlan had been a knockout. No wonder that Fae asshole had pursued her to the point where she'd bailed. Long black hair framed a face that could have been on a billboard: freckled skin, full lips, and high cheekbones that made the dark, depthless eyes above them striking.

It was Bryce's face—the coloring was just different. An equally attractive brown-skinned, dark-haired human male stood beside her, arm slung around her slim shoulders, grinning like a fiend at whoever was behind the camera. Hunt could just barely make out the writing on the silver dog tags dipping over the man's gray button-up.

Well, holy shit.

Randall Silago was Bryce's adoptive father? The legendary war hero and sharpshooter? He had no idea how he'd missed that fact in her file, though he supposed he had been skimming when he'd read it years ago.

No wonder his daughter was so fearless. And there, to the right of Ember, stood Bryce.

She was barely past three, that red hair pulled high into two floppy pigtails. Ember was looking at her daughter—the expression a bit exasperated—as if Bryce was *supposed* to be in the nice clothes that the two adults were wearing. But there she was, giving her mother an equally sassy look, hands on her chubby hips, legs set apart in an unmistakable fighting stance. Covered head to toe in mud.

Hunt snickered and turned to the other photo on the dresser.

It was a beautiful shot of two women—girls, really—sitting on some red rocks atop a desert mountain, their backs to the camera, shoulder-to-shoulder as they faced the scrub and sand far below. One was Bryce—he could tell from her sheet of red hair. The other was in a familiar leather jacket, the back painted with those words in the Republic's most ancient language. *Through love, all is possible.*

It had to be Bryce and Danika. And—that was Danika's jacket that Bryce now wore.

She had no other photos of Danika in the apartment.

Through love, all is possible. It was an ancient saying, dating back to some god he couldn't remember. Cthona, probably—what with all the mother-goddess stuff she presided over. Hunt had long since stopped visiting temples, or paying much attention to the overzealous priestesses who popped up on the morning talk shows every now and then. None of the five gods had ever helped him—or anyone he cared about. Urd, especially, had fucked him over often enough.

Danika's blond ponytail draped down Bryce's back as she leaned her head against her friend's shoulder. Bryce wore a loose white T-shirt, showing a bandaged arm braced on her knee. Bruises peppered her body. And gods—that was a sword lying to Danika's left. Sheathed and clean, but—he knew that sword.

Sabine had gone ballistic searching for it when it was discovered to be missing from the apartment where her daughter had been murdered. Apparently it was some wolf heirloom. But there it lay, beside Bryce and Danika in the desert.

Sitting there on those rocks, perched over the world, they seemed like two soldiers who had just walked through the darkest halls of Hel and were taking a well-earned break.

Hunt turned from the picture and rubbed at the tattoo on his brow. A flick of his power had the heavy gray curtains sliding shut over the floor-to-ceiling windows on a chill wind. He peeled off his clothes one by one, and found the bathroom was just as spacious as the bedroom.

Hunt showered quickly and fell into bed with his skin still drying. The last thing he saw before sleep overtook him was the photo of Bryce and Danika, frozen forever in a moment of peace.

28

Hunt woke the moment he scented a male in his room, his fingers wrapping around the knife under his pillow. He opened an eye, grip tightening on the hilt, remembering every window and doorway, every possible would-be weapon that he could wield to his advantage—

He found Syrinx sitting on the pillow beside his, the chimera's smooshed-up face peering into his own.

Hunt groaned, a breath exploding out of him. Syrinx just swatted at his face.

Hunt rolled out of reach. "Good morning to you, too," he mumbled, scanning the room. He'd *definitely* shut the door last night. It now gaped wide open. He glanced at the clock.

Seven. He hadn't noticed Bryce get up for work—hadn't heard her buzzing about the apartment or the music he knew she liked to play.

Granted, he hadn't heard his own door open, either. He'd slept like the dead. Syrinx rested his head on Hunt's shoulder, and huffed a mournful sigh.

Solas spare him. "Why do I get the feeling that if I give you breakfast, it'll actually be your second or third meal of the day?"

An innocent blink of those round eyes.

Unable to help himself, Hunt scratched the little beast behind his silly ears.

The sunny apartment beyond his room was silent, the light warming the pale wood floors. He eased from the bed, hauling on his pants. His shirt was a wreck from last night's events, so he left it on the floor, and— Shit. His phone. He grabbed it from the bedside table and flicked through the messages. Nothing new, no *missions* from Micah, thank the gods.

He left the phone on the dresser beside the door and padded into the great room.

No sign or sound. If Quinlan had just *left*—

He stormed across the space, to the hall on the other side. Her bedroom door was cracked, as if Syrinx had seen himself out, and—

Sound asleep. The heap of blankets had been twisted and tossed around, and Quinlan lay belly-down on the bed, wrapped around a pillow. The position was almost identical to the one she'd been in last night in the club, flung over Juniper.

Hunt was pretty sure most people would consider the low-backed gray nightgown, edged with pale pink lace, to be a shirt. Syrinx trotted past, leaping on the bed and nosing her bare shoulder.

The tattoo down her back—scrolling, beautiful lines in some alphabet he didn't recognize—rose and fell with each deep breath. Bruises he hadn't noted last night peppered her golden skin, already greenish thanks to the Fae blood in her.

And he was staring at her. Like a fucking creep.

Hunt twisted for the hall, his wings suddenly too big, his skin too tight, when the front door swung open. A smooth movement had his knife angled behind him—

Juniper breezed in, a brown bag of what smelled like chocolate pastries in one hand, a spare set of keys in another. She stopped dead as she spied him in the bedroom hallway.

Her mouth popped open in a silent *Oh*.

She looked him over—not in the way some females did until they noted the tattoos, but in the way that told him she realized a half-naked *male* stood in Bryce's apartment at seven in the morning.

He opened his mouth to say it wasn't how it looked, but Juniper just strutted past, her delicate hooves clipping on the wood floors. She shoved into the bedroom, jostling the bag, and Syrinx went wild, curly tail wagging as Juniper trilled, "I brought chocolate croissants, so get that bare ass out of bed and into some pants."

Bryce lifted her head to see Juniper, then Hunt in the hall. She didn't bother to tug the hem of her nightgown over her teal lace underwear as she squinted. "What?"

Juniper strode to the bed and looked like she was about to plop onto it, but glanced at him.

Hunt stiffened. "It's not what it seems."

Juniper gave him a sweet smile. "Then some privacy would be nice."

He backed down the hall, into the kitchen. Coffee. That sounded like a good plan.

He opened a cabinet, fishing out some mugs. Their voices flitted out to him anyway.

"I tried calling you, but your phone wasn't on—I figured you probably lost it," Juniper said.

Blankets rustled. "Are you all right?"

"Totally fine. News reports are still speculating, but they think human rebels from Pangera did it, wanting to start trouble here. There's video footage from the loading dock that shows their insignia on a case of wine. They think that's how the bomb got in."

So the theory had held overnight. Whether it was truly connected to the Horn remained to be seen. Hunt made a note to check with Isaiah about the request to meet with Briggs as soon as Juniper left.

"Is the Raven totally wrecked?"

A sigh. "Yeah—really bad. No idea when it'll be open again. I finally got a hold of Fury last night, and she said Riso's mad enough that he put a bounty on the head of whoever was responsible."

No surprise there. Hunt had heard that despite his laughing nature, when the butterfly shifter got pissed, he went all in. Juniper went on, "Fury's probably coming home because of it. You know she can't resist a challenge."

Burning Solas. Throwing Fury Axtar into this mess was a bad

fucking idea. Hunt spooned coffee beans into the gleaming chrome machine built into the kitchen wall.

Quinlan asked tightly, "So she'll come back home for a bounty, but not to see us?"

A silence. Then, "You weren't the only one who lost Danika that night, B. We all dealt with it in different ways. Fury's answer to her pain was to bail."

"Your therapist tell you that?"

"I'm not fighting with you about this again."

More silence. Juniper cleared her throat. "B, I'm sorry for what I did. You've got a bruise—"

"It's fine."

"No, it's not—"

"It is. I get it, I—"

Hunt turned on the machine's coffee grinder to give them some privacy. He might have ground the beans into a fine powder instead of rough shards, but when he finished, Juniper was saying, "So, the gorgeous angel who's making you coffee right now—"

Hunt grinned at the coffee machine. It had been a long, long while since anyone had bothered describing him as anything but *Umbra Mortis, the Knife of the Archangels.*

"No, no, and no," Bryce cut her off. "Jesiba is having me do a classified job, and Hunt was assigned to protect me."

"Is being shirtless in your house part of that assignment?"

"You know how these Vanir males are. They live to show off their muscles."

Hunt rolled his eyes as Juniper laughed. "I'm shocked you're even letting him stay here, B."

"I didn't really have a choice."

"Hmmm."

A thump of bare feet on the ground. "You know he's listening, right? His feathers are probably so puffed up he won't be able to fit through the door."

Hunt leaned against the counter, the coffee machine doing the growling for him as Bryce stalked into the hallway. "Puffed up?"

She certainly hadn't bothered to fulfill her friend's pants request.

Each step had the pale pink lace of the nightgown's hem brushing against her upper thighs, tugging up slightly to reveal that thick, brutal scar on the left leg. His stomach twisted at the sight of what he'd done to her.

"Eyes up here, Athalar," she drawled. Hunt scowled.

But Juniper was following closely on Bryce's heels, her hooves clopping lightly on the wood floors as she held up the pastry bag. "I just wanted to drop these off. I've got rehearsal in . . ." She fished her phone from the pocket of her tight black leggings. "Oh shit. *Now.* Bye, B." She rushed to the door, chucking the pastry bag on the table with impressive aim.

"Good luck—call me later," Bryce said, already going to inspect her friend's peace offering.

Juniper lingered in the doorway long enough to say to him, "Do your job, *Umbra.*"

Then she was gone.

Bryce slid into one of the white leather chairs at the glass table and sighed as she pulled out a chocolate croissant. She bit in and moaned. "Do legionaries eat croissants?"

He remained leaning against the counter. "Is that an actual question?"

Crunch-munch-swallow. "Why are you up so early?"

"It's nearly seven thirty. Hardly early by anyone's count. But your chimera nearly sat on my face, so how could I *not* be up? And how many people, exactly, have keys to this place?"

She finished off her croissant. "My parents, Juniper, and the doorman. Speaking of which . . . I need to give those keys back—and get another copy made."

"And get me a set."

The second croissant was halfway to her mouth when she set it down. "Not going to happen."

He held her stare. "Yes, it is. And you'll change the enchantments so I can get access—"

She bit into the croissant. "Isn't it *exhausting* to be an alphahole all the time? Do you guys have a handbook for it? Maybe secret support groups?"

"An alpha-*what*?"

"Alphahole. Possessive and aggressive." She waved a hand at his bare torso. "You know—you males who rip your shirt off at the slightest provocation, who know how to kill people in twenty different ways, who have females falling over themselves to be with you; and when you finally bang one, you go full-on mating-frenzy with her, refusing to let another male look at or talk to her, deciding what and when she needs to eat, what she should wear, when she sees her friends—"

"What the *fuck* are you talking about?"

"Your favorite hobbies are brooding, fighting, and roaring; you've perfected about thirty different types of snarls and growls; you've got a cabal of hot friends, and the moment one of you mates, the others fall like dominoes, too, and gods help you when you all start having babies—"

He snatched the croissant out of her hand. That shut her up.

Bryce gaped at him, then at the pastry, and Hunt wondered if she'd bite him as he lifted it to his mouth. Damn, but it was good.

"One," he told her, yanking over a chair and turning it backward for him to straddle. "The *last* thing I want to do is fuck you, so we can take the whole Sex, Mating, and Baby option off the table. *Two,* I don't have friends, so there sure as fuck will be no couples-retreat lifestyle anytime soon. *Three,* if we're complaining about people who are clothing-optional . . ." He finished the croissant and gave her a pointed look. "I'm not the one who parades around this apartment in a bra and underwear every morning while getting dressed."

He'd worked hard to forget that particular detail. How after her morning run, she did her hair and makeup in a routine that took her more than an hour from start to finish. Wearing only what seemed to be an extensive, and rather spectacular, assortment of lingerie.

Hunt supposed if he looked the way she did, he'd wear that shit, too.

Bryce only glared at him—his mouth, his hand—and grumbled, "That was my croissant."

The coffee machine beeped, but he kept his ass planted in the chair. "You're going to get me a new set of keys. And add me to the enchantments. Because it's part of my *job*, and being assertive isn't the first sign of being an *alphahole*—it's a sign of me wanting to make sure you don't wind up *dead*."

"Stop cursing so much. You're upsetting Syrinx."

He leaned close enough to note gold flecks in her amber eyes. "You have the dirtiest mouth I've ever heard, sweetheart. And from the way *you* act, I think *you* might be the alphahole here."

She hissed.

"See?" he drawled. "What was it you said? An assortment of snarls and growls?" He waved a hand. "Well, there you go."

She tapped her dusk-sky nails on the glass table. "Don't ever eat my croissant again. And stop calling me sweetheart."

Hunt threw her a smirk and rose. "I need to head to the Comitium for my clothes. Where are you going to be?"

Bryce scowled and said nothing.

"The answer," Hunt went on, "is with me. Anywhere you or I go, we go together from now on. Got it?"

She flipped him off. But she didn't argue further.

29

Micah Domitus might have been an asshole, but at least he gave his triarii the weekend off—or its equivalent if a particular duty required them to work through it.

Jesiba Roga, no surprise, didn't seem to believe in weekends. And since Quinlan was expected at work, Hunt had decided they'd hit the barracks at the Comitium during lunch, while most people were distracted.

The thick veils of morning mist hadn't burned off by the time Hunt trailed Bryce on her way to work. No new updates had been delivered to him on the bombing, and there was no mention of further attacks that matched the kristallos's usual methods.

But Hunt still kept his focus sharp, assessing every person who passed the redhead below. Most people spotted Syrinx, prancing at the end of his leash, and gave her a healthy berth. Chimeras were volatile pets—prone to small magics and biting. No matter that Syrinx seemed more interested in whatever food he could swindle out of people.

Bryce wore a little black dress today, her makeup more subdued, heavier on the eyes, lighter on the lipstick . . . Armor, he realized as she and Syrinx wound through other commuters and tourists, dodging cars already honking with impatience at the usual Old

Square traffic. The clothes, the hair, the makeup—they were like the leather and steel and guns he donned every morning.

Except he didn't wear lingerie beneath it.

For whatever reason, he found himself dropping onto the cobblestones behind her. She didn't so much as flinch, her sky-high black heels unfaltering. Impressive as Hel, for her to walk on the ancient streets without snapping an ankle. Syrinx huffed his greeting and kept trotting, proud as an imperial parade horse. "Your boss ever give you a day off?"

She sipped from the coffee she balanced in her free hand. She drank a surely illegal amount of the stuff throughout the day. Starting with no less than three cups before they'd left the apartment. "I get Sundays off," she said. Palm fronds hissed in the chill breeze above them. The tan skin of her legs pebbled with the cold. "Many of our clients are busy enough that they can't come in during the workweek. Saturday is their day of leisure."

"Do you get holidays off at least?"

"The store is closed on the major ones." She idly jangled the triknot amulet around her neck.

An Archesian charm like that had to cost . . . Burning Solas, it had to cost a fuck-ton. Hunt thought about the heavy iron door to the archives. Perhaps it hadn't been put there to keep thieves out . . . but to keep things *in*.

He had a feeling she wouldn't tell him any details about why the art required her to wear such an amulet, so he instead asked, "What's the deal with you and your cousin?" Who would be arriving at the gallery at some point this morning.

Bryce gently pulled on Syrinx's leash when he lunged for a squirrel scampering up a palm tree. "Ruhn and I were close for a few years when I was a teenager, and then we had a big fight. I stopped speaking to him after that. And things have been . . . well, you see how things are now."

"What'd you fight about?"

The morning mist swirled past as she fell quiet, as if debating what to reveal. She said, "It started off as a fight about his father.

What a piece of shit the Autumn King is, and how Ruhn was wrapped around his finger. It devolved into a screaming match about each other's flaws. I walked out when Ruhn said that I was flirting with his friends like a shameless hussy and to stay away from them."

Ruhn had said far worse than that, Hunt recalled. At Luna's Temple, he'd heard Bryce refer to him calling her a *half-breed slut*. "I've always known Danaan was an asshole, but even for him, that's low."

"It was," she admitted softly, "But . . . honestly, I think he was being protective of me. That's what the argument was about, really. He was acting like every other domineering Fae asshole out there. And just like my father."

Hunt asked, "You ever have contact with him?" There were a few dozen Fae nobles that might be monstrous enough to have prompted Ember Quinlan to bail all those years ago.

"Only when I can't avoid it. I think I hate him more than anyone else in Midgard. Except for Sabine." She sighed skyward, watching angels and witches zoom past above the buildings around them. "Who's number one on your shit list?"

Hunt waited until they'd passed a reptilian-looking Vanir typing on their phone before he replied, mindful of every camera mounted on the buildings or hidden in trees or garbage cans. "Sandriel."

"Ah." Only Sandriel's first name was necessary for anyone on Midgard. "From what I've seen on TV, she seems . . ." Bryce grimaced.

"Whatever you've seen is the pleasant version. The reality is ten times worse. She's a sadistic monster." To say the least. He added, "I was forced to . . . work for her for more than half a century. Until Micah." He couldn't say the word—*owned*. He'd never let Sandriel have that kind of power over him. "She and the commander of her triarii, Pollux, take cruelty and punishment to new levels." He clenched his jaw, shaking off the blood-soaked memories. "They're not stories to tell on a busy street." Or at all.

But she eyed him. "You ever want to talk about it, Athalar, I'm here."

She said it casually, but he could read the sincerity in her face. He nodded. "Likewise."

They passed the Old Square Gate, tourists already queued to take photos or touch the disk on the dial pad, gleefully handing over a drop of their power as they did so. None seemed aware of the body that had been found a few blocks away. In the drifting mist, the quartz Gate was almost ethereal, like it had been carved from ancient ice. Not one rainbow graced the buildings around it—not in the fog.

Syrinx sniffed at a trash can overflowing with food waste from the stands around the square. "You ever touch the disk and make a wish?" Bryce asked.

He shook his head. "I thought it was something only kids and tourists did."

"It is. But it's fun." She tossed her hair over a shoulder, smiling to herself. "I made a wish here when I was thirteen—when I visited the city for the first time. Ruhn took me."

Hunt lifted a brow. "What'd you wish for?"

"For my boobs to get bigger."

A laugh burst out of him, chasing away any lingering shadows that talk of Sandriel dragged up. But Hunt avoided looking at Bryce's chest as he said, "Seems your wish paid off, Quinlan." Understatement. Big, fucking, lace-covered understatement.

She chuckled. "Crescent City: Where dreams come true."

Hunt elbowed her ribs, unable to stop himself from making physical contact.

She batted him away. "What would you wish for, if you knew it'd come true?"

For his mother to be alive and safe and happy. For Sandriel and Micah and all the Archangels and Asteri to be dead. For his bargain with Micah to be over and the halo and slave tattoos removed. For the rigid hierarchies of the malakim to come crashing down.

But he couldn't say any of that. Wasn't ready to say those things aloud to her.

So Hunt said, "Since I'm perfectly happy with the size of *my* assets, I'd wish for you to stop being such a pain in my ass."

"Jerk." But Bryce grinned, and damn if the morning sun didn't finally make an appearance at the sight of it.

The library beneath Griffin Antiquities would have made even the Autumn King jealous.

Ruhn Danaan sat at the giant worktable in its heart, still needing a moment to take in the space—and the fire sprite who'd batted her eyelashes and asked if all his piercings had hurt.

Bryce and Athalar sat on the other side of the table, the former typing at a laptop, the latter leafing through a pile of old tomes. Lehabah lay on what seemed to be a doll's fainting couch, a digital tablet propped up before her, watching one of the more popular Vanir dramas.

"So," Bryce said without glancing up from the computer, "are you going to look around or sit there and gawk?"

Athalar snickered, but said nothing, his finger tracing over a line of text.

Ruhn glared at him. "What are you doing?"

"Researching the kristallos," Hunt said, his dark eyes lifting from the book. "I've killed about a dozen Type-Six demons over the centuries, and I want to see if there are any similarities."

"Is the kristallos a Type-Six?" Ruhn asked.

"I'm assuming it is," Hunt replied, studying the book again. "Type-Seven is only for the princes themselves, and given what this thing can do, I'd bet it'd be deemed a Six." He drummed his fingers on the ancient page. "I haven't seen any similarities, though."

Bryce hummed. "Maybe you're looking in the wrong spot. Maybe . . ." She angled her laptop toward Athalar, fingers flying. "We're looking for info on something that hasn't entered this world in fifteen thousand years. The fact that no one could ID it suggests it might not have made it into many of the history books, and only a handful of those books survived this long. But . . ." More typing, and Ruhn craned his neck to see the database she pulled up. "Where are we right now?" she asked Athalar.

"A library."

"An *antiquities* gallery, dumbass." A page loaded, full of images of ancient vases and amphorae, mosaics, and statues. She'd typed *demon + Fae* into the search bar. Bryce slid the laptop to Hunt. "Maybe we can find the kristallos in ancient art."

Hunt grumbled, but Ruhn noted the impressed gleam in his eyes before he began scanning through the pages of results.

"I've never met a prince before," Lehabah sighed from the couch.

"They're overrated," Ruhn said over a shoulder.

Athalar grunted his agreement.

"What is it like," the sprite asked, propping her fiery head on a burning fist, "to be the Chosen One?"

"Boring," Ruhn admitted. "Beyond the sword and some party tricks, there's not much to it."

"Can I see the Starsword?"

"I left it at home. I didn't feel like having to deal with tourists stopping me on every block, wanting to take pictures."

"Poor little prince," Bryce cooed.

Hunt grunted his agreement again, and Ruhn bit out, "You got something to say, Athalar?"

The angel's eyes lifted from the laptop. "She said it all."

Ruhn snarled, but Bryce asked, surveying them, "What's the deal with you two?"

"Oh, do tell," Lehabah pleaded, pausing her show to perk up on the couch.

Hunt went back to perusing the results. "We beat the shit out of each other at a party. Danaan's still sore about it."

Bryce's grin was the definition of shit-eating. "Why'd you fight?"

Ruhn snapped, "Because he's an arrogant asshole."

"Likewise," Hunt said, mouth curling in a half smile.

Bryce threw Lehabah a knowing look. "Boys and their pissing contests."

Lehabah made a prim little sound. "Not nearly as advanced as us ladies."

Ruhn rolled his eyes, surprised to find Athalar doing the same.

Bryce gestured to the endless shelves that filled the library. "Well, cousin," she said, "have at it. Let your Starborn powers guide you to enlightenment."

"Funny," he said, but began walking toward the shelves, scanning the titles. He paused at the various tanks and terrariums built into the bookcases, the small animals within wholly uninterested in his presence. He didn't dare ask if the rumors about them were true, especially not when Lehabah called over from her couch, "The tortoise is named Marlene."

Ruhn gave his sister an alarmed look, but Bryce was doing something on her phone.

Music began playing a moment later, trickling in from speakers hidden in the wood panels. Ruhn listened to the first strains of the song—just a guitar and two soaring, haunting female voices. "You're still into this band?" As a kid, she'd been obsessed with the sister folk duo.

"Josie and Laurel keep making good music, so I keep listening." She swiped at her phone.

Ruhn continued his idle browsing. "You always had really good taste." He tossed it out there—a rope into the stormy sea that was their relationship.

She didn't look up, but she said a shade quietly, "Thanks."

Athalar, wisely, didn't say a word.

Ruhn scanned the shelves, waiting to feel a tug toward anything beyond the sister who'd spoken more to him in the past few days than she had in nine years. The titles were in the common language, the Old Language of the Fae, the mer, and a few other alphabets he didn't recognize. "This collection is amazing."

Ruhn reached for a blue tome whose spine glittered with gold foil. *Words of the Gods*.

"Don't touch it," Lehabah warned. "It might bite."

Ruhn snatched back his hand as the book stirred, rumbling on the shelf. His shadows murmured inside him, readying to strike. He willed them to settle. "Why does the book *move*?"

"Because they're special—" Lehabah began.

"Enough, Lele," Bryce warned. "Ruhn, don't touch anything without permission."

"From you or the book?"

"Both," she said. As if in answer, a book high up on the shelf rustled. Ruhn craned his head to look, and saw a green tome . . . shining. Beckoning. His shadows murmured, as if in urging. All right, then.

It was a matter of moments to drag over the brass ladder and scale it. Bryce said, seemingly to the library itself, "Don't bother him," before Ruhn pulled the book from its resting place. He rolled his eyes at the title. *Great Romances of the Fae.*

Starborn power indeed. Tucking the book into the crook of his arm, he descended the ladder and returned to the table.

Bryce choked on a laugh at the title. "You sure that Starborn power isn't for finding smut?" She called to Lehabah, "This one's right up your alley."

Lehabah burned to a raspberry pink. "BB, you're horrible."

Athalar winked at him. "Enjoy."

"I will," Ruhn shot back, flipping open the book. His phone buzzed before he could begin. He fished it from his back pocket and glanced at the screen. "Dec's got the intel you wanted."

Bryce and Athalar went still. Ruhn opened the email, then his fingers hovered over the forwarding screen. "I, uh . . . is your email still the same?" he asked her. "And I don't have yours, Athalar."

Hunt rattled his off, but Bryce frowned at Ruhn for a long moment, as if weighing whether she wanted to open yet another door into her life. She then sighed and answered, "Yes, it's the same."

"Sent," Ruhn said, and opened up the attachment Declan had emailed over.

It was full of coordinates and their correlating locations. Danika's daily routine as Alpha of the Pack of Devils had her moving throughout the Old Square and beyond. Not to mention her healthy social life after sundown. The list covered everything from the apartment, the Den, the City Head office at the Comitium, a tattoo parlor, a burger joint, too many pizza places to count, bars, a concert venue, the CCU sunball arena, hair salons, the gym . . . Fuck, had she ever gotten any sleep? The list dated back two weeks prior to her death. From the silence around the table, he knew Bryce and Hunt were also skimming over the locations. Then—

Surprise lit Hunt's dark eyes as he looked to her. Bryce murmured, "Danika wasn't merely on duty near Luna's Temple around that time—this says Danika was stationed *at* the temple for the two days before the Horn was stolen. And during the night of the blackout."

Hunt asked, "You think she saw whoever took it and they killed her to cover it up?"

Could it be that easy? Ruhn prayed it was.

Bryce shook her head. "If Danika saw the Horn being stolen, she would have reported it." She sighed again. "Danika wasn't usually stationed at the temple, but Sabine often switched her schedule around for spite. Maybe Danika had some of the Horn's scent on her from being on duty and the demon tracked her down."

"Go through it again," Ruhn urged. "Maybe there's something you're missing."

Bryce's mouth twisted to the side, the portrait of skepticism, but Hunt said, "Better than nothing." Bryce held the angel's stare for longer than most people deemed wise.

Nothing good could come of it—Bryce and Athalar working together. Living together.

But Ruhn kept his mouth shut, and began reading.

"Any good sex scenes yet?" Bryce asked Ruhn idly, going over Danika's location data for the third time. The first few of those locations, she'd realized, had been to Philip Briggs's bomb lab just outside the city walls. Including the night of the bust itself.

She still remembered Danika and Connor limping into the apartment that night, after making the bust on Briggs and his Keres group two years ago. Danika had been fine, but Connor had sported a split lip and black eye that screamed some shit had gone down. They never told her what, and she hadn't asked. She'd just made Connor sit at that piece-of-shit kitchen table and let her clean him up.

He'd kept his eyes fixed on her face, her mouth, the entire time she'd gently dabbed his lip. She'd known then and there that it was coming—that Connor was done waiting. That five years of friendship, of dancing around each other, was now going to change, and he'd make his move soon. It didn't matter that she'd been dating Reid. Connor had let her take care of him, his eyes near-glowing, and she'd known it was time.

When Ruhn didn't immediately respond to her taunting, Bryce looked up from the laptop. Her brother had kept reading—and didn't seem to hear her. "Ruhn."

Hunt halted his own searching through the gallery database. "Danaan."

Ruhn snapped his head up, blinking. Bryce asked, "You found something?"

"Yes and no," Ruhn said, sitting back in his chair. "This is just a three-page account of Prince Pelias and his bride, Lady Helena. But I didn't realize that Pelias was actually the high general for a Fae Queen named Theia when they entered this world during the Crossing—and Helena was her daughter. From what it sounds like, Queen Theia was *also* Starborn, and her daughter possessed the same power. Theia had a younger daughter with the same gift, but only Lady Helena gets mentioned." Ruhn cleared his throat and read, "*Night-haired Helena, from whose golden skin poured starlight and shadows*. It seems like Pelias was one of several Fae back then with the Starborn power."

Bryce blinked. "So? What does it have to do with the Horn?"

"It mentions here that the sacred objects were made only for Fae like them. That the Horn worked only when that starlight flowed through it, when it was filled with power. This claims that the Starborn magic, in addition to a bunch of other crap, can be channeled through the sacred objects—bringing them to life. I sure as fuck have never been able to do anything like that, even with the Starsword. But it says that's why the Prince of the Pit had to steal Pelias's blood to make the kristallos to hunt the Horn—it contained that essence. I think the Horn could have been wielded by any of them, though."

Hunt said, "But if the Prince of the Pit had gotten his hands on the Horn, he wouldn't be able to use it unless he had a Starborn Fae to operate it." He nodded to Ruhn. "Even if whoever wants the Horn now finds it, they'd have to use you."

Ruhn considered. "But let's not forget that whoever is summoning the demon to track the Horn—and kill these people—doesn't *have* the Horn. Someone else stole it. So we're essentially looking for two different people: the killer and whoever has the Horn."

"Well, the Horn is broken anyway," Bryce said.

Ruhn tapped the book. "Permanently broken, apparently. It says here that once it was cracked, the Fae claimed it could only be repaired by *light that is not light; magic that is not magic*. Basically a convoluted way of saying there's no chance in Hel of it ever working again."

Hunt said, "So we need to find out why someone would want it, then." He frowned at Ruhn. "Your father wants it for what—some Fae PR campaign about the good old days of Faedom?"

Ruhn snorted, and Bryce smiled slightly. With lines like that, Athalar was in danger of becoming one of her favorite people. Ruhn said, "Basically, yeah. The Fae have been *declining*, according to him, for the past several thousand years. He claims our ancestors could burn entire forests to ash with half a thought—while he can probably torch a grove, and not much more." Ruhn's jaw tightened. "It drives him nuts that my Chosen One powers are barely more than a kernel."

Bryce knew her own lack of power had been part of her father's disgust with her.

Proof of the Fae's failing influence.

She felt Hunt's eyes on her, as if he could sense the bitterness that rippled through her. She half lied to him, "My own father never had a lick of interest in me for the same reason."

"Especially after your visit to the Oracle," Ruhn said.

Hunt's brows rose, but Bryce shook her head at him, scowling. "It's a long story."

Hunt again looked at her in that considering, all-seeing way. So

Bryce peered over at Ruhn's tome, skimmed a few lines, and then looked back up at Ruhn. "This whole section is about your fancy Avallen cousins. Shadow-walking, mind-reading . . . I'm surprised they don't claim they're Starborn."

"They wish they were," Ruhn muttered. "They're a bunch of pricks."

She had a vague memory of Ruhn telling her the details about why, exactly, he felt that way, but asked, "No mind-reading for you?"

"It's mind-speaking," he grumbled, "and it has nothing to do with the Starborn stuff. Or this case."

Hunt, apparently, seemed to agree, because he cut in, "What if we asked the Oracle about the Horn? Maybe she could see why someone would want a broken relic."

Bryce and Ruhn straightened. But she said, "We'd be better off going to the mystics."

Hunt cringed. "The mystics are some dark, fucked-up shit. We'll try the Oracle first."

"Well, I'm not going," Bryce said quickly.

Hunt's eyes darkened. "Because of what happened at your visit?"

"Right," she said tightly.

Ruhn cut in and said to Hunt, "You go, then."

Hunt snickered. "You have a bad experience, too, Danaan?"

Bryce found herself carefully watching her brother. Ruhn had never mentioned the Oracle to her. But he just shrugged and said, "Yeah."

Hunt threw up his hands. "Fine, assholes. I'll go. I've never been. It always seemed too gimmicky."

It wasn't. Bryce blocked out the image of the golden sphinx who'd sat before the hole in the floor of her dim, black chamber—how that human woman's face had monitored her every breath.

"You'll need an appointment," she managed to say.

Silence fell. A buzzing interrupted it, and Hunt sighed as he pulled out his phone. "I gotta take this," he said, and didn't wait for them to reply before striding up the stairs out of the library. A moment later, the front door to the gallery shut.

With Lehabah still watching her show behind them, Ruhn quietly said to Bryce, "Your power levels never mattered to me, Bryce. You know that, right?"

She went back to looking through Danika's data. "Yeah. I know." She lifted an eyebrow. "What's your deal with the Oracle?"

His face shuttered. "Nothing. She told me everything the Autumn King wanted to hear."

"What—you're upset that it wasn't something as disastrous as mine?"

Ruhn rose from his seat, piercings glittering in the firstlights. "Look, I've got an Aux meeting this afternoon that I need to prep for, but I'll see you later."

"Sure."

Ruhn paused, as if debating saying something else, but continued toward the stairs and out.

"Your cousin is dreamy," Lehabah sighed from her couch.

"I thought Athalar was your one true love," Bryce said.

"Can't they both be?"

"Considering how terrible they are at sharing, I don't think it'll end well for any of you."

Her email pinged on the laptop. Since her phone was in shards in the rubble of the Raven, Hunt had emailed, *Saw your cousin leave. We're heading to the Comitium in five minutes.*

She wrote back, *Don't give me orders, Athalar.*

Four minutes, sweetheart.

I told you: don't call me sweetheart.

Three minutes.

Growling, she stood from the table, rubbing her leg. Her heels were already killing her, and knowing Athalar, he'd make her walk the entire Comitium complex. Her dress would look ridiculous with a different set of shoes, but fortunately, she kept a change of clothes in the bottom drawer of the library desk, mostly in case of a rainy day that threatened to ruin whatever she was wearing.

Lehabah said, "It's nice—to have company down here."

Something in Bryce's chest wrenched, but she said, "I'll be back later."

30

Hunt kept a casual distance from Bryce as she walked beside him through the Comitium lobby to the bank of elevators that would take them up to the 33rd's barracks. The other elevator bays dispersed through the centralized, glass-enclosed atrium led to the four other towers of the complex: one for the City Heads' meeting rooms and the running of Lunathion, one for Micah as both residence and official office, one for general administrative bullshit, and one for public meetings and events. Thousands upon thousands of people lived and worked within its walls, but even with the bustling lobby, Quinlan somehow managed to stand out.

She'd changed into red suede flats and a button-up white blouse tucked into tight jeans, and tied her silken mass of hair into a high ponytail that swayed sassily with every step she took, matching Hunt stride for stride.

He placed his palm against the round disk next to the elevator doors, clearing him for access to his floor thirty levels up. Usually, he flew to the barracks' landing balcony—half for ease, half to avoid the busybodies who were now gawking at them across the lobby floor, no doubt wondering if Hunt was bringing Quinlan here to fuck her or interrogate her.

The legionary who lounged on a low-lying couch wasn't particularly skilled in stealing covert glances at her ass. Bryce looked over a shoulder, as if some extra sense told her someone was watching, and gave the soldier a smile.

The legionary stiffened. Bryce bit her lower lip, her lashes lowering slightly.

Hunt punched the elevator button, hard, even as the male gave Bryce a half smile Hunt was pretty sure the bastard threw at any female who came his way. As low-level grunts in a very large machine, legionaries—even those in the famed 33rd—couldn't be picky.

The elevator doors opened, and legionaries and business types filed out, those without wings careful not to step on anyone's feathers. And all of them careful not to look Hunt in the eye.

It wasn't that he was unfriendly. If someone offered him a smile, he usually made an attempt at returning it. But they'd all heard the stories. All knew whom he worked for—every one of his *masters*—and what he did for them.

They'd be more comfortable getting into an elevator with a starved tiger.

So Hunt kept back, minimizing any chance of contact. Bryce whirled to face the elevator, that ponytail nearly whipping him in the face.

"Watch that thing," Hunt snapped as the elevator finally emptied and they walked in. "You'll take my eye out."

She leaned nonchalantly against the far glass wall. Mercifully, no one got inside with them. Hunt wasn't stupid enough to think that it was by pure chance.

They'd made only one stop on their way here, to buy her a replacement phone for the one she'd lost at the club. She'd even coughed up a few extra marks for a standard protection spell package on the phone.

The glass-and-chrome store had been mostly empty, but he hadn't failed to notice how many would-be shoppers spied him through the windows and kept far away. Bryce hadn't seemed to notice, and while they'd waited for the employee to bring out a new phone for her, she'd asked him for his own, so she could trawl the news feeds for any updates on the club attack. Somehow, she'd wound up going through his photos. Or lack of them.

"There are thirty-six photos on this phone," she said flatly.

Hunt had frowned. "So?"

She scrolled through the paltry collection. "Going back *four years*." To when he'd arrived in Lunathion and gotten his first phone and taste of life without a monster ruling over him. Bryce had gagged as she opened a photo of a severed leg on a bloody carpet. "What the *fuck*?"

"I sometimes get called to crime scenes and have to snap a few for evidence."

"Are any of these people from your bargain with—"

"No," he said. "I don't take pictures of them."

"There are thirty-six photos on your four-year-old phone, and all of them are of dismembered bodies," she said. Someone gasped across the store.

Hunt gritted his teeth. "Say it a little louder, Quinlan."

She frowned. "You never take any others?"

"Of what?"

"Oh, I don't know—of *life*? A pretty flower or good meal or something?"

"What's the point?"

She'd blinked, then shook her head. "Weirdo."

And before he could stop her, she'd angled his phone in front of her, beamed from ear to ear, and snapped a photo of herself before she handed it back to him. "There. One non-corpse photo."

Hunt had rolled his eyes, but pocketed the phone.

The elevator hummed around them, shooting upward. Bryce watched the numbers rise. "Do you know who that legionary was?" she asked casually.

"Which one? There was the one drooling on the Traskian carpet, the one with his tongue rolled out on the floor, or the one who was staring at your ass like it was going to talk to him?"

She laughed. "They must keep you all starved for sex in these barracks if the presence of one female sends them into such a tizzy. So—do you know his name? The one who wanted to have a chat with my ass."

"No. There are three thousand of us in the 33rd alone." He

glanced at her sidelong, watching her monitor the rising floor numbers. "Maybe some guy that checks out your ass before he says hello isn't someone worth knowing."

Her brows lifted as the elevator stopped and the doors opened. "That is *precisely* the kind of person I'm looking for." She stepped into the simple hallway, and he followed her—realizing as she paused that *he* knew where they were going, and she only faked it.

He turned left. Their footsteps echoed off the tan granite tile of the long corridor. The stone was cracked and chipped in spots—from dropped weapons, magical pissing contests, actual brawls—but still polished enough that he could see both their reflections.

Quinlan took in the hall, the names on each door. "Males only, or are you mixed?"

"Mixed," he told her. "Though there are more males than females in the 33rd."

"Do you have a girlfriend? Boyfriend? Someone whose ass *you* gawk at?"

He shook his head, trying to fight the ice in his veins as he stopped before his door, opened it, and let her inside. Trying to block out the image of Shahar plunging to the earth, Sandriel's sword through her sternum, both angels' white wings streaming blood. Both sisters screaming, faces nearly mirror images of each other. "I was born a bastard." He shut the door behind them, watching her survey the small room. The bed was big enough to fit his wings, but there wasn't space for much else beyond an armoire and dresser, a desk stacked with books and papers, and discarded weapons.

"So?"

"So my mother had no money, and no distinguished bloodline that might have made up for it. I don't exactly have females lining up for me, despite this face of mine." His laugh was bitter as he opened the cheap pine armoire and pulled out a large duffel. "I had someone once, someone who didn't care about status, but it didn't end well." Each word singed his tongue.

Bryce wrapped her arms around herself, nails digging into the filmy silk of her shirt. She seemed to realize whom he'd alluded to.

She glanced around, as if casting for things to say, and somehow settled on, "When did you make the Drop?"

"I was twenty-eight."

"Why then?"

"My mother had just died." Sorrow filled her eyes, and he couldn't stand the look, couldn't stand to open up the wound, so he added, "I was reeling afterward. So I got a public Anchor and made the Drop. But it didn't make a difference. If I'd inherited the power of an Archangel or a dormouse, once the tattoos got inked on me five years later, it cut me off at the knees."

He could hear her hand stroke his blanket. "You ever regret the angels' rebellion?"

Hunt glanced over a shoulder to find her leaning against the bed. "No one's ever asked me that." No one dared. But she held his stare. Hunt admitted, "I don't know what I think."

He let his stare convey the rest. *And I wouldn't say a fucking word about it in this place.*

She nodded. Then looked at the walls—no artwork, no posters. "Not one to decorate?"

He stuffed clothes into the duffel, remembering she had a washing machine in the apartment. "Micah can trade me whenever he wants. It's asking for bad luck to put down roots like that."

She rubbed her arms, even though the room was warm, almost stuffy. "If he'd died that night, what would have happened to you? To every Fallen and slave he owns?"

"Our deed of ownership passes on to whoever replaces him." He hated every word out of his mouth. "If he doesn't have anyone listed, the assets get divided among the other Archangels."

"Who wouldn't honor his bargain with you."

"Definitely not." Hunt started on the weapons stashed in his desk drawers.

He could feel her watching his every movement, as if counting each blade and gun he pulled out. She asked, "If you achieved your freedom, what would you do?"

Hunt checked the ammo for the guns he had on his desk, and

she wandered over to watch. He tossed a few into his bag. She picked up a long knife as if it were a dirty sock. “I heard your lightning is unique among the angels—even the Archangels can’t produce it.”

He tucked in his wings. “Yeah?”

A shrug. “So why is Isaiah the Commander of the 33rd?”

He took the knife from her and set it in his bag. “Because I piss off too many people and don’t give a shit that I do.” It had been that way even before Mount Hermon. Yet Shahar had seen it as a strength. Made him her general. He’d tried and failed to live up to that honor.

Bryce gave him a conspirator’s smile. “We have something in common after all, Athalar.”

Fine. The angel wasn’t so bad. He had patched her up after the bombing with no male swaggering. And he had one Hel of a reason to want this case solved. And he pissed Ruhn off to no end.

As he’d finished packing, he’d gotten a call from Isaiah, who said that their request to see Briggs had been approved—but that it would take a few days to get Briggs cleaned up and brought over from Adrestia Prison. Bryce had chosen to ignore what, exactly, that implied about Briggs’s current state.

The only bright spot was that Isaiah informed Hunt that the Oracle had made room for him on her schedule first thing tomorrow.

Bryce eyed Hunt as they boarded the elevator once again, her stomach flipping as they plunged toward the central lobby of the Comitium. Whatever clearance Hunt had, it somehow included overriding the elevator commands to stop at other floors. Sweet.

She’d never really known any of the malakim beyond seeing the legionaries on patrol, or their rich elite strutting like peacocks around town. Most preferred the rooftop lounges in the CBD. And since half-breed sluts weren’t allowed into those, she’d never had a chance to take one home.

Well, now she *was* taking one home, though not in the way she’d once imagined while ogling their muscles. She and Danika had once spent two solid summer weeks of lunch breaks sitting on a rooftop adjacent to a legion training space. With the heat, the male angels had stripped down to their pants while they sparred. And then got sweaty. Very, very sweaty.

She and Danika would have kept going every lunch hour if they hadn't been caught by the building's janitor, who called them perverts and permanently locked access to the roof.

The elevator slowed to a stop, setting her stomach flipping again. The doors opened, and they were greeted by a wall of impatient-looking legionaries—who all made sure to rearrange their expressions to carefully noncommittal when they beheld Hunt.

The Shadow of Death. She'd spied the infamous helmet in his room, sitting beside his desk. He'd left it behind, thank the gods.

The Comitium lobby beyond the elevators was packed. Full of wings and halos and those enticing muscled bodies, all facing the front doors, craning their necks to see over each other but none launching into the atrium airspace—

Hunt went rigid at the edge of the crowd that had nearly blocked off the barracks elevator bank. Bryce made it all of one step toward him before the elevator to their right opened and Isaiah rushed out, halting as he spied Hunt. "I just heard—"

The ripple of power at the other end of the lobby made her legs buckle.

As if that power had knocked the crowd to the ground, everyone knelt and bowed their heads.

Leaving the three of them with a perfect view of the Archangel who stood at the giant glass doors of the atrium, Micah at her side.

31

Sandriel turned toward Hunt, Bryce, and Isaiah at the same moment Micah did. Recognition flared in the dark-haired female's eyes as that gaze landed on Hunt, skipped Bryce entirely, and took in Isaiah.

Bryce recognized her, of course. She was on television often enough that no one on the planet wouldn't recognize her.

A step ahead, Hunt was a trembling live wire. She'd never seen him like this.

"Get down," Isaiah murmured, and knelt.

Hunt didn't move. Wouldn't, Bryce realized. People looked over their shoulders as they remained on their knees.

Isaiah muttered, "Pollux isn't with her. Just fucking kneel." Pollux—the Hammer. Some of the tension went out of Hunt, but he remained standing.

He looked lost, stranded, somewhere between rage and terror. Not even a flicker of lightning at his fingertips. Bryce stepped closer to his side, flicking her ponytail over a shoulder. She took her brand-new phone out of her pocket, making sure the sound was cranked up.

So everyone could hear the loud *click click click* as she snapped photos of the two Archangels, then turned, angling herself and the phone, to get a shot with herself *and* the Governors in the background—

People murmured in shock. Bryce tilted her head to the side, smiling wide, and snapped another.

Then she turned to Hunt, who was still trembling, and said as flippantly as she could muster, "Thanks for bringing me to see them. Shall we?"

She didn't give Hunt the chance to do anything as she looped her arm through his, turned them both around before taking a photo with him and the stone-faced Archangels and the gawking crowd in the background, and then tugged him back toward the elevator bank.

That's why some legionaries had been rushing to get on. To flee.

Maybe there was another exit beyond the wall of glass doors. The crowd rose to their feet.

She pushed the button, praying it gave her access to any of the tower's floors. Hunt was still shaking. Bryce gripped his arm tight, tapping her foot on the tiles as—

"Explain yourself." Micah stood behind them, blocking the crowd from the elevator bank.

Hunt closed his eyes.

Bryce swallowed and turned, nearly whipping Hunt in the face with her hair again. "Well, I heard that you had a special guest, so I asked Hunt to bring me so I could get a photo—"

"Do not lie."

Hunt opened his eyes, then slowly turned to the Governor. "I had to pick up supplies and clothes. Isaiah gave me the go-ahead to bring her here."

As if speaking his name had summoned him, the Commander of the 33rd pushed through the line of guards. Isaiah said, "It's true, Your Grace. Hunt was grabbing necessities, and didn't want to risk leaving Miss Quinlan alone while he did it."

The Archangel looked at Isaiah, then Hunt. Then her.

Micah's gaze roved over her body. Her face. She knew that gaze, that slow study.

Too fucking bad that Micah was about as warm as a fish at the bottom of a mountain lake.

Too fucking bad he'd used Hunt like a weapon, dangling his freedom like a dog treat.

Too fucking bad he often worked with her father on city matters, and on House business—too bad he *reminded* her of her father.

Boo. Fucking. Hoo.

She said to Micah, "It was nice to see you again, Your Grace." Then the elevator doors opened, as if some god had willed them to make a good exit.

She nudged Hunt inside, and was following him in when a cold, strong hand gripped her elbow. She batted her eyelashes up at Micah as he stopped her between the elevator doors. Hunt didn't seem to be breathing.

As if he were waiting for the Governor to rescind his deal.

But Micah purred, "I would like to take you to dinner, Bryce Quinlan."

She pulled out of his grip, joining Hunt in the elevator. And as the doors closed, she looked the Archangel of Valbara full in the face. "Not interested," she said.

Hunt had known Sandriel was coming, but running into her today . . . She must have wanted to surprise them all, if Isaiah hadn't known. Wanted to catch the Governor and the legion off guard and see what this place was like *before* the pomp and circumstance made their defenses seem stronger, their wealth deeper. *Before* Micah could call in one of his other legions to make them look that much more impressive.

What piss-poor fucking luck that they'd run into her.

But at least Pollux hadn't been there. Not yet.

The elevator shot up again, and Bryce stayed silent. Holding herself.

Not interested.

He doubted Micah Domitus had ever heard those words before.

He doubted Sandriel ever had someone snap photos of her like that.

All he'd been able to think about while he beheld Sandriel was the weight of his knife at his side. All he could smell was the reek of her arena, blood and shit and piss and sand—

Then Bryce had made her move. Played that irreverent, vapid party girl she wanted them to believe she was, that he'd believed she was, snapping those photos, giving him an out—

Hunt placed his hand against the disk beside the button panel and punched in a different floor, overriding wherever the elevator had been taking them. "We can leave from the landing." His voice was like gravel. He always forgot—just how similar Sandriel and Shahar looked. Not identical twins, but their coloring and build had been nearly the same. "I'll have to carry you, though."

She twirled the silken length of her ponytail around a wrist, unaware that she bared the golden column of her throat to him with the movement.

Not interested.

She'd sounded certain. Not gleeful, not gloating, but . . . firm.

Hunt didn't dare consider how this rejection might affect his bargain with Micah—to wonder if Micah would somehow blame Hunt for it.

Bryce asked, "No back door?"

"There is, but we'd have to go down again."

He could feel her questions bubbling up, and before she could ask any of them he said, "Sandriel's Second, Pollux, is even worse than she is. When he arrives, avoid him at all costs."

He couldn't bring himself to dredge up the list of horrors Pollux had inflicted on innocents.

Bryce clicked her tongue. "Like my path will ever cross theirs if I can help it."

After that show in the lobby, it might. But Hunt didn't tell her that Sandriel wasn't above petty revenge for slights and minor offenses. Didn't tell her that Sandriel would likely never forget Bryce's face. Might already be asking Micah who she was.

The doors opened onto a quiet upper level. The halls were dim, hushed, and he led her into a labyrinth of gym equipment. A broad path cut through the gear directly to the wall of windows—and the launch balcony beyond. There was no railing, just an open jut of stone. She balked.

"I've never dropped anyone," he promised.

She gingerly followed him outside. The dry wind whipped at them. Far below, the city street was packed with onlookers and news vans. Above them, angels were flying, some fleeing outright, some circling the five spires of the Comitium to get a glimpse of Sandriel from afar.

Hunt bent, sliding a hand under Bryce's knees, bracing another on her back, and picked her up. Her scent filled his senses, washing away the last of the memory of that reeking dungeon.

"Thank you," he said, meeting her stare. "For bailing me out back there."

She shrugged as best she could in his grip, but winced as he stepped closer to the edge.

"That was fast thinking," he went on. "Ridiculous on so many levels, but I owe you."

She slid her arms around his neck, her grip near-strangling. "You helped me out last night. We're even."

Hunt didn't give her a chance to change her mind as he beat his wings in a powerful push and leapt off the edge. She clung to him, tight enough to hurt, and he held her firmly, the duffel strapped across his chest awkwardly banging against his thigh.

"Are you even watching?" he asked over the wind as he sent them sailing hard and fast, flying up, up, up the side of the adjacent skyscraper in the Central Business District.

"Absolutely not," she said in his ear.

He chuckled as they leveled out, cruising above the reaching pinnacles of the CBD, the Istros a winding sparkle to their right, the mist-shrouded isle of the Bone Quarter looming behind it. To the left, he could just make out the walls of the city, and then the wide-open land beyond the Angels' Gate. No houses or buildings or roads out there. Nothing but the aerialport. But at the Gate to their right—the Merchants' Gate in the Meat Market—the broad, pale line of the Western Road shot into the rolling, cypress-dotted hills.

A pleasant, beautiful city—in the midst of pleasant, beautiful countryside.

In Pangera, the cities were little more than pens for the Vanir to trap and feed on the humans—and their children. No wonder the humans had risen up. No wonder they were shredding that territory with their chemical bombs and machines.

A shiver of rage ran down his spine at the thought of those children, and he made himself look toward the city again. The Central Business District was separated from the Old Square by the clear dividing line of Ward Avenue. The sunlight glowed off the white stones of Luna's Temple—and, as if in a mirror reflection directly across from it, seemed to be absorbed by the black-domed Oracle's Temple. His destination tomorrow morning.

But Hunt looked beyond the Old Square, to where the green of Five Roses sparkled in the muggy haze. Towering cypresses and palms rose up, along with glittering bursts of magic. In Moonwood, more oak trees—less magic frills. Hunt didn't bother looking anywhere else. Asphodel Meadows wasn't much to behold. Yet the Meadows was a luxury development compared to the human districts in Pangera.

"Why'd you want to live in the Old Square?" he asked after several minutes of flying in silence, with only the song of the wind to listen to.

She still wasn't looking, and he began a gentle descent toward her little section of the Old Square, just a block off the river and a few blocks from the Heart Gate. Even from that distance, he could see it, the clear quartz glinting like an icy spear toward the gray sky.

"It's the heart of the city," she said, "why not be there?"

"FiRo is cleaner."

"And full of Fae peacocks who sneer at *half-breeds*." She spat out the term.

"Moonwood?"

"Sabine's territory?" A harsh laugh, and she pulled back to look at him. Her smattering of freckles crinkled as she scrunched her face. "Honestly, the Old Square is about the only safe place for someone like me. Plus, it's close to work *and* I've got my pick of restaurants, music halls, and museums. I never need to leave."

"But you do—you go all over the city on your morning runs. Why a different route so often?"

"Keeps it fresh and fun."

Her building became clearer, the roof empty. A firepit, some lounge chairs, and a grill occupied most of it. Hunt banked, circling back, and smoothly landed, carefully setting her down. She clung to him long enough to get her legs steady, then stepped back.

He adjusted the duffel, heading for the roof door. He held it open for her, firstlight warming the stairwell beyond. "Did you mean what you said—to Micah?"

She plunked down the stairs, the ponytail bobbing. "Of course I did. Why the Hel would I want to go out with him?"

"He's the Governor of Valbara."

"So? Just because I saved his life, that doesn't mean I'm destined to be his girlfriend. It'd be like banging a statue anyway."

Hunt smirked. "In all fairness, the females who have been with him say otherwise."

She unlocked her door, mouth twisting. "Like I said, not interested."

"You sure it's not because you're just avoiding—"

"See, that right there is the problem. You and the whole rest of the world seem to think I exist *just* to find someone like him. That *of course* I can't be genuinely *not* interested, because why *wouldn't* I want a big, strong male to protect me? Surely if I'm pretty and single, the second *any* powerful Vanir shows interest, I'm *bound* to drop my panties. In fact, I didn't even have a *life* until he showed up—never had good sex, never felt *alive*—"

Darkest Hel, this woman. "You've got a real chip on your shoulder there, you know."

Bryce snickered. "You make it really fucking easy, *you know*."

Hunt crossed his arms. She crossed hers.

That stupid fucking ponytail seemed to cross its proverbial arms, too.

"So," Hunt said through his teeth as he dumped his duffel on the ground, clothes and weapons thumping hard. "You gonna come with me to the Oracle tomorrow or what?"

"Oh no, Athalar." Her purred words ran over his skin, and her smile was pure wickedness. Hunt braced himself for whatever was about to come out of her mouth. Even as he found himself looking forward to it. "You get to deal with her alone."

32

After dropping off his gear at the apartment, Hunt trailed Bryce back to work, where she said she intended to look through Danika's location data from Declan and cross-reference it with her own list—and the murder scenes so far.

But the thought of sitting underground for another few hours grated enough that he found himself sitting on the roof instead. He needed the fresh, open air. Even if angels were still flying past—leaving the city. He made a point not to look toward the Comitium, looming at his back.

Just before sundown, Syrinx in tow, Bryce emerged from the gallery with a grim expression that matched Hunt's own.

"Nothing?" he asked, landing on the sidewalk beside her.

"Nothing," she confirmed.

"We'll look tomorrow with fresh eyes." Maybe there was something they were missing. Today had been long and awful and weird, and he was more than ready to collapse on her couch.

He asked as casually as he could, "There's a big sunball game on tonight. You mind if I watch it?"

She glanced at him sidelong, her brows rising.

"What?" he asked, unable to keep the corner of his mouth from twitching upward.

"It's just . . . you're such . . . a *guy*." She waved a hand at him. "With the sports and stuff."

"Females like sports as much as males."

She rolled her eyes. "This sunball-watching person doesn't fit with my mental image of the Shadow of Death."

"Sorry to disappoint." Hunt's turn to lift a brow. "What *do* you think I do with my spare time?"

"I don't know. I assumed you cursed at the stars and brooded and plotted revenge on all your enemies."

She didn't know the half of it. But Hunt let out a low chuckle. "Again, sorry to disappoint."

Her eyes crinkled with amusement, the last of the day's sun lighting them into liquid gold. He forced himself to monitor the streets around them.

They were a block from Bryce's apartment when Hunt's phone rang. She tensed, peering at his screen the same moment he did.

The phone rang a second time. They both stared at the name that popped up, pedestrians streaming past.

"You gonna answer it?" Bryce asked quietly.

It rang a third time.

Hunt knew. Before he hit the button, he knew.

Which was why he stepped away from Quinlan, putting the phone to his ear just as he said blandly, "Hi, boss."

"I have work for you tonight," Micah said.

Hunt's gut twisted. "Sure."

"I hope I'm not interrupting your fun with Miss Quinlan."

"We're good," Hunt said tightly.

Micah's pause was loaded. "What occurred in the lobby this morning is never to happen again. Understood?"

"Yes." He bit out the word. But he said it—and meant it—because the alternative to Micah was now staying at the Governor's residence in the Comitium. Because Sandriel would have drawn out his punishment for refusing to bow, for embarrassing her, for days, weeks. Months.

But Micah would give him this warning, and make him do this job tonight to remind him where the fuck he stood in the pecking order, and then that would be that.

"Good," Micah said. "The file's waiting at your room in the barracks." He paused, as if sensing the question now burning through Hunt. "The offer still stands, Athalar. Don't make me reconsider." The call ended.

Hunt clenched his jaw hard enough to hurt.

Quinlan's forehead wrinkled with concern. "Everything okay?"

Hunt slid the phone into his pocket. "It's fine." He resumed walking. "Just legion business." Not a lie. Not entirely.

The glass doors to her building opened. Hunt nodded toward the lobby. "You head up. I've got something to do. I'll call if we get the date and time for Briggs."

Her amber eyes narrowed. Yeah, she saw right through it. Or rather, heard everything he wasn't saying. Knew what Micah had ordered him to do.

But she said, "All right." She turned toward the lobby, but added over her shoulder, "Good luck."

He didn't bother answering before he shot into the skies, phone already to his ear as he called Justinian to ask him to play sentry for a few hours. Justinian whined about missing the sunball game, but Hunt pulled rank, earning a grumbled promise that the angel would be at the adjacent rooftop in ten minutes.

Justinian arrived in eight. Leaving his brother-in-arms to it, Hunt sucked in a breath of dusty, dry air, the Istros a teal ribbon to his left, and went to do what he did best.

"Please."

It was always the same word. The only word people tended to say when the Umbra Mortis stood before them.

Through the blood splattered on his helmet, Hunt regarded the male cougar shifter cowering before him. His clawed hands shook as he left them upraised. "Please," the man sobbed.

Every utterance dragged Hunt further away. Until the arm he

outstretched was distant, until the gun he aimed at the male's head was just a bit of metal.

A death for a death.

"Please."

The male had done horrible things. Unspeakable things. He deserved this. Deserved worse.

"Pleasepleaseplease."

Hunt was nothing but a shadow, a wisp of life, an instrument of death.

He was nothing and no one at all.

"Ple—"

Hunt's finger curled on the trigger.

Hunt returned early. Well, early for him.

Thankfully, no one was in the barracks bathroom while he showered off the blood. Then sat under the scalding spray for so long that he lost track of time.

He would have stayed longer had he not known that Justinian was waiting.

So he patched himself up, pieced himself together. Half crawled out of the boiling-hot shower and into the person he was when he wasn't forced to put a bullet between someone's eyes.

He made a few stops before getting back to Bryce's apartment. But he made it back, relieving Justinian from his duties, and walked through Bryce's door at eleven.

She was in her bedroom, the door shut, but Syrinx let out a little yowl of welcome from within. Her scolding hush was proof that she'd heard Hunt return. Hunt prayed she wouldn't come into the hall. Words were still beyond him.

Her doorknob turned. But Hunt was already at his room, and didn't dare look across the expanse of the great room as she said tightly, "You're back."

"Yeah," he choked out.

Even across the room, he could feel her questions. But she said softly, "I recorded the game for you. If you still want to watch it."

Something tightened unbearably in his chest. But Hunt didn't look back.

He slipped into his room with a mumbled "Night," and shut the door behind him.

33

The Oracle's black chamber reeked of sulfur and roasted meat—the former from the natural gases rising from the hole in the center of the space, the latter from the pile of bull bones currently smoldering atop the altar against the far wall, an offering to Ogenas, Keeper of Mysteries.

After last night, what he'd done, a sacred temple was the last place he wanted to be. The last place he deserved to be.

The twenty-foot doors shut behind Hunt as he strode across the silent chamber, aiming for the hole in the center and wall of smoke behind it. His eyes burned with the various acrid scents, and he summoned a wind to keep them out of his face.

Behind the smoke, a figure moved. "I wondered when the Shadow of Death would darken my chamber," a lovely voice said. Young, full of light and amusement—and yet tinged with ancient cruelty.

Hunt halted at the edge of the hole, avoiding the urge to peer into the endless blackness. "I won't take much of your time," he said, his voice swallowed by the room, the pit, the smoke.

"I shall give you what time Ogenas offers." The smoke parted, and he sucked in a breath at the being that emerged.

Sphinxes were rare—only a few dozen walked the earth, and all of them had been called to the service of the gods. No one knew how old they were, and this one before him . . . She was so beautiful he forgot what to do with his body. The golden lioness's form moved with fluid grace, pacing the other side of the hole, weaving in and out of the mist. Golden wings lay folded against the slender body, shimmering as if they were crafted from molten metal. And above that winged lion's body . . . the golden-haired woman's face was as flawless as Shahar's had been.

No one knew her name. She was simply her title: Oracle. He wondered if she was so old that she'd forgotten her true name.

The sphinx blinked large brown eyes at him, lashes brushing against her light brown cheeks. "Ask me your question, and I shall tell you what the smoke whispers to me." The words rumbled over his bones, luring him in. Not in the way he sometimes let himself be lured in by beautiful females, but in the manner that a spider might lure a fly to its web.

Maybe Quinlan and her cousin had a point about not wanting to come here. Hel, Quinlan had refused to even set foot in the park surrounding the black-stoned temple, opting to wait on a bench at its edge with Ruhn.

"What I say here is confidential, right?" he asked.

"Once the gods speak, I become the conduit through which their words pass." She arranged herself on the floor before the hole, folding her front paws, claws glinting in the dim light of the braziers smoldering to either side of them. "But yes—this shall be confidential."

It sounded like a whole bunch of bullshit, but he blew out a breath, meeting those large brown eyes, and said, "Why does someone want Luna's Horn?"

He didn't ask who had taken it—he knew from the reports that she had already been asked that question two years ago and had refused to answer.

She blinked, wings rustling as if in surprise, but settled herself. Breathed in the fumes rising from the hole. Minutes passed, and Hunt's head began to throb with the various scents—especially the reeking sulfur.

Smoke swirled, masking the sphinx from sight even though she sat only ten feet away.

Hunt forced himself to keep still.

A rasping voice slithered out of the smoke. "To open the doorway between worlds." A chill seized Hunt. "They wish to use the Horn to reopen the Northern Rift. The Horn's purpose wasn't merely to close doors—it opens them, too. It depends on what the bearer wishes."

"But the Horn is broken."

"It can be healed."

Hunt's heart stalled. "How?"

A long, long pause. Then, "It is veiled. I cannot see. None can see."

"The Fae legends say it can't be repaired."

"Those are legends. This is truth. The Horn can be repaired."

"Who wants to do this?" He had to ask, even if it was foolish.

"This, too, is veiled."

"Helpful."

"Be grateful, Lord of Lightning, that you learned anything at all." That voice—that title . . . His mouth went dry. "Do you wish to know what I see in your future, Orion Athalar?"

He recoiled at the sound of his birth name like he'd been punched in the gut. "No one has spoken that name in two hundred years," he whispered.

"The name your mother gave you."

"Yes," he ground out, his gut twisting at the memory of his mother's face, the love that had always shone in her eyes for him. Utterly undeserved, that love—especially when he had not been there to protect her.

The Oracle whispered, "Shall I tell you what I see, Orion?"

"I'm not sure I want to know."

The smoke peeled back enough for him to see her sensuous lips part in a cruel smile that did not wholly belong in this world. "People come from across Midgard to plead for my visions, yet you do not wish to know?"

The hair on the back of his neck stood. "I thank you, but no." Thanks seemed wise—like something that might appease a god.

Her teeth shone, her canines long enough to shred flesh. "Did Bryce Quinlan tell you what occurred when she stood in this chamber twelve years ago?"

His blood turned to ice. "That's Quinlan's business."

That smile didn't falter. "You do not wish to know what I saw for her, either?"

"No." He spoke from his heart. "It's her business," he repeated. His lightning rose within him, rallying against a foe he could not slay.

The Oracle blinked, a slow bob of those thick lashes. "You remind me of that which was lost long ago," she said quietly. "I had not realized it might ever appear again."

Before Hunt dared ask what that meant, her lion's tail—a larger version of Syrinx's—swayed over the floor. The doors behind him opened on a phantom wind, his dismissal clear. But the Oracle said before stalking into the vapors, "Do yourself a favor, Orion Athalar: keep well away from Bryce Quinlan."

34

Bryce and Ruhn had waited at the edge of the Oracle's Park for Hunt, each minute dripping by. And when he'd emerged again, eyes searching every inch of her face . . . Bryce knew it was bad. Whatever he'd learned.

Hunt waited until they'd walked down a quiet residential block bordering the park before he told them what the Oracle had said about the Horn.

His words were still hanging in the bright morning air around them as Bryce blew out a breath. Hunt did the same beside her and then said, "If someone has learned how to repair the Horn after so long, then they can do the opposite of what Prince Pelias did. They can *open* the Northern Rift. It seems like one Hel of a motive to kill anyone who might rat them out."

Ruhn ran a hand over the buzzed side of his hair. "Like the acolyte at the temple—either as a warning to us to stay the fuck away from the Horn or to keep her from saying anything, if she'd found out somehow."

Hunt nodded. "Isaiah questioned the others at the temple—they said the girl was the only acolyte on duty the night the Horn was stolen, and was interviewed then, but claimed she didn't know anything about it."

Guilt twisted and writhed within Bryce.

Ruhn said, "Maybe she was scared to say anything. And when we showed up . . ."

Hunt finished, "Whoever is looking for the Horn doesn't want us anywhere near it. They could have learned she'd been on duty that night and gone to extract information from her. They'd have wanted to make sure she didn't reveal what she knew to anyone else—to make sure she stayed silent. Permanently."

Bryce added the girl's death to the list of others she'd repay before this was finished.

Then she asked, "If that mark on the crate really was the Horn, maybe the Ophion—or even just the Keres sect—is seeking the Horn to aid in their rebellion. To open a portal to Hel, and bring the demon princes back here in some sort of alliance to overthrow the Asteri." She shuddered. "Millions would die." At their chilled silence, she went on, "Maybe Danika caught on to their plans about the Horn—and was killed for it. And the acolyte, too."

Hunt rubbed the back of his neck, his face ashen. "They'd need help from a Vanir to summon a demon like that, but it's a possibility. There are some Vanir pledged to their cause. Or maybe one of the witches summoned it. The new witch queen could be testing her power, or something."

"Unlikely that a witch was involved," Ruhn said a shade tightly, piercings along his ear glinting in the sun. "The witches obey the Asteri—they've had millennia of unbroken loyalty."

Bryce said, "But the Horn can only be used by a Starborn Fae—by you, Ruhn."

Hunt's wings rustled. "So maybe they're looking for some way around the Starborn shit."

"Honestly," Ruhn said, "I'm not sure I *could* use the Horn. Prince Pelias possessed what was basically an ocean of starlight at his disposal." Her brother's brow furrowed, and a pinprick of light appeared at his fingertip. "This is about as good as it gets for me."

"Well, you're not going to use the Horn, even if we find it, so it won't matter," Bryce said.

Ruhn crossed his arms. "If someone can repair the Horn . . . I don't even know how that would be possible. I read some mentions of the Horn having a sort of sentience to it—almost like it was alive. Maybe a healing power of some sort would be applicable? A medwitch might have some insight."

Bryce countered, "They heal people, not objects. And the book you found in the gallery's library said the Horn could only be repaired by light that is not light, magic that is not magic."

"Legends," said Hunt. "Not truth."

"It's worth looking into," Ruhn said, and halted, glancing between Bryce and Hunt, who was watching her warily from the corner of his eye. Whatever the fuck that meant. Ruhn said, "I'll look up a few medwitches and pay some discreet visits."

"Fine," she said. When he stiffened, she amended, "That sounds good."

Even if nothing else about this case did.

Bryce tuned out the sound of Lehabah watching one of her dramas and tried to concentrate on the map of Danika's locations. Tried but failed, since she could feel Hunt's eyes lingering on her from across the library table. For the hundredth time in that hour alone. She met his stare, and he looked away quickly. "What?"

He shook his head and went back to his research.

"You've been staring at me all afternoon with that weird fucking look on your face."

He drummed his fingers on the table, then blurted, "You want to tell me why the Oracle warned me to stay the Hel away from you?"

Bryce let out a short laugh. "Is that why you seemed all freaked when you left the temple?"

"She said she'd reveal her vision for you—like she has a damned bone to pick with you."

A shiver crawled down Bryce's spine at that. "I don't blame her if she's still pissed."

Hunt paled, but Bryce said, "In Fae culture, there's a custom: when girls get their cycle for the first time, or when they turn thirteen, they go to an Oracle. The visit provides a glimpse toward what sort of power they might ascend to when mature, so their parents can plan unions years before the actual Drop. Boys go, too—at age thirteen. These days, if the parents are progressive, it's just an old tradition to figure out a career for their children. Soldiers or healers or whatever Fae do if they can't afford to lounge around eating grapes all day."

"The Fae and malakim might hate each other, but they have a lot of bullshit in common."

Bryce hummed her agreement. "My cycle started when I was a few weeks shy of thirteen. And my mom had this . . . I don't know. Crisis? This sudden fear that she'd shut me off from a part of my heritage. She got in touch with my biological father. Two weeks later, the documents showed up, declaring me a full civitas. It came with a catch, though: I had to claim Sky and Breath as my House. I refused, but my mom actually insisted I do it. She saw it as some kind of . . . protection. I don't know. Apparently, she was convinced enough of his intention to protect me that she asked if he wanted to meet me. For the first time. And I eventually cooled down enough from the whole House allegiance thing to realize I wanted to meet him, too."

Hunt read her beat of silence. "It didn't go well."

"No. That visit was the first time I met Ruhn, too. I came here—stayed in FiRo for the summer. I met the Autumn King." The lie was easy. "Met my father, too," she added. "In the initial few days, the visit wasn't as bad as my mother had feared. I liked what I saw. Even if some of the other Fae children whispered that I was a half-breed, I knew what I was. I've never not been proud of it—being human, I mean. And I knew my father had invited me, so he at least wanted me there. I didn't mind what others thought. Until the Oracle."

He winced. "I have a bad feeling about this."

"It was catastrophic." She swallowed against the memory. "When the Oracle looked into her smoke, she screamed. Clawed at her eyes." There was no point hiding it. The event had been known in some circles. "I heard later that she went blind for a week."

"Holy shit."

Bryce laughed to herself. "Apparently, my future is *that* bad."

Hunt didn't smile. "What happened?"

"I returned to the petitioners' antechamber. All you could hear was the Oracle screaming and cursing me—the acolytes rushed in."

"I meant with your father."

"He called me a worthless disgrace, stormed out of the temple's VIP exit so no one could know who he was to me, and by the time I caught up, he'd taken the car and left. When I got back to his house, I found my bags on the curb."

"Asshole. Danaan had nothing to say about him kicking his cousin to the curb?"

"The king forbade Ruhn to interfere." She examined her nails. "Believe me, Ruhn tried to fight. But the king bound him. So I got a cab to the train station. Ruhn managed to shove money for the fares into my hand."

"Your mom must have gone ballistic."

"She did." Bryce paused a moment and then said, "Seems like the Oracle's still pissed."

He threw her a half smile. "I'd consider it a badge of honor."

Bryce, despite herself, smiled back. "You're probably the only one who thinks that." His eyes lingered on her face again, and she knew it had nothing to do with what the Oracle had said.

Bryce cleared her throat. "Find anything?"

Catching her request to drop the subject, Hunt pivoted the laptop toward her. "I've been looking at this ancient shit for days—and this is all I've found."

The terra-cotta vase dated back nearly fifteen thousand years. After Prince Pelias by about a century, but the kristallos hadn't yet faded from common memory. She read the brief catalog copy and said, "It's at a gallery in Mirsia." Which put it a sea and two thousand miles beyond that from Lunathion. She pulled the computer to her and clicked on the thumbnail. "But these photos should be enough."

"I might have been born before computers, Quinlan, but I do know how to use them."

"I'm just trying to spare you from further ruining your badass image as the Umbra Mortis. We can't have word getting out that you're a computer nerd."

"Thanks for your concern." His eyes met hers, the corner of his mouth kicking up.

Her toes might have curled in her heels. Slightly.

Bryce straightened. "All right. Tell me what I'm looking at."

"A good sign." Hunt pointed at the image, rendered in black paint against the burnt orange of the terra-cotta, of the kristallos demon roaring as a sword was driven through its head by a helmeted male warrior.

She leaned toward the screen. "How so?"

"That the kristallos can be killed the old-fashioned way. As far as I can tell, there's no magic or special artifact being used to kill it here. Just plain brute force."

Her gut tightened. "This vase could be an artistic interpretation. That thing killed Danika and the Pack of Devils, and knocked Micah on his ass, too. And you mean to tell me some ancient warrior killed it with just a sword through the head?"

Though Lehabah's show kept playing, Bryce knew the sprite was listening to every word.

Hunt said, "Maybe the kristallos had the element of surprise on its side that night."

She tried and failed to block out the red pulped piles, the spray of blood on the walls, the way her entire body had seemed to plummet downward even while standing still as she stared at what was left of her friends. "Or maybe this is just a bullshit rendering by an artist who heard an embellished song around a fire and did their own take on it." She began tapping her foot under the table, as if it'd somehow calm her staccato heartbeat.

He held her stare, his black eyes stark and honest. "All right." She waited for him to push, to pry, but Hunt slid the computer back to his side of the table. He squinted. "That's odd. It says the vase is originally from Parthos." He angled his head. "I thought Parthos was a myth. A human fairy tale."

"Because humans were no better than rock-banging animals until the Asteri arrived?"

"Tell me you don't believe that conspiracy crap about an ancient library in the heart of a pre-existing human civilization?" When she didn't answer, Hunt challenged, "If something like that *did* exist, where's the evidence?"

Bryce zipped her amulet along its chain and nodded toward the image on the screen.

"This vase was made by a nymph," he said. "Not some mythical, enlightened human."

"Maybe Parthos hadn't been wiped off the map entirely at that point."

Hunt looked at her from under lowered brows. "Really, Quinlan?" When she again didn't answer, he jerked his chin at her digital tablet. "Where are you with the data about Danika's locations?"

Hunt's phone buzzed before she could reply, but Bryce said, reeling herself back together as that image of the slain kristallos bled with what had been done to Danika, what had been left of her, "I'm still ruling out the things that were likely unconnected, but . . . Really, the only outlier here is the fact that Danika was on sentry duty at Luna's Temple. She was sometimes stationed in the general area, but never specifically at the temple itself. And somehow, days before she died, she got put on watch there? And data shows her being *right there* when the Horn was stolen. The acolyte was *also* there that night. It's all got to tie together somehow."

Hunt set down his phone. "Maybe Philip Briggs will enlighten us tonight."

Her head snapped up. "Tonight?"

Lehabah completely stopped watching her show at that.

"Just got the message from Viktoria. They transferred him from Adrestia. We're meeting him in an hour in a holding cell under the Comitium." He surveyed the data spread before them. "He's going to be difficult."

"I know."

He leaned back in the chair. "He's not going to have nice things to say about Danika. You sure you can handle hearing his kind of venom?"

"I'm fine."

"Really? Because that vase just set you off, and I doubt coming face-to-face with this guy is going to be any easier."

The walls began swelling around her. "Get out." Her words cut between them. "Just because we're working together doesn't mean you're entitled to push into my personal matters."

Hunt merely looked her over. Saw all of that. But he said roughly, "I want to head to the Comitium in twenty. I'll wait for you outside."

Bryce trailed Hunt out, making sure he didn't touch any of the books and that they didn't grab for him, then shut the door before he'd fully walked onto the street beyond.

She sank against the iron until she sat on the carpet, and braced her forearms on her knees.

They were gone—all of them. Thanks to that demon depicted on an ancient vase. They were gone, and there would be no more wolves in her life. No more hanging out in the apartment. No more drunken, stupid dancing on street corners, or blasting music at three in the morning until their neighbors threatened to call the 33rd.

No friends who would say *I love you* and mean it. Syrinx and Lele came creeping in, the chimera curling up beneath her bent legs, the sprite lying belly-down on Bryce's forearm.

"Don't blame Athie. I think he wants to be our friend."

"I don't give a shit what Hunt Athalar wants."

"June is busy with ballet, and Fury is as good as gone. Maybe it's time for more friends, BB. You seem sad again. Like you were two winters ago. Fine one minute, then not fine the next. You don't dance, you don't hang out with anyone, you don't—"

"Leave it, Lehabah."

"Hunt is nice. And Prince Ruhn is nice. But Danika was never nice to me. Always biting and snarling. Or she ignored me."

"*Watch it.*"

The sprite crawled off her arm and floated in front of her, arms wrapping across her round belly. "You can be cold as a Reaper,

Bryce." Then she was gone, whizzing off to stop a thick leather-bound tome from crawling its way up the stairs.

Bryce blew out a long breath, trying to piece the hole in her chest together.

Twenty minutes, Hunt had said. She had twenty minutes before going to question Briggs. Twenty minutes to get her shit together. Or at least pretend she had.

35

The fluorescent wands of firstlight hummed through the white-paneled, pristine corridor far beneath the Comitium. Hunt was a storm of black and gray against the shining white tiles, his steps unfaltering as he aimed for one of the sealed metal doors at the end of the long hall.

A step behind him, Bryce simply watched Hunt move—the way he cut through the world, the way the guards in the entry room hadn't so much as checked his ID before waving them through.

She hadn't realized that this place existed beneath the five shining towers of the Comitium. That they had cells. Interrogation rooms.

The one she'd been in the night Danika had died had been five blocks from here. A facility governed by protocols. But this place . . . She tried not to think about what this place was for. What laws stopped applying once one crossed over the threshold.

The lack of any scent except bleach suggested it was scrubbed down often. The drains she noted every few feet suggested—

She didn't want to know what the drains suggested.

They reached a room without windows, and Hunt laid a palm against the circular metal lock to its left. A hum and hiss, and he shouldered open the door, peering inside before nodding to her.

The firstlights above droned like hornets. What would her own firstlight go toward, small mote that it would be? With Hunt, the explosion of energy-filled light that had probably erupted from him when he'd made the Drop had likely gone toward fueling an entire city.

She sometimes wondered about it: whose firstlight was powering her phone, or the stereo, or her coffee machine.

And now was not the time to think about random shit, she chided herself as she followed Hunt into the cell and beheld the pale-skinned man sitting there.

Two seats had been set before the metal table in the center of the room—where Briggs's shackles were currently chained. His white jumpsuit was pristine, but—

Bryce beheld the state of his gaunt, hollow face and willed herself not to flinch. His dark hair was buzzed close to his scalp, and though not a bruise or scratch marred his skin, his deep blue eyes . . . empty and hopeless.

Briggs said nothing as she and Hunt claimed the seats across the table. Cameras blinked red lights in every corner, and she had no doubt someone was listening in a control room a few doors down.

"We won't take much of your time," Hunt said, as if noting those haunted eyes as well.

"Time is all I have now, angel. And being here is better than being . . . there."

There, where they kept him in Adrestia Prison. Where they did the things to him that resulted in those broken, awful eyes.

Bryce could feel Hunt silently urging her to ask the first of their questions, and she took a breath, bracing herself to fill this humming, too-small room with her voice.

But Briggs asked, "What month is it? What's today's date?"

Horror coiled in her gut. This man had wanted to kill people, she reminded herself. Even if it seemed he hadn't killed Danika, he had planned to kill plenty of others, to ignite a larger-scale war between the human and Vanir. To overthrow the Asteri. It was why he remained behind bars.

"It's the twelfth of April," Hunt said, his voice low, "in the year 15035."

"It's only been two years?"

Bryce swallowed against the dryness in her mouth. "We came to ask you about some things related to two years ago. As well as some recent events."

Briggs looked at her then. Really looked. "Why?"

Hunt leaned back, a silent indication that this was now her show to run. "The White Raven nightclub was bombed a few days ago. Considering that it was one of your prime targets a few years ago, evidence points toward Keres being active again."

"And you think I'm behind it?" A bitter smile curved the angular, harsh face. Hunt tensed. "I don't know what *year* it is, girl. And you think I'm somehow able to make outside contact?"

"What about your followers?" Hunt said carefully. "Would they have done it in your name?"

"Why bother?" Briggs reclined in his chair. "I failed them. I failed our people." He nodded toward Bryce. "And failed people like you—the undesirables."

"You never represented me," Bryce said quietly. "I abhor what you tried to do."

Briggs laughed, a broken rasp. "When the Vanir tell you you're not good enough for any job because of your human blood, when males like this asshole next to you just see you as a piece of ass to be fucked and then discarded, when you see your mother—it is a human mother for you, isn't it? It always is—being treated like trash . . . You'll find those self-righteous feelings fading real fast."

She refused to reply. To think about the times she'd seen her mother ignored or sneered at—

Hunt said, "So you're saying you're not behind this bombing."

"Again," Briggs said, tugging on his shackles, "the only people I see on a daily basis are the ones who take me apart like a cadaver, and then stitch me up again before nightfall, their medwitches smoothing everything away."

Her stomach churned. Even Hunt's throat bobbed as he swallowed.

"Your followers wouldn't have considered bombing the nightclub in revenge?"

Briggs demanded, "Against who?"

"Us. For investigating Danika Fendyr's murder and looking for Luna's Horn."

Briggs's blue eyes shuttered. "So the assholes in the 33rd finally realized I didn't kill her."

"You haven't been officially cleared of anything," Hunt said roughly.

Briggs shook his head, staring at the wall to his left. "I don't know anything about Luna's Horn, and I'm sure as shit no Keres soldier did either, but I liked Danika Fendyr. Even when she busted me, I liked her."

Hunt stared at the gaunt, haunted man—a shell of the powerfully built adult he'd been two years ago. What they were doing to him in that prison . . . Fucking Hel.

Hunt could take a few guesses about the manner of torture. The memories of it being inflicted upon him still dragged him from sleep.

Bryce was blinking at Briggs. "What do you mean, you *liked* her?"

Briggs smiled, savoring Quinlan's surprise. "She circled me and my agents for weeks. She even met with me twice. Told me to stop my plans—or else she'd have to bring me in. Well, that was the first time. The second time she warned me that she had enough evidence against me that she *had* to bring me in, but I could get off easy if I admitted to my plotting and ended it then and there. I didn't listen then, either. That third time . . . She brought her pack, and that was that."

Hunt reined in his emotions, setting his features into neutrality.

"Danika went easy on you?" Bryce's face had drained of color. It took a surprising amount of effort not to touch her hand.

"She tried to." Briggs ran gnarled fingers down his pristine jumpsuit. "For a Vanir, she was fair. I don't think she necessarily disagreed with us. With my methods, yes, but I thought she might have been a sympathizer." He surveyed Bryce again with a starkness that had Hunt's hackles rising.

Hunt suppressed a growl at the term. "Your followers knew this?"

"Yes. I think she even let some of them get away that night."

Hunt blew out a breath. "That is a big fucking claim to make against an Aux leader."

"She's dead, isn't she? Who cares?"

Bryce flinched. Enough so that Hunt didn't hold back his growl this time.

"Danika wasn't a rebel sympathizer," Bryce hissed.

Briggs looked down his nose at her. "Not yet, maybe," he agreed, "but Danika could have been starting down that path. Maybe *she* saw how her pretty, half-breed friend was treated by others and didn't like it too much, either." He smiled knowingly when Bryce blinked at his correct guess regarding her relationship to Danika. The emotions he'd probably read in her face.

Briggs went on, "My followers knew Danika was a potential asset. We'd discussed it, right up until the raid. And that night, Danika and her pack were fair with us. We fought, and even managed to get in a few good blows on that Second of hers." He whistled. "Connor Holstrom." Bryce went utterly rigid. "Guy was a bruiser." From the cruel curve of his lips, he'd clearly noticed how stiff she'd gone at the mention of Connor's name. "Was Holstrom your boyfriend? Pity."

"That's none of your business." The words were flat as Briggs's eyes.

They tightened something in Hunt's chest, her words. The vacancy in her voice.

Hunt asked him, "You never mentioned any of this when you were initially arrested?"

Briggs spat, "Why the *fuck* would I ever rat out a potentially sympathetic, incredibly powerful Vanir like Danika Fendyr? I might have been headed for *this*"—he gestured to the cell around them—"but the cause would live on. It *had* to live on, and I knew that someone like Danika could be a mighty ally to have on our side."

Hunt cut in, "But why not mention any of this during your murder trial?"

"My trial? You mean that two-day sham they televised? With that *lawyer* the Governor assigned me?" Briggs laughed and laughed. Hunt had to remind himself that this was an imprisoned man, enduring unspeakable torture. And not someone he could punch in the face. Not even for the way his laugh made Quinlan shift in her seat. "I knew they'd pin it on me no matter what. Knew that even if I told the truth, I'd wind up here. So on the chance that Danika might have friends still living who shared her sentiments, I kept her secrets to myself."

"You're ratting her out now," Bryce said.

But Briggs didn't reply to that, and instead studied the dented metal table. "I said it two years ago, and I'll say it again now: Keres didn't kill Danika or the Pack of Devils. The White Raven bombing, though—they might have managed that. Good for them if they did."

Hunt ground his teeth. Had he been this out of touch with reality when he'd followed Shahar? Had it been this level of fanaticism that prompted him to lead the angels of the 18th to Mount Hermon? In those last days, would he have even *listened* to anyone if they'd advised against it?

A hazy memory surfaced, of Isaiah doing just that, screaming in Hunt's war tent. Fuck.

Briggs asked, "Did a lot of Vanir die in the bombing?"

Disgust curdled Bryce's face. "No," she said, standing from her chair. "Not a single one." She spoke with the imperiousness of a queen. Hunt could only rise with her.

Briggs tsked. "Too bad."

Hunt's fingers balled into fists. He'd been so wildly in love with Shahar, with the cause—had he been no better than this man?

Bryce said tightly, "Thank you for answering our questions." Without waiting for Briggs to reply, she hurried for the door. Hunt kept a step behind her, even with Briggs anchored to the table.

That she'd ended the meeting so quickly showed Hunt that Bryce shared his opinion: Briggs truly hadn't killed Danika.

He'd nearly reached the open doorway when Briggs said to him, "You're one of the Fallen, huh?" Hunt paused. Briggs smiled.

"Tons of respect for you, man." He surveyed Hunt from head to toe. "What part of the 18th did you serve in?"

Hunt said nothing. But Briggs's blue eyes shone. "We'll bring the bastards down someday, brother."

Hunt glanced toward Bryce, already halfway down the hallway, her steps swift. Like she couldn't stand to breathe the same air as the man chained to the table, like she had to get out of this awful place. Hunt himself had been here, interrogated people, more often than he cared to remember.

And the kill he'd made last night . . . It had lingered. Ticked off another life-debt, but it had lingered.

Briggs was still staring at him, waiting for Hunt to speak. The agreement that Hunt would have voiced weeks ago now dissolved on his tongue.

No, he'd been no better than this man.

He didn't know where that put him.

"So Briggs and his followers are off the list," Bryce said, folding her feet beneath her on her living room couch. Syrinx was already snoring beside her. "Unless you think he was lying?"

Hunt, seated at the other end of the sectional, frowned at the sunball game just starting on TV. "He was telling the truth. I've dealt with enough . . . prisoners to sense when someone's lying."

The words were clipped. He'd been on edge since they'd left the Comitium through the same unmarked street door they'd used to enter. No chance of running into Sandriel that way.

Hunt pointed to the papers Bryce had brought from the gallery, noting some of Danika's movements and the list of names she'd compiled. "Remind me who's the next suspect on your list?"

Bryce didn't answer as she observed his profile, the light of the screen bouncing off his cheekbones, deepening the shadow beneath his strong jaw.

He truly was pretty. And really seemed to be in a piss-poor mood. "What's wrong?"

"Nothing."

"Says the guy who's grinding his teeth so hard I can hear them."

Hunt cut her a glare and spread a muscled arm along the back of the couch. He'd changed when they'd returned thirty minutes ago, having grabbed a quick bite at a noodles-and-dumplings food cart just down the block, and now wore a soft gray T-shirt, black sweats, and a white sunball cap turned backward.

It was the hat that had proven the most confusing—so ordinary and . . . *guy-ish,* for lack of a better word, that she'd been stealing glances at him for the past fifteen minutes. Stray locks of his dark hair curled around the edges, the adjustable band nearly covered the tattoo over his brow, and she had no idea why, but it was all just . . . Disgustingly distracting.

"What?" he asked, noting her gaze.

Bryce reached forward, her long braid slipping over a shoulder, and grabbed his phone from the coffee table. She snapped a photo of him and sent a copy to herself, mostly because she doubted anyone would believe her that Hunt fucking Athalar was sitting on her couch in casual clothes, sunball hat on backward, watching TV and drinking a beer.

The Shadow of Death, everyone.

"That's annoying," he said through his teeth.

"So is your face," she said sweetly, tossing the phone to him. Hunt picked it up, snapped a photo of *her,* and then set it down, eyes on the game again.

She let him watch for another minute before she said, "You've been broody since Briggs."

His mouth twisted toward the side. "Sorry."

"Why are you apologizing?"

His fingers traced a circle along the couch cushion. "It brought up some bad shit. About—about the way I helped lead Shahar's rebellion."

She considered, retracing every horrid word and exchange in that cell beneath the Comitium.

Oh. *Oh.* She said carefully, "You're nothing like Briggs, Hunt."

His dark eyes slid toward her. "You don't know me well enough to say that."

"Did you willingly and gleefully risk innocent lives to further your rebellion?"

His mouth thinned. "No."

"Well, there you have it."

Again, his jaw worked. Then he said, "But I was blind. About a lot of things."

"Like what?"

"Just a lot," he hedged. "Looking at Briggs, what they're doing to him . . . I don't know why it bothered me this time. I've been down there often enough with other prisoners that—I mean . . ." His knee bounced. He said without looking at her, "You know what kinda shit I have to do."

She said gently, "Yeah."

"But for whatever reason, seeing Briggs like that today, it just made me remember my own . . ." He trailed off again and swigged from his beer.

Icy, oily dread filled her stomach, twisting with the fried noodles she'd inhaled thirty minutes ago. "How long did they do that to you—after Mount Hermon?"

"Seven years."

She closed her eyes as the weight of those words rippled through her.

Hunt said, "I lost track of time, too. The Asteri dungeons are so far beneath the earth, so lightless, that days are years and years are days and . . . When they let me out, I went right to the Archangel Ramuel. My first . . . *handler.* He continued the pattern for two years, got bored with it, and realized that I'd be more useful dispatching demons and doing his bidding than rotting away in his torture chambers."

"Burning Solas, Hunt," she whispered.

He still didn't look at her. "By the time Ramuel decided to let me serve as his assassin, it had been nine years since I'd seen sunlight. Since I'd heard the wind or smelled the rain. Since I'd seen grass, or a river, or a mountain. Since I'd flown."

Her hands shook enough that she crossed her arms, tucking her fingers tight to her body. "I—I am so sorry."

His eyes turned distant, glazed. "Hatred was the only thing that fueled me through it. Briggs's kind of hatred. Not hope, not love. Only unrelenting, raging hatred. For the Archangels. For the Asteri. For all of it." He finally looked at her, his eyes as hollow as Briggs's had been. "So, yeah. I might not have ever been willing to kill innocents to help Shahar's rebellion, but that's the only difference between me and Briggs. Still is."

She didn't let herself reconsider before she took his hand.

She hadn't realized how much bigger Hunt's hand was until hers coiled around it. Hadn't realized how many calluses lay on his palms and fingers until they rasped against her skin.

Hunt glanced down at their hands, her dusk-painted nails contrasting with the deep gold of his skin. She found herself holding her breath, waiting for him to snatch his hand back, and asked, "Do you still feel like hatred is all that gets you through the day?"

"No," he said, eyes lifting from their hands to scan her face. "Sometimes, for some things, yes, but . . . No, Quinlan."

She nodded, but he was still watching her, so she reached for the spreadsheets.

"You have nothing else to say?" Hunt's mouth twisted to the side. "You, the person who has an opinion on everything and everyone, have nothing else to say about what I just told you?"

She pushed her braid over her shoulder. "You're not like Briggs," she said simply.

He frowned. And began to withdraw his hand from hers.

Bryce clamped her fingers around his. "You might see yourself that way, but I see you, too, Athalar. I see your kindness and your . . . whatever." She squeezed his hand for emphasis. "I see all the shit you conveniently forget. Briggs is a bad person. He might have once gotten into the human rebellion for the right reasons, but he is a *bad person*. You aren't. You will never be. End of story."

"This bargain I've got with Micah suggests otherwise—"

"You're not like him."

The weight of his stare pressed on her skin, warmed her face.

She withdrew her hand as casually as she could, trying not to note how his own fingers seemed hesitant to let go. But she leaned forward, stretching out her arm, and flicked his hat. "What's up with this, by the way?"

He batted her away. "It's a hat."

"It doesn't fit with your whole predator-in-the-night image."

For a heartbeat, he was utterly silent. Then he laughed, tipping back his head. The strong tan column of his throat worked with the movement, and Bryce crossed her arms again.

"Ah, Quinlan," he said, shaking his head. He swept the hat off his head and plunked it down atop her own. "You're merciless."

She grinned, twisting the cap backward the way he'd worn it, and primly shuffled the papers. "Let's look this over again. Since Briggs was a bust, and the Viper Queen's out . . . maybe there's something with Danika at Luna's Temple the night the Horn was stolen that we're missing."

He drifted closer, his thigh grazing her bent knee, and peered at the papers in her lap. She watched his eyes slide over them as he studied the list of locations. And tried not to think about the warmth of that thigh against her leg. The solid muscle of it.

Then he lifted his head.

He was close enough that she realized his eyes weren't black after all, but rather a shade of darkest brown. "We're idiots."

"At least you said *we*."

He snickered, but didn't pull back. Didn't move that powerful leg of his. "The temple has exterior cameras. They would have been recording the night the Horn was stolen."

"You make it sound as if the 33rd didn't check that two years ago. They said the blackout rendered any footage essentially useless."

"Maybe we didn't run the right tests on the footage. Look at the right fields. Ask the right people to examine it. If Danika was there that night, why didn't anyone know that? Why didn't *she* come forward about being at the temple when the Horn was stolen? Why didn't the acolyte say anything about her presence?"

Bryce chewed on her lip. Hunt's eyes dipped to it. She could have sworn they darkened. That his thigh pressed harder into hers. As if in challenge—a dare to see if she'd back down.

She didn't, but her voice turned hoarse as she said, "You think

Danika might have known who took the Horn—and she tried to hide it?" She shook her head. "Danika wouldn't have done that. She barely seemed to care that the Horn had been stolen at all."

"I don't know," he said. "But let's start by looking at the footage, even if it's a whole lot of nothing. And send it to someone who can give us a more comprehensive analysis." He swiped his hat off her head, and put it back on his own—still backward, still with those little curling pieces of hair peeking around the edges. As if for good measure, he tugged the end of her braid, then folded his hands behind his head as he went back to watching the game.

The absence of his leg against hers was like a cold slap. "Who do you have in mind?"

His mouth just curved upward.

36

The three-level shooting range in Moonwood catered to a lethal, creative clientele. Occupying a converted warehouse that stretched four city blocks along the Istros, it boasted the only sniper-length gallery in the city.

Hunt stopped by every few weeks to keep his skills sharp, usually in the dead of night when no one could gawk at the Umbra Mortis donning a pair of earmuffs and military-grade glasses as he walked through the concrete hallways to one of the private galleries.

It had been late when he'd gotten the idea for this meeting, and then Jesiba had slammed Quinlan with work the next day, so they'd decided to wait until nightfall to see where their quarry wound up. Hunt had bet Bryce a gold mark it'd be a tattoo parlor, and she'd raised him to two gold marks that it'd be a fake-grungy rock bar. But when she'd gotten the reply to her message, it had led them here.

The sniper gallery lay on the northern end of the building, accessible through a heavy metal door that sealed off any sound. They grabbed electronic earmuffs that would stifle the boom of the guns—but still allow them to hear each other's voices—on the way in. Before he entered the gallery, Hunt glanced over a shoulder at Bryce, checking that her earmuffs were in place.

She noted his assessing look and chuckled. "Mother hen."

"I wouldn't want your pretty little ears to get blown out, Quinlan." He didn't give her the chance to reply as he opened the door, thumping music blasting to greet them, and beheld the three males lined up along a waist-high glass barrier.

Lord Tristan Flynn had a sniper rifle aimed toward a person-shaped paper target at the far, far end of the space, so distant a mortal could barely make it out. He'd opted out of using the scope, instead relying on his keen Fae eyesight as Danaan and Declan Emmet stood near him, their own rifles hanging off their shoulders.

Ruhn nodded their way, and motioned to wait a moment.

"He's gonna miss," Emmet observed over the bumping bass of the music, barely sparing Hunt and Bryce a glance. "Off by a half inch."

"Screw you, Dec," Flynn muttered, and fired. The gunshot erupted through the space, the sound absorbed by the padding along the ceiling and walls, and at the far end of the gallery, the piece of paper swayed, the torso rippling.

Flynn lowered the rifle. "Straight shot to the balls, dickbags." He held out his palm toward Ruhn. "Pay up."

Ruhn rolled his eyes and slammed a gold coin into it as he turned to Hunt and Bryce.

Hunt glanced at the prince's two friends, who were now sizing him up as they pulled off their earmuffs and eye gear. He and Bryce followed suit.

He didn't expect the tinge of envy curdling in his gut at the sight of the friends together. A glance at Quinlan's stiff shoulders had him wondering if she felt the same—if she was remembering nights with Danika and the Pack of Devils when they'd had nothing better to do than give each other grief over nonsense.

Bryce shook it off faster than Hunt did as she drawled, "Sorry to interrupt you boys playing commando, but we have some adult things to discuss."

Ruhn set his rifle on the metal table to his left and leaned against the glass barrier. "You could have called."

Bryce strode to the table to examine the gun her cousin had set down. Her nails glimmered against the matte black. Stealth weapons, designed to blend into shadows and not give away their bearer with a gleam. "I didn't want this intel out there in the networks."

Flynn flashed a grin. "Cloak-and-dagger shit. Nice." He sidled up to her at the table, close enough that Hunt found himself tensing. "Color me intrigued."

Quinlan's gift of looking down her nose at males who towered above her usually grated on Hunt to no end. But seeing it used on someone else was a true delight.

Yet that imperious look only seemed to make Flynn's grin grow wider, especially as Bryce said, "I'm not here to talk to you."

"You wound me, Bryce," Flynn drawled.

Declan Emmet snickered. "You up to do some more hacking shit?" Quinlan asked him.

"Call it shit again, Bryce, and see if I help you," Declan said coolly.

"Sorry, sorry. Your technology . . . stuff." She waved a hand. "We need analysis of some footage from Luna's Temple the night the Horn was stolen."

Ruhn went still, his blue eyes flaring as he said to Hunt, "You've got a lead on the Horn?"

Hunt said, "Just laying out the puzzle pieces."

Declan rubbed his neck. "All right. What are you looking for exactly?"

"Everything," Hunt said. "Anything that might come up on the audio or thermal, or if there's a way to make the video any clearer despite the blackout."

Declan set down his rifle beside Ruhn's. "I might have some software that can help, but no promises. If the investigators didn't find anything two years ago, the odds are slim I'll find any anomalies now."

"We know," Bryce said. "How long would it take you to look?"

He seemed to do some mental calculations. "Give me a few days. I'll see what I can find."

"Thank you."

Flynn let out an exaggerated gasp. "I think that's the first time you've ever said those words to us, B."

"Don't get used to it." She surveyed them again with that cool, mocking indifference that made Hunt's pulse begin to pound as drivingly as the beat of the music playing through the chamber's speakers. "Why are you three even here?"

"We do actually work for the Aux, Bryce. That requires the occasional bit of training."

"So where's the rest of your unit?" She made a show of looking around. Hunt didn't bother to hide his mirth. "Or was this a roomies-only kind of thing?"

Declan chuckled. "This was an invite-only session."

Bryce rolled her eyes and said to Ruhn, "I'm sure the Autumn King told you he wants reports on our movements." She crossed her arms. "Keep this"—she gestured to all of them—"quiet for a few days."

"You're asking me to lie to my king," Ruhn said, frowning.

"I'm asking you not to tell him about this for the moment," Bryce said.

Flynn lifted a brow. "Are you saying the Autumn King is one of your suspects?"

"I'm saying I want shit kept quiet." She grinned at Ruhn, showing all her white teeth, the expression more savage than amused. "I'm saying if you three morons leak any of this to your Aux buddies or drunken hookups, I am going to be *very* unhappy."

Honestly, Hunt would have liked nothing more than to grab some popcorn and a beer, kick back in a chair, and watch her verbally fillet these assholes.

"Sounds like a whole lot of big talk," Ruhn said, then indicated the target at the back of the room. "Why don't you put on a little demonstration for Athalar, Bryce?"

She smirked. "I don't need to prove I can handle a big gun to run with the boys' club." Hunt's skin tightened at the feral delight in her eyes as she said *big gun*. Other parts of him tightened, too.

Tristan Flynn said, "Twenty gold marks says we outshoot you."

"Only rich-ass pieces of shit have twenty gold marks to blow on bullshit contests," Bryce said, amber eyes dancing with amusement as she winked at Hunt. His blood thrummed, his body tensing as surely as if she'd gripped his cock. But her gaze already drifted to the distant target.

She snapped the earmuffs over her arched ears.

Flynn rubbed his hands together. "Here we fuckin' go."

Bryce popped on the glasses, adjusted her ponytail, and hefted Ruhn's rifle into her hands. She weighed it in her arms, and Hunt couldn't drag his eyes away from the way her fingers brushed over the chassis, stroking all the way down to the butt plate.

He swallowed hard, but she merely fitted the gun to her shoulder, each movement as comfortable as he'd expect from someone raised by a legendary sharpshooter. She clicked off the safety and didn't bother to use the scope as she said to none of them in particular, "Allow me to demonstrate why you all can kiss my fucking ass."

Three shots cracked over the music, one after another, her body absorbing the kickback of the gun like a champ. Hunt's mouth dried out entirely.

They all peered up at the screen with the feed of the target.

"You only landed one," Flynn snorted, eyeing the hole through the heart of the target.

"No, she didn't," Emmet murmured, just as Hunt saw it, too: the circle wasn't perfect. No, two of its edges bulged outward—barely noticeable.

Three shots, so precise that they'd passed through the same small space.

A chill skittered down Hunt's body that had nothing to do with fear as Bryce merely reset the safety, placed the rifle on the table, and removed the earmuffs and glasses.

She turned, and her eyes met Hunt's again—a new sort of vulnerability shining beneath the self-satisfied narrowing. A challenge thrown down. Waiting to see how he'd react.

How many males had run from this part of her, their alphahole egos threatened by it? Hunt hated them all merely for putting the question in her eyes.

He didn't hear whatever shit Flynn was saying as he put on the earmuffs and eye gear and took up the rifle Bryce had set down, the metal still warm from her body. He didn't hear Ruhn asking him something as he lined up his shot.

No, Hunt only met Bryce's stare as he clicked off the safety.

That click reverberated between them, loud as a thunderclap. Her throat bobbed.

Hunt pulled his gaze from hers and fired one round. With his eagle-sharp vision, he didn't need the scope to see the bullet pass through the hole she'd made.

When he lowered the gun, he found Bryce's cheeks flushed, her eyes like warm whiskey. A quiet sort of light shone in them.

He still didn't hear any of what the males were saying, only had the vague notion of even Ruhn cursing with appreciation. Hunt just held Bryce's stare.

I see you, Quinlan, he silently conveyed to her. *And I like all of it.*

Right back at you, her half smile seemed to say.

Hunt's phone rang, dragging his eyes from the smile that made the floor a little uneven. He fished it from his pocket with fingers that were surprisingly shaky. *Isaiah Tiberian* flashed on the screen. He answered instantly. "What's up?"

Hunt knew Bryce and the Fae males could hear every word as Isaiah said, "Get your asses over to Asphodel Meadows. There's been another murder."

37

Where?" Hunt demanded into the phone, one eye on Quinlan, her arms crossed tight as she listened. All that light had vanished from her eyes.

Isaiah told him the address. A good two miles away. "We've got a team already setting up camp," the commander said.

"We'll be there in a few," Hunt answered, and hung up.

The three Fae males, having heard as well, began packing their gear with swift efficiency. Well trained. Total pains in his ass, but they were well trained.

But Bryce fidgeted, hands twitching at her sides. He'd seen that stark look before. And the fake-ass calm that crept over her as Ruhn and his friends glanced at her.

Then, Hunt had bought into it, essentially bullied her into going to that other murder scene.

Hunt said without looking at the males, "I take it you heard the address." He didn't wait for any of them to confirm before he ordered, "We'll meet you there." Quinlan's eyes flickered, but Hunt didn't take his focus off her as he walked closer. He sensed Danaan, Flynn, and Emmet leaving the gallery, but didn't look to confirm as he halted before her.

The cold emptiness of the sniper range yawned around them.

Again, Quinlan's hands curled, fingers wiggling at her sides.

Like she could shake the dread and pain away. Hunt said calmly, "You want me to handle it?"

Color crept over her freckled cheeks. She pointed to the door with a shaking finger. "Someone *died* while we were dicking around tonight."

Hunt wrapped his hand around her finger. Lowered it to the space between them. "This guilt isn't on you. It's on whoever is doing this."

People like him, butchering in the night.

She tried to yank her finger back, and he let go, remembering her wariness of male Vanir. Of alphaholes.

Bryce's throat bobbed, and she peered around his wing. "I want to go to the scene of the crime." He waited for the rest of it. She blew out an uneven breath. "I need to go," she said, more to herself. Her foot tapped on the concrete floor, in time to the beat of the still-thumping music. She winced. "But I don't want Ruhn or his friends seeing me like this."

"Like what?" It was normal, expected, to be screwed up by what she'd endured.

"Like a fucking mess." Her eyes glowed.

"Why?"

"Because it's none of their business, but they'll make it their business if they see. They're Fae males—sticking their noses into places they don't belong is an art form for them."

Hunt huffed a laugh. "True."

She exhaled again. "Okay," she murmured. "Okay." Her hands still shook, as if her bloody memories swarmed her.

It was instinct to take her hands in his own.

They trembled like glasses rattling on a shelf. Felt as delicate, even with the slick, clammy sweat coating them.

"Take a breath," Hunt said, squeezing her fingers gently.

Bryce closed her eyes, head bowing as she obeyed.

"Another," he commanded.

She did.

"Another."

So Quinlan breathed, Hunt not letting go of her hands until the sweat dried. Until she lifted her head. "Okay," she said again, and this time, the word was solid.

"You good?"

"As good as I'll ever be," she said, but her gaze had cleared.

Unable to help himself, he brushed back a loose tendril of her hair. It slid like cool silk against his fingers as he hooked it behind her arched ear. "You and me both, Quinlan."

Bryce let Hunt fly her to the crime scene. The alley in the Asphodel Meadows was about as seedy as they came: overflowing dumpster, suspect puddles of liquid gleaming, rail-thin animals rooting through the trash, broken glass sparkling in the firstlight from the rusting lamppost.

Glowing blue magi-screens already blocked off the alley entrance. A few technicians and legionaries were on the scene, Isaiah Tiberian, Ruhn, and his friends among them.

The alley lay just off Main Street, in the shadow of the North Gate—the Mortal Gate, most people called it. Apartment buildings loomed, most of them public, all in dire need of repairs. The noises from the cramped avenue beyond the alley echoed off the crumbling brick walls, the cloying reek of trash stuffing itself up her nose. Bryce tried not to inhale too much.

Hunt surveyed the alley and murmured, a strong hand on the small of her back, "You don't need to look, Bryce."

What he'd done for her just now in that shooting range . . . She'd never let anyone, even her parents, see her like that before. Those moments when she couldn't breathe. She usually went into a bathroom or bailed for a few hours or went for a run.

The instinct to flee had been nearly as overwhelming as the panic and dread searing her chest, but . . . she'd seen Hunt come in from his mission the other night. Knew he of all people might get it.

He had. And hadn't balked for one second.

Just as he hadn't balked from seeing her shoot that target, and instead answered it with a shot of his own. Like they were two of a kind, like she could throw anything at him and he'd catch it. Would meet every challenge with that wicked, feral grin.

She could have sworn the warmth from his hands still lingered on her own.

Whatever conversation they'd been having with Isaiah over, Flynn and Declan strode for the magi-screen. Ruhn stood ten feet beyond them, talking to a beautiful, dark-haired medwitch. No doubt asking about what she'd assessed.

Peering around the glowing blue edge to the body hidden beyond, Flynn and Declan swore.

Her stomach bottomed out. Maybe coming here had been a bad idea. She leaned slightly into Hunt's touch.

His fingers dug into her back in silent reassurance before he murmured, "I can look for us."

Us, like they were a unit against this fucking mess of a world.

"I'm fine," she said, her voice mercifully calm. But she didn't move toward the screen.

Flynn pulled away from the blocked-off body and asked Isaiah, "How fresh is this kill?"

"We're putting the TOD at thirty minutes ago," Isaiah answered gravely. "From the remains of the clothes, it looks like it was one of the guards at Luna's Temple. He was on his way home."

Silence rippled around them. Bryce's stomach dropped.

Hunt swore. "I'm gonna take a guess and say he was on duty the night the Horn was stolen?"

Isaiah nodded. "It was the first thing I checked."

Bryce swallowed and said, "We have to be getting close to something, then. Or the murderer is already one step ahead of us, interrogating and then killing anyone who might have known where the Horn disappeared to."

"None of the cameras caught anything?" Flynn asked, his handsome face unusually serious.

"Nothing," Isaiah said. "It's like it knew where they were. Or whoever summoned it did. It stayed out of sight."

Hunt ran his hand up the length of her spine, a solid, calming sweep, and then stepped toward the Commander of the 33rd, his voice low as he said, "To know every camera in this city, especially the hidden ones, would require some clearance." His words hung there, none of them daring to say more, not in public. Hunt asked, "Did anyone report a sighting of a demon?"

A DNA technician emerged from the screen, blood staining the knees of her white jumpsuit. Like she'd knelt in it while she gathered the sample kit dangling from her gloved fingers.

Bryce glanced away again, back toward Main Street.

Isaiah shook his head. "No reports from civilians or patrols yet."

Bryce barely heard him as the facts poured into her mind. Main Street.

She pulled out her phone, drawing up the map of the city. Her location pinged, a red dot on the network of streets.

The males were still talking about the scant evidence when she placed a few pins in the map, then squinted at the ground beneath them. Ruhn had drifted over, falling into conversation with his friends as she tuned them out.

But Hunt noted her focus and turned toward her, his dark brows high. "What?"

She leaned into the shadow of his wing, and could have sworn he folded it more closely around her. "Here's a map of where all the murders happened."

She allowed Ruhn and his friends to prowl near. Even deigned to show them her screen, her hands shaking slightly.

"This one," she said, pointing to the blinking dot, "is us." She pointed to another, close by. "This is where Maximus Tertian died." She pointed to another, this one near Central Avenue. "This is the acolyte's murder." Her throat constricted, but she pushed past it as she pointed to the other dot, a few blocks due north. "Here's where . . ." The words burned. Fuck. Fuck, she had to say it, voice it—

"Danika and the Pack of Devils were killed," Hunt supplied.

Bryce threw him a grateful glance. "Yes. Do you see what I see?"

"No?" Flynn said.

"Didn't you go to some fancy Fae prep school?" she asked. At

Flynn's scowl, she sighed, zooming out on the screen. "Look: all of them took place within steps of one of the major avenues. On top of the ley lines—natural channels for the firstlight to travel through the city."

"Highways of power," Hunt said, his eyes shining. "They flow right through the Gates." Yeah, Athalar got it. He aimed for where Isaiah stood twenty feet away, talking to a tall, blond nymph in a forensics jacket.

Bryce said to the Fae males, to her wide-eyed brother, "Maybe whoever is summoning this demon is drawing upon the power of these ley lines under the city to have the strength to summon it. If all the murders take place near them, maybe that's how the demon appeared."

One of the Aux team called Ruhn's name, and her brother merely gave her an impressed nod before going over to them. She ignored what that admiration did to her, turning her gaze to Hunt instead as he kept walking down the alley, the powerful muscles of his legs shifting. She heard him call to Isaiah as he walked toward the commander, "Have Viktoria run a search on the cameras along Main, Central, and Ward. See if they catch any blip of power—any small surge or drop in temperature that might happen if a demon were summoned." The kristallos might stay out of sight, but surely the cameras would pick up a slight disturbance in the power flow or temperature. "And have her look at the firstlight grid around those times, too. See if anything registered."

Declan watched the angel stride off, then said to Bryce, "You know what he does, right?"

"Look really good in black?" she said sweetly.

Declan growled. "That demon-hunting is a front. He does the Governor's dirty work." His chiseled jaw clenched for a second. "Hunt Athalar is bad news."

She batted her eyelashes. "Good thing I like bad boys."

Flynn let out a low whistle.

But Declan shook his head. "The angels don't give a shit about anyone, B. His goals are not *your* goals. Athalar's goals might not even be the same as Micah's. Be careful."

She nodded to where her brother was again speaking with the stunning medwitch. "I already got the pep talk from Ruhn, don't worry."

Down the alley, Hunt was saying to Isaiah, "Call me if Viktoria gets any video of it." Then he added, as if not quite used to it, "Thanks."

In the distance, clouds gathered. Rain had been predicted for the middle of the night, but it seemed it was arriving sooner.

Hunt stalked back toward them. "They're on it."

"We'll see if the 33rd follows through this time," Declan muttered. "I'm not holding my breath."

Hunt straightened. Bryce waited for his defense, but the angel shrugged. "Me neither."

Flynn jerked his head toward the angels working the scene. "No loyalty?"

Hunt read a message that flashed on his phone's screen, then pocketed it. "I don't have any choice but to be loyal."

And to tick off those deaths one by one. Bryce's stomach twisted.

Declan's amber eyes dropped to the tattoo on Hunt's wrist. "It's fucked up."

Flynn grumbled his agreement. At least her brother's friends were on the same page as her regarding the politics of the Asteri.

Hunt looked the males over again. Assessing. "Yeah," he said quietly. "It is."

"Understatement of the century." Bryce surveyed the murder scene, her body tightening again, not wanting to look. Hunt met her eyes, as if sensing that tightening, the shift in her scent. He gave her a subtle nod.

Bryce lifted her chin and declared, "We're going now."

Declan waved. "I'll call you soon, B."

Flynn blew her a kiss.

She rolled her eyes. "Bye." She caught Ruhn's stare and motioned her farewell. Her brother threw her a wave, and continued talking to the witch.

They made it all of one block before Hunt said, a little too casually, "You and Tristan Flynn ever hook up?"

Bryce blinked. "Why would you ask that?"

He tucked in his wings. "Because he flirts with you nonstop."

She snorted. "You wanna tell me about everyone you've ever hooked up with, Athalar?"

His silence told her enough. She smirked.

But then the angel said, as if he needed something to distract him from the pulped remains they'd left behind, "None of my *hookups* are worth mentioning." He paused again, taking a breath before continuing. "But that's because Shahar ruined me for anyone else."

Ruined me. The words clanged through Bryce.

Hunt went on, eyes swimming with memory, "I grew up in Shahar's territory in the southeast of Pangera, and as I worked my way up the ranks of her legions, I fell in love with her. With her vision for the world. With her ideas about how the angel hierarchies might change." He swallowed. "Shahar was the only one who ever suggested to me that I'd been denied anything by being born a bastard. She promoted me through her ranks, until I served as her right hand. Until I was her lover." He blew out a long breath. "She led the rebellion against the Asteri, and I led her forces—the 18th Legion. You know how it ended."

Everyone in Midgard did. The Daystar would have led the angels—maybe everyone—to a freer world, but she'd been extinguished. Another dreamer crushed under the boot heel of the Asteri.

Hunt said, "So you and Flynn . . . ?"

"You tell me this tragic love story and expect me to answer it with my bullshit?" His silence was answer enough. She sighed. But—fine. She, too, needed to talk about *something* to shake off that murder scene. And to dispel the shadows that had filled his eyes when he'd spoken of Shahar.

For that alone she said, "No. Flynn and I never hooked up." She smiled slightly. "When I visited Ruhn as a teenager, I was barely able to *function* in Flynn's and Declan's presence." Hunt's mouth curled upward. "They indulged my outrageous flirting, and for a while, I had a fanatic's conviction that Flynn would be my husband one day."

Hunt snickered, and Bryce elbowed him. "It's true. I wrote *Lady Bryce Flynn* on all my school notebooks for two years straight."

He gaped. "You did not."

"I so did. I can prove it: I still have all my notebooks at my parents' house because my mom refuses to throw anything away." Her amusement faltered. She didn't tell him about that time senior year of college when she and Danika ran into Flynn and Declan at a bar. How Danika had gone home with Flynn, because Bryce hadn't wanted to mess up anything between him and Ruhn.

"Want to hear my worst hookup?" she asked, throwing him a forced grin.

He chuckled. "I'm half-afraid to hear it, but sure."

"I dated a vampyr for like three weeks. My first and only hookup with anyone in Flame and Shadow."

The vamps had worked hard to get people to forget the tiny fact that they'd all come from Hel, lesser demons themselves. That their ancestors had defected from their seven princes during the First Wars, and fed the Asteri Imperial Legions vital intel that aided in their victory. Traitors and turncoats—who still held a demon's craving for blood.

Hunt lifted a brow. "And?"

Bryce winced. "And I couldn't stop wondering what part of me he wanted more: blood or . . . you know. And then he suggested eating *while* eating, if you know what I mean?"

It took Hunt a second to sort it out. Then his dark eyes widened. "Oh fuck. *Really?*" She didn't fail to note his glance to her legs—between them. The way his eyes seemed to darken further, something within them sharpening. "Wouldn't that hurt?"

"I didn't want to find out."

Hunt shook his head, and she wondered if he was unsure whether to cringe or laugh. But the light had come back to his eyes. "No more vamps after that?"

"Definitely not. He claimed the finest pleasure was always edged in pain, but I showed him the door."

Hunt grunted his approval. Bryce knew she probably shouldn't, but asked carefully, "You still have a thing for Shahar?"

A muscle feathered in his jaw. He scanned the skies. "Until the day I die."

No longing or sorrow graced the words, but she still wasn't entirely sure what to do with the dropping sensation in her stomach.

Hunt's eyes slid to hers at last. Bleak and lightless. "I don't see how I can move on from loving her when she gave up *everything* for me. For the cause." He shook his head. "Every time I hook up, I remember it."

"Ah." No arguing with that. Anything she said against it would sound selfish and whiny. And maybe she was dumb, for letting herself read into his leg touching hers or the way he'd looked at her at the shooting range or coaxed her through her panic or any of it.

He was staring at her. As if seeing all of that. His throat bobbed. "Quinlan, that isn't to say that I'm not—"

His words were cut off by a cluster of people approaching from the other end of the street.

She glimpsed silvery blond hair and couldn't breathe. Hunt swore. "Let's get airborne—"

But Sabine had spotted them. Her narrow, pale face twisted in a snarl.

Bryce hated the shaking that overtook her hands. The trembling in her knees.

Hunt warned Sabine, "Keep moving, Fendyr."

Sabine ignored him. Her stare was like being pelted with shards of ice. "I heard you've been showing your face again," she seethed at Bryce. "Where the *fuck* is my sword, Quinlan?"

Bryce couldn't think of anything to say, any retort or explanation. She just let Hunt lead her past Sabine, the angel a veritable wall of muscle between them.

Hunt's hand rested on Bryce's back as he nudged her along. "Let's go."

"Stupid slut," Sabine hissed, spitting at Bryce's feet as she passed.

Hunt stiffened, a growl slipping out, but Bryce gripped his arm in a silent plea to let it go.

His teeth gleamed as he bared them over a shoulder at Sabine, but Bryce whispered, "Please."

He scanned her face, mouth opening to object. She made them keep walking, even as Sabine's sneer branded itself into her back.

"Please," Bryce whispered again.

His chest heaved, as if it took every bit of effort to reel in his rage, but he faced forward. Sabine's low, smug laugh rippled toward them.

Hunt's body locked up, and Bryce squeezed his arm tighter, misery coiling around her gut.

Maybe he scented it, maybe he read it on her face, but Hunt's steps evened out. His hand again warmed her lower back, a steady presence as they walked, finally crossing the street.

They were halfway across Main when Hunt scooped her into his arms, not saying a word as he launched into the brisk skies.

She leaned her head against his chest. Let the wind drown out the roaring in her mind.

They landed on the roof of her building five minutes later, and she would have gone right down to the apartment had he not gripped her arm to stop her.

Hunt again scanned her face. Her eyes.

Us, he'd said earlier. A unit. A team. A two-person pack.

Hunt's wings shifted slightly in the wind off the Istros. "We're going to find whoever is behind all this, Bryce. I promise."

And for some reason, she believed him.

She was brushing her teeth when her phone rang.

Declan Emmet.

She spat out her toothpaste before answering. "Hi."

"You still have my number saved? I'm touched, B."

"Yeah, yeah, yeah. What's up?"

"I found something interesting in the footage. The taxpaying residents of this city should revolt at how their money's being blown on second-rate analysts instead of people like me."

Bryce padded into the hall, then into the great room—then to

Hunt's door. She knocked on it once, and said to Declan, "Are you going to tell me or just gloat about it?"

Hunt opened the door.

Burning. Fucking. Solas.

He wasn't wearing a shirt, and from the look of it, had been in the middle of brushing his teeth, too. But she didn't give a shit about his dental hygiene when he looked like *that*.

Muscles upon muscles upon muscles, all covered by golden-brown skin that glowed in the firstlights. It was outrageous. She'd seen him shirtless before, but she hadn't noticed—not like this.

She'd seen more than her fair share of cut, beautiful male bodies, but Hunt Athalar's blew them all away.

He was pining for a lost love, she reminded herself. Had made that *very* clear earlier tonight. Through an effort of will, she lifted her eyes and found a shit-eating smirk on his face.

But his smug-ass smile faded when she put Declan on speaker. Dec said, "I don't know if I should tell you to sit down or not."

Hunt stepped into the great room, frowning. "Just tell me," Bryce said.

"Okay, so I'll admit someone could easily have made a mistake. Thanks to the blackout, the footage is just darkness with some sounds. Ordinary city sounds of people reacting to the blackout. So I pulled apart each audio thread from the street outside the temple. Amped up the ones in the background that the government computers might not have had the tech to hear. You know what I heard? People giggling, goading each other to *touch it*."

"Please tell me this isn't going to end grossly," Bryce said. Hunt snorted.

"It was people at the Rose Gate. I could hear people at the Rose Gate in FiRo daring each other to touch the disk on the dial pad in the blackout, to see if it still worked. It did, by the way. But I could also hear them *ooh*ing about the night-blooming flowers on the Gate itself."

Hunt leaned in, his scent wrapping around her, dizzying her, as he said into the phone, "The Rose Gate is halfway across the city from Luna's Temple."

Declan chuckled. "Hey, Athalar. Enjoying playing houseguest with Bryce?"

"Just tell us," Bryce said, grinding her teeth. Taking a big, careful step away from Hunt.

"Someone swapped the footage of the temple during the time of the Horn's theft. It was clever fucking work—they patched it right in so that there isn't so much as a flicker in the time stamp. They picked audio footage that was a near-match for what it would have sounded like at the temple, with the angle of the buildings and everything. Really smart shit. But not smart enough. The 33rd should have come to me. I'd have found an error like that."

Bryce's heart pounded. "Can you find who did this?"

"I already did." Any smugness faded from Declan's voice. "I looked at who was responsible for heading up the investigation of the video footage that night. They'd be the only one with the clearance to make a swap like that."

Bryce tapped her foot on the ground, and Athalar brushed his wing against her shoulder in quiet reassurance. "Who *is* it, Dec?"

Declan sighed. "Look, I'm not saying it's this person one hundred percent . . . but the official who headed up that part of the investigation was Sabine Fendyr."

PART III
THE CANYON

38

It makes sense," Hunt said carefully, watching Bryce where she sat on the rolled arm of her sofa, chewing on her lower lip. She'd barely thanked Declan before hanging up.

Hunt said, "The demon has been staying out of view of the cameras in the city. Sabine would know where those cameras are, especially if she had the authority to oversee the video footage of criminal cases."

Sabine's behavior earlier tonight . . . He'd wanted to kill her.

He'd seen Bryce laugh in the face of the Viper Queen, go toe-to-toe with Philip Briggs, and taunt three of the most lethal Fae warriors in this city—and yet she'd trembled before Sabine.

He hadn't been able to stand it, her fear and misery and guilt.

When Bryce didn't reply, he said again, "It makes sense that Sabine could be behind this." He sat beside her on the sectional. He'd put on a shirt a moment ago, even though he'd enjoyed the look of pure admiration on Bryce's face as she got an eyeful of him.

"Sabine wouldn't have killed her own daughter."

"You really believe that?"

Bryce wrapped her arms around her knees. "No." In a pair of sleeping shorts and an oversize, worn T-shirt, she looked young. Small. Tired.

Hunt said, "Everyone knows that the Prime was considering skipping over Sabine to tap Danika to be his heir. That seems like a good fucking motive to me." He considered again, an old memory snagging his attention. He pulled out his phone and said, "Hold on."

Isaiah answered on the third ring. "Yeah?"

"How easily can you access your notes from the observation room the night Danika died?" He didn't let Isaiah reply before he said, "Specifically, did you write down what Sabine said to us?"

Isaiah's pause was fraught. "Tell me you don't think Sabine killed her."

"Can you get me the notes?" Hunt pushed. Isaiah swore, but a moment later he said, "All right, I've got it." Hunt moved closer to Quinlan so she could hear the commander's voice as he said, "You want me to recite this whole thing?"

"Just what she said about Danika. Did you catch it?"

He knew Isaiah had. The male took extensive notes on everything.

"Sabine said, *Danika couldn't stay out of trouble.*" Bryce stiffened, and Hunt laid his free hand on her knee, squeezing once. "*She could never keep her mouth* shut *and know when to be quiet around her enemies. And look what became of her. That stupid little bitch in there is still breathing, and Danika is* not. *Danika should have known better.* Hunt, you then asked her what Danika should have known better about, and Sabine said, *All of it. Starting with that slut of a roommate.*"

Bryce flinched, and Hunt rubbed his thumb over her knee. "Thanks, Isaiah."

Isaiah cleared his throat. "Be careful." The call ended.

Bryce's wide eyes glimmered. "What Sabine said could be construed a lot of ways," she admitted. "But—"

"It sounds like Sabine wanted Danika to keep quiet about something. Maybe Danika threatened to talk about the Horn's theft, and Sabine killed her for it. "

Bryce's throat bobbed as she nodded. "Why wait two years, though?"

"I suppose that's what we'll find out from her."

"What would Sabine want with a broken artifact? And even if she knew how to repair it, what would she do with it?"

"I don't know. And I don't know if someone else has it and she wants it, but—"

"If Danika saw Sabine steal it, it'd make sense that Danika never said anything. Same with the guard and the acolyte. They were probably too scared to come forward."

"It would explain why Sabine swapped the footage. And why it freaked her out when we showed up at the temple, causing her to kill anyone who might have seen anything that night. The bomb at the club was probably a way to either intimidate us or kill us while making it look like humans were behind it."

"But . . . I don't think she has it," Bryce mused, toying with her toes. They were painted a deep ruby. Ridiculous, he told himself. Not the alternative. The one that had him imagining tasting each and every one of those toes before slowly working his way up those sleek, bare legs of hers. Bare legs that were mere inches from him, golden skin gleaming in the firstlights. He forced himself to withdraw his hand from her knee, even as his fingers begged to move, to stroke along her thigh. Higher.

Bryce went on, oblivious to his filthy train of thoughts, "I don't see why Sabine would have the Horn and still summon the kristallos."

Hunt cleared his throat. It'd been a long fucking day. A weird one, if this was where his thoughts had drifted. Honestly, they'd been drifting in this direction since the gun range. Since he'd seen her hold that gun like a gods-damned pro.

He forced himself to focus. Consider the conversation at hand and not contemplate whether Quinlan's legs would feel as soft beneath his mouth as they looked. "Don't forget that Sabine hates Micah's guts. Beyond silencing the victims, the killings now could also be to undermine him. You saw how tied up he is about getting this solved before the Summit. Murders like these, caused by an unknown demon, when Sandriel is here? It'll make a mockery of him. Maximus Tertian was high profile enough to create a political headache for Micah—Tertian's death might have just been to fuck with Micah's standing. For fuck's sake, she and Sandriel might even be in on it together, hoping to weaken him in the Asteri's eyes, so they appoint Sandriel to Valbara instead. She could easily make Sabine the Prime of all Valbaran shifters—not just wolves."

Bryce's face blanched. No such title existed, but it was within a Governor's right to create it. "Sabine isn't that type. She's power hungry, but not on that scale. She thinks petty—*is* petty. You heard her bitching about Danika's missing sword." Bryce idly braided her long hair. "We shouldn't waste our breath guessing her motives. It could be anything."

"You're right. We've got a damn good reason for thinking she killed Danika, but nothing solid enough to explain these new murders." He watched her long, delicate fingers twine through her hair. Made himself look at the darkened television screen instead. "Catching her with the demon would prove her involvement."

"You think Viktoria can find that footage we requested?"

"I hope so," he said. Hunt mulled it over. Sabine—fuck, if it was her . . .

Bryce rose from the couch. "I'm going for a run."

"It's one in the morning."

"I need to run for a bit, or I won't be able to fall asleep."

Hunt shot to his feet. "We just came from the scene of a murder, and Sabine was out for your blood, Bryce—"

She aimed for her bedroom and didn't look back.

She emerged two minutes later in her exercise clothes and found him standing by the door in workout gear of his own. She frowned. "I want to run alone."

Hunt opened the door and stepped into the hall. "Too fucking bad."

There was her breathing, and the pounding of her feet on the slick streets, and the blaring music in her ears. She'd turned it up so loud it was mostly just noise. Deafening noise with a beat. She never played it this loud during her morning runs, but with Hunt keeping a steady pace beside her, she could blast her music and not worry about some predator taking advantage of it.

So she ran. Down the broad avenues, the alleys, and side streets. Hunt moved with her, every motion graceful and rippling with power. She could have sworn lightning trailed in their wake.

Sabine. Had she killed Danika?

Bryce couldn't wrap her mind around it. Each breath was like shards of glass.

They needed to catch her in the act. Find evidence against her.

Her leg began to ache, an acidic burn along her upper thighbone. She ignored it.

Bryce cut toward Asphodel Meadows, the route so familiar that she was surprised her footprints hadn't been worn into the cobblestones. She rounded a corner sharply, biting down on the groan of pain as her leg objected. Hunt's gaze snapped to her, but she didn't look at him.

Sabine. Sabine. Sabine.

Her leg burned, but she kept going. Through the Meadows. Through FiRo.

Kept running. Kept breathing. She didn't dare stop.

Bryce knew Hunt was making a concerted effort to keep his mouth shut when they finally returned to her apartment an hour later. She had to grip the doorway to keep upright.

His eyes narrowed, but he said nothing. He didn't mention that her limp had been so bad she'd barely been able to run the last ten blocks. Bryce knew the limp and pain would be worse by morning. Each step drew a cry to her throat that she swallowed down and down and down.

"All right?" he asked tightly, lifting his shirt to wipe the sweat from his face. She had a too-brief glimpse of those ridiculous stomach muscles, gleaming with sweat. He'd stayed by her side the entire time—hadn't complained or spoken. Had just kept pace.

Bryce made a point not to lean on the wall as she walked toward her bedroom.

"I'm fine," she said breathlessly. "Just needed to run it out."

He reached for her leg, a muscle ticking in his jaw. "That happen often?"

"No," she lied.

Hunt just gave her a look.

She couldn't stop her next limping step. "Sometimes," she amended, wincing. "I'll ice it. It'll be fine by morning." If she'd been full-blooded Fae, it would have healed in an hour or two. Then again, if she were full-blooded Fae, the injury wouldn't have lingered like this.

His voice was hoarse as he asked, "You ever get it checked out?"

"Yep," she lied again, and rubbed at her sweaty neck. Before he could call her on it, she said, "Thanks for coming."

"Yeah." Not quite an answer, but Hunt mercifully said nothing else as she limped down the hallway and shut the door to her room.

39

Despite its entrance facing the bustle of the Old Square, Ruhn found the medwitch clinic blissfully quiet. The white-painted walls of the waiting room glowed with the sunshine leaking through the windows that looked onto the semipermanent traffic, and the trickle of a small quartz fountain atop the white marble counter blended pleasantly with the symphony playing through the ceiling's speakers.

He'd been waiting for five minutes now, while the witch he'd come to see finished up with a patient, and had been perfectly content to bask in the tendrils of lavender-scented steam from the diffuser on the small table beside his chair. Even his shadows slumbered inside him.

Magazines and pamphlets had been spread across the white oak coffee table before him, the latter advertising everything from fertility treatments to scar therapy to arthritis relief.

A door down the narrow hallway beyond the counter opened, and a dark head of softly curling hair emerged, a musical voice saying, "Please do call if you have any further symptoms." The door clicked shut, presumably to give the patient privacy.

Ruhn stood, feeling out of place in his head-to-toe black clothes in the midst of the soft whites and creams of the clinic, and kept himself perfectly still as the medwitch approached the counter.

At the crime scene last night, he'd gone over to inquire as to whether she'd noted anything interesting about the corpse. He'd been impressed enough by her clear-eyed intelligence that he'd asked to stop by this morning.

The medwitch smiled slightly as she reached the other side of the counter, her dark eyes lighting with welcome.

Then there was that. Her arresting face. Not the cultivated beauty of a movie star or model—no, this was beauty in its rawest form, from her large brown eyes to her full mouth to her high cheekbones, all in near-perfect symmetry. All radiating a cool serenity and awareness. He'd been unable to stop looking at her, even with a splattered corpse behind them.

"Good morning, Prince." And there was that, too. Her fair, beautiful voice. Fae were sensitive about sounds, thanks to their heightened hearing. They could hear notes within notes, chords within chords. Ruhn had once nearly run from a date with a young nymph when her high-pitched giggling had sounded more like a porpoise's squeal. And in bed . . . fuck, how many partners had he never called again not because the sex had been bad, but because the sounds they'd made had been unbearable? Too many to count.

Ruhn offered the medwitch a smile. "Hi." He nodded toward the hall. "I know you're busy, but I was hoping you could spare a few minutes to chat about this case I'm working on."

Clad in loose navy pants and a white cotton shirt with quarter-length sleeves that brought out her glowing brown skin, the medwitch stood with an impressive level of stillness.

They were a strange, unique group, the witches. Though they looked like humans, their considerable magic and long lives marked them as Vanir, their power mostly passed through the female line. All of them deemed civitas. The power was inherited, from some ancient source that the witches claimed was a three-faced goddess, but witches did pop up in non-magical families every now and then. Their gifts were varied, from seers to warriors to potion-makers, but healers were the most visible in Crescent City. Their schooling was thorough and long enough that the young witch before him was unusual. She had to be skilled to be already working in a clinic when she couldn't have been a day over thirty.

"I have another patient coming soon," she said, glancing over his shoulder to the busy street beyond. "But I have lunch after that. Do you mind waiting half an hour?" She gestured to the hall behind her, where sunlight leaked in through a glass door at its other end. "We have a courtyard garden. The day is fine enough that you could wait out there."

Ruhn agreed, glancing to the nameplate on the counter. "Thank you, Miss Solomon."

She blinked, those thick, velvety lashes bobbing in surprise. "Oh—I am not . . . This is my sister's clinic. She went on holiday, and asked me to cover for her while she's gone." She gestured again to the hallway, graceful as a queen.

Ruhn followed her down the hall, trying not to breathe in her eucalyptus-and-lavender scent too deeply.

Don't be a fucking creep.

The sunlight tangled in her thick night-dark hair as she reached the courtyard door and shouldered it open, revealing a slate-covered patio surrounded by terraced herb gardens. The day was indeed lovely, the river breeze making the plants rustle and sway, spreading their soothing fragrances.

She pointed to a wrought-iron table and chairs set by a bed of mint. "I'll be out shortly."

"Okay," he said, and she didn't wait for him to take a seat before disappearing inside.

The thirty minutes passed quickly, mostly thanks to a flurry of calls he got from Dec and Flynn, along with a few of his Aux captains. By the time the glass door opened again, he had just set down his phone, intending on enjoying a few minutes of sweet-smelling silence.

He shot to his feet at the sight of the heavy tray the witch bore, laden with a steaming teapot, cups, and a plate of cheese, honey, and bread. "I thought that if I'm stopping for lunch, we might as well eat together," she said as Ruhn took the tray.

"You didn't need to bring me anything," he said, careful not to upset the teapot as he set the tray on the table.

"It was no trouble. I don't like to eat alone anyway." She took the seat across from him, and began distributing the silverware.

"Where's your accent from?" She didn't speak with the fast-paced diction of someone in this city, but rather like someone who selected each word carefully.

She spread some cheese onto a slice of bread. "My tutors were from an old part of Pelium—by the Rhagan Sea. It rubbed off on me, I suppose."

Ruhn poured himself some of the tea, then filled her cup. "All of that area is old."

Her brown eyes gleamed. "Indeed."

He waited until she'd taken a sip of tea before saying, "I've spoken about this to a few other medwitches around town, but no one's been able to give me an answer. I'm fully aware that I might be grasping at straws here. But before I say anything, I'd like to ask for your . . . discretion."

She pulled a few grapes and dates onto her plate. "You may ask what you wish. I will not speak a word of it."

He inhaled the scent of his tea—peppermint and licorice and something else, a whisper of vanilla and something . . . woodsy. He leaned back in his chair. "All right. I know your time is limited, so I'll be direct: can you think of any way a magical object that was broken might be repaired when no one—not witches, not the Fae, not the Asteri themselves—has been able to fix it? A way it might be . . . healed?"

She drizzled honey atop her cheese. "Was the object made from magic, or was it an ordinary item that was imbued with power afterward?"

"Legend says it was made with magic—and could only be used with the Starborn gifts."

"Ah." Her clear eyes scanned him, noting his coloring. "So it is a Fae artifact."

"Yes. From the First Wars."

"You speak of Luna's Horn?" None of the other witches had gotten to it so quickly.

"Maybe," he hedged, letting her see the truth in his eyes.

"Magic and the power of the seven holy stars could not repair it," she said. "And far wiser witches than I have looked at it and found it an impossible task."

Disappointment dropped in his stomach. "I just figured that the medwitches might have some idea how to heal it, considering your field of expertise."

"I see why you might think that. This clinic is full of marvels that I did not know existed—that my tutors did not know existed. Lasers and cameras and machines that can peer inside your body in the same way my magic can." Her eyes brightened with each word, and for the life of him, Ruhn couldn't look away. "And maybe . . ." She angled her head, staring into a swaying bed of lavender.

Ruhn kept his mouth shut, letting her think. His phone buzzed with an incoming message, and he quickly silenced it.

The witch went still. Her slender fingers contracted on the table. Just one movement, one ripple of reaction, to suggest something had clicked in that pretty head of hers. But she said nothing.

When she met his stare again, her eyes were dark. Full of warning. "It is possible that with all the medical advancements today, someone might have found a way to repair a broken object of power. To treat the artifact not as something inert, but as a living thing."

"So, what—they'd use some sort of laser to repair it?"

"A laser, a drug, a skin graft, a transplant . . . current research has opened many doors."

Shit. "Would it ring any bells if I said the ancient Fae claimed the Horn could only be repaired by light that was not light, magic that was not magic? Does it sound like any modern tech?"

"In that, I will admit I am not as well-versed as my sisters. My knowledge of healing is rooted in our oldest ways."

"It's all right," he said, and rose from his chair. "Thanks for your time."

She met his eyes with a surprising frankness. Utterly unafraid of or impressed by him. "I am certain you will do so already, but I'd advise you to proceed with caution, Prince."

"I know. Thanks." He rubbed the back of his neck, bracing himself. "Do you think your queen might have an answer?"

The medwitch's head angled again, all that glorious hair spilling over her shoulder. "My . . . Oh." He could have sworn sorrow clouded her eyes. "You mean the new queen."

"Hypaxia." Her name shimmered on his tongue. "I'm sorry about the loss of your old queen."

"So am I," the witch said. For a moment, her shoulders seemed to curve inward, her head bowing under a phantom weight. Hecuba had been beloved by her people—her loss would linger. The witch blew out a breath through her nose and straightened again, as if shaking off the mantle of sorrow. "Hypaxia has been in mourning for her mother. She will not receive visitors until she makes her appearance at the Summit." She smiled slightly. "Perhaps you can ask her yourself then."

Ruhn winced. On the one hand, at least he didn't have to go see the woman his father wanted him to marry. "Unfortunately, this case is pressing enough that it can't wait until the Summit."

"I will pray to Cthona that you find your answers elsewhere, then."

"Hopefully she'll listen." He took a few steps toward the door.

"I hope to see you again, Prince," the medwitch said, returning to her lunch.

The words weren't a come-on, some not-so-subtle invitation. But even later, as he sat in the Fae Archives researching medical breakthroughs, he still pondered the tone and promise of her farewell.

And realized he'd never gotten her name.

40

It took Viktoria two days to find anything unusual on the city cameras and the power grid. But when she did, she didn't call Hunt. No, she sent a messenger.

"Vik told me to get your ass to her office—the one at the lab," Isaiah said by way of greeting as he landed on the roof of the gallery.

Leaning against the doorway that led downstairs, Hunt sized up his commander. Isaiah's usual glow had dimmed, and shadows lay beneath his eyes. "It's that bad with Sandriel there?"

Isaiah folded in his wings. Tightly. "Micah's keeping her in check, but I was up all night dealing with petrified people."

"Soldiers?"

"Soldiers, staff, employees, nearby residents . . . She's rattled them." Isaiah shook his head. "She's keeping the timing of Pollux's arrival quiet, too, to put us all on edge. She knows what kind of fear he drags up."

"Maybe we'll get lucky and that piece of shit will stay in Pangera."

"We're never that lucky, are we?"

"No. We're not." Hunt let out a bitter laugh. "The Summit's still a month away." A month of enduring Sandriel's presence. "I . . . If you need anything from me, let me know."

Isaiah blinked, surveying Hunt from head to boot tip. It shouldn't have shamed him, that surprise on the commander's face at his offer. Isaiah's gaze shifted to the tiled roof beneath their matching boots, as if contemplating what or who might be responsible for his turn toward the altruistic. But Isaiah just asked, "Do you think Roga really turns her exes and enemies into animals?"

Having observed the creatures in the small tanks throughout the library, Hunt could only say, "I hope not." Especially for the sake of the assistant who had been pretending she wasn't falling asleep at her desk when he'd called to check in twenty minutes ago.

Since Declan had dropped the bomb about Sabine, she'd been broody. Hunt had advised her to be cautious about going after the future Prime, and she'd seemed inclined to wait for Viktoria to find any hint of the demon's patterns—any proof that Sabine was indeed using the power of the ley lines to summon it, since her own power levels weren't strong enough. Most shifters' powers weren't, though Danika had been an exception. Another reason for her mother's jealousy—and motive.

They'd heard nothing from Ruhn, only a message yesterday about doing more research on the Horn. But if Vik had found something . . . Hunt asked, "Vik can't come here with the news?"

"She wanted to show you in person. And I doubt Jesiba will be pleased if Vik comes here."

"Considerate of you."

Isaiah shrugged. "Jesiba is assisting us—we need her resources. It'd be stupid to push her limits. I have no interest in seeing any of you turned into pigs if we step on her toes too much."

And there it was. The meaningful, too-long glance.

Hunt held up his hands with a grin. "No need to worry on my front."

"Micah will come down on you like a hammer if you jeopardize this."

"Bryce already told Micah she wasn't interested."

"He won't forget that anytime soon." Fuck, Hunt certainly knew that. The kill Micah had ordered last week as punishment for Hunt and Bryce embarrassing him in the Comitium lobby . . . It had lingered. "But I don't mean that. I meant if we don't find out who's behind this, if it turns out you're wrong about Sabine—not only will your reduced sentence be off the table, but Micah will find *you* responsible."

"Of course he will." Hunt's phone buzzed, and he pulled it from his pocket.

He choked. Not just at the message from Bryce: *The gallery roof isn't a pigeon roost, you know,* but what she'd changed her contact name to, presumably when he'd gone to the bathroom or showered or just left his phone on the coffee table: *Bryce Rocks My Socks.*

And there, beneath the ridiculous name, she'd added a photo to her contact: the one she'd snapped of herself in the phone store, grinning from ear to ear.

Hunt suppressed a growl of irritation and typed back, *Shouldn't you be working?*

Bryce Rocks My Socks wrote back a second later, *How can I work when you two are thumping around up there?*

He wrote back, *How'd you get my password?* She hadn't needed it to activate the camera feature, but to have gotten into his contacts, she would have needed the seven-digit combination.

I paid attention. She added a second later, *And might have observed you typing it in a few times while you were watching some dumb sunball game.*

Hunt rolled his eyes and pocketed his phone without replying. Well, at least she was coming out of that quiet cloud she'd been in for days.

He found Isaiah watching him carefully. "There are worse fates than death, you know."

Hunt looked toward the Comitium, the female Archangel lurking in it. "I know."

Bryce frowned out the gallery door. "The forecast didn't call for rain." She scowled at the sky. "*Someone* must be throwing a tantrum."

"It's illegal to interfere with the weather," Hunt recited from beside her, thumbing a message into his phone. He hadn't changed the new contact name she'd given herself, Bryce had noticed. Or erased that absurd photo she'd added to her contact listing.

She silently mimicked his words, then said, "I don't have an umbrella."

"It's not a far flight to the lab."

"It'd be easier to call a car."

"At this hour? In the rain?" He sent off his message and pocketed his phone. "It'll take you an hour just to cross Central Avenue."

The rain swept through the city in sheets. "I could get electrocuted up there."

Hunt's eyes glittered as he offered her a hand. "Good thing I can keep you safe."

With all that lightning in his veins, she supposed it was true.

Bryce sighed and frowned at her dress, the black suede heels that would surely be ruined. "I'm not in flying-appropriate attire—"

The word ended on a yelp as Hunt hauled her into the sky.

She clung to him, hissing like a cat. "We have to go back before closing for Syrinx."

Hunt soared over the congested, rain-battered streets as Vanir and humans ducked into doorways and under awnings to escape the weather. The only ones on the streets were those with umbrellas or magical shields up. Bryce buried her face against his chest, as if it'd shield her from the rain—and the terrible drop. What it amounted to was a face full of his scent and the warmth of his body against her cheek.

"Slow down," she ordered, fingers digging into his shoulders and neck.

"Don't be a baby," he crooned in her ear, the richness of his voice skittering over every bone of her body. "Look around, Quinlan. Enjoy the view." He added, "I like the city in the rain."

When she kept her head ducked against his chest, he gave her a squeeze. "Come on," he teased over the honking horns and splash of tires through puddles. He added, voice nearly a purr, "I'll buy you a milkshake if you do."

Her toes curled in her shoes at the low, coaxing voice.

"Only for ice cream," she muttered, earning a chuckle from him, and cracked open an eye. She forced the other one open, too. Clutching his shoulders nearly hard enough to pierce through to his skin, working against every instinct that screamed for her body to lock up, she squinted through the water lashing her face at the passing city.

In the rain, the marble buildings gleamed like they were made from moonstone, the gray cobblestone streets appeared polished a silvery blue splashed with the gold of the firstlight lamps. To her right, the Gates in the Old Square, Moonwood, and FiRo rose through the sprawl, like the humped spine of some twining beast breaking the surface of a lake, their crystal gleaming like melting ice. From this high, the avenues that linked them all—the ley lines beneath them—shot like spears through the city.

The wind rattled the palms, tossing the fronds to and fro, their hissing almost drowning out the cranky honking of drivers now in a traffic standstill. The whole city, in fact, seemed to have stopped for a moment—except for them, swiftly passing above it all.

"Not so bad, huh?"

She pinched Athalar's neck, and his answering laugh brushed over her ear. She might have pressed her body a little harder against the solid wall of his. He might have tightened his grip, too. Just a bit.

In silence, they watched the buildings shift from ancient stone and brick to sleek metal and glass. The cars turned fancier, too—worn taxis exchanged for black sedans with tinted windows, uniformed drivers idling in the front seats while they waited in lines outside the towering high-rises. Fewer people occupied the much-cleaner streets—certainly there was no music or restaurants overflowing with food and drink and laughter. This was a sanitized, orderly pocket of the city, where the point was not to look around, but to look *up*. High in the rain-veiled gloom that wreathed the upper portions of the buildings, lights and shimmering whorls of color stained the mists. A splotch of red gleamed to her left, and she didn't need to look to know it came from Redner Industries' headquarters. She hadn't seen or heard from Reid in the two years since Danika's murder—he'd never even sent his condolences afterward. Even though Danika herself had worked part-time at the company. Prick.

Hunt steered for a solid concrete building that Bryce had tried to block from her memory, landing smoothly on a second-story balcony. Hunt was opening the glass doors, flashing some sort of entry ID into a scanner, when he said to her, "Viktoria's a wraith."

She almost said *I know*, but only nodded, following him inside. She and Hunt had barely spoken about that night. About what she remembered.

The air-conditioning was on full blast, and she instantly wrapped her arms around herself, teeth chattering at the shock of going from the storm into crisp cold.

"Walk fast" was the only help Hunt offered, wiping the rain off his face.

A cramped elevator ride and two hallways later, Bryce found herself shivering in the doorway of a spacious office overlooking a small park.

Watching as Hunt and Viktoria clasped hands over the wraith's curved glass desk.

Hunt gestured to her, "Bryce Quinlan, this is Viktoria Vargos."

Viktoria, to her credit, pretended to be meeting her for the first time.

So much of that night was a blur. But Bryce remembered the sanitized room. Remembered Viktoria playing that recording.

At least Bryce could now appreciate the beauty before her: the dark hair and pale skin and stunning green eyes were all Pangeran heritage, speaking of vineyards and carved marble palaces. But the grace with which Viktoria moved . . . Viktoria must have been old as Hel to have that sort of fluid beauty. To be able to steer her body so smoothly.

A halo had been tattooed on her brow as well. Bryce hid her surprise—her memory had failed to provide that detail. She knew the sprites had fought in the angels' rebellion, but hadn't realized any other non-malakim had marched under Shahar's Daystar banner.

Warmth glowed in Viktoria's eyes as she purred, "Pleasure."

Somehow, Athalar only looked better soaked with rain, his shirt clinging to every hard, sculpted muscle. Bryce was all too aware, as she extended a hand, of how her hair now lay flat on her head thanks to the rain, of the makeup that had probably smeared down her face.

Viktoria took Bryce's hand, her grip firm but friendly, and smiled. Winked.

Hunt grumbled, "She does that flirty smile with everyone, so don't bother being flattered."

Bryce settled into one of the twin black leather seats on the other side of the desk, batting her eyelashes at Hunt. "Does she do it for you, too?"

Viktoria barked a laugh, the sound rich and lovely. "You earned that one, Athalar."

Hunt scowled, dropping into another chair—one with the back cut low, Bryce realized, to accommodate anyone with wings.

"Isaiah said you found something," Hunt said, crossing an ankle over a knee.

"Yes, though not quite what you requested." Viktoria came around the desk and handed a file to Bryce. Hunt leaned in to peer over her shoulder. His wing brushed against the back of Bryce's head, but he didn't remove it.

Bryce squinted at the grainy photo, the sole clawed foot in the lower right corner. "Is that—"

"Spotted in Moonwood just last night. I was tracking temperature fluctuations around the main avenues like you said, and noticed a dip—just for two seconds."

"A summoning," Hunt said.

"Yes," Viktoria said. "The camera only got this tiny image of the foot—it mostly stayed out of sight. But it was just off a main avenue, like you suspected. We have a few more grainy captures from other locations last night, but those show it even less—a talon, rather than this entire foot."

The photo was blurry, but there it was—those shredding claws she'd never forget.

It was an effort not to touch her leg. To remember the clear teeth that had ripped into it.

Both of them looked to her. Waiting. Bryce managed to say, "That's a kristallos demon."

Hunt's wing spread a little farther around her, but he said nothing.

"I couldn't find temperature fluctuations from the night of every murder," Vik said, face turning grim. "But I did find one from when Maximus Tertian died. Ten minutes and two blocks away from him. No video footage, but it was the same seventy-seven-degree dip, made in the span of two seconds."

"Did it attack anyone last night?" Bryce's voice had turned a bit distant—even to her ears.

"No," Viktoria said. "Not as far as we know."

Hunt kept studying the image. "Did the kristallos go anywhere specific?"

Viktoria handed over another document. It was a map of Moonwood, full of sprawling parks and riverfront walkways, palatial villas and complexes for Vanir and a few wealthy humans, peppered with the best schools and many of the fanciest restaurants in town. In its heart: the Den. About six red dots surrounded it. The creature had crawled around its towering walls. Right in the heart of Sabine's territory.

"Burning Solas," Bryce breathed, a chill slithering along her spine.

"It would have found a way inside the Den's walls if what it hunts was there," Hunt mused quietly. "Maybe it was just following an old scent."

Bryce traced a finger between the various dots. "No bigger pattern, though?"

"I ran it through the system and nothing came up beyond what you two figured out about the proximity to the ley lines beneath those roads and the temperature dips." Viktoria sighed. "It seems like it was looking for something. Or someone."

Blood and bone and gore, sprayed and shredded and in chunks—

Glass ripping into her feet; fangs ripping into her skin—

A warm, strong hand gently gripped her thigh. Squeezed once.

But when Bryce looked over at Hunt, his attention was upon Viktoria—even as his hand remained upon her bare leg, his wing still slightly curved around her. "How'd you lose track of it?"

"It was simply there one moment, and gone the next."

Hunt's thumb stroked her leg, just above her knee. An idle, reassuring touch.

One that was far too distracting as Viktoria leaned forward to tap another spot on the map, her green eyes lifting from it only to note Hunt's hand as well. Wariness flooded her stare, but she said, "This was its last known location, at least as far as what our cameras could find." The Rose Gate in FiRo. Nowhere near Sabine's territory. "As I said, one moment it was there, then it was gone. I've had two different units and one Auxiliary pack hunting for it all day, but no luck."

Hunt's hand slid from her leg, leaving a cold spot in its wake. A glance at his face and she saw the cause: Viktoria now held his gaze, her own full of warning.

Bryce tapped her dusky nails on the chrome arm of the chair.

Well, at least she knew what they were doing after dinner tonight.

41

The rain didn't halt.

Hunt couldn't decide if it was a blessing, since it kept the streets mostly empty of all save Vanir affiliated with water, or if it was shit-poor luck, since it certainly wiped away any chance of a scent from the demon prowling the streets.

"Come . . . *on*," Bryce grunted.

Leaning against the wall beside the front door of the gallery, sunset mere minutes away, Hunt debated pulling out his phone to film the scene before him: Syrinx with his claws embedded in the carpet, yowling his head off, and Bryce trying to haul him by the back legs toward the door.

"It's. Just. *Water!*" she gritted out, tugging again.

"Eeettzzz!" Syrinx wailed back.

Bryce had declared that they were dropping off Syrinx at her apartment before going out to FiRo to investigate.

She grunted again, legs straining as she heaved the chimera. "We. Are. Going. *Home!*"

The green carpet began to lift, nails popping free as Syrinx clung for dear life.

Cthona spare him. Snickering, Hunt did Jesiba Roga a favor before Syrinx started on the wood panels, and wrapped a cool breeze around the chimera. Brow scrunching with concentration, he hoisted Syrinx from the carpet, floating him on a storm-wind straight to Hunt's open arms.

Syrinx blinked at him, then bristled, his tiny white teeth bared.

Hunt said calmly, "None of that, beastie."

Syrinx harrumphed, then went boneless.

Hunt found Bryce blinking, too. He threw her a grin. "Any more screeching from you?"

She grumbled, her words muffled by the rain-blasted night. Syrinx tensed in Hunt's arms as they emerged into the wet evening, Bryce shutting and locking the door behind them. She limped slightly. As if her tug-of-war with the chimera had strained her thigh again.

Hunt kept his mouth shut as he handed Syrinx over to her, the chimera practically clawing holes in Bryce's dress. He knew her leg bothered her. Knew he'd been the cause, with his battlefield stapling. But if she was going to be stupid and not get it looked at, then fine. Fine.

He didn't say any of that as Bryce wrapped her arms around Syrinx, hair already plastered to her head, and stepped closer to him. Hunt was keenly aware of every part of his body that met every part of hers as he scooped her into his arms, flapped his wings, and shot them into the storming skies, Syrinx huffing and hissing.

Syrinx forgave them both by the time they stood, dripping water, in the kitchen, and Bryce earned redemption points for the additional food she dumped into his bowl.

An outfit change for Bryce into athletic gear, and thirty minutes later, they stood in front of the Rose Gate. Its roses, wisteria, and countless other flowers gleamed with rain in the firstlight from lampposts flanking the traffic circle beyond it. A few cars wound past to disperse either into the city streets or along Central Avenue, which crossed through the Gate and became the long, dark expanse of the Eastern Road.

Hunt and Bryce squinted through the rain to peer at the square, the Gate, the traffic circle.

No hint of the demon that had been creeping through Vik's feeds.

From the corner of his eye, he watched Bryce rub her upper

thigh, reining in her wince. He ground his teeth, but bit back his reprimand.

He didn't feel like getting another lecture on domineering alphahole behavior.

"Right," Bryce said, the ends of her ponytail curling in the damp. "Since you're the sicko with dozens of crime scene photos on your phone, I'll let you do the investigating."

"Funny." Hunt pulled out his phone, snapped a photo of her standing in the rain and looking pissy, and then pulled up a photo he'd taken of the printouts Vik had made.

Bryce pressed closer to study the photo on his phone, the heat of her body a beckoning song. He kept perfectly still, refusing to heed it, as she lifted her head. "That camera there," she said, pointing to one of the ten mounted on the Gate itself. "That's the one that got the little blur."

Hunt nodded, surveying the Rose Gate and its surroundings. No sign of Sabine. Not that he expected the future Prime to be standing out in the open, summoning demons like some city-square charlatan. Especially not in such a public place, usually packed with tourists.

In the centuries since the Fae had decided to cover their Gate with flowers and climbing plants, the Rose Gate had become one of the biggest tourist draws, with thousands of people flocking there each day to give a drop of power to make a wish on its dial pad, nearly hidden beneath ivy, and to snap photos of the stunning little creatures who now made their nests and homes within the tangle of green. But at this hour, in this weather, even the Rose Gate was quiet. Dark.

Bryce rubbed her gods-damned thigh again. He swallowed down his annoyance and asked, "You think the demon headed out of the city?"

"I'm praying it didn't." The broad Eastern Road speared into dark, rolling hills and cypresses. A few golden firstlights gleamed among them, the only indication of the farms and villas interspersed throughout the vineyards, grazing lands, and olive groves. All good places to hide.

Bryce kept close as they crossed the street, into the heart of the small park in the center of the traffic circle. She scanned the rain-slick trees around them. "Anything?"

Hunt began to shake his head, but paused. He saw something on the other side of the marble circle on which the Gate stood. He took out his phone, the screen light bouncing off the strong planes of his face. "Maybe we were wrong. About the ley lines."

"What do you mean?"

He showed her the map of the city he'd pulled up, running a finger over Ward Avenue. Then Central. Main. "The kristallos appeared near all these streets. We thought it was because they were close to the ley lines. But we forgot what lies right beneath the streets, allowing the demon to appear and vanish without anyone noticing. The perfect place for Sabine to summon something and order it to move around the city." He pointed to the other side of the Gate. To a sewer grate.

Bryce groaned. "You've got to be kidding."

"Gods, it reeks," Bryce hissed over the rushing water below, pressing her face into her elbow as she knelt beside Hunt and peered into the open sewer. "What the fuck."

Soaked from the rain and kneeling in Ogenas knew what on the sidewalk, Hunt hid his smile as the beam of his flashlight skimmed over the slick bricks of the tunnel below in a careful sweep, then over the cloudy, dark river, surging thanks to the waterfalls of rain that poured in through the grates. "It's a sewer," he said. "What did you expect?"

She flipped him off. "You're the warrior-investigator-whatever. Can't you go down there and find some clues?"

"You really think Sabine left an easy trail like that?"

"Maybe there are claw marks or whatever." She surveyed the ancient stone. Hunt didn't know why she bothered. There were claw marks and scratches *everywhere*. Likely from whatever lowlifes had dwelled and hunted down here for centuries.

"This isn't some crime-scene investigative drama, Quinlan. It's not that easy."

"No one likes a condescending asshole, *Athalar.*"

His mouth curved upward. Bryce studied the gloom below, mouth tightening as if she'd will the kristallos or Sabine to appear. He'd already sent a message to Isaiah and Vik to get extra cameras on the Gate and the sewer grate, along with any others in the vicinity. If one so much as shifted an inch, they'd know. He didn't dare ask them to follow Sabine. Not yet.

"We should go down there," Bryce declared. "Maybe we can pick up her scent."

He said carefully, "You haven't made the Drop."

"Spare me the protective bullshit."

Dark Hel, this woman. "I'm not going down there unless we have a fuck-ton more weapons." He only had two guns and a knife. "Demon aside, if Sabine's down there . . ." He might outrank Sabine in terms of power, but with the witches' spells hobbling most of his might through the halo's ink, he had his proverbial hands tied.

So it'd come down to brute strength, and while he had the advantage there, too, Sabine was lethal. Motivated. And mean as an adder.

Bryce scowled. "I can handle myself." After the shooting range, he certainly knew that.

"It's not about you, sweetheart. It's about *me* not wanting to wind up dead."

"Can't you use your lightning-thing to protect us?"

He suppressed another smile at *lightning-thing*, but he said, "There's water down there. Adding lightning to the mix doesn't seem wise."

She cut him a glare. Hunt gave one right back.

Hunt had the feeling he'd passed some test when she smiled slightly.

Avoiding that little smile, Hunt scanned the river of filth running below. "All sewers lead to the Istros. Maybe the Many Waters folk have seen something."

Bryce's brows rose. "Why would they?"

"A river's a good place to dump a corpse."

"The demon left remains, though. It—or Sabine—doesn't seem

to be interested in hiding them. Not if she wants to do this as part of some scheme to jeopardize Micah's image."

"That's only a theory right now," Hunt countered. "I have a Many Waters contact who might have intel."

"Let's head to the docks, then. We'll be less likely to be noticed at night anyway."

"But twice as likely to encounter a predator searching for a meal. We'll wait until daylight." The gods knew they'd already risked enough in coming down here. Hunt placed the metal lid back on the sewer with a *thud*. He got one look at her annoyed, dirty face and chuckled. Before he could reconsider, he said, "I have fun with you, Quinlan. Despite how terrible this case is, despite all of it, I haven't had fun like this in a while." In *ever*.

He could have sworn she blushed. "Hang with me, Athalar," she said, trying to wipe the grime off her legs and hands from kneeling at the grate entrance, "and you might get rid of that stick up your ass after all."

He didn't answer. There was just a *click*.

She whirled toward him to find his phone out. Snapping a photo of her.

Hunt's grin was a slash of white in the rainy gloom. "I'd rather have a stick up my ass than look like a drowned rat."

Bryce used the spigot on the roof to wash off her shoes, her hands. She had no desire to track the filth of the street into her house. She went so far as to make Hunt take off his boots in the hallway, and didn't look to see if he was planning on taking a shower before she ran for her own room and had the water going in seconds.

She left her clothes in a pile in the corner, turned the heat as high as she could tolerate, and began a process of scrubbing and foaming and scrubbing some more. Remembering how she'd knelt on the filthy city street and breathed in a face full of sewer air, she scrubbed herself again.

Hunt knocked twenty minutes later. "Don't forget to clean between your toes."

Even with the shut door, she covered herself. "Fuck off."

His chuckle rumbled to her over the sound of the water. He said, "The soap in the guest room is out. Do you have another bar?"

"There's some in the hall linen closet. Just take whatever."

He grunted his thanks, and was gone a heartbeat later. Bryce washed and lathered herself again. Gross. This city was so gross. The rain only made it worse.

Then Hunt knocked again. "Quinlan."

His grave tone had her shutting off the water. "What's wrong?"

She whipped a towel around herself, sliding across the marble tiles as she reached the door. Hunt was shirtless, leaning against the doorjamb to her bedroom. She might have ogled the muscles the guy was sporting if his face hadn't been serious as Hel. "You want to tell me something?"

She gulped, scanning him from head to toe. "About what?"

"About what the fuck this is?" He extended his hand. Opened up his big fist.

A purple glittery unicorn lay in it.

She snatched the toy from his hand. His dark eyes lit with amusement as Bryce demanded, "Why are you snooping through my things?"

"Why do you have a box of unicorns in your linen closet?"

"This one is a unicorn-*pegasus*." She stroked the lilac mane. "Jelly Jubilee."

He just stared at her. Bryce shoved past him into the hall, where the linen closet door was still ajar, her box of toys now on one of the lower shelves. Hunt followed a step behind. Still shirtless.

"The soap is *right there*," she said, pointing to the stack directly at his eye level. "And yet you took down a box from the highest shelf?"

She could have sworn color stained his cheeks. "I saw purple glitter."

She blinked at him. "You thought it was a sex toy, didn't you?"

He said nothing.

"You think I keep my vibrator in my *linen closet*?"

He crossed his arms. "What I want to know is why you have a box of these things."

"Because I love them." She gently set Jelly Jubilee in the box, but pulled out an orange-and-yellow toy. "This is my pegasus, Peaches and Dreams."

"You're twenty-five years old."

"And? They're sparkly and squishy." She gave P&D a little squeeze, then put her back in the box and pulled out the third one, a slender-legged unicorn with a mint-green coat and rose-colored mane. "And this is Princess Creampuff." She almost laughed at the juxtaposition as she held up the sparkly toy in front of the Umbra Mortis.

"That name doesn't even match her coloring. What's up with the food names?"

She ran a finger over the purple glitter sprayed across the doll's flank. "It's because they're so cute you could eat them. Which I did when I was six."

His mouth twitched. "You didn't."

"Her name was Pineapple Shimmer and her legs were all squishy and glittery and I couldn't resist anymore and just . . . took a bite. Turns out the inside of them really is jelly. But not the edible kind. My mom had to call poison control."

He surveyed the box. "And you still have these because . . . ?"

"Because they make me happy." At his still-bemused look she added, "All right. If you want to get deep about it, Athalar, playing with them was the first time the other kids didn't treat me like a total freak. The Starlight Fancy horses were the number one toy on every girl's Winter Solstice wish list when I was five. And they were *not* all made equal. Poor Princess Creampuff here was common as a hoptoad. But Jelly Jubilee . . ." She smiled at the purple unicorn-pegasus, the memory it summoned. "My mom left Nidaros for the first time in years to buy her from one of the big towns two hours away. She was the ultimate Starlight Fancy conquest. Not just a unicorn, not just a pegasus—but *both.* I flashed this baby at school and was instantly accepted."

His eyes shone as she gently set the box on the high shelf. "I'll never laugh at them again."

"Good." She turned back to him, remembering that she still

wore only her towel, and he was still shirtless. She grabbed a box of soap and shoved it toward him. "Here. Next time you want to check out my vibrators, just ask, Athalar." She inclined her head toward her bedroom door and winked. "They're in the left nightstand."

Again, his cheeks reddened. "I wasn't—you're a pain in the ass, you know that?"

She shut the linen closet door with her hip and sauntered back to her bedroom. "I'd rather be a pain in the ass," she said slyly over her bare shoulder, "than a snooping pervert."

His snarl followed her all the way back into the bathroom.

42

In the midmorning light, the Istros River gleamed a deep blue, its waters clear enough to see the detritus sprinkled among the pale rocks and waving grasses. Centuries of Crescent City artifacts rusted away down there, picked over again and again by the various creatures who eked out a living by scavenging the crap hurled into the river.

Rumor had it that city officials had once tried to institute heavy fines for anyone caught dumping things in the river, but the scavengers had caught wind of it and put up such a fuss that the River Queen had no choice but to shut the bill down when it was officially proposed.

Overhead, angels, witches, and winged shifters soared by, keeping clear of the misty gloom of the Bone Quarter. Last night's rain had cleared to a pleasant spring day—no hint of the flickering lights that often drifted beneath the river's surface, visible only once night fell.

Bryce frowned down at a crustacean—some type of mammoth blue crab—picking its way along the floor beside the quay's stone block, sorting through a pile of beer bottles. The remnants of last night's drunken revels. "Have you ever been down to the mer-city?"

"No." Hunt rustled his wings, one brushing against her

shoulder. "Happy to stay above the surface." The river breeze drifted past, chill despite the warm day. "You?"

She rubbed her hands down her arms along the smooth leather of Danika's old jacket, trying to coax some warmth into them. "Never got an invite."

Most never would. The river folk were notoriously secretive, their city beneath the surface—the Blue Court—a place few who dwelled on land would ever see. One glass sub went in and out per day, and those on it traveled by invitation only. And even if they possessed the lung capacity or artificial means, no one was stupid enough to swim down. Not with what prowled these waters.

An auburn head of hair broke the surface a couple hundred yards out, and a partially scaled, muscled arm waved before vanishing, fingers tipped in sharp gray nails glinting in the sun.

Hunt glanced to Bryce. "Do you know any mer?"

Bryce lifted a corner of her mouth. "One lived down the hall my freshman year at CCU. She partied harder than all of us combined."

The mer could shift into fully human bodies for short periods of time, but if they went too long, the shift would be permanent, their scales drying up and flaking away into dust, their gills shrinking to nothing. The mer down the hall had been granted an oversize tub in her dorm room so she didn't need to interrupt her studies to return to the Istros once a day.

By the end of the first month of school, the mer had turned it into a party suite. Parties that Bryce and Danika gleefully attended, Connor and Thorne in tow. At the end of that year, their entire floor had been so wrecked that every one of them was slapped with a hefty fine for damages.

Bryce made sure she intercepted the letter before her parents got it out of the mailbox and quietly paid the fine with the marks she earned that summer scooping ice cream at the town parlor.

Sabine had gotten the letter, paid the fine, and made Danika spend the whole summer picking up trash in the Meadows.

Act like trash, Sabine had told her daughter, *and you can spend your days with it.*

Naturally, the following fall, Bryce and Danika had dressed as trash cans for the Autumnal Equinox.

The water of the Istros was clear enough for Bryce and Hunt to see the powerful male body swim closer, the reddish-brown scales of his long tail catching the light like burnished copper. Black stripes slashed through them, the pattern continuing up his torso and along his arms. Like some sort of aquatic tiger. The bare skin of his upper arms and chest was heavily tanned, suggesting hours spent near the surface or basking on the rocks of some hidden cove along the coast.

The male's head broke the water, and his taloned hands brushed back his jaw-length auburn hair as he flashed Hunt a grin. "Long time no see."

Hunt smiled at the mer male treading water. "Glad you weren't too busy with your fancy new title to say hello."

The mer waved a hand in dismissal, and Hunt beckoned Bryce forward. "Bryce, this is Tharion Ketos." She stepped closer to the concrete edge of the quay. "An old friend."

Tharion grinned at Hunt again. "Not as old as you."

Bryce gave the male a half smile. "Nice to meet you."

Tharion's light brown eyes glittered. "The pleasure, Bryce, is all mine."

Gods spare him. Hunt cleared his throat. "We're here on official business."

Tharion swam the remaining few feet to the quay's edge, knocking the crustacean into the drifting blue with a careless brush of his tail. Planting his talon-tipped hands on the concrete, he easily heaved his massive body from the water, the gills beneath his ears sealing in as he switched control of his breathing to his nose and mouth. He patted the now-wet concrete next to him and winked at Bryce. "Take a seat, Legs, and tell me all about it."

Bryce huffed a laugh. "You're trouble."

"It's my middle name, actually."

Hunt rolled his eyes. But Bryce sat beside the male, apparently not caring that the water would surely soak into the green dress she wore beneath the leather jacket. She pulled off her beige heels and dipped her feet in the water, splashing softly. Normally, he'd have dragged her away from the river's edge, and told her she'd be lucky to lose just the leg if she put a foot in the water. But with Tharion beside them, none of the river's denizens would dare approach.

Tharion asked Bryce, "Are you in the 33rd or the Auxiliary?"

"Neither. I'm working with Hunt as a consultant on a case."

Tharion hummed. "What does your boyfriend think of you working with the famed Umbra Mortis?"

Hunt sat down on the male's other side. "Real subtle, Tharion."

Yet Bryce's mouth bloomed into a full smile.

It was a near-twin to the one she'd given him this morning, when he'd popped his head into her room to see if she was ready to leave. Of course, his eyes had gone directly to the left nightstand. And then that smile had turned feral, like she knew exactly what he was wondering about.

He certainly had not been looking for any of her sex toys when he'd opened up the linen closet last night. But he'd spied a flash of purple sparkles, and—fine, maybe the thought had crossed his mind—he'd just pulled down the box before he could really think.

And now that he knew where they were, he couldn't help but look at that nightstand and imagine her there, in that bed. Leaning against the pillows and—

It might have made sleeping a shade uncomfortable last night.

Tharion leaned back on his hands, displaying his muscled abdomen as he asked innocently, "What did I say?"

Bryce laughed, making no attempt to hide her blatant ogling of the mer's cut body. "I don't have a boyfriend. You want the job?"

Tharion smirked. "You like to swim?"

And that was about as much as Hunt could take with only one cup of coffee in his system. "I know you're busy, Tharion," he said through his teeth with just enough edge that the mer peeled his attention away from Bryce, "so we'll keep this quick."

"Oh, take your time," Tharion said, eyes dancing with pure male challenge. "The River Queen gave me the morning off, so I'm all yours."

"You work for the River Queen?" Bryce asked.

"I'm a lowly peon in her court, but yes."

Hunt leaned forward to catch Bryce's stare. "Tharion's just been promoted to her Captain of Intelligence. Don't let the charm and irreverence fool you."

"Charm and irreverence happen to be my two favorite traits," Bryce said with a wink for Tharion this time.

The mer's smile deepened. "Careful, Bryce. I might decide I like you and bring you Beneath."

Hunt gave Tharion a warning look. Some of the darker mer had done just that, long ago. Carried human brides down to their undersea courts and kept them there, trapped within the massive air bubbles that contained parts of their palaces and cities, unable to reach the surface.

Bryce waved off the awful history. "We have a few questions for you, if that's all right."

Tharion gestured lazily with a claw-tipped, webbed hand. The markings on the mer were varied and vibrant: different coloring, stripes or specks or solids, their tails long-finned or short or wispy. Their magic mostly involved the element in which they lived, though some could summon tempests. The River Queen, part mer, part river-spirit, could summon far worse, they said. Possibly wash away all of Lunathion, if provoked.

She was a daughter of Ogenas, according to legend, born from the mighty river-that-encircles-the-world, and sister to the Ocean Queen, the reclusive ruler of the five great seas of Midgard. There was a fifty-fifty chance the goddess thing was true of the River Queen, Hunt supposed. But regardless, the residents of this city did their best not to piss her off. Even Micah maintained a healthy, respectful relationship with her.

Hunt asked, "You see anything unusual lately?"

Tharion's tail idly stirred the sparkling water. "What kind of case is this? Murder?"

"Yes," Hunt said. Bryce's face tightened.

Tharion's claws clicked on the concrete. "Serial killer?"

"Just answer the question, asshole."

Tharion peered at Bryce. "If he talks to you like that, I hope you kick him in the balls."

"She'd enjoy it," Hunt muttered.

"Hunt has learned his lesson about pissing me off," Bryce said sweetly.

Tharion's smile was sly. "*That* is a story I'd like to hear."

"Of course you would," Hunt grumbled.

"Does this have to do with the Viper Queen pulling in her people the other week?"

"Yes," Hunt said carefully.

Tharion's eyes darkened, a reminder that the male could be lethal when the mood struck him, and that there was a good reason the creatures of the river didn't fuck with the mer. "Some bad shit's going down, isn't it."

"We're trying to stop it," Hunt said.

The mer nodded gravely. "Let me ask around."

"Covertly, Tharion. The less people who know something's happening the better."

Tharion slipped back into the water, again disturbing the poor crab who'd clawed his way back to the quay. The mer's powerful tail thrashed, keeping him effortlessly in place as he surveyed Hunt and Bryce. "Do I tell my queen to pull in our people, too?"

"Doesn't fit the pattern so far," Hunt said, "but it wouldn't hurt to give a warning."

"What should I be warning her about?"

"An old-school demon called the kristallos," Bryce said softly. "A monster straight from the Pit, bred by the Star-Eater himself."

For a moment, Tharion said nothing, his tan face going pale. Then, "Fuck." He ran a hand through his wet hair. "I'll ask around," he promised again. Far down the river, motion drew Hunt's eye. A black boat drifted toward the mist of the Bone Quarter.

On the Black Dock, jutting from the city's bright shoreline

like a dark sword, a group of mourners huddled beneath the inky arches, praying for the boat to safely bear the veiled pine coffin across the water.

Around the wooden vessel, broad, scaled backs broke the river's surface, writhing and circling. Waiting for final judgment—and lunch.

Tharion followed his line of sight. "Five marks says it tips."

"That's disgusting," Bryce hissed.

Tharion swished his tail, playfully splashing Bryce's legs with water. "I won't bet on your Sailing, Legs. I promise." He flicked some water toward Hunt. "And we already know *your* boat is going to tip right the fuck over before it's even left the shore."

"Funny."

Behind them, an otter in a reflective yellow vest loped past, a sealed wax message tube held in its fanged mouth. It barely glanced their way before leaping into the river and vanishing. Bryce bit her lip, a high-pitched squeal cracking from her.

The fearless, fuzzy messengers were hard to resist, even for Hunt. While true animals and not shifters, they possessed an uncanny level of intelligence, thanks to the old magic in their veins. They'd found their place in the city by relaying tech-free communication between those who lived in the three realms that made up Crescent City: the mer in the river, the Reapers in the Bone Quarter, and the residents of Lunathion proper.

Tharion laughed at the naked delight on Bryce's face. "Do you think the Reapers fall to pieces over them, too?"

"I bet even the Under-King himself squeals when he sees them," Bryce said. "They were part of why I wanted to move here in the first place."

Hunt lifted a brow. "Really?"

"I saw them when I was a kid and thought they were the most magical thing I'd ever seen." She beamed. "I still do."

"Considering your line of work, that's saying something."

Tharion angled his head at them. "What manner of work is that?"

"Antiquities," Bryce said. "If you ever find anything interesting in the depths, let me know."

"I'll send an otter right to you."

Hunt got to his feet, offering a hand to help Bryce rise. "Keep us posted."

Tharion gave him an irreverent salute. "I'll see you when I see you," he said, gills flaring, and dove beneath the surface. They watched him swim out toward the deep heart of the river, following the same path as the otter, then plunge down, down—to those distant, twinkling lights.

"He's a charmer," Bryce murmured as Hunt hauled her to her feet, his other hand coming to her elbow.

Hunt's hand lingered, the heat of it searing her even through the leather of the jacket. "Just wait until you see him in his human form. He causes riots."

She laughed. "How'd you even meet him?"

"We had a string of mer murders last year." Her eyes darkened in recognition. It'd been all over the news. "Tharion's little sister was one of the victims. It was high-profile enough that Micah assigned me to help out. Tharion and I worked on the case together for the few weeks it lasted."

Micah had traded him three whole *debts* for it.

She winced. "It was you two who caught the killer? They never said on the news—just that he'd been apprehended. Nothing more—not even who it was."

Hunt let go of her elbow. "We did. A rogue panther shifter. I handed him over to Tharion."

"I'm assuming the panther didn't make it down to the Blue Court."

Hunt surveyed the shimmering expanse of water. "No, he didn't."

"Is Bryce being nice to you, Athie?"

Seated at the front desk of the gallery showroom, Bryce

muttered, "Oh please," and kept clicking through the paperwork Jesiba had sent over.

Hunt, sprawled in the chair across the desk from her, the portrait of angelic arrogance, merely asked the fire sprite lurking in the open iron door, "What would you do if I said she wasn't, Lehabah?"

Lehabah floated in the archway, not daring to come into the showroom. Not when Jesiba would likely see. "I'd burn all her lunches for a month."

Hunt chuckled, the sound sliding along her bones. Bryce, despite herself, smiled.

Something heavy thumped, audible even a level above the library, and Lehabah zoomed down the stairs, hissing, "*Bad!*"

Bryce looked at Hunt as he sifted through the photos of the demon from a few nights ago. His hair hung over his brow, the sable strands gleaming like black silk. Her fingers curled on the keyboard.

Hunt lifted his head. "We need more intel on Sabine. The fact that she swapped the footage of the Horn's theft from the temple is suspicious, and what she said in the observation room that night is pretty suspicious, too, but they don't necessarily mean she's a murderer. I can't approach Micah without concrete proof."

She rubbed the back of her neck. "Ruhn hasn't gotten any leads on finding the Horn, either, so that we can lure the kristallos."

Silence fell. Hunt crossed an ankle over a knee, then stretched out a hand to where she'd discarded Danika's jacket on the chair beside him, too lazy to bother hanging it. "I saw Danika wearing this in the photo in your guest room. Why'd you keep it?"

Bryce let out a long breath, thankful for his shift in subject. "Danika used to store her stuff in the supply closet here, rather than bothering to go back to the apartment or over to the Den. She'd stashed the jacket here the day . . ." She blew out a breath and glanced toward the bathroom in the back of the space, where Danika had changed only hours before her death. "I didn't want Sabine to have it. She would have read the back of it and thrown it in the trash."

Hunt picked up the jacket and read, "Through love, all is possible."

Bryce nodded. "The tattoo on my back says the same thing. Well, in some fancy alphabet that she dug up online, but . . . Danika had a thing about that phrase. It was all the Oracle told her, apparently. Which makes no sense, because Danika was one of the least lovey-dovey people I've ever met, but . . ." Bryce toyed with the amulet around her neck, zipping it along the chain. "Something about it resonated with her. So after she died, I kept the jacket. And started wearing it."

Hunt carefully set the jacket back on the chair. "I get it—about the personal effects." He seemed like he wasn't going to say more, but then he continued, "That sunball hat you made fun of?"

"I didn't make fun of it. You just don't seem like the kind of male who *wears* such a thing."

He chuckled again—in that same way that slid over her skin. "That hat was the first thing I bought when I came here. With the first paycheck I ever received from Micah." The corner of his mouth turned upward. "I saw it in an athletic shop, and it just seemed so ordinary. You have no idea how different Lunathion is from the Eternal City. From anything in Pangera. And that hat just . . ."

"Represented that?"

"Yeah. It seemed like a new beginning. A step toward a more normal existence. Well, as normal an existence as someone like me can have."

She made an effort not to look at his wrist. "So you have your hat—and I have Jelly Jubilee."

His smile lit up the dimness of the gallery. "I'm surprised you don't have a tattoo of Jelly Jubilee somewhere." His eyes skimmed over her, lingering on the short, tight green dress.

Her toes curled. "Who says I don't have a tattoo of her somewhere you can't see, Athalar?"

She watched him sort through everything he had *already* seen. Since he'd moved in, she'd stopped parading about the apartment in her underwear while getting dressed, but she knew he'd spotted her through the window in the days before. Knew he realized there was a limited, very intimate, number of places where another tattoo might be hidden.

She could have sworn his voice dropped an octave or two as he asked, "Do you?"

With any other male, she would have said, *Why don't you come find out?*

With any other male, she would have already been on the other side of the desk. Crawling into his lap. Unbuckling his belt. And then sinking down onto his cock, riding him until they were both moaning and breathless and—

She made herself go back to her paperwork. "There are a few males who can answer that question, if you're so curious." How her voice was so steady, she had no idea.

Hunt's silence was palpable. She didn't dare look over her computer screen.

But his eyes remained focused on her, burning her like a brand.

Her heart thundered throughout her body. Dangerous, stupid, reckless—

Hunt let out a long, tight breath. The chair he sat in groaned as he shifted in it, his wings rustling. She still didn't dare look. She honestly didn't know what she'd do if she looked.

But then Hunt said, his voice gravelly, "We need to focus on Sabine."

Hearing her name was like being doused with ice water.

Right. Yes. Of course. Because hooking up with the Umbra Mortis wasn't a possibility. The reasons for that started with him pining for a lost love and ended with the fact that he was owned by the gods-damned Governor. With a million other obstacles in between.

She still couldn't look at him as Hunt asked, "Any thoughts on how we can get more intel on her? Even just a glimpse into her current state of mind?"

Needing something to do with her hands, her too-warm body, Bryce printed out, then signed and dated, the paperwork Jesiba had sent. "We can't bring in Sabine for formal questioning without making her aware that we're onto her," Bryce said, at last looking at Hunt.

His face was flushed, and his eyes . . . Fucking Solas, his black eyes glittered, wholly fixed on her face. Like he was thinking of touching her.

Tasting her.

"Okay," he said roughly, running a hand through his hair. His eyes settled, the dark fire in them banking. Thank the gods.

An idea dawned upon her, and Bryce said in a strangled voice, her stomach twisting with dread, "So I think we have to bring the questions to Sabine."

43

The wolves' Den in Moonwood occupied ten entire city blocks, a sprawling villa built around a wild tangle of forest and grass that legend claimed had grown there since before anyone had touched these lands. Through the iron gates built into the towering limestone arches, Bryce could see through to the private park, where morning sunlight coaxed drowsy flowers into opening up for the day. Wolf pups bounded, pouncing on each other, chasing their tails, watched over by gray-muzzled elders whose brutal days in the Aux were long behind them.

Her gut twisted, enough to make her grateful she'd forgone breakfast. She'd barely slept last night, as she considered and reconsidered this plan. Hunt had offered to do it himself, but she'd refused. She had to come here—had to step up. For Danika.

In his usual battle-suit, Hunt stood a step away, silent as he'd been on the walk over here. As if he knew she could barely keep her legs from shaking. She wished she'd worn sneakers. The steep angle of her heels had irritated the wound in her thigh. Bryce clenched her jaw against the pain as they stood before the Den.

Hunt kept his dark eyes fixed upon the four sentries stationed at the gates.

Three females, one male. All in humanoid form, all in black, all armed with guns and sheathed swords down their backs. A tattoo of an onyx rose with three claw marks slashed through its petals adorned the sides of their necks, marking them as members of the Black Rose Wolf Pack.

Her stomach roiled at the hilts peeking over their armored shoulders. But she pushed away the memory of a braid of silvery-blond hair streaked with purple and pink, constantly snagging in the hilt of an ancient, priceless blade.

Though young, the Pack of Devils had been revered, the most talented wolves in generations. Led by the most powerful Alpha to grace Midgard's soil.

The Black Rose Pack was a far cry from that. A far fucking cry.

Their eyes lit with predatory delight as they spotted Bryce.

Her mouth went dry. And turned positively arid as a fifth wolf appeared from the glass security vestibule to the left of the gate.

The Alpha's dark hair had been pulled into a tight braid, accentuating the sharp angles of her face as she sneered toward Bryce and Hunt. Athalar's hand casually drifted to the knife at his thigh.

Bryce said as casually as she could, "Hi, Amelie."

Amelie Ravenscroft bared her teeth. "What the fuck do you want?"

Hunt bared his teeth right back. "We're here to see the Prime." He flashed his legion badge, the gold twinkling in the sun. "On behalf of the Governor."

Amelie flicked her gold eyes to Hunt, over his tattooed halo. Over his hand on the knife and the *SPQM* she surely knew was tattooed on the other side of his wrist. Her lip curled. "Well, at least you picked interesting company, Quinlan. Danika would have approved. Hel, you might have even done him together." Amelie leaned a shoulder against the vestibule's side. "You used to do that, right? I heard about you guys and those two daemonaki. Classic."

Bryce smiled blandly. "It was three daemonaki, actually."

"Stupid slut," Amelie snarled.

"Watch it," Hunt growled back.

Amelie's pack members lingered behind her, eyeing Hunt and keeping back. The benefit of hanging with the Umbra Mortis, apparently.

Amelie laughed, a sound filled with loathing. Not merely hatred for her, Bryce realized. But for the angels. The Houses of Earth and Blood and Sky and Breath were rivals on a good day, enemies on a bad one. "Or what? You'll use your lightning on me?" she said to Hunt. "If you do, you'll be in such deep shit that your *master* will bury you alive in it." A little smile at the tattoo across his brow.

Hunt went still. And as interesting as it would have been to finally see how Hunt Athalar killed, they had a reason for being here. So Bryce said to the pack leader, "You're a delight, Amelie Ravenscroft. Radio your boss that we're here to see the Prime." She flicked her brows in emphasis of the dismissal she knew would make the Alpha see red.

"Shut that mouth of yours," Amelie said, "before I rip out your tongue."

A brown-haired male wolf standing behind Amelie taunted, "Why don't you go fuck someone in a bathroom again, Quinlan?"

She blocked out every word. But Hunt huffed a laugh that promised broken bones. "I told you to watch it."

"Go ahead, angel," Amelie sneered. "Let's see what you can do."

Bryce could barely move around the panic and dread pushing in, could barely breathe, but Hunt said quietly, "There are six pups playing in sight of this gate. You really want to expose them to the kind of fight we'd have, Amelie?"

Bryce blinked. Hunt didn't so much as glance her way as he continued addressing a seething Amelie. "I'm not going to beat the shit out of you in front of children. So either you let us in, or we'll come back with a warrant." His gaze didn't falter. "I don't think Sabine Fendyr would be particularly happy with Option B."

Amelie held his stare, even as the others tensed. That haughty arrogance had made Sabine tap her as Alpha of the Black Rose Pack, even over Ithan Holstrom, now Amelie's Second. But Sabine had wanted someone just like herself, regardless of Ithan's higher power ranking. And perhaps someone a little less Alpha, too—so she'd have them firmly under her claws.

Bryce waited for Amelie to call Hunt's bluff about the warrant. Waited for a snide remark or the appearance of fangs.

Yet Amelie plucked the radio from her belt and said into it, "Guests are here for the Prime. Come get them."

She had once breezed through the doors beyond Amelie's dark head, had spent hours playing with the pups in the grass and trees beyond it whenever Danika had been given babysitting duty.

She shut out the memory of what it had been like—to watch Danika playing with the fuzzy pups or shrieking children, who had all worshipped the ground she walked upon. Their future leader, their protector, who would take the wolves to new heights.

Bryce's chest constricted to the point of pain. Hunt glanced her way then, his brows rising.

She couldn't do this. Be here. Enter this place.

Amelie smiled, as if realizing that. Scenting her dread and pain.

And the sight of the fucking bitch standing there, where Danika had once been . . . Red washed over Bryce's vision as she drawled, "It's good to see that crime has gone down so much, if all you have to do with your day, Amelie, is play guard at the front door."

Amelie smiled slowly. Footsteps sounded on the other side of the gate, just before they swung open, but Bryce didn't dare look. Not as Amelie said, "You know, sometimes I think I should thank you—they say if Danika hadn't been so distracted by messaging you about your drunk bullshit, she might have anticipated the attack. And then I wouldn't be where I am, would I."

Bryce's nails cut into her palms. But her voice, thank the gods, was steady as she said, "Danika was a thousand times the wolf you are. No matter *where you are,* you'll never be where *she* was."

Amelie went white with rage, her nose crinkling, lips pulling back to expose her now-lengthening teeth—

"Amelie," a male voice growled from the shadows of the gate archway.

Oh gods. Bryce curled her fingers into fists to keep from shaking as she looked toward the young male wolf.

But Ithan Holstrom's eyes darted between her and Amelie as he approached his Alpha. "It's not worth it." The unspoken words simmered in his eyes. *Bryce isn't worth it.*

Amelie snorted, turning back to the vestibule, a shorter, brown-haired female following her. The pack's Omega, if memory served. Amelie sneered over a shoulder to Bryce, "Go back to the dumpster you crawled out of."

Then she shut the door. Leaving Bryce standing before Connor's younger brother.

There was nothing kind on Ithan's tan face. His golden-brown hair was longer than the last time she'd seen him, but he'd been a sophomore playing sunball for CCU then.

This towering, muscled male before them had made the Drop. Had stepped into his brother's shoes and joined the pack that had replaced Connor's.

A brush of Hunt's velvet-soft wings against her arm had her walking. Every step toward the wolf ratcheted up her heartbeat.

"Ithan," Bryce managed to say.

Connor's younger brother said nothing as he turned toward the pillars flanking the walkway.

She was going to puke. All over everything: the limestone tiles, the pale pillars, the glass doors that opened into the park in the center of the villa.

She shouldn't have let Athalar come. Should have made him stay on the roof somewhere so he couldn't witness the spectacular meltdown that she was three seconds away from having.

Ithan Holstrom's steps were unhurried, his gray T-shirt pulling across the considerable expanse of his muscled back. He'd been a cocky twenty-year-old when Connor died, a history major like Danika and the star of CCU's sunball team, rumored to be going pro as soon as his brother gave the nod. He could have gone pro right after high school, but Connor, who had raised Ithan since their parents had died five years earlier, had insisted that a degree came first, sports second. Ithan, who had idolized Connor, had always folded on it, despite Bronson's pleas with Connor to let the kid go pro.

Connor's Shadow, they'd teased Ithan.

He'd filled out since then. At last started truly resembling his older brother—even the shade of his golden-brown hair was like a spike through her chest.

I'm crazy about you. I don't want anyone else. I haven't for a long while.

She couldn't breathe. Couldn't stop seeing, hearing those words, feeling the giant fucking rip in the space-time continuum where Connor should have been, in a world where nothing bad could ever, ever happen—

Ithan stopped before another set of glass doors. He opened one, the muscles in his long arm rippling as he held it for them.

Hunt went first, no doubt scanning the space in the span of a blink.

Bryce managed to look up at Ithan as she passed.

His white teeth shone as he bared them at her.

Gone was the cocky boy she'd teased; gone was the boy who'd tried out flirting on her so he could use the techniques on Nathalie, who had laughed when Ithan asked her out but told him to wait a few more years; gone was the boy who had relentlessly questioned Bryce about when she'd finally start dating his brother and wouldn't take *never* for an answer.

A honed predator now stood in his place. Who had surely not forgotten the leaked messages she'd sent and received that horrible night. That she'd been fucking some random in the club bathroom while Connor—Connor, who had just spilled his heart to her—was slaughtered.

Bryce lowered her eyes, hating it, hating every second of this fucked-up visit.

Ithan smiled, as if savoring her shame.

He'd dropped out of CCU after Connor had died. Quit playing sunball. She only knew because she'd caught a game on TV one night two months later and the commentators had still been discussing it. No one, not his coaches, not his friends, not his packmates, could convince him to return. He'd walked away from the sport and never looked back, apparently.

She hadn't seen him since the days right before the murders.

Her last photo of him was the one Danika had taken at his game, playing in the background. The one she'd tortured herself with last night for hours while bracing herself for what the dawn would bring.

Before that, though, there had been hundreds of photos of the two of them together. They still sat on her phone like a basket full of snakes, waiting to bite if she so much as opened the lid.

Ithan's cruel smile didn't waver as he shut the door behind them. "The Prime's taking a nap. Sabine will meet with you."

Bryce glanced at Hunt, who gave her a shallow nod. Precisely as they'd planned.

Bryce was aware of Ithan's every breath at her back as they aimed for the stairs that Bryce knew would take them up a level to Sabine's office. Hunt seemed aware of Ithan, too, and let enough lightning wreathe his hands, his wrists, that the young wolf took a step away.

At least alphaholes were good for something.

Ithan didn't leave. No, it seemed he was to be their guard and silent tormentor for the duration of this miserable trip.

Bryce knew every step toward Sabine's office on the second level, but Ithan led the way: up the sprawling limestone stairs marred with so many scratches and gouges no one bothered to fix them anymore; down the high-ceilinged, bright hall whose windows overlooked the busy street outside; and finally to the worn wood door. Danika had grown up here—and moved out as soon as she'd gone to CCU. After graduation, she'd stayed only during formal wolf events and holidays.

Ithan's pace was leisurely. As if he could scent Bryce's misery, and wanted to make her endure it for every possible second.

She supposed she deserved it. *Knew* she deserved it.

She tried to block out the memory that flashed.

The twenty-one ignored calls from Ithan, all in the first few days following the murder. The half-dozen audiomails. The first had been sobbing, panicked, left in the hours afterward. *Is it true, Bryce? Are they dead?*

And then the messages had shifted to worry. *Where are you? Are you okay? I called the major hospitals and you're not listed, but no one is talking. Please call me.*

And then, by the end, that last audiomail from Ithan, nothing but razor-sharp coldness. *The Legion inspectors showed me all the messages. Connor practically told you that he loved you, and you finally agreed to go out with him, and then you fucked some stranger in the Raven bathroom? While he was* dying? *Are you kidding me with this shit? Don't come to the Sailing tomorrow. You're not welcome there.*

She'd never written back, never sought him out. Hadn't been able to endure the thought of facing him. Seeing the grief and pain in his face. Loyalty was the most prized of all wolf traits. In their eyes, she and Connor had been inevitable. Nearly mated. Just a question of time. Her hookups before that hadn't mattered, and neither had his, because nothing had been declared yet.

Until he'd asked her out at last. And she had said yes. Had started down that road.

To the wolves, she was Connor's, and he was hers.

Message me when you're home safe.

Her chest tightened and tightened, the walls pushing in, squeezing—

She forced herself to take a long breath. To inhale to the point where her ribs strained from holding it in. Then to exhale, pushing-pushing-pushing, until she was heaving out the pure gut-shredding panic that burned through her whole body like acid.

Bryce wasn't a wolf. She didn't play by their rules of courtship. And she'd been stupid and scared of what agreeing to that date had meant, and Danika certainly didn't care one way or another if Bryce had some meaningless hookup, but—Bryce hadn't ever worked up the nerve to explain to Ithan after she'd seen and heard his messages.

She'd kept them all. Listening to them was a solid central arc of her emotional death-spiral routine. The culmination of it, of course, being Danika's last, foolishly happy messages.

Ithan knocked on Sabine's door, letting it swing wide to reveal a sunny white office whose windows looked into the verdant greenery of the Den's park. Sabine sat at her desk, her corn-silk hair near-glowing in the light. "You have some nerve coming here."

Words dried up in Bryce's throat as she took in the pale face, the slender hands interlaced on the oak desk, the narrow shoulders that belied her tremendous strength. Danika had been pure wildfire; her mother was solid ice. And if Sabine had killed her, if Sabine had done this . . .

Roaring began in Bryce's head.

Hunt must have sensed it, scented it, because he stepped up to Bryce's side, Ithan lingering in the hall, and said, "We wanted to meet with the Prime."

Irritation flickered in Sabine's eyes. "About?"

"About your daughter's murder."

"Stay the fuck out of our business," Sabine barked, setting the glass on her table rattling. Bile burned Bryce's throat, and she focused on not screaming or launching herself at the woman.

Hunt's wing brushed Bryce's back, a casual gesture to anyone watching, but that warmth and softness steadied her. Danika. For Danika, she'd do this.

Sabine's eyes blazed. "Where the Hel is my sword?"

Bryce refused to answer, to even snap that the sword was and would always be Danika's, and said, "We have intel that suggests Danika was stationed at Luna's Temple the night the Horn was stolen. We need the Prime to confirm." Bryce kept her eyes on the carpet, the portrait of terrified, shameful submission, and let Sabine dig her own grave.

Sabine demanded, "What the fuck does this have to do with her death?"

Hunt said calmly, "We're putting together a picture of Danika's movements before the kristallos demon killed her. Who she might have met, what she might have seen or done."

Another bit of bait: to see her reaction to the demon's breed, when it hadn't yet been made public. Sabine didn't so much as blink. Like she was already familiar with it—perhaps because she'd been summoning it all along. Though she might just not have cared, Bryce supposed. Sabine hissed, "Danika wasn't at the temple that night. She had nothing to do with the Horn being stolen."

Bryce avoided the urge to close her eyes at the lie that confirmed everything.

Claws slid from Sabine's knuckles, embedding in her desk. "Who told you Danika was at the temple?"

"No one," Bryce lied. "I thought I might have remembered her mentioning—"

"You *thought*?" Sabine sneered, voice rising to imitate Bryce's. "It's hard to remember, isn't it, when you were high, drunk, and fucking strangers."

"You're right," Bryce breathed, even as Hunt growled. "This was a mistake." She didn't give Hunt time to object before she turned on a heel and left, gasping for breath.

How she kept her back straight, her stomach inside her body, she had no idea.

She barely heard Hunt as he fell into step behind her. Couldn't stand to look at Ithan as she entered the hallway and found him waiting against the far wall.

Back down the stairs. She didn't dare look at the wolves she passed.

She knew Ithan trailed, but she didn't care, didn't care—

"Quinlan." Hunt's voice cut through the marble stairwell. She made it down another flight when he said again, "*Quinlan*."

It was sharp enough that she paused. Looked up over a shoulder. Hunt's eyes scanned her face—worry, not triumph at Sabine's blatant lie, shining there.

But Ithan stood between them on the steps, eyes hard as stones. "Tell me what this is about."

Hunt drawled, "It's classified, asshole."

Ithan's snarl rumbled through the stairwell.

"It's starting again," Bryce said quietly, aware of all the cameras, of Micah's order to keep this quiet. Her voice was rasping. "We're trying to figure out why and who's behind it. Three murders so far. The same way. Be careful—warn your pack to be careful."

Ithan's face remained unreadable. That had been one of his assets as a sunball player—his ability to keep from broadcasting moves to his opponents. He'd been brilliant, and cocky as fuck, yes, but that arrogance had been well earned through hours of practice and brutal discipline.

Ithan's face remained cold. "I'll let you know if I hear anything."

"Do you need our numbers?" Hunt asked coolly.

Ithan's lip curled. "I have hers." She struggled to meet his stare, especially as he asked, "Are you going to bother to reply this time?"

She turned on her heel and rushed down the stairs into the reception hall.

The Prime of the wolves stood in it now. Talking to the receptionist, hunched over his redwood cane, Danika's grandfather lifted his withered face as she came to an abrupt halt in front of him.

His warm brown eyes—those were Danika's eyes, staring out at her.

The ancient male offered her a sad, kind smile. It was worse than any of the sneers or snarls.

Bryce managed to bow her head before she bolted through the glass doors.

She made it to the gates without running into anyone else. Had almost made it onto the street when Ithan caught up to her, Hunt a step behind. Ithan said, "You never deserved him."

He might as well have drawn the knife she knew was hidden in his boot and plunged it into her chest. "I know," she rasped.

The pups were still playing, bounding through the high grasses. He nodded to the second level, to where Sabine's office overlooked the greenery. "You made some dumb fucking choices, Bryce, but I never pegged you for stupid. She wants you dead." Another confirmation, perhaps.

The words snapped something in her. "Likewise." She pointed to the gates, unable to stop the rage boiling in her as she realized that all signs pointed toward Sabine. "Connor would be ashamed of you for letting Amelie run rampant. For letting a piece of shit like that be your Alpha."

Claws glinted at Ithan's knuckles. "Don't you *ever* say his name again."

"Walk away," Hunt said softly to him. Lightning licked along his wings.

Ithan looked inclined to rip out his throat, but Hunt was already at Bryce's side, following her onto the sun-drenched street. She didn't dare look at Amelie or her pack at the gates, sneering and snickering at them.

"You're trash, Quinlan!" Amelie shouted as they passed by, and her friends roared with laughter.

Bryce couldn't bear to see if Ithan laughed with them.

44

Sabine lied about Danika not being at the temple. But we need a solid plan for catching her if she's summoning this demon," Hunt said to Bryce twenty minutes later over lunch. The angel devoured no less than three bowls of cereal, one after another. She hadn't spoken on the way back to the apartment. Had needed the entire walk here to reel herself back together.

Bryce pushed at the puffed rice floating around in her own bowl. She had zero interest in eating. "I'm sick of waiting. Just arrest her."

"She's the unofficial Head of Moonwood and basically the Prime of the wolves," Hunt cautioned. "If not in title, then in every other way. We have to be careful how we approach this. The fallout could be catastrophic."

"Sure." Bryce poked at her cereal again. She knew she should be screaming, knew she should be marching back to the Den to kill that fucking bitch. Bryce ground her teeth. They'd had no word from Tharion or Ruhn, either.

Hunt tapped a finger on the glass table, weighing her expression. Then he mercifully switched subjects. "I get Ithan's history, but what's Amelie's problem with you?"

Maybe Bryce was just tired, but she wound up saying, "Did you ever see them—the messages from that night? Every newspaper had them on the front page after they leaked."

Hunt stilled. "Yeah," he said gently. "I did."

She shrugged, swirling the cereal in her bowl. Around and around.

"Amelie had . . . a thing. For Connor. Since they were kids. I think she still does."

"Ah."

"And—you know about me and Connor."

"Yeah. I'm sorry."

She hated those two words. Had heard them so many times she just fucking *hated* them. She said, "When she saw the messages from that night, I think Amelie finally realized why he had never returned her feelings."

He frowned. "It's been two years."

"So?" It sure as shit hadn't done anything to help her feel better about it.

Hunt shook his head. "People still bring them up? Those messages?"

"Of course." She snorted, shaking her head. "Just look me up online, Athalar. I had to shut down every account I had." The thought made her stomach churn, nauseating panic tightening every muscle and vein in her body. She'd gotten better about managing it—that feeling—but not by much. "People hate me. Literally *hate* me. Some of the wolf packs even wrote a song and put it online—they called it 'I Just Hooked Up with Someone in the Bathroom, Don't Tell Connor.' They sing it whenever they see me."

His face had gone cold as ice. "Which packs?"

She shook her head. She certainly wouldn't name them, not with that murderous expression on his face. "It doesn't matter. People are assholes."

It was as simple as that, she'd learned. Most people were assholes, and this city was rife with them.

She sometimes wondered what they'd say if they knew about that time two winters ago when someone had sent a thousand printed-out lyric sheets of the song to her new apartment, along with mock album artwork taken from the photos she'd snapped that night. If they knew she had gone up to the roof to burn them all—but instead wound up staring over the ledge. She wondered what would have happened if Juniper, on a whim, hadn't called just to check in that night. Right as Bryce had braced her hands on the rail.

Only that friendly voice on the other end of the line kept Bryce from walking right off the roof.

Juniper had kept Bryce on the phone—babbling about nothing. Right until her cab had pulled up in front of the apartment. Juniper refused to hang up until she was on the roof with Bryce, laughing it off. She'd only known where to find her because Bryce had mumbled something about sitting there. And perhaps she'd rushed over because of how hollow Bryce's voice had been when she'd said it.

Juniper had stayed to burn the copies of the song, then gone downstairs to the apartment, where they'd watched TV in bed until they fell asleep. Bryce had risen at one point to turn off the TV and use the bathroom; when she'd come back, Juniper had been awake, waiting.

Her friend didn't leave her side for three days.

They'd never spoken of it. But Bryce wondered if Juniper had later told Fury how close it had been, how hard she'd worked to keep that phone call going while she raced over without alerting Bryce, sensing that something was wrong-wrong-wrong.

Bryce didn't like to think about that winter. That night. But she would never stop being grateful for Juniper for that sense—that love that had kept her from making such a terrible, stupid mistake.

"Yeah," Hunt said, "people are assholes."

She supposed he'd had it worse than her. A lot worse.

Two centuries of slavery that was barely disguised as some sort of twisted path to redemption. Micah's bargain with him, reduced or no, was a disgrace.

She made herself take a bite of her now-soggy cereal. Made herself ask something, anything, to clear her head a bit. "Did you make up your nickname? The Shadow of Death?"

Hunt set down his spoon. "Do I look like the sort of person who needs to make up nicknames for myself?"

"No," Bryce admitted.

"They only call me that because I'm ordered to do that sort of shit. And I do it well." He shrugged. "They'd be better off calling me Slave of Death."

She bit her lip and took another bite of cereal.

Hunt cleared his throat. "I know that visit today was hard. And I know I didn't act like it at first, Quinlan, but I'm glad you got put on this case. You've been . . . really great."

She tucked away what his praise did to her heart, how it lifted the fog that had settled on her. "My dad was a Dracon captain in the 25th Legion. They stationed him at the front for the entire three years of his military service. He taught me a few things."

"I know. Not about you being taught, I mean. But about your dad. Randall Silago, right? He's the one who taught you to shoot."

She nodded, an odd sort of pride wending its way through her.

Hunt said, "I never fought beside him, but I heard of him the last time I was sent to the front—around twenty-six years ago. Heard about his sharpshooting, I mean. What does he think about . . ." A wave of his hand to her, the city around them.

"He wants me to move back home. I had to go to the mat with him—literally—to win the fight about going to CCU."

"You physically fought him?"

"Yeah. He said if I could pin him, then I knew enough about defense to hold my own in the city. Turns out, I'd been paying more attention than I'd let him believe."

Hunt's low laugh skittered over her skin. "And he taught you how to shoot a sniper rifle?"

"Rifles, handguns, knives, swords." But guns were Randall's specialty. He'd taught her ruthlessly, over and over and over again.

"You ever use any outside of practice?"

I love you, Bryce.

Close your eyes, Danika.

"When I had to," she rasped. Not that it had made a difference when it mattered.

Her phone buzzed. She glanced at the message from Jesiba and groaned.

A client is coming in thirty minutes. Be there or you've got a one-way ticket to life as a vole.

Bryce set down her spoon, aware of Hunt watching her, and began to type. *I'll be at—*

Jesiba added another message before Bryce could reply. *And where is that paperwork from yesterday?*

Bryce deleted what she'd written, and began writing, *I'll get it—*

Another message from Jesiba: *I want it done by noon.*

"Someone's pissed off," Hunt observed, and Bryce grimaced, grabbing up her bowl and hurrying to the sink.

The messages kept coming in on the walk over, along with half a dozen threats to turn her into various pathetic creatures, suggesting someone had indeed royally pissed off Jesiba. When they reached the gallery door, Bryce unlocked the physical and magical locks and sighed. "Maybe you should stay on the roof this afternoon. She's probably going to be monitoring me on the cameras. I don't know if she's seen you inside before, but . . ."

He clapped a hand on her shoulder. "Got it, Quinlan." His black jacket buzzed, and he pulled out his phone. "It's Isaiah," he murmured, and nodded to the now-open door of the gallery, through which they could see Syrinx scratching at the library door, yowling his greeting to Lehabah. "I'll check in later," he said.

He waited to fly to the roof, she knew, until she'd locked the gallery door behind herself. A message from him appeared fifteen minutes later. *Isaiah needs me for an opinion on a different case. Heading over now. Justinian's watching you. I'll be back in a few hours.*

She wrote back, *Is Justinian hot?*

He answered, *Who's the pervert now?*

A smile pulled at her mouth.

Her thumbs were hovering over the keyboard to reply when her phone rang. Sighing, she raised it to her ear to answer.

"Why aren't you ready for the client?" Jesiba demanded.

This morning had been a wreck. Standing guard on the roof of the gallery hours later, Hunt couldn't stop thinking it. Yes, they'd caught Sabine in her lie, and all signs pointed toward her as the murderer, but . . . Fuck. He hadn't realized how rough it'd be on Quinlan, even knowing Sabine hated her. Hadn't realized the other wolves had it out for Bryce, too. He should never have brought her. Should have gone himself.

The hours ticked by, one by one, as he mulled it all over.

Hunt made sure no one was flying over the roof before he pulled up the video footage, accessed from the 33rd's archives. Someone had compiled the short reel, no doubt an attempt to get a better image of the demon than a toe or a claw.

The kristallos was a gray blur as it exploded from the front door of the apartment building. They hadn't been able to get footage of it actually entering the building, which suggested it had either been summoned on-site or had snuck through the roof, and no nearby cameras had picked it up, either. But here it was, shattering the front door, so fast it was just gray smoke.

And then—there *she* was. Bryce. Hurtling through the door, barefoot and running on shards of glass, table leg in her hand, pure rage twisting her face.

He'd seen the footage two years ago, but it made slightly more sense now, knowing that Randall Silago had trained her. Watching her leap over cars, careening down streets, as fast as a Fae male. Her face was smeared with blood, her lips curled in a snarl he couldn't hear.

But even in the grainy video footage, her eyes were hazy. Still fighting those drugs.

She definitely didn't remember that he'd been in that interrogation room with her, if she'd asked about the messages during lunch. And, fuck—he'd known everything from her phone had leaked, but he'd never thought about what it must have been like.

She was right: people were assholes.

Bryce cleared Main Street, sliding over the hood of a car, and then the footage ended.

Hunt blew out a breath. If it really was Sabine behind this . . . Micah had given him permission to take out the culprit. But Bryce might very well do it herself.

Hunt frowned toward the wall of fog just visible across the river, the mists impenetrable even in the afternoon sunlight. The Bone Quarter.

No one knew what went on in the Sleeping City. If the dead roamed through the mausoleums, if the Reapers patrolled and ruled like kings, if it was merely mist and carved stone and silence. No one flew over it—no one dared.

But Hunt sometimes felt like the Bone Quarter watched them, and some people claimed that their beloved dead could communicate through the Oracle or cheap market psychics.

Two years ago, Bryce hadn't been at Danika's Sailing. He'd looked. The most important people in Crescent City had gone, but she hadn't been there. Either to avoid Sabine killing her on sight, or for reasons of her own. After what he'd seen today, his money was on the former.

So she hadn't witnessed Sabine pushing the ancient black boat into the Istros, the gray silk-shrouded box—all that remained of Danika's body—in its center. Hadn't counted the seconds as it drifted into the muddy waters, holding her breath with all those on shore to see if the boat would be picked up by that swift current that would bring it to the shores of the Bone Quarter, or if it would overturn, Danika's unworthy remains given to the river and the beasts who swam within it.

But Danika's boat headed straight for the mist-shrouded island across the river, the Under-King deeming her worthy, and more than one person had heaved a sigh. The audio from the apartment building's shitty hall camera of Danika begging for mercy had leaked a day before.

Hunt had suspected that half the people who'd come to her Sailing hoped Danika's begging meant she'd be given to the river, that they could deem the haughty and wild former Alpha a coward.

Sabine, clearly aware of those anticipating such an outcome, had only waited until the river gates opened to reveal the swirling mists of the Bone Quarter, the boat tugged inside by invisible hands, and then left. She didn't wait to see the Sailings for the rest of the Pack of Devils.

But Hunt and everyone else had. It had been the last time he'd seen Ithan Holstrom. Weeping as he pushed his brother's remains into the blue waters, so distraught his sunball teammates had been forced to hold him up. The cold-eyed male who'd served as escort today was a wholly different person from that boy.

Talented, Hunt had heard Naomi say of Ithan in her endless running commentary about the Aux packs and how they stacked up to the 33rd. Beyond his skill on the sunball field, Ithan Holstrom was a gifted warrior, who had made the Drop and come within spitting distance of Connor's power. Naomi always said that despite being cocky, Ithan was a solid male: fair-minded, smart, and loyal.

And a fucking prick, it seemed.

Hunt shook his head, again staring toward the Bone Quarter.

Did Danika Fendyr roam that misty island? Or part of her, at least? Did she remember the friend who, even so long after her death, took no shit from anyone who insulted her memory? Did she know that Bryce would do anything, possibly descend to the level of rage forever preserved in the video, to destroy her killer? Even if that killer was Danika's own mother?

Loyal unto death and beyond.

Hunt's phone rang, Isaiah's name popping up again, but Hunt didn't immediately answer. Not as he glanced at the gallery roof beneath his boots and wondered what it was like—to have a friend like that.

45

So do you think you'll get promoted to principal after the season?" Her shoulder wedging her phone against her ear, Bryce toed off her shoes at her apartment door and strode for the wall of windows. Syrinx, freed of his leash, ran for his food bowl to await his dinner.

"Doubtful," Juniper said, her voice soft and quiet. "Eugenie is really killing it this year. I think she'll be tapped for principal next. I've been a little off in some of my solos, I can feel it."

Bryce peered out the window, spotted Hunt precisely where he said he'd wait until she signaled that she was safe and sound in her apartment, and waved. "You know you've been awesome. Don't pretend that you're not killing it, too."

Hunt lifted a hand and launched skyward, winking at her as he flew past the window, then headed to the Munin and Hugin.

He hadn't been able to convince her to join his triarii companions at the bar, and had made her swear on all five gods that she wouldn't leave her apartment or open the door for anyone while he was gone.

Well, for *almost* anyone.

From their brief conversation, she'd gleaned that Hunt was invited often to the bar, but had never gone. Why he was going tonight for the first time . . . Maybe she was driving him nuts. She hadn't sensed that, but maybe he just needed a night off.

"I've been doing all right, I guess," Juniper admitted.

Bryce clicked her tongue. "You're so full of shit with that 'all right' crap."

"I was thinking, B," Juniper said carefully. "My instructor mentioned that she's starting a dance class that's open to the general public. You could go."

"Your instructor is the most in-demand teacher in this city. No way I'd get in," Bryce deflected, watching the cars and pedestrians stream past below her window.

"I know," Juniper said. "That's why I asked her to save you a spot."

Bryce stilled. "I've got a lot going on right now."

"It's a two-hour class, twice a week. After work hours."

"Thanks, but I'm good."

"You were, Bryce. You were *good*."

Bryce clenched her teeth. "Not fucking good enough."

"It didn't matter to you before Danika died. Just go to the class. It's not an audition—it's literally just a class for people who love to dance. Which you do."

"Which I *did*."

Juniper's breath rattled the phone. "Danika would be heartbroken to hear you don't dance anymore. Even for fun."

Bryce made a show of humming with consideration. "I'll think about it."

"Good," Juniper said. "I'm sending you the details."

Bryce changed the subject. "You wanna come over and watch some trashy TV? *Beach House Hookup* is on tonight at nine."

Juniper asked slyly, "Is the angel there?"

"He's out for beers with his little cabal of killers."

"They're called the triarii, Bryce."

"Yeah, just ask them." Bryce turned from the window and aimed for the kitchen. Syrinx still waited at his food bowl, lion's tail wagging. "Would it make a difference if Hunt was here?"

"I'd be over a Hel of a lot faster."

Bryce laughed. "Shameless." She scooped Syrinx's food into his bowl. His claws clicked as he pranced in place, counting each kibble piece. "Unfortunately for you, I think he's hung up on someone."

"Unfortunately for *you*."

"Please." She opened the fridge and pulled out an assortment of food. A grazer's dinner it was. "I met a mer the other day who was so hot you could have fried an egg on his ten billion abs."

"None of what you said makes any sort of sense, but I think I get the point."

Bryce laughed again. "Should I get a veggie burger warmed up for you, or what?"

"I wish I could, but—"

"But you have to practice."

Juniper sighed. "I'm not going to be made principal by lounging on a couch all night."

"You'll get injured if you push yourself too hard. You're already doing eight shows a week."

The soft voice sharpened. "I'm fine. Maybe Sunday, okay?" The only day the dance company didn't perform.

"Sure," Bryce said. Her chest tightened, enough that she said, "Call me when you're free."

"Will do."

Their goodbyes were quick, and Bryce had barely hung up when she dialed another number.

Fury's phone went right to audiomail. Not bothering to leave a message, Bryce set down her phone and pried open the container of hummus, then leftover noodles, then some possibly rotten pork stew. Magic kept most of the food in her fridge fresh, but there were rational limits.

Grunting, she dumped the stew into the trash. Syrinx frowned up at her.

"Even you wouldn't eat that, my friend," she said.

Syrinx waggled his tail again and bounded for the couch.

The silence of her apartment grew heavy.

One friend—that was what her social circle had become. Fury had made it clear she had no interest in bothering with her anymore.

So now, with her solitary friend too busy with her career to hang out on a reliable schedule, especially in the upcoming summer months when the company performed throughout the week . . . Bryce supposed she was down to zero.

Bryce half-heartedly ate the hummus, dipping slightly slimy carrots into the spread. The crunch of them filled the silence of the apartment.

That too-familiar surge of self-pity came creeping in, and Bryce chucked the carrots and hummus in the garbage before padding for the couch.

She flipped through the channels until she found the local news. Syrinx peered up at her expectantly. "Just you and me tonight, bud," she said, plopping down next to him.

On the news, Rigelus, Bright Hand of the Asteri, appeared, giving some speech on new trade laws at a gilded podium. Behind him, the five other Asteri sat enthroned in their crystal chamber, cold-faced and radiating wealth and power. As always, the seventh throne sat empty in honor of their long-dead sister. Bryce changed the channel again, this time to another news station, blasting footage of lines of human-built mech-suits going toe-to-toe with elite Imperial Legions on a muddy battlefield. Another channel showed starving humans lined up for bread in the Eternal City, their children wailing with hunger.

Bryce switched to a show about buying vacation houses unseen and watched without really processing it.

When was the last time she'd read a book? Not for work or research, but for pleasure? She'd read loads before everything with Danika, but that part of her brain had just turned off afterward.

She'd wanted to drown out any sort of calm and quiet. The blaring television had become her companion to drive the silence away. The dumber the show, the better.

She nestled into the cushions, Syrinx curling up tightly against her leg as she scratched at his velvet-soft ears. He wriggled in a request for more.

The silence pushed in, tighter and thicker. Her mouth dried out, her limbs going light and hollow. The events at the Den threatened to begin looping, Ithan's cold face at the forefront.

She peered at the clock. Barely five thirty.

Bryce blew out a long breath. Lehabah was wrong—this wasn't like that winter. Nothing could ever be as bad as that first winter without Danika. She wouldn't let it.

She stood, Syrinx huffing with annoyance at being disturbed.

"I'll be back soon," she promised, pointing toward the hall and his crate.

Throwing her a baleful look, the chimera saw himself into his cage, yanking the metal door shut with a hooked claw.

Bryce locked it, reassuring him again that she wouldn't be out for long, and slipped back into her heels. She'd promised Hunt she would stay put—had sworn it on the gods.

Too bad the angel didn't know that she no longer prayed to any of them.

Hunt had drunk all of half a beer when his phone rang.

He knew exactly what had happened before he picked up. "She left, didn't she?"

Naomi let out a quiet laugh. "Yeah. All glammed up, too."

"That's how she usually is," he grumbled, rubbing his temple.

Down the carved oak bar, Vik arched a graceful eyebrow, her halo shifting with the movement. Hunt shook his head and reached for his wallet. He shouldn't have come out tonight. The offer had been thrown to him so many times these past four years, and he'd never gone, not when it had felt so much like being in the 18th again. But this time, when Isaiah had called with his standard caveat (*I know you'll say no, but . . .*) he'd said yes.

He didn't know why, but he'd gone.

Hunt asked, "Where'd she head?"

"I'm tracking her now," Naomi said, the wind rustling on her end of the line. She hadn't asked questions when Hunt had called her an hour ago to ask that she guard Bryce—and give up her spot in tonight's hangout. "Looks like she's headed toward FiRo."

Maybe she was seeking out her cousin for an update. "Stay close, and keep your guard up," he said. He knew he didn't need to say it. Naomi was one of the most talented warriors he'd ever encountered, and took no shit from anyone. One look at her tightly braided black hair, the colorful tattoo that covered her hands, and the array of weapons on her muscled body and most people didn't dare to tangle with her. Maybe even Bryce would have obeyed an order to stay put, if Naomi had been the one to give it. "Send me your coordinates."

"Will do." The line went dead.

Hunt sighed. Viktoria said, "You should have known better, friend."

Hunt ran his hands through his hair. "Yeah."

Beside him, Isaiah swigged from his beer. "You could let Naomi handle her."

"I have a feeling that would result in them unleashing Hel together, and I'd still need to go end their fun."

Vik and Isaiah chuckled, and Hunt dropped a silver mark on the bar. Viktoria held up a hand in protest, but Hunt ignored it. They might all be slaves, but he could pay for his own damn drink. "I'll see you two later."

Isaiah raised his beer in salute, and Viktoria gave him a knowing smile before Hunt elbowed his way through the packed bar. Justinian, playing pool in the back, lifted a hand in farewell. Hunt had never asked why all of them preferred the tight quarters of the street-level bar to one of the rooftop lounges most angels frequented. He supposed he wouldn't get the chance to learn why tonight.

Hunt wasn't surprised that Bryce had bailed. Frankly, the only thing that surprised him was that she'd waited this long.

He shouldered through the leaded glass door and out onto the muggy street beyond. Patrons drank at reclaimed oak barrels, and a raucous group of some sort of shifter pack—perhaps wolves or one of the big cats—puffed away on cigarettes.

Hunt scowled at the reek that chased him into the sky, then frowned again at the clouds rolling in from the west, the heavy scent of rain already on the wind. Fantastic.

Naomi sent over her coordinates in Five Roses, and a five-minute flight had Hunt arriving at one of the night gardens, just beginning to awaken with the fading light. Naomi's black wings were a stain against the creeping darkness as she hovered in place above a fountain filled with moon lilies, the bioluminescent flowers already open and glowing pale blue.

"That way," Naomi said, the harsh planes of her face gilded by the soft light from the plants.

Hunt nodded to the angel. "Thanks."

"Good luck." The words were enough to set him on edge, and Hunt didn't bother saying goodbye before soaring down the path. Star oaks lined it, their leaves glittering in a living canopy overhead. The gentle illumination danced on Bryce's hair as she ambled down the stone path, night-blooming flowers opening around her. Jasmine lay heavy in the twilight air, sweet and beckoning.

"You couldn't give me an hour of peace?"

Bryce didn't flinch as he dropped into step beside her. "I wanted some fresh air." She admired an unfurling fern, its fronds lit from within to illuminate every vein.

"Were you going somewhere in particular?"

"Just—out."

"Ah."

"I'm waiting for you to start yelling." She continued past beds of night crocuses, their purple petals shimmering amid the vibrant moss. The garden seemed to awaken for her, welcome her.

"I'll yell when I find out what was so important that you broke your promise."

"Nothing."

"Nothing?"

"Nothing is important."

She said the words with enough quiet that he watched her carefully. "You all right?"

"Yeah." Definitely *no*, then.

She admitted, "The quiet bothers me sometimes."

"I invited you to the bar."

"I didn't want to go to a bar with a bunch of triarii."

"Why not?"

She cut him a sidelong glance. "I'm a civilian. They wouldn't be able to relax."

Hunt opened his mouth to deny it, but she gave him a look. "Fine," he admitted. "Maybe."

They walked in silence for a few steps. "You could go back to your drinking, you know. That ominous-looking angel you sent to babysit me can handle it."

"Naomi left."

"She looks intense."

"She is."

Bryce threw him a hint of a smile. "You two . . . ?"

"No." Though Naomi had hinted about it on occasion. "It'd complicate things."

"Mmm."

"Were you on your way to meet your friends?"

She shook her head. "Just the one friend these days, Athalar. And she's too busy."

"So you were going out alone. To do what?"

"Walk through this garden."

"Alone."

"I knew you'd send a babysitter."

Hunt moved before he could think, gripping her elbow.

She peered up into his face. "Is this the part where you start yelling?"

Lightning cracked through the sky, and echoed in his veins as he leaned closer and purred, "Would you like me to yell, Bryce Quinlan?"

Her throat bobbed, her eyes glowing with golden fire. "Maybe?"

Hunt let out a low laugh. Didn't try to stop the heat that flooded him. "That can be arranged."

All of his focus narrowed on the dip of her eyes to his mouth. The blush that bloomed over her freckled cheeks, inviting him to taste every rosy inch.

No one and nothing existed but this—but her.

He never heard the night-dark bushes behind him rustling. Never heard the branches cracking.

Not until the kristallos crashed into him and sank its teeth into his shoulder.

46

The kristallos slammed into Hunt with the force of an SUV.

Bryce knew he only had enough time to either draw a weapon or shove her out of the way. Hunt chose her.

She hit the asphalt several feet from him, bones barking, and froze. Angel and demon went down, the kristallos pinning Hunt with a roar that sent the night garden shuddering.

It was worse. So much worse than that night.

Blood sprayed, and a knife glinted as Hunt pulled it from its sheath and plunged it into the grayish, near-translucent hide.

Veins of lightning wreathed Hunt's hands—and faded into blackness.

People screamed and bolted down the path, cries to *run!* ringing through the glowing flora. Bryce barely heard them as she climbed to her knees.

Hunt rolled, flipping the creature off him and onto the pathway, wrenching his knife free in the process. Clear blood dripped down the blade as Hunt angled it in front of himself, his shredded arm outflung to protect Bryce. Lightning flared and sputtered at his fingertips.

"Call for backup," he panted without taking his focus off the demon, who paced a step, a clawed hand—crystalline talons glinting—going to the wound in its side.

She'd never seen anything like it. Anything so unearthly, so primal and raging. Her memory of that night was fogged with rage and grief and drugs, so this, the real, undiluted thing—

Bryce reached for her phone, but the creature lunged for Hunt.

The angel's blade drove home. It made no difference.

They again toppled to the path, and Hunt bellowed as the demon's jaws wrapped around his forearm and *crunched*.

His lightning died out entirely.

Move. *Move*, she had to *move*—

Hunt's free fist slammed into the creature's face hard enough to crack bone, but the crystal teeth remained clamped.

This thing pinned him down so easily. Had it done just this to Danika? Shredding and shredding?

Hunt grunted, brow bunched in pain and concentration. His lightning had vanished. Not one flicker of it rose again.

Every part of her shook.

Hunt punched the demon's face again, "*Bryce—*"

She scrambled into movement. Not for her phone, but for the gun holstered at Hunt's hip.

The blind demon sensed her, its nostrils flaring as her fingers wrapped around the handgun. She freed the safety, hauling it up as she uncoiled to her feet.

The creature released Hunt's arm and leapt for her. Bryce fired, but too slow. The demon lunged to the side, dodging her bullet. Bryce fell back as it roared and leapt for her again—

Its head snapped to the side, clear blood spraying like rain as a knife embedded itself to the hilt just above its mouth.

Hunt was upon it again, drawing another long knife from a hidden panel down the back of his battle-suit and plunging the blade right into the skull and toward the spine.

The creature struggled, snapping for Bryce, its clear teeth stained red with Hunt's blood. She'd wound up on the pavement somehow, and crawled backward as it tried to lunge for her. Failed to, as Hunt wrapped his hands around the blade and *twisted*.

The crack of its severing neck was muffled by the moss-shrouded trees.

Bryce still aimed the handgun. "Get out of the way."

Hunt released his grip, letting the creature slump to the mossy path. Its black tongue lolled from its clear-fanged mouth.

"Just in case," Bryce said, and fired. She didn't miss this time.

Sirens wailed, and wings filled the air. Ringing droned in her head.

Hunt withdrew his blade from the creature's skull and brought it down with a mighty, one-armed sweep. The severed head tumbled away. Hunt moved again, and the head split in half. Then quarters.

Another plunge and the hateful heart was skewered, too. Clear blood leaked everywhere, like a spilled vial of serum.

Bryce stared and stared at its ruined head, the horrible, monstrous body.

Powerful forms landed among them, that black-winged malakh instantly at Hunt's side. "Holy shit, Hunt, what—"

Bryce barely heard the words. Someone helped her to her feet. Blue light flared, and a magi-screen encompassed the site, blocking it from the view of any who hadn't yet fled. She should have been screaming, should have been leaping for the demon, ripping apart its corpse with her bare hands. But only a thrumming silence filled her head.

She looked around the park, stupidly and slowly, as if she might see Sabine there.

Hunt groaned, and she whirled as he tumbled face-first to the ground. The dark-winged angel caught him, her powerful body easily bearing his weight. "Get a medwitch here *now*!"

His shoulder was gushing blood. So was his forearm. Blood, and some sort of silvery slime.

She knew the burn of that slime, like living fire.

A head of sleek black curls streamed past, and Bryce blinked as a curvy young woman in a medwitch's blue jumpsuit unhooked the bag across her chest and slid to her knees beside Hunt.

He was bent over, a hand at his forearm, panting heavily. His gray wings sagged, splattered with both clear and red blood.

The medwitch asked him something, the broom-and-bell insignia on her right arm catching the blue light of the screens. Her brown hands didn't falter as she used a pair of tweezers to extract what looked to be a small worm from a glass jar full of damp moss and set it on Hunt's forearm.

He winced, teeth flashing.

"Sucking out the venom," a female voice explained beside Bryce. The dark-winged angel. Naomi. She pointed a tattooed finger toward Hunt. "They're mithridate leeches."

The leech's black body swiftly swelled. The witch set another on Hunt's shoulder wound. Then another on his forearm.

Bryce said nothing.

Hunt's face was pale, his eyes shut as he seemed to focus on his breathing. "I think the venom nullified my power. As soon as it bit me . . ." He hissed at whatever agony worked through his body. "I couldn't summon my lightning."

Recognition jolted through her. It explained so much. Why the kristallos had been able to pin Micah, for one thing. If it had ambushed the Archangel and gotten a good bite, he would have been left with only physical strength. Micah had probably never even realized what happened. Had likely written it off as shock or the swiftness of the attack. Perhaps the bite had nullified the preternatural strength of Danika and the Pack of Devils, too.

"Hey." Naomi put a hand on Bryce's shoulder. "You hurt?"

The medwitch peeled a poison-eating leech from Hunt's shoulder, threw it back in the glass jar, then replaced it with another. Pale light wreathed her hands as she assessed Hunt's other injuries, then began the process of healing them. She didn't bother with the vials of firstlight glowing in her bag—a cure-all for many medics. As if she preferred using the magic in her own veins.

"I'm fine."

Hunt's body might have been able to heal itself, but it would have taken longer. With the venom in those wounds, Bryce knew too well that it might not really heal at all.

Naomi ran a hand over her inky hair. "You should let that medwitch examine you."

"No."

Her onyx eyes sharpened. "If Hunt can let the medwitch work on him, then you—"

Vast, cold power erupted through the site, the garden, the whole quarter of the city. Naomi whirled as Micah landed. Silence fell, Vanir of all types backing away as the Archangel prowled toward the fallen demon and Hunt.

Naomi was the only one with enough balls to approach him. "I was on watch right before Hunt arrived and there was no sign—"

Micah stalked past her, his eyes pinned on the demon. The medwitch, to her credit, didn't halt her ministrations, but Hunt managed to lift his head to meet Micah's interrogation.

"What happened."

"Ambush," Hunt said, his voice gravelly.

Micah's white wings seemed to glow with power. And for all the ringing silence in Bryce's head, all the distance she now felt between her body and what remained of her soul, she stepped up. Like Hel would this jeopardize Micah's bargain with Hunt. Bryce said, "It came out of the shadows."

The Archangel raked his eyes over her. "Which one of you did it attack?"

Bryce pointed to Hunt. "Him."

"And which one of you killed it?"

Bryce began to repeat "Him," but Hunt cut in, "It was a joint effort." Bryce shot him a look to keep quiet, but Micah had already pivoted to the demon's corpse. He toed it with his boot, frowning.

"We can't let the press get wind of this," Micah ordered. "Or the others coming in for the Summit." The unspoken part of that statement lingered. *Sandriel doesn't hear a word.*

"We'll keep it out of the papers," Naomi promised.

But Micah shook his head, and extended a hand.

Before Bryce could so much as blink, white flame erupted around the demon and its head. Within a second, it was nothing more than ash.

Hunt started. "We needed to examine it for evidence—"

"No press," Micah said, then turned toward a cluster of angel commanders.

The medwitch began removing her leeches and bandaging Hunt. Each of the silk strips was imbued with her power, willing the skin and muscle to knit back together and staving off infection. They'd dissolve once the wounds had healed, as if they'd never existed.

The pile of ashes still lay there, mockingly soft considering the true terror the kristallos had wrought. Had this demon been the one to kill Danika, or merely one of thousands waiting on the other side of the Northern Rift?

Was the Horn here, in this park? Had she somehow, unwittingly, come near it? Or maybe whoever was looking for it—Sabine?—simply sent the kristallos as another message. They were nowhere near Moonwood, but Sabine's patrols took her all over the city.

The sting of the gun still bit into Bryce's palms, its kickback zinging along her bones.

The medwitch removed her bloody gloves. A crackle of lightning at Hunt's knuckles showed his returning power. "Thanks," he said to the witch, who waved him off. Within a few seconds, she'd packed the poison-swollen leeches in their jars and swept behind the magi-screens.

Hunt's stare met Bryce's. The ashes and busy officials and warriors around them faded away into white noise.

Naomi approached, braid swaying behind her. "Why'd it target you?"

"Everyone wants to take a bite out of me," Hunt deflected.

Naomi gave them both a look that told Bryce she didn't buy it for one second, but moved off to talk to a Fae female in the Aux.

Hunt tried to ease to his feet, and Bryce stepped in to offer a hand up. He shook his head, grimacing as he braced a hand on his knee and rose. "I guess we hit a nerve with Sabine," he said. "She must have figured out we're onto her. This was either a warning like the club bombing or a failed attempt to take care of a problem like she did with the acolyte and guard."

She didn't answer. A wind drifted by, stirring the ashes.

"Bryce." Hunt stepped closer, his dark eyes clear despite his injury.

"It doesn't make any sense," she whispered at last. "You—we killed it so quickly."

Hunt didn't reply, giving her the space to think through it, to say it.

She said, "Danika was strong. Connor was strong. Either one of them could have taken on that demon and walked away. But the entire Pack of Devils was there that night. Even if its venom nullified some of their powers, the entire pack could have . . ." Her throat tightened.

"Even Mic—" Hunt caught himself, glancing toward the Archangel still talking to commanders off to the side. "He didn't walk away from it."

"But I did. Twice now."

"Maybe it's got some Fae weakness."

She shook her head. "I don't think so. It just . . . it's not adding up."

"We'll lay it all out tomorrow." Hunt nodded toward Micah. "I think tonight just proved it's time to tell him our suspicions about Sabine."

She was going to be sick. But she nodded back.

They waited until most of Micah's commanders had peeled off on their various assignments before approaching, Hunt wincing with each step.

Hunt grunted, "We need to talk to you."

Micah only crossed his arms. And then Hunt, briskly and efficiently, told him. About the Horn, about Sabine, about their suspicions. About the Horn possibly being repaired—though they still didn't know why she'd want or need to open a portal to another world.

Micah's eyes went from annoyed to enraged to outright glacial.

When Hunt was done, the Governor looked between them. "You need more evidence."

"We'll get it," Hunt promised.

Micah surveyed them, his face dark as the Pit. "Come to me when you have concrete proof. Or if you find that Horn. If someone's gone to so much trouble over it, there's a damn good chance they've found a way to repair it. I won't have this city endangered by a power-hungry bitch." Bryce could have sworn the thorns tattooed across Hunt's brow darkened as his eyes met the Archangel's. "Don't fuck this up for me, Athalar." Without a further word, he flapped his wings and shot into the night sky.

Hunt blew out a breath, staring at the pile of ashes. "Prick."

Bryce rubbed her hands over her arms. Hunt's eyes darted toward her, noting the movement. The cold creeping over her that had nothing to do with the spring night. Or the storm that was moments from unleashing itself.

"Come on," he said gently, rotating his injured arm to test its strength. "I think I can manage flying us back to your place."

She surveyed the busy crew, the tracker shifters already moving off into the trees to hunt for prints before the rain wiped them away. "Don't we need to answer questions?"

He extended a hand. "They know where to find us."

Ruhn got to the night garden moments after his sister and Athalar left, according to Naomi Boreas, captain of the 33rd's infantry. The take-no-shit angel had merely said both of them were fine, and pivoted to receive an update from a unit captain under her command.

All that was left of the kristallos was a burnt stain and a few sprayed drops of clear blood, like beaded rainwater on the stones and moss.

Ruhn approached a carved boulder just off the path. Squatting, he freed the knife in his boot and angled the blade toward a splash of the unusual blood clinging to some ancient moss.

"I wouldn't do that."

He knew that fair voice—its steady, calm cadence. He peered over his shoulder to find the medwitch from the clinic standing behind him, her curly dark hair loose around her striking face. But her eyes were upon the blood. "Its venom lies in its saliva," she said, "but we don't know what other horrors might be in the blood itself."

"It hasn't affected the moss," he said.

"Yes, but this was a demon bred for specific purposes. Its blood might be harmless to non-sentient life, but be dangerous to everything else."

Ruhn started. "You recognized the demon?"

The witch blinked, as if she'd been caught. "I had very old tutors, as I told you. They required me to study ancient texts."

Ruhn rose to his feet. "We could have used you years ago."

"I had not completed my training then." A nonanswer. Ruhn's brow furrowed. The witch took a step back. "I was thinking, Prince," she said, continuing her retreat. "About what you asked me. I looked into it, and there is some potential . . . research. I have to leave the city for a few days to attend to a personal matter, but when I return and fully review it, I will send it to you."

"Ruhn!" Flynn's shout cut through the chaos of the investigatory team around them.

Ruhn glanced over a shoulder to tell his friend to wait for two gods-damned seconds, but motion from the witch caught his eye.

He hadn't seen the broom she'd stashed beside the tree, but he certainly saw it now as she shot into the night sky, her hair a dark curtain behind her.

"Who was that?" Flynn asked, nodding toward the vanishing witch.

"I don't know," Ruhn said quietly, staring after her into the night.

47

The storm hit when they were two blocks from Bryce's building, soaking them within seconds. Pain lanced through Hunt's forearm and shoulder as he landed on the roof, but he swallowed it down. Bryce was still shaking, her face distant enough that he didn't immediately let go when he set her upon the rain-soaked tiles.

She peered up at him when his arms remained around her waist.

Hunt couldn't help the thumb he swept over her ribs. Couldn't stop himself from doing it a second time.

She swallowed, and he tracked every movement of her throat. The raindrop that ran over her neck, her pulse pounding delicately beneath it.

Before he could react, she leaned forward, wrapping her arms around him. Held him tightly. "Tonight sucked," she said against his soaked chest.

Hunt slid his arms around her, willing his warmth into her trembling body. "It did."

"I'm glad you're not dead."

Hunt chuckled, letting himself bury his face against her neck. "So am I."

Bryce's fingers curled against his spine, exploring and gentle.

Every single one of his senses narrowed to that touch. Came roaring awake. "We should get out of the rain," she murmured.

"We should," he replied. And made no move.

"Hunt."

He couldn't tell if his name was a warning or a request or something more. Didn't care as he grazed his nose against the rain-slick column of her neck. Fuck, she smelled good.

He did it again, unable to help himself or get enough of that scent. She tipped her chin up slightly. Just enough to expose more of her neck to him.

Hel, yes. Hunt almost groaned the words as he let himself nuzzle into that soft, delicious neck, as greedy as a fucking vampyr to be there, smell her, taste her.

It overrode every instinct, every pained memory, every vow he'd sworn.

Bryce's fingers tightened on his back—then began stroking. He nearly purred.

He didn't let himself think, not as he brushed his lips over the spot he'd nuzzled. She arched slightly against him. Into the hardness that ached behind the reinforced leather of his battle-suit.

Swallowing another groan against her neck, Hunt tightened his arms around her warm, soft body, and ran his hands downward, toward that perfect, sweet ass that had tortured him since day fucking one, and—

The metal door to the roof opened. Hunt already had his gun drawn and aimed toward it as Sabine stepped out and snarled, "*Back the fuck up.*"

48

Hunt weighed his options carefully.

He had a gun pointed at Sabine's head. She had a gun pointed at Bryce's heart.

Which of them was faster? The question buzzed in his skull.

Bryce obeyed Sabine's command, her hands raised. Hunt could only follow, stepping behind Bryce so she was up against his chest, so he could snake his free hand around her waist, pinning her against him. Could he get into the air fast enough to avoid a bullet?

Bryce wouldn't survive a close-range shot to the heart. She'd be dead in seconds.

Bryce managed to ask over the drumming rain, "Where's your little demon friend?"

Sabine kicked the door to the roof shut. The cameras had all been disabled, he realized. They had to be, or the legion would already be here, having been tipped off by Marrin. The feeds had to be looping on harmless footage—just as she'd done at Luna's Temple. Which meant no one, absolutely no one, knew what was happening.

Hunt slowly began to bring his good arm up Bryce's shaking, soaked body.

Sabine spat. "Don't fucking think about it, Athalar."

He stopped his arm before it could cover Bryce's breasts—the heart beating beneath them. His battle-suit had enough armor to deflect a bullet. To let him absorb the impact. Better for him to lose an arm that he could regrow than for her to—

He couldn't think the last word.

Sabine hissed, "I told you to stay away from this. And yet you just couldn't listen—you had to show up at the Den, asking questions you have *no right* to ask."

Bryce snarled, "We were asking those questions because you killed Danika, you fucking psycho."

Sabine went wholly still. Nearly as still as the Fae could go. "You think I did *what*?"

Hunt knew Sabine wore every emotion on her face and had never once bothered to hide it. Her shock was genuine. Rain dripped off the narrow angles of her face as she seethed, "You think I killed my own daughter?"

Bryce was shaking so hard that Hunt had to tighten his grip, and she snapped, "You killed her because she was going to take your place as future Prime, you stole the Horn to undermine her, and you've been using that demon to kill anyone who might have seen you and to humiliate Micah before the Summit—"

Sabine laughed, low and hollow. "What utter bullshit."

Hunt growled, "You wiped the footage of the Horn's theft from the temple. We have it confirmed. You lied to us about Danika being there that night. And ranted about your daughter not keeping her mouth shut the night she died. All we need to prove you killed Danika is to tie you to the kristallos demon."

Sabine lowered her gun, putting the safety back on. She trembled with barely restrained rage. "I didn't steal anything, you stupid fucks. And I didn't kill my daughter."

Hunt didn't dare lower his gun. Didn't dare let go of Bryce.

Not as Sabine said, cold and joyless, "I was protecting her. *Danika* stole the Horn."

49

Danika didn't steal anything," Bryce whispered, cold lurching through her. Only Hunt's arm around her middle kept her upright, his body a warm wall at her back.

Sabine's light brown eyes—the same shade Danika's had been but void of their warmth—were merciless. "Why do you think I swapped the footage? She thought the blackout would hide her, but was too dumb to consider that there might be audio still rolling that picked up each one of her disappearing footsteps as she left her post to steal the Horn, then reappeared a minute later, going back on patrol, as if she hadn't spat in our goddess's face. Whether she caused the blackout to steal it or if she took advantage of an opportunity, I don't know."

"Why would she take it?" Bryce could barely get the words out.

"Because Danika was a brat who wanted to see what she could get away with. As soon as I got the alert that the Horn had been stolen, I looked into the videos and swapped the footage on every database." Sabine's smile was a cruel slash. "I cleaned up her mess—just like I did for her entire life. And you two, in asking your *questions*, have threatened the shred of a legacy that she stands to leave."

Hunt's wings flared slightly. "You sent that demon after us tonight—"

Sabine's pale brows snapped together. "What demon? I've been waiting for you here all night. I thought about your stupid fucking visit to *my* Den, and decided you needed a real reminder to stay the Hel out of this case." She bared her teeth. "Amelie Ravenscroft is standing across the street, waiting to make the call if you step out of line, Athalar. She says you two were putting on quite the show a moment ago." A vicious, knowing smile.

Bryce flushed, and let Hunt look to confirm. From the way he tensed, she knew it was true.

Sabine said, "And as for what I said the night she died: Danika *couldn't* keep her mouth shut—about anything. I knew she'd stolen the Horn, and knew someone probably killed her for it because she couldn't keep it quiet." Another cold laugh. "Everything I did was to protect my daughter. My reckless, arrogant daughter. Everything *you* did encouraged the worst in her."

Hunt's growl rent the night. "Careful, Sabine."

But the Alpha just snorted. "You'll regret crossing me." She strolled for the edge of the roof, her power thrumming in a faint glow around her as she assessed the same leap that Bryce had so stupidly considered a year and a half ago. Only, Sabine would be able to gracefully land on the pavement. Sabine looked back over a thin shoulder, her lengthening teeth gleaming as she said, "I didn't kill my daughter. But if you jeopardize her legacy, I will kill *you*."

And then she jumped, shifting with a soft flash of light as she went. Hunt sprinted for the edge, but Bryce knew what he'd see: a wolf landing lightly on the pavement and streaking away into the darkness.

50

Hunt didn't realize just how badly Sabine's bombshell had hit Bryce until the next morning. She didn't run. Nearly didn't get up in time for work.

She drank a cup of coffee but refused the eggs he made. Barely said three words to him.

He knew she wasn't mad at him. Knew that she was just . . . processing.

Whether that processing also had to do with what they'd done on the roof, he didn't dare ask. It wasn't the time. Even though he'd had to take a cold, cold shower afterward. And take matters into his own hands. It was to Bryce's face, the memory of her scent and that breathy moan she'd made as she arched against him, that he'd come, hard enough he'd seen stars.

But it was the least of his concerns, this thing between them. Whatever it was.

Mercifully, nothing had leaked to the press about the attack in the park.

Bryce barely spoke after work. He'd made her dinner and she'd poked at it, then gone to sleep before nine. There sure as fuck were no more hugs that led to nuzzling.

The next day was the same. And the next.

He was willing to give her space. The gods knew he'd sometimes needed it. Every time he killed for Micah he needed it.

He knew better than to suggest Sabine could be lying, since there was no easier person to accuse than a dead one. Sabine was a monster, but Hunt had never known her to be a liar.

The investigation was full of dead ends, and Danika had died—for what? For an ancient artifact that didn't work. That hadn't worked in fifteen thousand years and never would again.

Had Danika herself wanted to repair and use the Horn? Though why, he had no idea.

He knew those thoughts weighed on Bryce. For five fucking days, she barely ate. Just went to work, slept, and went to work again.

Every morning he made her breakfast. Every morning she ignored the plate he laid out.

Micah called only once, to ask if they'd gotten proof on Sabine. Hunt had merely said, "It was a dead end," and the Governor had hung up, his rage at the unsolved case palpable.

That had been two days ago. Hunt was still waiting for the other shoe to drop.

"I thought hunting for ancient, deadly weapons would be exciting," Lehabah groused from where she sat on her little divan, half watching truly inane daytime television.

"Me too," Bryce muttered.

Hunt looked up from the evidence report he'd been skimming and was about to answer when the front doorbell rang. Ruhn's face appeared on the camera feed, and Bryce let out a long, long sigh before silently buzzing him in.

Hunt rotated his stiff shoulder. His arm still throbbed a bit, an echo of the lethal venom that had ripped his magic right from his body.

The prince's black boots appeared on the green carpeted steps seconds later, apparently taking a hint about their location thanks to the open library door. Lehabah was instantly zooming across the space, sparks in her wake, as she beamed and said, "*Your Highness!*"

Ruhn offered her a half smile, his eyes going right to Quinlan.

They missed none of the quiet, brooding exhaustion. Or the tone in Bryce's voice as she said, "To what do we owe this pleasure?"

Ruhn slid into a seat across from them at the book-strewn table. The Starsword sheathed down his back didn't reflect the lights in the library. "I wanted to check in. Anything new?"

Neither of them had told him about Sabine. And apparently Declan hadn't, either.

"No," Bryce said. "Anything about the Horn?"

Ruhn ignored her question. "What's wrong?"

"Nothing." Her spine stiffened.

Ruhn looked ready to get into it with his cousin, so Hunt did both of them—and himself, if he was being honest—a favor and said, "We've been waiting on a Many Waters contact to get back to us about a possible pattern with the demon attacks. Have you come across any information about the kristallos negating magic?" Days later, he couldn't stop thinking about it—how it'd felt for his power to just sputter and die in his veins.

"No. I still haven't found anything about the creation of the kristallos except that it was made from the blood of the first Starborn Prince and the essence of the Star-Eater himself. Nothing about it negating magic." Ruhn nodded at him. "You've never come across a demon that can do that?"

"Not one. Witch spells and gorsian stones negate magic, but this was different." He'd dealt with both. Before they'd bound him using the witch-ink on his brow, they'd shackled him with manacles hewn from the gorsian stones of the Dolos Mountains, a rare metal whose properties numbed one's access to magic. They were used on high-profile enemies of the empire—the Hind herself was particularly fond of using them as she and her interrogators broke the Vanir among the rebel spies and leaders. But for years now, rumors had swirled in the 33rd's barracks that rebels were experimenting with ways to render the metal into a spray that could be unleashed upon Vanir warriors on the battlefields.

Ruhn motioned to the ancient book he'd left on the table days ago, still open to a passage about the Starborn Fae. "If the Star-Eater himself put his essence in the kristallos, that's probably what gave the demon the ability to eat magic. Just as Prince Pelias's blood gave it the ability to look for the Horn."

Bryce frowned. "So that Chosen One sense of yours hasn't detected a trace of the Horn?"

Ruhn tugged at the silver ring through his bottom lip. "No. But I got a message this morning from a medwitch I met the other day—the one who stitched up Hunt in the night garden. It's a shot in the dark, but she mentioned that there's a relatively new drug on the market that's just starting to come into use. It's a synthetic healing magic." Hunt and Bryce straightened. "It can have some wicked side effects if not carefully controlled. She didn't have access to its exact formula or the trials, but she said research showed it capable of healing at rates nearly double that of firstlight."

Bryce said, "You think something like that could repair the Horn?"

"It's a possibility. It'd fit with that stupid riddle about light that's not light, magic that's not magic repairing the Horn. That's kind of what a synthetic compound like that is."

Her eyes flickered. "And it's . . . readily available?"

"It entered the market at some point in the past few years, apparently. No one has tested it on inanimate objects, but who knows? If real magic couldn't heal it, maybe a synthetic compound could."

"I've never heard of synthetic magic," Hunt said.

"Neither have I," Ruhn admitted.

"So we have a potential way to repair the Horn," Bryce mused, "but not the Horn itself." She sighed. "And we still don't know if Danika stole the Horn on a lark or for some actual purpose."

Ruhn started. "Danika did *what*?"

Bryce winced, then filled the prince in on all they'd learned. When she finished, Ruhn leaned back in his chair, shock written on every line of his face.

Hunt said into the silence, "Regardless of whether Danika stole the Horn for fun or to do something with it, the fact remains that she stole it."

Ruhn asked carefully, "Do you think she wanted it for herself? To repair it and use it?"

"No," Bryce said quietly. "No, Danika might have kept things from me, but I knew her heart. She never would have sought a weapon as dangerous as the Horn—something that could jeopardize the world like that." She ran her hands over her face. "Her killer is still out there. Danika must have taken the Horn to keep them from getting it. They killed her for it, but they must not have found it, if they're still using the kristallos to search for it." She waved a hand at Ruhn's sword. "That thing can't help you find it? I still think luring the killer with the Horn is probably the most surefire way to find them."

Ruhn shook his head. "The sword doesn't work like that. Aside from being picky about who draws it, the sword has no power without the knife."

"The knife?" Hunt asked.

Ruhn drew the sword, the metal whining, and laid it on the table between them. Bryce leaned back, away from it, as a bead of starlight sang down the fuller and sparkled at the tip.

"Fancy," Hunt said, earning a glare from Ruhn, who had raised a brow at Bryce, no doubt expecting some kind of reverence from her at a sword that was older than this city, older than the Vanir's first step in Midgard.

"The sword was part of a pair," Ruhn said to him. "A long-bladed knife was forged from the iridium mined from the same meteorite, which fell on our old world." The world the Fae had left to travel through the Northern Rift and into Midgard. "But we lost the knife eons ago. Even the Fae Archives have no record of how it might have been lost, but it seems to have been sometime during the First Wars."

"It's another of the Fae's countless inane prophecies," Bryce muttered. "*When knife and sword are reunited, so shall our people be.*"

"It's literally carved above the Fae Archives entrance—whatever the fuck it means," Ruhn said. Bryce gave a small smile at that.

Hunt grinned. Her little smile was like seeing the sun after days of rain.

Bryce pretended not to notice his grin, but Ruhn gave him a sharp look.

Like he knew every filthy thing Hunt had thought about Bryce, everything he'd done to pleasure himself while imagining it was her mouth around him, her hands, her soft body.

Shit—he was in such deep, unrelenting shit.

Ruhn only snorted, as if he knew that, too, and sheathed the sword again.

"I'd like to see the Fae Archives," Lehabah sighed. "Think of all that ancient history, all those glorious objects."

"Kept locked away, only for their pure-blooded heirs to see," Bryce finished with a pointed glance at Ruhn.

Ruhn held up his hands. "I've tried to get them to change the rules," he said. "No luck."

"They let in visitors on the major holidays," Lehabah said.

"Only from an approved list," Bryce said. "And fire sprites are *not* on it."

Lehabah rolled over onto her side, propping her head up with a fiery hand. "They would let me in. I am a descendant of Queen Ranthia Drahl."

"Yeah, and I'm the seventh Asteri," Bryce said dryly.

Hunt was careful not to react at the tone. The first bit of spark he'd seen in days.

"I am," Lehabah insisted, turning to Ruhn. "She was my six-times-great-grandmother, dethroned in the Elemental Wars. Our family was cast from favor—"

"The story changes every time," Bryce told Hunt, whose lips twitched.

"It does not," Lehabah whined. Ruhn was smiling now, too. "We stood a chance at earning back our title, but my great-great-grandmother was booted from the Eternal City for—"

"Booted."

"Yes, *booted*. For a completely false accusation of trying to steal the royal consort from the impostor queen. She'd be thrashing in her ashes if she knew what had become of her last scion. Little more than a bird in a cage."

Bryce sipped from her water. "This is the point, boys, where she solicits you for cash to purchase her freedom."

Lehabah turned crimson. "That is *not* true." She pointed her finger at Bryce. "My *great*-grandmother fought with Hunt against the angels—and *that* was the end of my entire people's freedom."

The words cracked through Hunt. All of them looked at him now. "I'm sorry." He had no other words in his head.

"Oh, Athie," Lehabah said, zooming over to him and turning rose pink. "I didn't mean to . . ." She cupped her cheeks in her hands. "I do not blame *you*."

"I led everyone into battle. I don't see how there's anyone else to blame for what happened to your people because of it." His words sounded as hollow as they felt.

"But Shahar led *you*," Danaan said, his blue eyes missing nothing.

Hunt bristled at the sound of her name on the prince's lips. But he found himself looking to Quinlan, to torture himself with the damning agreement he'd find on her face.

Only sorrow lay there. And something like understanding. Like she saw him, as he'd seen her in that shooting gallery, marked every broken shard and didn't mind the jagged bits. Under the table, the toe of her high heel brushed against his boot. A little confirmation that yes—she saw his guilt, the pain, and she wouldn't shy from it. His chest tightened.

Lehabah cleared her throat and asked Ruhn, "Have you ever visited the Fae Archives on Avallen? I heard they're grander than what was brought over here." She twirled her curl of flame around a finger.

"No," Ruhn said. "But the Fae on that misty island are even less welcoming than the ones here."

"They do like to hoard all their wealth, don't they," Lehabah said, eyeing Bryce. "Just like you, BB. Only spending on yourself, and never anything nice for me."

Bryce removed her foot. "Do I not buy you strawberry shisha every other week?"

Lehabah crossed her arms. "That's barely a gift."

"Says the sprite who hotboxes herself in that little glass dome and burns it all night and tells me not to bother her until she's done." She leaned back in her chair, smug as a cat, and Hunt nearly grinned again at the spark in her eyes.

Bryce grabbed his phone from the table and snapped a photo of him before he could object. Then one of Lehabah. And another of Syrinx.

If Ruhn noticed she didn't bother with a photo of him, he said nothing. Though Hunt could have sworn the shadows in the room deepened.

"All I want, BB," Lehabah said, "is a little appreciation."

"Gods spare me," Bryce muttered. Even Ruhn smiled at that.

The prince's phone rang, and he picked up before Hunt could see who it was. "Flynn."

Hunt heard Flynn's voice faintly. "You're needed at the barracks. Some bullshit fight broke out about somebody's girlfriend sleeping with someone else and I honestly don't give two fucks about it, but they bloodied each other up pretty damn good."

Ruhn sighed. "I'll be there in fifteen," he said, and hung up.

Hunt asked, "You really have to moderate petty fights like that?"

Ruhn ran a hand down the hilt of the Starsword. "Why not?"

"You're a prince."

"I don't understand why you make that sound like an insult," Ruhn growled.

Hunt said, "Why not do . . . bigger shit?"

Bryce answered for him. "Because his daddy is scared of him."

Ruhn shot her a warning look. "He outranks me power-wise *and* title-wise."

"And yet he made sure to get you under his thumb as early as possible—as if you were some sort of animal to be tamed." She said the words mildly, but Ruhn tensed.

"It was going well," Ruhn said tightly, "until you came along."

Hunt braced himself for the brewing storm.

Bryce said, "He was alive the last time a Starborn Prince appeared, you know. You ever ask what happened to him? Why he died before he made the Drop?"

Ruhn paled. "Don't be stupid. That was an accident during his Ordeal."

Hunt kept his face neutral, but Bryce just leaned back in her chair. "If you say so."

"You still believe this shit you tried to sell me as a kid?"

She crossed her arms. "I wanted your eyes open to what he really is before it was too late for you, too."

Ruhn blinked, but straightened, shaking his head as he rose from the table. "Trust me, Bryce, I've known for a while what he is. I had to fucking live with him." Ruhn nodded toward the messy table. "If I hear anything new about the Horn or this synthetic healing magic, I'll let you know." He met Hunt's stare and added, "Be careful."

Hunt gave him a half smile that told the prince he knew exactly what that *be careful* was about. And didn't give a shit.

Two minutes after Ruhn left, the front door buzzed again.

"What does he fucking want now?" Bryce muttered, grabbing the tablet Lehabah had been using to watch her trash TV and pulling up the video feed for the front cameras.

A squeal escaped her. An otter in a reflective yellow vest stood on its hind legs, a little paw on the lower buzzer she'd had Jesiba install for shorter patrons. Out of the hope that one day, somehow, she'd find a fuzzy, whiskery messenger standing on the doorstep.

Bryce bolted from her chair a second later, her heels eating up the carpet as she ran upstairs.

The message the otter bore from Tharion was short and sweet.

I think you'll find this of interest. Kisses, Tharion

"Kisses?" Hunt asked.

"They're for you, obviously," Bryce said, still smiling about the otter. She'd handed him a silver mark, for which she'd earned a twitch of the whiskers and a little fanged grin.

Easily the highlight of her day. Week. Year.

Honestly, her entire life.

At the desk in the showroom, Bryce removed Tharion's letter from the top of the pile, while Hunt began to leaf through some of the pages beneath.

The blood rushed from her face at a photograph in Hunt's hand. "Is that a body?"

Hunt grunted. "It's what's left of one after Tharion pried it from a sobek's lair."

Bryce couldn't stop the shudder down her spine. Clocking in at more than twenty-five feet and nearly three thousand pounds of scale-covered muscle, sobeks were among the worst of the apex predators who prowled the river. Mean, strong, and with teeth that could snap you in two, a full-grown male sobek could make most Vanir back away. "He's insane."

Hunt chuckled. "Oh, he most certainly is."

Bryce frowned at the gruesome photo, then read through Tharion's notes. "He says the bite marks on the torso aren't consistent with sobek teeth. This person was already dead when they were dumped into the Istros. The sobek must have seen an easy meal and hauled it down to its lair to eat later." She swallowed the dryness in her mouth and again looked at the body. A dryad female. Her chest cavity had been ripped open, heart and internal organs removed, and bite marks peppered—

"These wounds look like the ones you got from the kristallos. And the mer's lab figured this body was probably five days old, judging by the level of decay."

"The night we were attacked."

Bryce studied the analysis. "There was clear venom in the wounds. Tharion says he could feel it inside the corpse even before the mer did tests on it." Most of those in the House of Many Waters could sense what flowed in someone's body—illnesses and weaknesses and, apparently, venom. "But when they tested it . . ." She blew out a breath. "It negated magic." It had to be the kristallos. Bryce cringed, reading on, "He looked into records of all unidentified bodies the mer found in the past couple years. They found two with identical wounds and this clear venom right around the time of . . ." She swallowed. "Around when Danika and the pack died.

A dryad and a fox shifter male. Both reported missing. This month, they've found *five* with these marks and the venom. All reported missing, but a few weeks after the fact."

"So they're people who might not have had many close friends or family," Hunt said.

"Maybe." Bryce again studied the photograph. Made herself look at the wounds. Silence fell, interrupted only by the distant sounds of Lehabah's show downstairs.

She said quietly, "That's not the creature that killed Danika."

Hunt ran a hand through his hair. "There might have been multiple kristallos—"

"No," she insisted, setting down the papers. "The kristallos isn't what killed Danika."

Hunt's brow furrowed. "You were on the scene, though. You saw it."

"I saw it in the hall, not in the apartment. Danika, the pack, and the other three recent victims were in *piles*." She could barely stand to say it, to think about it again.

These past five days had been . . . not easy. Putting one foot in front of the other had been the only thing to get her through it after the disaster with Sabine. After the bomb she'd dropped about Danika. And if they'd been looking for the wrong fucking thing all this time . . .

Bryce held up the photo. "These wounds aren't the same. The kristallos wanted to get at your heart, your organs. Not turn you into a—a heap. Danika, the Pack of Devils, Tertian, the acolyte and temple guard—*none* of them had wounds like this. And *none* had this venom in their system." Hunt just blinked at her. Bryce's voice cracked. "What if something else came through? What if the kristallos was summoned to look for the Horn, but something worse was also there that night? If you had the power to summon the kristallos, why not summon multiple types of demons?"

Hunt considered. "I can't think of a demon that demolishes its victims like that, though. Unless it's another ancient horror straight from the Pit." He rubbed his neck. "If the kristallos killed this dryad—killed these people whose bodies washed into the river through the sewers—then *why* summon two kinds of demons? The kristallos is already lethal as Hel." Literally.

Bryce threw up her hands. "I have no idea. But if everything we know about Danika's death is wrong, then we need to figure out *how* she died. We need someone who can weigh in."

He rubbed his jaw. "Any ideas?"

She nodded slowly, dread curling in her gut. "Promise me you won't go ballistic."

51

Summoning a demon is a bad fucking idea," Hunt breathed as night fell beyond the apartment's shut curtains. "Especially considering that's what started this mess in the first place."

They stood in her great room, lights dimmed and candles flickering around them, Syrinx bundled in blankets and locked in his crate in Bryce's bedroom, surrounded by a protective circle of white salt.

What lay around and before them on the pale floors, reeking of mold and rotten earth, was the opposite of that.

Bryce had ground the block of obsidian salt down at some point—presumably using her fucking food processor. For something she'd dropped ten grand on, Bryce didn't treat it with any particular reverence. She'd chucked it into a kitchen cabinet as if it were a bag of chips.

He hadn't realized she'd only been biding her time until she needed it.

Now, she'd crafted two circles with the obsidian salt. The one near the windows was perhaps five feet in diameter. The other was big enough to hold herself and Hunt.

Bryce said, "I'm not going to waste my time snooping around town for answers about what kind of demon killed Danika. Going right to the source will save me a headache."

"Going right to the source will get you splattered on a wall. And if not, arrested for summoning a demon into a residential zone." Shit. *He* should arrest her, shouldn't he?

"No one likes a narc, Athalar."

"I *am* a narc."

A dark red eyebrow arched. "Could've fooled me, Shadow of Death." She joined him in the salt circle. Her long ponytail pooled in the collar of her leather jacket, the candlelight gilding the red strands.

His fingers twitched, as if they'd reach for that silken length of hair. Run it between them. Wrap it around his fist and draw her head back, exposing that neck of hers again to his mouth. His tongue. Teeth.

Hunt growled, "You do know that it is my *job* to stop these demons from entering this world."

"We're not setting the demon loose," she hissed back. "This is as safe as a phone call."

"Are you going to summon it with its unholy number, then?" Many demons had numbers associated with them, like some sort of ancient email address.

"No, I don't need it. I know how to find this demon." He started to answer, but she cut him off. "The obsidian salt will hold it."

Hunt eyed the circles she'd made, then sighed. Fine. Even though arguing with her was nearly as enticing as foreplay, he didn't feel like wasting time, either.

But then the temperature in the room began to drop. Rapidly.

And as Hunt's breath began to cloud the air, as a humanoid male appeared, thrumming with dark power that made his stomach roil . . .

Bryce grinned up at Hunt as his heart stopped dead. "Surprise."

She'd lost her fucking mind. He would kill her for this—if they weren't both killed in the next few seconds.

"Who is that?" Ice formed in the room. No clothing could protect against the cold this demon brought with him. It pierced through every layer, snatching the breath from Hunt's chest with clawed fingers. A shuddering inhale was the only sign of Bryce's discomfort as she remained facing the circle on the other side of the room. The male now contained inside its dark border.

"Aidas," she said softly.

Hunt had always imagined the Prince of the Chasm as similar to the lower-level demons he'd hunted over the centuries: scales or fangs or claws, brute muscle and snarling with blind animal rage.

Not this slender, pale-skinned . . . pretty boy.

Aidas's blond hair fell to his shoulders in soft waves, loose, yet well cut around his fine-boned face. Undoubtedly to show off the eyes like blue opals, framed by thick, golden lashes. Those lashes bobbed once in a cursory blink. Then his full, sensuous mouth parted in a smile to reveal a row of too-white teeth. "Bryce Quinlan."

Hunt's hand drifted to his gun. The Prince of the Chasm knew her name—her face. And the way he'd spoken her name was as much greeting as it was question, his voice velvet-soft.

Aidas occupied the fifth level of Hel—the Chasm. He yielded only to two others: the Prince of the Abyss, and the Prince of the Pit, the seventh and mightiest of the demon princes. The Star-Eater himself, whose name was never uttered on this side of the Northern Rift.

No one would dare say his name, not after the Prince of the Pit became the first and only being to ever kill an Asteri. His butchering of the seventh holy star—Sirius, the Wolf Star—during the First Wars remained a favorite ballad around war-camp fires. And what he'd done to Sirius after slaying her had earned him that awful title: Star-Eater.

"You appeared as a cat the last time" was all Bryce said.

All. She. Said.

Hunt dared take his eyes off the Prince of the Chasm to find Bryce bowing her head.

Aidas slid his slender hands into the pockets of his closely tailored jacket and pants—the material blacker than the Chasm in which he resided. "You were very young then."

Hunt had to plant his feet to keep from swaying. She'd met the prince before—how?

His shock must have been written on his face because she shot him a look that he could only interpret as *Calm the fuck down*, but said, "I was thirteen—not *that* young."

Hunt reined in his grunt that would have suggested otherwise.

Aidas tilted his head to one side. "You were very sad then as well."

It took Hunt a moment to process it—the words. The bit of history, and the bit of now.

Bryce rubbed her hands together. "Let's talk about *you*, Your Highness."

"I am always happy to do so."

The cold burned Hunt's lungs. They could last only minutes at this temperature before their healing abilities started churning. And despite Bryce's Fae blood, there was a good chance that she might not recover at all. Without having made the Drop, the frostbite would be permanent for Bryce. As would any digits or limbs lost.

She said to the demon prince, "You and your colleagues seem to be getting restless in the dark."

"Is that so?" Aidas frowned at his polished leather shoes as if he could see all the way down to the Pit. "Perhaps you summoned the wrong prince, for this is the first I've heard of it."

"Who is summoning the kristallos demon to hunt through this city?" Flat, cutting words. "And what killed Danika Fendyr?"

"Ah yes, we heard of that—how Danika screamed as she was shredded apart."

Bryce's beat of silence told Hunt enough about the internal wound that Aidas had pressed. From the smile gracing Aidas's face, the Prince of the Chasm knew it as well.

She went on, "Do you know what demon did it?"

"Despite what your mythologies claim, I am not privy to the movements of every being in Hel."

She said tightly, "Do you know, though? Or know who summoned it?"

His golden lashes shimmered as he blinked. "You believe I dispatched it?"

"You would not be standing there if I did."

Aidas laughed softly. "No tears from you this time."

Bryce smiled slightly. "You told me not to let them see me cry. I took the advice to heart."

What the Hel had gone on during that meeting twelve years ago?

"Information is not free."

"What is your price?" A bluish tint crept over her lips. They'd have to cut the connection soon.

Hunt kept perfectly still as Aidas studied her. Then his eyes registered Hunt.

He blinked—once. As if he had not really marked his presence until this moment. As if he hadn't cared to notice, with Bryce before him. Hunt tucked away that fact, just as Aidas murmured, "Who are you."

A command.

"He's eye candy," Bryce said, looping her arm through Hunt's and pressing close. For warmth or steadiness, he didn't know. She was shaking. "And he is not for sale." She pointed to the halo across Hunt's brow.

"My pets like to rip out feathers—it would be a good trade."

Hunt leveled a stare at the prince. Bryce threw Hunt a sidelong glare, the effect of which was negated by her chattering teeth.

Aidas smiled, looking him over again. "A Fallen warrior with the power of . . ." Aidas's groomed brows lifted in surprise. His blue opal eyes narrowed to slits—then simmered like the hottest flame. "What are *you* doing with a black crown around your brow?"

Hunt didn't dare let his surprise at the question show. He'd never heard it called that before—a black crown. Halo, witch-ink, mark-of-shame, but never that.

Aidas looked between them now. Carefully. He didn't bother to let Hunt answer his question before that awful smile returned. "The seven princes dwell in darkness and do not stir. We have no interest in your realm."

"I'd believe it if you and your brethren hadn't been rattling the

Northern Rift for the past two decades," Hunt said. "And if I hadn't been cleaning up after it."

Aidas sucked in a breath, as if tasting the air on which Hunt's words had been delivered to him. "You do realize that it might not be my people? The Northern Rift opens to other places—other realms, yes, but other planets as well. What is Hel but a distant planet bound to yours by a ripple in space and time?"

"Hel is a planet?" Hunt's brows lowered. Most of the demons he'd killed and dealt with hadn't been able to or inclined to speak.

Aidas shrugged with one shoulder. "It is as real a place as Midgard, though most of us would have you believe it wasn't." The prince pointed to him. "Your kind, Fallen, were made in Midgard by the Asteri. But the Fae, the shifters, and many others came from their own worlds. The universe is massive. Some believe it has no end. Or that our universe might be one in a multitude, as bountiful as the stars in the sky or the sand on a beach."

Bryce threw Hunt a look that told him she, too, was wondering what the Hel the demon prince was smoking in the Chasm. "You're trying to distract us," Bryce said, arms crossing. Hoarfrost crept across the floors. "You're not rattling the Northern Rift?"

"The lesser princes do that—levels one through four," Aidas said, head angling again. "Those of us in the true dark have no need or interest in sunshine. But even they did not send the kristallos. Our plans do not involve such things."

Hunt growled, "Your kind wanted to live here, once upon a time. Why would that change?"

Aidas chuckled. "It is dreadfully amusing to hear the stories the Asteri have spun for you." He smiled at Bryce. "What blinds an Oracle?"

All color leached from Bryce's face at the mention of her visit to the Oracle. How Aidas knew about it, Hunt could only guess, but she countered, "What sort of cat visits an Oracle?"

"Winning first words." Aidas slid his hands into his pockets again. "I did not know what you might prefer now that you are grown." A smirk at Hunt. "But I may appear more like that, if it pleases you, Bryce Quinlan."

"Better yet: don't appear again at all," Hunt said to the demon prince.

Bryce squeezed his arm. He stepped on her foot hard enough to get her to cut it out.

But Aidas chuckled. "Your temperature drops. I shall depart."

"Please," Bryce said. "Just tell me if you know what killed Danika. Please."

A soft laugh. "Run the tests again. Find what is in-between."

He began to fade, as if a phone call were indeed breaking up.

"Aidas," she blurted, stepping right to the edge of their circle. Hunt fought the urge to tuck her to his side. Especially as darkness frayed the edges of Aidas's body. "Thank you. For that day."

The Prince of the Chasm paused, as if clinging to this world. "Make the Drop, Bryce Quinlan." He flickered. "And find me when you are done."

Aidas had nearly vanished into nothing when he added, the words a ghost slithering through the room, "The Oracle did not see. But I did."

Silence pulsed in his wake as the room thawed, frost vanishing.

Hunt whirled on Bryce. "First of all," he seethed, "*fuck you* for that surprise."

She rubbed her hands together, working warmth back into them. "You never would have let me summon Aidas if I'd told you first."

"Because we should be fucking *dead* right now!" He gaped at her. "Are you insane?"

"I knew he wouldn't hurt me. Or anyone with me."

"You want to tell me how you *met* Aidas when you were thirteen?"

"I . . . I told you how badly things ended between me and my biological father after my Oracle visit." His anger banked at the lingering pain in her face. "So afterward, when I was crying my little heart out on one of the park benches outside the temple, this white cat appeared next to me. It had the most unnatural blue eyes. I knew, even before it spoke, that it wasn't a cat—and wasn't a shifter."

"Who summoned him that time?"

"I don't know. Jesiba told me that the princes can sneak through cracks in either Rift, taking the form of common animals. But then they're confined to those forms—with none of their own power, save the ability to speak. And they can only stay for a few hours at a time."

A shudder worked its way down his gray wings. "What did Aidas say?"

"He asked me: *What blinds an Oracle?* And I replied: *What sort of cat visits an Oracle?* He'd heard the screaming on his way in. I suppose it intrigued him. He told me to stop crying. Said it would only satisfy those who had wronged me. That I shouldn't give them the gift of my sorrow."

"Why was the Prince of the Chasm at the Oracle?"

"He never told me. But he sat with me until I worked up the nerve to walk back to my father's house. By the time I remembered to thank him, he was gone."

"Strange." And—fine, he could understand why she hadn't balked from summoning him, if he'd been kind to her in the past.

"Perhaps some of the feline body wore off on him and he was merely curious about me."

"Apparently, he's missed you." A leading question.

"Apparently," she hedged. "Though he barely gave us anything to go on."

Her gaze turned distant as she looked at the empty circle before them, then took her phone out of her pocket. Hunt caught a glimpse of who she dialed—*Declan Emmet*.

"Hi, B." In the background, music thumped and male laughter roared.

Bryce didn't bother with niceties. "We've been tipped off that we should run various tests again—I'm assuming that means the ones on the victims and crime scenes a few years ago. Can you think of anything that should be reexamined?"

In the background, Ruhn asked, *Is that Bryce?* But Declan said, "I'd definitely run a scent diagnostic. You'll need clothes."

Bryce said, "They must have done a scent diagnostic two years ago."

Declan said, "Was it the common one, or the Mimir?"

Hunt's stomach tightened. Especially as Bryce said, "What's the difference?"

"The Mimir is better. It's relatively new."

Bryce looked at Hunt, and he shook his head slowly. She said quietly into the phone, "No one did a Mimir test."

Declan hesitated. "Well . . . it's Fae tech mostly. We loan it out to the legion for their major cases." A pause. "Someone should have said something."

Hunt braced himself. Bryce asked, "You had access to this sort of thing two years ago?"

Declan paused again. "Ah—shit." Then Ruhn came on the line. "Bryce, a direct order was given not to pursue it through those channels. It was deemed a matter that the Fae should stay out of."

Devastation, rage, grief—all exploded across her face. Her fingers curled at her sides.

Hunt said, knowing Ruhn could hear it, "The Autumn King is a real prick, you know that?"

Bryce snarled, "I'm going to tell him just that." She hung up.

Hunt demanded, "What?" But she was already running out of the apartment.

52

Bryce's blood roared as she sprinted through the Old Square, down rain-soaked streets, all the way to Five Roses. The villas glowed in the rain, palatial homes with immaculate lawns and gardens, all fenced with wrought iron. Stone-faced Fae or shifter sentries from the Auxiliary were posted at every corner.

As if the residents here lived in abject terror that the peregrini and few slaves of Crescent City were poised to loot at any moment.

She hurtled past the marble behemoth that was the Fae Archives, the building covered in drooping veils of flowers that ran down its many columns. Roses, jasmine, wisteria—all in perpetual bloom, no matter the season.

She sprinted all the way to the sprawling white villa covered in pink roses, and to the wrought-iron gate around it guarded by four Fae warriors.

They stepped into her path as she skidded to a halt, the flagstone street slick with rain.

"Let me in," she said through her teeth, panting.

They didn't so much as blink. "Do you have an appointment with His Majesty?" one asked.

"Let me in," she said again.

He'd known. Her father had known there were tests to assess

what had killed Danika and had done *nothing*. Had deliberately stayed out of it.

She had to see him. Had to hear it from him. She didn't care what time it was.

The polished black door was shut, but the lights were on. He was home. He had to be.

"Not without an appointment," said the same guard.

Bryce took a step toward them and rebounded—hard. A wall of heat surrounded the compound, no doubt generated by the Fae males before her. One of the guards snickered. Her face grew hot, her eyes stinging.

"Go tell your *king* that Bryce Quinlan needs a word. *Now*."

"Come back when you have an appointment, half-breed," one of the sentries said.

Bryce smacked her hand against their shield. It didn't so much as ripple. "*Tell him—*"

The guards stiffened as power, dark and mighty, pulsed from behind her. Lightning skittered over the cobblestones. The guards' hands drifted to their swords.

Hunt said, voice like thunder, "The lady wants an audience with His Majesty."

"His Majesty is unavailable." The guard who spoke had clearly noted the halo at Hunt's brow. The sneer that spread across his face was one of the most hideous things Bryce had ever seen. "Especially for Fallen scum and half-human skanks."

Hunt took a step toward them. "Say that again."

The guard's sneer remained. "Once wasn't enough?"

Hunt's hand fisted at his side. He'd do it, she realized. He'd pummel these assholes into dust for her, fight his way inside the gates so she could have a chat with the king.

Down the block, Ruhn appeared, wreathed in shadow, his black hair plastered to his head. Flynn and Declan followed close behind him. "Stand down," Ruhn ordered the guards. "Stand the fuck down."

They did no such thing. "Even you, Prince, are not authorized to order that."

Ruhn's shadows swirled at his shoulders like a phantom pair of wings, but he said to Bryce, "There are other battles worth fighting with him. This isn't one of them."

Bryce stalked a few feet from the gate, even though the guards could likely hear every word. "He deliberately chose not to help with what happened to Danika."

Hunt said, "Some might consider that to be interference with an imperial investigation."

"Fuck off, Athalar," Ruhn growled. He reached for Bryce's arm, but she stepped back. He clenched his jaw. "You are considered a member of this court, you know. You were involved in a colossal mess. He decided the best thing for your safety was to let the case drop, not dig further."

"As if he's ever given two shits about my safety."

"He gave enough of a shit about you to want me to be your live-in guard. But you wanted Athalar to play sexy roomie."

"He wants to find the Horn for *himself*," she snapped. "It has *nothing* to do with me." She pointed to the house beyond the iron fence. "You go in there and tell that piece of shit that I won't forget this. *Ever.* I doubt he'll care, but you tell him."

Ruhn's shadows stilled, draping from his shoulders. "I'm sorry, Bryce. About Danika—"

"Do *not*," she seethed, "ever say her name to me. Never say her name to me again."

She could have sworn hurt that even his shadows couldn't hide flashed across her brother's face, but she turned, finding Hunt watching with crossed arms. "I'll see you at the apartment," she said to him, and didn't bother to say more before launching back into a run.

It had been fucked up to not warn Hunt whom she was summoning. She'd admit it.

But not as fucked up as the Fae tests her father had *declined* to provide access to.

Bryce didn't go home. Halfway there, she decided she'd head

somewhere else. The White Raven was shut down, but her old favorite whiskey bar would do just fine.

Lethe was open and serving. Which was good, because her leg throbbed mercilessly and her feet were blistered from running in her stupid flats. She took them off the moment she hopped onto the leather stool at the bar, and sighed as her bare feet touched the cool brass footrest running the length of the dark wood counter.

Lethe hadn't changed in the two years since she'd last set foot on the floor that lent itself to an optical illusion, painted with black, gray, and white cubes. The cherrywood pillars still rose like trees to form the carved, arched ceiling high above, looming over a bar made from fogged glass and black metal, all clean lines and square edges.

She'd messaged Juniper five minutes ago, inviting her for a drink. She still hadn't heard back. So she'd watched the news on the screen above the bar, flashing to the muddy battlefields in Pangera, the husks of mech-suits littering them like broken toys, bodies both human and Vanir sprawled for miles, the crows already feasting.

Even the human busboy had stopped to look, his face tight as he beheld the carnage. A barked order from the bartender had kept him moving, but Bryce had seen the gleam in the young man's brown eyes. The fury and determination.

"What the Hel," she muttered, and knocked back a mouthful of the whiskey in front of her.

It tasted as acrid and vile as she remembered—burned all the way down. Precisely what she wanted. Bryce took another swig.

A bottle of some sort of purple tonic plunked onto the counter beside her tumbler. "For your leg," Hunt said, sliding onto the stool beside hers. "Drink up."

She eyed the glass vial. "You went to a medwitch?"

"There's a clinic around the corner. I figured you weren't leaving here anytime soon."

Bryce sipped her whiskey. "You guessed right."

He nudged the tonic closer. "Have it before you finish the rest."

"No comment about breaking my No Drinking rule?"

He leaned on the bar, tucking in his wings. "It's your rule—you can end it whenever you like."

Whatever. She reached for the tonic, uncorking and knocking it back. She grimaced. "Tastes like grape soda."

"I told her to make it sweet."

She batted her eyelashes. "Because I'm so sweet, Athalar?"

"Because I knew you wouldn't drink it if it tasted like rubbing alcohol."

She lifted her whiskey. "I beg to differ."

Hunt signaled the bartender, ordered a water, and said to Bryce, "So, tonight went well."

She chuckled, sipping the whiskey again. Gods, it tasted awful. Why had she ever guzzled this stuff down? "Superb."

Hunt drank from his water. Watched her for a long moment before he said, "Look, I'll sit here while you get stupid drunk if that's what you want, but I'll just say this first: there are better ways to deal with everything."

"Thanks, Mom."

"I mean it."

The bartender set another whiskey before her, but Bryce didn't drink.

Hunt said carefully, "You're not the only person to have lost someone you love."

She propped her head on a hand. "Tell me all about her, Hunt. Let's hear the full, unabridged sob story at last."

He held her gaze. "Don't be an asshole. I'm trying to talk to you."

"And I'm trying to drink," she said, lifting her glass to do so.

Her phone buzzed, and both of them glanced at it. Juniper had finally written back.

Can't, sorry. Practice. Then another buzz from Juniper. *Wait—why are you drinking at Lethe? Are you drinking again? What happened?*

Hunt said quietly, "Maybe your friend is trying to tell you something, too."

Bryce's fingers curled into fists, but she set her phone facedown on the glowing, fogged glass. "Weren't you going to tell me your heartbreaking story about your amazing girlfriend? What would *she* think about the way you manhandled me and practically devoured my neck the other night?"

She regretted the words the moment they were out. For so many reasons, she regretted them, the least of which being that she hadn't been able to stop thinking about that moment of insanity on the roof, when his mouth had been on her neck and she'd started to completely unravel.

How good it had felt—*he* had felt.

Hunt stared her down for a long moment. Heat rose to her face.

But all he said was "I'll see you at home." The word echoed between them as he set another purple tonic on the counter. "Drink that one in thirty minutes."

Then he was gone, prowling through the empty bar and onto the street beyond.

Hunt had just settled onto the couch to watch the sunball game when Bryce walked into the apartment, two bags of groceries in her hands. About fucking time.

Syrinx flung himself off the couch and bounded to her, rising onto his back legs to demand kisses. She obliged him, ruffling his golden fur before looking up at where Hunt sat on the couch. He just sipped from his beer and gave her a terse nod.

She nodded back, not quite meeting his eyes, and strode for the kitchen. The limp was better, but not wholly gone.

He'd sent Naomi to monitor the street outside that fancy whiskey bar while he hit the gym to work off his temper.

Manhandled. The word had lingered. Along with the truth: he hadn't thought about Shahar for a second while they'd been on the roof. Or in the days following. And when he'd had his hand wrapped around his cock in the shower that night, and every night since, it hadn't been the Archangel he'd thought of. Not even close.

Quinlan had to know that. She had to know what wound she'd hit.

So the options had been to yell at her, or to exercise. He'd picked the latter.

That had been two hours ago. He'd cleaned up all the obsidian salt, walked and fed Syrinx, and then sat on the couch to wait.

Bryce set her bags onto the counter, Syrinx lingering at her feet to inspect every purchase. In between plays, Hunt stole glances at what she unpacked. Vegetables, fruits, meat, oat milk, cow's milk, rice, a loaf of brown bread—

"Are we having company?" he asked.

She yanked out a skillet and plunked it on the burner. "I figured I'd make a late dinner."

Her back was stiff, her shoulders straight. He might have thought she was pissed, but the fact that she was making dinner for them suggested otherwise. "Is it wise to cook when you've been pounding whiskey?"

She shot him a glare over a shoulder. "I'm trying to do something nice, and you're not making it easy."

Hunt held up his hands. "All right. Sorry."

She went back to the stove, adjusted the heat, and opened a package of some sort of ground meat. "I wasn't pounding whiskey," she said. "I left Lethe soon after you did."

"Where'd you go?"

"Out to a storage unit near Moonwood." She began gathering spices. "I stashed a lot of Danika's stuff there. Sabine was going to chuck it, but I took it before she did." She dumped some ground meat in the skillet and gestured to a third bag she'd left by the door. "I just wanted to make sure there was no hint of the Horn there, anything I might not have noticed at the time. And to grab some of Danika's clothes—ones that were in my bedroom that night that Evidence didn't take. I know they already have clothes from before, but I thought . . . Maybe there's something on these, too."

Hunt opened his mouth to say something—what, exactly, he didn't know—but Bryce went on. "After that, I went to the market. Since condiments aren't food, apparently."

Hunt brought his beer with him as he padded to the kitchen. "Want help?"

"No. This is an apology meal. Go watch your game."

"You don't need to apologize."

"I acted like an asshole. Let me cook something for you to make up for it."

"Based on how much chili powder you just dumped into that pan, I'm not sure I want to accept this particular apology."

"Fuck, I forgot to add the cumin!" She whirled toward the skillet, turning down the heat and adding the spice, stirring it into what smelled like ground turkey. She sighed. "I'm a mess."

He waited, letting her gather her words.

She began cutting an onion, her motions easy and smooth.

"Honestly, I was a bit of a mess before what happened to Danika, and . . ." She sliced the onion into neat rings. "It didn't get any better."

"Why were you a mess before she died?"

Bryce slid the onion into the skillet. "I'm a half-human with a near-useless college degree. All my friends were going somewhere, doing something with themselves." Her mouth quirked to the side. "I'm a glorified secretary. With no long-term plan for anything." She stirred the onion around. "The partying and stuff—it was the only time when the four of us were on equal footing. When it didn't matter that Fury's some kind of merc or Juniper's so amazingly talented or Danika would one day be this all-powerful wolf."

"They ever hold that against you?"

"No." Her amber eyes scanned his face. "No, they would never have done that. But I couldn't ever forget it."

"Your cousin said you used to dance. That you stopped after Danika died. You never wanted to follow that road?"

She pointed to the sweep of her hips. "I was told my half-human body was *too clunky*. I was also told that my boobs were too big, and my ass could be used as an aerialport landing pad."

"Your ass is perfect." The words slipped out. He refrained from commenting on just how much he liked the other parts of her, too. How much he wanted to worship them. Starting with that ass of hers.

Color bloomed on her cheeks. "Well, thank you." She stirred the contents of the skillet.

"But you don't dance for fun anymore?"

"No." Her eyes went cold at that. "I don't."

"And you never thought of doing anything else?"

"Of course I have. I've got ten job applications hidden on my work computer, but I can't focus enough to finish them. It's been so long since I saw the job postings that they're probably filled by now anyway. It doesn't even matter that I'd also have to find some way to convince Jesiba that I'll keep paying off my debt to her." She kept stirring. "A human life span seems like a long time to fill, but an immortal one?" She hooked her hair behind an ear. "I have no idea what to do."

"I'm two hundred thirty-three years old, and I'm still figuring it out."

"Yeah, but you—you *did* something. You fought for something. You *are* someone."

He tapped the slave tattoo on his wrist. "And look where I wound up."

She turned from the stove. "Hunt, I really am sorry for what I said about Shahar."

"Don't worry about it."

Bryce jerked her chin toward Hunt's open bedroom door, the photo of her and Danika just barely visible on the dresser. "My mom took that the day we got out of the hospital in Rosque."

He knew she was building to something, and was willing to play along. "Why were you in the hospital?"

"Danika's senior thesis was on the history of the illegal animal trade. She uncovered a real smuggling ring, but no one in the Aux or the 33rd would help her, so she and I went to deal with it ourselves." Bryce snorted. "The operation was run by five asp shifters, who caught us trying to free their stock. We called them asp-holes, and things went downhill from there."

Of course they did. "How downhill?"

"A motorcycle chase and crash, my right arm broken in three places, Danika's pelvis fractured. Danika got shot twice in the leg."

"Gods."

"You should have seen the asp-holes."

"You killed them?"

Her eyes darkened, nothing but pure Fae predator shining

there. "Some. The ones who shot Danika . . . I took care of them. The police got the rest." Burning Solas. He had a feeling there was far more to the story. "I know people think Danika was a reckless partier with mommy issues, I know Sabine thinks that, but . . . Danika went to free those animals because she literally couldn't sleep at night knowing they were in cages, terrified and alone."

The Party Princess, Hunt and the triarii had mocked her behind her back.

Bryce went on, "Danika was always doing that kind of thing—helping people Sabine thought were beneath them. Some part of her might have done it to piss off her mom, yeah, but most of it was because she wanted to help. That's why she went easy on Philip Briggs and his group, why she gave him so many chances." She let out a long breath. "She was difficult, but she was good."

"And what about you?" he asked carefully.

She ran a hand through her hair. "Most days, I feel cold as it was in here with Aidas. Most days, all I want is to go back. To how it was before. I can't bear to keep going forward."

Hunt gazed at her for a long moment. "There were some of the Fallen who accepted the halo and slave tattoo, you know. After a few decades, they accepted it. Stopped fighting it."

"Why have you never stopped?"

"Because we were right then, and we're still right now. Shahar was only the spear point. I followed her blindly into a battle we could never have won, but I believed in what she stood for."

"If you could do it over, march under Shahar's banner again—would you?"

Hunt considered that. He didn't normally let himself dwell too long on what had happened, what had occurred since then. "If I hadn't rebelled with her, I'd probably have been noticed by another Archangel for my lightning. I'd likely now be serving as a commander in one of Pangera's cities, hoping to one day earn enough to buy my way out of service. But they'd never let someone with my gifts go. And I had little choice but to join a legion. It was the path I was pushed onto, and the lightning, the killing—I never asked to be good at it. I'd give it up in a heartbeat if I could."

Her eyes flickered with understanding. "I know." He lifted a brow. She clarified, "The being good at something you don't want to be good at. That talent you'd let go of in a heartbeat." He angled his head. "I mean, look at me: I'm *amazing* at attracting assholes."

Hunt huffed a laugh. She said, "You didn't answer my question. Would you still rebel if you knew what would happen?"

Hunt sighed. "That's what I was starting to say: even if I hadn't rebelled, I'd wind up in a sugarcoated version of my life now. Because I'm still a legionary being used for my so-called gifts—just now *officially* a slave, rather than being forced into service by a lack of other options. The only other difference is that I'm serving in Valbara, in a fool's bargain with an Archangel, hoping to one day be forgiven for my supposed sins."

"You don't think they were sins."

"No. I think the angel hierarchies are bullshit. We were right to rebel."

"Even though it cost you everything?"

"Yeah. So I guess that's my answer. I'd still do it, even knowing what would happen. And if I ever get free . . ." Bryce halted her stirring. Met his stare unblinkingly as Hunt said, "I remember every one of them who was there on the battlefield, who brought down Shahar. And all the angels, the Asteri, the Senate, the Governors—all of them, who were there at our sentencing." He leaned against the counter behind them and swigged from his beer, letting her fill in the rest.

"And after you've killed them all? What then?"

He blinked at the lack of fear, of judgment. "Assuming I live through it, you mean."

"Assuming you live through taking on the Archangels and Asteri, what then?"

"I don't know." He gave her a half smile. "Maybe you and I can figure it out, Quinlan. We'll have centuries to do it."

"If I make the Drop."

He started. "You would choose not to?" It was rare—so, so rare for a Vanir to refuse to make the Drop and live only a mortal life span.

She added more vegetables and seasoning to the pan before throwing a packet of instant rice into the microwave. "I don't know. I'd need an Anchor."

"What about Ruhn?" Her cousin, even if neither of them would admit it, would take on every beast in the Pit itself to protect her.

She threw him a look dripping with disdain. "No fucking way."

"Juniper, then?" Someone she truly trusted, loved.

"She'd do it, but it doesn't feel right. And using one of the public Anchors isn't for me."

"I used one. It was fine." He spied the questions brimming in her eyes and cut her off before she could voice them. "Maybe you'll change your mind."

"Maybe." She chewed on her lip. "I'm sorry you lost your friends."

"I'm sorry you lost yours."

Bryce nodded her thanks, going back to stirring. "I know people don't get it. It's just . . . a light went out inside me when it happened. Danika wasn't my sister, or my lover. But she was the one person I could be myself around and never feel judged. The one person that I knew would always pick up the phone, or call me back. She was the one person who made me feel brave because no matter what happened, no matter how bad or embarrassing or shitty it was, I knew that I had her in my corner. That if it all went to Hel, I could talk to her and it would be fine."

Her eyes gleamed, and it was all he could do to not cross the few feet between them and grab her hand as she continued. "But it . . . It's not fine. I will *never* talk to her again. I think people expect me to be over it by now. But I can't. Anytime I get anywhere close to the truth of my new reality, I want to space out again. To not have to *be* me. I can't fucking dance anymore because it reminds me of her—of all the dancing we did together in clubs or on the streets or in our apartment or dorm. I *won't* let myself dance anymore because it brought me joy, and . . . And I didn't, I don't, want to feel those things." She swallowed. "I know it sounds pathetic."

"It's not," he said quietly.

"I'm sorry I dumped my baggage in your lap."

A corner of his mouth turned up. "You can dump your baggage in my lap anytime, Quinlan."

She snorted, shaking her head. "You made it sound gross."

"You said it first." Her mouth twitched. Damn, if the smile didn't make his chest tighten.

But Hunt just said, "I know you'll keep going forward, Quinlan—even if it sucks."

"What makes you so sure of it?"

His feet were silent as he crossed the kitchen. She tipped back her head to hold his stare. "Because you pretend to be irreverent and lazy, but deep down, you don't give up. Because you know that if you do, then they win. All the asp-holes, as you called them, win. So living, and living well—it's the greatest *fuck you* that you can ever give them."

"That's why you're still fighting."

He ran a hand over the tattoo on his brow. "Yes."

She let out a *hmm*, stirring the mixture in the pan again. "Well then, Athalar. I guess it'll be you and me in the trenches for a while longer."

He smiled at her, more openly than he'd dared do with anyone in a long while. "You know," he said, "I think I like the sound of that."

Her eyes warmed further, a blush stealing across her freckled cheeks. "You said *home* earlier. At the bar."

He had. He'd tried not to think about it.

She went on, "I know you're supposed to live in the barracks or whatever Micah insists on, but if we somehow solve this case . . . that room is yours, if you want it."

The offer rippled through him. And he couldn't think of a single word beyond "Thanks." It was all that was necessary, he realized.

The rice finished cooking, and she divvied it into two bowls before dumping the meat mixture on top of it. She extended one to him. "Nothing gourmet, but . . . here. I'm sorry for earlier."

Hunt studied the steaming heap of meat and rice. He'd seen dogs served fancier meals. But he smiled slightly, his chest inexplicably tightening again. "Apology accepted, Quinlan."

* * *

A cat was sitting on her dresser.

Exhaustion weighed her eyelids, so heavily she could barely raise them.

Eyes like the sky before dawn pinned her to the spot.

What blinds an Oracle, Bryce Quinlan?

Her mouth formed a word, but sleep tugged her back into its embrace.

The cat's blue eyes simmered. *What blinds an Oracle?*

She fought to keep her eyes open at the question, the urgency.

You know, she tried to say.

The Autumn King's only daughter—thrown out like rubbish.

The cat had either guessed it at the temple all those years ago, or followed her home to confirm whose villa she had tried to enter.

He'll kill me if he knows.

The cat licked a paw. *Then make the Drop.*

She tried to speak again. Sleep held her firm, but she finally managed, *And what then?*

The cat's whiskers twitched. *I told you. Come find me.*

Her eyelids drooped—a final descent toward sleep. *Why?*

The cat angled its head. *So we can finish this.*

53

It was still raining the next morning, which Bryce decided was an omen.

Today would suck. Last night had sucked.

Syrinx refused to emerge from under the sheets, even though Bryce tried to coax him with the promise of breakfast *before* his walk, and by the time Bryce finally hauled him to the street below, Hunt monitoring from the windows, the rain had gone from a pleasant patter to an outright deluge.

A fat hoptoad squatted in the corner of the building doorway, under the slight overhang, waiting for any small, unfortunate Vanir to fly past. He eyed Bryce and Syrinx as they splashed by, earning a whiskery huff from the latter, and sidled closer to the side of the building.

"Creep," she murmured above the drumming rain on the hood of her coat, feeling the hoptoad watch them down the block. For a creature no bigger than her fist, they found ways to be menaces. Namely to all manner of sprites. Even confined to the library, Lehabah loathed and dreaded them.

Despite her navy raincoat, her black leggings and white T-shirt were soon soaked. As if the rain somehow went *up* from the ground. It pooled in her green rain boots, too, squelching with every step she made through the lashing rain, the palms swaying and hissing overhead.

The rainiest spring on record, the news had proclaimed last night. She didn't doubt it.

The hoptoad was still there when they returned, Syrinx having completed his morning routine in record time, and Bryce might or might not have gone out of her way to stomp in a nearby puddle.

The hoptoad had stuck out his tongue at her, but flopped away.

Hunt was standing at the stove, cooking something that smelled like bacon. He glanced over his shoulder while she removed her raincoat, dripping all over the floor. "You hungry?"

"I'm good."

His eyes narrowed. "You should eat something before we go."

She waved him off, scooping food into Syrinx's bowl.

When she stood, she found Hunt extending a plate toward her. Bacon and eggs and thick brown toast. "I watched you pick at your food for five days this past week," he said roughly. "We're not starting down that road again."

She rolled her eyes. "I don't need a male telling me when to eat."

"How about a friend telling you that you had an understandably rough night, and you get mean as shit when you're hungry?"

Bryce scowled. Hunt just kept holding out the plate.

"It's all right to be nervous, you know," he said. He nodded toward the paper bag she'd left by the door—Danika's clothes, folded and ready for analysis. She'd overheard Hunt calling Viktoria thirty minutes ago, asking her to get the Mimir tech from the Fae. She'd said Declan already sent it.

Bryce said, "I'm not nervous. They're just clothes." He only stared at her. Bryce growled. "I'm not. Let them lose the clothes in Evidence or whatever."

"Then eat."

"I don't like eggs."

His mouth twitched upward. "I've seen you eat about three dozen of them."

Their gazes met and held. "Who taught you to cook, anyway?"

He sure as Hel was a better cook than she was. The pitiful dinner she'd made him last night was proof.

"I taught myself. It's a useful skill for a soldier. Makes you a popular person in any legion camp. Besides, I've got two centuries under my belt. It'd be pathetic not to know how to cook at this point." He held the plate closer. "Eat up, Quinlan. I won't let anyone lose those clothes."

She debated throwing the plate in his face, but finally took it and plunked into the seat at the head of the dining table. Syrinx trotted over to her, already gazing expectantly at the bacon.

A cup of coffee appeared on the table a heartbeat later, the cream still swirling inside.

Hunt smirked at her. "Wouldn't want you to head out to the world without the proper provisions."

Bryce flipped him off, took his phone from where he'd left it on the table, and snapped a few pictures: the breakfast, the coffee, his stupid smirking face, Syrinx sitting beside her, and her own scowl. But she drank the coffee anyway.

By the time she put her mug into the sink, Hunt finishing up his meal at the table behind her, she found her steps feeling lighter than they had in a while.

"Don't lose those," Hunt warned Viktoria as she sifted through the bag on her desk.

The wraith looked up from the faded gray band T-shirt with a wailing, robed figure on the front. *The Banshees*. "We've got clothes in Evidence for Danika Fendyr and the other victims."

"Fine, but use these, too," Hunt said. Just in case someone had tampered with the evidence here—and to let Quinlan feel as if she'd helped with this. Bryce was at the gallery dealing with some snooty customer, with Naomi watching. "You got the Mimir tech from Declan?"

"As I said on the phone: yes." Vik peered into the bag again. "I'll give you a call if anything comes up."

Hunt stretched a piece of paper across the desk. "See if traces of any of these come up, too."

Viktoria took one look at the words on it and went pale, her halo stark over her brow. "You think it's one of these demons?"

"I hope not."

He'd made a list of potential demons that might be working in conjunction with the kristallos, all ancient and terrible, his dread deepening with each new name he added. Many of them were nightmares that prowled bedtime stories. All of them were catastrophic if they entered Midgard. He'd faced two of them before—and barely made it through the encounters.

Hunt nodded toward the bag again. "I mean it: don't lose those clothes," he said again.

"Going soft, Athalar?"

Hunt rolled his eyes and aimed for the doorway. "I just like my balls where they are."

Viktoria notified Hunt that evening that she was still running the diagnostic. The Fae's Mimir tech was thorough enough that it'd take a good while to run.

He prayed the results wouldn't be as devastating as he expected.

He'd messaged Bryce about it while she finished up work, chuckling when he saw that she'd again changed her contact information in his phone: *Bryce Is a Queen*.

They stayed up until midnight binge-watching a reality show about a bunch of hot young Vanir working at a beach club in the Coronal Islands. He'd refused at first—but by the end of the first hour, he'd been the one pressing play on the next episode. Then the next.

It hadn't hurt that they'd gone from sitting on opposite ends of the sectional to being side by side, his thigh pressed against hers. He might have toyed with her braid. She might have let him.

The next morning, Hunt was just following Bryce toward the apartment elevator when his phone rang. He took one look at the number and grimaced before picking up. "Hi, Micah."

"My office. Fifteen minutes."

Bryce pressed the elevator button, but Hunt pointed to the roof door. He'd fly her to the gallery, then head to the CBD. "All right," he said carefully. "Do you want Miss Quinlan to join us?"

"Just you." The line went dead.

54

Hunt took a back entrance into the tower, careful to avoid any area that Sandriel might be frequenting. Isaiah hadn't picked up, and he knew better than to keep calling until he did.

Micah was staring out the window when he arrived, his power already a brewing storm in the room. "Why," the Archangel asked, "are you running Fae tests on old evidence down at the lab?"

"We have good reason to think the demon we identified isn't the one behind Danika Fendyr's death. If we can find what actually did kill her, it might lead us to whoever summoned it."

"The Summit is in two weeks."

"I know. We're working as hard as we can."

"Are you? Drinking at a whiskey bar with Bryce Quinlan counts as working?"

Asshole. "We're on it. Don't worry."

"Sabine Fendyr called my office, you know. To rip my head off about being a *suspect*." There was nothing humane behind those eyes. Only cold predator.

"It was a mistake, and we'll own up to that, but we had sufficient cause to believe—"

"Get. The. Job. Done."

Hunt gritted out, "We will."

Micah surveyed him coolly. Then he said, "Sandriel has

been asking about you—about Miss Quinlan, too. She's made me a few generous offers to trade again." Hunt's stomach became leaden. "I've turned her down so far. I told her that you're too valuable to me."

Micah threw a file on the table, then turned back to the window. "Don't make me reconsider, Hunt."

Hunt read through the file—the silent order it conveyed. His punishment. For Sabine, for taking too long, for just existing. A death for a death.

He stopped at the barracks to pick up his helmet.

Micah had written a note in the margin of the list of targets, their crimes. *No guns.*

So Hunt grabbed a few more of his black-hilted daggers, and his long-handled knife, too.

Every movement was careful. Deliberate. Every shift of his body as he donned his black battle-suit quieted his mind, pulling him farther and farther from himself.

His phone buzzed on his desk, and he glanced at it only long enough to see that *Bryce Is a Queen* had written to him: *Everything okay?*

Hunt slid on his black gloves.

His phone buzzed again.

I'm going to order in dumpling soup for lunch. Want some?

Hunt turned the phone over, blocking the screen from view. As if it'd somehow stop her from learning what he was doing. He gathered his weapons with centuries of efficiency. And then donned the helmet.

The world descended into cool calculations, its colors dimmed.

Only then did he pick up his phone and write back to Bryce, *I'm good. I'll see you later.*

She'd written back by the time he reached the barracks landing pad. He'd watched the typing bubble pop up, vanish, then pop up again. Like she'd written out ten different replies before settling on *Okay.*

Hunt shut off his phone as he shouldered his way through the doors and into the open air.

He was a stain against the brightness. A shadow standing against the sun.

A flap of his wings had him skyborne. And he did not look back.

Something was wrong.

Bryce had known it the moment she realized she hadn't heard from him after an hour in the Comitium.

The feeling had only worsened at his vague response to her message. No mention of why he'd been called in, what he was up to.

As if someone else had written it for him.

She'd typed out a dozen different replies to that not-Hunt message.

Please tell me everything is okay.

Type 1 if you need help.

Did I do something to upset you?

What's wrong?

Do you need me to come to the Comitium?

Turning down an offer of dumpling soup—did someone steal this phone?

On and on, writing and deleting, until she'd written, *I'm worried. Please call me.* But she had no right to be worried, to demand those things of him.

So she'd settled with a pathetic *Okay*.

And had not heard back from him. She'd checked her phone obsessively the whole workday.

Nothing.

Worry was a writhing knot in her stomach. She didn't even order the soup. A glance at the roof cameras showed Naomi sitting there all day, her face tight.

Bryce had gone up there around three. "Do you have any idea where he might have gone?" she asked, her arms wrapped tightly around herself.

Naomi looked her over. "Hunt is fine," she said. "He . . ." She stopped herself, reading something on Bryce's face. Surprise flickered in her eyes. "He's fine," the angel said gently.

By the time Bryce got home, with Naomi stationed on the adjacent rooftop, she had stopped believing her.

So she'd decided to Hel with it. To Hel with caution or looking cool or any of it.

Standing in her kitchen as the clock crept toward eight, she wrote to Hunt, *Please call me. I'm worried about you.*

There. Let it shoot into the ether or wherever the messages floated.

She walked Syrinx one final time for the night, her phone clutched in her hand. As if the harder she gripped it, the more likely he'd be to respond.

It was eleven by the time she broke, and dialed a familiar number. Ruhn picked up on the first ring. "What's wrong?"

How he knew, she didn't care. "I . . ." She swallowed.

"Bryce." Ruhn's voice sharpened. Music was playing in the background, but it began to shift, as if he were moving to a quieter part of wherever he was.

"Have you seen Hunt anywhere today?" Her voice sounded thin and high.

In the background, Flynn asked, "Is everything okay?"

Ruhn just asked her, "What happened?"

"Like, have you seen Hunt at the gun range, or anywhere—"

The music faded. A door slammed. "Where are you?"

"Home." It hit her then, the rush of how stupid this was, calling him, asking if Ruhn, of all people, knew what the Governor's personal assassin was doing.

"Give me five minutes—"

"No, I don't need you here. I'm fine. I just . . ." Her throat burned. "I can't find him." What if Hunt was lying in a pile of bones and flesh and blood?

When her silence dragged on, Ruhn said with quiet intensity, "I'll put Dec and Flynn on it right—"

The enchantments hummed, and the front door unlocked.

Bryce went still as the door slowly opened. As Hunt, clad in battle-black and wearing that famed helmet, walked in.

Every step seemed like it took all of his concentration. And his scent—

Blood.

Not his own.

"Bryce?"

"He's back," she breathed into the phone. "I'll call you tomorrow," she said to her brother, and hung up.

Hunt paused in the center of the room.

Blood stained his wings. Shone on his leather suit. Splattered the visor of his helmet.

"What—what happened?" she managed to get out.

He began walking again. Walked straight past her, the scent of all that blood—several different types of blood—staining the air. He didn't say a word.

"Hunt." Any relief that had surged through her now transformed into something sharper.

He headed for his room and did not stop. She didn't dare to move. He was a wraith, a demon, a—a shadow of death.

This male, helmeted and in his battle clothes . . . she didn't know him.

Hunt reached his room, not even looking at her as he shut the door behind him.

He couldn't stand it.

He couldn't stand the look of pure, knee-wobbling relief on her face when he'd walked into the apartment. He'd come right back here after he'd finished because he thought she'd be asleep and he could wash off the blood without having to go back to the Comitium barracks first, but she'd been just standing in the living room. Waiting for him.

And as he'd stepped into the apartment and she'd seen and smelled the blood . . .

He couldn't stand the horror and pain on her face, either.

You see what this life has done to me? he wanted to ask. But he had been beyond words. There had been only screaming until now. From the three males he'd spent hours ending, all of it done to Micah's specifications.

Hunt strode for the bathroom and turned the shower up to scalding. He removed the helmet, the bright lights stinging his eyes without the visor's cooling tones. Then he removed his gloves.

She had looked so horrified. It was no surprise. She couldn't have really understood what he was, who he was, until now. Why people shied away from him. Didn't meet his eyes.

Hunt peeled his suit off, his bruised skin already healing. The drug lords he'd ended tonight had gotten in a few blows before he'd subdued them. Before he'd pinned them to the ground, impaled on his blades.

And left them there, shrieking in pain, for hours.

Naked, he stepped into the shower, the white tiles already sweating with steam.

The scalding water blasted his skin like acid.

He swallowed his scream, his sob, his whimper, and didn't balk from the boiling torrent.

Didn't do anything as he let it burn everything away.

Micah had sent him on a mission. Had ordered Hunt to kill someone. Several people, from the different scents on him. Did each one of those lives count toward his hideous *debt*?

It was his job, his path to freedom, what he did for the Governor, and yet . . . And yet Bryce had never really considered it. What it did to him. What the consequences were.

It wasn't a path to freedom. It was a path to Hel.

Bryce lingered in the living room, waiting for him to finish showering. The water kept running. Twenty minutes. Thirty. Forty.

When the clock crept up on an hour, she found herself knocking on his door. "Hunt?"

No answer. The water continued.

She cracked the door, peering into the dim bedroom. The

bathroom door stood open, steam wafting out. So much steam that the bedroom had turned muggy.

"Hunt?" She pushed forward, craning her neck to see into the bright bathroom. No sign of him in the shower—

A hint of a soaked gray wing rose from behind the shower glass.

She moved, not thinking. Not caring.

She was in the bathroom in a heartbeat, his name on her lips, bracing for the worst, wishing she'd grabbed her phone from the kitchen counter—

But there he was. Sitting naked on the floor of the shower, his head bowed between his knees. Water pounded into his back, his wings, dripping off his hair. His gold-dusted brown skin gleamed an angry red.

Bryce took one step into the shower and hissed. The water was scalding. Burning hot.

"Hunt," she said. He didn't so much as blink.

She glanced between him and the showerhead. His body was healing the burns—healing and then scalding, healing and scalding. It had to be torturous.

She bit down on her yelp as she reached into the shower, the near-boiling water soaking her shirt, her pants, and lowered the temperature.

He didn't move. Didn't even look at her. He'd done this many times, she realized. Every time Micah had sent him out, and for all the Archangels he'd served before that.

Syrinx came to investigate, sniffed at the bloody clothes, then sprawled himself on the bath mat, head on his front paws.

Hunt made no indication that he knew she stood there.

But his breathing deepened. Became easier.

And she couldn't explain why she did it, but she grabbed a bottle of shampoo and the block of lavender soap from the nook in the tiles. Then knelt before him.

"I'm going to clean you off," she said quietly. "If that's all right."

A slight but terribly clear nod was his only response. Like words were still too hard.

So Bryce poured the shampoo into her hands, and then laced

her fingers into his hair. The thick strands were heavy, and she gently scrubbed, tipping his head back to rinse it. His eyes lifted at last. Met hers, as his head leaned back into the stream of water.

"You look how I feel," she whispered, her throat tight. "Every day."

He blinked, his only sign that he'd heard.

She removed her hands from his hair, and picked up the bar of soap. He was naked, she realized, having somehow forgotten. Utterly naked. She didn't let herself contemplate it as she began lathering his neck, his powerful shoulders, his muscled arms. "I'll leave your bottom half for you to enjoy," she said, her face heating.

He was just watching her with that raw openness. More intimate than any touch of his lips on her neck. Like he indeed saw everything she was and had been and might yet become.

She scrubbed down his upper body as best she could. "I can't clean your wings with you sitting against the wall."

Hunt rose to his feet in a mighty, graceful push.

She kept her eyes averted from what, exactly, this brought into her direct line of vision. The very considerable something that he didn't seem to notice or care about.

So she wouldn't care about it, either. She stood, water splattering her, and gently turned him. She didn't let herself admire the view from behind, either. The muscles and perfection of him.

Your ass is perfect, he'd said to her.

Likewise, she could now attest.

She soaped his wings, now dark gray in the water.

He towered over her, enough that she had to rise to her toes to reach the apex of his wings. In silence, she washed him, and Hunt braced his hands against the tiles, his head hanging. He needed rest, and the comfort of oblivion. So Bryce rinsed off the soap, making sure each and every feather was clean, and then reached around the angel to turn off the shower.

Only the dribbling of water eddying into the drain filled the steamy bathroom.

Bryce grabbed a towel, keeping her eyes up as Hunt turned to face her. She slung it around his hips, yanked a second towel off the bar just outside the shower stall, and ran it over his tan skin. Gently patted his wings dry. Then rubbed his hair.

"Come on," she murmured. "Bed."

His face became more alert, but he didn't object when she tugged him from the shower, dripping water from her sodden clothes and hair. Didn't object when she led him into the bedroom, to the chest of drawers where he'd put his things.

She pulled out a pair of black undershorts and stooped down, eyes firmly on the ground as she stretched out the waistband. "Step in."

Hunt obeyed, first one foot and then the other. She rose, sliding the shorts up his powerful thighs and releasing the elastic waist with a soft snap. Bryce snatched a white T-shirt from another drawer, frowned at the complicated slats on the back to fit his wings, and set it down again. "Underwear it is," she declared, pulling back the blanket on the bed he so dutifully made each morning. She patted the mattress. "Get some sleep, Hunt."

Again, he obeyed, sliding between the sheets with a soft groan.

She shut off the bathroom light, darkening the bedroom, and returned to where he now lay, still staring at her. Daring to stroke his damp hair away from his brow, Bryce's fingers grazed over the hateful tattoo. His eyes closed.

"I was so worried about you," she whispered, stroking his hair again. "I . . ." She couldn't finish the sentence. So she made to step back, to head to her room and change into dry clothes and maybe get some sleep herself.

But a warm, strong hand gripped her wrist. Halted her.

She looked back, and found Hunt staring at her again. "What?"

A slight tug on her wrist told her everything.

Stay.

Her chest squeezed to the point of pain. "Okay." She took a breath. "Okay, sure."

And for some reason, the thought of going all the way to her bedroom, of leaving him for even a moment, seemed too risky. Like he might vanish again if she left to change.

So she grabbed the white T-shirt she'd intended to give him, and twisted away, peeling off her own shirt and bra and chucking them into the bathroom. They landed with a slap on the tiles, drowning out the rustle of his soft shirt as she slid it over herself. It hung down to her knees, providing enough coverage that she shucked off her wet sweats and underwear and threw them into the bathroom, too.

Syrinx had leapt into the bed, curling at the foot. And Hunt had moved over, giving her ample room. "Okay," she said again, more to herself.

The sheets were warm, and smelled of him—rain-kissed cedar. She tried not to breathe it in too obviously as she took up a sitting position against the headboard. And she tried not to look too shocked when he laid his head on her thigh, his arm coming across her to rest on the pillow.

A child laying his head on his mother's lap. A friend looking for any sort of reassuring contact to remind him that he was a living being. A good person, no matter what they made him do.

Bryce tentatively brushed the hair from his brow again.

Hunt's eyes closed, but he leaned slightly into the touch. A silent request.

So Bryce continued stroking his hair, over and over, until his breathing deepened and steadied, until his powerful body grew limp beside hers.

It smelled like paradise. Like home and eternity and like exactly where he was meant to be.

Hunt opened his eyes to feminine softness and warmth and gentle breathing.

In the dim light, he found himself half-sprawled across Bryce's lap, the woman herself passed out against the headboard, head lolling to the side. Her hand still lingered in his hair, the other in the sheets by his arm.

The clock read three thirty. It wasn't the time that surprised him, but the fact that he was clearheaded enough to notice.

She'd taken care of him. Washed and clothed and soothed him. He couldn't remember the last time anyone had done that.

Hunt carefully peeled his face from her lap, realizing that her legs were bare. That she wasn't wearing anything beneath his T-shirt. And his face had been mere inches away.

His muscles protested only slightly as he rose upward. Bryce didn't so much as stir.

She'd put him in his underwear, for fuck's sake.

His cheeks warmed, but he eased from the bed, Syrinx opening an eye to see what the commotion was about. He waved the beastie off and padded to Bryce's side of the mattress.

She stirred only slightly as he scooped her into his arms and carried her to her own room. He laid her on her bed, and she grumbled, protesting at the cool sheets, but he swiftly tossed the down comforter over her and left before she could awaken.

He was halfway across the living area when her phone, discarded on the kitchen counter, glared with light. Hunt looked at it, unable to help himself.

A chain of messages from Ruhn filled the screen, all from the past few hours.

Is Athalar all right? Later, *Are you all right?*

Then, an hour ago, *I called the front desk of your building, and the doorman reassured me that you're both up there, so I'm assuming you two are fine. But call me in the morning.*

And then from thirty seconds ago, as if it were an afterthought, *I'm glad you called me tonight. I know things are fucked up between us, and I know a lot of that is my fault, but if you ever need me, I'm here. Anytime at all, Bryce.*

Hunt glanced toward her bedroom hallway. She'd called Ruhn—that's who she'd been on the phone with when he got back. He rubbed at his chest.

He fell back asleep in his own bed, where the scent of her still lingered, like a phantom, warming touch.

55

The golden rays of dawn coaxed Bryce awake. The blankets were warm, and the bed soft, and Syrinx was still snoring—

Her room. Her bed.

She sat up, jostling Syrinx awake. He yowled in annoyance and slithered deeper under the covers, kicking her in the ribs with his hind legs for good measure.

Bryce left him to it, sliding from bed and leaving her room within seconds. Hunt must have moved her at some point. He'd been in no shape to do anything like that, and if he'd somehow been forced to go back out again—

She sighed as she glimpsed a gray wing draped over the guest room bed. The golden-brown skin of a muscled back. Rising and falling. Still asleep.

Thank the gods. Rubbing her hands over her face, sleep a lost cause, she padded for the kitchen and began to make coffee. She needed a strong cup of it, then a quick run. She let muscle memory take over, and as the coffee maker buzzed and rattled away, she scooped up her phone from the counter.

Ruhn's messages occupied most of her alerts. She read through them twice.

He would have dropped everything to come over. Put his friends on the task of finding Hunt. Would have done it without question. She knew that—had made herself forget it.

She knew why, too. Had been well aware that her reaction to their argument years ago had been justified, but overblown. He'd tried to apologize, and she had only used it against him. And he must have felt guilty enough that he'd never questioned why she'd cut him out of her life. That he'd never realized that it hadn't just been some slight hurt that had forced her to shut him off from her life, but fear. Absolute terror.

He'd wounded her, and it had scared the Hel out of her that he held such power. That she had wanted so many things from him, imagined so many things with her brother—adventures and holidays and ordinary moments—and he had the ability to rip it all away.

Bryce's thumbs hovered over the keyboard on her phone, as if searching for the right words. *Thank you* would be good. Or even *I'll call you later* would suffice, since maybe she should actually say those words aloud.

But her thumbs remained aloft, the words slipping and tumbling past.

So she let them fall by, and turned to the other message she'd received—from Juniper.

Madame Kyrah told me that you never showed up to her class. What the Hel, Bryce? I had to beg her to hold that spot for you. She was really mad.

Bryce ground her teeth. She wrote back, *Sorry. Tell her I'm in the middle of working on something for the Governor and got called away.*

Bryce set down the phone and turned to the coffee machine. Her phone buzzed a second later. Juniper had to be on her way to morning practice, then.

This woman does not peddle in excuses. I worked hard to get her to like me, Bryce.

June was definitely pissed if she was calling her *Bryce* instead of *B*.

Bryce wrote back, *I'm sorry, okay? I told you I was a maybe. You shouldn't have let her think I'd be there.*

Juniper sniped back, *Whatever. I gotta go.*

Bryce blew out a breath, forcing herself to unclench her fingers from around her phone. She cradled her mug of hot coffee.

"Hey."

She whirled to find Hunt leaning a hip against the marble island. For someone heavily muscled and winged, the angel was stealthy, she had to admit. He'd put on a shirt and pants, but his hair was still sleep-mussed.

She rasped, her knees wobbling only slightly, "How are you feeling?"

"Fine." The word held no bite, only a quiet resignation and a request not to push. So Bryce fished out another mug, set it in the coffee machine, and hit a few buttons that had it brewing.

His gaze brushed over every part of her like a physical touch. She peered down at herself and realized why. "Sorry I took one of your shirts," she said, bunching the white fabric in a hand. Gods, she wasn't wearing any underwear. Did he know?

His eyes dipped toward her bare legs and went a shade darker. He definitely knew.

Hunt pushed off the island, stalking toward her, and Bryce braced herself. For what, she didn't know, but—

He just strode past. Right to the fridge, where he pulled out eggs and the slab of bacon. "At the risk of sounding like an alphahole cliché," he said without looking at her as he set the skillet on the stove, "I like seeing you in my shirt."

"Total alphahole cliché," she said, even as her toes curled on the pale wood floor.

Hunt cracked the eggs into a bowl. "We always seem to end up in the kitchen."

"I don't mind," Bryce said, sipping her coffee, "as long as you're cooking."

Hunt snorted, then stilled. "Thanks," he said quietly. "For what you did."

"Don't mention it," she said, taking another sip of coffee. Remembering the one she'd brewed for him, she reached for the now-full mug.

Hunt turned from the stove as she extended the coffee to him. Glanced between the outstretched mug and her face.

And as his large hand wrapped around the mug, he leaned in,

closing the space between them. His mouth brushed over her cheek. Brief and light and sweet.

"Thank you," he said again, pulling back and returning to the stove. As if he didn't notice that she couldn't move a single muscle, couldn't find a single word to utter.

The urge to grab him, to pull his face down to hers and taste every part of him practically blinded her. Her fingers twitched at her sides, nearly able to feel those hard muscles beneath them.

He had a long-lost love he was still holding a torch for. And she'd just gone too long without sex. Cthona's tits, it'd been weeks since that hookup with the lion shifter in the Raven's bathroom. And with Hunt here, she hadn't dared open up her left nightstand to take care of herself.

Keep telling yourself all that, a small voice said.

The muscles in Hunt's back stiffened. His hands paused whatever they were doing.

Shit, he could smell this kind of thing, couldn't he? Most Vanir males could. The shifts in a person's scent: fear and arousal being the two big ones.

He was the Umbra Mortis. Off-limits in ten million ways. And the Umbra Mortis didn't date—no, it'd be all or nothing with him.

Hunt asked, voice like gravel, "What are you thinking about?" He didn't turn from the stove.

You. Like a fucking idiot, I'm thinking about you.

"There's a sample sale at one of the designer stores this afternoon," she lied.

Hunt glanced over his shoulder. Fuck, his eyes were dark. "Is that so?"

Was that a purr in his voice?

She couldn't help the step she took back, bumping into the kitchen island. "Yes," she said, unable to look away.

Hunt's eyes darkened further. He said nothing.

She couldn't breathe properly with that stare fixed on her. That stare that told her he scented everything going on in her body.

Her nipples pebbled under that stare.

Hunt went preternaturally still. His eyes dipped downward. Saw her breasts. The thighs she now clamped together—as if it'd stop the throbbing beginning to torture her between them.

His face went positively feral. A mountain cat ready to pounce. "I didn't know clothing sales got you so hot and bothered, Quinlan."

She nearly whimpered. Forced herself to keep still. "It's the little things in life, Athalar."

"Is that what you think about when you open up that left nightstand? Clothing sales?" He faced her fully now. She didn't dare let her gaze drop.

"Yes," she breathed. "All those clothes, all over my body." She had no idea what the fuck was coming out of her mouth.

How was it possible all the air in the apartment, the city, had been sucked out?

"Maybe you should buy some new underwear," he murmured, nodding to her bare legs. "Seems like you're out."

She couldn't stop it—the image that blazed over her senses: Hunt putting those big hands on her waist and hoisting her onto the counter currently pressing into her spine, shoving her T-shirt over her midriff—his T-shirt, actually—and spreading her legs wide. Fucking her with his tongue, then his cock, until she was sobbing in pleasure, screaming with it, she didn't care just so long as he was touching her, inside her—

"Quinlan." He seemed to be shaking now. As if only a tether of pure will kept him in place. As if he'd seen the same burning image and was just waiting for her nod.

It'd complicate everything. The investigation, whatever he felt for Shahar, her own life—

To fucking Hel with all that. They'd figure it out later. They'd—

Burning smoke filled the air between them. Gross, nose-stinging smoke.

"Fuck," Hunt hissed, whirling to the stove and the eggs he'd left on the burner.

As if a witch spell had snapped, Bryce blinked, the dizzying heat vanishing. Oh gods. His emotions had to be all over the place after last night, and hers were a mess on a good day, and—

"I have to get dressed for work," she managed to say, and hurried toward her bedroom before he could turn from the burning breakfast.

She'd lost her mind, she told herself in the shower, in the bathroom, on the too-quiet walk to work with Syrinx, Hunt trailing overhead. Keeping his distance. As if he realized the same thing.

Let someone in, give them the power to hurt you, and they'd do exactly that, in the end.

She couldn't do it. Endure it.

Bryce had resigned herself to that fact by the time she reached the gallery. A glance upward showed Hunt making his descent as Syrinx yipped happily, and the thought of a day in an enclosed space with him, with only Lehabah as a buffer . . .

Thank fucking Urd, her phone rang as she opened the gallery door. But it wasn't Ruhn calling to check in, and it wasn't Juniper with an earful about missing the dance class. "Jesiba."

The sorceress didn't bother with pleasantries. "Get the back door open. Now."

"Oh, it's horrible, BB," Lehabah whispered in the dimness of the library. "Just horrible."

Staring up at the massive, dimly lit tank, Bryce felt her arm hair stand on end as she watched their new addition explore its environment. Hunt crossed his arms and peered into the gloom. Any thoughts of getting naked with him had vanished an hour ago.

A dark, scaled hand slapped against the thick glass, ivory claws scraping. Bryce swallowed. "I want to know where anyone even found a nøkk in these waters." From what she'd heard, they existed only in the icy seas of the north, and mostly in Pangera.

"I preferred the kelpie," Lehabah whispered, shrinking behind her little divan, her flame a quivering yellow.

As if it had heard them, the nøkk paused before the glass and smiled.

At more than eight feet long, the nøkk might have very well been the Helish twin to a mer male. But instead of humanoid features, the nøkk presented a jutting lower jaw with a too-wide, lipless mouth, full of needle-thin teeth. Its overlarge eyes were milky, like some of the fishes of the deep. Its tail was mostly translucent—bony and sharp—and above it, a warped, muscled torso rose.

No hair covered its chest or head, and its four-fingered hands ended in daggerlike claws.

With the tank spanning the entire length of one side of the library, there would be no escaping its presence, unless the nøkk went down to the cluster of dark rocks at the bottom. The creature dragged those claws over the glass again. The inked *SPQM* gleamed stark white on his greenish-gray wrist.

Bryce lifted her phone to her ear. Jesiba picked up on the first ring. "Yes?"

"We have a problem."

"With the Korsaki contract?" Jesiba's voice was low, as if she didn't want to be overheard.

"No." Bryce scowled at the nøkk. "The creep in the aquarium needs to go."

"I'm in a meeting."

"Lehabah is scared as Hel."

Air was lethal to nøkks—if one was exposed for more than a few seconds, its vital organs would begin shutting down, its skin peeling away as if burned. But Bryce had still gone up the small stairwell to the right of the tank to ensure that the feeding hatch built into the grate atop the water was thoroughly locked. The hatch itself was a square platform that could be raised and lowered into the water, operated by a panel of controls in the rear of the space atop the tank, and Bryce had triple-checked that the machine was completely turned off.

When she'd returned to the library, she'd found Lehabah curled into a ball behind a book, the sprite's flame a sputtering yellow.

Lehabah whispered from her couch, "He's a hateful, horrible creature."

Bryce shushed her. "Can't you gift him to some macho loser in Pangera?"

"I'm hanging up now."

"But he's—"

The line went dead. Bryce slumped into her seat at the table. "Now she'll just keep him forever," she told the sprite.

"What are you going to feed it?" Hunt asked as the nøkk again tested the glass wall, feeling with those terrible hands.

"It loves humans," Lehabah whispered. "They drag swimmers under the surface of ponds and lakes and drown them, then slowly feast on their corpses over days and days—"

"Beef," Bryce said, her stomach turning as she glanced at the small door to access the stairwell to the top of the tank. "He'll get a few steaks a day."

Lehabah cowered. "Can't we put up a curtain?"

"Jesiba will just rip it down."

Hunt offered, "I could pile some books on this table—block your view of him instead."

"He'll still know where I am, though." Lehabah pouted at Bryce. "I can't sleep with it in here."

Bryce sighed. "What if you just pretend he's an enchanted prince or something?"

The sprite pointed toward the tank. To the nøkk hovering in the water, tail thrashing. Smiling at them. "A prince from Hel."

"Who would want a nøkk for a pet?" Hunt asked, sprawling himself across from Bryce at the desk.

"A sorceress who chose to join Flame and Shadow and turns her enemies into animals." Bryce motioned to the smaller tanks and terrariums built into the shelves around them, then rubbed at the persistent ache in her thigh beneath her pink dress. When she'd finally worked up the nerve to emerge from her bedroom this morning after the kitchen fiasco, Hunt had looked at her for a long, long moment. But he'd said nothing.

"You should see a medwitch about that leg," he said now. Hunt didn't look up from where he was leafing through some report Justinian had sent over that morning for a second opinion. She'd asked what it was, but he'd told her it was classified, and that was that.

"My leg is fine." She didn't bother to turn from where she once again began typing in the details for the Korsaki contract Jesiba was so eager to have finalized. Mindless busywork, but work that had to be done at some point.

Especially since they were again at a dead end. No word had arrived from Viktoria about the Mimir test results. Why Danika had stolen the Horn, who wanted it so badly that they'd kill her for it . . . Bryce still had no idea. But if Ruhn was right about a method to heal the Horn . . . It all had to tie together somehow.

And she knew that while they'd killed the one kristallos demon, there were other kristallos waiting in Hel that could still be summoned to hunt the Horn. And if its kind had failed so far, when the breed had literally been created by the Princes of Hel to track the Horn . . . How could she even hope to find it?

Then there was the matter of those gruesome, pulping killings . . . which hadn't been done by a kristallos. Hunt had already put in a request to have the footage checked again, but nothing had come through.

Hunt's phone buzzed, and he fished it from his pocket, glimpsed at the screen, then put it away. From across the desk, she could just barely make out the text box of a message on the screen.

"Not going to write back?"

His mouth twisted to the side. "Just one of my colleagues, busting my balls." His eyes flickered when he looked at her, though. And when she smiled at him, shrugging, his throat bobbed—just slightly.

Hunt said a bit roughly, "I gotta head out for a while. Naomi will come to stand guard. I'll pick you up when you're ready to leave."

Before she could ask about it, he was gone.

* * *

"I know it's been a while," Bryce said, her phone wedged between her shoulder and ear.

Hunt had been waiting outside the gallery while she locked up, smiling at Syrinx scratching at the door. The chimera yowled in protest when he realized Bryce wasn't bringing him along yet, and Hunt stooped to scratch his fuzzy golden head before Bryce shut the door, locking him in.

"I'll have to look at my calendar," Bryce was saying, nodding her hello to Hunt.

She looked beautiful today, in a rose-pink dress, pearls at her ears, and hair swept back on either side with matching pearl combs.

Fuck, *beautiful* wasn't even the right word for it.

She'd emerged from her bedroom and he'd been struck stupid.

She hadn't seemed to notice that *he'd* noticed, though he supposed she knew that she looked gorgeous every day. Yet there was a light to her today, a color that hadn't been there before, a glow in her amber eyes and flush to her skin.

But that pink dress . . . It had distracted him all day.

So had their encounter in the kitchen this morning. He'd done his best to ignore it—to forget about how close he'd come to begging her to touch him, to let him touch her. It hadn't stopped him from being in a state of semi-arousal all day.

He had to get his shit together. Considering that their investigation had slowed this past week, he couldn't afford distractions. Couldn't afford to ogle her every time she wasn't looking. This afternoon, she'd been rising up onto her toes, arm straining to grab some book on a high shelf in the library, and it was like that color pink was the fucking Horn, and he was a kristallos demon.

He'd been out of his chair in an instant, at her side a heartbeat after that, and had pulled the book off the shelf for her.

She'd stood there, though, when he'd held the book out. Hadn't backed up a step as she looked between the outstretched book and his face. His blood had begun pounding in his ears, his skin becoming too tight. Just like it had this morning when he'd seen her breasts peak, and had scented how filthy her own thoughts had turned.

But she'd just taken the book and walked away. Unfazed and unaware of his sheer stupidity.

It hadn't improved as the hours had passed. And when she'd smiled at him earlier . . . He'd been half-relieved to be called away from the gallery a minute later. It was while he was heading back, breathing in the brisk air off the Istros, that Viktoria sent him a message: *I found something. Meet me at Munin and Hugin in 15.*

He debated telling the wraith to wait. To delay the inevitable bad news coming their way, to go just a few more days with that beautiful smile on Bryce's face and that desire starting to smolder in her eyes, but . . . Micah's warnings rang in his ears. The Summit was still two weeks away, but Hunt knew Sandriel's presence had stretched Micah's patience thinner than usual. That if he delayed much longer, he'd find his bargain null and void.

So whatever intel Vik had, however bad . . . he'd find a way to deal with it. He called *Bryce Kicks Ass* and told her to get *her* ass outside to meet him.

"I don't know, Mom," Bryce was saying into her phone, falling into step with Hunt as they started down the street. The setting sun bathed the city in gold and orange, gilding even the puddles of filth. "Of course I miss you, but maybe next month?"

They passed an alley a few blocks away, neon signs pointing to the small tea bars and ancient food stalls cramming its length. Several tattoo shops lay interspersed, some of the artists or patrons smoking outside before the evening rush of drunken idiots.

"What—*this* weekend? Well, I have a guest—" She clicked her tongue. "No, it's a long story. He's like . . . a roommate? His name? Uh, Athie. *No,* Mom." She sighed. "This weekend *really* doesn't work. No, I'm not blowing you guys off again." She gritted her teeth. "What about a video chat, then? Mmhmm, yeah, of course I'll make the time." Bryce winced again. "Okay, Mom. Bye."

Bryce turned to him, grimacing.

"Your mom seems . . . insistent," Hunt said carefully.

"I'm video chatting with my parents at seven." She sighed at the sky. "They want to meet you."

Viktoria was at the bar when they arrived, a glass of whiskey in front of her. She offered them both a grave smile, then slid a file over as they seated themselves to her left.

"What did you find?" Bryce asked, opening the cream-colored folder.

"Read it," Viktoria said, then glanced toward the cameras in the bar. Recording everything.

Bryce nodded, taking the warning, and Hunt leaned closer as her head dipped to read, unable to stop himself from stretching out his wing, ever so slightly, around her back.

He forgot about it, though, when he beheld the test results. "This can't be right," he said quietly.

"That's what I said," Viktoria said, her narrow face impassive.

There, on the Fae's Mimir screening, lay the results: small bits of something synthetic. Not organic, not technological, not magic—but a combination of all three.

Find what is in-between, Aidas had said.

"Danika freelanced for Redner Industries," Bryce said. "They do all sorts of experiments. Would that explain this?"

"It might," Viktoria said. "But I'm running the Mimir on every other sample we have—from the others. Initial tests also came up positive on Maximus Tertian's clothes." The tattoo on Viktoria's brow bunched as she frowned. "It's not pure magic, or tech, or organic. It's a hybrid, with its other traces causing it to be canceled out in the other categories. A cloaking device, almost."

Bryce frowned. "What is it, exactly?"

Hunt knew Viktoria well enough to read the caution in the wraith's eyes. She said to Bryce, "It's some sort of . . . drug. From what I can find, it looks like it's mostly used for medical purposes in very small doses, but might have leaked onto the streets—which led to doses that are far from safe."

"Danika wouldn't have taken a drug like that."

"Of course not," Viktoria said quickly. "But she was exposed to it—all her clothes were. Whether that was upon her death or before it, however, is unclear. We're about to run the test on the samples we took from the Pack of Devils and the two most recent victims."

"Tertian was in the Meat Market," Hunt murmured. "He might have taken it."

But Bryce demanded, "What's it called? This thing?"

Viktoria pointed to the results. "Exactly what it sounds like. Synth."

Bryce whipped her head around to look at Hunt. "Ruhn said that medwitch mentioned a synthetic healing compound that could possibly repair . . ." She didn't finish the statement.

Hunt's eyes were dark as the Pit, a haunted look in them. "It might be the same one."

Viktoria held up her hands. "Again, I'm still testing the other victims, but . . . I just thought you should know."

Bryce hopped off the stool. "Thanks."

Hunt let her reach the front door before he murmured to the wraith, "Keep it quiet, Vik."

"Already wiped the files from the legion database," Vik said.

They barely spoke while they returned to the gallery, grabbed Syrinx, and headed home. Only when they stood in her kitchen, Hunt leaning against the counter, did he say, "Investigations can take time. We're getting closer. That's a good thing."

She dumped food in Syrinx's bowl, face unreadable. "What do you think about this synth?"

Hunt considered his words carefully. "As you said, it could have just been exposure Danika had at Redner. Tertian could have just taken it as a recreational drug right before he died. And we're still waiting to find out if it shows up on the clothes of the remaining victims."

"I want to know about it," she said, pulling out her phone and dialing.

"It might not be worth our—"

Ruhn picked up. "Yeah?"

"That synthetic healing drug you heard about from the medwitch. What do you know about it?"

"She sent over some research a couple days ago. A lot of it's been redacted by Redner Industries, but I'm going through it. Why?"

Bryce glanced toward Hunt's open bedroom door—to the photo of her and Danika on the dresser, Hunt realized. "There were traces of something called synth on Danika's clothes—it's a relatively new synthetic medicine. And it sounds like it's leaked onto the streets and is being used in higher concentrations as an illegal substance. I'm wondering if it's the same thing."

"Yeah, this research is on synth." Pages rustled in the background. "It can do some pretty amazing things. There's a list of ingredients here—again, a lot of it was redacted, but . . ."

Ruhn's silence was like a bomb dropping.

"But what?" Hunt said into the phone, leaning close enough to hear Bryce's thundering heart.

"Obsidian salt is listed as one of the ingredients."

"Obsidian . . ." Bryce blinked at Hunt. "Could the synth be used to summon a demon? If someone didn't have the power on their own, could the obsidian salt in the drug let them call on something like the kristallos?"

"I'm not sure," Ruhn said. "I'll read through this and let you know what I find."

"Okay." Bryce blew out a breath, and Hunt pulled a step away as she began pacing again. "Thanks, Ruhn."

Ruhn's pause was different this time. "No problem, Bryce." He hung up.

Hunt met her stare. She said, "We need to figure out who's selling this stuff. Tertian must have known before he died. We're going to the Meat Market." Because if there was one place in this city where a drug like that might be available, it'd be in that cesspit.

Hunt swallowed. "We need to be *careful*—"

"I want answers." She aimed for the front closet.

Hunt stepped into her path. "We'll go tomorrow." She drew up short, mouth opening. But Hunt shook his head. "Take tonight off."

"It can't—"

"Yes, it can wait, Bryce. Talk to your parents tonight. I'll put on some real clothes," he added, gesturing to his battle-suit. "And then tomorrow, we'll go to the Meat Market to ask around. It can wait." Hunt, despite himself, grabbed her hand. Ran his thumb over the back of it. "Enjoy talking to your parents, Bryce. They're *alive.* Don't miss out on a moment of it. Not for this." She still looked like she'd object, insist they go hunt down the synth, so he said, "I wish I had that luxury."

She looked down at his hand, gripping hers, for a second—for a lifetime. She asked, "What happened to your parents?"

He said, throat tight, "My mother never told me who my father is. And she . . . She was a low-ranking angel. She cleaned the villas of some of the more powerful angels, because they didn't trust humans or other Vanir to do it." His chest ached at the memory of his mother's beautiful, gentle face. Her soft smile and dark, angular eyes. The lullabies he could still hear, more than two hundred years later.

"She worked day and night to keep me fed and never once complained, because she knew that if she did, she'd be out of a job and she had me to think about. When I was a foot soldier, and sending home every copper I made, she refused to spend it. Apparently, someone heard I was doing that, thought she had tons of money hidden in her apartment, and broke in one night. Killed her and took the money. All five hundred silver marks she'd amassed over her life, and the fifty gold marks I'd managed to send her after five years in service."

"I am so sorry, Hunt."

"None of the angels—the powerful, adored angels—that my mother worked for bothered to care that she'd been killed. No one investigated who did it, and no one granted me leave to mourn. She was nothing to them. But she was . . . she was everything to me." His throat ached. "I made the Drop and joined Shahar's cause soon after that. I battled on Mount Hermon that day for her—my mother. In her memory." Shahar had taken those memories and made them into weapons.

Bryce's fingers pressed his. "It sounds like she was a remarkable person."

"She was." He pulled his hand away at last.

But she still smiled at him, his chest tightening to the point of pain as she said, "All right. I'll video chat my parents. Playing legionary with you can wait."

Bryce spent most of the evening cleaning. Hunt helped her, offering to fly over to the nearest apothecary and get an insta-clean spell, but Bryce waved him off. Her mom was such a neat freak, she claimed, that she could tell the difference between magically cleaned bathrooms and hand-scrubbed ones. Even on video chat.

It's that bleach smell that tells me it's been done properly, Bryce, her daughter had imitated to Hunt in a flat, no-nonsense voice that made him just a little nervous.

Bryce had used his phone throughout, snapping photos of him cleaning, of Syrinx taking the toilet paper rolls from their container and shredding them on the carpet they'd just vacuumed, of herself with Hunt stooped over his toilet behind her, brushing down the inside.

By the time he'd snatched the phone out of her gloved hands, she'd again changed her contact name, this time to *Bryce Is Cooler Than Me*.

But despite the smile it brought to his face, Hunt kept hearing Micah's voice, threats both spoken and implied. *Find who is behind this. Get. The. Job. Done. Don't make me reconsider our bargain. Before I take you off this case. Before I sell you back to Sandriel. Before I make you and Bryce Quinlan regret it.*

Once he solved this case, it would be over, wouldn't it? He'd still have ten kills left for Micah, which could easily take years to fulfill. He'd have to go back to the Comitium. To the 33rd.

He found himself looking at her while they cleaned. Taking out his phone and snapping some photos of her as well.

He knew too much. Had learned too much. About all of it. About what he might have had, without the halo and slave tattoos.

"I can open a bottle of wine, if you need some liquid courage," Bryce was saying as they sat before her computer at the kitchen island, the video chat service dialing her parents. She'd bought a bag of pastries from the corner market on their way home—a stress-coping device, he assumed.

Hunt just scanned her face. This—calling her parents, sitting thigh-to-thigh with her . . . Fucking Hel.

He was on a one-way collision course. He couldn't bring himself to stop it.

Before Hunt could open his mouth to suggest that this might be a mistake, a female voice said, "And why exactly would he need liquid courage, Bryce Adelaide Quinlan?"

56

A stunning woman in her mid-forties appeared on the screen, her sheet of black hair still untouched by gray, her freckled face just beginning to show the signs of a mortal life span.

From what Hunt could see, Ember Quinlan was seated on a worn green couch situated against oak-paneled walls, her long, jeans-clad legs folded beneath her.

Bryce rolled her eyes. "I'd say most people need liquid courage when dealing with you, Mom." But she smiled. One of those broad smiles that did funny things to Hunt's sense of balance.

Ember's dark eyes shifted toward Hunt. "I think Bryce is confusing me with herself."

Bryce waved off the comment. "Where's Dad?"

"He had a long day at work—he's making some coffee so he doesn't fall asleep."

Even through the video feed, Ember possessed a grounded sort of presence that commanded attention. She said, "You must be Athie."

Before he could answer, a male eased onto the couch beside Ember.

Bryce beamed in a way Hunt hadn't seen before. "Hey, Dad."

Randall Silago held two coffees, one of which he handed to Ember as he grinned back at his daughter. Unlike his wife, the years or the war had left their mark on him: his black braided hair was streaked with silver, his brown skin marred with a few brutal scars. But his dark eyes were friendly as he sipped from his mug—a chipped white one that said *Insert Cliché Dad Joke Here*. "I'm still scared of that fancy coffee machine you bought us for Winter Solstice," he said by way of greeting.

"I've shown you how to use it literally three times."

Her mother chuckled, toying with a silver pendant around her neck. "He's old-school."

Hunt had looked up how much the built-in machine in this apartment cost—if Bryce had bought them anything remotely similar, she must have dumped a considerable portion of her paycheck on it. Money she did not have. Not with her debt to Jesiba.

He doubted her parents knew that, doubted they'd have accepted that machine if they'd known the money could have gone toward paying back her debts to the sorceress.

Randall's eyes shifted to Hunt, the warmth cooling to something harder. The eyes of the fabled sharpshooter—the man who'd taught his daughter how to defend herself. "You must be Bryce's sort-of roommate." Hunt saw the man notice his tattoos—on his brow, on his wrist. Recognition flared across Randall's face.

Yet he didn't sneer. Didn't cringe.

Bryce elbowed Hunt in the ribs, reminding him to actually *speak*. "I'm Hunt Athalar," he said, glancing at Bryce. "Or Athie, as she and Lehabah call me."

Randall slowly set down his coffee. Yeah, that had been recognition in the man's face a moment ago. But Randall narrowed his eyes at his daughter. "You were going to mention this when, exactly?"

Bryce rootled through the pastry bag on the counter and pulled out a chocolate croissant. She bit in and said around it, "He's not as cool as you think, Dad."

Hunt snorted. "Thanks."

Ember said nothing. Didn't even move. But she watched every bite Bryce took.

Randall met Hunt's stare through the feed. "You were stationed at Meridan when I was over there. I was running recon the day you took on that battalion."

"Rough battle" was all Hunt said.

Shadows darkened Randall's eyes. "Yeah, it was."

Hunt shut out the memory of that one-sided massacre, of how many humans and their few Vanir allies hadn't walked away from his sword or lightning. He'd been serving Sandriel then, and her orders had been brutal: no prisoners. She'd sent him and Pollux out that day, ahead of her legion, to intercept the small rebel force camped in a mountain pass.

Hunt had worked around her order as best he could. He'd made the deaths quick.

Pollux had taken his time. And enjoyed every second of it.

And when Hunt could no longer listen to people screaming for Pollux's mercy, he'd ended their lives, too. Pollux had raged, the brawl between them leaving both angels spitting blood onto the rocky earth. Sandriel had been delighted by it, even if she'd thrown Hunt into her dungeons for a few days as punishment for ending Pollux's fun too soon.

Beneath the counter, Bryce brushed her crumb-covered hand over Hunt's. There had been no one, after that battle, to wash away the blood and put him in bed. Would it have been better or worse to have known Bryce then? To have fought, knowing he could return to her?

Bryce squeezed his fingers, leaving a trail of buttery flakes, and opened the bag for a second croissant.

Ember watched her daughter dig through the pastries and again toyed with the silver pendant—a circle set atop two triangles. The Embrace, Hunt realized. The union of Solas and Cthona. Ember frowned. "Why," she asked Bryce, "is Hunt Athalar your roommate?"

"He was booted from the 33rd for his questionable fashion sense," she said, munching on the croissant. "I told him his boring black clothes don't bother me, and let him stay here."

Ember rolled her eyes. The exact same expression he'd seen on Bryce's face moments before. "Do you ever manage to get a straight answer out of her, Hunt? Because I've known her for twenty-five years and she's never given me one."

Bryce glared at her mother, then turned to Hunt. "Do not feel obligated to answer that."

Ember let out an outraged click of her tongue. "I wish I could say that the big city corrupted my lovely daughter, but she was this rude even before she left for university."

Hunt couldn't help his low chuckle. Randall leaned back on the couch. "It's true," Randall said. "You should have seen their fights. I don't think there was a single person in Nidaros who didn't hear them hollering at each other. It echoed off the gods-damned mountains."

Both Quinlan women scowled at him. That expression was the same, too.

Ember seemed to peer over their shoulders. "When was the last time you cleaned, Bryce Adelaide Quinlan?"

Bryce stiffened. *"Twenty minutes ago."*

"I can see dust on that coffee table."

"You. Can. Not."

Ember's eyes danced with devilish delight. "Does Athie know about JJ?"

Hunt couldn't stop himself from going rigid. JJ—an ex? She hadn't ever mentioned—Oh. Right. Hunt smirked. "Jelly Jubilee and I are good friends."

Bryce grumbled something he chose not to hear.

Ember leaned closer to the screen. "All right, Hunt. If she showed you JJ, then she's got to like you." Bryce, mercifully, refrained from mentioning to her parents how he'd discovered her doll collection in the first place. Ember continued, "So tell me about yourself."

Randall said flatly to his wife. "He's Hunt Athalar."

"I know," Ember said. "But all I've heard are horrible war stories. I want to know about the real male. And get a straight answer about why you're living in my daughter's guest room."

Bryce had warned him while they cleaned: *Do* not *say a word about the murders.*

But he had a feeling that Ember Quinlan could sniff out lies like a bloodhound, so Hunt smudged the truth. "Jesiba is working with my boss to find a stolen relic. With the Summit happening in two weeks, the barracks are overloaded with guests, so Bryce generously offered me a room to make working together easier."

"Sure," Ember said. "My daughter, who never once shared her precious Starlight Fancy toys with a single kid in Nidaros, but only let them *look* at the stupid things, offered up the entire guest room of her own goodwill."

Randall nudged his wife with a knee, a silent warning, perhaps, of a man used to keeping the peace between two highly opinionated women.

Bryce said, "This is why I told him to have a drink before we dialed you."

Ember sipped from her coffee. Randall picked up a newspaper from the table and began to flip through it. Ember asked, "So you won't let us come visit this weekend because of this case?"

Bryce winced. "Yes. It's not the sort of thing you guys could tag along on."

A hint of the warrior shone through as Randall's eyes sharpened. "It's dangerous?"

"No," Bryce lied. "But we need to be a little stealthy."

"And bringing along two humans," Ember said testily, "is the opposite of that?"

Bryce sighed at the ceiling. "Bringing along my *parents*," she countered, "would undermine my image as a cool antiquities dealer."

"*Assistant* antiquities dealer," her mother corrected.

"Ember," Randall warned.

Bryce's mouth tightened. Apparently, this was a conversation they'd had before. He wondered if Ember saw the flicker of hurt in her daughter's eyes.

It was enough that Hunt found himself saying, "Bryce knows more people in this city than I do—she's a pro at navigating all this. She's a real asset to the 33rd."

Ember considered him, her gaze frank. "Micah is your boss, isn't he?"

A polite way of putting what Micah was to him.

"Yeah," Hunt said. Randall was watching him now. "The best I've had."

Ember's stare fell on the tattoo across his brow. "That's not saying much."

"Mom, can we not?" Bryce sighed. "How's the pottery business?"

Ember opened her mouth, but Randall nudged her knee again, a silent plea to let it drop. "Business," Ember said tightly, "is going great."

Bryce knew her mother was a brewing tempest.

Hunt was kind to them, friendly even, well aware that her mom was now on a mission to figure out why he was here, and what existed between them. But he asked Randall about his job as co-head of an organization to help humans traumatized by their military service and asked her mom about her roadside stand selling pottery of fat babies lolling in various beds of vegetables.

Her mom and Hunt were currently debating which sunball players were best this season, and Randall was still flipping through the newspaper and chiming in every now and then.

It had gutted her to hear what had happened to Hunt's own mother. She kept the call going longer than usual because of it. Because he was right. Rubbing her aching leg beneath the table—she'd strained it again at some point during their cleaning—Bryce dug into her third croissant and said to Randall, "This still isn't as good as yours."

"Move back home," her dad said, "and you could have them every day."

"Yeah, yeah," she said, eating another mouthful. She massaged her thigh. "I thought you were supposed to be the cool parent. You've become even worse than Mom with the nagging."

"I was always worse than your mother," he said mildly. "I was just better at hiding it."

Bryce said to Hunt, "This is why my parents have to ambush me if they want to visit. I'd never let them through the door."

Hunt just glanced at her lap—her thigh—before he asked Ember, "Have you tried to get her to a medwitch for that leg?"

Bryce froze at exactly the same heartbeat as her mother.

"What's wrong with her leg?" Ember's eyes dropped to the lower half of her screen as if she could somehow see Bryce's leg beneath the camera's range, Randall following suit.

"Nothing," Bryce said, glaring at Hunt. "A busybody angel, that's what."

"It's the wound she got two years ago," Hunt answered. "It still hurts her." He rustled his wings, as if unable to help the impatient gesture. "And she still insists on running."

Ember's eyes filled with alarm. "Why would you do that, Bryce?"

Bryce set down her croissant. "It's none of anyone's business."

"Bryce," Randall said. "If it bothers you, you should see a medwitch."

"It doesn't bother me," Bryce said through her teeth.

"Then why have you been rubbing your leg under the counter?" Hunt drawled.

"Because I was trying to convince it not to kick you in the face, asshole," Bryce hissed.

"*Bryce*," her mother gasped. Randall's eyes widened.

But Hunt laughed. He rose, picking up the empty pastry bag and squishing it into a ball before tossing it into the trash can with the skill of one of his beloved sunball players. "I think the wound still has venom lingering from the demon who attacked her. If she doesn't get it checked out before the Drop, she'll be in pain for centuries."

Bryce shot to her feet, hiding her wince at the ripple of pain in her thigh. They'd never discussed it—that the kristallos's venom might indeed still be in her leg. "I don't need you deciding what is best for me, you—"

"Alphahole?" Hunt supplied, going to the sink and turning on the water. "We're partners. Partners look out for each other. If you won't listen to me about your gods-damned leg, then maybe you'll listen to your parents."

"How bad is it?" Randall asked quietly.

Bryce whirled back to the computer. "It's *fine*."

Randall pointed to the floor behind her. "Balance on that leg and tell me that again."

Bryce refused to move. Filling a glass of water, Hunt smiled, pure male satisfaction.

Ember reached for her phone, which she'd discarded on the cushions beside her. "I'll find the nearest medwitch and see if she can squeeze you in tomorrow—"

"I am not going to a medwitch," Bryce snarled, and grabbed the rim of the laptop. "It was great chatting with you. I'm tired. Good night."

Randall began to object, eyes shooting daggers at Ember, but Bryce slammed the laptop shut.

At the sink, Hunt was the portrait of smug, angelic arrogance. She aimed for her bedroom.

Ember, at least, waited two minutes before video-calling Bryce on her phone.

"Is your father behind this *case*?" Ember asked, venom coating each word. Even through the camera, her rage was palpable.

"Randall is not behind this," Bryce said dryly, flopping onto her bed.

"Your *other* father," Ember snapped. "This sort of arrangement reeks of him."

Bryce kept her face neutral. "No. Jesiba and Micah are working together. Hunt and I are mere pawns."

"Micah Domitus is a monster," Ember breathed.

"All the Archangels are. He's an arrogant ass, but not that bad."

Ember's eyes simmered. "Are you being careful?"

"I'm still taking birth control, yes."

"Bryce Adelaide Quinlan, you know what I mean."

"Hunt has my back." Even if he'd thrown her under the bus by mentioning her leg to them.

Her mom was having none of it. "I have no doubt that sorceress would push you into harm's way if it made her more money. Micah's no better. Hunt might have your back, but don't forget that these Vanir only look out for themselves. He's Micah's personal assassin, for fuck's sake. And one of the Fallen. The Asteri *hate* him. He's a slave because of it."

"He's a slave because we live in a fucked-up world." Hazy wrath fogged her vision, but she blinked it away.

Her dad called out from the kitchen, asking where the microwave popcorn was. Ember hollered back that it was in the same exact place it always was, her eyes never leaving the phone's camera. "I know you'll bite my head off for it, but let me just say this."

"Gods, Mom—"

"Hunt might be a good roommate, and he might be nice to look at, but remember that he's a Vanir male. A very, *very* powerful Vanir male, even with those tattoos keeping him in line. He and every male like him is lethal."

"Yeah, and you never let me forget it." It was an effort not to look at the tiny scar on her mom's cheekbone.

Old shadows banked the light in her mom's eyes, and Bryce winced. "Seeing you with an older Vanir male—"

"I'm not *with* him, Mom—"

"It brings me back to that place, Bryce." She ran a hand through her dark hair. "I'm sorry."

Her mom might as well have punched her in the heart.

Bryce wished she could reach through the camera and wrap her arms around her, breathing in her honeysuckle-and-nutmeg scent.

Then Ember said, "I'll make some calls and get that medwitch appointment for your leg."

Bryce scowled. "No, thanks."

"You're going to that appointment, Bryce."

Bryce turned the phone and stretched out her leg over the covers so her mother could see. She rotated her foot. "See? No problems."

Her mother's face hardened to steel that matched the wedding band on her finger. "Just because Danika died doesn't mean you need to suffer, too."

Bryce stared at her mother, who was always so good at cutting to the heart of everything, at rendering her into rubble with a few words. "It doesn't have anything to do with that."

"*Bullshit*, Bryce." Her mom's eyes glazed with tears. "You think

Danika would want you limping in pain for the rest of your existence? You think she would've wanted you to stop dancing?"

"I don't want to talk about Danika." Her voice trembled.

Ember shook her head in disgust. "I'll message the medwitch's address and number when I get the appointment for you. Good night."

She hung up without another word.

57

Thirty minutes later, Bryce had changed into her sleep shorts and was brooding on her bed when a knock thumped on the door. "You're a fucking traitor, Athalar," she called.

Hunt opened the door and leaned against its frame. "No wonder you moved here, if you and your mom fight so much."

The instinct to strangle him was overwhelming, but she said, "I've never seen my mom back down from a fight. It rubbed off, I guess." She scowled at him. "What do you want?"

Hunt pushed off the door and approached. The room became too small with each step closer. Too airless. He stopped at the foot of her mattress. "I'll go to the medwitch appointment with you."

"I'm not going."

"Why?"

She sucked in a breath. And then it all burst out. "Because once that wound is gone, once it stops hurting, then *Danika* is gone. The Pack of Devils is gone." She shoved back the blankets, revealing her bare legs, and hitched up her silk sleep shorts so the full, twisting scar was visible. "It will all be some memory, some dream that happened for a flash and then was gone. But this scar and the pain . . ." Her eyes stung. "I can't let it be erased. I can't let *them* be erased."

Hunt slowly sat beside her on the bed, as if giving her time to object. His hair skimmed his brow, the tattoo, as he studied the scar. And ran a calloused finger over it.

The touch left her skin prickling in its wake.

"You're not going to erase Danika and the pack if you help yourself."

Bryce shook her head, looking toward the window, but his fingers closed around her chin. He gently turned her face back to his. His dark, depthless eyes were soft. Understanding.

How many people ever saw those eyes this way? Ever saw *him* this way?

"Your mother loves you. She cannot—literally, on a biological level, Bryce—bear the thought of you in pain." He let go of her chin, but his eyes remained on hers. "Neither can I."

"You barely know me."

"You're my friend." The words hung between them. His head dipped again, as if he could hide the expression on his face as he amended, "If you would like me to be."

For a moment, she stared at him. The offer thrown out there. The quiet vulnerability. It erased any annoyance still in her veins.

"Didn't you know, Athalar?" The tentative hope in his face nearly destroyed her. "We've been friends from the moment you thought Jelly Jubilee was a dildo."

He tipped back his head and laughed, and Bryce scooted back on the bed. Propped up the pillows and turned on the TV. She patted the space beside her.

Grinning, eyes full of light in a way she'd never seen before, he sat beside her. Then he pulled out his phone and snapped a picture of her.

Bryce blew out a breath, her smile fading as she surveyed him. "My mom went through a lot. I know she's not easy to deal with, but thanks for being so cool with her."

"I like your mom," Hunt said, and she believed him. "How'd she and your dad meet?"

Bryce knew he meant Randall. "My mom ran from my biological father before he found out she was pregnant. She wound up at a temple to Cthona in Korinth, and knew the priestesses there would take her in—shield her—since she was a holy pregnant vessel or whatever." Bryce snorted. "She gave birth to me there, and I spent the first three years of my life cloistered behind the temple walls. My mom did their laundry to earn our keep. Long story short, my biological father heard a rumor that she had a child and sent goons to hunt her down." She ground her teeth. "He told them that if there was a child that was undoubtedly his, they were to bring me to him. At any cost."

Hunt's mouth thinned. "Shit."

"They had eyes at every depot, but the priestesses got us out of the city—with the hope of getting us all the way to the House of Earth and Blood headquarters in Hilene, where my mom could beg for asylum. Even my father wouldn't dare infringe on their territory. But it's a three-day drive, and none of the Korinth priestesses had the ability to defend us against Fae warriors. So we drove the five hours to Solas's Temple in Oia, partially to rest, but also to pick up our holy guard."

"Randall." Hunt smiled. But he arched a brow. "Wait—Randall was a sun-priest?"

"Not quite. He'd gotten back from the front a year before, but the stuff he did and saw while he was serving . . . It messed with him. Really badly. He didn't want to go home, couldn't face his family. So he'd offered himself as an acolyte to Solas, hoping that it'd somehow atone for his past. He was two weeks away from swearing his vows when the High Priest asked him to escort us to Hilene. Many of the priests are trained warriors, but Randall was the only human, and the High Priest guessed my mother wouldn't trust a Vanir male. Right before we reached Hilene, my father's people caught up with us. They expected to find a helpless, hysterical female." Bryce smiled again. "What they found was a legendary sharpshooter and a mother who would move the earth itself to keep her daughter."

Hunt straightened. "What happened?"

"What you might expect. My parents dealt with the mess afterward." She glanced at him. "Please don't tell that to anyone. It . . . There were never any questions about the Fae that didn't return to Crescent City. I don't want any to come up now."

"I won't say a word."

Bryce smiled grimly. "After that, the House of Earth and Blood literally deemed my mother a vessel for Cthona and Randall a vessel for Solas, and blah blah religious crap, but it basically amounted to an official order of protection that my father didn't dare fuck with. And Randall finally went home, bringing us with him, and obviously didn't swear his vows to Solas." Her smile warmed. "He proposed by the end of the year. They've been disgustingly in love ever since."

Hunt smiled back. "It's nice to hear that sometimes things work out for good people."

"Yeah. Sometimes." A taut silence stretched between them. In her bed—they were in her bed, and just this morning, she'd fantasized about him going down on her atop the kitchen counter—

Bryce swallowed hard. "*Fangs and Bangs* is on in five minutes. You want to watch?"

Hunt smiled slowly, as if he knew precisely why she'd swallowed, but lay back on the pillows, his wings sprawled beneath him. A predator content to wait for his prey to come to him.

Fucking Hel. But Hunt winked at her, tucking an arm behind his head. The motion made the muscles down his biceps ripple. His eyes glittered, as if he was well aware of that, too. "Hel yes."

Hunt hadn't realized how badly he needed to ask it. How badly he'd needed her answer.

Friends. It didn't remotely cover whatever was between them, but it was true.

He leaned against the towering headboard, the two of them watching the raunchy show. But by the time they reached the halfway point of the episode, she'd begun to make comments about the inane plot. And he'd begun to join her.

Another show came on, a reality competition with different Vanir performing feats of strength and agility, and it felt only natural to watch that, too. All of it felt only natural. He let himself settle into the feeling.

And wasn't that the most dangerous thing he'd ever done.

58

Her mother messaged while she was dressing for work the next morning, with the time and location of a medwitch appointment. *Eleven today. It's five blocks from the gallery. Please go.*

Bryce didn't write back. She certainly wouldn't be going to the appointment.

Not when she had another one scheduled with the Meat Market.

Hunt had wanted to wait until night, but Bryce knew that the vendors would be much more likely to chat during the quieter daytime hours, when they wouldn't be trying to entice the usual evening buyers.

"You're quiet again today," Bryce murmured as they wove through the cramped pathways of the warehouse. This was the third they'd visited so far—the other two had quickly proven fruitless.

No, the vendors didn't know anything about drugs. No, that was a stereotype of the Meat Market that they did not appreciate. No, they did not know anyone who might help them. No, they were not interested in marks for information, because they really did not know anything useful at all.

Hunt had stayed a few stalls away during every discussion, because no one would talk with a legionary and Fallen slave.

Hunt held his wings tucked in tight. "Don't think I've forgotten that we're missing that medwitch appointment right now."

She never should have mentioned it.

"I don't remember giving you permission to shove your nose into my business."

"We're back to that?" He huffed a laugh. "I'd think cuddling in front of the TV allowed me to at least be able to *voice* my opinions without getting my head bitten off."

She rolled her eyes. "We didn't cuddle."

"What is it you want, exactly?" Hunt asked, surveying a stall full of ancient knives. "A boyfriend or mate or husband who will just sit there, with no opinions, and agree to everything you say, and never dare to ask you for anything?"

"Of course not."

"Just because I'm male and have an opinion doesn't make me into some psychotic, domineering prick."

She shoved her hands into the pockets of Danika's leather jacket. "Look, my mom went through a lot thanks to some psychotic, domineering pricks."

"I know." His eyes softened. "But even so, look at her and your dad. He voices his opinions. And he seems pretty damn psychotic when it comes to protecting both of you."

"You have no idea," Bryce grumbled. "I didn't go on a single date until I got to CCU."

Hunt's brows rose. "Really? I would have thought . . ." He shook his head.

"Thought what?"

He shrugged. "That the human boys would have been crawling around after you."

It was an effort not to glance at him, with the way he said *human boys*, as if they were some other breed than him—a full-grown malakh male.

She supposed they were, technically, but that hint of masculine arrogance . . . "Well, if they wanted to, they didn't dare show it. Randall was practically a god to them, and though he never said anything, they all got it into their heads that I was firmly off-limits."

"That wouldn't have been a good enough reason for me to stay away."

Her cheeks heated at the way his voice lowered. "Well, idolizing Randall aside, I was also different." She gestured to her pointed ears. Her tall body. "Too Fae for humans. Woe is me, right?"

"It builds character," he said, examining a stall full of opals of every color: white, black, red, blue, green. Iridescent veins ran through them, like preserved arteries from the earth itself.

"What are these for?" he asked the black-feathered, humanoid female at the stall. A magpie.

"They're luck charms," the magpie said, waving a feathery hand over the trays of gems. "White is for joy; green for wealth; red for love and fertility; blue for wisdom . . . Take your pick."

Hunt asked, "What's the black for?"

The magpie's onyx-colored mouth curved upward. "For the opposite of luck." She tapped one of the black opals, kept contained within a glass dome. "Slip it under the pillow of your enemy and see what happens to them."

Bryce cleared her throat. "Interesting as that may be—"

Hunt held out a silver mark. "For the white."

Bryce's brows rose, but the magpie swept up the mark, and plunked the white opal into Hunt's awaiting palm. They left, ignoring her gratitude for their business.

"I didn't peg you for superstitious," Bryce said.

But Hunt paused at the end of the row of stalls and took her hand. He pressed the opal into it, the stone warm from his touch. The size of a crow's egg, it shimmered in the firstlights high above.

"You could use some joy," Hunt said quietly.

Something bright sparked in her chest. "So could you," she said, attempting to press the opal back into his palm.

But Hunt stepped away. "It's a gift."

Bryce's face warmed again, and she looked anywhere but at him as she smiled. Even though she could feel his gaze lingering on her face while she slid the opal into the pocket of her jacket.

* * *

The opal had been stupid. Impulsive.

Likely bullshit, but Bryce had pocketed it, at least. She hadn't commented on how rusty his skills were, since it had been two hundred years since he'd last thought to buy something for a female.

Shahar would have smiled at the opal—and forgotten about it soon after. She'd had troves of jewels in her alabaster palace: diamonds the size of sunballs; solid blocks of emerald stacked like bricks; veritable bathtubs filled with rubies. A small white opal, even for joy, would have been like a grain of sand on a miles-long beach. She'd have appreciated the gift but, ultimately, let it disappear into a drawer somewhere. And he, so dedicated to their cause, would probably have forgotten about it, too.

Hunt clenched his jaw as Bryce strode for a hide stall. The teenager—a feline shifter from her scent—was in her lanky humanoid form and watched them approach from where she perched on a stool. Her brown braid draped over a shoulder, nearly grazing the phone idly held in her hands.

"Hey," Bryce said, pointing toward a pile of shaggy rugs. "How much for one of them?"

"Twenty silvers," the shifter said, sounding as bored as she looked.

Bryce smirked, running a hand over the white pelt. Hunt's skin tightened over his bones. He'd felt that touch the other night, stroking him to sleep. And could feel it now as she petted the sheepskin. "Twenty silvers for a snowsheep hide? Isn't that a little low?"

"My mom makes me work weekends. It'd piss her off to sell it for what it's actually worth."

"Loyal of you," Bryce said, chuckling. She leaned in, her voice dropping. "This is going to sound *so* random, but I have a question for you."

Hunt kept back, watching her work. The irreverent, down-to-earth party girl, merely looking to score some new drugs.

The shifter barely looked up. "Yeah?"

Bryce said, "You know where I can get anything . . . fun around here?"

The girl rolled her chestnut-colored eyes. "All right. Let's hear it."

"Hear what?" Bryce asked innocently.

The shifter lifted her phone, typing away with rainbow-painted nails. "That fake-ass act you gave everyone else here, and in the two other warehouses." She held up her phone. "We're all on a group chat." She gestured to everyone in the market around them. "I got, like, ten warnings you two would be coming through here, asking cheesy questions about drugs or whatever."

It was, perhaps, the first time Hunt had seen Bryce at a loss for words. So he stepped up to her side. "All right," he said to the teenager. "But *do* you know anything?"

The girl looked him over. "You think the Vipe would allow shit like that synth in here?"

"She allows every other depravity and crime," Hunt said through his teeth.

"Yeah, but she's not dumb," the shifter said, tossing her braid over a shoulder.

"So you've heard of it," Bryce said.

"The Vipe told me to tell you that it's nasty, and she doesn't deal in it, and never will."

"But someone does?" Bryce said tightly.

This was bad. This would not end well at all—

"The Vipe also told me to say you should check the river." She went back to her phone, presumably to tell *the Vipe* that she'd conveyed the message. "That's the place for that kinda shit."

"What do you mean?" Bryce asked.

A shrug. "Ask the mer."

"We should lay out the facts," Hunt said as Bryce stormed for the Meat Market's docks. "Before we run to the mer, accusing them of being drug dealers."

"Too late," Bryce said.

He hadn't been able to stop her from sending a message via otter to Tharion twenty minutes ago, and sure as Hel hadn't been able to stop her from heading for the river's edge to wait.

Hunt gripped her arm, the dock mere steps away. "Bryce, the mer do *not* take kindly to being falsely accused—"

"Who said it's false?"

"Tharion isn't a drug dealer, and he sure as shit isn't selling something as bad as synth seems to be."

"He might know someone who is." She shrugged out of his grasp. "We've been dicking around for long enough. I want answers. Now." She narrowed her eyes. "Don't you want to get this over with? So you can have your *sentence* reduced?"

He did, but he said, "The synth probably has *nothing* to do with this. We shouldn't—"

But she'd already reached the wood slats of the dock, not daring to look into the eddying water beneath. The Meat Market's docks were notorious dumping grounds. And feeding troughs for aquatic scavengers.

Water splashed, and then a powerful male body was sitting on the end of the dock. "This part of the river is gross," Tharion said by way of greeting.

Bryce didn't smile. Didn't say anything other than, "Who's selling synth in the river?"

The grin vanished from Tharion's face. Hunt began to object, but the mer said, "Not in, Legs." He shook his head. "*On* the river."

"So it's true, then. It's—it's what? A healing drug that leaked from a lab? Who's behind it?"

Hunt stepped up to her side. "Tharion—"

"Danika Fendyr," Tharion said, his eyes soft. Like he knew who Danika had been to her. "The intel came in a day before her death. She was spotted doing a deal on a boat just past here."

59

What do you mean, *Danika* was selling it?"

Tharion shook his head. "I don't know if she was selling it or buying it or what, but right before synth started appearing on the streets, she was spotted on an Auxiliary boat in the dead of night. There was a crate of synth on board."

Hunt murmured, "It always comes back to Danika."

Above the roaring in her head, Bryce said, "Maybe she was confiscating it."

"Maybe," Tharion admitted, then ran a hand through his auburn hair. "But that synth—it's some bad shit, Bryce. If Danika was involved in it—"

"She wasn't. She never would have done something like that." Her heart was racing so fast she thought she'd puke. She turned to Hunt. "But it explains why there were traces of it on her clothes, if she had to confiscate it for the Aux."

Hunt's face was grim. "Maybe."

She crossed her arms. "What is it, exactly?"

"It's synthetic magic," Tharion said, eyes darting between them. "It started off as an aid for healing, but someone apparently realized that in super-concentrated doses, it can give humans strength greater than most Vanir. For short bursts, but it's potent. They've tried to make it for centuries, but it seemed impossible. Most people thought it was akin to alchemy—just as unlikely as turning something into gold. But apparently modern science made it work this time." He angled his head. "Does this have to do with the demon you were hunting?"

"It's a possibility," Hunt said.

"I'll let you know if I get any other reports," Tharion said, and didn't wait for a farewell before diving back into the water.

Bryce stared out at the river in the midday sun, gripping the white opal in her pocket.

"I know it wasn't what you wanted to hear," Hunt said cautiously beside her.

"Was she killed by whoever is creating the synth? If she was on that boat to seize their shipment?" She tucked a strand of hair behind her ear. "Could the person selling the synth and the person searching for the Horn be the same, if the synth can possibly repair the Horn?"

He rubbed his chin. "I guess. But this could also be a dead end."

She sighed. "I don't get why she never mentioned it."

"Maybe it wasn't worth mentioning," he suggested.

"Maybe," she murmured. "Maybe."

Bryce waited until Hunt hit the gym in her apartment building before she dialed Fury.

She didn't know why she bothered. Fury hadn't taken a call from her in months.

The call nearly went to audiomail before she answered. "Hey."

Bryce slumped against her bed and blurted, "I'm shocked you picked up."

"You caught me between jobs."

Or maybe Juniper had bitten Fury's head off about bailing.

Bryce said, "I thought you were coming back to hunt down whoever was behind the Raven's bombing."

"I thought so, too, but it turned out I didn't need to cross the Haldren to do it."

Bryce leaned against her headboard, stretching out her legs. "So it really was the human rebellion behind it?" Maybe that *C* on the crates Ruhn thought was the Horn was just that: a letter.

"Yeah. Specifics and names are classified, though."

Fury had said that to her so many times in the past that she'd lost count. "At least tell me if you found them?"

There was a good chance that Fury was sharpening her arsenal of weapons on the desk of whatever fancy hotel she was holed up in right now. "I said I was between jobs, didn't I?"

"Congratulations?"

A soft laugh that still freaked Bryce the fuck out. "Sure." Fury paused. "What's up, B."

As if that somehow erased two years of near-silence. "Did Danika ever mention synth to you?"

Bryce could have sworn something heavy and metallic clunked in the background. Fury said softly, "Who told you about synth?"

Bryce straightened. "I think it's getting spread around here. I met a mer today who said Danika was seen on an Aux boat with a crate of it, right before she died." She blew out a breath.

"It's dangerous, Bryce. Really dangerous. Don't fuck around with it."

"I'm not." Gods. "I haven't touched any drugs in two years." Then she added, unable to stop herself, "If you'd bothered to take my calls or visit, you would have known that."

"I've been busy."

Liar. Fucking liar and coward. Bryce ground out, "Look, I wanted to know if Danika had ever mentioned synth to you before she died, because she didn't mention it to me."

Another one of those pauses.

"She did, didn't she." Even now, Bryce wasn't sure why jealousy seared her chest.

"She might have said that there was some nasty shit being sold," Fury said.

"You never thought to mention it to anyone?"

"I did. To you. At the White Raven the night Danika died. Someone tried to sell it to you then, for fuck's sake. I told you to stay the Hel away from it."

"And you still didn't find the chance to mention then or after Danika died that she warned you about it in the first place?"

"A demon ripped her to shreds, Bryce. Drug busts didn't seem connected to it."

"And what if it was?"

"How?"

"I don't know, I just . . ." Bryce tapped her foot on the bed. "Why wouldn't she have told me?"

"Because . . ." Fury stopped herself.

"Because *what*?" Bryce snapped.

"All right," Fury said, her voice sharpening. "Danika didn't want to tell you because she didn't want you getting near it. Even *thinking* about trying synth."

Bryce shot to her feet. "Why the *fuck* would I ever—"

"Because we have literally seen you take everything."

"You've been right there, taking everything with me, you—"

"Synth is *synthetic magic*, Bryce. To replace *real* magic. Of which you have *none*. It gives humans Vanir powers and strength for like an hour. And then it can seriously fuck you up. Make you addicted and worse. For the Vanir, it's even riskier—a crazy high and superstrength, but it can easily turn bad. Danika didn't want you even knowing something like that existed."

"As if I'm so desperate to be like you big, tough Vanir that I'd take something—"

"Her goal was to protect you. *Always*. Even from yourself."

The words struck like a slap to the face. Bryce's throat closed up.

Fury blew out a breath. "Look, I know that came out harsh. But take my word for it: don't mess with synth. If they've actually managed to mass-produce the stuff outside of an official lab and make it in even stronger concentrations, then it's bad news. Stay away from it, and anyone who deals in it."

Bryce's hands shook, but she managed to say "All right" without sounding like she was one breath away from crying.

"Look, I gotta go," Fury said. "I've got something to do tonight. But I'll be back in Lunathion in a few days. I'm wanted at the

Summit in two weeks—it's at some compound a few hours outside the city."

Bryce didn't ask why Fury Axtar would attend a Summit of various Valbaran leaders. She didn't really care that Fury would be coming back at all.

"Maybe we can grab a meal," Fury said.

"Sure."

"Bryce." Her name was both a reprimand and an apology. Fury sighed. "I'll see you."

Her throat burned, but she hung up. Took a few long breaths. Fury could go to Hel.

Bryce waited to call her brother until she'd plunked her ass down on the couch, opened her laptop, and pulled up the search engine. He answered on the second ring. "Yeah?"

"I want you to spare me the lectures and the warnings and all that shit, okay?"

Ruhn paused. "Okay."

She put the call on speaker and leaned her forearms on her knees, the cursor hanging over the search bar.

Ruhn asked, "What's going on with you and Athalar?"

"Nothing," Bryce said, rubbing her eyes. "He's not my type."

"I was asking about why he's not on the call, not whether you're dating, but that's good to know."

She gritted her teeth and typed *synthetic magic* in the search bar. As the results filtered in, she said, "*Athalar* is off making those muscles of his even nicer." Ruhn huffed a laugh.

She skimmed the results: small, short articles about the uses of a synthetic healing magic to aid in human healing. "That medwitch who sent you the information about synthetic magic—did she offer any thoughts on why or how it got onto the streets?"

"No. I think she's more concerned about its origins—and an antidote. She told me she actually tested some of the kristallos venom she got out of Athalar from the other night against the synth, trying to formulate one. She thinks her healing magic can act like some kind of stabilizer for the venom to make the antidote, but she needs more of the venom to keep testing it out. I don't know. It sounded like some complex shit." He added wryly, "If you run into a kristallos, ask it for some venom, would you?"

"Got a crush, Ruhn?"

He snorted. "She's done us a huge favor. I'd like to repay her in whatever way we can."

"All right." She clicked through more results, including a patent filing from Redner Industries for the drug, dating back ten years. Way before Danika's time working there.

"The research papers say only tiny amounts are released, even for the medwitches and their healing. It's incredibly expensive and difficult to make."

"What if . . . what if the formula and a shipment leaked two years ago from Redner, and Danika was sent out to track it down. And maybe she realized whoever wanted to steal the synth planned to use it to repair the Horn, and she stole the Horn before they could. And then they killed her for it."

"But why keep it a secret?" Ruhn asked. "Why not bust the person behind it?"

"I don't know. It's just a theory." Better than nothing.

Ruhn went quiet again. She had the feeling a Serious Talk was coming and braced herself. "I think it's admirable, Bryce. That you still care enough about Danika and the Pack of Devils to keep looking into this."

"I was ordered to by my boss and the Governor, remember?"

"You would have looked once you heard it wasn't Briggs anyway." He sighed. "You know, Danika nearly beat the shit out of me once."

"No she didn't."

"Oh, she did. We ran into each other in Redner Tower's lobby when I went to meet up with Declan after some fancy meeting he was having with their top people. Wait—you dated that prick son of Redner's, didn't you?"

"I did," she said tightly.

"Gross. Just gross, Bryce."

"Tell me about Danika wiping the floor with your pathetic ass."

She could nearly hear his smile through the phone. "I don't know how we got into it about you, but we did."

"What'd you say?"

"Why are you assuming I did the instigating? Did you ever meet Danika? She had a mouth on her like I've never seen." He clicked his tongue, the admiration in the noise making Bryce's chest clench. "Anyway, I told her to tell you that I was sorry. She told me to go fuck myself, and fuck my apology."

Bryce blinked. "She never told me she ran into you."

"*Ran into* is an understatement." He whistled. "She hadn't even made the Drop, and she nearly kicked my balls across the lobby. Declan had to . . . involve himself to stop it."

It sounded like Danika all right. Even if everything else she'd learned lately didn't.

60

It's a stretch," Hunt said an hour later from his spot beside her on the sectional. She'd filled him in on her latest theory, his brows rising with each word out of her mouth.

Bryce clicked through the pages on Redner Industries' website. "Danika worked part-time at Redner. She rarely talked about the shit she did for them. Some kind of security division." She pulled up the login page. "Maybe her old work account still has info on her assignments."

Her fingers shook only slightly as she typed in Danika's username, having seen it so many times on her phone in the past: *dfendyr.*

DFendyr—Defender. She'd never realized it until now. Fury's harsh words rang through her head. Bryce ignored them.

She typed in one of Danika's usual half-assed passwords: 1234567. Nothing.

"Again," Hunt said warily, "it's a stretch." He leaned back against the cushions. "We're better off doubling down with Danaan on looking for the Horn, not chasing down this drug."

Bryce countered, "Danika was involved in this synth stuff and never said a word. You don't think that's weird? You don't think there might be something more here?"

"She also didn't tell you the truth about Philip Briggs," Hunt said carefully. "Or that she stole the Horn. Keeping things from you could have been standard for her."

Bryce just typed in another password. Then another. And another.

"We need the full picture, Hunt," she said, trying again. *She* needed the full picture. "It all ties together somehow."

But every password failed. Every one of Danika's usual combinations.

Bryce shut her eyes, foot bouncing on the carpet as she recited, "The Horn could possibly be healed by the synth in a large enough dose. Synthetic magic has obsidian salt as one of its ingredients. The kristallos can be summoned by obsidian salt . . ." Hunt remained silent as she thought it through. "The kristallos was bred to track the Horn. The kristallos's venom can eat away at magic. The medwitch wants some venom to test if it's possible to create an antidote to synth with her magic or something."

"What?"

Her eyes opened. "Ruhn told me." She filled him in on Ruhn's half-joking request for more venom to give the medwitch.

Hunt's eyes darkened. "Interesting. If the synth is on the verge of becoming a deadly street drug . . . we should help her get the venom."

"What about the Horn?"

His jaw tightened. "We'll keep looking. But if this drug explodes—not just in this city but across the territory, the world . . . that antidote is vital." He scanned her face. "How can we get our hands on some venom for her?"

Bryce breathed, "If we summon a kristallos—"

"We don't take that risk," Hunt snarled. "We'll figure out how to get the venom another way."

"I can handle myself—"

"*I* can't fucking handle myself, Quinlan. Not if you might be in danger."

His words rippled between them. Emotion glinted in his eyes, if she dared to read what was there.

But Hunt's phone buzzed, and he lifted his hips off the couch to pull it from the back pocket of his pants. He glanced at the screen, and his wings shifted, tucking in slightly.

"Micah?" she dared ask.

"Just some legion shit," he murmured, and stood. "I gotta head out for a few. Naomi will take watch." He gestured to the computer. "Keep trying if you want, but let's *think*, Bryce, before we do anything drastic to get our hands on that venom."

"Yeah, yeah."

It was apparently acceptance enough for Hunt to leave, but not before ruffling her hair and leaning down to whisper, his lips brushing the curve of her ear, "JJ would be proud of you." Her toes curled in her slippers, and stayed that way long after he'd left.

After trying another few password options, Bryce sighed and shut the computer. They were narrowing in on it—the truth. She could feel it.

But would she be ready for it?

Her cycle arrived the next morning like a gods-damned train barreling into her body, which Bryce decided was fitting, given what day it was.

She stepped into the great room to find Hunt making breakfast, his hair still mussed with sleep. He stiffened at her approach, though. Then he turned, his eyes darting over her. His preternatural sense of smell missed nothing. "You're bleeding."

"Every three months, like clockwork." Pure-blooded Fae rarely had a cycle at all; humans had it monthly—she'd somehow settled somewhere in between.

She slid onto a stool at the kitchen counter. A glance at her phone showed no messages from Juniper or Fury. Not even a message from her mom biting her head off about bailing on the medwitch appointment.

"You need anything?" Hunt extended a plate of eggs and bacon toward her. Then a cup of coffee.

"I took something for the cramps." She sipped her coffee. "But thanks."

He grunted, going back to plating his own breakfast. He stood on the other side of the counter and wolfed down a few bites before he said, "Beyond the synth stuff and the antidote, I think the Horn ties everything together. We should concentrate on looking for it. There hasn't been a murder since the temple guard, but I doubt the person has dropped the search for it since they've already gone to such trouble. If we get our hands on the Horn, I still feel like the killer will save us the trouble of looking for them and come right to us."

"Or maybe they found wherever Danika hid it already." She took another bite. "Maybe they're just waiting until the Summit or something."

"Maybe. If that's the case, then we need to figure out who has it. Immediately."

"But even Ruhn can't find it. Danika didn't leave any hint of where she hid it. None of her last known locations were likely hiding spots."

"So maybe today we go back to square one. Look at everything we've learned and—"

"I can't today." She finished off her breakfast and brought the plate over to the sink. "I've got some meetings."

"Reschedule them."

"Jesiba needs them held today."

He looked at her for a long moment, as if he could see through everything she'd said, but finally nodded.

She ignored the disappointment and concern in his face, his tone, as he said, "All right."

Lehabah sighed. "You're being mean today, BB. And don't blame it on your cycle."

Seated at the table in the heart of the gallery's library, Bryce massaged her brows with her thumb and forefinger. "Sorry."

Her phone lay dark and quiet on the table beside her.

"You didn't invite Athie down here for lunch."

"I didn't need the distraction." The lie was smooth. Hunt hadn't called her on the other lie, either—that Jesiba was watching the gallery cameras today, so he should stay on the roof.

But despite needing him, needing everyone, at arm's length today, and despite claiming she couldn't look for the Horn, she'd been combing over various texts regarding it for hours now. There was nothing in them but the same information, over and over.

A faint scratching sound stretched across the entire length of the library. Bryce pulled over Lehabah's tablet and cranked up the volume on the speakers, blasting music through the space.

A loud, angry *thump* sounded. From the corner of her eye, she watched the nøkk swim off, its translucent tail slashing through the dim water.

Pop music: Who would have thought it was such a strong deterrent for the creature?

"He wants to kill me," Lehabah whispered. "I can tell."

"I doubt you'd make a very satisfying snack," Bryce said. "Not even a mouthful."

"He knows that if I'm submerged in water, I'm dead in a heartbeat."

It was another form of torture for the sprite, Bryce had realized early on. A way for Jesiba to keep Lehabah in line down here, caged within a cage, as surely as all the other animals throughout the space. No better way to intimidate a fire sprite than to have a hundred-thousand-gallon tank looming.

"He wants to kill you, too," Lehabah whispered. "You ignore him, and he hates that. I can see the rage and hunger in his eyes when he looks at you, BB. Be careful when you feed him."

"I am." The feeding hatch was too small for it to fit through anyway. And since the nøkk wouldn't dare bring its head above the water for fear of the air, only its arms were a threat if the hatch was opened and the feeding platform was lowered into the water. But it kept to the bottom of the tank, hiding among the rocks whenever she dumped in the steaks, letting them drift lazily down.

It wanted to hunt. Wanted something big, juicy, and frightened.

Bryce glanced toward the dim tank, illuminated by three

built-in spotlights. "Jesiba will get bored with him soon and gift him to a client," she lied to Lehabah.

"Why does she collect us at all?" the sprite whispered. "Am I not a person, too?" She pointed to the tattoo on her wrist. "Why do they insist on this?"

"Because we live in a republic that has decided that threats to its order have to be punished—and punished so thoroughly that it makes others hesitate to rebel, too." Her words were flat. Cold.

"Have you ever thought of what it might be like—without the Asteri?"

Bryce shot her a look. "Be quiet, Lehabah."

"But BB—"

"Be *quiet*, Lehabah." There were cameras everywhere in this library, all with audio. They were exclusive to Jesiba, yes, but to speak of it here . . .

Lehabah drifted to her little couch. "Athie would talk to me about it."

"Athie is a slave with little left to lose."

"Don't say such things, BB," Lehabah hissed. "There is *always* something left to lose."

Bryce was in a foul spirit. Maybe there was something going on with Ruhn or Juniper. Hunt had seen her checking her phone frequently this morning, as if waiting for a call or message. None had come. At least, as far as he could tell on the walk to the gallery. And, judging by the distant, sharp look still on her face as she left just before sunset, none had come in during the day, either.

But she didn't head home. She went to a bakery.

Hunt kept to the rooftops nearby, watching while she walked into the aqua-painted interior and walked out three minutes later with a white box in her hands.

Then she turned her steps toward the river, dodging workers and tourists and shoppers all enjoying the end of the day. If she was aware that he followed, she didn't seem to care. Didn't even look up once as she aimed for a wooden bench along the river walkway.

The setting sun gilded the mists veiling the Bone Quarter. A few feet down the paved walkway, the dark arches of the Black Dock loomed. No mourning families stood beneath them today, waiting for the onyx boat to take their coffin.

Bryce sat on the bench overlooking the river and the Sleeping City, the white bakery box beside her, and checked her phone again.

Sick of waiting until she deigned to talk to him about whatever was eating her up, Hunt landed quietly before sliding onto the bench's wooden planks, the box between them. "What's up?"

Bryce stared out at the river. She looked drained. Like that first night he'd seen her, in the legion's holding center.

She still wasn't looking at him when she said, "Danika would have been twenty-five today."

Hunt went still. "It's . . . Today's Danika's birthday."

She glanced to her phone, discarded at her side. "No one remembered. Not Juniper or Fury—not even my mom. Last year, they remembered, but . . . I guess it was a onetime thing."

"You could have asked them."

"I know they're busy. And . . ." She ran a hand through her hair. "Honestly, I thought they'd remember. I *wanted* them to remember. Even just a message saying something bullshitty, like *I miss her* or whatever."

"What's in the box?"

"Chocolate croissants," she said hoarsely. "Danika always wanted them on her birthday. They were her favorite."

Hunt looked from the box to her, then to the looming Bone Quarter across the river. How many croissants had he seen her eating these weeks? Perhaps in part because they connected her to Danika the same way that scar on her thigh did. When he looked back at her, her mouth was a tight, trembling line.

"It sucks," she said, her voice thick. "It sucks that everyone just . . . moves on, and forgets. They expect me to forget. But I can't." She rubbed at her chest. "I *can't* forget. And maybe it's fucking weird that I bought my dead friend a bunch of birthday croissants. But the world moved on. Like she never existed."

He watched her for a long moment. Then he said, "Shahar was that for me. I'd never met anyone like her. I think I loved her from the moment I laid eyes on her in her palace, even though she was so high above me that she might as well have been the moon. But she saw me too. And somehow, she picked me. Out of all of them, she picked me." He shook his head, the words creaking from him as they crept from that box he'd locked them in all this while. "I would have done anything for her. I *did* anything for her. Anything she asked. And when it all went to Hel, when they told me it was over, I refused to believe it. How could she be gone? It was like saying the sun was gone. It just . . . there was nothing left if she wasn't there." He ran a hand through his hair. "This won't be a consolation, but it took me about fifty years before I really believed it. That it was over. Yet even now . . ."

"You still love her that much?"

He held her gaze, unflinching. "After my mother died, I basically fell into my grief. But Shahar—she brought me out of that. Made me feel alive for the first time. Aware of myself, of my potential. I'll always love her, if only for that."

She looked to the river. "I never realized it," she murmured. "That you and I are mirrors."

He hadn't, either. But a voice floated back to him. *You look how I feel every day*, she'd whispered when she'd cleaned him up after Micah's latest assignment. "Is it a bad thing?"

A half smile tugged at a corner of her mouth. "No. No, it isn't."

"No issue with the Umbra Mortis being your emotional twin?"

But her face grew serious again. "That's what they call you, but that's not who you are."

"And who am I?"

"A pain in my ass." Her smile was brighter than the setting sun on the river. He laughed, but she added, "You're my friend. Who watches trashy TV with me and puts up with my shit. You're the person I don't need to explain myself to—not when it matters. You see everything I am, and you don't run away from it."

He smiled at her, let it convey everything that glowed inside him at her words. "I like that."

Color stained her cheeks, but she blew out a breath as she turned toward the box. "Well, Danika," she said. "Happy birthday."

She peeled off the tape and flipped back the top.

Her smile vanished. She shut the lid before Hunt could see what was inside.

"What is it?"

She shook her head, making to grab the box—but Hunt grabbed it first, pulling it onto his lap and opening the lid.

Inside lay half a dozen croissants, carefully arranged in a pile. And on the top one, artfully written in a chocolate drizzle, was one word: *Trash*.

It wasn't the hateful word that tore through him. No, it was the way Bryce's hands shook, the way her face turned red, and her mouth became a thin line.

"Just throw it out," she whispered.

No hint of the loyal defiance and anger. Just exhausted, humiliated pain.

His head went quiet. Terribly, terribly quiet.

"Just throw it out, Hunt," she whispered again. Tears shone in her eyes.

So Hunt took the box. And he stood.

He had a good idea of who had done it. Who'd had the message altered. Who had shouted that same word—*trash*—at Bryce the other week, when they'd left the Den.

"Don't," Bryce pleaded. But Hunt was already airborne.

Amelie Ravenscroft was laughing with her friends, swigging from a beer, when Hunt exploded into the Moonwood bar. People screamed and fell back, magic flaring.

But Hunt only saw her. Saw her claws form as she smirked at him. He set the pastry box on the wooden bar with careful precision.

A phone call to the Aux had given him the info he needed about the shifter's whereabouts. And Amelie seemed to have been waiting for him, or at least Bryce, when she leaned back against the bar and sneered, "Well, isn't this—"

Hunt pinned her against the wall by the throat.

The growls and attempted attacks of her pack against the wall of rippling lightning he threw up were background noise. Fear gleamed in Amelie's wide, shocked eyes as Hunt snarled in her face.

But he said softly, "You don't speak to her, you don't go near her, you don't even fucking *think* about her again." He sent enough of his lightning through his touch that he knew pain lashed through her body. Amelie choked. "Do you understand me?"

People were on their phones, dialing for the 33rd Legion or the Auxiliary.

Amelie scratched at his wrists, her boots kicking at his shins. He only tightened his grip. Lightning wrapped around her throat. "Do you understand?" His voice was frozen. Utterly calm. The voice of the Umbra Mortis.

A male approached his periphery. Ithan Holstrom.

But Ithan's eyes were on Amelie as he breathed, "What did you do, Amelie?"

Hunt only said, snarling again in Amelie's face, "Don't play dumb, Holstrom."

Ithan noticed the pastry box on the bar then. Amelie thrashed, but Hunt held her still as her Second opened the lid and looked inside. Ithan asked softly, "What is this?"

"Ask your Alpha," Hunt ground out.

Ithan went utterly still. But whatever he was thinking wasn't Hunt's concern, not as he met Amelie's burning stare again. Hunt said, "You leave her the fuck alone. *Forever.* Got it?"

Amelie looked like she'd spit on him, but he sent another casual zap of power into her, flaying her from the inside out. She winced, hissing and gagging. But nodded.

Hunt immediately released her, but his power kept her pinned against the wall. He surveyed her, then her pack. Then Ithan, whose face had gone from horror to something near grief as he must have realized what day it was and pieced enough of it together—thought about who had always wanted chocolate croissants on this day, at least.

Hunt said, "You're all pathetic."

And then he walked out. Took a damn while flying home.

Bryce was waiting for him on the roof. A phone in her hand. "No," she was saying to someone on the line. "No, he's back."

"Good," he heard Isaiah say, and it sounded like the male was about to add something else when she hung up.

Bryce wrapped her arms around herself. "You're a fucking idiot."

Hunt didn't deny it.

"Is Amelie dead?" There was fear—actual fear—in her face.

"No." The word rumbled from him, lightning hissing in its wake.

"You . . ." She rubbed at her face. "I didn't—"

"Don't tell me I'm an alphahole, or possessive and aggressive or whatever terms you use."

She lowered her hands, her face stark with dread. "You'll get in so much trouble for this, Hunt. There's no way you won't—"

It was fear *for* him. Terror for *him*.

Hunt crossed the distance between them. Took her hands. "You're my mirror. You said so yourself."

He was shaking. For some reason, he was shaking as he waited for her to respond.

Bryce looked at her hands, gripped in his, as she answered, "Yes."

The next morning, Bryce messaged her brother. *What's your medwitch's number?*

Ruhn sent it immediately, no questions asked.

Bryce called her office a minute later, hands shaking. The fair-voiced medwitch could squeeze her in—immediately. So Bryce didn't give herself the time to reconsider as she slid on her running shorts and a T-shirt, then messaged Jesiba:

Medical appointment this morning. Be at the gallery by lunch.

She found Hunt making breakfast. His brows rose when she just stared at him.

"I know where we can get kristallos venom for the medwitch's antidote tests," she said.

61

The medwitch's immaculately clean white clinic was small, not like the larger practices Bryce had visited in the past. And rather than the standard blue neon sign that jutted over nearly every other block in this city, the broom-and-bell insignia had been rendered in loving care on a gilded wooden sign hanging outside. About the only old-school-looking thing about the place.

The door down the hallway behind the counter opened, and the medwitch appeared, her curly dark hair pulled back into a bun that showed off her elegant brown face. "You must be Bryce," the woman said, her full smile instantly setting Bryce at ease. She glanced to Hunt, giving him a shallow nod of recognition. But she made no mention of their encounter in the night garden before she said to Bryce, "Your partner can come back with you if you would like. The treatment room can accommodate his wings."

Hunt looked at Bryce, and she saw the question in his expression: *Do you want me with you?*

Bryce smiled at the witch. "My partner would love to come."

The white treatment room, despite the clinic's small size, contained all the latest technology. A bank of computers sat against one wall, the long mechanical arm of a surgical light was set against the other.

The third wall held a shelf of various tonics and potions and powders in sleek glass vials, and a chrome cabinet on the fourth wall likely possessed the actual surgical instruments.

A far cry from the wood-paneled shops Hunt had visited in Pangera, where witches still made their own potions in iron cauldrons that had been passed down through the generations.

The witch idly patted the white leather examination table in the center of the room. Hidden panels gleamed in its plastic sides, extensions for Vanir of all shapes and sizes.

Hunt claimed the lone wooden chair by the cabinet as Bryce hopped onto the table, her face slightly pale.

"You said on the phone that you received this wound from a kristallos demon, and it was never healed—the venom is still in you."

"Yes," Bryce said quietly. Hunt hated every bit of pain that laced that word.

"And you give me permission to use the venom I extract in my experiments as I search for a synth antidote?"

Bryce glanced at him, and he nodded his encouragement. "An antidote to synth seems pretty damn important to have," she said, "so yes, you have my permission."

"Good. Thank you." The medwitch rifled through a chart, presumably the one Bryce had filled out on the woman's website, along with the medical records that were tied to her file as a civitas. "I see that the trauma to your leg occurred nearly two years ago?"

Bryce fiddled with the hem of her shirt. "Yes. It, um—it closed up, but still hurts. When I run or walk too much, it burns, right along my bone." Hunt refrained from grunting his annoyance.

The witch's brow creased, and she looked up from the file to glance at Bryce's leg. "How long has the pain been present?"

"Since the start," Bryce said, not looking at him.

The medwitch glanced at Hunt. "Were you there for this attack as well?"

Bryce opened her mouth to answer, but Hunt said, "Yes." Bryce whipped her head around to look at him. He kept his eyes on the witch. "I arrived three minutes after it occurred. Her leg was ripped open across the thigh, courtesy of the kristallos's teeth." The words tumbled out, the confession spilling from his lips. "I used one of the legion's medical staplers to seal the wound as best I could." Hunt went on, unsure why his heart was thundering, "The medical note about the injury is from me. She didn't receive any treatment after that. It's why the scar . . ." He swallowed against the guilt working its way up his throat. "It's why it looks the way it does." He met Bryce's eyes, letting her see the apology there. "It's my fault."

Bryce stared at him. Not a trace of damnation on her face—just raw understanding.

The witch glanced between them, as if debating whether to give them a moment. But she asked Bryce, "So you did not see a med-witch after that night?"

Bryce still held Hunt's gaze as she said to the woman, "No."

"Why?"

Her eyes still didn't leave his as she rasped, "Because I wanted to hurt. I wanted it to remind me every day." Those were tears in her eyes. Tears forming, and he didn't know why.

The witch kindly ignored her tears. "Very well. The *why*s and *how*s aren't as important as what remains in the wound." She frowned. "I can treat you today, and if you stick around afterward, you're welcome to watch me test your sample. The venom, in order to be an effective antidote, needs to be stabilized so it can interact with the synth and reverse its effects. My healing magic can do that, but I need to be present in order to hold that stability. I'm trying to find a way for the magic to permanently hold the stabilization so it can be sent out into the world and widely used."

"Sounds like some tricky stuff," Bryce said, looking away from Hunt at last. He felt the absence of her stare as if a warm flame had been extinguished.

The witch lifted her hands, white light shining at her fingertips then fading away, as if giving a quick check of her magic's readiness. "I was raised by tutors versed in our oldest forms of magic. They taught me an array of specialized knowledge."

Bryce let out a breath through her nose. "All right. Let's get on with it, then."

But the witch's face grew grave. "Bryce, I have to open the wound. I can numb you so you don't feel that part, but the venom, if it's as deep as I suspect . . . I cannot use mithridate leeches to extract it." She gestured to Hunt. "With his wound the other night, the poison had not yet taken root. With an injury like yours, deep and old . . . The venom is a kind of organism. It feeds off you. It won't want to go easily, especially after so long meshing itself to your body. I shall have to use my own magic to pull it from your body. And the venom might very well try to convince you to get me to stop. Through pain."

"It's going to hurt her?" Hunt asked.

The witch winced. "Badly enough that the local anesthesia cannot help. If you like, I can get a surgical center booked and put you under, but it could take a day or two—"

"We do it today. Right now," Bryce said, her eyes meeting Hunt's again. He could only offer her a solid nod in return.

"All right," the witch said, striding gracefully to the sink to wash her hands. "Let's get started."

The damage was as bad as she'd feared. Worse.

The witch was able to scan Bryce's leg, first with a machine, then with her power, the two combining to form an image on the screen against the far wall.

"You see the dark band along your femur?" The witch pointed to a jagged line like forked lightning through Bryce's thigh. "That's the venom. Every time you run or walk too long, it creeps into the surrounding area and hurts you." She pointed to a white area above it. "That's all scar tissue. I need to cut through it first, but that should be fast. The extraction is what might take a while."

Bryce tried to hide her trembling as she nodded. She'd already signed half a dozen waivers.

Hunt sat in the chair, watching.

"Right," the witch said, washing her hands again. "Change into a gown, and we can begin." She reached for the metal cabinet near Hunt, and Bryce removed her shorts. Her shirt.

Hunt looked away, and the witch helped Bryce step into a light cotton shift, tying it at the back for her.

"Your tattoo is lovely," the medwitch said. "I don't recognize the alphabet, though—what does it say?"

Bryce could still feel every needle prick that had made the scrolling lines of text on her back. "*Through love, all is possible.* Basically: my best friend and I will never be parted."

A hum of approval as the medwitch looked between Bryce and Hunt. "You two have such a powerful bond." Bryce didn't bother to correct her assumption that the tattoo was about Hunt. The tattoo that Danika had drunkenly insisted they get one night, claiming that putting the vow of eternal friendship in another language would make it less cheesy.

Hunt turned back to them, and the witch asked him, "Does the halo hurt you?"

"Only when it went on."

"What witch inked it?"

"Some imperial hag," Hunt said through his teeth. "One of the Old Ones."

The witch's face tightened. "It is a darker aspect of our work—that we bind individuals through the halo. It should be halted entirely."

He threw her a half smile that didn't reach his eyes. "Want to take it off for me?"

The witch went wholly still, and Bryce's breath caught in her throat. "What would you do if I did?" the witch asked softly, her dark eyes glimmering with interest—and ancient power. "Would you punish those who have held you captive?"

Bryce opened her mouth to warn them that this was a dangerous conversation, but Hunt thankfully said, "I'm not here to talk about my tattoo."

It lay in his eyes, though—his answer. The confirmation. Yes, he'd kill the people who'd done this. The witch inclined her head slightly, as if she saw that answer.

She turned back to Bryce and patted the examination table. "Very well. Lie on your back, Miss Quinlan."

Bryce began shaking as she obeyed. As the witch strapped down her upper body, then her legs, and adjusted the arm of the surgical light. A cart rattled as the witch hauled over a tray of various gleaming silver instruments, cotton pads, and an empty glass vial.

"I'm going to numb you first," the witch said, and then a needle was in her gloved hands.

Bryce shook harder.

"Deep breaths," the witch said, tapping the air bubbles from the needle.

A chair scraped, and then a warm, calloused hand wrapped around Bryce's.

Hunt's eyes locked on hers. "Deep breath, Bryce."

She sucked one in. The needle sank into her thigh, its prick drawing tears. She squeezed Hunt's hand hard enough to feel bones grinding. He didn't so much as flinch.

The pain swiftly faded, numbness tingling over her leg. Deep inside it.

"Do you feel this?" the witch asked.

"Feel what?"

"Good," the witch declared. "I'm starting now. I can put up a little curtain if you—"

"No," Bryce gritted out. "Just do it."

No delays. No waiting.

She saw the witch lift the scalpel, and then a slight, firm pressure pushed against her leg. Bryce shook again, blasting a breath through her clenched teeth.

"Steady now," the witch said. "I'm cutting through the scar tissue."

Hunt's dark eyes held hers, and she forced herself to think of him instead of her leg. He had been there that night. In the alley.

The memory surfaced, the fog of pain and terror and grief clearing slightly. Strong, warm hands gripping her. Just as he held her hand now. A voice speaking to her. Then utter stillness, as if his voice had been a bell. And then those strong, warm hands on her thigh, holding her as she sobbed and screamed.

I've got you, he'd said over and over. *I've got you.*

"I believe I can remove most of this scar tissue," the witch observed. "But . . ." She swore softly. "Luna above, look at this."

Bryce refused to look, but Hunt's eyes slid to the screen behind her, where her bloody wound was on display. A muscle ticked in his jaw. It said enough about what was inside the wound.

"I don't understand how you're walking," the witch murmured. "You said you weren't taking painkillers to manage it?"

"Only during flare-ups," Bryce whispered.

"Bryce . . ." The witch hesitated. "I'm going to need you to hold very still. And to breathe as deeply as you can."

"Okay." Her voice sounded small.

Hunt's hand clasped hers. Bryce took a steadying breath—

Someone poured acid into her leg, and her skin was sizzling, bones melting away—

In and out, out and in, her breath sliced through her teeth. Oh gods, oh gods—

Hunt interlaced their fingers, squeezing.

It burned and burned and burned and burned—

"When I got to the alley that night," he said above the rush of her frantic breathing, "you were bleeding everywhere. Yet you tried to protect him first. You wouldn't let us get near until we showed you our badges and proved we were from the legion."

She whimpered, her breathing unable to outrun the razor-sharp digging, digging, digging—

Hunt's fingers stroked over her brow. "I thought to myself, *There's someone I want guarding my back. There's a friend I'd like to have.* I think I gave you such a hard time when we met up again because . . . because some part of me knew that, and was afraid of what it'd mean."

She couldn't stop the tears sliding down her face.

His eyes didn't waver from hers. "I was there in the interrogation room, too." His fingers drifted through her hair, gentle and calming. "I was there for all of it."

The pain struck deep, and she couldn't help the scream that worked its way out of her.

Hunt leaned forward, putting his cool brow against hers. "I've known who you were this whole time. I never forgot you."

"I'm beginning extraction and stabilization of the venom," the witch said. "It will worsen, but it's almost over."

Bryce couldn't breathe. Couldn't think beyond Hunt and his words and the pain in her leg, the scar across her very soul.

Hunt whispered, "You've got this. You've got this, Bryce."

She didn't. And the Hel that erupted in her leg had her arching against the restraints, her vocal cords straining as her screaming filled the room.

Hunt's grip never wavered.

"It's almost out," the witch hissed, grunting with effort. "Hang on, Bryce."

She did. To Hunt, to his hand, to that softness in his eyes, she held on. With all she had.

"I've got you," he murmured. "Sweetheart, I've got you."

He'd never said it like that before—that word. It had always been mocking, teasing. She'd always found it just this side of annoying.

Not this time. Not when he held her hand and her gaze and everything she was. Riding out the pain with her.

"Breathe," he ordered her. "You can do it. We can get through this."

Get through it—together. Get through this mess of a life together. Through this mess of a world. Bryce sobbed, not entirely from pain this time.

And Hunt, as if he sensed it, too, leaned forward again. Brushed his mouth against hers.

Just a hint of a kiss—a feather-soft glancing of his lips over hers.

A star bloomed inside her at that kiss. A long-slumbering light began to fill her chest, her veins.

"Burning Solas," the witch whispered, and the pain ceased.

Like a switch had been flipped, the pain was gone. It was startling enough that Bryce turned away from Hunt and peered at her body, the blood on it, the gaping wound. She might have fainted at the sight of a good six inches of her leg lying open were it not for the thing that the witch held between a set of pincers, as if it were indeed a worm.

"If my magic wasn't stabilizing the venom like this, it'd be liquid," the witch said, carefully moving the venom—a clear, wriggling worm with black flecks—toward a glass jar. It writhed, like a living thing.

The witch deposited it in the jar and shut the lid, magic humming. The poison instantly dissolved into a puddle within, but still vibrated. As if looking for a way out.

Hunt's eyes were still on Bryce's face. As they'd been the entire time. Had never left.

"Let me clean you out and stitch you up, and then we'll test the antidote," the witch said.

Bryce barely heard the woman as she nodded. Barely heard anything beyond Hunt's lingering words. *I've got you.*

Her fingers curled around his. She let her eyes tell him everything her ravaged throat couldn't. *I've got you, too.*

Thirty minutes later, Bryce was sitting up, Hunt's arm and wing around her, both of them watching as the witch's glowing, pale magic wrapped around the puddle of venom in the vial and warped it into a thin thread.

"You'll forgive me if my method of antidote testing fails to qualify as a proper medical experiment," she declared as she walked over to where an ordinary white pill sat in a clear plastic box. Lifting the lid, she dropped the thread of venom in. It fluttered like a ribbon, hovering above the pill before the witch shut the lid again. "What is being used on the street is a much more potent version of this," she said, "but I want to see if this amount of my healing magic, holding the venom in place and merging with it, will do the trick against the synth."

The witch carefully let the thread of the magic-infused venom alight on the tablet. It vanished within a blink, sucked into the pill.

But the witch's face remained bunched in concentration. As if focused on whatever was happening within the pill.

Bryce asked, "So your magic is currently stabilizing the venom in that tablet? Making it stop the synth?"

"Essentially," the witch said distantly, still focused on the pill. "It takes most of my concentration to keep it stable long enough to halt the synth. Which is why I'd like to find a way to remove myself from the equation—so it can be used by anyone, even without me."

Bryce fell silent after that, letting the witch work in peace.

Nothing happened. The pill merely sat there.

One minute passed. Two. And just as it was nearing three minutes—

The pill turned gray. And then dissolved into nothing but minuscule particles that then faded away, too. Until there was nothing left.

Hunt said into the silence, "It worked?"

The witch blinked at the now-empty box. "It would appear so." She turned to Bryce, sweat gleaming on her brow. "I'd like to continue testing this, and try to find some way for the antidote to work without my magic stabilizing the venom. I can send over a vial for you when I'm finished, though, if you'd like. Some people want to keep such reminders of their struggles."

Bryce nodded blankly. And realized she had absolutely no idea what to do next.

62

Jesiba hadn't seemed to care when Bryce explained that she needed the rest of the day off. She'd just demanded that Bryce be in first thing tomorrow or be turned into a donkey.

Hunt flew her home from the medwitch's office, going so far as to carry her down the stairs from the roof of the apartment building and through her door. He deposited her on the couch, where he insisted she stay for the remainder of the day, curled up beside him, snuggled into his warmth.

She might have stayed there all afternoon and evening if Hunt's phone hadn't rung.

He'd been in the midst of making her lunch when he picked up. "Hi, Micah."

Even from across the room, Bryce could hear the Archangel's cold, beautiful voice. "My office. Immediately. Bring Bryce Quinlan with you."

While he dressed in his battle-suit and gathered his helmet and weapons, Hunt debated telling Bryce to get on a train and get the fuck out of the city. He knew this meeting with Micah wasn't going to be pleasant.

Bryce was limping, her wound still tender enough that he'd

grabbed her a pair of loose workout pants and helped her put them on in the middle of the living room. She'd registered for a follow-up appointment in a month, and it only now occurred to Hunt that he might not be there to see it.

Either because this case had wrapped up, or because of whatever the fuck was about to go down in the Comitium.

Bryce tried to take all of one step before Hunt picked her up, carrying her out of the apartment and into the skies. She barely spoke, and neither did he. After this morning, what use were words? That too-brief kiss he'd given her had said enough. So had the light he could have sworn glowed in her eyes as he'd pulled away.

A line had been crossed, one from which there was no walking away.

Hunt landed on a balcony of the Governor's spire—the central of the Comitium's five. The usually bustling hall of his public office was hushed. Bad sign. He carried Bryce toward the chamber. If people had run, or Micah ordered them out . . .

If he saw Sandriel right now, if she realized Bryce was injured . . .

Hunt's temper became a living, deadly thing. His lightning pushed against his skin, coiling through him, a cobra readying to strike.

He gently set Bryce down before the shut fogged-glass office doors. Made sure she was steady on her feet before he let go, stepping back to study every inch of her face.

Worry shone in her eyes, enough of it that he leaned in, brushing a kiss over her temple. "Chin up, Quinlan," he murmured against her soft skin. "Let's see you do that fancy trick where you somehow look down your nose at people a foot taller than you."

She chuckled, smacking him lightly on the arm. Hunt pulled away with a half smile of his own before opening the doors and guiding Bryce through with a hand on her back. He knew it would likely be his last smile for a long while. But he'd be damned if he let Quinlan know it. Even as they beheld who stood in Micah's office.

To the left of the Governor's desk stood Sabine, arms crossed and spine rigid, the portrait of cold fury. A tight-faced Amelie lingered at her side.

He knew precisely what this meeting was about.

Micah stood at the window, his face glacial with distaste. Isaiah and Viktoria flanked his desk. The former's eyes flashed with warning.

Bryce glanced between them all and hesitated.

Hunt said quietly to Micah, to Sabine, "Quinlan doesn't need to be here for this."

Sabine's silvery blond hair shimmered in the firstlight lamps as she said, "Oh, she does. I want her here for every second."

"I won't bother asking if it's true," Micah said to Hunt as he and Bryce stopped in the center of the room. The doors shut behind them. Locking.

Hunt braced himself.

Micah said, "There were six cameras in the bar. They all captured what you did and said to Amelie Ravenscroft. She reported your behavior to Sabine, and Sabine brought it directly to me."

Amelie flushed. "I just mentioned it to her," she amended. "I didn't howl like a pup about it."

"It is unacceptable," Sabine hissed to Micah. "You think you can set your assassin on a member of one of *my* packs? My heir?"

"I will tell you again, Sabine," Micah said, bored, "I did not set Hunt Athalar upon her. He acted of his own free will." A glance at Bryce. "He acted on behalf of his companion."

Hunt said quickly, "Bryce had nothing to do with this. Amelie pulled a bullshit prank and I decided to pay her a visit." He bared his teeth at the young Alpha, who swallowed hard.

Sabine snapped, "You assaulted my captain."

"I told Amelie to stay the fuck away," Hunt bit out. "To leave her alone." He angled his head, unable to stop the words. "Or are you unaware that Amelie has been gunning for Bryce since your daughter died? Taunting her about it? Calling her trash?"

Sabine's face didn't so much as flinch. "What does it matter, if it's true?"

Hunt's head filled with roaring. But Bryce just stood there. And lowered her eyes.

Sabine said to Micah, "This cannot go unpunished. You fumbled the investigation of my daughter's murder. You allowed these two to poke their noses into it, to accuse *me* of killing her. And now this. I'm one breath away from telling this city how your *slaves* cannot even stay in line. I'm sure your current guest will be highly interested in that little fact."

Micah's power rumbled at the mention of Sandriel. "Athalar will be punished."

"Now. Here." Sabine's face was positively lupine. "Where I can see it."

"Sabine," Amelie murmured. Sabine growled at her young captain.

Sabine had been hoping for this moment—had used Amelie as an excuse. No doubt dragged the wolf here. Sabine had sworn they'd pay for accusing her of murdering Danika. And Sabine was, Hunt supposed, a female of her word.

"Your position among the wolves," Micah said with terrifying calm, "does not entitle you to tell a Governor of the Republic what to do."

Sabine didn't back down. Not an inch.

Micah just loosed a long breath. He met Hunt's eyes, disappointed. "You acted foolishly. I'd have thought you, at least, would know better."

Bryce was shaking. But Hunt didn't dare touch her.

"History indicates that a slave assaulting a free citizen should automatically forfeit their life."

Hunt suppressed a bitter laugh at her words. Wasn't that what he'd been doing for the Archangels for centuries now?

"Please," Bryce whispered.

And perhaps it was sympathy that softened the Archangel's face as Micah said, "Those are old traditions. For Pangera, not Valbara." Sabine opened her mouth, objecting, but Micah lifted a hand. "Hunt Athalar will be punished. And he shall die—in the way that angels die."

Bryce lurched a limping step toward Micah. Hunt grabbed her by the shoulder, halting her.

Micah said, "The Living Death."

Hunt's blood chilled. But he bowed his head. He had been ready to face the consequences since he'd shot into the skies yesterday, pastry box in his hands.

Bryce looked at Isaiah, whose face was grim, for an explanation. The commander said to her, to the confused Amelie, "The Living Death is when an angel's wings are cut off."

Bryce shook her head. "No, please—"

But Hunt met Micah's rock-solid stare, read the fairness in it. He lowered himself to his knees and removed his jacket, then his shirt.

"I don't need to press charges," Amelie insisted. "Sabine, *I don't want this.* Let it go."

Micah stalked toward Hunt, a shining double-edged sword appearing in his hand.

Bryce flung herself in the Archangel's path. "Please—*please*—" The scent of her tears filled the office.

Viktoria instantly appeared at her side. Holding her back. The wraith's whisper was so quiet Hunt barely heard it. "They will grow back. In several weeks, his wings will grow back."

But it would hurt like Hel. Hurt so badly that Hunt now took steadying, bracing breaths. Plunged down into himself, into that place where he rode out everything that had ever been done to him, every task he'd been assigned, every life he'd been ordered to take.

"Sabine, *no,*" Amelie insisted. "It's gone far enough."

Sabine said nothing. Just stood there.

Hunt spread his wings and lifted them, holding them high over his back so the slice might be clean.

Bryce began shouting something, but Hunt only looked at Micah. "Do it."

Micah didn't so much as nod before his sword moved.

Pain, such as Hunt had not experienced in two hundred years, raced through him, short-circuiting every—

* * *

Hunt jolted into consciousness to Bryce screaming.

It was enough of a summons that he forced his head to clear, even around the agony down his back, his soul.

He must have blacked out only for a moment, because his wings were still spurting blood from where they lay like two fallen branches on the floor of Micah's office.

Amelie looked like she was going to be sick; Sabine was smirking, and Bryce was now at his side, his blood soaking her pants, her hands, as she sobbed, "*Oh gods, oh gods—*"

"We're settled," Sabine said to Micah, who punched a button on his phone to call for a medwitch.

He'd paid for his actions, and it was over, and he could go home with Bryce—

"You are a disgrace, Sabine." Bryce's words speared through the room as she bared her teeth at the Prime Apparent. "You are a disgrace to every wolf who has ever walked this planet."

Sabine said, "I don't care what a half-breed thinks of me."

"You didn't deserve Danika," Bryce growled, shaking. "You didn't deserve her for one second."

Sabine halted. "I didn't deserve a selfish, spineless brat for a daughter, but that's not how it turned out, is it?"

Dimly, from far away, Bryce's snarl cut through Hunt's pain. He couldn't reach her in time, though, as she surged to her feet, wincing in agony at her still-healing leg.

Micah stepped in front of her. Bryce panted, sobbing through her teeth. But Micah stood there, immovable as a mountain. "Take Athalar out of here," the Archangel said calmly, the dismissal clear. "To your home, the barracks, I don't care."

But Sabine, it seemed, had decided to stay. To give Bryce a piece of her vicious mind.

Sabine said to her, low and venomous, "I sought out the Under-King last winter, did you know that? To get answers from my daughter, with whatever speck of her energy lives on in the Sleeping City."

Bryce stilled. The pure stillness of the Fae. Dread filled her eyes.

"Do you know what he told me?" Sabine's face was inhuman.

"He said that Danika would not come. She would not obey my summons. My pathetic daughter would not even deign to meet me in her afterlife. For the *shame* of what she did. How she died, helpless and screaming, begging like one of *you*." Sabine seemed to hum with rage. "And do you know what the Under-King told me when I demanded again that he summon her?"

No one else dared speak.

"He told me that *you*, you piece of trash, had made a bargain with him. For *her*. That *you* had gone to him after her death and traded your spot in the Bone Quarter in exchange for Danika's passage. That you worried she would be denied access because of her cowardly death and *begged* him to take her in your stead."

Even Hunt's pain paused at that.

"That wasn't why I went!" Bryce snapped. "Danika wasn't a coward for one *fucking* moment of her life!" Her voice broke as she shouted the last words.

"You had *no right*," Sabine exploded. "She *was* a coward, and died like one, and deserved to be dumped into the river!" The Alpha was screaming. "And now she is left with eons of *shame* because of you! Because she should not *be there*, you *stupid* whore. And now she must *suffer* for it!"

"That's enough," Micah said, his words conveying his order. *Get out*.

Sabine just let out a dead, cold laugh and turned on her heel.

Bryce was still sobbing when Sabine strutted out, a stunned Amelie on her heels. The latter murmured as she shut the door, "I'm sorry."

Bryce spat at her.

It was the last thing Hunt saw before darkness swept in again.

She would never forgive them. Any of them.

Hunt remained unconscious while the medwitches worked on him in Micah's office, stitching him up so that the stumps where his wings had been stopped spurting blood onto the floor, then dressing the wounds in bandages that would promote quick growth.

No firstlight—apparently, its aid in healing wasn't allowed for the Living Death. It would delegitimize the punishment.

Bryce knelt with Hunt the entire time, his head in her lap. She didn't hear Micah telling her how the alternative was Hunt being dead—officially and irrevocably dead.

She stroked Hunt's hair as they lay in her bed an hour later, his breathing still deep and even. *Give him the healing potion every six hours*, the medwitch ordered her. *It will stave off the pain, too.*

Isaiah and Naomi had carried them home, and she'd barely let them lay Hunt facedown on her mattress before she'd ordered them to get out.

She hadn't expected Sabine to understand why she'd given up her place in the Bone Quarter for Danika. Sabine never listened when Danika spoke about how she'd one day be buried there, in full honor, with all the other great heroes of her House. Living on, as that small speck of energy, for eternity. Still a part of the city she loved so much.

Bryce had seen people's boats tip. Would never forget Danika's half-muffled pleading on the audio of the apartment building's hall camera.

Bryce hadn't been willing to make the gamble that the boat might not reach the far shore. Not for Danika.

She'd tossed a Death Mark into the Istros, payment to the Under-King—a coin of pure iron from an ancient, long-gone kingdom across the sea. Passage for a mortal on a boat.

And then she'd knelt on the crumbling stone steps, the river mere feet behind her, the arches of the bone gates above her, and waited.

The Under-King, veiled in black and silent as death, had appeared moments later.

It has been an age since a mortal dared set foot on my isle.

The voice had been old and young, male and female, kind and full of hatred. She'd never heard anything so hideous—and beckoning.

I wish to trade my place.

I know why you are here, Bryce Quinlan. Whose passage you seek to barter. An amused pause. *Do you not wish to one day dwell here among the honored dead? Your balance remains skewed toward acceptance—continue on your path, and you shall be welcomed when your time comes.*

I wish to trade my place. For Danika Fendyr.

Do this and know that no other Quiet Realms of Midgard shall be open to you. Not the Bone Quarter, not the Catacombs of the Eternal City, not the Summer Isles of the north. None, Bryce Quinlan. To barter your resting place here is to barter your place everywhere.

I wish to trade my place.

You are young, and you are weighed with grief. Consider that your life may seem long, but it is a mere flutter of eternity.

I wish to trade my place.

Are you so certain Danika Fendyr will be denied welcome? Have you so little faith in her actions and deeds that you must make this bargain?

I wish to trade my place. She'd sobbed the words.

There is no undoing this.

I wish to trade my place.

Then say it, Bryce Quinlan, and let the trade be done. Say it a seventh and final time, and let the gods and the dead and all those between hear your vow. Say it, and it shall be done.

She hadn't hesitated, knowing this was the ancient rite. She'd looked it up in the gallery archives. Had stolen the Death Mark from there, too. It had been given to Jesiba by the Under-King himself, the sorceress had told her, when she'd sworn fealty to the House of Flame and Shadow.

I wish to trade my place.

And so it had been done.

Bryce had not felt any different afterward, when she'd been sent back over the river. Or in the days after that. Even her mother had not been able to tell—hadn't noticed that Bryce had snuck from her hotel room in the dead of night.

In the two years since, Bryce had sometimes wondered if she'd dreamed it, but then she'd look through the drawer in the gallery where all the old coins were kept and see the empty, dark spot where the Death Mark had been. Jesiba had never noticed it was gone.

Bryce liked to think of her chance at eternal rest as missing with it. To imagine the coins nestled in their velvet compartments in the drawer as all the souls of those she loved, dwelling together forever. And there was hers—missing and drifting, wiped away the moment she died.

But what Sabine had claimed about Danika suffering in the Bone Quarter . . . Bryce refused to believe it. Because the alternative—No. Danika had deserved to go to the Bone Quarter, had nothing to be ashamed about, whether Sabine or the other assholes disagreed or not. Whether the Under-King or whoever the Hel deemed their souls *worthy* disagreed or not.

Bryce ran her hand through Hunt's silken hair, the sounds of his breathing filling the room.

It sucked. This stupid fucking world they lived in.

It sucked, and it was full of awful people. And the good ones always paid for it.

She pulled her phone from the nightstand and began typing out a message.

She fired it off a moment later, not giving herself time to reconsider what she'd written to Ithan. Her first message to him in two years. His frantic messages from that horrible night, then his cold order to stay away, were still the last things in a thread that went back five years before that.

You tell your Alpha that Connor never bothered to notice her because he always knew what a piece of shit she was. And tell Sabine that if I see her again, I will kill her.

Bryce lay down next to Hunt, not daring to touch his ravaged back.

Her phone buzzed. Ithan had written, *I had no part in what went down today.*

Bryce wrote back, *You disgust me. All of you.*

Ithan didn't reply, and she put her phone on silent before she let out a long breath and leaned her brow against Hunt's shoulder.

She'd find a way to make this right. Somehow. Someday.

* * *

Hunt's eyes cracked open, pain a steady throb through him. Its sharpness was dulled—likely by some sort of potion or concoction of drugs.

The steady counterweight that should have been on his back was gone. The emptiness hit him like a semitruck. But soft, feminine breathing filled the darkness. A scent like paradise filled his nose, settled him. Soothed the pain.

His eyes adjusted to the dark enough to know that he was in Bryce's bedroom. That she was lying beside him. Medical supplies and vials lay next to the bed. All for him, many looking used. The clock read four in the morning. How many hours had she sat up, tending to him?

Her hands were tucked in at her chest, as if she had fallen asleep beseeching the gods.

He mouthed her name, his tongue as dry as sandpaper.

Pain rippled through his body, but he managed to stretch out an arm. Managed to slide it over her waist and tuck her into him. She made a soft sound and nuzzled her head into his neck.

Something deep in him shifted and settled. What she'd said and done today, what she'd revealed to the world in her pleading for him . . . It was dangerous. For both of them. So, so dangerous.

If he were wise, he'd find somehow to pull away. Before this thing between them met its inevitable, horrible end. As all things in the Republic met a horrible end.

And yet Hunt couldn't bring himself to remove his arm. To avoid the instinct to breathe in her scent and listen to her soft breathing.

He didn't regret it, what he'd done. Not one bit of it.

But there might come a day when that wouldn't be true. A day that might dawn very soon.

So Hunt savored the feel of Bryce. Her scent and breathing.

Savored every second of it.

63

Is Athie okay, BB?"

Bryce rubbed her eyes as she studied the computer screen in the gallery library. "He's sleeping it off."

Lehabah had cried this morning when Bryce had trudged in to tell her what had occurred. She'd barely noticed that her leg had no pain—not a whisper. She'd wanted to stay home, to care for Hunt, but when she'd called Jesiba, the answer had been clear: *No.*

She'd spent the first half of the morning filling out job applications.

And had sent each and every one of them in.

She didn't know where the Hel she would end up, but getting out of this place was the first step. Of many.

She'd taken a few more today.

Ruhn had picked up on the first ring, and come right over to the apartment.

Hunt had still been asleep when she'd left him in her brother's care. She didn't want anyone from that fucking legion in her house. Didn't want to see Isaiah or Viktoria or any of the triarii anytime soon.

Ruhn had taken one glance at Hunt's mutilated back and gagged. But he'd promised to stay on the pills-and-wound-care schedule she laid out for him.

"Micah went easy on him," Ruhn said when she stopped by at lunch, toying with one of his earrings. "Really fucking easy. Sabine had the right to call for his death." As a slave, Hunt had no rights whatsoever. None.

"I will never forget it as long as I live," Bryce answered, her voice dull. The flash of Micah's sword. Hunt's scream, as if his soul was being shredded. Sabine's smile.

"I should have been the one to shut Amelie up." Shadows flickered in the room.

"Well, you weren't." She measured the potion for Ruhn to give Hunt at the top of the hour.

Ruhn stretched an arm over the back of the sofa. "I'd like to be, Bryce."

She met her brother's gaze. "Why?"

"Because you're my sister."

She didn't have a response—not yet.

She could have sworn hurt flashed in his eyes at her silence. She was out of her apartment in another minute, and barely reached the gallery before Jesiba had called, raging about how Bryce wasn't ready for the two o'clock meeting with the owl shifter who was ready to buy a marble statuette worth three million gold marks.

Bryce executed the meeting, and the sale, and didn't hear half of what was said.

Sign, stamp, goodbye.

She returned to the library by three. Lehabah warmed her shoulder as she opened her laptop. "Why are you on Redner Industries' site?"

Bryce just stared at the two small fields:

Username. Password.

She typed in *dfendyr.* The cursor hovered over the password.

Someone might be tipped off that she was trying to get in. And if she did get access, someone might very well receive an alert. But . . . It was a risk worth taking. She was out of options.

Lehabah read the username. "Does this somehow tie in to the Horn?"

"Danika knew something—something big," Bryce mused.

Password. What would Danika's password be?

Redner Industries would have told her to write something random and full of symbols.

Danika would have hated being told what to do, and would have done the opposite.

Bryce typed in *SabineSucks*.

No luck. Though she'd done it the other day, she again typed in Danika's birthday. Her own birthday. The holy numbers. Nothing.

Her phone buzzed, and a message from Ruhn lit up her screen.

He woke up, took his potions like a good boy, and demanded to know where you were.

Ruhn added, *He's not a bad male.*

She wrote back, *No, he's not.*

Ruhn replied, *He's sleeping again, but seemed in good enough spirits, all things considered.*

A pause, and then her brother wrote, *He told me to tell you thanks. For everything.*

Bryce read the messages three times before she looked at the interface again. And typed in the only other password she could think of. The words written on the back of a leather jacket she'd worn constantly for the last two years. The words inked on her own back in an ancient alphabet. Danika's favorite phrase, whispered to her by the Oracle on her sixteenth birthday.

The Old Language of the Fae didn't work. Neither did the formal tongue of the Asteri.

So she wrote it in the common language.

Through love, all is possible.

The login screen vanished. And a list of files appeared.

Most were reports on Redner's latest projects: improving tracking quality on phones; comparing the speed at which shifters could change forms; analyzing the healing rates of witch magic versus Redner medicines. Boring everyday science.

She'd almost given up when she noticed a subfolder: *Party Invites*.

Danika had never been organized enough to keep such things, let alone put them in a folder. She either deleted them right away or let them rot in her inbox, unanswered.

It was enough of an anomaly that Bryce clicked on it and found a list of folders within. Including one titled *Bryce*.

A file with her name on it. Hidden in another file. Exactly as Bryce had hidden her own job applications on this computer.

"What is that?" Lehabah whispered at her shoulder.

Bryce opened the file. "I don't know. I never sent invites to her work address."

The folder contained a single photo.

"Why does she have a picture of her old jacket?" Lehabah asked. "Was she going to sell it?"

Bryce stared and stared at the image. Then she moved, logging out of the account before running up the stairs to the showroom, where she grabbed the leather jacket from her chair.

"It was a clue," she said breathlessly to Lehabah as she flew back down the stairs, fingers running and pawing over every seam of the jacket. "The photo is a fucking clue—"

Something hard snagged her fingers. A lump. Right along the vertical line of the *L* in *love*.

"Through love, all is possible," Bryce whispered, and grabbed a pair of scissors from the cup on the table. Danika had even tattooed the hint on Bryce's fucking *back*, for fuck's sake. Lehabah peered over her shoulder as Bryce cut into the leather.

A small, thin metal rectangle fell onto the table. A flash drive.

"Why would she hide that in her coat?" Lehabah asked, but Bryce was already moving again, hands shaking as she fitted the drive into the slot on her laptop.

Three unmarked videos lay within.

She opened the first video. She and Lehabah watched in silence.

Lehabah's whisper filled the library, even over the scratching of the nøkk.

"Gods spare us."

64

Hunt had managed to get out of bed and prove himself alive enough that Ruhn Danaan had finally left. He had no doubt the Fae Prince had called his cousin to inform her, but it didn't matter: Bryce was home in fifteen minutes.

Her face was white as death, so ashen that her freckles stood out like splattered blood. No sign of anything else amiss, not one thread on her black dress out of place.

"What." He was instantly at the door, wincing as he surged from where he'd been on the couch watching the evening news coverage of Rigelus, Bright Hand of the Asteri, giving a pretty speech about the rebel conflict in Pangera. It'd be another day or two before he could walk without pain. Another several weeks until his wings grew back. A few days after that until he could test out flying. Tomorrow, probably, the insufferable itching would begin.

He remembered every miserable second from the first time he'd had his wings cut off. All the surviving Fallen had endured it. Along with the insult of having their wings displayed in the crystal palace of the Asteri as trophies and warnings.

But she first asked, "How are you feeling?"

"Fine." Lie. Syrinx pranced at his feet, showering his hand with kisses. "What's wrong?"

Bryce wordlessly closed the door. Shut the curtains. Yanked out her phone from her jacket pocket, pulled up an email—from herself to herself—and clicked on an attached file. "Danika had a flash drive hidden in the lining of her jacket," Bryce said, voice shaking, and led him back to the couch, helping him to sit as the video loaded. Syrinx leapt onto the cushions, curling up beside him. Bryce sat on his other side, so close their thighs pressed together. She didn't seem to notice. After a heartbeat, Hunt didn't, either.

It was grainy, soundless footage of a padded cell.

At the bottom of the video, a ticker read: *Artificial Amplification for Power Dysfunction, Test Subject 7.*

A too-thin human female sat in the room in a med-gown. "What the fuck is this?" Hunt asked. But he already knew.

Synth. These were the synth research trials.

Bryce grunted—*keep watching.*

A young draki male in a lab coat entered the room, bearing a tray of supplies. The video sped up, as if someone had increased the speed of the footage for the sake of urgency. The draki male took her vitals and then injected something into her arm.

Then he left. Locked the door.

"Are they . . ." Hunt swallowed. "Did he just inject her with synth?"

Bryce made a small, confirming noise in her throat.

The camera kept rolling. A minute passed. Five. Ten.

Two Vanir walked into the room. Two large serpentine shifters who sized up the human female locked in alone with them. Hunt's stomach turned. Turned further at the slave tattoos on their arms, and knew that they were prisoners. Knew, from the way they smiled at the human female shrinking against the wall, why they had been locked up.

They lunged for her.

But the human female lunged, too.

It happened so fast that Hunt could barely track it. The person who had edited the footage went back and slowed it, too.

So he watched, blow by blow, as the human female launched herself at the two Vanir males.

And ripped them to pieces.

It was impossible. Utterly impossible. Unless—

Tharion had said synth could temporarily grant humans powers greater than most Vanir. Powers enough to kill.

"Do you know how badly the human rebels would want this?" Hunt said. Bryce just jerked her chin toward the screen. Where the footage kept going.

They sent in two other males. Bigger than the last. And they, too, wound up in pieces.

Piles.

Oh gods.

Another two. Then three. Then five.

Until the entire room was red. Until the Vanir were clawing at the doors, begging to be let out. Begging as their companions, then they themselves, were slaughtered.

The human female was screaming, her head tilted to the ceiling. Screaming in rage or pain or what, he couldn't tell without the sound.

Hunt knew what was coming next. Knew, and couldn't stop himself from watching.

She turned on herself. Ripped herself apart. Until she, too, was a pile on the floor.

The footage cut out.

Bryce said softly, "Danika must have figured out what they were working on in the labs. I think someone involved in these tests . . . Could they have sold the formula to some drug boss? Whoever killed Danika and the pack and the others must have been high on this synth. Or injected someone with it and sicced them on the victims."

Hunt shook his head. "Maybe, but how does it tie in to the demons and the Horn?"

"Maybe they summoned the kristallos for the antidote in its venom—and nothing more. They wanted to try to make an antidote of their own, in case the synth ever turned on them. Maybe it doesn't connect to the Horn at all," Bryce said. "Maybe this is what we were meant to find. There are two other videos like this, of two different human subjects. Danika left them for *me*. She must have known someone was coming for her. Must have known when she was on that Aux boat, confiscating that crate of synth, that they'd come after her soon. There was no second type of demon hunting alongside the kristallos. Just a person—from *this* world. Someone who was high on the synth and used its power to break through our apartment's enchantments. And then had the strength to kill Danika and the whole pack."

Hunt considered his next words carefully, fighting against his racing mind. "It could work, Bryce. But the Horn is still out there, with a drug that might be able to repair it, coincidence or no. And we're no closer to finding it." No, this just led them a Hel of a lot closer to trouble. He added, "Micah already demonstrated what it means to set one foot out of line. We need to go slow on the synth hunt. Make sure we're certain this time. And careful."

"*None* of you were able to find out anything like this. Why should I go slow with the only clue I have about who killed Danika and the Pack of Devils? This ties in, Hunt. I know it does."

And because she was opening her mouth to object again, he said what he knew would stop her. "Bryce, if we pursue this and we're wrong, if Micah learns about another fuckup, forget the bargain being over. I might not walk away from his next punishment."

She flinched.

His entire body protested as he reached a hand to touch her knee. "This synth shit is horrific, Bryce. I . . . I've never seen anything like it." It changed everything. *Everything*. He didn't even know where to begin sorting out all he'd seen. He should make some phone calls—*needed* to make some phone calls about this. "But to find the murderer and maybe the Horn, and to make sure there's an afterward for you and me"—because there would be a *you and me* for them; he'd do whatever it took to ensure it—"we need to be *smart*." He nodded to the footage. "Forward that to me. I'll make sure it gets to Vik on our encrypted server. See what she can dig up about these trials."

Bryce scanned his face. The openness in her expression nearly sent him to his knees before her. Hunt waited for her to argue, to defy him. To tell him he was an idiot.

But she only said, "Okay." She let out a long breath, slumping back against the cushions.

She was so fucking beautiful he could barely stand it. Could barely stand to hear her ask quietly, "What sort of an afterward for you and me do you have in mind, Athalar?"

He didn't balk from her searching gaze. "The good kind," he said with equal quiet.

She didn't ask, though. About how it would be possible. How any of it would be possible for him, for them. What he'd do to make it so.

Her lips curved upward. "Sounds like a plan to me."

For a moment, an eternity, they stared at each other.

And despite what they'd just watched, what lurked in the world beyond the apartment, Hunt said, "Yeah?"

"Yeah." She toyed with the ends of her hair. "Hunt. You kissed me—at the medwitch's office."

He knew he shouldn't, knew it was ten kinds of stupid, but he said, "What about it?"

"Did you mean it?"

"Yes." He'd never said anything more true. "Did you want me to mean it?"

His heart began to race, fast enough that he nearly forgot the pain along his back as she said, "You know the answer to that, Athalar."

"Do you want me to do it again?" Fuck, his voice had dropped an octave.

Her eyes were clear, bright. Fearless and hopeful and everything that had always made it impossible for him to think about anything else if she was around. "*I* want to do it." She added, "If that's all right with you."

Hel, yes. He made himself throw her a half smile. "Do your worst, Quinlan."

She let out a breathy little laugh and turned her face up toward his. Hunt didn't so much as inhale too deeply for fear of startling her. Syrinx, apparently taking the hint, saw himself into his crate.

Bryce's hands shook as they lifted to his hair, brushed back a strand, then ran over the band of the halo.

Hunt gripped her trembling fingers. "What's this about?" he murmured, unable to help himself from pressing his mouth to the dusky nails. How many times had he thought about these hands on him? Caressing his face, stroking down his chest, wrapped around his cock?

Her swallow was audible. He pressed another kiss to her fingers.

"This wasn't supposed to happen—between us," she whispered.

"I know," he said, kissing her shaking fingers again. He gently unfurled them, exposing the heart of her palm. He pressed his mouth there, too. "But thank fucking Urd it did."

Her hands stopped shaking. Hunt lifted his eyes from her hand to find her own lined with silver—and full of fire. He interlaced their fingers. "For fuck's sake, just kiss me, Quinlan."

She did. Dark Hel, she did. His words had barely finished sounding when she slid her hand over his jaw, around his neck, and hauled his lips to hers.

The moment Hunt's lips met her own, Bryce erupted.

She didn't know if it was weeks without sex or Hunt himself, but she unleashed herself. That was the only way to describe it as she drove her hands into his hair and slanted her mouth against his.

No tentative, sweet kisses. Not for them. Never for them.

Her mouth opened at that first contact, and his tongue swept in, tasting her in savage, unrelenting strokes. Hunt groaned at that first taste—and the sound was kindling.

Rising onto her knees, fingers digging into his soft hair, she couldn't get enough, taste enough of him—rain and cedar and salt and pure lightning. His hands skimmed over her hips, slow and steady despite the mouth that ravaged hers with fierce, deep kisses.

His tongue danced with her own. She whimpered, and he let out a dark laugh as his hand wandered under the back of her dress, down the length of her spine, his calluses scraping. She arched into the touch, and he tore his mouth away.

Before she could grab his face back to hers, his lips found her neck. He pressed openmouthed kisses to it, nipped at the sensitive skin beneath her ears. "Tell me what you want, Quinlan."

"All of it." There was no doubt in her. None.

Hunt dragged his teeth along the side of her neck, and she panted, her entire consciousness narrowing to the sensation. "All of it?"

She slid her hand down his front. To his pants—the hard, considerable length straining against them. Urd spare her. She palmed his cock, eliciting a hiss from him. "All of it, Athalar."

"Thank fuck," he breathed against her neck, and she laughed.

Her laugh died as he put his mouth on hers again, as if he needed to taste the sound, too.

Tongues and teeth and breath, his hands artfully unhooking her bra under her dress. She wound up straddling his lap, wound up grinding herself over that beautiful, perfect hardness in his lap. Wound up with her dress peeled down to her waist, her bra gone, and then Hunt's mouth and teeth were around her breast, suckling and biting and kissing, and nothing, nothing, nothing had ever felt this good, this right.

Bryce didn't care that she was moaning loud enough for every demon in the Pit to hear. Not as Hunt switched to her other breast, sucking her nipple deep into his mouth. She drove her hips down on his, release already a rising wave in her. "Fuck, Bryce," he murmured against her breast.

She only dove her hand beneath the waist of his pants. His hand wrapped around her wrist, though. Halted her millimeters from what she'd wanted in her hands, her mouth, her body for weeks.

"Not yet," he growled, dragging his tongue along the underside of her breast. Content to feast on her. "Not until I've had my turn."

The words short-circuited every logical thought. And any objections died as he slipped a hand up her dress, running it over her thigh. Higher. His mouth found her neck again as a finger explored the lacy front of her underwear.

He hissed again as he found it utterly soaked, the lace doing nothing to hide the proof of just how badly she wanted this, wanted him. He ran his finger down the length of her—and back up again.

Then that finger landed on that spot at the apex of her thighs. His thumb gently pressed on it over the fabric, drawing a moan deep from her throat.

She felt him smile against her neck. His thumb slowly circled, every sweep a torturous blessing.

"Hunt." She didn't know if his name was a plea or a question.

He just tugged aside her underwear and put his fingers directly on her.

She moaned again, and Hunt stroked her, two fingers dragging up and down with teeth-grinding lightness. He licked up the side of her throat, fingers playing mercilessly with her. He whispered against her skin, "Do you taste as good as you feel, Bryce?"

"Please find out immediately," she managed to gasp.

His laugh rumbled through her, but his fingers didn't halt their leisurely exploration. "Not yet, Quinlan."

One of his fingers found her entrance and lingered, circling. "Do it," she said. If she didn't feel him inside her—his fingers or his cock, anything—she might start begging.

"So bossy," Hunt purred against her neck, then claimed her mouth again. And as his lips settled over hers, nipping and taunting, he slid that finger deep into her.

Both of them groaned. "Fuck, Bryce," he said again. "Fuck."

Her eyes nearly rolled back into her head at the feeling of that finger. She rocked her hips, desperate to drive him deeper, and he obliged her, pulling out his finger nearly all the way, adding a second, and plunging both back into her.

She bucked, her nails digging into his chest. His thunderous heartbeat raged against her palms. She buried her face in his neck, biting and licking, starving for any taste of him while he pumped his hand into her again.

Hunt breathed into her ear, "I am going to fuck you until you can't remember your gods-damned name."

Gods, yes. "Likewise," she croaked.

Release shimmered in her, a wild and reckless song, and she rode his hand toward it. His other hand cupped her backside. "Don't think I've forgotten this particular asset," he murmured, squeezing for emphasis. "I have plans for this beautiful ass, Bryce. Filthy, filthy plans."

She moaned again, and his fingers stroked into her, over and over.

"Come for me, sweetheart," he purred against her breast, his tongue flicking over her nipple just as one of his fingers curled inside her, hitting that gods-damned spot.

Bryce did. Hunt's name on her lips, she tipped her head back and let go, riding his hand with abandon, driving them both into the couch cushions.

He groaned, and she swallowed the sound with an openmouthed kiss as every nerve in her body exploded into glorious starlight.

Then there was only breathing, and him—his body, his scent, that strength.

The starlight receded, and she opened her eyes to find him with his head tipped back, teeth bared.

Not in pleasure. In pain.

She'd driven him into the cushions. Shoved his wounded back right up against the couch.

Horror lurched through her like ice water, dousing any heat in her veins. "Oh gods. I am so sorry—"

He cracked his eyes open. That groan he'd made as she came had been *pain*, and she'd been so fucking wild for him that she hadn't noticed—

"Are you hurt?" she demanded, hoisting herself up from his lap, reaching to remove his fingers, still deep inside her.

He halted her with his other hand on her wrist. "I'll survive." His eyes darkened as he looked at her bare breasts, still inches from his mouth. The dress shoved halfway down her body. "I have other things to distract me," he murmured, leaning down for her peaked nipple.

Or trying to. A grimace passed over his face.

"Dark Hel, Hunt," she barked, yanking out of his grip, off his fingers, nearly falling from his lap. He didn't even fight her as she grabbed his shoulder and peered at his back.

Fresh blood leaked through his bandages.

"Are you out of your mind?" she shouted, searching for anything in the immediate vicinity to press against the blood. "Why didn't you tell me?"

"As you like to say," he panted, shaking slightly, "it's my body. I decide its limits."

She reined in the urge to strangle him, grabbing for her phone. "I'm calling a medwitch."

He gripped her wrist again. "We're not done here."

"Oh yes we fucking are," she seethed. "I'm not having sex with you when you're spouting blood like a fountain." An exaggeration, but still.

His eyes were dark—burning. So Bryce poked his back, a good six inches beneath his wound. His answering wince of pain settled the argument.

Setting her underwear to rights and sliding her dress back over her chest and arms, she dialed the public medwitch number.

The medwitch arrived and was gone within an hour. Hunt's wound was fine, she'd declared, to Bryce's knee-wobbling relief.

Then Hunt had the nerve to ask if he was cleared for sex.

The witch, to her credit, didn't laugh. Just said, *When you're able to fly again, then I'd say it's safe for you to be sexually active as well.* She nodded toward the couch cushions—the bloodstain that would require a magi-spell to erase. *I'd suggest whatever . . . interaction caused tonight's injury also be postponed until your wings are healed.*

Hunt had looked ready to argue, but Bryce had hurried the witch out of the apartment. And then helped him to his bed. For all his questions, he swayed with each step. Nearly collapsed onto his bed. He answered a few messages on his phone, and was asleep before she'd shut off the lights.

Cleared for sex, indeed.

Bryce slept heavily in her own bed, despite what she'd learned and seen about the synth.

But she woke at three. And knew what she had to do.

She fired off an email with her request, and regardless of the late hour, received one back within twenty minutes: she'd need to wait until her request was approved by the 33rd. Bryce frowned. She didn't have time for that.

She crept from her room. Hunt's door was shut, his room dark beyond it. He didn't so much as come to investigate as she slipped out of the apartment.

And headed for her old one.

She hadn't been on this block in two years.

But as she rounded the corner and saw the flashing lights and terrified crowds, she knew.

Knew what building burned midway down the block.

Someone must have noticed that she'd logged on to Danika's account at Redner Industries today. Or perhaps someone had been monitoring her email account—and seen the message she'd sent to the building's landlord. Whoever had done this must have acted quickly, realizing that she'd wanted to come hunt for any other clues Danika might have left around the apartment.

There had to be more. Danika was smart enough to not have put everything she'd discovered in one place.

Terrified, weeping people—her old neighbors—had clustered on the street, hugging each other and gazing up at the blaze in disbelief. Fire licked at every windowsill.

She'd done this—brought this upon the people watching their homes burn. Her chest tightened, the pain barely eased by overhearing a passing water nymph announce to her firefighting squad that every resident was accounted for.

She had caused this.

But—it meant she was getting close. *Look toward where it hurts the most,* the Viper Queen had advised her all those weeks ago. She'd thought the shifter meant what hurt her. But maybe it had been about the murderer all along.

And by circling in on the synth . . . Apparently, she'd hit a nerve.

Bryce was halfway home when her phone buzzed. She pulled it from her hastily repaired jacket, the white opal in the pocket clinking against the screen, already bracing herself for Hunt's questions.

But it was from Tharion.

There's a deal going down on the river right now. A boat is out there, signaling. Just past the Black Dock. Be there in five and I can get you out to see it.

She clenched the white opal in her fist and wrote back, *A synth deal?*

Tharion answered, *No, a cotton candy deal.*

She rolled her eyes. *I'll be there in three.*

And then she broke into a run. She didn't call Hunt. Or Ruhn.

She knew what they'd say. *Do not fucking go there without me, Bryce. Wait.*

But she didn't have time to waste.

65

Bryce gripped Tharion's waist so hard it was a wonder he didn't have difficulty breathing. Beneath them, the wave skimmer bobbed on the river's current. Only the occasional passing glow under the dark surface indicated that there was anything or anyone around them.

She'd hesitated when the mer arrived at the pier, the matte black wave skimmer idling. *It's either this or swimming, Legs,* he'd informed her.

She'd opted for the wave skimmer, but had spent the last five minutes regretting it.

"Up there," the mer male murmured, cutting the already quiet engine. It must have been a stealth vehicle from the River Queen's stash. Or Tharion's own, as her Captain of Intelligence.

Bryce beheld the small barge idling on the river. Mist drifted around them, turning the few firstlights on the barge into bobbing orbs.

"I count six people," Tharion observed.

She peered into the gloom ahead. "I can't make out what they are. Humanoid shapes."

Tharion's body hummed, and the wave skimmer drifted forward, carried on a current of his own making.

"Neat trick," she murmured.

"It always gets the ladies," he muttered back.

Bryce might have chuckled had they not neared the barge. "Keep downwind so they can't scent us."

"I know how to remain unseen, Legs." But he obeyed her.

The people on the boat were hooded against the misting rain, but as they drifted closer—

"It's the Viper Queen," Bryce said, her voice hushed. No one else in this city would have the swagger to wear that ridiculous purple raincoat. "Lying *asshole*. She said she didn't deal in synth."

"No surprise," Tharion growled. "She's always up to shady shit."

"Yeah, but is she buying or selling this time?"

"Only one way to find out."

They drifted closer. The barge, they realized, was painted with a pair of snake eyes. And the crates piled on the rear of the barge . . . "Selling," Tharion observed. He jerked his chin to a tall figure facing the Viper Queen, apparently in a heated discussion with someone beside them. "Those are the buyers." A nod to the person half-hidden in the shadows, arguing with the tall figure. "Disagreeing about what it's worth, probably."

The Viper Queen was selling synth. Had it really been her this entire time? Behind Danika and the pack's deaths, too, despite that alibi? Or had she merely gotten her hands on the substance once it leaked from the lab?

The arguing buyer shook their head with clear disgust. But their associate seemed to ignore whatever was said and chucked the Viper Queen what looked like a dark sack. She peered inside, and pulled something out. Gold flashed in the mist.

"That is a fuck-ton of money," Tharion murmured. "Enough for that entire shipment, I bet."

"Can you get closer so we can hear?"

Tharion nodded, and they drifted again. The barge loomed, the attention of all aboard fixed on the deal going down rather than the shadows beyond it.

The Viper Queen was saying to them, "I think you'll find this to be sufficient for your goals."

Bryce knew she should call Hunt and Ruhn and get every

legionary and Aux member over here to shut this down before more synth flooded the streets or wound up in worse hands. In the hands of fanatics like Philip Briggs and his ilk.

She pulled her phone from her jacket pocket, flicking a button to keep the screen from lighting up. A push of another button had the camera function appearing. She snapped a few photos of the boat, the Viper Queen, and the tall, dark figure she faced. Human, shifter, or Fae, she couldn't tell with the jacket and hood.

Bryce pulled up Hunt's number.

The Viper Queen said to the buyers, "I think this is the start of a beautiful friendship, don't you?"

The tallest buyer didn't reply. Just stiffly turned back to their companions, displeasure written in every movement as the first-lights illuminated the face beneath the hood.

"Holy fuck," Tharion whispered.

Every thought eddied out of Bryce's head.

There was nothing left in her but roaring silence as Hunt's face became clear.

66

Bryce didn't know how she wound up on the barge. What she said to Tharion to make him pull up. How she climbed off the wave skimmer and onto the boat itself.

But it happened fast. Fast enough that Hunt had made it only three steps before Bryce was there, soaked and wondering if she'd puke.

Guns clicked, pointing at her. She didn't see them.

She only saw Hunt whirl toward her, his eyes wide.

Of course she hadn't recognized him from a distance. He had no wings. But the powerful build, the height, the angle of his head . . . That was all him.

And his colleague behind him, the one who'd handed over the money—Viktoria. Justinian emerged from the shadows beyond them, his wings painted black to conceal them in the moonlight.

Bryce was distantly aware of Tharion behind her, telling the Viper Queen that she was under arrest on behalf of the River Queen. Distantly aware of the Viper Queen chuckling.

But all she heard was Hunt breathe, "Bryce."

"What the fuck is this?" she whispered. Rain slashed her face. She couldn't hear, couldn't get any air down, couldn't think as she said again, her voice breaking, "What the *fuck* is this, Hunt?"

"It is exactly what it looks like," a cold, deep voice said behind her.

In a storm of white wings, Micah emerged from the mists and landed, flanked by Isaiah, Naomi, and six other angels, all armed to the teeth and in legion black. But they made no move to incapacitate the Viper Queen or her cronies.

No, they all faced Hunt and his companions. Aimed their guns toward them.

Hunt looked at the Governor—then at the Viper Queen. He snarled softly, "You fucking bitch."

The Viper Queen chuckled. She said to Micah, "You owe me a favor now, Governor."

Micah jerked his chin in confirmation.

Viktoria hissed at her, halo crinkling on her brow, "You set us up."

The Viper Queen crossed her arms. "I knew it would be worth my while to see who came sniffing around for this shit when word leaked that I got my hands on a shipment," she said, motioning toward the synth. Her smile was pure poison as she looked at Hunt. "I was hoping it'd be you, Umbra Mortis."

Bryce's heart thundered. "What are you talking about?"

Hunt pivoted to her, his face bleak in the floodlights. "It wasn't supposed to go down like this, Bryce. Maybe at first, but I saw that video tonight and I tried to stop it, stop them, but they wouldn't fucking *listen*—"

"These three thought synth would be an easy way to regain what was taken from them," the Viper Queen said. A vicious pause. "The power to overthrow their masters."

The world shifted beneath her. Bryce said, "I don't believe you."

But the flicker of pain in Hunt's eyes told her that her blind, stupid faith in his innocence had gutted him.

"It's true," Micah said, his voice like ice. "These three learned of the synth days ago, and have since been seeking a way to purchase it—and to distribute it among their fellow would-be rebels. To attain its powers long enough to break their halos, and finish what Shahar started on Mount Hermon." He nodded toward the Viper Queen. "She was gracious enough to inform me of this plan, after Justinian tried to recruit a female under her . . . influence."

Bryce shook her head. She was trembling so hard that Tharion gripped her around the waist.

"I told you I'd figure out your asking price, Athalar," the Viper Queen said.

Bryce began crying. She hated every tear, every shuddering, stupid gasp. Hated the pain in Hunt's eyes as he stared at her, only her, and said, "I'm sorry."

But Bryce just asked, "*Days* ago?"

Silence.

She said again, "You knew about the synth *days* ago?"

Her heart—it was her stupid fucking heart that was cracking and cracking and cracking . . .

Hunt said, "Micah assigned me some targets. Three drug lords. They told me that two years ago, a small amount of synth leaked from the Redner lab and onto the streets. But it ran out fast—too fast. They said that finally, after two years of trying to replicate it, someone had figured out the formula at last, and it was now being made—and would be capable of amping up our power. I didn't think it had anything to do with the case—not until recently. I didn't know the truth of what the Hel it could even *do* until I saw that footage of the trials."

"How." Her word cut through the rain. "How did it leak?"

Hunt shook his head. "It doesn't matter."

Micah said coldly, "Danika Fendyr."

Bryce backed up a step, into Tharion's grip. "That's not possible."

Hunt said with a gentleness that decimated her, "Danika sold it, Bryce. It's why she was spotted on that boat with the crate of it. I figured it out nearly a week ago. She stole the formula for it, sold the stock, and—" He stopped himself.

"And *what*?" Bryce whispered. "And *what*, Hunt?"

"And Danika used it herself. Was addicted to it."

She was going to be sick. "Danika would *never* have done that. She never would have done *any* of this."

Hunt shook his head. "She did, Bryce."

"No."

When Micah didn't interrupt them, Hunt said, "Look at the

evidence." His voice was sharp as knives. "Look at the last messages between you. The drugs we found in your system that night—that was standard shit for you two. So what was one more kind of drug? One that in small doses could give an even more intense high? One that could take the edge off for Danika after a long day, after Sabine had ripped her apart yet again? One that gave her a taste of what it'd be like to be Prime of the wolves, *gave* her that power, since she was waiting to make the Drop with you?"

"*No.*"

Hunt's voice cracked. "She took it, Bryce. All signs point to her killing those two CCU students the night the Horn was stolen. They saw her stealing the Horn and she chased them down and killed them."

Bryce remembered Danika's pallor when she'd told her about the students' deaths, her haunted eyes.

"It's not true."

Hunt shook his head. As if he could undo it, unlearn it. "Those drug lords I killed said Danika was seen around the Meat Market. Talking about synth. It was how Danika knew Maximus Tertian—he was an addict like her. His girlfriend had no idea."

"No."

But Hunt looked to Micah. "I assume we're going now." He held out his wrists. For cuffs. Indeed, those were gorsian stones—thick, magic-killing manacles—gleaming in Isaiah's hands.

The Archangel said, "Aren't you going to tell her the rest?"

Hunt stilled. "It's not necessary. Let's go."

"Tell me what," Bryce whispered. Tharion's hands tightened on her arms in warning.

"That he already knows the truth about Danika's murder," the Archangel said coldly. Bored. As if he'd done this a thousand times, in a thousand variations. As if he'd already guessed.

Bryce looked at Hunt and saw it in his eyes. She began shaking her head, weeping. "No."

Hunt said, "Danika took the synth the night she died. Took too much of it. It drove her out of her mind. She slaughtered her own pack. And then herself."

Only Tharion's grip was keeping her upright. "No, no, no—"

Hunt said, "It's why there was never any audio of the killer, Bryce."

"She was begging for her life—"

"She was begging herself to stop," Hunt said. "The only snarls on the recording were hers."

Danika. Danika had killed the pack. Killed Thorne. Killed Connor.

And then ripped herself to shreds.

"But the Horn—"

"She must have stolen it just to piss off Sabine. And then probably sold it on the black market. It had nothing to do with any of this. It was always about the synth for her."

Micah cut in, "I have it on good authority that Danika stole footage of the synth trials from Redner's lab."

"But the kristallos—"

"A side effect of the synth, when used in high doses," Micah said. "The surge of powerful magic it grants the user also brings the ability to open portals, thanks to the obsidian salt in its formula. Danika did just that, accidentally summoning the kristallos. The black salt in the synth can have a mind of its own. A sentience. Its measurement in the synth's formula matches the unholy number of the kristallos. With high doses of synth, the power of the salt gains control and can summon the kristallos. That's why we've been seeing them recently—the drug is on the streets now, in doses often higher than recommended. Like you suspected, the kristallos feeds on vital organs, using the sewers to deposit bodies into the waterway. The two recent murder victims—the acolyte and the temple guard—were the unfortunate victims of someone high on the synth."

Silence fell again. And Bryce turned once more to Hunt. "You knew."

He held her stare. "I'm sorry."

Her voice rose to a scream. "*You knew!*"

Hunt lunged—one step toward her.

A gun gleamed in the dark, pressed against his head, and halted him in his tracks.

Bryce knew that handgun. The engraved silver wings on the black barrel.

"You move, angel, and you fucking die."

Hunt held up his hands. But his eyes did not leave Bryce as Fury Axtar emerged from the shadows beyond the crates of synth.

Bryce didn't question how Fury had arrived without even Micah noticing or how she knew to come. Fury Axtar was liquid night—she'd made herself infamous for knowing the world's secrets.

Fury edged around Hunt, backing up to Bryce's side. She pocketed the gun in the holster at her thigh, her usual skintight black suit gleaming with rain and her chin-length black hair dripping with it, but said to the Viper Queen, "Get the fuck out of my sight."

A sly smile. "It's my boat."

"Then go somewhere I can't see your face."

Bryce didn't have it in her to be shocked that the Viper Queen obeyed Fury's order.

Didn't have it in her to do anything but stare at Hunt. "You knew," she said again.

Hunt's eyes scanned hers. "I never wanted you to be hurt. I never wanted you to know—"

"You knew, you knew, you knew!" He'd figured out the truth, and for nearly a week, he'd said nothing to her. Had let her go on and on about how much she loved her friend, how great Danika had been, and had led her in fucking *circles*. "All your talk about the synth being a waste of my time to look into . . ." She could barely get the words out. "Because you realized the truth already. Because you *lied*." She threw out an arm to the crates of drugs. "Because you learned the truth and then realized you wanted the synth for yourself? And when you wanted to help the medwitch find an antidote . . . It was for *yourself*. And all of this for what—to rebel again?"

Hunt slid to his knees, as if he'd beg her forgiveness. "At first, yes, but it was all just based on a rumor of what it could do. Then tonight I saw that footage you found, and I wanted to pull out from the deal. I knew it wasn't right—any of it. Even with the antidote, it was too dangerous. I realized *all* this was the wrong path. But you and me, Bryce . . . *You* are where I want to end up. A life—with *you*. *You* are my fucking path." He pointed to Justinian and Viktoria, stone-faced and handcuffed. "I messaged them that it was over, but they got spooked, contacted the Viper Queen, and insisted it was going down *tonight*. I swear, I came here only to stop it, to put a fucking *end* to it before it became a disaster. I *never*—"

She grabbed the white opal from her pocket and hurled it at him.

Hurled it so hard it slammed into Hunt's head. Blood flowed from his temple. As if the halo itself were bleeding.

"I never want to see you again," she whispered as Hunt gazed at the blood-splattered opal on the deck.

"That won't be a problem," Micah said, and Isaiah stepped forward, gorsian stone manacles gleaming like amethyst fire. The same as those around Viktoria's and Justinian's wrists.

Bryce couldn't stop shaking as she leaned back into Tharion, Fury a silent force beside her.

"Bryce, I'm sorry," Hunt said as a grim-looking Isaiah clapped the shackles on him. "I couldn't bear the thought of you—"

"That's enough," Fury said. "You've said and done enough." She looked to Micah. "She's done with you. All of you." She tugged Bryce toward her wave skimmer idling beside Tharion's, the mer male guarding their backs. "You bother her again and I'll pay *you* a visit, Governor."

Bryce didn't notice as she was eased onto the wave skimmer. As Fury got on in front of her and gunned the engine. As Tharion slipped onto his and trailed, to guard the way back to shore.

"Bryce," Hunt tried again as she wrapped her arms around Fury's tiny waist. "Your heart was already so broken, and the last thing I ever wanted to do was—"

She didn't look back at him as the wind whipped her hair and the wave skimmer launched into the rain and darkness.

"*BRYCE!*" Hunt roared.

She didn't look back.

67

Ruhn was in the apartment lobby when Fury dropped her off. Tharion left them at the docks, saying he was going to help haul in the seized synth shipment, and Fury departed fast enough that Bryce knew she was heading out to make sure the Viper Queen didn't abscond with any of it, either.

Ruhn said nothing as they rode the elevator.

But she knew Fury had told him. Summoned him here.

Her friend had been messaging someone on the walk back from the docks. And she'd spied Flynn and Declan standing guard on the rooftops of her block, armed with their long-range rifles.

Her brother didn't speak until they were in the apartment, the place dark and hollow and foreign. Every piece of clothing and gear belonging to Hunt was like an asp, ready to strike. That bloodstain on the couch was the worst of all.

Bryce made it halfway across the great room before she puked all over the carpet.

Ruhn was instantly there, his arms and shadows around her.

She could feel her sobs, hear them, but they were distant. The entire world was distant as Ruhn picked her up and carried her to the couch, keeping away from that spot where she'd yielded herself entirely to Hunt. But he made no comment about the bloodstain or any lingering scent.

It wasn't true. It couldn't be true.

No better than a bunch of drug addicts. That's what Hunt had implied. She and Danika had been no better than two addicts, inhaling and snorting everything they could get their hands on.

It wasn't like that. Hadn't ever been like that. It had been stupid, but it had been for fun, for distraction and release, never for something dark—

She was shaking so hard she thought her bones might snap.

Ruhn's grip on her tightened, like he could keep her together.

Hunt must have known she was getting close to learning the truth when she'd shown him the trial videos. So he'd spun her lies about a happy ending for the two of them, a *future* for them, had distracted her with his mouth and hands. And then, as one of the triarii, he'd gotten the alert from her old landlord about her request to visit the apartment—and snuck out, letting her think he was asleep. A bolt of his lightning had probably sparked the flame.

She remembered the water nymph saying that there hadn't been any casualties—had some shred of decency in Hunt made him trigger the fire alarms in an attempt to warn people? She had to believe it.

But once Hunt had burned the building down so there was no hint of evidence left, he'd met with the Viper Queen to barter for what he needed to fuel his rebellion. She didn't believe his bullshit about pulling out of the deal. Not for a heartbeat. He knew the world of hurt about to come down on him. He'd have said anything.

Danika had killed the Pack of Devils. Killed Thorne and Connor. And then herself.

And now Danika lived on, in shame, among the mausoleums of the Sleeping City. Suffering. Because of Bryce.

It wasn't true. It couldn't be true.

By the time Fury came back, Bryce had been staring at the same spot on the wall for hours. Ruhn left her on the couch to talk to the assassin in the kitchen.

Bryce heard their whispering anyway.

Athalar's in one of the holding cells under the Comitium, Fury said.

Micah didn't execute him?

No. Justinian and Viktoria . . . He crucified the angel, and did some fucked-up shit to the wraith.

They're dead?

Worse. Justinian's still bleeding out in the Comitium lobby. They gave him some shit to slow his healing. He'll be dead soon enough if he's lucky.

What about the wraith?

Micah ripped her from her body and shoved her essence into a glass box. Put it at the base of Justinian's crucifix. Rumor says he's going to dump the box—Viktoria—into the Melinoë Trench and let her fall right to the bottom of the sea to go insane from the isolation and darkness.

Fucking Hel. You can't do anything?

They're traitors to the Republic. They were caught conspiring against it. So, no.

But Athalar's not crucified beside Justinian?

I think Micah came up with a different punishment for him. Something worse.

What could be worse than what the other two are enduring?

A long, horrible pause. *A lot of things, Ruhn Danaan.*

Bryce let the words wash over her. She sat on the couch and stared at the dark screen of the television. And stared into the black pit inside herself.

PART IV

THE RAVINE

68

For some reason, Hunt had expected a stone dungeon.

He didn't know why, since he'd been in these holding cells beneath the Comitium countless times to deposit the few enemies Micah wanted left alive, but he'd somehow pictured his capture to be the mirror of what had gone down in Pangera: the dark, filthy dungeons of the Asteri, the ones that were so similar in Sandriel's palace.

Not this white cell, the chrome bars humming with magic to nullify his own. A screen on the wall of the hallway showed a feed of the Comitium atrium: the one body spiked to the iron crucifix in its center, and the glass box, covered in dripping blood, sitting at its feet.

Justinian still groaned every now and then, his toes or fingers twitching as he slowly asphyxiated, his body trying and failing to heal his taxed lungs. His wings had already been cut off. Left on the marble floor beneath him.

Viktoria, her essence invisible within that glass box, was forced to watch. To endure Justinian's blood dripping on the lid of her container.

Hunt had sat on the small cot and watched every second of what had been done to them. How Viktoria had screamed while Micah ripped her from that body she'd been trapped in for so long. How

Justinian had fought, even as they held down his brutalized body on the crucifix, even as the iron spikes went into him. Even as they raised the crucifix, and he'd begun screaming at the pain.

A door clanged open down the hallway. Hunt didn't rise from the cot to see who approached. The wound on his temple had healed, but he hadn't bothered to wash away the blood streaking down his cheek and jaw.

The footsteps down the hall were steady, unhurried. Isaiah.

Hunt remained seated as his old companion paused before the bars.

"Why." There was nothing charming, nothing warm on the handsome face. Just anger, exhaustion, and fear.

Hunt said, aware of every camera and not caring, "Because it has to stop at some point."

"It stops when you're *dead*. When *everyone we love* is dead." Isaiah pointed to the screen behind him, to Justinian's ravaged body and Viktoria's blood-soaked box. "Does this make you feel like you're on the right path, Hunt? Was this worth it?"

When he'd gotten Justinian's message that the deal was going down, as he climbed into bed, he'd realized it *wasn't* worth it. Not even with the medwitch's antidote. Not after these weeks with Bryce. Not after what they'd done on that couch. But Hunt said, because it was still true, "Nothing's changed since Mount Hermon, Isaiah. Nothing has gotten better."

"How long have you three been planning this shit?"

"Since I killed those three drug lords. Since they told me about the synth and what it could do. Since they told me what kind of power it gave Danika Fendyr when she took it in the right doses. We decided it was time. No more fucking bargains with Micah. No more deaths for deaths. Just the ones *we* choose."

The three of them had known there was one place, one person, who might get the synth. He'd paid the Viper Queen a private visit a few days ago. Had found her in her den of poisons and told her what he wanted. Vik had the gold, thanks to the paychecks she'd saved up for centuries.

It hadn't occurred to him that the snake would be in the Archangel's pocket. Or looking for a way into it.

Isaiah shook his head. "And you thought that *you*, you and Vik and Justinian and whatever idiots would follow you, could take the synth and do what? Kill Micah? Sandriel? All of them?"

"That was the idea." They'd planned to do it at the Summit. And afterward, they'd make their way to Pangera. To the Eternal City. And finish what was started so long ago.

"What if it turned on you—what if you took too much and ripped yourself to shreds instead?"

"I was working on getting my hands on an antidote." Hunt shrugged. "But I've already confessed to everything, so spare me the interrogation."

Isaiah banged a hand on the cell bars. Wind howled in the corridor around him. "You couldn't have let it go, couldn't serve and prove yourself and—"

"I tried to stop it, for fuck's sake. I was on that barge because I realized . . ." He shook his head. "It makes no difference at this point. But I did try. I saw that footage of what it really did to someone who took it, and even with an antidote, it was too fucking dangerous. But Justinian and Vik refused to quit. By the time Vik gave the Viper Queen the gold, I just wanted us to go our separate ways."

Isaiah shook his head in disgust.

Hunt spat, "You might be able to accept the bit in your mouth, but I *never* will."

"I don't," Isaiah hissed. "But I have a reason to work for my freedom, Hunt." A flash of his eyes. "I thought you did, too."

Hunt's stomach twisted. "Bryce had nothing to do with this."

"Of course she didn't. You shattered her fucking heart in front of everyone. It was obvious she had no idea."

Hunt flinched, his chest aching. "Micah won't go after her to—"

"No. You're lucky as fuck, but no. He won't crucify her to punish you. Though don't be naïve enough to believe the thought didn't cross his mind."

Hunt couldn't stop his shudder of relief.

Isaiah said, "Micah knows that you tried to stop the deal. Saw the messages between you and Justinian about it. That's why they're in the lobby right now and you're here."

"What's he going to do with me?"

"He hasn't declared it yet." His face softened slightly. "I came down to say goodbye. Just in case we can't later on."

Hunt nodded. He'd accepted his fate. He'd tried, and failed, and would pay the price. Again.

It was a better end than the slow death of his soul as he took one life after another for Micah. "Tell her I'm sorry," Hunt said. "Please."

At the end of the day, despite Vik and Justinian, despite the brutal end that would come his way, it was the sight of Bryce's face that haunted him. The sight of the tears he'd caused.

He'd promised her a future and then brought that pain and despair and sorrow to her face. He'd never hated himself more.

Isaiah's fingers lifted toward the bars, as if he'd reach for Hunt's hand, but then lowered back to his side. "I will."

"It's been three days," Lehabah said. "And the Governor hasn't announced what he's doing with Athie."

Bryce looked up from the book she was reading in the library. "Turn off that television."

Lehabah did no such thing, her glowing face fixed on the tablet's screen. The news footage of the Comitium lobby and the now-rotting corpse of the triarii soldier crucified there. The blood-crusted glass box beneath it. Despite the endless bullshitting by the news anchors and analysts, no information had leaked regarding why two of Micah's top soldiers had been so brutally executed. *A failed coup* was all that had been suggested. No mention of Hunt. Whether he lived.

"He's alive," Lehabah whispered. "I know he is. I can feel it."

Bryce ran a finger over a line of text. It was the tenth time she'd attempted to read it in the twenty minutes since the messenger had left, dropping off a vial of the antidote from the medwitch who'd taken the kristallos venom from her leg. Apparently, she'd found the way to make the antidote work without her being present. But Bryce didn't marvel. Not when the vial was just a silent reminder of what she and Hunt had shared that day.

She'd debated throwing it out, but had opted to lock the antidote in the safe in Jesiba's office, right next to that six-inch golden bullet for the Godslayer Rifle. Life and death, salvation and destruction, now entombed there together.

"Violet Kappel said on the morning news that there might be more would-be rebels—"

"Turn off that screen, Lehabah, before I throw it in the fucking tank."

Her sharp words cut through the library. The rustling creatures in their cages stilled. Even Syrinx stirred from his nap.

Lehabah dimmed to a faint pink. "Are you sure there's nothing we can—"

Bryce slammed the book shut and hauled it with her, aiming for the stairs.

She didn't hear Lehabah's next words over the front door's buzzer. Work had proved busier than usual, a grand total of six shoppers wasting her time asking about shit they had no interest in buying. If she had to deal with one more idiot today—

She glanced at the monitors. And froze.

The Autumn King surveyed the gallery, the showroom stocked with priceless artifacts, the door that led up to Jesiba's office and the window in it that overlooked the floor. He stared at the window for long enough that Bryce wondered if he could somehow see through the one-way glass, all the way to the Godslayer Rifle mounted on the wall behind Jesiba's desk. Sense its deadly presence, and that of the golden bullet in the wall safe beside it. But his eyes drifted on, to the iron door sealed to her right, and finally, finally to Bryce herself.

He'd never come to see her. In all these years, he'd never come. Why bother?

"There are cameras everywhere," she said, staying seated behind her desk, hating every whiff of his ashes-and-nutmeg scent that dragged her back twelve years, to the weeping thirteen-year-old she'd been the last time she'd spoken to him. "In case you're thinking of stealing something."

He ignored the taunt and slid his hands into the pockets of his black jeans, still conducting his silent survey of the gallery. He was gorgeous, her father. Tall, muscled, with an impossibly beautiful face beneath that long red hair, the exact same shade and silken texture as her own. He looked just a few years older than her, too—dressed like a young man, with those black jeans and a matching long-sleeved T-shirt. But his amber eyes were ancient and cruel as he said at last, "My son told me what occurred on the river on Wednesday night."

How he managed to make that slight emphasis on *my son* into an insult was beyond her.

"Ruhn is a good dog."

"*Prince* Ruhn deemed it necessary that I know, since you might be . . . in peril."

"And yet you waited three days? Were you hoping I'd be crucified, too?"

Her father's eyes flashed. "I have come to tell you that your security has been assured, and that the Governor knows you were innocent in the matter and will not dare to harm you. Even to punish Hunt Athalar."

She snorted. Her father stilled. "You are incredibly foolish if you think that would not be enough to break Athalar at last."

Ruhn must have told him about that, too. The disaster that had been this thing between her and Hunt. Whatever it had been. Whatever using her like that could be called.

"I don't want to talk about this." Not with him, not with anyone. Fury had disappeared again, and while Juniper had messaged, Bryce kept the conversation brief. Then the calls from her mother and Randall had started. And the big lies had begun.

She didn't know why she'd lied about Hunt's involvement. Maybe because explaining her own idiocy in letting Hunt in—being so fucking *blind* to the fact that he'd led her around when everyone had warned her, that he'd even *told her* he would love Shahar until the day he died—was too much. It gutted her to know he'd chosen the Archangel and their rebellion over her, over *them* . . . She couldn't talk to her mom about it. Not without completely losing what was left of her ability to function.

So Bryce had gone back to work, because what else was there to do? She'd heard nothing from the places where she'd applied for new jobs.

"I'm *not* talking about this," she repeated.

"You will talk about this. With your king." A crackling ember of his power set the firstlights guttering.

"You are not my king."

"Legally, I am," her father said. "You are listed as a half-Fae citizen. That places you under my jurisdiction both in this city and as a member of the House of Sky and Breath."

She clicked her nails together. "So what is it you want to talk about, *Your Majesty*?"

"Have you stopped looking for the Horn?"

She blinked. "Does it matter now?"

"It is a deadly artifact. Just because you learned the truth regarding Danika and Athalar doesn't mean whoever wishes to use it is done."

"Didn't Ruhn tell you? Danika stole the Horn on a lark. Ditched it somewhere in one of her flying-high-as-a-fucking-kite moments. It was a dead end." At her father's frown, she explained, "The kristallos were all accidentally summoned by Danika and the others who took synth, thanks to the black salt in it. We were wrong in even looking for the Horn. There was no one pursuing it."

She couldn't decide whom she hated more: Hunt, Danika, or herself for not seeing their lies. Not *wanting* to see any of it. It haunted every step, every breath, that loathing. Burned deep inside.

"Even if no enemy seeks it, it is worth ensuring that the Horn does not fall into the wrong hands."

"Only Fae hands, right?" She smiled coldly. "I thought your Chosen One son was put on its tail."

"He is otherwise occupied." Ruhn must have told him to go fuck himself.

"Well, if you can think where Danika unloaded it in her synth-high stupor, I'm all ears."

"It is no trivial matter. Even if the Horn is long defunct, it still holds a special place in Fae history. It will mean a great deal to my people if it is recovered. I'd think with your *professional expertise*, such a search would be of interest to you. And your employer."

She looked back at her computer screen. "Whatever."

He paused, and then his power buzzed, warping every audio feed before he said, "I loved your mother very much, you know."

"Yeah, so much you left a scar on her face."

She could have sworn he flinched. "Do not think I have not spent every moment since then regretting my actions. Living in shame."

"Could have fooled me."

His power rumbled through the room. "You are so much like her. More than you know. She never forgave anyone for anything."

"I take that as a compliment." That fire burned and raged inside her head, her bones.

Her father said quietly, "I would have made her my queen. I had the paperwork ready."

She blinked. "How surprisingly un-elitist of you." Her mother had never suggested, never hinted at it. "She would have hated being queen. She would have said no."

"She loved me enough to have said yes." Absolute certainty laced his words.

"You think that somehow erases what you did?"

"No. Nothing shall ever erase what I did."

"Let's skip the woe-is-me bullshit. You came here after all these years to tell me this crap?"

Her father looked at her for a long moment. Then strode for the door, opening it in silence. But he said before he stepped into the street, his red hair gleaming in the afternoon sunlight, "I came here after all these years to tell you that you may be like your mother, but you are also more like me than you realize." His amber eyes—her own—flickered. "And that is not a good thing."

The door shut, the gallery darkening. Bryce stared at the computer screen before her, then typed in a few words.

There was still nothing on Hunt. No mention of him in the news. Not a whisper about whether the Umbra Mortis was imprisoned or tortured or alive or dead.

As if he had never existed. As if she had dreamed him up.

69

Hunt ate only because his body demanded it, slept because there was nothing else to do, and watched the TV screen in the hall beyond his cell bars because he'd brought this upon himself and Vik and Justinian and there was no undoing it.

Micah had left the latter's body up. Justinian would hang there for seven full days and then be pulled off the crucifix—and dumped into the Istros. No Sailings for traitors. Just the bellies of the river beasts.

Viktoria's box had already been dumped into the Melinoë Trench.

The thought of her trapped on the seafloor, the deepest place in Midgard, nothing but dark and silence and that tight, tight space . . .

Dreams of her suffering had launched Hunt over to the toilet, puking up his guts.

And then the itching began. Deep in his back, radiating through the framework now beginning to regrow, it itched and itched and itched. His fledgling wings remained sore enough that scratching them resulted in near-blinding pain, and as the hours ticked by, each new bit of growth had him clenching his jaw against it.

A waste, he silently told his body. A big fucking waste to

regrow his wings, when he was likely hours or days away from an execution.

He'd had no visitors since Isaiah six days ago. He'd tracked the time by watching the sunlight shift in the atrium on the TV feed.

Not a whisper from Bryce. Not that he dared hope she'd somehow find a way to see him, if only to let him beg on his knees for her forgiveness. To tell her what he needed to say.

Maybe Micah would let him rot down here. Let him go mad like Vik, buried beneath the earth, unable to fly, unable to feel fresh air on his face.

The doors down the hall hissed, and Hunt blinked, rising from his silence. Even his miserably itching wings halted their torture.

But the female scent that hit him a heartbeat later was not Bryce's.

It was a scent he knew just as well—would never forget as long as he lived. A scent that stalked his nightmares, whetted his rage into a thing that made it impossible to think.

The Archangel of northwestern Pangera smiled as she appeared before his cell. He'd never get used to it: how much she looked like Shahar. "This seems familiar," Sandriel said. Her voice was soft, beautiful. Like music. Her face was, too.

And yet her eyes, the color of fresh-tilled soil, gave her away. They were sharp, honed by millennia of cruelty and near-unchecked power. Eyes that delighted in pain and bloodshed and despair. That had always been the difference between her and Shahar—their eyes. Warmth in one; death in the other.

"I heard you want to kill me, Hunt," the Archangel said, crossing her thin arms. She clicked her tongue. "Are we really back to that old game?"

He said nothing. Just sat on his cot and held her gaze.

"You know, when you had your belongings confiscated, they found some interesting things, which Micah was kind enough to share." She pulled an object from her pocket. His phone. "This in particular."

She waved a hand and his phone screen appeared on the TV behind her, its wireless connection showing every movement of her fingers through the various programs. "Your email, of course, was dull as dirt. Do you never delete anything?" She didn't wait for his response before she went on. "But your messages . . ." Her lips curled, and she clicked on the most recent chain.

Bryce had changed her contact name one last time, it seemed.

Bryce Thinks Hunt Is the Best had written:

I know you're not going to see this. I don't even know why I'm writing to you.

She'd messaged a minute after that, *I just . . .* Then another pause. *Never mind. Whoever is screening this, never mind. Ignore this.*

Then nothing. His head became so, so quiet.

"And you know what I found absolutely fascinating?" Sandriel was saying, clicking away from the messages and going into his photos. "These." She chuckled. "*Look* at all of this. Who knew you could act so . . . *commonly*?"

She hit the slideshow function. Hunt just sat there as photos began appearing on the screen.

He'd never looked through them. The photos that he and Bryce had taken these weeks.

There he was, drinking a beer on her couch, petting Syrinx while watching a sunball game.

There he was, making her breakfast because he'd come to enjoy knowing that he could take care of her like that. She'd snapped another photo of him working in the kitchen: of his ass. With her own hand in the foreground, giving a thumbs-up of approval.

He might have laughed, might have smiled, had the next photo not popped up. A photo he'd taken this time, of her mid-sentence.

Then one of him and her on the street, Hunt looking notably annoyed at having his photo taken, while she grinned obnoxiously.

The photo he'd snapped of her dirty and drenched by the sewer grate, spitting mad.

A photo of Syrinx sleeping on his back, limbs splayed. A photo of Lehabah in the library, posing like a pinup girl on her little couch. Then a photo he'd gotten of the river at sunset as he flew overhead. A photo of Bryce's tattooed back in the bathroom mirror, while she gave a saucy wink over her shoulder. A photo he'd taken of an otter in its yellow vest, then one he'd managed to grab a second later of Bryce's delighted face.

He didn't hear what Sandriel was saying.

The photos had begun as an ongoing joke, but they'd become real. Enjoyable. There were more of the two of them. And more photos that Hunt had taken, too. Of the food they'd eaten, interesting graffiti along the alleys, of clouds and things he normally never bothered to notice but had suddenly wanted to capture. And then ones where he looked into the camera and smiled.

Ones where Bryce's face seemed to glow brighter, her smile softer.

The dates drew closer to the present. There they were, on her couch, her head on his shoulder, smiling broadly while he rolled his eyes. But his arm was around her. His fingers casually tangled in her hair. Then a photo he'd taken of her in his sunball hat. Then a ridiculous medley she'd taken of Jelly Jubilee and Peaches and Dreams and Princess Creampuff tucked into his bed. Posed on his dresser. In his bathroom.

And then some by the river again. He had a vague memory of her asking a passing tourist to snap a few. One by one, the various shots unfolded.

First, a photo with Bryce still talking and him grimacing.

Then one with her smiling and Hunt looking at her.

The third was of her still smiling—and Hunt still looking at her. Like she was the only person on the planet. In the galaxy.

His heart thundered. In the next few, her face had turned toward him. Their eyes had met. Her smile had faltered.

As if realizing how he was looking at her.

In the next, she was smiling at the ground, his eyes still on her. A secret, soft smile. Like she knew, and didn't mind one bit.

And then in the last, she had leaned her head against his chest, and wrapped her arms around his middle. He'd put his arm and wing around her. And they had both smiled.

True, broad smiles. Belonging to the people they might have been without the tattoo on his brow and the grief in her heart and this whole stupid fucking world around them.

A life. These were the photos of someone with a *life*, and a good one at that. A reminder of what it had felt like to have a home, and someone who cared whether he lived or died. Someone who made him smile just by entering a room.

He'd never had that before. With anyone.

The screen went dark, and then the photos began again.

And he could see it, this time. How her eyes—they had been so cold at the start. How even with her ridiculous pictures and poses, that smile hadn't reached her eyes. But with each photo, more light had crept into them. Brightened them. Brightened his eyes, too. Until those last photos. When Bryce was near-glowing with joy.

She was the most beautiful thing he had ever seen.

Sandriel was smirking like a cat. "Is this really what you wanted in the end, Hunt?" She gestured to the photos. To Bryce's smiling face. "To be freed one day, to marry the girl, to live out some ordinary, basic life?" She chuckled. "Whatever would Shahar say?"

Her name didn't clang. And the guilt he thought would sear him didn't so much as sizzle.

Sandriel's full lips curved upward, a mockery of her twin's smile. "Such simple, sweet wishes, Hunt. But that's not how these things work out. Not for people like you."

His stomach twisted. The photos were torture, he realized. To remind him of the life he might have had. What he'd tasted on the couch with Bryce the other night. What he'd pissed away.

"You know," Sandriel said, "if you had played the obedient dog, Micah would have eventually petitioned for your freedom." The words pelted him. "But you couldn't be patient. Couldn't be smart. Couldn't choose this"—she gestured to their photos—"over your own petty revenge." Another snake's smile. "So here we are. Here *you* are." She studied a photo Hunt had taken of Bryce with Syrinx, the chimera's pointed little teeth bared in something terrifyingly close to a grin. "The girl will probably cry her little heart out for a while. But then she'll forget you, and she'll find someone else. Maybe there will be some Fae male who can stomach an inferior pairing."

Hunt's senses pricked, his temper stirring.

Sandriel shrugged. "Or she'll wind up in a dumpster with the other half-breeds."

His fingers curled into fists. There was no threat in Sandriel's words. Just the terrible practicality of how their world treated people like Bryce.

"The point is," Sandriel continued, "she will go on. And you and I will go on, Hunt."

At last, at last, he dragged his eyes from Bryce and the photos of the life, the home, they'd made. The life he still so desperately, stupidly wanted. His wings resumed their itching. "What."

Sandriel's smile sharpened. "Didn't they tell you?"

Dread curled as he looked at his phone in her hands. As he realized why he'd been left alive, and why Sandriel had been allowed to take his belongings.

They were *her* belongings now.

Bryce entered the near-empty bar just after eleven. The lack of a brooding male presence guarding her back was like a phantom limb, but she ignored it, made herself forget about it as she spotted Ruhn sitting at the counter, sipping his whiskey.

Only Flynn had joined him, the male too busy seducing the female currently playing billiards with him to give Bryce more than a wary, pitying nod. She ignored it and slid onto the stool beside Ruhn, her dress squeaking against the leather. "Hi."

Ruhn glanced sidelong at her. "Hey."

The bartender strode over, brows raised in silent question. Bryce shook her head. She didn't plan to be here long enough for a drink, water or otherwise. She wanted this over with as quickly as possible so she could go back home, take off her bra, and put on her sweats.

Bryce said, "I wanted to come by to say thanks." Ruhn only stared at her. She watched the sunball game on the TV above the bar. "For the other day. Night. For looking out for me."

Ruhn squinted at the tiled ceiling.

"What?" she asked.

"I'm just checking to see if the sky's falling, since you're thanking me for something."

She shoved his shoulder. "Asshole."

"You could have called or messaged." He sipped from his whiskey.

"I thought it'd be more adultlike to do it face-to-face."

Her brother surveyed her carefully. "How are you holding up?"

"I've been better." She admitted, "I feel like a fucking idiot."

"You're not."

"Oh yeah? Half a dozen people warned me, you included, to be on my guard around Hunt, and I laughed in all your faces." She blew out a breath. "I should have seen it."

"In your defense, I didn't think Athalar was still that ruthless." His blue eyes blazed. "I thought his priorities had shifted lately."

She rolled her eyes. "Yeah, you and dear old Dad."

"He visited you?"

"Yep. Told me I'm just as big a piece of shit as he himself is. Like father, like daughter. Like calls to like or whatever."

"You're nothing like him."

"Don't bullshit a bullshitter, Ruhn." She tapped the bar. "Anyway, that's all I came to say." She noted the Starsword hanging at his side, its black hilt not reflecting the firstlights in the room. "You on patrol tonight?"

"Not until midnight." With his Fae metabolism, the whiskey would be out of his system long before then.

"Well . . . good luck." She hopped off the stool, but Ruhn halted her with a hand on her elbow.

"I'm having some people over at my place in a couple weeks to watch the big sunball game. Why don't you come over?"

"Pass."

"Just come for the first period. If it isn't your thing, no problem. Leave when you want."

She scanned his face, weighing the offer there. The hand extended.

"Why?" she asked quietly. "Why keep bothering?"

"Why keep pushing me away, Bryce?" His voice strained. "It wasn't just about that fight."

She swallowed, her throat thick. "You were my best friend," she said. "Before Danika, you were my best friend. And I . . . It doesn't matter now." She'd realized back then that the truth didn't matter—she wouldn't *let* it matter. She shrugged, as if it'd help lighten the crushing weight in her chest. "Maybe we could start over. On a trial basis *only*."

Ruhn started to smile. "So you'll come watch the game?"

"Juniper was supposed to come over that day, but I'll see if she's up for it." Ruhn's blue eyes twinkled like stars, but Bryce cut in, "No promises, though."

He was still grinning when she rose from her barstool. "I'll save a seat for you."

70

Fury was sitting on the couch when Bryce returned from the bar. In the exact spot where she'd gotten used to seeing Hunt.

Bryce chucked her keys onto the table beside the front door, loosed Syrinx upon her friend, and said, "Hey."

"Hey, yourself." Fury gave Syrinx a look that stopped him in his tracks. That made him sit his fluffy butt down on the carpet, lion's tail swaying, and wait until she deigned to greet *him*. Fury did so after a heartbeat, ruffling his velvety, folded ears.

"What's up?" Bryce toed off her heels, rotated her aching feet a few times, and reached back to tug at the zipper to her dress. Gods, it was incredible to have no pain in her leg—not even a flicker. She padded for her bedroom before Fury could answer, knowing she'd hear anyway.

"I got some news," Fury said casually.

Bryce peeled off her dress, sighing as she took off her bra, and changed into a pair of sweats and an old T-shirt before pulling her hair into a ponytail. "Let me guess," she said from the bedroom, shoving her feet into slippers, "you finally realized that black all the time is boring and want me to help you find some real-person clothes?"

A quiet laugh. "Smart-ass." Bryce emerged from the bedroom, and Fury eyed her with that swift assassin's stare. So unlike Hunt's.

Even when she and Fury had been out partying, Fury never really lost that cold gleam. That calculation and distance. But Hunt's stare—

She shut out the thought. The comparison. That roaring fire in her veins flared.

"Look," Fury said, standing from the couch. "I'm heading out a few days early to the Summit. So I just thought you should know something before I go."

"You love me and you'll write often?"

"Gods, you're the worst," Fury said, running a hand through her sleek bob. Bryce missed the long ponytail her friend had worn in college. The new look made Fury seem even more lethal, somehow. "Ever since I met you in that dumb-ass class, you've been the worst."

"Yeah, but you find it delightful." Bryce aimed for the fridge.

A huff. "Look, I'm going to tell you this, but I want you to first promise me that you won't do anything stupid."

Bryce froze with her fingers grasping the handle of the fridge. "As you've told me so often, *stupid* is my middle name."

"I mean it this time. I don't even think anything can be done, but I need you to promise."

"I promise."

Fury studied her face, then leaned against the kitchen counter. "Micah gave Hunt away."

That fire in her veins withered to ash. "To whom?"

"Who do you think? Fucking Sandriel, that's who."

She couldn't feel her arms, her legs. "When."

"You said you wouldn't do anything stupid."

"Is asking for details stupid?"

Fury shook her head. "This afternoon. That bastard knew giving Hunt back to Sandriel was a bigger punishment than publicly crucifying him or shoving his soul into a box and dumping it into the sea."

It was. For so many reasons.

Fury went on, "She and the other angels are heading to the Summit tomorrow afternoon. And I have it on good authority that once the meeting's done next week, she'll go back to Pangera to keep dealing with the Ophion rebels. With Hunt in tow."

And he'd never be free again. What Sandriel would do to him . . . He deserved it. He fucking deserved *everything*.

Bryce said, "If you're so concerned I'll do something stupid, why tell me at all?"

Fury's dark eyes scanned her again. "Because . . . I just thought you should know."

Bryce turned to the fridge. Yanked it open. "Hunt dug his own grave."

"So you two weren't . . ."

"No."

"His scent is on you, though."

"We lived in this apartment together for a month. I'd think it'd be on me."

She'd handed over a hideous number of silver marks to have his blood removed from the couch. Along with all traces of what they'd done there.

A small, strong hand slammed the fridge door shut. Fury glared up at her. "Don't bullshit me, Quinlan."

"I'm not." Bryce let her friend see her true face. The one her father had talked about. The one that did not laugh and did not care for anybody or anything. "Hunt is a liar. He *lied* to me."

"Danika did some fucked-up stuff, Bryce. You know that. You always knew it and laughed it off, looked the other way. I'm not so sure Hunt was lying about that."

Bryce bared her teeth. "I'm over it."

"Over what?"

"All of it." She yanked open the fridge again, nudging Fury out of the way. To her surprise, Fury let her. "Why don't you go back to Pangera and ignore me for another two years?"

"I didn't ignore you."

"You fucking *did*," Bryce spat. "You talk to June all the time, and yet you dodge my calls and barely reply to my messages?"

"June is different."

"Yeah, I know. The special one."

Fury blinked at her. "You nearly *died* that night, Bryce. And Danika *did* die." The assassin's throat bobbed. "I gave you drugs—"

"I bought that mirthroot."

"And I bought the lightseeker. I don't fucking care, Bryce. I got too close to all of you, and *bad things* happen when I do that with people."

"And yet you can still talk to Juniper?" Bryce's throat closed up. "I wasn't worth the risk to you?"

Fury hissed, "Juniper and I have something that is *none* of your fucking business." Bryce refrained from gaping. Juniper had never hinted, never suggested—"I could no sooner stop talking to her than I could rip out my own fucking heart, okay?"

"I get it, I get it," Bryce said. She blew out a long breath. "Love trumps all."

Too fucking bad Hunt hadn't realized that. Or he had, but he'd just chosen the Archangel who still held his heart and their *cause*. Too fucking bad Bryce had still been stupid enough to believe nonsense about love—and let it blind her.

Fury's voice broke. "You and Danika were my friends. You were these two stupid fucking *puppies* that came bounding into my perfectly fine life, and then one of you was slaughtered." Fury bared her teeth. "And. I. Couldn't. Fucking. Deal."

"I needed you. I needed you *here*. Danika died, but it was like I lost you, too." Bryce didn't fight the burning in her eyes. "You walked away like it was nothing."

"It wasn't." Fury blew out a breath. "Fuck, did Juniper not tell you *anything*?" At Bryce's silence, she swore again. "Look, she and I have been working through a lot of my shit, okay? I know it was fucked up that I bailed like that." She dragged her fingers through her hair. "It's all just . . . it's more fucked than you know, Bryce."

"Whatever."

Fury angled her head. "Do I need to call Juniper?"

"No."

"Is this a repeat of two winters ago?"

"No." Juniper must have told her about that night on the roof. They told each other everything, apparently.

Bryce grabbed a jar of almond butter, screwed off the lid, and dug in with a spoon. "Well, have fun at the Summit. See you in another two years."

Fury didn't smile. "Don't make me regret telling you all this."

She met her friend's dark stare. "I'm over it," she said again.

Fury sighed. "All right." Her phone buzzed and she peered at the screen before saying, "I'll be back in a week. Let's hang then, okay? Maybe without screaming at each other."

"Sure."

Fury stalked for the door, but paused on the threshold. "It'll get better, Bryce. I know the past two years have been shit, but it will get better. I've been there, and I promise you it does."

"Okay." Bryce added, because real concern shone on Fury's normally cold face, "Thanks."

Fury had the phone to her ear before she'd shut the door. "Yeah, I'm on my way," she said. "Well, why don't you shut the fuck up and let me drive so I can get there on time, dickbag?"

Through the peephole, Bryce watched her get onto the elevator. Then crossed the room and watched from the window as Fury climbed into a fancy black sports car, gunned the engine, and roared off into the streets.

Bryce peered at Syrinx. The chimera wagged his little lion's tail.

Hunt had been given away. To the monster he hated and feared above all others.

"I *am* over it," she said to Syrinx.

She looked toward the couch, and could nearly see Hunt sitting there, that sunball cap on backward, watching a game on TV. Could nearly see his smile as he looked over his shoulder at her.

That roaring fire in her veins halted—and redirected. She wouldn't lose another friend.

Especially not Hunt. Never Hunt.

No matter what he had done, what and who he'd chosen, even if this was the last she would ever see of him . . . she wouldn't let this happen. He could go to Hel afterward, but she would do this. For him.

Syrinx whined, pacing in a circle, claws clicking on the wood floor.

"I promised Fury not to do anything *stupid*," Bryce said, her eyes on Syrinx's branded-out tattoo. "I didn't say I wouldn't do something smart."

71

Hunt had a night to puke out his guts.

One night in that cell, likely the last bit of security he'd have for the rest of his existence.

He knew what would happen after the Summit. When Sandriel took him back to her castle in the misty, mountainous wilds of northwestern Pangera. To the gray-stoned city in its heart.

He'd lived it for more than fifty years, after all.

She'd left the photo feed up on the hallway TV screen, so he could see Bryce over and over and over. See the way Bryce had looked at him by the end, like he wasn't a complete waste of life.

It wasn't just to torture him with what he'd lost.

It was a reminder. Of who would be targeted if he disobeyed. If he resisted. If he fought back.

By dawn, he'd stopped puking. Had washed his face in the small sink. A change of clothes had arrived for him. His usual black armor. No helmet.

His back itched incessantly as he dressed, the cloth scraping against the wings that were taking form. Soon they'd be fully regenerated. A week of careful physical therapy after that and he'd be in the skies.

If Sandriel ever let him out of her dungeons.

She'd lost him once, to pay off her debts. He had few illusions that she'd allow it to happen again. Not until she found a way to break him for how he'd targeted her forces on Mount Hermon. How he and Shahar had come so close to destroying her completely.

It wasn't until nearly sunset that they came for him. As if Sandriel wanted him stewing all day.

Hunt let them shackle him again with the gorsian stones. He knew what the stones would do if he so much as moved wrong. Disintegration of blood and bone, his brain turned into soup before it leaked out his nose.

The armed guard, ten deep, led him from the cell and into the elevator. Where Pollux Antonius, the golden-haired commander of Sandriel's triarii, waited, a smile on his tan face.

Hunt knew that dead, cruel smile well. Had tried his best to forget it.

"Miss me, Athalar?" Pollux asked, his clear voice belying the monster lurking within. The Hammer could smash through battlefields and delighted in every second of carnage. Of fear and pain. Most Vanir never walked away. No humans ever had.

But Hunt didn't let his rage, his hatred for that smirking, handsome visage so much as flicker across his face. A glimmer of annoyance flashed in Pollux's cobalt eyes, his white wings shifting.

Sandriel waited in the Comitium lobby, the last of the sunlight shining in her curling hair.

The lobby. Not the landing pad levels above. So he might see—

Might see—

Justinian still hung from the crucifix. Rotting away.

"We thought you might want to say goodbye," Pollux purred in his ear as they crossed the lobby. "The wraith, of course, is at the bottom of the sea, but I'm sure she knows you'll miss her."

Hunt let the male's words flow through him, out of him. They would only be the start. Both from the Malleus and from Sandriel herself.

The Archangel smiled at Hunt as they approached, the cruelty on her face making Pollux's smirk look downright pleasant. But she said nothing as she turned on her heel toward the lobby doors.

An armed transport van idled outside, back doors flung wide. Waiting for him, since he sure as fuck couldn't fly. From the mocking gleam in Pollux's eyes, Hunt had a feeling he knew who would be accompanying him.

Angels from the Comitium's five buildings filled the lobby.

He noted Micah's absence—coward. The bastard probably didn't want to sully himself by witnessing the horror he'd inflicted. But Isaiah stood near the heart of the gathered crowd, his expression grim. Naomi gave Hunt a grave nod.

It was all she dared, the only farewell they could make.

The angels silently watched Sandriel. Pollux. Him. They hadn't come to taunt, to witness his despair and humiliation. They, too, had come to say goodbye.

Every step toward the glass doors was a lifetime, was impossible. Every step was abhorrent.

He had done this, brought this upon himself and his companions, and he would pay for it over and over and—

"*Wait!*" The female voice rang out from across the lobby.

Hunt froze. Everyone froze.

"*Wait!*"

No. No, she couldn't be here. He couldn't bear for her to see him like this, knees wobbling and a breath away from puking again. Because Pollux strode beside him, and Sandriel prowled in front of him, and they would destroy her—

But there was Bryce. Running toward them. Toward him.

Fear and pain tightened her face, but her wide eyes were trained on him as she shouted again, to Sandriel, to the entire lobby full of angels, "*Wait!*"

She was breathless as the crowd parted. Sandriel halted, Pollux and the guards instantly on alert, forcing Hunt to pause with them, too.

Bryce skidded to a stop before the Archangel. "Please," she

panted, bracing her hands on her knees, her ponytail drooping over a shoulder as she tried to catch her breath. No sign of that limp. "Please, wait."

Sandriel surveyed her like she would a gnat buzzing about her head. "Yes, Bryce Quinlan?"

Bryce straightened, still panting. Looked at Hunt for a long moment, for eternity, before she said to the Archangel of northwestern Pangera, "Please don't take him."

Hunt could barely stand to hear the plea in her voice. Pollux let out a soft, hateful laugh.

Sandriel was not amused. "He has been gifted to me. The papers were signed yesterday."

Bryce pulled something from her pocket, causing the guards around them to reach for their weapons. Pollux's sword was instantly in his hand, angled toward her with lethal efficiency.

But it wasn't a gun or a knife. It was a piece of paper.

"Then let me buy him from you."

Utter silence.

Sandriel laughed then, the sound rich and lilting. "Do you know how much—"

"I'll pay you ninety-seven million gold marks."

The floor rocked beneath Hunt. People gasped. Pollux blinked, eyeing Bryce again.

Bryce extended a piece of paper toward Sandriel, though the malakh didn't take it. Even from a few feet behind the Archangel, Hunt's sharp eyesight could make out the writing.

Proof of funds. A check from the bank, made out to Sandriel. For nearly a hundred million marks.

A check from Jesiba Roga.

Horror sluiced through him, rendering him speechless. How many years had Bryce added to her debt?

He didn't deserve it. Didn't deserve her. Not for a heartbeat. Not in a thousand years—

Bryce waved the check toward Sandriel. "Twelve million more than his asking price when you sold him, right? You'll—"

"I know how to do the mathematics."

Bryce remained with her arm outstretched. Hope in her beautiful face. Then she reached up, Pollux and the guards tensing again. But it was to just unclasp the golden amulet from around her neck. "Here. To sweeten the deal. An Archesian amulet. It's fifteen thousand years old, and fetches around three million gold marks on the market."

That tiny necklace was worth three *million* gold marks?

Bryce extended both the necklace and the paper, the gold glinting. "Please."

He couldn't let her do it. Not even for what remained of his soul. Hunt opened his mouth, but the Archangel took the dangling necklace from Bryce's fingers. Sandriel glanced between them. Read everything on Hunt's face. A snake's smile curled her mouth. "Your loyalty to my sister was the one good thing about you, Athalar." She clenched her fist around the amulet. "But it seems those photographs did not lie."

The Archesian amulet melted into streams of gold on the floor.

Something ruptured in Hunt's chest at the devastation that crumpled Bryce's face.

He said quietly to her, his first words all day, "Get out of here, Bryce."

But Bryce pocketed the check. And slid to her knees.

"Then take me."

Terror rocked him, so violently he had no words when Bryce looked up at Sandriel, tears filling her eyes as she said, "Take me in his place."

A slow grin spread across Pollux's face.

No. She'd already traded her eternal resting place in the Bone Quarter for Danika. He couldn't let her trade her mortal life for him. Not for him—

"Don't you dare!" The male bellow cracked across the space. Then Ruhn was there, wreathed in shadows, Declan and Flynn flanking him. They weren't foolish enough to reach for their guns as they sized up Sandriel's guards. Realized that Pollux Antonius, the

Malleus, stood there, sword angled to punch through Bryce's chest if Sandriel so much as gave the nod.

The Crown Prince of the Fae pointed at Bryce. "Get off the floor."

Bryce didn't move. She just repeated to Sandriel, "Take me in his place."

Hunt snapped at Bryce, "*Be quiet*," just as Ruhn snarled at the Archangel, "Don't listen to a word she says—"

Sandriel took a step toward Bryce. Another. Until she stood before her, peering down into Bryce's flushed face.

Hunt pleaded, "Sandriel—"

"You offer your life," Sandriel said to Bryce. "Under no coercion, no force."

Ruhn lunged forward, shadows unfurling around him, but Sandriel raised a hand and a wall of wind held him in check. It choked off the prince's shadows, shredding them into nothing.

It held Hunt in check, too, as Bryce met Sandriel's stare and said, "Yes. In exchange for Hunt's freedom, I offer myself in his place." Her voice shook, cracking. She knew how he'd suffered at the Archangel's hands. Knew what awaited her would be even worse.

"Everyone here would call me a fool to take this bargain," Sandriel mused. "A half-breed with no true power or hope to come into it—in exchange for the freedom of one of the most powerful malakim to ever darken the skies. The only warrior on Midgard who can wield lightning."

"Sandriel, *please*," Hunt begged. The air ripping from his throat choked off his words.

Pollux smiled again. Hunt bared his teeth at him as Sandriel stroked a hand over Bryce's cheek, wiping away her tears. "But I know your secret, Bryce Quinlan," Sandriel whispered. "I know what a prize you are."

Ruhn cut in, "That is *enough*—"

Sandriel stroked Bryce's face again. "The only daughter of the Autumn King."

Hunt's knees wobbled.

"Holy fuck," Tristan Flynn breathed. Declan had gone pale as death.

Sandriel purred at Bryce, "Yes, what a prize you would be to possess."

Her cousin's face was stark with terror.

Not cousin. *Brother.* Ruhn was her brother. And Bryce was . . .

"What does your father think of his bastard daughter borrowing such a vast amount from Jesiba Roga?" Sandriel went on, chuckling as Bryce began crying in earnest now. "What shame it would bring upon his royal household, knowing you sold your life away to a half-rate sorceress."

Bryce's pleading eyes met his. The amber eyes of the Autumn King.

Sandriel said, "You thought you were safe from *me*? That after you pulled your little stunt when I arrived, I wouldn't look into your history? My spies are second to none. They found what could not be found. Including your life span test from twelve years ago, and whom it exposed as your father. Even though he paid steeply to bury it."

Ruhn stepped forward, either pushing past Sandriel's wind or being allowed to do so. He grabbed Bryce under the arm and hauled her to her feet. "She is a female member of the Fae royal household and a full civitas of the Republic. I lay claim to her as my sister and kin."

Ancient words. From laws that had never been changed, though public sentiment had.

Bryce whirled on him. *"You have no right—"*

"Based upon the laws of the Fae, as approved by the Asteri," Ruhn charged on, "she is *my* property. My father's. And I do not permit her to trade herself in exchange for Athalar."

Hunt's legs almost gave out with relief. Even as Bryce shoved at Ruhn, clawed at him, and growled, "I'm no property of yours—"

"You are a Fae female of my bloodline," Ruhn said coldly. "You are my property and our father's until you marry."

She looked to Declan, to Flynn, whose solemn faces must have told her she'd find no allies among them. She hissed at Ruhn, "I will *never* forgive you. I will *never*—"

"We're done here," Ruhn said to Sandriel.

He tugged Bryce away, his friends falling into formation around them, and Hunt tried to memorize her face, even with despair and rage twisting it.

Ruhn tugged her again, but she thrashed against him.

"Hunt," she pleaded, stretching a hand for him, "I'll find a way."

Pollux laughed. Sandriel just began to turn from them, bored.

But Bryce continued to reach for him, even as Ruhn tried to drag her toward the doors.

Hunt stared at her outstretched fingers. The desperate hope in her eyes.

No one had ever fought for him. No one had ever cared enough to do so.

"*Hunt*," Bryce begged, shaking. Her fingers strained. *"I'll find a way to save you."*

"*Stop it*," Ruhn ordered, and grabbed for her waist.

Sandriel walked toward the lobby doors and the awaiting motorcade. She said to Ruhn, "You should have slit your sister's throat when you had the chance, Prince. I speak from personal experience."

Bryce's wrenching sobs ripped at Hunt as Pollux shoved him into movement.

She'd never stop fighting for him, would never give up hope. So Hunt went in for the kill as he passed her, even as each word broke him apart, "I owe you nothing, and you owe me nothing. Don't ever come looking for me again."

Bryce mouthed his name. As if he were the sole person in the room. The city. The planet.

And it was only when Hunt was loaded onto the armored truck, when his chains were anchored to the metal sides and Pollux was smirking across from him, when the driver had embarked on the five-hour drive to the town in the heart of the Psamathe Desert where the Summit would be held in five days, that he let himself take a breath.

* * *

Ruhn watched as Pollux loaded Athalar into that prison van. Watched as it rumbled to life and sped off, watched as the crowd in the lobby dispersed, marking the end of this fucking disaster.

Until Bryce wrenched out of his grip. Until Ruhn let her. Pure, undiluted hatred twisted her features as she said again, "I will *never* forgive you for this."

Ruhn said coldly, "Do you have any idea what Sandriel does to her slaves? Do you know that was Pollux Antonius, the fucking *Hammer*, with her?"

"Yes. Hunt told me everything."

"Then you're a fucking idiot." She advanced on him, but Ruhn seethed, "I will not apologize for protecting you—not from her, and not from yourself. I get it, I do. Hunt was your—whatever he was to you. But the last thing he would ever want is—"

"Go fuck yourself." Her breathing turned jagged. *"Go fuck yourself, Ruhn."*

Ruhn jerked his chin toward the lobby doors in dismissal. "Cry about it to someone else. You'll have a hard time finding anyone who'll agree with you."

Her fingers curled at her sides. As if she'd punch him, claw him, shred him.

But she just spat at Ruhn's feet and stalked away. Bryce reached her scooter and didn't look back as she zoomed off.

Flynn said, voice low, "What the fuck, Ruhn."

Ruhn sucked in a breath. He didn't even want to think about what kind of bargain she'd struck with the sorceress to get that kind of money.

Declan was shaking his head. And Flynn . . . disappointment and hurt flickered on his face. "Why didn't you tell us? Your *sister*, Ruhn?" Flynn pointed to the glass doors. "She's our fucking *princess*."

"She is not," Ruhn growled. "The Autumn King has not recognized her, nor will he ever."

"Why?" Dec demanded.

"Because she's his bastard child. Because he doesn't like her.

I don't fucking know," Ruhn spat. He couldn't—wouldn't—ever tell them his own motivations for it. That deep-rooted fear of what the Oracle's prophecy might mean for Bryce should she ever be granted a royal title. For if the royal bloodline was to end with Ruhn, and Bryce was officially a princess of their family . . . She would have to be out of the picture for it to come to pass. Permanently. He'd do whatever was necessary to keep her safe from that particular doom. Even if the world hated him for it.

Indeed, at his friends' disapproving frowns, he snapped, "All I know is that I was given an order never to reveal it, even to you."

Flynn crossed his arms. "You think we would have told anyone?"

"No. But I couldn't take the risk of him finding out. And *she* didn't want anyone to know." And now wasn't the time or place to speak about this. Ruhn said, "I need to talk to her."

What came *after* he spoke with Bryce, he didn't know if he could handle.

Bryce rode to the river. To the arches of the Black Dock.

Darkness had fallen by the time she chained her scooter to a lamppost, the night balmy enough that she was grateful for Danika's leather jacket keeping her warm as she stood on the dark dock and stared across the Istros.

Slowly, she sank to her knees, bowing her head. "It's so fucked," she whispered, hoping the words would carry across the water, to the tombs and mausoleums hidden behind the wall of mist. "It is all so, so fucked, Danika."

She'd failed. Utterly and completely failed. And Hunt was . . . he was . . .

Bryce buried her face in her hands. For a while, the only sounds were the wind hissing through the palms and the lapping of the river against the dock.

"I wish you were here," Bryce finally allowed herself to say. "Every day, I wish that, but today especially."

The wind quieted, the palms going still. Even the river seemed to halt.

A chill crept toward her, through her. Every sense, Fae and human, went on alert. She scanned the mists, waiting, praying for a black boat. She was so busy looking that she didn't see the attack coming.

Didn't twist to see a kristallos demon leaping from the shadows, jaws open, before it tackled her into the eddying waters.

72

Claws and teeth were everywhere. Ripping at her, snatching her, dragging her down.

The river was pitch-black, and there was no one, no one at all, who'd seen or would know—

Something burned along her arm, and she screamed, water rushing down her throat.

Then the claws splayed. Loosened.

Bryce kicked, shoving blindly away, the surface somewhere—in any direction—oh gods, she was going to pick wrong—

Something grabbed her by the shoulder, dragging her away, and she would have screamed if there had been any air left in her lungs—

Air broke around her face, open and fresh, and then there was a male voice at her ear saying, "I've got you, I've got you."

She might have sobbed, if she hadn't spewed water, hadn't launched into a coughing fit. Hunt had said those words to her, and now Hunt was gone, and the male voice at her ear—Declan Emmet.

Ruhn shouted from a few feet away, "It's down."

She thrashed, but Declan held her firm, murmuring, "It's all right."

It wasn't fucking all right. Hunt should have been there. He should have been with her, he should have been freed, and she should have found a way to help him—

It took half a moment for Declan to heave her out of the water. Ruhn, his face grim, hauled her the rest of the way, cursing up a storm while she shuddered on the dock.

"What the fucking fuck," Tristan Flynn was panting, rifle aimed at the black water, ready to unload a hail of bullets at the slightest ripple.

"Are you all right?" Declan asked, water streaming down his face, red hair plastered to his head.

Bryce drew back into herself enough to survey her body. A gash sliced down her arm, but it had been made with claws, not those venomous teeth. Other slices peppered her, but . . .

Declan didn't wait before kneeling before her, hands wreathed in light as he held them over the gash in her arm. It was rare—the Fae healing gift. Not as powerful as the talent of a medwitch, but a valuable strength to possess. She'd never known Dec had the ability.

Ruhn asked, "Why the *fuck* were you standing on the Black Dock after sundown?"

"I was kneeling," she muttered.

"Same fucking question."

She met her brother's gaze as her wounds healed shut. "I needed a breather."

Flynn muttered something.

"What?" She narrowed her eyes at him.

Flynn crossed his arms. "I said I've known that you're a princess for all of an hour and you're already a pain in my ass."

"I'm not a princess," she said at the same moment Ruhn snapped, "She's not a princess."

Declan snorted. "Whatever, assholes." He pulled back from Bryce, healing complete. "We should have realized. You're the only one who even comes close to getting under Ruhn's skin as easily as his father does."

Flynn cut in, "Where did that thing come from?"

"Apparently," she said, "people who take large quantities of synth can inadvertently summon a kristallos demon. It was probably a freak accident."

"Or a targeted attack," Flynn challenged.

"The case is over," Bryce said flatly. "It's done."

The Fae lord's eyes flashed with a rare show of anger. "Maybe it isn't."

Ruhn wiped the water off his face. "On the chance Flynn's right, you're staying with me."

"Over my dead fucking body." Bryce stood, water pouring off her. "Look, thanks for rescuing me. And thanks for royally fucking me and Hunt over back there. But you know what?" She bared her teeth and pulled out her phone, wiping water from it, praying the protective spell she'd paid good money for had held. It had. She scrolled through screens until she got to Ruhn's contact info. She showed it to him. "You?" She swiped her finger, and it was deleted. "Are *dead* to me."

She could have sworn her brother, her fuck-you-world brother, flinched.

She looked at Dec and Flynn. "Thanks for saving my ass."

They didn't come after her. Bryce could barely stop shaking long enough to steer her scooter home, but she somehow made it. Made it upstairs, walked Syrinx.

The apartment was too quiet without Hunt in it. No one had come to take his things. If they had, they'd have found that sunball hat missing. Hidden in the box alongside Jelly Jubilee.

Exhausted, Bryce peeled off her clothes and stared at herself in the bathroom mirror. She lifted a palm to her chest, where the weight of the Archesian amulet had been for the past three years.

Red, angry lines marred her skin where the kristallos had swiped, but with Declan's magic still working on her, they'd be faded to nothing by morning.

She twisted, bracing herself to see the damage to the tattoo on her back. This last shred of Danika. If that fucking demon had wrecked it . . .

She nearly wept to see it intact. To look at the lines in that ancient, unreadable alphabet and know that even with everything gone to Hel, this still remained: The words Danika had insisted they ink there, with Bryce too plastered to object. Danika had picked the alphabet out of some booklet at the shop, though it sure as fuck didn't look like any Bryce recognized. Maybe the artist had just made it up, and told them it said what Danika had wanted:

Through love, all is possible.

The same words on the jacket in a pile at her feet. The same words that had been a clue—to her Redner account, to finding that flash drive.

Nonsense. It was all fucking nonsense. The tattoo, the jacket, losing that amulet, losing Danika, losing Connor and the Pack of Devils, losing Hunt—

Bryce tried and failed to wrest herself from the cycle of thoughts, the maelstrom that brought them around and around and around, until they all eddied together.

73

The last Summit Hunt had attended had been in an ancient, sprawling palace in Pangera, bedecked in the riches of the empire: silk tapestries and sconces of pure gold, goblets twinkling with precious stones, and succulent meats crusted in the rarest spices.

This one was held in a conference center.

The glass and metal space was sprawling, its layout reminding Hunt of a bunch of shoeboxes stacked beside and atop each other. Its central hall rose three stories high, the stairs and escalators at the back of the space adorned with the crimson banners of the Republic, the long pathway leading to them carpeted in white.

Each territory in Midgard held their own Summit every ten years, attended by various leaders within their borders, along with a representative of the Asteri and a few visiting dignitaries relevant to whatever issues would be discussed. This one was no different, save for its smaller scope: Though Valbara was far smaller than Pangera, Micah held four different Summit meetings, each for a separate quadrant of his realm. This one, for the southeastern holdings—with Lunathion's leaders at its heart—was the first.

The site, located in the heart of the Psamathe Desert, a good five-hour drive from Crescent City—an hour for an angel at top flying speeds or a mere half hour by helicopter—had its own holding cells for dangerous Vanir.

He'd spent the last five days there, marking them by the shift in his food: breakfast, lunch, dinner. At least Sandriel and Pollux had not come to taunt him. At least he had that small reprieve. He'd barely listened to the Hammer's attempts to bait him during the drive. He'd barely felt or heard anything at all.

Yet this morning, a set of black clothes had arrived with his breakfast tray. No weapons, but the uniform was clear enough. So was the message: he was about to be displayed, a mockery of an imperial Triumphus parade, for Sandriel to gloat about regaining ownership of him.

But he'd obediently dressed, and let Sandriel's guards fit the gorsian manacles on him, rendering his power null and void.

He followed the guards silently, up through the elevator, and into the grand lobby itself, bedecked in imperial regalia.

Vanir of every House filled the space, most dressed in business clothes or what had once been known as courtly attire. Angels, shifters, Fae, witches . . . Delegations flanked either side of the red runner leading toward the stairs. Fury Axtar stood among the crowd, clad in her usual assassin leathers, watching everyone. She didn't look his way.

Hunt was led toward a delegation of angels near the staircase—members of Sandriel's 45th Legion. Her triarii. Pollux stood in front of them, his commander status marked by his gold armor, his cobalt cape, his smirking face.

That smirk only grew as Hunt took up his position nearby, wedged between her guards.

Her other triarii were nearly as bad as the Hammer. Hunt would never forget any of them: the thin, pale-skinned, dark-haired female known as the Harpy; the stone-faced, black-winged male called the Helhound; and the haughty, cold-eyed angel named the Hawk. But they ignored him. Which, he'd learned, was better than their attention.

No sign of the Hind, the final member of the triarii—though maybe her work as a spy-breaker in Pangera was too valuable to the Asteri for Sandriel to be allowed to drag her here.

Across the runner stood Isaiah and the 33rd. What remained

of its triarii. Naomi was stunning in her uniform, her chin high and right hand on the hilt of her formal legion sword, its winged cross guard glinting in the morning light.

Isaiah's eyes drifted over to his. Hunt, in his black armor, was practically naked compared to the full uniform of the Commander of the 33rd: the bronze breastplate, the epaulets, the greaves and vambraces . . . Hunt still remembered how heavy it was. How stupid he'd always felt decked out in the full regalia of the Imperial Army. Like some prize warhorse.

The Autumn King's Auxiliary forces stood to the left of the angels, their armor lighter but no less ornate. Across from them were the shifters, in their finest clothes. Amelie Ravenscroft didn't so much as dare look in his direction. Smaller groups of Vanir filled the rest of the space: mer and daemonaki. No sign of any humans. Certainly no one with mixed heritage, either.

Hunt tried not to think of Bryce. Of what had gone down in the lobby.

Princess of the Fae. Bastard princess was more like it, but she was still the only daughter of the Autumn King.

She might have been furious at him for lying, but she'd lied plenty to him as well.

Drummers—fucking Hel, the gods-damned drummers—sounded the beat. The trumpeters began a moment later. The rolling, hateful anthem of the Republic filled the cavernous glass space. Everyone straightened as a motorcade pulled up beyond the doors.

Hunt sucked in a breath as Jesiba Roga emerged first, clad in a thigh-length black dress cut to her curvy body, ancient gold glittering at her ears and throat, a diaphanous midnight cape flowing behind her on a phantom wind. Even in towering high heels, she moved with the eerie smoothness of the House of Flame and Shadow.

Maybe she'd been the one who told Bryce how to sell her soul to the ruler of the Sleeping City.

The blond sorceress kept her gray eyes on the three flags hanging above the stairs as she moved toward them: on the left, the flag of Valbara; on the right, the insignia of Lunathion with its crescent moon bow and arrow. And in the center, the *SPQM* and its twin branches of stars—the flag of the Republic.

The witches came next, their steps ringing out. A young, brown-skinned female in flowing azure robes strode down the carpet, her braided black hair gleaming like spun night.

Queen Hypaxia. She'd worn her mother's gold-and-red crown of cloudberries for barely three months, and though her face was unlined and beautiful, there was a weariness to her dark eyes that spoke volumes about her lingering grief.

Rumor had it that Queen Hecuba had raised her deep in the boreal forest of the Heliruna Mountains, far from the corruption of the Republic. Hunt might have expected that such a person would shy from the gathered crowd and imperial splendor, or at least gape a little, but her chin remained high, her steps unfaltering. As if she had done this a dozen times.

She was to be formally recognized as Queen of the Valbaran Witches when the Summit officially began. Her final bit of pageantry before truly inheriting her throne. But—

Hunt got a look at her face as she neared.

He knew her: the medwitch from the clinic. She acknowledged Hunt with a swift sidelong glance as she passed.

Had Ruhn known? Who he'd met with, who had fed him research about the synth?

The mer leaders arrived, Tharion in a charcoal suit beside a female in a flowing, gauzy teal gown. Not the River Queen—she rarely left the Istros. But the beautiful, dark-skinned female might as well have been her daughter. Probably was her daughter, in the way that all mer claimed the River Queen as their mother.

Tharion's red-brown hair was slicked back, with a few escaped strands hanging over his brow. He'd swapped his fins for legs, but they didn't falter as his eyes slid toward Hunt. Sympathy shone there.

Hunt ignored it. He hadn't forgotten just who had brought Bryce to the barge that night.

Tharion, to his credit, didn't balk from Hunt's stare. He just gave him a sad smile and looked ahead, following the witches to the mezzanine level and open conference room doors beyond.

Then came the wolves. Sabine walked beside the hunched figure of the Prime, helping the old male along. His brown eyes were milky with age, his once-strong body bent over his cane. Sabine, clad in a dove-gray suit, sneered at Hunt, steering the ancient Prime toward the escalator rather than the steps.

But the Prime halted upon seeing where she planned to bring him. Drew her to the stairs. And began the ascent, step by painful step.

Proud bastard.

The Fae left their black cars, stalking onto the carpet. The Autumn King emerged, an onyx crown upon his red hair, the ancient stone like a piece of night even in the light of morning.

Hunt didn't know how he hadn't seen it before. Bryce looked more like her father than Ruhn did. Granted, plenty of the Fae had that coloring, but the coldness on the Autumn King's face . . . He'd seen Bryce make that expression countless times.

The Autumn King, not some prick lordling, had been the one to go with her to the Oracle that day. The one to kick a thirteen-year-old to the curb.

Hunt's fingers curled at his sides. He couldn't blame Ember Quinlan for running the moment she'd seen the monster beneath the surface. Felt its cold violence.

And realized she was carrying its child. A potential heir to the throne—one that might complicate things for his pure-blooded, Chosen One son. No wonder the Autumn King had hunted them down so ruthlessly.

Ruhn, a step behind his father, was a shock to the senses. In his princely raiment, the Starsword at his side, he could have very well been one of the first Starborn with that coloring of his. Might have been one of the first through the Northern Rift, so long ago.

They passed Hunt, and the king didn't so much as glance his way. But Ruhn did.

Ruhn looked to the shackles on Hunt's wrists, the 45th's triarii around him. And subtly shook his head. To any observer, it was in disgust, in reprimand. But Hunt saw the message.

I'm sorry.

Hunt kept his face unmoved, neutral. Ruhn moved on, the circlet of gilded birch leaves atop his head glinting.

And then the atrium seemed to inhale. To pause.

The angels did not arrive in cars. No, they dropped from the skies.

Forty-nine angels in the Asterian Guard, in full white-and-gold regalia, marched into the lobby, spears in their gloved hands and white wings shining. Each had been bred, hand-selected, for this life of service. Only the whitest, purest of wings would do. Not one speck of color on them.

Hunt had always thought they were swaggering assholes.

They took up spots along the carpet, standing at attention, wings high and spears pointing at the glass ceiling, their snowy capes draping to the floor. The white plumes of horsehair on their golden helmets gleamed as if freshly brushed, and the visors remained down.

They'd been sent from Pangera as a reminder to all of them, the Governors included, that the ones who held their leashes still monitored everything.

Micah and Sandriel arrived next, side by side. Each in their Governor's armor.

The Vanir sank to a knee before them. Yet the Asterian Guard—who would bow only for their six masters—remained standing, their spears like twin walls of thorns that the Governors paraded between.

No one dared speak. No one dared breathe as the two Archangels passed by.

They were all fucking worms at their feet.

Sandriel's smile seared Hunt as she breezed past. Almost as badly as Micah's utter disappointment and weariness.

Micah had picked his method of torture well, Hunt would give him that. There was no way Sandriel would let him die quickly. The torment when he returned to Pangera would last decades. No chance of a new death-bargain or a buyout.

And if he so much as stepped out of line, she'd know where to strike first. Who to strike.

The Governors swept up the stairs, their wings nearly touching. Why the two of them hadn't become a mated pair was beyond Hunt. Micah was decent enough that he likely found Sandriel as abhorrent as everyone else did. But it was still a wonder the Asteri hadn't ordered the bloodlines merged. It wouldn't have been unusual. Sandriel and Shahar had been the result of such a union.

Though perhaps the fact that Sandriel had likely killed her own parents to seize power for her and her sister had made the Asteri put a halt to the practice.

Only when the Governors reached the conference room did those assembled in the lobby move, first the angels peeling off for the stairs, the rest of the assembly falling into line behind them.

Hunt was kept wedged between two of the 45th's triarii—the Helhound and the Hawk, who both sneered at him—and took in as many details as he could when they entered the meeting room.

It was cavernous, with rings of tables flowing down to a central floor and round table where the leaders would sit.

The Pit of Hel. That's what it was. It was a wonder none of its princes stood there.

The Prime of Wolves, the Autumn King, the two Governors, the River Queen's fair daughter, Queen Hypaxia, and Jesiba all took seats at that central table. Their seconds—Sabine, Ruhn, Tharion, an older-looking witch—all claimed spots in the ring of tables around them. No one else from the House of Flame and Shadow had come with Jesiba, not even a vampyr. The ranks fell into place beyond that, each ring of tables growing larger and larger, seven in total. The Asterian Guard lined the uppermost level, standing against the wall, two at each of the room's three exits.

The seven levels of Hel indeed.

Vidscreens were interspersed throughout the room, two hanging from the ceiling itself, and computers lined the tables, presumably for references. Fury Axtar, to his surprise, took up a spot in the third circle, leaning back in her chair. No one else accompanied her.

Hunt was led to a spot against the wall, nestled between two Asterian Guards who ignored him completely. Thank fuck the angle blocked his view of Pollux and the rest of Sandriel's triarii.

Hunt braced himself as the vidscreens flicked on. The room went quiet at what appeared.

He knew those crystal halls, torches of firstlight dancing on the carved quartz pillars rising toward the arched ceiling stories above. Knew the seven crystal thrones arranged in a curve on the golden dais, the one empty throne at its far end. Knew the twinkling city beyond them, the hills rolling away into the dimming light, the Tiber a dark band wending between them.

Everyone rose from their seats as the Asteri came into view. And everyone knelt.

Even from nearly six thousand miles away, Hunt could have sworn their power rippled into the conference room. Could have sworn it sucked out the warmth, the air, the life.

The first time he'd been before them, he'd thought he'd never experienced anything worse. Shahar's blood had still coated his armor, his throat had still been ravaged from screaming during the battle, and yet he had never encountered anything so horrific. So unearthly. As if his entire existence were but a mayfly, his power but a wisp of breeze in the face of their hurricane. As if he'd been hurled into deep space.

They each held the power of a sacred star, each could level this planet to dust, yet there was no light in their cold eyes.

Through lowered lashes, Hunt marked who else dared to lift their eyes from the gray carpet as the six Asteri surveyed them: Tharion and Ruhn. Declan Emmet. And Queen Hypaxia.

No others. Not even Fury or Jesiba.

Ruhn met Hunt's stare. And a quiet male voice said in his head, *Bold move*.

Hunt held in his shock. He'd known there were occasional telepaths out there among the Fae, especially the ones who dwelled in

Avallen. But he'd never had a conversation with one. Certainly not inside his head. *Neat trick.*

A gift from my mother's kin—one I've kept quiet.

And you trust me with this secret?

Ruhn was silent for a moment. *I can't be seen talking to you. If you need anything, let me know. I'll do what I can for you.*

Another shock, as physical as his lightning zapping through him. *Why would you help me?*

Because you would have done everything in your power to keep Bryce from trading herself to Sandriel. I could see it on your face. Ruhn hesitated, then added, a shade uncertainly, *And because I don't think you're quite as much of an asshole now.*

The corner of Hunt's mouth lifted. *Likewise.*

Is that a compliment? Another pause. *How are you holding up, Athalar?*

Fine. How is she?

Back at work, according to the eyes I have on her.

Good. He didn't think he could endure any more talk of Bryce without completely falling apart, so he said, *Did you know that med-witch was Queen Hypaxia?*

No. I fucking didn't.

Ruhn might have gone on, but the Asteri began to speak. As one, like they always did. Telepaths in their own regard. "You have converged to discuss matters pertaining to your region. We grant you our leave." They looked to Hypaxia.

Impressively, the witch didn't flinch, didn't so much as tremble as the six Asteri looked upon her, the world watching with them, and said, "We formally recognize you as the heir of the late Queen Hecuba Enador, and with her passing, now anoint you Queen of the Valbaran Witches."

Hypaxia bowed her head, her face grave. Jesiba's face revealed nothing. Not even a hint of sorrow or anger for the heritage she'd walked away from. So Hunt dared a look at Ruhn, who was frowning.

The Asteri again surveyed the room, none more haughtily than

Rigelus, the Bright Hand. That slim teenage boy's body was a mockery of the monstrous power within. As one the Asteri continued, "You may begin. May the blessings of the gods and all the stars in the heavens shine upon you."

Heads bowed further, in thanks for merely being allowed to exist in their presence.

"It is our hope that you discuss a way to end this inane war. Governor Sandriel will prove a valuable witness to its destruction." A slow, horrible scan through the room followed. And Hunt knew their eyes were upon him as they said, "And there are others here who may also provide their testimony."

There was only one testimony to provide: that the humans were wasteful and foolish, and the war was their fault, their fault, their fault, and must be ended. Must be avoided here at all costs. There was to be no sympathy for the human rebellion, no hearing of the humans' plight. There was only the Vanir side, the good side, and no other.

Hunt held Rigelus's dead stare on the central screen. A zap of icy wind through his body courtesy of Sandriel warned him to avert his eyes. He did not. He could have sworn the Head of the Asteri smiled. Hunt's blood turned to ice, not just from Sandriel's wind, and he lowered his eyes.

This empire had been built to last for eternity. In more than fifteen thousand years, it had not broken. This war would not be the thing that ended it.

The Asteri said together, "Farewell." Another small smile from all of them—the worst being Rigelus's, still directed at Hunt. The screens went dark.

Everyone in the room, the two Governors included, blew out a breath. Someone puked, by the sound and reek from the far corner. Sure enough, a leopard shifter bolted through the doors, a hand over his mouth.

Micah leaned back in his chair, his eyes on the wood table before him. For a moment, no one spoke. As if they all needed to reel themselves back in. Even Sandriel.

Then Micah straightened, his wings rustling, and declared in a deep, clear voice, "I hereby commence this Valbaran Summit. All hail the Asteri and the stars they possess."

The room echoed the words, albeit half-heartedly. As if everyone remembered that even in this land across the sea from Pangera, so far from the muddy battlefields and the shining crystal palace in a city of seven hills, even here, there was no escaping.

74

Bryce tried not to dwell on the fact that Hunt and the world knew what and who she really was. At least the press hadn't caught wind of it, for whatever small mercy that was.

As if being a bastard princess meant anything. As if it said anything about her as a person. The shock on Hunt's face was precisely why she hadn't told him.

She'd torn up Jesiba's check, and with it the centuries of debts.

None of it mattered now anyway. Hunt was gone.

She knew he was alive. She'd seen the news footage of the Summit's opening procession. Hunt had looked just as he had before everything went to shit. Another small mercy.

She'd barely noticed the others arriving: Jesiba, Tharion, her sire, her brother . . . No, she'd just kept her eyes on that spot in the crowd, those gray wings that had now regrown.

Pathetic. She was utterly pathetic.

She would have done it. Would have gladly traded places with Hunt, even knowing what Sandriel would do to her. What Pollux would do to her.

Maybe it made her an idiot, as Ruhn said. Naïve.

Maybe she was lucky to have walked out of the Comitium lobby still breathing.

Maybe being attacked by that kristallos was payment for her fuckups.

She'd spent the past few days looking through the laws to see if there was anything to be done for Hunt. There wasn't. She'd done the only two things that might have granted him his freedom: offered to buy him, and offered herself in his stead.

She didn't believe Hunt's bullshit last words to her. She would have said the same had she been in his place. Would have been as nasty as she could, if it would have gotten him to safety.

Bryce sat at the front desk in the showroom, staring at the blank computer screen. The city had been quiet these past two days. As if everyone's attention was on the Summit, even though only a few of Crescent City's leaders and citizens had gone.

She'd watched the news recaps only to catch another glimpse of Hunt—without any luck.

She slept in his room every night. Had put on one of his T-shirts and crawled between the sheets that smelled of him and pretended he was lying in the dark beside her.

An envelope with the Comitium listed as its return address had arrived at the gallery three days ago. Her heart had thundered as she'd ripped it open, wondering if he'd been able to get a message out—

The white opal had fallen to the desk. Isaiah had written a reserved note, as if aware that every piece of mail was read:

Naomi found this on the barge. Thought you might want it back.

Then he'd added, as if on second thought, *He's sorry.*

She'd slid the stone into her desk drawer.

Sighing, Bryce opened it now, peering at the milky gem. She ran her finger over its cool surface.

"Athie looks miserable," Lehabah observed, floating by Bryce's head. She pointed to the tablet, where Bryce had paused her third replay of the opening procession on Hunt's face. "So do you, BB."

"Thank you."

At her feet, Syrinx stretched out, yawning. His curved claws glinted.

"So what do we do now?"

Bryce's brow furrowed. "What do you mean?"

Lehabah wrapped her arms around herself, floating in midair. "We just go back to normal?"

"Yes."

Her flickering eyes met Bryce's. "What is *normal*, anyway?"

"Seems boring to me."

Lehabah smiled slightly, turning a soft rose color.

Bryce offered one in return. "You're a good friend, Lele. A really good friend." She sighed again, setting the sprite's flame guttering. "I'm sorry if I haven't been such a good one to you at times."

Lehabah waved a hand, going scarlet. "We'll get through this, BB." She perched on Bryce's shoulder, her warmth seeping into skin Bryce hadn't realized was so cold. "You, me, and Syrie. Together, we'll get through this."

Bryce held up a finger, letting Lehabah take it in both of her tiny, shimmering hands. "Deal."

75

Ruhn had anticipated that the Summit would be intense, vicious, flat-out dangerous—each moment spent wondering whether someone's throat would be ripped out. Just as it was at every one he'd attended.

This time, his only enemy seemed to be boredom.

It had taken Sandriel all of two hours to tell them that the Asteri had ordered more troops to the front from every House. There was no point in arguing. It wasn't going to change. The order had come from the Asteri.

Talk turned to the new trade proposals. And then circled and circled and circled, even Micah getting caught in the semantics of who did what and got what and on and on until Ruhn was wondering if the Asteri had come up with this meeting as some form of torture.

He wondered how many of the Asterian Guard were sleeping behind their masks. He'd caught a few of the lesser members of the various delegations nodding off. But Athalar was alert—every minute, the assassin seemed to be listening. Watching.

Maybe that was what the Governors wanted: all of them so bored and desperate to end this meeting that they eventually agreed to terms that weren't to their advantage.

There were a few holdouts, still. Ruhn's father being one, along with the mer and the witches.

One witch in particular.

Queen Hypaxia spoke little, but he noticed that she, too, listened to every word being bandied about, her rich brown eyes full of wary intelligence despite her youth.

It had been a shock to see her the first day—that familiar face in this setting, with her crown and royal robes. To know he'd been talking to his would-be betrothed for weeks now with no fucking idea.

He'd managed to slip between two of her coven members as they filed into the dining hall the first day, and, like an asshole, demanded, "Why didn't you say anything? About who you really are?"

Hypaxia held her lunch tray with a grace better suited to holding a scepter. "You didn't ask."

"What the Hel were you doing in that shop?"

Her dark eyes shuttered. "My sources told me that evil was stirring in the city. I came to see for myself—discreetly." It was why she'd been at the scene of the temple guard's murder, he realized. And there the night Athalar and Bryce had been attacked in the park. "I also came to see what it was like to be . . . ordinary. Before this." She waved with a hand toward her crown.

"Do you know what my father expects of you? And me?"

"I have my suspicions," she said coolly. "But I am not considering such . . . changes in my life right now." She gave him a nod before walking away. "Not with anyone."

And that was it. His ass had been handed to him.

Today, at least, he'd tried to pay attention. To not look at the witch who had absolutely zero interest in marrying him, thank fuck. With her healing gifts, could she sense whatever was wrong inside him that would mean he was the last of the bloodline? He didn't want to find out. Ruhn shoved away the memory of the Oracle's prophecy. He wasn't the only one ignoring Hypaxia, at least. Jesiba Roga hadn't spoken one word to her.

Granted, the sorceress hadn't said much, other than to assert that the House of Flame and Shadow thrived on death and chaos, and had no quarrel with a long, devastating war. Reapers were always happy to ferry the souls of the dead, she said. Even the Archangels had looked disconcerted at that.

As the clock struck nine and all took their seats in the room, Sandriel announced, "Micah has been called away, and will be joining us later."

Only one person—well, six of them—could summon Micah away from this meeting. Sandriel seemed content to rule over the day's proceedings, and declared, "We will begin with the mer explaining their shortsighted resistance to the building of a canal for the transportation of our tanks and the continuation of the supply lines."

The River Queen's daughter bit her bottom lip, hesitating. But it was Captain Tharion Ketos who drawled to Sandriel, "I'd say that when your war machines rip up our oyster beds and kelp forests, it's not shortsighted to say that it will destroy our fishing industry."

Sandriel's eyes flashed. But she said sweetly, "You will be compensated."

Tharion didn't back down. "It is not just about the money. It is about the care of this planet."

"War requires sacrifice."

Tharion crossed his arms, muscles rippling beneath his black long-sleeved T-shirt. After the initial parade and that first day of endless meetings, most of them had donned far less formal wear for the rest of the talks. "I know the costs of war, Governor."

Bold male, to say that, to look Sandriel dead in the eye.

Queen Hypaxia said, her voice soft but unflinching, "Tharion's concern has merit. And precedent." Ruhn straightened as all eyes slid toward the witch-queen. She, too, did not back down from the storms in Sandriel's eyes. "Along the eastern borders of the Rhagan Sea, the coral and kelp beds that were destroyed in the Sorvakkian Wars two thousand years ago have still not returned. The mer who farmed them were compensated, as you claim. But only for a few seasons." Utter silence in the meeting room. "Will you pay, Governor, for a thousand seasons? Two thousand seasons? What of the creatures who make their homes in places you propose to destroy? How shall you pay them?"

"They are Lowers. Lower than the Lowers," Sandriel said coldly, unmoved.

"They are children of Midgard. Children of Cthona," the witch-queen said.

Sandriel smiled, all teeth. "Spare me your bleeding-heart nonsense."

Hypaxia didn't smile back. She just held Sandriel's stare. No challenge in it, but frank assessment.

To Ruhn's eternal shock, it was Sandriel who looked away first, rolling her eyes and shuffling her papers. Even his father blinked at it. And assessed the young queen with a narrowed gaze. No doubt wondering how a twenty-six-year-old witch had the nerve. Or what Hypaxia might have on Sandriel to make an Archangel yield to her.

Wondering if the witch-queen would indeed be a good bride for Ruhn—or a thorn in his side.

Across the table, Jesiba Roga smiled slightly at Hypaxia. Her first acknowledgment of the young witch.

"The canal," Sandriel said tightly, setting down her papers, "we shall discuss later. The supply lines . . ." The Archangel launched into another speech about her plans to streamline the war.

Hypaxia went back to the papers before her. But her eyes lifted to the second ring of tables.

To Tharion.

The mer male gave her a slight, secret smile—gratitude and acknowledgment.

The witch-queen nodded back, barely a dip of her chin.

The mer male just casually lifted his paper, flashing what looked like about twenty rows of markings—counting something.

Hypaxia's eyes widened, bright with reproach and disbelief, and Tharion lowered the paper before anyone else noticed. Added another slash to it.

A flush crept over the witch-queen's cheeks.

His father, however, began speaking, so Ruhn ignored their antics and squared his shoulders, trying his best to look like he was paying attention. Like he cared.

None of it would matter, in the end. Sandriel and Micah would get what they wanted.

And everything would remain the same.

Hunt was so bored he honestly thought his brain was going to bleed out his ears.

But he tried to savor these last days of calm and relative comfort, even with Pollux monitoring everything from across the room. Waiting until he could stop appearing civilized. Hunt knew Pollux was counting down the hours until he'd be unleashed upon him.

So every time the asshole smiled at him, Hunt grinned right back.

Hunt's wings, at least, had healed. He'd been testing them as much as he could, stretching and flexing. If Sandriel allowed him to get airborne, he knew they'd carry him. Probably.

Standing against the wall, dissecting each word spoken, was its own form of torture, but Hunt listened. Paid attention, even when it seemed like so many others were fighting sleep.

He hoped the delegations who held out—the Fae, the mer, the witches—would last until the end of the Summit before remembering that control was an illusion and the Asteri could simply issue an edict regarding the new trade laws. Just as they had with the war update.

A few more days, that was all Hunt wanted. That's what he told himself.

76

Bryce had camped out in the gallery library for the past three days, staying well after closing and returning at dawn. There was no point in spending much time at the apartment, since her fridge was empty and Syrinx was always with her. She figured she might as well be at the office until she stopped feeling like her home was just an empty shell.

Jesiba, busy with the Summit, didn't check the gallery video feeds. Didn't see the takeout containers littering every surface of the library, the mini fridge mostly full of cheese, or the fact that Bryce had started wearing her athletic clothes into the office. Or that she'd begun showering in the bathroom in the back of the library. Or that she'd canceled all their client meetings. And taken a new Archesian amulet right from the wall safe in Jesiba's office—the very last one in the territory. One of five left in the entire world.

It was only a matter of time, however, until Jesiba got bored and pulled up the dozens of feeds to see everything. Or looked at their calendar and saw all the rescheduled appointments.

Bryce had heard back about two potential new jobs, and had interviews lined up. She'd need to invent some excuse to feed Jesiba, of course. A medwitch appointment or teeth cleaning or something else normal but necessary. And if she got one of those jobs, she'd have to come up with a plan for repaying her debt for Syrinx—something that would please Jesiba's ego enough to keep her from transforming Bryce into some awful creature just for asking to leave.

Bryce sighed, running a hand over an ancient tome full of legal jargon that required a degree to decipher. She'd never seen so many *ergo*s and *therefore*s and *hence the following*s and *shall be included but not limited to*s. But she kept looking.

So did Lehabah. "What about this, BB?" The sprite flared, pointing to a page before her. "It says here, *A criminal's sentence may be commuted to service if—*"

"We saw that one two days ago," Bryce said. "It leads us right back to slavery."

A faint scratching filled the room. Bryce glanced at the nøkk from under her lashes, careful not to let him see her attention.

The creature was grinning at her anyway. Like it knew something she didn't.

She found out why a moment later.

"There's another case beneath it," Lehabah said. "The human woman was freed after—"

Syrinx growled. Not at the tank. At the green-carpeted stairs.

Casual footsteps thudded. Bryce was instantly standing, reaching for her phone.

A pair of boots, then dark jeans, and then—

Snow-white wings. An unfairly beautiful face.

Micah.

Every thought short-circuited as he stepped into the library, surveying its shelves and the stairs leading to the brass mezzanines and alcoves, the tank and the nøkk who was still grinning, the exploding-sun light high above.

He couldn't be down here. Couldn't see these books—

"Your Grace," Bryce blurted.

"The front door was open," he said. The sheer power behind his stare was like being hit in the face with a brick.

Of course the locks and enchantments hadn't kept him out. Nothing could ever keep him out.

She calmed her racing heart enough to say, "I'd be happy to meet with you upstairs, Your Grace, if you want me to phone Jesiba."

Jesiba, who is at the Summit where you *are currently supposed to be.*

"Down here is fine." He slowly stalked over to one of the towering shelves.

Syrinx was shaking on the couch; Lehabah hid behind a small stack of books. Even the animals in their various cages and small tanks cowered. Only the nøkk kept smiling.

"Why don't you have a seat, Your Grace?" Bryce said, scooping takeout containers into her arms, not caring if she got chili oil on her white T-shirt, only that Micah got the fuck away from the shelves and those precious books.

He ignored her, examining the titles at eye level.

Urd save her. Bryce dumped the takeout containers into the overflowing trash can. "We have some fascinating art upstairs. Perhaps you can tell me what you're looking for." She glanced at Lehabah, who had turned a startling shade of cyan, and shook her head in a silent warning to be careful.

Micah folded his wings, and turned to her. "What I'm looking for?"

"Yes," she breathed. "I—"

He pinned her with those icy eyes. "I'm looking for you."

Today's meeting was by far the worst. The slowest.

Sandriel delighted in leading them in circles, lies and half-truths spewing from her lips, as if savoring the kill soon to come: the moment they yielded everything to her and the Asteri's wishes.

Hunt leaned against the wall, standing between the Asterian Guards in their full regalia, and watched the clock inch toward four. Ruhn looked like he'd fallen asleep half an hour ago. Most of the lower-level parties had been dismissed, leaving the room barely occupied. Even Naomi had been sent back to Lunathion to make sure the 33rd remained in shape. Only skeleton staff and their leaders remained. As if everyone now knew this was over. That this *republic* was a sham. Either one ruled or one bowed.

"Opening a new port along the eastern coastline of Valbara," Sandriel said for the hundredth time, "would allow us to build a secure facility for our aquatic legion—"

A phone buzzed.

Jesiba Roga, to his surprise, pulled it from an inner pocket of the gray blazer she wore over a matching dress. She shifted in her seat, angling the phone away from the curious male to her left.

A few of the other leaders had noticed Roga's change in attention. Sandriel kept talking, unaware, but Ruhn had stirred at the sound and was looking at the woman. So was Fury, seated two rows behind her.

Jesiba's thumbs flew over her phone, her red-painted mouth tightening as she lifted a hand. Even Sandriel shut up.

Roga said, "I'm sorry to interrupt, Governor, but there's something that you—that all of us—need to see."

He had no rational reason for the dread that began to curl in his stomach. Whatever was on her phone could have been about anything. Yet his mouth dried up.

"What?" Sabine demanded from across the room.

Jesiba ignored her, and glanced to Declan Emmet. "Can you link what's on my phone to these screens?" She indicated the array of them throughout the room.

Declan, who had been half-asleep in the circle behind Ruhn, instantly straightened. "Yeah, no problem." He was smart enough to look to Sandriel first—and the Archangel rolled her eyes but nodded. Declan's laptop was open a heartbeat later. He frowned at what popped up on the laptop, but then he hit a button.

And revealed dozens of different video feeds—all from Griffin Antiquities. In the lower right corner, in a familiar library . . . Hunt forgot to breathe entirely.

Especially as Jesiba's phone buzzed again, and a message—a continuation of a previous conversation, it seemed—popped up on the screens. His heart stalled at the name: *Bryce Quinlan.*

His heart wholly stopped at the message. *Are the feeds on yet?*

"What the fuck?" Ruhn hissed.

Bryce was standing in front of the camera, pouring what seemed to be a glass of wine. And behind her, seated at the main table of the library, was Micah.

Sandriel murmured, "He said he had a meeting . . ."

The camera was hidden inside one of the books, just above Bryce's head.

Declan hit a few keys on his computer, pulling up that particular feed. Another keystroke and its audio filled the conference room.

Bryce was saying over her shoulder, throwing Micah a casual smile, "Would you like some food with your wine? Cheese?"

Micah lounged at the table, surveying a spread of books. "That would be appreciated."

Bryce hummed, covertly typing on her phone as she fiddled on the refreshment cart.

The next message to Jesiba blared across the conference room screens.

One word that had Hunt's blood going cold.

Help.

It was not a cheeky, charming plea. Not as Bryce lifted her gaze to the camera.

Fear shone there. Stark, bright fear. Every instinct in Hunt went on roaring alert.

"Governor," the Autumn King said to Sandriel, "I would like an explanation."

But before Sandriel could reply, Ruhn quietly ordered, with eyes glued to the feeds, "Flynn, send an Aux unit to Griffin Antiquities. Right now."

Flynn instantly had his phone out, fingers flying.

"Micah has not done anything wrong," Sandriel snapped at the Fae Prince. "Except demonstrate his poor choice in females."

Hunt's snarl ripped from him.

It would have earned him a whip of cold wind from Sandriel, he knew, had the sound not been hidden by matching snarls from Declan and Ruhn.

Tristan Flynn was snapping at someone, "Get over to Griffin Antiquities right now. Yes, in the Old Square. No—just go. That is a *fucking* order."

Ruhn barked another command at the Fae lord, but Micah began speaking again.

"You've certainly been busy." Micah motioned to the table. "Looking for a loophole?"

Bryce swallowed as she began assembling a plate for Micah. "Hunt is my friend."

Those were—those were law books on the table. Hunt's stomach dropped to his feet.

"Ah yes," Micah said, leaning back in his chair. "I admire that about you."

"What the fuck is going on?" Fury bit out.

"Loyal unto death—and beyond," Micah continued. "Even with all the proof in the world, you still didn't believe Danika was little better than a drug-addicted whore."

Sabine and several wolves growled. Hunt heard Amelie Ravenscroft say to Sabine, "We should send a wolf pack."

"All the top packs are here," Sabine murmured, eyes fixed on the feed. "Every top security force is here. I only left a few behind."

But like a struck match, Bryce's entire countenance shifted. Fear pivoted into bright, sharp anger. Hunt ordinarily thrilled to see that blazing look. Not now.

Use your fucking head, he silently begged her. *Be smart.*

Bryce let Micah's insult settle, surveying the platter of cheese and grapes she was assembling. "Who knows what the truth is?" she asked blandly.

"The philosophers in this library certainly had opinions on the matter."

"On Danika?"

"Don't play stupid." Micah's smile widened. He gestured to the books around them. "Do you know that harboring these volumes earns you a one-way ticket to execution?"

"Seems like a lot of fuss over some books."

"Humans died for these books," Micah purred, motioning to the shelves towering around them. "Banned titles, if I'm not mistaken, many of them supposed to only exist in the Asteri Archives. Evolution, mathematics, theories to disprove the superiority of the

Vanir and Asteri. Some from philosophers people claimed existed *before* the Asteri arrived." A soft, awful laugh. "Liars and heretics, who admitted they were wrong when the Asteri tortured them for the truth. They were burned alive with the heretical works used as kindling. And yet here, they survive. All the knowledge of the ancient world. Of a world before Asteri. And theories of a world in which the Vanir are not your masters."

"Interesting," Bryce said. She still did not turn to face him.

Ruhn said to Jesiba, "What, exactly, is in that library?"

Jesiba said nothing. Absolutely nothing. Her gray eyes promised cold death, though.

Micah went on, unwittingly answering the prince's question. "Do you even know what you are surrounded by, Bryce Quinlan? This is the Great Library of Parthos."

The words clanged through the room. Jesiba refused to so much as open her mouth.

Bryce, to her credit, said, "Sounds like a lot of conspiracy theory crap. Parthos is a bedtime story for humans."

Micah chuckled. "Says the female with the Archesian amulet around her neck. The amulet of the priestesses who once served and guarded Parthos. I think you know what's here—that you spend your days in the midst of all that remains of the library after most of it burned at Vanir hands fifteen thousand years ago."

Hunt's stomach turned. He could have sworn a chill breeze drifted from Jesiba.

Micah went on idly, "Did you know that during the First Wars, when the Asteri gave the order, it was at Parthos that a doomed human army made its final stand against the Vanir? To save proof of what they were before the Rifts opened—to save the *books*. A hundred thousand humans marched that day knowing they would die, and lose the war." Micah's smile grew. "All to buy the priestesses time to grab the most vital volumes. They loaded them onto ships and vanished. I am curious to learn how they landed with Jesiba Roga."

The sorceress watching her truth unfold on the screens still did not speak. To acknowledge what had been suggested. Did it have something to do with why she'd left the witches? Or why she'd joined the Under-King?

Micah leaned back in his seat, wings rustling. "I've long suspected that the remains of Parthos were housed here—a record of two thousand years of human knowledge before the Asteri arrived. I took one look at some of the titles on the shelves and knew it to be true."

No one so much as blinked as the truth settled. But Jesiba pointed to the screens and said to Tristan Flynn, to Sabine, her voice shaking, "Tell the Aux to move their fucking asses. Save those books. I *beg* you."

Hunt ground his teeth. Of course the books were more important to her than Bryce.

"The Aux shall do no such thing," Sandriel said coldly. She smiled at Jesiba as the female went rigid. "And whatever Micah has in mind for your little assistant is going to look mild compared to what the Asteri do to *you* for harboring that lying rubbish—"

But Bryce picked up the cheese tray and glass of wine. "Look, I only work here, Governor."

She faced Micah at last. She was wearing athletic clothes: leggings and a long-sleeved white T-shirt. Her neon-pink sneakers shone like firstlight in the dim library.

"Run," Flynn urged to the screen, as if Bryce could hear him. "Fucking *run*, Bryce."

Sandriel glared at the Fae warrior. "You dare accuse a Governor of foul play?" But doubt shone in her eyes.

The Fae lord ignored her, his eyes again on the screens.

Hunt couldn't move. Not as Bryce set down the cheese platter, the wine, and said to Micah, "You came here looking for me, and here I am." A half smile. "That Summit must have been a real bore." She crossed her arms behind her back, the portrait of casualness. She winked. "Are you going to ask me out again?"

Micah didn't see the angle of the second feed that Declan pulled up—how her fingers began flicking behind her back. Pointing to the stairs. A silent, frantic order to Lehabah and Syrinx to flee. Neither moved.

“As you once said to me,” Micah replied smoothly, “I’m not interested.”

“Too bad.” Silence throbbed in the conference room.

Bryce gestured again behind her back, her fingers shaking now. *Please,* those hands seemed to say. *Please run. While he’s distracted by me.*

“Have a seat,” Micah said, gesturing to the chair across the table. “We might as well be civilized about it.”

Bryce obeyed, batting her eyelashes. “About what?”

“About you giving me Luna’s Horn.”

77

Bryce knew there was little chance of this ending well.

But if Jesiba had seen her messages, maybe it wouldn't be in vain. Maybe everyone would know what had happened to her. Maybe they could save the books, if the protective spells on them held out against an Archangel's wrath. Even if the gallery's enchantments had not.

Bryce said smoothly to Micah, "I have no idea where the Horn is."

His smile didn't waver. "Try again."

"I have no idea where the Horn is, *Governor*?"

He braced his powerful forearms on the table. "Do you want to know what I think?"

"No, but you're going to tell me anyway?" Her heart raced and raced.

Micah chuckled. "I think you figured it out. Likely at the same moment I did a few days ago."

"I'm flattered you think I'm that smart."

"Not you." Another cold laugh. "Danika Fendyr was the smart one. She stole the Horn from the temple, and you knew her well enough to finally realize what she did with it."

"Why would Danika have ever wanted the Horn?" Bryce asked innocently. "It's broken."

"It was cleaved. And I'm guessing you already learned what could repair it at last." Her heart thundered as Micah growled, "*Synth*."

She got to her feet, her knees shaking only slightly. "Governor or not, this is private property. If you want to burn me at the stake with all these books, you'll need a warrant."

Bryce reached the steps. Syrinx and Lehabah hadn't moved, though.

"Hand over the Horn."

"I told you, I don't know where it is."

She put one foot on the steps, and then Micah was there, his hand at the collar of her shirt. He hissed, "*Do not lie*."

Hunt staggered all of one step down the stairs before Sandriel stopped him, her wind shoving him back against the wall. It snaked down his throat, clamping on to his vocal cords. Rendering him silent to watch what unfolded on the screens.

Micah growled in Bryce's ear, more animal than angel, "Do you want to know how I figured it out?"

She trembled as the Governor ran a possessive hand down the curve of her spine.

Hunt saw red at that touch, the entitlement in it, the sheer dread that widened her eyes.

Bryce wasn't stupid enough to try to run as Micah ran his fingers back up her spine, intent in every stroke.

Hunt's jaw clenched so hard it hurt, his breath coming out in great, bellowing pants. He'd kill him. He'd find a way to get free of Sandriel, and fucking *kill* Micah for that touch—

Micah trailed his fingers over the delicate chain of her necklace. A new one, Hunt realized.

Micah purred, unaware of the camera mere feet away, "I saw the footage of you in the Comitium lobby. You gave your Archesian amulet to Sandriel. And she destroyed it." His broad hand clamped around her neck, and Bryce squeezed her eyes shut. "That's how I realized. How you realized the truth, too."

"I don't know what you're talking about," Bryce whispered.

Micah's hand tightened, and it might as well have been his hand on Hunt's throat for all the difficulty he had breathing. "For three years, you wore that amulet. Every single day, every single hour. Danika knew that. Knew you were without ambition, too, and would never have the drive to leave this job. And thus never take off the amulet."

"You're insane," Bryce managed to say.

"Am I? Then explain to me why, within an hour after you took off the amulet, that kristallos demon attacked you."

Hunt stilled. A demon had *attacked* her that day? He found Ruhn's stare, and the prince nodded, his face deathly pale. *We got to her in time* was all Danaan said to him, mind-to-mind.

"Bad luck?" Bryce tried.

Micah didn't so much as smile, his hand still clamped on her neck. "You don't just have the Horn. You *are* the Horn." His hand again ran down her back. "You became its bearer the night Danika had it ground into a fine powder, mixed it with witch-ink, and then got you so drunk you didn't ask questions when she had it tattooed onto your back."

"*What?*" Fury Axtar barked.

Holy fucking gods. Hunt bared his teeth, still forbidden from speaking.

But Bryce said, "Cool as that sounds, Governor, this tattoo says—"

"The language is beyond that of this world. It is the language of *universes*. And it spells out a direct command to activate the Horn through a blast of raw power upon the tattoo itself. Just as it once did for the Starborn Prince. You may not possess his gifts like your brother, but I believe your bloodline and the synth shall compensate for it when I use my power upon you. To fill the tattoo—to fill *you*—with power is, in essence, to blow the Horn."

Bryce's nostrils flared. "Blow *me*, asshole." She snapped her head back, fast enough that even Micah couldn't stop the collision of her skull with his nose. He stumbled, buying her time to twist and flee—

His hand didn't let go, though.

And with a shove, her shirt ripping down the back, Micah hurled her to the floor.

Hunt's shout was lodged in his throat, but Ruhn's echoed through the conference room as Bryce skidded across the carpet.

Lehabah screamed as Syrinx roared, and Bryce managed to snap, "*Hide.*"

But the Archangel halted, surveying the woman sprawled on the floor before him.

The tattoo down her back. Luna's Horn contained within its dark ink.

Bryce scrambled to her feet, as if there were anywhere to go, anywhere to hide from the Governor and his terrible power. She made it across the room, to the steps up to the mezzanine—

Micah moved fast as the wind. He wrapped a hand around her ankle and tossed her across the room.

Bryce's scream as she collided with the wood table and it shattered beneath her was the worst sound Hunt had ever heard.

Ruhn breathed, "He's going to fucking kill her."

Bryce crawled backward through the debris of the table, blood running from her mouth as she whispered to Micah, "You killed Danika and the pack."

Micah smiled. "I enjoyed every second of it."

The conference room shook. Or maybe that was just Hunt himself.

And then the Archangel was upon her, and Hunt couldn't bear it, the sight of him grabbing Bryce by the neck and throwing her across the room again, into those shelves.

"Where is the *fucking* Aux?" Ruhn screamed at Flynn. At Sabine.

But her eyes were wide. Stunned.

So slowly, Bryce crawled backward, up the mezzanine stairs again, clawing at the books to heave herself along. A gash leaked blood onto her leggings, bone gleaming beneath a protruding shard of wood. She panted, half sobbing, "Why?"

Lehabah had crept to the metal bathroom door in the back of the library and managed to open it, as if silently signaling Bryce to get there—so they could lock themselves inside until help arrived.

"Did you learn, in all your research, that I am an investor in Redner Industries? That I have access to all its experiments?"

"Oh fuck," Isaiah said from across the pit.

"And did you ever learn," Micah went on, "what Danika *did* for Redner Industries?"

Bryce still crawled backward up the stairs. There was nowhere to go, though. "She did part-time security work."

"Is that how she sanitized it for you?" He smirked. "Danika tracked down the people that Redner wanted her to find. People who didn't want to be found. Including a group of Ophion rebels who had been experimenting with a formula for synthetic magic—to assist in the humans' treachery. They'd dug into long-forgotten history and learned that the kristallos demons' venom nullified magic—*our* magic. So these clever rebels decided to look into why, isolating the proteins that were targeted by that venom. The source of magic. Redner's human spies tipped him off, and out Danika went to bring in the research—and the people behind it."

Bryce gasped for breath, still slowly crawling upward. No one spoke in the conference room as she said, "The Asteri don't approve of synthetic magic. How did Redner even get away with doing the research on it?"

Hunt shook. She was buying herself time.

Micah seemed all too happy to indulge her. "Because Redner knew the Asteri would shut down any synthetic magic research, that *I* would shut their experiments down, they spun synth experiments as a drug for healing. Redner invited me to invest. The earliest trials were a success: with it, humans could heal faster than with any medwitch or Fae power. But later trials did not go according to plan. Vanir, we learned, went out of their minds when given it. And humans who took too much synth . . . well. Danika used her security clearance to steal footage of the trials—and I suspect she left it for you, didn't she?"

Burning Solas. Up and up, Bryce crawled along the stairs, fingers scrabbling over those ancient, precious books. "How did she learn what you were really up to?"

"She always stuck her nose where it didn't belong. Always wanting to protect the meek."

"From monsters like *you*," Bryce spat, still inching upward. Still buying herself time.

Micah's smile was hideous. "She made no secret that she kept an eye on the synth trials, because she was keen to find a way to help her weak, vulnerable, half-human friend. You, who would inherit no power—she wondered if it might give you a fighting chance against the predators who rule this world. And when she saw the horrors the synth could bring about, she became *concerned* for the test subjects. Concerned for what it'd do to humans if it leaked into the world. But Redner's employees said Danika had her own research there, too. No one knew what, but she spent time in their labs outside of her own duties."

All of it had to be on the flash drive Bryce had found. Hunt prayed she'd put it somewhere safe. Wondered what other bombshells might be on it.

Bryce said, "She was never selling the synth on that boat, was she?"

"No. By that point, I'd realized I needed someone with unrestricted access to the temple to take the Horn—I would be too easily noticed. So when she stole the synth trial footage, I had my chance to use her."

Bryce made it up another step. "You dumped the synth into the streets."

Micah kept trailing her. "Yes. I knew Danika's constant need to be the hero would send her running after it, to save the lowlifes of Lunathion from destroying themselves with it. She got most of it, but not all. When I told her I'd seen her on the river, when I claimed no one would believe the Party Princess was trying to get drugs off the streets, her hands were tied. I told her I'd forget about it, if she did one little favor for me, at just the right moment."

"You caused the blackout that night she stole the Horn."

"I did. But I underestimated Danika. She'd been wary of my interest in the synth long before I leaked it onto the streets, and when I blackmailed her into stealing the Horn, she must have realized the connection between the two. That the Horn could be repaired by synth."

"So you killed her for it?" Another step, another question to buy herself time.

"I killed her because she hid the Horn before I could repair it with the synth. And thus help my people."

"I'd think your power alone would be enough for that," Bryce said, as if trying flattery to save herself.

The Archangel looked truly sad for a moment. "Even my power is not enough to help them. To keep war from Valbara's shores. For that, I need help from beyond our own world. The Horn will open a portal—and allow me to summon an army to decimate the human rebels and end their wanton destruction."

"What world?" Bryce asked, blanching. "Hel?"

"Hel would resist kneeling to me. But ancient lore whispers of other worlds that exist that would bow to a power like mine—and bow to the Horn." He smiled, cold as a deep-sea fish. "The one who possesses the Horn at full power can do anything. Perhaps establish oneself as an Asteri."

"Their power is born, not made," Bryce snapped, even as her face turned ashen.

"With the Horn, you would not need to inherit a star's might to rule. And the Asteri would recognize that. Welcome me as one of them." Another soft laugh.

"You killed those two CCU students."

"No. They were slaughtered by a satyr high on synth—while Danika was busy stealing the Horn that night. I'm sure the guilt of it ate her up."

Bryce was shaking. Hunt was, too. "So you went to the apartment and killed her and the Pack of Devils?"

"I waited until Philip Briggs was released."

She murmured, "He had the black salt in his lab that would incriminate him."

"Yes. Once he was again on the streets, I went to Danika's apartment—your apartment—disabled the Pack of Devils with my power, and injected her with the synth. And watched as she ripped them apart before turning on herself."

Bryce was crying in earnest now. "She didn't tell you, though. Where the Horn was."

Micah shrugged. "She held out."

"And what—you summoned the kristallos afterward to cover your tracks? Let it attack you in the alley to keep your triarii from suspecting you? Or just to give yourself a reason to monitor this case so closely without raising any eyebrows? And then you waited two fucking years?"

He frowned. "I have spent these past two years looking for the Horn, calling kristallos demons to track it down for me, but I couldn't find a trace of it. Until I realized *I* didn't have to do the legwork. Because you, Bryce Quinlan, were the key to finding the Horn. I knew Danika had hidden it somewhere, and *you*, if I gave you a chance for vengeance, would lead me to it. All my power couldn't find it, but you—you loved her. And the power of your love would bring the Horn to me. Would fuel your need for justice and lead you right to it." He snorted. "But there was a chance you might not get that far—not alone. So I planted a seed in the mind of the Autumn King."

Everyone in the room looked to the stone-faced Fae male.

Ruhn growled at his father, "He played you like a fucking fiddle."

The Autumn King's amber eyes flashed with white-hot rage. But Micah went on before he could speak. "I knew a bit of taunting about the Fae's waning power, about the loss of the Horn, would rankle his pride *just* enough for him to order his Starborn son to look for it."

Bryce let out a long breath. "So if I couldn't find it, then Ruhn might."

Ruhn blinked. "I—every time I went to look for the Horn . . ." He paled. "I always had the urge to go to Bryce." He twisted in his seat to meet Hunt's stare and said to him mind-to-mind, *I thought it was the gallery, some knowledge in there, but . . . fuck, it was her.*

Your Starborn connection to her and the Horn must have overcome even the masking power of the Archesian amulet, Hunt answered. *That's quite a bond, Prince.*

Bryce demanded, "And summoning the kristallos these months? The murders?"

Micah drawled, "I summoned the kristallos to nudge you both along, making sure it kept just enough out of camera range, knowing its connection to the Horn would lead you toward it. Injecting Tertian, the acolyte, and the temple guard with the synth—letting them rip themselves apart—was also to prompt you. Tertian, to give us an excuse to come to you for this investigation, and the others to keep pointing you toward the Horn. I targeted two people from the temple that were on duty the night Danika stole it."

"And the bombing at the White Raven, with an image of the Horn on the crate? Another *nudge*?"

"Yes, and to raise suspicions that humans were behind everything. I planted bombs throughout the city, in places I thought you might go. When Athalar's phone location pinged at the club, I knew the gods were helping me along. So I remotely detonated it."

"I could have died."

"Maybe. But I was willing to bet Athalar would shield you. And why not cause a little chaos, to stir more resentment between the humans and Vanir? It would only make it easier to convince others of the wisdom of my plan to end this conflict. Especially at a cost most would deem too high."

Hunt's head swam. No one in the room spoke.

Bryce slowed her retreat as she winced in pain, "And the apartment building? I thought it was Hunt, but it wasn't, was it? It was you."

"Yes. Your landlord's request went to all of my triarii. And to me. I knew Danika had left nothing there. But by that time, Bryce Quinlan, I was enjoying watching you squirm. I knew Athalar's plan to acquire the synth would soon be exposed—and I took a guess that you'd be willing to believe the worst of him. That he'd used the lightning in his veins to endanger innocent people. He's a killer. I thought you might need a reminder. That it played into Athalar's guilt was an unexpected boon."

Hunt ignored the eyes that glanced his way. The fucking asshole had never planned to honor his bargain. If he'd solved the case, Micah would have killed him. Killed them both. He'd been played like a fucking fool.

Bryce asked, voice raw, "When did you start to think it was me?"

"That night it attacked Athalar in the garden. I realized only later that he'd probably come into contact with one of Danika's personal items, which must have come into contact with the Horn."

Hunt had touched Danika's leather jacket that day. Gotten its scent on him.

"Once I got Athalar off the streets, I summoned the kristallos again—and it went right to you. The only thing that had changed was that you finally, finally took that amulet off. And then . . ." He chuckled. "I looked at Hunt Athalar's photos of your time together. Including that one of your back. The tattoo you had inked there, days before Danika's death, according to the list of Danika's last locations Ruhn Danaan sent to you and Athalar—whose account is easily accessible to me."

Bryce's fingers curled into the carpet, as if she'd sprout claws. "How do you know the Horn will even work now that it's in my back?"

"The Horn's physical shape doesn't matter. Whether it is fashioned as a horn or a necklace or a powder mixed with witch-ink, its power remains."

Hunt silently swore. He and Bryce had never visited the tattoo parlor. Bryce had said she knew why Danika was there.

Micah went on, "Danika knew the Archesian amulet would hide you from any detection, magical or demonic. With that amulet, you were *invisible* to the kristallos, bred to hunt the Horn. I suspect she knew that Jesiba Roga has similar enchantments upon this gallery, and perhaps Danika placed some upon your apartments—your old one and the one she left to you—to make sure you would be even more veiled from it."

Hunt scanned the gallery camera feeds from the street. Where the fuck was the Aux?

Bryce spat, "And you thought no one would figure this out? What about Briggs's testimony?"

"Briggs is a raving fanatic who'd been caught by Danika before a planned bombing. No one would listen to his pleas of innocence." Especially when his lawyer had been provided by Micah.

Bryce glanced up at the camera. As if checking that it was on.

Sabine whispered, "She's been leading him along to get a full confession."

Despite the terror tightening his body, pride flared through Hunt.

Micah smiled again. "So here we are."

"You're a piece of shit," Bryce said.

But then Micah reached into his jacket pocket. Pulled out a needle. Full of clear liquid. "Calling me names isn't going to stop me from using the Horn."

Hunt's breath sawed through his chest.

Micah advanced on her. "The Horn's remnants are now embedded in your flesh. When I inject you with synth, the healing properties in it will target and fix whatever it finds to be broken. And the Horn will again be whole. Ready for me to learn if it works at last."

"You'd risk opening a portal to another fucking world in the middle of Crescent City," she spat, inching farther away, "just to *learn if it works*?"

"If I am correct, the benefits shall far outweigh any casualties," Micah answered mildly as a bead of liquid gleamed on the syringe's tip. "Too bad you will not survive the synth's side effects in order to see for yourself."

Bryce lunged for a book on a low-lying shelf along the stairs, but Micah halted her with a leash of wind.

Her face crumpled as the Archangel knelt over her. "*No*."

This couldn't happen; Hunt couldn't *let* this happen.

But Bryce could do nothing, Hunt could do nothing, as Micah stabbed the needle into her thigh. Drained it to the hilt. She screamed, thrashing, but Micah stepped back.

His power must have lessened its hold on her, because she sagged to the carpeted steps.

The bastard glanced at the clock. Assessing how much time remained until she tore herself apart. And slowly, the wounds on her battered body began to seal. Her split lip healed fully—though the bone-deep gash in her thigh knit far more slowly.

Smiling, Micah reached for the tattoo on her exposed back. "Shall we?"

But Bryce moved again—and this time Micah's power didn't catch her before she grabbed a book from the shelf and clutched it tight.

Golden light erupted from the book, a bubble against which Micah's hand bounced harmlessly off. He pushed. The bubble would not yield.

Thank the gods. If it could buy her just a few more minutes until help came . . . But what could an Aux pack do against an Archangel? Hunt strained against his invisible bonds. Scoured his memory for anything that could be done, anyone left in the fucking city who might help—

"Very well," Micah said, that smile remaining as he again tested the golden barrier. "There are other ways to get you to yield."

Bryce was shaking in her golden bubble. Hunt's heart stopped as Micah strode down the mezzanine steps. Heading straight for where Syrinx cowered behind the couch. "No," Bryce breathed. "*No—*"

The chimera thrashed, biting at the Archangel, who grabbed him by the scruff of his neck.

Bryce dropped the book. The golden bubble vanished. But when she tried to rise on her still-healing leg, it collapsed. Even the synth couldn't heal fast enough for it to bear weight.

Micah just carried Syrinx along. Over to the tank.

"*PLEASE,*" Bryce screamed. Again, she tried to move. Again, again, again.

But Micah didn't even falter as he opened the door to the small stairs that led to the top of the nøkk's tank. Bryce's screaming was unending.

Declan switched the feed over to a camera atop the tank—just as Micah flipped open the feeding hatch. And threw Syrinx into the water.

78

He couldn't swim.

Syrinx couldn't swim. He didn't stand a chance of getting out, getting free of the nøkk—

From her angle below, Bryce could only glimpse the bottoms of Syrinx's frantic, desperate legs as he struggled to stay at the surface. She dropped the book, the golden bubble rupturing, and tried to rise to her feet.

Micah emerged from the door to the tank stairwell. His power hit her a moment later.

It flipped her, pinning her facedown on the carpeted stairs. Exposing her back to him.

She writhed, the ebbing pain in her leg secondary to the tingling numbness creeping through her blood. Syrinx was drowning, he was—

Micah loomed over her. She stretched her arm out—toward the shelf. Her tingling fingers brushed over the titles. *On the Divine Number*; *The Walking Dead*; *The Book of Breathings*; *The Queen with Many Faces . . .*

Syrinx was thrashing and thrashing, still fighting so hard—

And then Micah sent a blast of white-hot flame straight into her back. Into the Horn.

She screamed, even as the fire didn't burn, but rather absorbed into the ink, raw power filling her, flame turning to ice and cracking through her blood like shifting glaciers.

The air in the room seemed to suck in on itself, tighter and tighter and tighter—

It blasted outward in a violent ripple. Bryce screamed, hoarfrost in her veins sizzling into burning agony. Upstairs, glass shattered. Then nothing.

Nothing. She shuddered on the ground, tingling ice and searing flame spasming through her.

Micah looked around. Waited.

Bryce could barely breathe, trembling as she waited for a portal to open, for some hole to another world to appear. But nothing occurred.

Disappointment flickered in Micah's eyes before he said, "Interesting."

The word told her enough: he'd try again. And again. It wouldn't matter if she was alive or a pile of self-destructed pulp. Her body would still bear the Horn's ink—the Horn itself. He'd lug around her corpse if he had to until he found a way to open a portal to another world.

She'd figured it out in the hours after the kristallos's attack at the docks, when she'd seen herself in the mirror. And began to suspect that the tattoo on her back was not in any alphabet she knew because it was *not* an alphabet. Not one from Midgard. She'd looked again at all the locations Danika had visited that last week, and saw that only the tattoo shop had gone unchecked. Then she'd realized the amulet was gone, and she had been attacked. Just as Hunt had been attacked by the kristallos in the park—after he'd touched Danika's jacket in the gallery. Touched Danika's scent, full of the Horn.

Bryce strained, hauling herself against the invisible grip of Micah's power. Her fingers brushed a dark purple book spine.

Syrinx, Syrinx, Syrinx—

"Maybe carving the Horn from you will be more effective," Micah murmured. A knife hummed free from its sheath at his thigh. "This will hurt, I'm afraid."

Bryce's finger hooked on the lip of the book's spine. *Please.*

It did not move. Micah knelt over her.

Please, she begged the book. *Please.*

It slid toward her fingers.

Bryce whipped the book from its shelf and splayed open its pages.

Greenish light blasted from it. Right into Micah's chest.

It sent him rocketing back across the library, a clear shot to the open entry to the bathroom.

To where Lehabah waited in the shadows of the bathroom door, a small book in her own hands, whose pages she opened to unleash another blast of power against the door, propelling it shut.

The book's power hissed over the bathroom door, sealing it tight. Locking the Archangel within.

Ruhn had not woken up this morning expecting to watch his sister die.

And his father . . . Ruhn's father said nothing at the horror that unfolded.

For three heartbeats, Bryce lay on the steps as the last of her leg stitched itself together, while she stared at the shut bathroom door. It might have been funny, the idea of locking a near-god inside a bathroom, had it not been so fucking terrifying.

A strangled voice growled behind Ruhn, "Help her."

Hunt. The muscles of his neck were bulging, fighting Sandriel's grip on him. Indeed, Hunt's eyes were on Sandriel as he snarled, "*Help her.*"

The metal bathroom door, even with the book's power sealing it, wouldn't hold Micah for long. Minutes, if that. And the synth in Bryce's system . . . How long did she have until she turned herself into bloody ribbons?

Lehabah rushed over to Bryce just as Hunt again growled at Sandriel, "*Go stop him.*"

No matter that even at ungodly speeds, it would take Sandriel an hour to fly there. Thirty minutes by helicopter.

A choking sound filled the air as Sandriel clamped down on her power, silencing Hunt's voice. "This is Micah's territory. I do not have the authority to intervene in his business."

Athalar still managed to get out, dark eyes blazing, "*Fuck. You.*"

All of Sandriel's triarii fixed their lethal attention on Hunt. He didn't seem to give a shit, though. Not as Bryce gasped to Lehabah, "*Get the tank's feeding dock running.*"

The gaping wound in her thigh finally sealed shut thanks to the synth shooting through her blood. And then Bryce was up and running.

The bathroom door shuddered. She didn't so much as look back as she sprinted, still limping, for the stairs to the tank. She grabbed a knife off the ground. Micah's knife.

Ruhn had to remind himself to take a breath as Bryce hit the stairs, ripping a piece from her torn shirt, wrapping it around her thigh to bind the knife to her. A makeshift sheath.

Declan switched the feed to the small chamber atop the tank, the water sloshing through the grated floor. A three-foot square in the center opened into the gloom, the small platform on a chain anchored to the top of the tank. Lehabah floated at the controls. "It's not attacking him," the sprite wept. "Syrie's just limp there, he's dead—"

Bryce knelt, and began taking swift, deep breaths. Fast, fast, fast—

"What's she doing?" Queen Hypaxia asked.

"She's hyperventilating," Tharion murmured back. "To get more air into her lungs."

"Bryce," Lehabah pleaded. "It's a—"

But then Bryce sucked in one last, mighty breath, and plunged beneath the surface.

Into the nøkk's lair. The feeding platform dropped with her, chain unraveling into the gloom, and as it raced past Bryce, she gripped the iron links, swimming down, down, down—

Bryce had no magic. No strength nor immortality to shield her. Not against the nøkk in the tank with her; not against the Archangel likely only a minute away from breaking through that bathroom door. Not against the synth that would destroy her if the rest didn't.

His sister, his brash, wild sister—knew all that and still went to save her friend.

"It's her Ordeal," Flynn murmured. "This is her fucking Ordeal."

79

The frigid water threatened to snatch the precious little breath from her lungs.

Bryce refused to think of the cold, of the lingering pain in her healed leg, of the two monsters in this library with her. One, at least, had been contained behind the bathroom door.

The other . . .

Bryce kept her focus upon Syrinx, refusing to let her terror take over, to let it rob her of breath as she reached the chimera's limp body.

She would not accept this. Not for a moment.

Her lungs began burning, a growing tightness that she fought against as she bore Syrinx back toward the feeding platform, her lifeline out of the water, away from the nøkk. Her fingers latched into the chain links as the dock rose back toward the surface.

Lungs constricting, Bryce held Syrinx on the platform, letting it propel them up, up—

From the shadows of the rocks at the bottom, the nøkk burst forth. It was already smiling.

The nøkk knew she'd come for Syrinx. It had been watching her in the library for weeks now.

But the feeding platform broke the surface, Bryce with it, and she gasped down sweet, life-saving air as she heaved Syrinx over the edge and gasped to Lehabah, "Chest compressions—"

Clawed hands wrapped around her ankles, slicing her skin as they yanked her back. Her brow smashed into the metal rim of the platform before the cold water swallowed her once more.

Hunt couldn't breathe as the nøkk slammed Bryce into the glass of the tank so hard it cracked.

The impact shook her from her stunned stupor, just as the nøkk snapped for her face.

She dodged left, but it still had its talons on her shoulders, cutting into her skin. She reached for the knife she'd tied to her thigh—

The nøkk grabbed the knife from her hands, tossing it into the watery gloom.

This was it. This was how she'd die. Not at Micah's hand, not from the synth in her body, but by being ripped to shreds by the nøkk.

Hunt could do nothing, nothing, nothing as it again snapped for her face—

Bryce moved again. Lunging not for a hidden weapon, but another sort of attack.

She punched her right hand low into the nøkk's abdomen—and dug inside the nearly invisible front fold. It happened so fast Hunt wasn't sure what she'd done. Until she twisted her wrist, and the nøkk arched in pain.

Bubbles leaked from Bryce's mouth as she wrenched its balls harder—

Every male in the pit flinched.

The nøkk let go, falling to the bottom. It was the opening Bryce needed. She drifted back against the cracked glass, braced her legs, and pushed.

It launched her into the open water. Blood from her head wound streamed in her wake, even as the synth healed the gash and prevented the blow from rendering her unconscious.

The platform dropped into the water again. Lehabah had sent

it down. A final lifeline. Bryce dolphin-kicked for it, her arms pointed in front of her. Blood swirled with each undulating kick.

At the rocky bottom of the tank, the nøkk had recovered—and now bared its teeth up at the fleeing woman. Molten rage gleamed in its milky eyes.

"*Swim, Bryce,*" Tharion growled. "Don't look back."

The platform hit its lowest level. Bryce swam, her teeth gritted. The instinct to take a breath had to be horrendous.

Come on, Hunt prayed. *Come on*.

Bryce's fingers wrapped around the bottom of the platform. Then the rim. The nøkk charged up from the depths, fury and death blazing in its monstrous face.

"Don't stop, Bryce," Fury Axtar warned the screen.

Bryce didn't. Hand by hand by hand, she climbed the ascending chain, fighting for each foot gained toward the surface.

Ten feet from the top. The nøkk reached the platform base.

Five. The nøkk shot up the chain, closing in on her heels.

Bryce broke the surface with a sharp gasp, her arms grappling, hauling, hauling—

She got her chest out. Her stomach. Her legs.

The nøkk's hands broke from the water, reaching.

But Bryce had cleared its range. And now panted, dripping water into the churning surface beneath the grated floor. Head healed without a trace.

The nøkk, unable to stand the touch of the air, dropped beneath the surface just as the feeding platform halted, sealing access to the water beneath.

"Fucking Hel," Fury whispered, running her shaking hands over her face. "Fucking Hel."

Bryce rushed to the unresponsive Syrinx and demanded from Lehabah, "Anything?"

"No, it's—"

Bryce began chest compressions, two fingers on the center of the chimera's sodden chest. She closed his jaws and blew into his nostrils. Did it again. Again. Again.

She didn't speak. Didn't beg any of the gods as she tried to resuscitate him.

On a feed across the room, the bathroom door fizzled beneath Micah's assaults. She had to get out. Had to run now, or she'd be ruptured into shards of bone—

Bryce stayed. Kept fighting for the chimera's life.

"Can you speak through the audio?" Ruhn asked Declan and Jesiba. "Can you patch us through?" He pointed to the screen. "Tell her to *get the fuck out now*."

Jesiba said quietly, her face ashen, "It's only one-way."

Bryce kept up the chest compressions, her soaking hair dripping, her skin bluish in the light from the tank, as if she were a corpse herself. And scrawled on her back, cut off only by her black sports bra—the Horn.

Even if she got free of the gallery, if she somchow survived the synth, Micah would . . .

Syrinx thrashed, vomiting water. Bryce let out a sob, but turned the chimera over, letting him cough it out. He convulsed, vomiting again, gasping for every breath.

Lehabah had dragged a shirt up the steps from one of the desk drawers. She handed it to her, and Bryce swapped it with her ruined shirt before gathering the still-weak Syrinx in her arms and trying to stand.

She moaned in pain, nearly dropping Syrinx as her leg gushed blood into the water below.

Hunt had been so focused on the head wound he hadn't seen the nøkk slash her calf—where the flesh visible through her leggings remained half-shredded. Still slowly healing. The nøkk must have dug its claws in to the bone if the injury was so severe the synth was still stitching it together.

Bryce said, "We have to run. Now. Before he gets out." She didn't wait for Lehabah to reply as she managed to get upright, carrying Syrinx.

She limped—badly. And she moved so, so slowly toward the stairs.

The bathroom door heated again, the metal red-hot as Micah attempted to melt his way through.

Bryce panted through her teeth, a controlled *hiss-hiss-hiss* with each step. Trying to master the pain the synth hadn't yet taken away. Trying to drag a thirty-pound chimera down a set of steps on a shredded leg.

The bathroom door pulsed with light, sparks flying from its cracks. Bryce reached the library, took a limping step toward the main stairs up to the showroom, and whimpered.

"Leave it," the Autumn King growled. "Leave the chimera."

Hunt knew, even before Bryce took another step, that she would not. That she'd rather have her back peeled off by an Archangel than leave Syrinx behind.

And he could see that Lehabah knew it, too.

Bryce was a third of the way up the stairs, sparks flying from the seams of the bathroom door across the library behind them, when she realized Lehabah was not with her.

Bryce halted, gasping around the pain in her calf that even the synth could not dull, and looked back at the base of the library stairs. "Forget the books, Lehabah," she pleaded.

If they survived, she'd kill Jesiba for even making the sprite hesitate. *Kill her.*

Yet Lehabah did not move. "Lehabah," Bryce said, the name an order.

Lehabah said softly, sadly, "You won't make it in time, BB."

Bryce took one step up, pain flaring up her calf. Each movement kept ripping it open, an uphill battle against the synth attempting to heal her. Before it'd rip apart her sanity. She swallowed her scream and said, "We have to try."

"Not we," Lehabah whispered. "You."

Bryce felt her face drain of any remaining color. "You can't." Her voice cracked.

"I can," Lehabah said. "The enchantments won't hold him much longer. Let me buy you time."

Bryce kept moving, gritting her teeth. "We can figure this out. We can get out together—"

"No."

Bryce looked back to find Lehabah smiling softly. Still at the base of the stairs. "Let me do this for you, BB. For you, and for Syrinx."

Bryce couldn't stop the sob that wrenched its way out of her. "You're free, Lehabah."

The words rippled through the library as Bryce wept. "I traded with Jesiba for your freedom last week. I have the papers in my desk. I wanted to throw a party for it—to surprise you." The bathroom door began warping, bending. Bryce sobbed, "I bought you, and now I set you free, Lehabah."

Lehabah's smile didn't falter. "I know," she said. "I peeked in your drawer."

And despite the monster trying to break loose behind them, Bryce choked on a laugh before she begged, "You are a free person—you do not have to do this. You are *free*, Lehabah."

Yet Lehabah remained at the foot of the stairs. "Then let the world know that my first act of freedom was to help my friends."

Syrinx shifted in Bryce's arms, a low, pained sound breaking from him. Bryce thought it might be the sound her own soul was making as she whispered, unable to bear this choice, this moment, "I love you, Lehabah."

The only words that ever mattered.

"And I will love you always, BB." The fire sprite breathed, "Go."

So Bryce did. Gritting her teeth, a scream breaking from her, Bryce heaved herself and Syrinx up the stairs. Toward the iron door at the top. And whatever time it'd buy them, if the synth didn't destroy her first.

The bathroom door groaned.

Bryce glanced back—just once. To the friend who had stayed by her when no one else had. Who had refused to be anything but cheerful, even in the face of the darkness that had swallowed Bryce whole.

Lehabah burned a deep, unfaltering ruby and began to move.

First, a sweep of her arm upward. Then an arc down. A twirl, hair spiraling above her head. A dance, to summon her power. Whatever kernel of it a fire sprite might have.

A glow spread along Lehabah's body.

So Bryce climbed. And with each painful step upward, she could hear Lehabah whisper, almost chanting, "I am a descendant of Ranthia Drahl, Queen of Embers. She is with me now and I am not afraid."

Bryce reached the top of the stairs.

Lehabah whispered, "My friends are behind me, and I will protect them."

Screaming, Bryce shoved the library door. Until it clanged shut, the enchantments sealing, cutting off Lehabah's voice with it, and Bryce leaned against it, sliding to the floor as she sobbed through her teeth.

Bryce had made it up to the showroom and locked the iron door behind her. Thank the gods for that—thank the fucking gods.

Yet Hunt couldn't take his eyes off the library feed, where Lehabah still moved, still summoned her power, repeating the words over and over:

"*I am a descendant of Ranthia Drahl, Queen of Embers. She is with me now and I am not afraid.*"

Lehabah glowed, bright as the heart of a star.

"*My friends are behind me, and I will protect them.*"

The top of the bathroom door began to curl open.

And Lehabah unleashed her power. Three blows. Perfectly aimed.

Not to the bathroom door and Archangel behind it. No, Lehabah couldn't slow Micah.

But a hundred thousand gallons of water would.

Lehabah's shimmering blasts of power slammed into the glass tank. Right on top of the crack that Bryce had made when the nøkk threw her into it.

The creature, sensing the commotion, rose from the rocks. And recoiled in horror as Lehabah struck again. Again. The glass cracked further.

And then Lehabah hurled herself against it. Pushed her tiny body against the crack.

She kept whispering the words over and over again. They morphed together into one sentence, a prayer, a challenge.

"My friends are with me and I am not afraid."

Hunt wrested control of his body enough that he was able to put a hand over his heart. The only salute he could make as Lehabah's words whispered through the speakers.

"My friends are with me and I am not afraid."

One by one, the angels in the 33rd rose to their feet. Then Ruhn and his friends. And they, too, put their hands on their hearts as the smallest of their House pushed and pushed against the glass wall, burning gold as the nøkk tried to flee to any place it might survive what was about to come.

Over and over, Lehabah whispered, *"My friends are with me and I am not afraid."*

The glass spiderwebbed.

Everyone in the conference room rose to their feet. Only Sandriel, her attention fixed on the screen, did not notice. They all stood, and bore witness to the sprite who brought her death down upon herself, upon the nøkk—to save her friends. It was all they could offer her, this final respect and honor.

Lehabah still pushed. Still shook with terror. Yet she did not stop. Not for one heartbeat.

"My friends are with me and I am not afraid."

The bathroom door tore open, metal curling aside to reveal Micah, glowing as if newly forged, as if he'd rend this world apart. He surveyed the library, eyes landing on Lehabah and the cracked tank wall.

The sprite whirled, back pressed against the glass. She hissed at Micah, "This is for Syrinx."

She slammed her little burning palm into the glass.

And a hundred thousand gallons of water exploded into the library.

80

Flashing red lights erupted, casting the world into flickering color. A roar rose from below, the gallery shuddering.

Bryce knew.

She knew the tank had exploded, and that Lehabah had been wiped away with it. Knew the nøkk, exposed to the air, had been killed, too. Knew that Micah would only be slowed for so long.

Syrinx was still whimpering in her arms. Glass littered the gallery floor, the window to Jesiba's office shattered a level above.

Lehabah was dead.

Bryce's fingers curled into claws at her side. The red light of the warning alarms washed over her vision. She welcomed the synth into her heart. Every destructive, raging, frozen ounce of it.

Bryce crawled for the front door, broken glass tinkling. Power, hollow and cold, thrummed at her fingertips.

She grabbed the handle and hoisted herself upright. Yanked the door open to the golden light of late afternoon.

But she did not go through it.

That was not what Lehabah had bought her time to do.

Hunt knew Lehabah was killed instantly, as surely as a torch plunged into a bucket of water.

The tidal wave threw the nøkk onto the mezzanine, where it thrashed, choking on the air as it ate away its skin. It even blasted Micah back into the bathroom.

Hunt just stared and stared. The sprite was gone.

"Shit," Ruhn was whispering.

"Where's Bryce?" Fury asked.

The main floor of the gallery was empty. The front door lay open, but—

"Holy fuck," Flynn whispered.

Bryce was sprinting up the stairs. To Jesiba's office. Only synth fueled that sprint. Only that kind of drug could override pain. And reason.

Bryce set Syrinx on the ground as she entered the office—and then leapt over the desk. To the disassembled gun mounted on the wall above it.

The Godslayer Rifle.

"She's going to kill him," Ruhn whispered. "She's going to kill him for what he did to Danika and the pack." Before she succumbed to the synth, Bryce would offer her friends nothing less than this. Her final moments of clarity. Of her life.

Sabine was silent as death. But she trembled wildly.

Hunt's knees buckled. He couldn't watch this. Wouldn't watch it.

Micah's power rumbled in the library. Parted the water as he plowed across the space.

Bryce grabbed the four parts of the Godslayer Rifle mounted on the wall and chucked them onto the desk. Unlocked the safe door and reached inside. She pulled out a glass vial and knocked back some sort of potion—another drug? Who knew what the sorceress kept in there?—and then pulled out a slender golden bullet.

It was six inches long, its surface engraved with a grinning, winged skull on one side. On the other, two simple words:

Memento Mori.

Remember that you will die. They now seemed more of a promise than the mild reminder from the Meat Market.

Bryce clenched the bullet between her teeth as she hauled the first piece of the rifle toward her. Fitted the second.

Micah surged up the stairs, death incarnate.

Bryce whirled toward the open interior window. She threw out a hand, and the third piece of the rifle—the barrel—flew from the desk into her splayed fingers, borne on magic she did not naturally possess, thanks to the synth coursing through her veins. A few movements had her locking it into place.

She ran for the shattered window, assembling the rifle as she went, summoning the final piece from the desk on an invisible wind, that golden bullet still clenched in her teeth.

Hunt had never seen anyone assemble a gun without looking at it, running toward a target. As if she had done it a thousand times.

She had, Hunt remembered.

Bryce might have been fathered by the Autumn King, but she was Randall Silago's daughter. And the legendary sharpshooter had taught her well.

Bryce clicked the last piece into place and dropped into a slide, finally loading the bullet. She careened into a stop before the gaping window, rising onto her knees as she braced the Godslayer against her shoulder.

And in the two seconds it took Bryce to line up her shot, in the two seconds it took for her to loose a steadying breath, Hunt knew those seconds were Lehabah's. Knew that's what the sprite's life had bought her friend. What Lehabah had offered to Bryce, and Bryce had accepted, understanding.

Not a chance to run. No, there would never be any escaping Micah.

Lehabah had offered Bryce the two extra seconds needed to kill an Archangel.

Micah exploded out of the iron door. Metal embedded in the wood paneling of the gallery. The Governor whirled toward the open front door. To the trap Bryce had laid in opening it.

So he wouldn't look up. So he didn't have time to even glance in Bryce's direction before her finger curled on the trigger.

And she shot that bullet right through Micah's fucking head.

81

Time warped and stretched.

Hunt had the distinct feeling of falling backward, even though he was already against a wall and hadn't so much as moved a muscle.

Yet the coffee in the mug on the nearest table tilted, the liquid endlessly rocking, rocking, rocking to one side—

The death of an Archangel, of a world power, could shudder through time and space. A second could last an hour. A day. A year.

So Hunt saw everything. Saw the endlessly slow movements of everyone in the room, the gaping shock that rippled, Sandriel's outrage, Pollux's white-faced disbelief, Ruhn's terror—

The Godslayer bullet was still burrowing through Micah's skull. Still twisting through bone and brain matter, dragging time in its wake.

Then Bryce stood at the office's blown-out window. A sword in both hands.

Danika's sword—she must have left it in the gallery on her last day alive. And Bryce must have stashed it in Jesiba's office, where it had stayed hidden for two years. Hunt saw every minute expression on Sabine's face, the widening of her pupils, the flow of her corn-silk hair as she reeled at the sight of the missing heirloom—

Bryce leapt from the window and into the showroom below. Hunt saw each movement of her body, arcing as she raised the sword above her head, then brought it back down as she fell.

He could have sworn the ancient steel cut the very air itself. And then it cut through Micah.

Sliced his head in two as Bryce drove it through, the sword cleaving a path into his body. Peeling him apart. Only Danika's sword would do for this task.

Hunt savored these final moments of her life, before the synth took over. Was this the first sign of it—this madness, this pure, frenzied rage?

Bryce. His Bryce. His friend and . . . everything they had that was more than that. She was his and he was hers, and he should have told her that, should have told her in the Comitium lobby that she was the only person who mattered, who would ever matter to him, and he'd find her again, even if it took him a thousand years, he'd find her and do everything Sandriel had mocked him about.

Bryce still leapt, still kept cutting through Micah's body. His blood rained upward.

In normal time, it would have splattered. But in this warped existence, the Archangel's blood rose like ruby bubbles, showering Bryce's face, filling her screaming mouth.

In this warped existence, he could see the synth heal every sliced, bruised place on Bryce as she cut her way down through Micah. Cut him in half.

She landed on the green carpet. Hunt expected to hear bone cracking. But her calf was wholly healed. The last gift of the synth before it destroyed her. Yet in her eyes . . . he saw no haze of insanity, of self-destructive frenzy. Only cold, glittering vengeance.

The two halves of Micah's body fell away from each other and Bryce moved again. Another swipe. Across his torso. And then another to his head.

The red alarm lights were still blaring, but there was no mistaking the blood on Bryce. The white shirt that was now crimson. Her eyes remained clear, though. Still the synth did not take control.

Hypaxia murmured, "The antidote is working. It's working on her."

Hunt swayed then. He said to the witch, "I thought you were only sending over the venom."

Hypaxia didn't take her eyes off the screen. "I figured out how to stabilize the venom without needing to be present, and—I sent the antidote to her instead. Just . . . just in case."

And they'd watched Bryce down it like a bottle of whiskey.

It had taken almost three minutes for the antidote to wholly destroy the synth in Hypaxia's clinic. Neither Hunt nor the witch-queen took their eyes off Bryce long enough to count the minutes until the synth had vanished from her body entirely.

Bryce walked calmly to the hidden supply closet. Pulled out a red plastic container. And dumped the entire gallon of gasoline on the Governor's dismembered corpse.

"Holy fuck," Ruhn whispered, over and over. "Holy fuck."

The rest of the room didn't so much as breathe too loudly. Even Sandriel had no words as Bryce grabbed a pack of matches from a drawer in her desk.

She struck one, and tossed it onto the Governor's body.

Flames erupted. The fireproofing enchantments on the art around her shimmered.

There would be no chance of salvation. Of healing. Not for Micah. Not after what he had done to Danika Fendyr. To the Pack of Devils. And Lehabah.

Bryce stared at the fire, her face still splattered with the Archangel's blood. And finally, she lifted her eyes. Right to the camera. To the world watching.

Vengeance incarnate. Wrath's bruised heart. She would bow for no one. Hunt's lightning sang at the sight of that brutal, beautiful face.

Time sped up, the flames devouring Micah's body, crisping his wings to cinders. They spat him out as ashes.

Sirens wailed outside the gallery as the Auxiliary pulled up at last.

Bryce slammed the front door shut as the first of the Fae units and wolf packs appeared.

No one, not even Sandriel, spoke a word as Bryce took out the vacuum from the supply closet. And erased the last trace of Micah from the world.

82

A gas explosion, she told the Aux through the intercom, who apparently hadn't been informed of the details by their superiors. She was fine. Just a private mess to deal with.

No mention of the Archangel. Of the ashes she'd vacuumed, then dumped in the bin out back.

She'd gone up to Jesiba's office afterward, to hold Syrinx, stroking his fur, kissing his still-damp head, whispering repeatedly, "It's okay. You're okay."

He'd eventually fallen asleep in her lap, and when she'd assured herself that his breathing was unlabored, she'd finally pulled her phone from the pocket in the back of her leggings.

She had seven missed calls, all from Jesiba. And a string of messages. She barely comprehended the earlier ones, but the one that had arrived a minute ago said, *Tell me that you are all right.*

Her fingers were distant, her blood pounded in her ears. But she wrote back, *Fine. Did you see what happened?*

Jesiba's reply came a moment later.

Yes. The entire thing. Then the sorceress added, *Everyone at the Summit did.*

Bryce just wrote back, *Good.*

She put her phone on silent, tucking it back in her pocket, and ventured down to the watery ruin of the archives.

There was no trace of Lehabah in the mostly submerged library. Not even a smudge of ash.

The nøkk's corpse lay sprawled on the mezzanine, its dried-out skin flaking away, one clawed hand still gripping the iron bars of the balcony rail.

Jesiba had enough spells on the library that the books and the small tanks and terrariums had been shielded from the wave, though their occupants were near-frantic, but the building itself . . .

The silence roared around her.

Lehabah was gone. There was no voice at her shoulder, grousing about the mess.

And Danika . . . She tucked away the truth Micah had revealed. The Horn on her back, healed and functional again. She felt no different—wouldn't have known it was awake were it not for the horrific blast the Archangel had unleashed. At least a portal hadn't opened. At least she had that.

She knew the world was coming. It would arrive on her doorstep soon.

And she might very well burn for what she'd just done.

So Bryce trudged back upstairs. Her leg was healed. Every ache was gone; the synth was cleansed from her system—

Bryce puked into the trash can beside her desk. The venom in the antidote had burned as fiercely as it had gone down, but she didn't stop. Not until there was nothing left but spittle.

She should call someone. Anyone.

Still, the doorbell did not ring. No one came to punish her for what she'd done. Syrinx was still sleeping, curled into a tight ball. Bryce crossed the gallery and opened the door for the world.

It was then that she heard the screaming. She grabbed Syrinx and ran toward it.

And when she arrived, she realized why no one had come for her, or for the Horn inked in her flesh.

They had far bigger problems to deal with.

* * *

Chaos reigned at the Summit. The Asterian Guard had flown off, presumably to get instructions from their masters, and Sandriel just gaped at the feed that had shown Bryce Quinlan casually vacuuming up the ashes of a Governor as if she'd spilled chips on the carpet.

She was distracted enough that Hunt was able to finally move. He slid into the empty seat beside Ruhn and Flynn. His voice was low. "This just went from bad to worse."

Indeed, the Autumn King had Declan Emmet and two other techs on six different computers, monitoring everything from the gallery to the news to the movements of the Aux through the city. Tristan Flynn was again on his phone, arguing with someone in the Fae command post.

Ruhn rubbed his face. "They'll kill her for this."

For murdering a Governor. For proving a sprite and a half-human woman could take on a Governor and win. It was absurd. As likely as a minnow slaying a shark.

Sabine still stared at the screens, unseeing as the ancient Prime, currently dozing in his chair beside her. A tired, weary wolf ready for his last slumber. Amelie Ravenscroft, still pale and shaky, handed Sabine a glass of water. The future Prime ignored it.

Across the room, Sandriel rose, a phone to her ear. She looked at none of them as she ascended the steps out of the pit and left, her triarii falling into rank around her, Pollux already mastering himself enough to recover his swagger.

Hunt's stomach churned as he wondered if Sandriel was moments away from being crowned Archangel of Valbara. Pollux was grinning widely enough to confirm the possibility. Fuck.

Ruhn glanced at Hunt. "We need to figure out a plan, Athalar."

For Bryce. To somehow shield her from the fallout of this. If such a thing were even possible. If the Asteri weren't already moving against her, already telling Sandriel what to do. To eliminate the threat Bryce had just made herself into, even without the Horn inked in her back.

At least Micah's *experiment* had failed. At least they had that.

Ruhn said again, more to himself, "They'll kill her for this."

Queen Hypaxia took a seat at Hunt's other side, giving him a warning look as she held up a key. She fitted it into Hunt's manacles and the gorsian stones thumped to the table. "I believe they have bigger issues at hand," she said, gesturing to the city cameras Declan had pulled up.

Quiet rippled through the conference room.

"Tell me that's not what I think it is," Ruhn said.

Micah's experiment with the Horn hadn't failed at all.

83

Bryce took one look at the Heart Gate in the Old Square and sprinted home, Syrinx in her arms.

Micah had indeed wielded the Horn successfully. And it had opened a portal right through the mouth of the Heart Gate, drawing upon the magic in its quartz walls. Bryce had taken one look at what sailed out of the void suspended in the Heart Gate and knew Micah had not opened a portal to unknown worlds, as he'd intended. This one went straight to Hel.

People screamed as winged, scaled demons soared out of the Gate—demons from the Pit itself.

At her building, she yelled at Marrin to get into the basement, along with any tenants he could bring with him. And to call his family, his friends, and warn them to get somewhere secure—the bomb shelters, if they could—and hunker down with whatever weapons were available.

She left Syrinx in the apartment, laid down a massive bowl of water, and took the lid off the food bin entirely. He could feed himself. She piled blankets on the couch, tucking him into them, and kissed him once on his furry head before she grabbed what she needed and ran out the door again.

She raced to the roof, shrugging on Danika's leather jacket, then tying the Fendyr family's sword across her back. She tucked one of

Hur•'s handguns into the waist of her jeans, shouldered his rifle, and slid as many packs of ammo as she could into her pockets. She surveyed the city and her blood turned to ice. It was worse—so much worse—than she'd imagined.

Micah hadn't just opened a portal to Hel in the Heart Gate. He'd opened one in *every* Gate. Every one of the seven quartz arches was a doorway to Hel.

Screams from below rose as the demons raced from the voids and into the defenseless city.

A siren wailed. A warning cry—and an order.

Bomb shelters opened, their automatic foot-thick doors sliding aside to let in those already gathered. Bryce lifted her phone to her ear.

Juniper, for once, picked up on the first ring. "Oh gods, Bryce—"

"Get somewhere safe!"

"I am, I am," Juniper sobbed. "We were having a dress rehearsal with some big donors, and we're all in the shelter down the block, and—" Another sob. "Bryce, they're saying they're going to shut the door early."

Horror lurched through her. "People need to get in. They need every moment you can spare."

Juniper wept. "I told them that, but they're frantic and won't listen. They won't let humans in."

"Fucking bastards," Bryce breathed, studying the shelter still open down her block—the people streaming inside. The shelters could be shut manually at any time, but all would close within an hour. Sealed until the threat was dealt with.

Juniper's voice crackled. "I'll *make* them hold the doors. But Bryce, it's—" Reception cut out as she presumably moved farther into the shelter, and Bryce glanced northward, toward the theaters. Mere blocks from the Heart Gate. "Mess of—" Another crackle. "Safe?"

"I'm safe," Bryce lied. "Stay in the shelter. Hold the doors for as long as you can."

But Juniper, sweet and determined and brave, wouldn't be able to calm a panicked crowd. Especially one draped in finery—and convinced of their right to live at the expense of all others.

Juniper's voice crackled again, so Bryce just said, "I love you, June." And hung up.

She fired off a message to Jesiba about the literal Hel being unleashed, and when she received no instantaneous reply, added another saying that she was heading out into it. Because someone had to.

Demons soared into the skies from the Moonwood Gate. Bryce could only pray the Den had gone into lockdown already. But the Den had guards by the dozen and powerful enchantments. Parts of this city had no protection at all.

It was enough to send her sprinting for the stairs off the roof. Down through the building.

And into the chaotic streets below.

"Demons are coming out of every Gate," Declan reported over the clamor of various leaders and their teams shouting into their phones. The Gates now held black voids within their archways. As if an invisible set of doors had been opened within them.

He could only see six of them on his screens, since the Bone Quarter had no cameras, but Declan supposed he could safely assume the Dead Gate across the Istros held the same darkness. Jesiba Roga made no attempt to contact the Under-King, but kept her eyes fixed on the feeds. Her face was ashen.

It didn't matter, Hunt thought, looking over Declan's shoulder. The denizens of the Bone Quarter were already dead.

Calls were going out—many weren't being answered. Sabine barked orders at Amelie, both of them pressing phones to their ears as they tried to reach the Alphas of the city packs.

On every screen in the conference center, cameras from around Crescent City revealed a land of nightmares. Hunt didn't know where to look. Each new image was more awful than the last. Demons he recognized with chilling clarity—the worst of the worst—poured into the city through the Gates. Demons that had been an effort for *him* to kill. The people of Lunathion didn't stand a chance.

Not the urbane, clever demons like Aidas. No, these were the grunts. The beasts of the Pit. Its wild dogs, hungry for easy prey.

In FiRo, the iridescent bubbles of the villas' defense enchantments already gleamed. Locking out anyone poor or unlucky enough to be on the streets. It was there, in front of the ironclad walls of the city's richest citizens, that the Aux had been ordered to go. To protect the already safe.

Hunt snarled at Sabine, "Tell your packs there are defenseless homes where they're needed—"

"These are the protocols," Sabine snarled back. Amelie Ravenscroft, at least, had the decency to flush with shame and lower her head. But she didn't dare speak out of turn.

Hunt growled, "Fuck the protocols." He pointed to the screens. "Those assholes have enchantments *and* panic rooms in their villas. The people on the streets have *nothing*."

Sabine ignored him. But Ruhn ordered his father, "Pull our forces from FiRo. Send them where they're needed."

The Autumn King's jaw worked. But he said, "The protocols are in place for a reason. We will not abandon them to chaos."

Hunt demanded, "Are you both fucking kidding me?"

The afternoon sun inched toward the horizon. He didn't want to think about how much worse it would get once night fell.

"I don't care if they don't want to," Tharion was yelling into his phone. "Tell them to *go to shore*." A pause. "*Then tell them to take anyone they can carry under the surface!*"

Isaiah was on the phone across the room. "No, that time warp was just some spell that went wrong, Naomi. Yeah, it caused the Gates to open. No, get the 33rd to the Old Square. *Get them to the Old Square Gate right now. I don't care if they all get ripped to shreds—*" Isaiah pulled his phone away from his ear, blinking at the screen.

Isaiah's eyes met Hunt's. "The CBD is under siege. The 33rd are being slaughtered." He didn't muse whether Naomi had just been one of them, or had merely lost her phone in the fight.

Ruhn and Flynn dialed number after number. No one answered. As if the Fae leaders left in the city were all dead, too.

Sabine got through. "Ithan—report."

Declan wordlessly patched Sabine's number through to the room's speakers. Ithan Holstrom's panting filled the space, his location pinging from outside the bespelled and impenetrable Den. Unearthly, feral growls that did not belong to wolves cut between his words. "They're fucking *everywhere*. We can barely keep them away—"

"Hold positions," Sabine commanded. *"Hold your positions and await further orders."*

Humans and Vanir alike were running, children in their arms, to any open shelter they could find. Many were already shut, sealed by the frantic people inside.

Hunt asked Isaiah, "How long until the 32nd can make it down from Hilene?"

"An hour," the angel replied, eyes on the screen. On the slaughter, on the panicking city. "They'll be too late." And if Naomi was down, either injured or dead . . . *Fuck*.

Flynn thundered at someone on the phone, "Get the Rose Gate surrounded *now*. You're just *handing* the city to them."

Hunt surveyed the bloodshed and sorted through the city's few options. They'd need armies to surround all seven Gates that opened to Hel—and find some way to close those portals.

Hypaxia had risen from her seat. She studied the screens with grim determination and said calmly into her phone, "Suit up and move out. We're heading in."

Everyone turned toward her. The young queen didn't seem to notice. She just ordered whoever was on the line, "To the city. Now."

Sabine hissed, "You'll all be slaughtered." And too late, Hunt didn't say.

Hypaxia ended the call and pointed to a screen on the left wall, its footage of the Old Square. "I would rather die like her than watch innocents die while I'm sitting in here."

Hunt turned to where she'd pointed, the hair on his neck rising. As if knowing what he'd see.

There, racing through the streets in Danika's leather jacket, sword in one hand and gun in the other, was Bryce.

Running not from the danger, but into it.

She roared something, over and over. Declan locked into the feeds, changing from camera to camera to follow her down the street. "I think I can pull up her audio and isolate her voice against the ambient noise," he said to no one in particular. And then—

"*Get into the shelters!*" she was screaming. Her words echoed off every part of the room.

Duck, slash, shoot. She moved like she'd trained with the Aux her entire life.

"*Get inside now!*" she bellowed, whirling to aim at a winged demon blotting out the mockingly golden afternoon sun. Her gun fired, and the creature screeched, careening into an alley. Declan's fingers flew on the keyboard as he kept her on-screen.

"Where the fuck is she going?" Fury said.

Bryce kept running. Kept firing. She did not miss.

Hunt looked at her surroundings, and realized where she was headed.

To the most defenseless place in Crescent City, full of humans with no magic. No preternatural gifts or strength.

"She's going to the Meadows," Hunt said.

It was worse than anything Bryce had imagined.

Her arm was numb from the bite of the gun every time she fired, reeking blood covered her, and there was no end to the snapping teeth; the leathery wings; the raging, lightless eyes. The afternoon bled toward a vibrant sunset, the sky soon matching the gore in the streets.

Bryce sprinted, her breath sharp as a knife in her chest.

Her handgun ran out. She didn't waste time feeling for ammo she didn't have left. No, she just hurled the gun at a winged black demon that swooped for her, knocking it off-kilter, and unslung the rifle from her shoulder. Hunt's rifle. His cedar-and-rain scent wrapped around her as she pumped the barrel, and by the time the demon had whirled back her way, jaws snapping, she'd fired.

Its head was blasted off in a spray of red.

Still she ran on, working her way into the city. Past the few still-open shelters, whose occupants were doing their best to defend the entrances. To buy others time to make it inside.

Another demon launched from a rooftop, curved claws reaching for her—

Bryce swiped Danika's sword upward, splitting the demon's mottled gray skin from gut to neck. It crashed into the pavement behind her, leathery wings snapping beneath it, but she was already moving again.

Keep going. She had to keep going.

All her training with Randall, every hour between the boulders and pines of the mountains around her home, every hour in the town rec hall, all of it had been for this.

84

Hunt couldn't take his eyes from the feed of Bryce battling her way through the city. Hypaxia's phone rang somewhere off to his left, and the witch-queen answered before the first ring had ended. Listened. "What do you mean, the brooms are destroyed?"

Declan patched her call through to the speakers, so they could all hear the shaking voice of the witch on the other end of the line. "They're all in splinters, Your Majesty. The conference center armory, too. The guns, the swords—the helicopters, too. The cars. All of it, wrecked."

Dread curdled in Hunt's gut as the Autumn King murmured, "Micah." The Archangel must have done it before he left, quietly and unseen. Anticipating keeping them at bay while he experimented with the Horn's power. With Bryce.

"I have a helicopter," Fury said. "I kept it off-site."

Ruhn got to his feet. "Then we move out now." It would still take thirty minutes to get there.

"The city is a slaughterhouse," Sabine was saying into the phone. "Hold your posts in Moonwood and FiRo!"

Every pack in the Aux was linked to the call, able to hear each other. With a few keystrokes, Declan had linked Sabine's phone to the system in the conference room so the Aux might hear them all as well. But some packs had stopped responding altogether.

Hunt snapped at Sabine, "*Get a fucking wolf pack to the Old Square now!*" Even with Fury's helicopter, he'd be too late. But if help could at least reach Bryce before she headed solo into the charnel house that would be the Meadows—

Sabine snapped back at him, "*There are no wolves left for the Old Square!*"

But the Prime of the wolves had stirred at last, and pointed an ancient, gnarled finger to the screen. To the feeds. And he said, "One wolf remains in the Old Square."

Everyone looked then. To where he'd pointed. Whom he'd pointed to.

Bryce raced through the carnage, sword glinting with each swipe and duck and slash.

Sabine choked. "That's Danika's sword you're sensing, Father—"

The Prime's age-worn eyes blinked unseeingly at the screen. His hand curled on his chest. "A wolf." He tapped his heart. Still Bryce fought onward toward the Meadows, still she ran interference for anyone fleeing for the shelters, buying them a path to safety. "A true wolf."

Hunt's throat tightened to the point of pain. He extended his hand to Isaiah. "Give me your phone."

Isaiah didn't question him, and didn't say a word as he handed it over. Hunt dialed a number he'd memorized, since he hadn't dared to store it in his contacts. The call rang and rang before it finally went through. "I'm guessing this is important?"

Hunt didn't bother to identify himself as he growled, "You owe me a gods-damned favor."

The Viper Queen only said, amusement coating her rich voice, "Oh?"

Two minutes later, Hunt had risen from his seat, intent on following Ruhn to Fury's helicopter, when Jesiba's phone rang. The sorceress announced, voice strained, "It's Bryce."

Hunt whipped his head to the camera feed, and sure enough, Bryce had tucked her phone into her bra strap over her shoulder, presumably leaving it on speaker. She wove around abandoned cars as she crossed the border into Asphodel Meadows. The sun began to set, as if Solas himself was abandoning them.

"Bring it up on the speakers and merge the call with the Aux lines," Jesiba ordered Declan, and answered the phone. "Bryce?"

Bryce's panting was labored. Her rifle cracked like breaking thunder. "Tell whoever's at the Summit that I need backup in the Meadows—I'm heading for the shelter near the Mortal Gate."

Ruhn vaulted down the stairs and ran right to the speaker in the center of the table. He said to it, "Bryce, it's a massacre. Get inside that shelter before they all shut—"

Her rifle boomed, and another demon went down. But more swept through the Gates and into the city, staining the streets with blood as surely as the vibrant sunset now stained the sky.

Bryce ducked behind a dumpster for cover as she fired again and again. Reloaded.

"There's no backup for Asphodel Meadows," Sabine said. "Every pack is stationed—"

"*There are children here!*" Bryce screamed. "There are *babies*!"

The room fell silent. A deeper sort of horror spread through Hunt like ink in water.

And then a male voice panted over the speakers, "I'm coming, Bryce."

Bryce's bloodied face crumpled as she whispered, "Ithan?"

Sabine snarled, "Holstrom, stay at your *fucking* post—"

But Ithan said again, more urgently this time, "Bryce, I'm coming. *Hang on.*" A pause. Then he added, "We're all coming."

Hunt's knees wobbled as Sabine bellowed at Ithan, "*You are disobeying a direct order from your—*"

Ithan cut off her call. And every wolf under his command ended their connection, too.

The wolves could be at the Meadows in three minutes.

Three minutes through Hel, through the slaughter and death.

Three minutes in a flat-out run, a sprint to save the most defenseless among them.

The human children.

The jackals joined them. The coyotes. The wild dogs and common dogs. The hyenas and dingoes. The foxes. It was who they were. Who they had always been. Defenders of those who could not protect themselves. Defenders of the small, the young.

Shifter or true animal, that truth lay etched in the soul of every canine.

Ithan Holstrom sprinted toward Asphodel Meadows with the weight of that history behind him, burning in his heart. He prayed he was not too late.

85

Bryce knew it was stupid luck that kept her alive. And pure adrenaline that made her focus her aim so clearly. Calmly.

But with each block she cleared as the sunset deepened, her legs moved more slowly. Her reactions lagged. Her arms ached, becoming leaden. Every pull of the trigger took a bit more effort.

Just a little longer—that was all she needed. Just a little longer, until she could make sure that everyone in Asphodel Meadows got into a shelter before they all closed. It wouldn't be long now.

The shelter halfway down the block remained open, figures holding the line in front of it while human families rushed in. The Mortal Gate lay a few blocks northward—still open to Hel.

So Bryce planted herself at the intersection, sheathing Danika's sword as she again raised Hunt's rifle to her shoulder. She had six rounds left.

Ithan would be here soon. Any moment now.

A demon surged from around a corner, taloned fingers gouging lines into the cobblestones. The rifle bit into her shoulder as she fired. The demon was still falling, sliding across the ground, when she angled the rifle and fired again. Another demon went down.

Four bullets left.

Behind her, humans screamed orders. *Hurry! Into the shelter! Drop the bag and run!*

Bryce fired at a demon soaring across the intersection, right for the shelter. The demon went down twenty feet from the entrance. The humans finished it off.

Inside the shelter's open mouth, children shrieked, babies wailed.

Bryce fired again. Again. Again.

Another demon barreled around the corner, sprinting for her. The trigger clicked.

Out. Done. Empty.

The demon leapt, jaws opening wide to reveal twin rows of dagger-sharp teeth. Aiming for her throat. Bryce barely had time to lift the rifle and wedge it between those gaping jaws. Metal and wood groaned, and the world tilted with the impact.

She and the demon slammed into the cobblestones, her bones barking in pain. The demon clamped down on the rifle. It snapped in two.

Bryce managed to hurl herself backward from under the demon as it spat out the pieces of the rifle. Maw leaking saliva on the bloodied streets, it advanced on her. Seemed to savor each step.

With her sheathed sword pinned beneath her, Bryce reached for the knife at her thigh. As if it would do anything, as if it would stop this—

The demon sank onto its haunches, readying for the kill.

The ground shook behind her as Bryce angled her wrist, blade tilting upward—

A sword plunged through the demon's gray head.

A massive sword, at least four feet long, borne by a towering, armored male figure. Blue lights glowed along the blade. More glared along sleek black body armor and a matching helmet. And across the male's chest, an emblem of a striking cobra glowed.

One of the Viper Queen's Fae bodyguards.

Six others raced past him, the cobblestones shaking beneath their feet, guns and swords drawn. No venom-addled stupor to be seen. Just lethal precision.

And with the Viper Queen's Fae guards, wolves and foxes and canines of every breed flowed by, launching into the fray.

Bryce scrambled to her feet, nodding to the warrior who'd saved her. The Fae male only whirled, his metal-encased hands grabbing a demon by the shoulders and wrenching it apart with a mighty yell. He tore the demon in two.

But more of Hel's worst thundered and soared for them. So Bryce freed Danika's sword again from across her back.

She willed strength to her arm, bracing her feet as another demon galloped down the street for her. Canine shifters engaged demons all around, forming a barrier of fur and teeth and claws between the oncoming horde and the shelter behind them.

Bryce feinted left, swiping her sword up as the demon fell for her fake-out. But the blade didn't break through bone and to the soft, vulnerable organs beneath. The creature roared, pivoting, and lunged again. She gritted her teeth, and lifted her sword in challenge, the demon too frenzied to notice that she'd let herself become the distraction.

While the massive gray wolf attacked from behind.

Ithan ripped into the demon in an explosion of teeth and claws, so fast and brutal it momentarily stunned her. She'd forgotten how enormous he was in this form—all the shifters were at least three times the size of normal animals, but Ithan had always been larger. Exactly like his brother.

Ithan spat out the demon's throat and shifted, wolf becoming a tall male in a flash of light. Blood coated his navy T-shirt and jeans as much as it did her own clothes, but before they could speak, his brown eyes flared with alarm. Bryce twisted, met by the rancid breath of a demon as it dive-bombed her.

She ducked and thrust the sword upward, the demon's shriek nearly bursting her ears as she let the beast drag its belly down the blade. Gutting it.

Gore splattered her sneakers, her torn leggings, but she made sure the demon's head was rolling before whirling to Ithan. Just as he drew a sword from a sheath on his back and split another demon apart.

Their stares held, and all the words she'd needed to say hung there. She saw them in his eyes, too, as he realized whose jacket and sword she bore.

But she offered a grim smile. Later. If they somehow survived this, if they could last another few minutes and get into the shelter . . . They'd speak then.

Ithan nodded, understanding.

Bryce knew it wasn't adrenaline alone that powered her as she launched back into the carnage.

"Shelters close in four minutes," Declan announced to the conference room.

"Why hasn't your helicopter arrived?" Ruhn asked Fury. He stood, Flynn rising with him.

Axtar checked her phone. "It's on its way over from—"

The doors at the top of the pit burst open, and Sandriel entered on a storm wind. And there was no sign of her triarii or Pollux as she strode down the stairs. No one spoke.

Hunt prepared himself as she glanced his way, seated between a now-standing Ruhn and Hypaxia. The gorsian manacles lay on the table before him.

But she merely returned to her seat at the lowermost table. She had bigger concerns at hand, he supposed. Her attention darting between the screens and feeds and updates, Sandriel said, "There is nothing we can do for the city with the Gates open to Hel. We are under orders to remain here."

Ruhn started. "We are *needed*—"

"We are to *remain here*." The words rumbled like thunder through the room. "The Asteri are sending help."

Hunt sagged in his seat, and Ruhn sank down beside him. "Thank fuck," the prince muttered, rubbing shaking hands over his face.

They must have dispatched the Asterian Guard, then. And further reinforcements. Perhaps Sandriel's triarii had gone to Lunathion. They might all be psychotic assholes, but at least they could hold their own in a fight. Fuck, the Hammer alone would be a blessing to the city right now.

"Three minutes until shelter lockdown," Declan said.

In the general chaos of the audio feed Declan had pulled up, a shifter's howl went out, warning everyone to get to safety. To abandon the boundary they'd established against the horde and run like Hel for the still-open metal door.

Humans were still fleeing, though. Adults carrying children and pets sprinted for the opening, hardly bigger than a single-car garage door. The Viper Queen's warriors and a few of the wolves remained at the intersection.

"Two minutes," Declan said.

Bryce and Ithan fought side by side. Where one stumbled, the other did not fail. Where one baited a demon, the other executed it.

A siren blared in the city. A warning. Still Bryce and Ithan held the corner.

"Thirty seconds," Declan said.

"Go," Hunt urged. "Go, Bryce."

She gutted a demon, whirling toward the shelter at last, Ithan moving with her. Good, she'd get inside, and could wait it out until the Asterian Guard arrived to wipe these fuckers away. Maybe they'd know how to seal the voids in the Gates.

The shelter door began closing.

"They're too far," Fury said quietly.

"They'll make it," Hunt ground out, even as he eyed the distance between the slowly closing door and the two figures racing for it, Bryce's red hair a banner behind her.

Ithan stumbled, and Bryce grabbed his hand before he could go down. A nasty gash gleamed in Ithan's side, blood soaking his T-shirt. How the male was even running—

The door was halfway closed. Losing inches every second.

A clawed, humanoid hand from inside wrapped around its edge. Multiple pairs.

And then a young, brown-haired wolf was there, her teeth gritted, her face lupine, roaring as she heaved against the inevitable. As every one of the wolves behind her grabbed the sliding door and tried to slow it.

"Fifteen seconds," Declan whispered.

Bryce ran and ran and ran.

One by one, the wolves of Ithan's pack lost their grip on the door.

Until only that one young female was holding it back, a foot braced against the concrete wall, bellowing in defiance—

Ithan and Bryce charged for the shelter, the wolf's focus solely on the shelter door.

Only three feet of space remained. Not enough room for both of them. Bryce's stare shot to Ithan's face. Sorrow filled her eyes. And determination.

"No," Hunt breathed. Knowing exactly what she'd do.

Bryce dropped behind just a step. Just enough to draw upon her Fae strength to shove Ithan forward. To save Connor Holstrom's brother.

Ithan twisted toward Bryce, eyes flaring with rage and despair and grief, hand outstretched, but too late.

The metal door shut with a boom that seemed to echo across the city.

That *was* echoed across the city, as every shelter door shut at last.

Her momentum was too great to slow. Bryce slammed into the metal door, grunting in pain.

She turned in place, face leached of color. Searching for options and coming up empty.

Hunt read it on her face, then. For the first time, Bryce had no idea what to do.

Every part of Bryce shook as she took cover in the slight alcove before the shelter, the sunset a vibrant wash of orange and ruby—like the final battle cry of the world before the oncoming night.

The demons had moved on, but more would be coming. Soon. As long as the Gates held those portals to Hel, they would never stop coming.

Someone—Ithan, probably—began pounding on the shelter door behind her. As if he'd claw his way through, open up a passage for her to get inside. She ignored the sound.

The Viper Queen's warriors were flashes of metal and light far down the street, still fighting. Some had fallen, heaps of steaming armor and blood.

If she could make it to her apartment, it had enchantments enough to protect her and any others she could get inside. But it was twenty blocks away. It might as well have been twenty miles.

An idea flared, and she weighed it, considering. She could try. She had to try.

Bryce took a bracing breath. In her hand, Danika's sword shook like a reed in the wind.

She could make it. Somehow, she'd find a way.

She leapt into the blood-slick streets, sword held ready to attack. She didn't look back at the shelter behind her as she began to run, blind memory of the city grid sinking in to guide her on the fastest route. A snarl rumbled from around a corner, and Bryce barely brought up her sword in time to intercept the demon. She partially severed its neck, and was running again before it fully hit the ground. She had to keep moving. Had to get to the Old Square—

Dead shifters and the Viper Queen's soldiers lay in the streets. Even more dead humans around them. Most in pieces.

Another demon barreled from the red sky—

She screamed as it knocked her back, slamming her into a car so hard the windows shattered. She had all of a second to wrench open the passenger-side door and climb in before it landed again. Attacked the car.

Bryce scrambled over the armrests and stick shift, fumbling for the driver's-side door. She yanked on the handle and half fell into the street, the demon so distracted with shredding the tires on the opposite side that it didn't see her lurch into a sprint.

The Old Square. If she could make it to the Old Square—

Two demons raced for her. The only thing she could do was run as the light began to fade.

Alone. She was alone out here.

86

The city was starting to go quiet. Every time Declan checked the audio in another district, more screams had diminished, cut off one by one.

Not from any calm or salvation, Hunt knew.

The voids in the Gates remained open. The sunset gave way to bruised purple skies. When true night fell, he could imagine what sort of horrors Hel would send through. The kind that did not like the light, that had been bred and learned to hunt in the dark.

Bryce was still out there. One mistake, one misstep, and she would be dead.

There would be no healing, no regeneration. Not without the Drop.

She made it over the border of the Old Square. But she didn't run for safety. No, she seemed to be running for the Heart Gate, where the flow of demons had halted. As if Hel were indeed waiting for true night to begin before its second round.

His heart thundered as she paused down the block from the Gate. As she ducked into the alcove of a nearby shelter. Illuminated by the firstlight lamp mounted outside it, she slid to the ground, her sword loosely gripped in one hand.

Hunt knew that position, that angle of the head.

A soldier who had fought a good, hard battle. A soldier who was exhausted, but would take this moment, this last moment, to rally before their final stand.

Hunt bared his teeth at the screen, "*Get up, Bryce.*"

Ruhn was shaking his head, terror stark on his face. The Autumn King said nothing. Did nothing as he watched his daughter on the feed Declan placed on the main screen.

Bryce reached into her shirt to pull out her phone. Her hands were shaking so hard she could barely hold it. But she hit a button on the screen and lifted it to her ear. Hunt knew what that was, too. Her final chance to say goodbye to her parents, her loved ones.

A faint ringing sounded in the conference room. From the table at its center. Hunt looked to Jesiba, but her phone remained dark. Ruhn's stayed dark as well. Everyone went silent as Sandriel pulled a phone from her pocket. Hunt's phone.

Sandriel glanced toward him, shock slackening her face. Every thought eddied from Hunt's head.

"Give him the phone," Ruhn said softly.

Sandriel just stared at the screen. Debating.

"*Give him the fucking phone*," Ruhn ordered her.

Sandriel, to Hunt's shock, did. With trembling hands, he picked up.

"Bryce?"

On the video feed, he could see her wide eyes. "Hunt?" Her voice was so raw. "I—I thought it would go to audiomail—"

"Help is coming soon, Bryce."

The stark terror on her face as she surveyed the last of the sunlight destroyed him. "No—no, it'll be too late."

"It won't. I need you to get up, Bryce. Get to a safer location. Do *not* go any closer to that Gate."

She bit her lip, trembling. "It's still wide open—"

"*Go to your apartment and stay there until help comes.*" The panicked terror on her face hardened into something calm at his order. Focused. Good.

"Hunt, I need you to call my mom."

"Don't start making those kinds of goodbyes—"

"I need you to call my mom," she said quietly. "I need you to tell her that I love her, and that everything I am is because of her. Her strength and her courage and her love. And I'm sorry for all the bullshit I put her through."

"Stop—"

"Tell my dad . . . ," she whispered. The Autumn King stiffened. Looked back toward Hunt. "Tell Randall," she clarified, "that I'm so proud I got to call him my father. That he was the only one that ever mattered."

Hunt could have sworn something like shame flitted across the Autumn King's face. But Hunt implored, "Bryce, you need to move to safer ground *now*."

She did no such thing. "Tell Fury I'm sorry I lied. That I would have told her the truth eventually." Across the room, the assassin had tears running down her face. "Tell Juniper . . ." Bryce's voice broke. "Tell her thank you—for that night on the roof." She swallowed a sob. "Tell her that I know now why she stopped me from jumping. It was so I could get here—to help today."

Hunt's heart cracked entirely. He hadn't known, hadn't guessed that things had ever been that bad for her—

From the pure devastation on Ruhn's face, her brother hadn't known, either.

"Tell Ruhn I forgive him," Bryce said, shaking again. Tears streamed down the prince's face.

"I forgave him a long time ago," Bryce said. "I just didn't know how to tell him. Tell him I'm sorry I hid the truth, and that I only did it because I love him and didn't want to take anything away from him. He'll always be the better one of us."

The agony on Ruhn's face turned to confusion.

But Hunt couldn't bear it. He couldn't take another word of this. "Bryce, please—"

"Hunt." The entire world went quiet. "I was waiting for you."

"Bryce, sweetheart, just get back to your apartment and give me an hour and—"

"No," she whispered, closing her eyes. She put her hand on her chest. Over her heart. "I was waiting for you—in here."

Hunt couldn't stop his own tears then. "I was waiting for you, too."

She smiled, even as she sobbed again.

"Please," Hunt begged. "Please, Bryce. You have to go *now*. Before more come through."

She opened her eyes and got to her feet as true night fell. Faced the Gate halfway down the block. "I forgive you—for the shit with the synth. For all of it. None of it matters. Not anymore." She ended the call and leaned Danika's sword against the wall of the shelter alcove. Placed her phone carefully on the ground next to it.

Hunt shot from his seat. "*BRYCE—*"

She ran for the Gate.

87

No," Ruhn was saying, over and over. "No, *no*—"

But Hunt heard nothing. Felt nothing. It had all crumbled inside him the moment she'd hung up.

Bryce leapt the fence around the Gate and halted before its towering archway. Before the terrible black void within it.

A faint white radiance began to glow around her.

"What is that?" Fury whispered.

It flickered, growing brighter in the night.

Enough to illuminate her slender hands cupping a sparkling, pulsing light before her chest.

The light was coming *from* her chest—had been pulled from inside it. Like it had dwelled inside her all along. Bryce's eyes were closed, her face serene.

Her hair drifted above her head. Bits of debris floated up around her, too. As if gravity had ceased to exist.

The light she held was so stark it cast the rest of the world into grays and blacks. Slowly, her eyes opened, amber blazing like the first pure rays of dawn. A soft, secret smile graced her mouth.

Her eyes lifted to the Gate looming above her. The light between her hands grew stronger.

Ruhn fell to his knees.

"I am Bryce Quinlan," she said to the Gate, to the void, to all of

Hel behind it. Her voice was serene—wise and laughing. "Heir to the Starborn Fae."

The ground slid out from under Hunt as the light between her hands, the star she'd drawn from her shattered heart, flared as bright as the sun.

Danika knelt on the asphalt, hands interlocked behind her blood-soaked hair. The two gunshot wounds to her leg had stopped leaking blood, but Bryce knew the bullets remained lodged in her upper thigh. The pain from kneeling had to be unbearable.

"You stupid cunt," the asp shifter spat at her, opening the chamber of his handgun with brutal precision. Bullets were on the way—as soon as his associate found them, that gun would be loaded.

The agony in Bryce's injured arm was secondary. All of it was secondary to that gun.

The motorcycle smoldered thirty feet away, the rifle thrown even farther into the arid scrub. Down the road, the semitruck idled, its cargo hold filled with all those petrified animals on their way to gods knew where.

They had failed. Their wild rescue attempt had failed.

Danika's caramel eyes met the asp shifter's. The leader of this horrific smuggling ring. The male responsible for this moment, when the shootout that had taken place at a hundred miles an hour had turned on them. Danika had been steering the motorcycle, an arm looped through Bryce's leg to hold her steady as she'd aimed her rifle. Taken out the asps' two sedans full of equally hateful males intent on hurting and selling those animals. They'd been nearing the racing semi when the male before them had managed a shot to the motorcycle's tires.

The motorcycle had flipped, and Danika had reacted with a wolf's speed. She had wrapped her body around Bryce. And taken the brunt of the impact.

Her shredded skin, the fractured pelvis—all thanks to that.

"Bryce," Danika whispered, tears running down her face now as the reality of this colossal fuckup set in. "Bryce, I love you. And I'm sorry."

Bryce shook her head. "I don't regret it." The truth.

And then the asp shifter's associate arrived, bullets in hand. Their clink as they loaded into the gun echoed through Bryce's bones.

Danika sobbed. "I love you, Bryce."

The words rippled between them. Cleaved Bryce's heart wide open.

"I love you," Danika said again.

Danika had never said those words to her. Not once in four years of college. Not once to anyone, Bryce knew. Not even Sabine.

Especially not Sabine.

Bryce watched the tears roll down Danika's proud, fierce face. A lock clicked open in Bryce's heart. Her soul.

"Close your eyes, Danika," she said softly. Danika just stared at her.

Only for this. Only for Danika would she do this, risk this.

The gravel around Bryce began to shiver. Began to float upward. Danika's eyes widened. Bryce's hair drifted as if underwater. In deep space.

The asp shifter finished loading the bullets and pointed the gun at Danika's face. His colleague smirked from a step behind him.

Bryce held Danika's stare. Did not look away as she said again, "Danika, close your eyes." Trembling, Danika obeyed. Squeezed them shut.

The asp shifter clicked off the gun's safety, not even glancing at Bryce and the debris that floated toward the sky. "Yeah, you'd better close your eyes, you—"

Bryce exploded. White, blinding light ruptured from her, unleashed from that secret place in her heart.

Right into the eyes of the asp shifter. He screamed, clawing at his face. Blazing bright as the sun, Bryce moved.

Pain forgotten, she had his arm in her hands in a heartbeat. Twisted it so he dropped the gun into her waiting palm. Another movement and he was sprawled on the asphalt.

Where she fired that bullet meant for Danika into his heart.

His accomplice was screaming, on his knees and clawing at his eyes. Bryce fired again.

He stopped screaming.

But Bryce did not stop burning. Not as she raced for the semi's cab—for the final asp now trying to start its engine. Danika trembled on the ground, hands over her head, eyes squeezed shut against the brightness.

The asp shifter gave up on the engine and fled the cab, sprinting down the road. Bryce took aim, just as Randall had taught her, and waited for the shot to come to her.

Another crack of the gun. The male dropped.

Bryce blazed for a long moment, the world bleached into blinding white.

Slowly, carefully, she spooled the light back into herself. Smothered it, the secret she and her parents had kept for so long. From her sire, from the Asteri, from Midgard.

From Ruhn.

The pure light of a star—from another world. From long, long ago. The gift of the ancient Fae, reborn again. Light, but nothing more than that. Not an Asteri, who possessed brute power of the stars. Just light.

It meant nothing to her. But the Starborn gifts, the title—they had always meant something to Ruhn. And that first time she'd met him, she'd intended to share her secret with him. He'd been kind, joyful at finding a new sister. She'd instantly known she could trust him with this secret, hidden thing.

But then she'd seen their father's cruelty. Seen how that Starborn gift gave her brother just the slightest edge against that fucking monster. Seen the pride her brother denied but undoubtedly felt at being Starborn, blessed and chosen by Urd.

She couldn't bring herself to tell Ruhn the truth. Even after things fell apart, she hid it. Would never tell anyone—anyone at all. Except Danika.

Blue skies and olive trees filtered back in, color returning to the world as Bryce hid the last of her starlight inside her chest. Danika still trembled on the asphalt.

"Danika," Bryce said.

Danika lowered her hands from her face. Opened her eyes. Bryce waited for the terror her mother had warned about, should someone learn what she bore. The strange, terrible light that had come from another world.

But there was only wonder on Danika's face.

Wonder—and love.

Bryce stood before the Gate, holding the star she'd kept hidden within her heart, and let the light build. Let it flow out of her chest, untethered and pure.

Even with the void mere feet away, Hel just a step beyond it, a strange sense of calm wended through her. She'd kept this light a secret for so long, had lived in such utter terror of anyone finding out, that despite everything, relief filled her.

There had been so many times these weeks when she was sure Ruhn would realize it at last. Her blatant disinterest in learning about anything related to the first Starborn, Prince Pelias and Queen Theia, had bordered on suspicious, she'd feared. And when he'd laid the Starsword on the table in the gallery library and it had hummed, shimmering, she'd had to physically pull back to avoid the instinct to touch it, to answer its silent, lovely song.

Her sword—it was her sword, and Ruhn's. And with that light in her veins, with the star that slumbered inside her heart, the Starsword had recognized her not as a royal, worthy Fae, but as *kin*. Kin to those who had forged it so long ago.

Like called to like. Even the kristallos's venom in her leg had not been able to stifle the essence of what she was. It had blocked her access to the light, but not what lay stamped in her blood. The moment the venom had come out of her leg, as Hunt's lips had met hers that first time, she'd felt it awaken again. Freed.

And now here she was, the starlight building within her hands.

It was a useless gift, she'd decided as a child. It couldn't do much at all beyond blinding people, as she'd done to her father's men when they came after her and her mother and Randall, as had happened to the Oracle when the seer peered into her future and beheld only her blazing light, as she'd done to those asp-hole smugglers.

Only her father's unfaltering Fae arrogance and snobbery had kept him from realizing it after her Oracle visit. The male was incapable of imagining anyone but pure Fae being blessed by fate.

Blessed—as if this gift made her something special. It didn't. It was an old power and nothing more. She had no interest in the throne or crown or palace that could come with it. None.

But Ruhn . . . He might have claimed otherwise, but the first time he'd told her about his Ordeal, when he'd won the sword from its ancient resting place in Avallen, she'd seen how his face had glowed with pride that he'd been able to draw the sword from its sheath.

So she'd let him have it, the title and the sword. Had tried to open Ruhn's eyes to their father's true nature as often as she could, even if it made her father resent her further.

She would have kept this burning, shining secret inside her until her dying day. But she'd realized what she had to do for her city. This world.

The dregs of the light flowed out of her chest, all of it now cupped between her palms.

She'd never done it before—wholly removed the star itself. She'd only glowed and blinded, never summoned its burning core from inside her. Her knees wobbled, and she gritted her teeth against the strain of holding the light in place.

At least she'd spoken to Hunt one last time. She hadn't expected him to be able to pick up. Had thought the phone would go right to audiomail where she could say everything she wanted. The words she still hadn't said aloud to him.

She didn't let herself think of it as she took the final step to the Gate's quartz archway.

She was Starborn, and the Horn lay within her, repaired and now filled with her light.

This had to work.

The quartz of the Gate was a conduit. A prism. Able to take light and power and refract them. She closed her eyes, remembering the rainbows this Gate had been adorned with on the last day of Danika's life, when they'd come here together. Made their wishes.

This had to work. A final wish.

"*Close*," Bryce whispered, shaking.

And she thrust her starlight into the Gate's clear stone.

88

Hunt had no words in his head, his heart, as Bryce shoved her burning starlight into the Gate.

White light blasted from the Gate's clear stone.

It filled the square, shooting outward for blocks. Demons caught in its path screamed as they were blinded, then fled. Like they remembered whom it had once belonged to. How the Starborn Prince had battled their hordes with it.

The Starborn line had bred true—twice.

Ruhn's face drained of color as he remained kneeling and beheld his sister, the blazing Gate. What she'd declared to the world. What she'd revealed herself to be.

His rival. A threat to all he stood to inherit.

Hunt knew what the Fae did to settle disputes to the throne.

Bryce possessed the light of a star, such as hadn't been witnessed since the First Wars. Jesiba looked like she'd seen a ghost. Fury gaped at the screen. When the flare dimmed, Hunt's breath caught in his throat.

The void within the Heart Gate was gone. She'd channeled her light through the Horn somehow—and sealed the portal.

In the stunned silence of the conference room, they watched Bryce pant, leaning against one side of the Gate before sliding to the slate tiles. The crystal archway still shone. A temporary haven that would make any demons think twice before approaching, fearful of a Starborn descendant.

But the rest of the Gates in the city remained open.

A phone rang—an outgoing call, linked to the room's speakers. Hunt scanned the room for the culprit and found the Autumn King with his phone in his hands. But the male was apparently too lost in the rage crinkling his face to care that the call was audible to everyone. Declan Emmet showed no sign of even trying to make the call private as Ember Quinlan picked up the phone and said, "Who is—"

"You've known she was Starborn Fae all these years and *lied* to me about it," the king bit out.

Ember didn't miss a beat. "I've been waiting for this call for more than twenty years."

"You *bitch*—"

A low, agonized laugh. "Who do you think ended your goons all those years ago? Not me and Randall. They had her in their grasp—by the neck. And they had *us* at gunpoint." Another laugh. "She realized what they were going to do to me. To Randall. And she fucking *blinded* them."

What blinds an Oracle?

Light. Light the way the Starborn had possessed it.

Bryce still sat against the archway, breathing hard. Like summoning that star, wielding the Horn, had taken everything out of her.

Ruhn murmured, more to himself than anyone, "Those books claimed there were multiple Starborn in the First Wars. I told her, and she . . ." He blinked slowly. "She already knew."

"She lied because she loves you," Hunt ground out. "So you could keep your title."

Because compared to the Starborn powers he'd seen from Ruhn . . . Bryce's were the real deal. Ruhn's ashen face contorted with pain.

"Who knew?" the Autumn King demanded of Ember. "Those fucking priestesses?"

"No. Only me and Randall," Ember said. "And Danika. She and

Bryce got into some serious trouble in college and it came out then. She blinded the males that time, too."

Hunt remembered the photo on the guest room dresser—taken in the aftermath of that. Their closeness and exhaustion the result not just of a battle fought and won but of a deadly secret revealed at last.

"Her tests showed no power," the Autumn King spat.

"Yes," Ember said quietly. "They were correct."

"*Explain.*"

"It is a gift of starlight. Light, and nothing more. It never meant anything to us, but to your people . . ." Ember paused. "When Bryce was thirteen, she agreed to visit you. To meet you—to see if you could be trusted to know what she possessed and not be threatened by it."

To see if he could handle that such a gift had gone to a half-human bastard and not Ruhn.

Hunt saw no fear on the prince's face, though. No envy or doubt. Only sorrow.

"But then she met your son. And she told me that when she saw his pride in his Chosen One status, she realized she couldn't take it away from him. Not when she also saw that was the only value *you* placed in him. Even if it meant she would be denied everything she was due, even if revealing herself would have meant she could lord it over you, she wouldn't do that to Ruhn. Because she loved him that much more than she hated you."

Ruhn's face crumpled.

Ember spat at the Autumn King, "*And then you left her on the curb like garbage.*" She let out another broken laugh. "I hope she finally returns the favor, you fucking asshole." She hung up.

The Autumn King hurled a pitcher of water before him across the room, so hard it shattered against the wall.

Hunt's blood thrummed through him as a conversation from weeks ago flitted back to him: how he'd spoken of having gifts he didn't really want. Bryce had agreed, to his surprise, and then seemed to catch herself before joking about attracting assholes. Deflecting, hiding the truth.

A soft female hand landed atop Hunt's. Queen Hypaxia. Her dark brown eyes glowed when he looked over in surprise. Her power was a song of warmth through him. It was a hammer to every wall and obstacle placed on him. And he felt that power focus on the halo's spell upon his brow.

She'd asked him weeks ago what he'd do if she removed it. Whom he'd kill.

His first target was in this room with them. His eyes darted toward Sandriel, and Hypaxia's chin dipped, as if in confirmation.

Still Bryce sat against the Gate. As if trying to rally herself. As if wondering how she could possibly do this six more times.

Demons in adjacent streets beheld the starlight still glowing from the Old Square Gate and stayed back. Yes, they remembered the Starborn. Or knew the myths.

Aidas had known. Had watched her all these years, waiting for her to reveal herself.

Hypaxia's power flowed silently and unnoticed into Hunt.

Sandriel slid her phone into her pocket. As if she'd been using it under the table.

Ruhn saw it, too. The Crown Prince of the Fae asked with savage quiet, "What did you do?"

Sandriel smiled. "I took care of a problem."

Hunt's power growled within him. She'd have told the Asteri all she'd seen. Not only what glowed in Bryce's veins—but about the Horn, too.

They were likely already moving on the information. Quickly. Before anyone else could ponder Bryce's gifts. What it might mean to the people of the world if they knew a half-human female, heir to the Starborn line, now bore the Horn in her very body. Able to be used only by her—

The truth clicked into place.

It was why Danika had inked it on Bryce. *Only* the Starborn line could use the Horn.

Micah had believed the synth and Bryce's bloodline would be enough to let him use the Horn, overriding the need for the true Starborn power. The Horn had indeed been healed—but it only worked because Bryce was heir to the Starborn line. Object and wielder had become one.

If Bryce willed it, the Horn could open a portal to any world, any realm. Just as Micah had wanted to do. But that kind of power—belonging to a half-human, no less—could endanger the sovereignty of the Asteri. And the Asteri would take out any threat to their authority.

A roar began building in Hunt's bones.

Ruhn snarled, "They *can't* kill her. She's the only one who can shut those fucking Gates."

Sandriel leaned back in her chair. "She hasn't made the Drop yet, Prince. So they most certainly can." She added, "And it looks like she's wholly drained anyway. I doubt she'll be able to close a second Gate, let alone six more."

Hunt's fingers curled.

Hypaxia met his stare again and smiled slightly. An invitation and challenge. Her magic shimmered through him, over his forehead.

Sandriel had informed the Asteri—so they'd kill Bryce.

His Bryce. Hunt's attention narrowed on the back of Sandriel's neck.

And he rose to his feet as Hypaxia's magic dissolved the halo from his brow.

89

The conference room shook.

Ruhn had kept Sandriel distracted, kept her talking while Queen Hypaxia had freed Hunt from the halo's grip. He'd sensed the ripple of her power down the table, then seen Athalar's halo begin to glow, and had understood what the witch, her hand on Hunt's, was doing.

There was nothing but cold death in Hunt's eyes as the halo tattoo flaked away from his brow. The true face of the Umbra Mortis.

Sandriel whirled, realizing too late who now stood at her back. No mark across his brow. Something like pure terror crossed the Archangel's face as Hunt bared his teeth.

Lightning gathered around his hands. The walls cracked. Debris rained from the ceiling.

Sandriel was too slow.

Ruhn knew Sandriel had signed her own death warrant when she didn't bring her triarii back with her. And stamped the official seal on it the moment she'd revealed that she'd put Bryce in the Asteri's line of fire.

Even her Archangel's might couldn't protect her from Athalar. From what he felt for Bryce.

Athalar's lightning skittered over the floors. Sandriel barely had time to lift her arms and summon a gale-force wind before Hunt was upon her.

Lightning erupted, the entire room cracking with it.

Ruhn threw himself under a table, grabbing Hypaxia with him. Slabs of stone slammed onto the surface above them. Flynn swore up a storm beside him, and Declan crouched low, curled around a laptop. A cloud of debris filled the space, choking them. Ether coated Ruhn's tongue.

Lightning flared, licking and crackling through the room.

Then time shifted and slowed, sliding by, by, by—

"*Fuck,*" Flynn was saying between pants, each word an eternity and a flash, the world tipping over again, slowing and dragging. "*Fuck.*"

Then the lightning stopped. The cloud of debris pulsed and hummed.

Time began its normal pace, and Ruhn crawled out from under the table. He knew what he'd find within the whirling, electrified cloud everyone gaped at. Fury Axtar had a gun pointed at where the Archangel and Hunt had stood, debris whitening her dark hair.

Hypaxia helped Ruhn to his feet. Her eyes were wide as they scanned the cloud. The witch-queen had undoubtedly known that Sandriel would kill her for freeing Hunt. She'd taken a gamble that the Umbra Mortis would be the one to walk away.

The cloud of debris cleared, lightning fading into the dust-choked air. Her gamble had paid off. Blood splattered Hunt's face as his feathers fluttered on a phantom wind.

And from his hand, gripped by the hair, dangled Sandriel's severed head.

Her mouth was still open in a scream, smoke rippling from her lips, the skin of her neck so damaged Ruhn knew Hunt had torn it off with his bare hands.

Hunt slowly lifted the head before him, as if he were one of the ancient heroes of the Rhagan Sea surveying a slain creature. A monster.

He let the Archangel's head drop. It thumped and lolled to

the side, smoke still trickling from the mouth, the nostrils. He'd flayed her with his lightning from the inside out.

The angels in the room all knelt on one knee. Bowed. Even a wide-eyed Isaiah Tiberian. No one on the planet had that sort of power. No one had seen it fully unleashed in centuries.

Two Governors dead in one day. Slain by his sister and his sister's . . . whatever Hunt was. From the awe and fear on his father's face, Ruhn knew the Autumn King was wondering about it. Wondering if Hunt would kill him next, for how he'd treated Bryce.

Bryce, his Starborn sister.

Ruhn didn't know what to think about it. That she'd thought he valued the Chosen One bullshit more than her. And when that fight had happened, had she let things rupture between them to keep him from ever learning what she was? She'd walked away from the privilege and honor and glory—for him.

And all those warnings she'd given him about the Autumn King, about their father killing the last Starborn . . . She'd lived with that fear, too.

Hunt threw the Autumn King a feral grin.

Ruhn felt a sick amount of satisfaction as his father went pale.

But then Hunt looked to Fury, who was pulling debris from her dark hair, and growled, "Fuck the Asteri. Get your gods-damned helicopter over here."

Every decision, every order flowed from a long-quiet place within Hunt.

He sizzled with power, the lightning in his veins roaring to crack free into the world, to burn and sunder. He suppressed it, promised it he'd allow it to flow unchecked as soon as they reached the city—but they had to reach the city first.

Fury shook slightly—as if even she had forgotten what he could do. What he'd done to Sandriel with primal satisfaction, sinking into a place of such rage that there had only been his lightning and his enemy and the threat she posed to Bryce. But Fury said, "The helicopter is landing on the roof now."

Hunt nodded and ordered the remaining angels without looking at them, "We move out."

Not one of them objected to his command. He hadn't given a shit that they'd bowed—whatever the fuck that meant. He'd only cared that they flew to Lunathion as fast as they could.

Fury was already at the exit, phone at her ear. Hunt strode after her, through the room full of rustling wings and stomping feet, but looked back over his shoulder. "Danaan, Ketos—you in?" He needed them.

Ruhn shot to his feet without question; Tharion waited until he got the nod from the River Queen's daughter before rising. Amelie Ravenscroft stepped forward, ignoring Sabine's glare, and said, "I'm going with you, too." Hunt nodded again.

Flynn was already moving, not needing to voice that he'd join his prince—to save his princess. Declan pointed to the screens. "I'll be your eyes in the field."

"Good," Hunt said, aiming for the door.

The Autumn King and the Prime of the wolves, the only City Heads present, remained in the pit, along with Sabine. Jesiba and Hypaxia would have to keep them honest. Neither of the females so much as acknowledged the other, but no animosity sparked between them, either. Hunt didn't care.

He silently scaled the stairs toward the roof, his companions behind him. They were thirty minutes by helicopter from the city. So much could go wrong before they reached it. And when they got there . . . it would be pure slaughter.

The helicopter's blades whipped Fury's black hair as she crossed the landing pad. Flynn trailed close behind, sizing up their ride, and let out an impressed whistle.

It wasn't a luxury transport. It was a military-grade helicopter. Complete with two gunners on either door and a cache of assorted guns and weapons in duffels strapped to the floor.

Fury Axtar had not come to this meeting expecting it to be

friendly. She grabbed the headset from the departing pilot before slinging her slender body into the cockpit.

"I'm with you," Hunt said, gesturing to the helicopter as the angels took off around them. "My wings can't handle the flight yet."

Ruhn leapt into the helicopter behind Flynn and Amelie, Tharion claiming the left gunner. Hunt remained on the roof, shouting orders to the departing angels. *Establish a perimeter around the city. Scout team: investigate the portal. Send survivors to triage at least five miles beyond city walls.* He didn't let himself think about how easy it was to slip back into a commander's role.

Then Hunt was in the helicopter, taking up the right gunner. Fury flicked switch after switch on the control panel. Hunt asked her, his voice hoarse, "Did you know about what happened on the roof with Bryce and Juniper?"

It had fucking gutted him to hear Bryce allude to it—that she'd considered jumping. To hear that he'd come so close to losing her before he even knew her. Ruhn turned toward them, his agonized face confirming that he felt the same.

Fury didn't stop her prep. "Bryce was a ghost for a long while, Hunt. She pretended she wasn't, but she was." The helicopter finally pulled into the air. "You brought her back to life."

90

Bryce's entire body trembled as she leaned against the glowing quartz of the Gate, exhaustion rooting her to the spot.

It had worked. Somehow, it had worked.

She didn't let herself marvel over it—or dread its implications, when her father and the Asteri found out. Not when she had no idea how long her starlight would remain glowing in the Gate. But maybe it would hold long enough for help to come. Maybe this had made a difference.

Maybe she had made a difference.

Each breath burned in her chest. Not much longer now. For help to come, for her end, she didn't know.

But it would be soon. Whichever way it ended, Bryce knew it would be soon.

"Declan says Bryce is still at the Old Square Gate," Fury reported over a shoulder.

Hunt just kept his eyes on the star-filled horizon. The city was a dark shadow, interrupted only by a faint glowing in its heart. The Old Square Gate. Bryce.

"And Hypaxia says Bryce can barely move," Fury added, a note of surprise in her flat voice. "It looks like she's drained. She's not going to be able to get to the next Gate without help."

"But the light from the Gate is keeping her safe?" Ruhn called over the wind.

"Until the demons stop fearing the Starborn light." Fury switched the call to the helicopter's speakers. "Emmet, radar's picking up three war machines from the west. Any read on them?"

Thank fuck. Someone else was coming to help after all. If they could bring Bryce to each Gate and she could just muster enough starlight to flow through the Horn, they'd stop the carnage.

Declan took a moment to reply, his voice crackling through the speakers above Hunt. "They're registering as imperial tanks." His pause had Hunt's grip tightening on the gunner.

Hypaxia clarified, "It's the Asterian Guard. With brimstone missile launchers." Her voice sharpened as she said to the Autumn King and Prime of the wolves, "*Get your forces out of the city.*"

The blood in Hunt's veins went cold.

The Asteri had sent someone to deal with the demons. And with Bryce.

They were going to blast the city into dust.

The brimstone missiles weren't ordinary bombs of chemicals and metal. They were pure magic, made by the Asterian Guard: a combination of their angelic powers of wind and rain and fire into one hyperconcentrated entity, bound with firstlight and fired through machinery. Where they struck, destruction bloomed.

To make them even deadlier, they were laced with spells to slow healing. Even for Vanir. The only comfort for any on their receiving end was that the missiles took a while to make, offering reprieve between rounds. A small, fool's comfort.

Fury flicked buttons on the switchboard. "Copy Asterian Units One, Two, and Three, this is Fury Axtar speaking. Pull back." No answer. "I repeat, *pull back*. Abort mission."

Nothing. Declan said, "They're the Asterian Guard. They won't answer to you."

The Autumn King's voice crackled through the speakers. "No one at Imperial Command is answering our calls."

Fury angled the helicopter, sweeping southward. Hunt saw them then. The black tanks breaking over the horizon, each as large as a small house. The imperial insignia painted on their flanks. All three gunning for Crescent City.

They halted just outside its border. The metal launchers atop them angled into position.

The brimstone missiles shot from the launchers and arced over the walls, blazing with golden light. As the first of them hit, he prayed that Bryce had left the Gate to find shelter.

Bryce choked on dust and debris, chest heaving. She tried to move—and failed. Her spine—

No, that was her leg, pinned in a tangle of concrete and iron. She'd heard the boom a minute ago, recognized the golden, arcing plume as brimstone thanks to news coverage of the Pangeran wars, and had sprinted halfway across the square, aiming for the open door of the brick music hall there, hoping it had a basement, when it hit.

Her ears were roaring, buzzing. Shrieking.

The Gate still stood, still shielded her with its light. Her light, technically.

The nearest brimstone missile had hit a neighborhood away, it seemed. It had been enough to trash the square, to reduce some buildings to rubble, but not enough to decimate it.

Move. She had to move. The other Gates still lay open. She had to find some way to get there; shut them, too.

She tugged at her leg. To her surprise, the minor wounds were already healing—far faster than she'd ever experienced. Maybe the Horn in her back helped speed it along.

She reached forward to haul the concrete slab off her. It didn't budge.

She panted through her teeth, trying again. They'd unleashed brimstone upon the city. The Asterian Guard had blindly fired it over the walls to either destroy the Gates or kill the demons. But they'd fired on their own people, not caring who they hit—

Bryce took deep, steadying breaths. It did nothing to settle her.

She tried again, fingernails cracking on the concrete. But short of cutting off her foot, she wasn't getting free.

The Asterian Guard was reloading their missile launchers atop the tanks. Hyperconcentrated magic flared around them, as if the brimstone was straining to be free of its firstlight constraints. Eager to unleash angelic ruin upon the helpless city.

"They're going to fire again," Ruhn whispered.

"The brimstone landed mostly in Moonwood," Declan told them. "Bryce is alive but in trouble. She's trapped under a piece of concrete. Struggling like Hel to free herself, though."

Fury screamed into the microphone, "*ABORT MISSION*."

No one answered. The launchers cocked skyward again, pivoting to new targets.

As if they knew Bryce still lived. They'd keep bombarding the city until she was dead, killing anything in their path. Perhaps hoping that if they took out the Gates, too, the voids would vanish.

An icy, brutal calm settled over Hunt.

He said to Fury, "Go high. High as the helicopter can handle."

She saw what he intended. He couldn't fly, not on weak wings. But he didn't need to.

"Grab something," Fury said, and angled the helicopter sharply. It went up, up, up, all of them gritting their teeth against the weight trying to shove them earthward.

Hunt braced himself, settling into that place that had seen him through battles and years in dungeons and Sandriel's arena.

"Get ready, Athalar," Fury called. The war machines halted, launchers primed.

The helicopter flew over Lunathion's walls. Hunt unstrapped himself from the gunner. The Bone Quarter was a misty swirl below as they crossed the Istros.

Gratitude shone in Danaan's eyes. Understanding what only Hunt could do.

The Old Square and glowing Gate at its heart became visible. The only signal he needed. There was no hesitation in Hunt. No fear.

Hunt leapt out of the helicopter, his wings tucked in tight. A one-way ticket. His last flight.

Far below, his sharp eyes could just make out Bryce as she curled herself into a ball, as if it'd save her from the death soon to blast her apart.

The brimstone missiles launched one after another after another, the closest arcing toward the Old Square, shimmering with lethal golden power. Even as Hunt plunged to the earth, he knew its angle was off—it'd strike probably ten blocks away. But it was still too close. Still left her in the blast zone, where all that compressed angelic power would splatter her apart.

The brimstone hit, the entire city bouncing beneath its unholy impact. Block after block ruptured in a tidal wave of death.

Wings splaying, lightning erupting, Hunt threw himself over Bryce as the world shattered.

91

She should be dead.

But those were her fingers, curling on the rubble. That was her breath, sawing in and out.

The brimstone had decimated the square, the city was now in smoldering ruins, yet the Gate still stood. Her light had gone out, though, the quartz again an icy white. Fires sputtered around her, lighting the damage in flickering relief.

Clumps of ashes rained down, mixing with the embers.

Bryce's ears buzzed faintly, yet not as badly as they had after the first blast.

It wasn't possible. She'd spied the shimmering golden brimstone missile arcing past, knew it'd strike a few blocks away, and that death would soon find her. The Gate must have shielded her, somehow.

Bryce eased into a kneeling position with a groan. The bombardment, at least, had ceased. Only a few buildings stood. The skeletons of cars still burned around her. The acrid smoke rose in a column that blotted out the first of the evening stars.

And—and in the shadows, those were stirring demons. Bile burned her throat. She had to get up. Had to move while they were down.

Her legs wouldn't cooperate. She wiggled her toes inside her sneakers, just to make sure they could work, but . . . she couldn't rise off the ground. Her body refused to obey.

A clump of ash landed on the torn knee of her leggings.

Her hands began to shake. It wasn't a piece of ash.

It was a gray feather.

Bryce twisted to look behind herself. Her head emptied out. A scream broke from her, rising from so deep that she wondered if it was the sound of the world shredding apart.

Hunt lay sprawled on the ground, his back a bloodied, burned mess, and his legs . . .

There was nothing left of them but ribbons. Nothing left of his right arm but splattered blood on pavement. And through his back, where his wings had been—

That was a bloody, gaping hole.

She moved on instinct, scrambling over concrete and metal and blood.

He'd shielded her against the brimstone. Had somehow escaped Sandriel and come here. To save her.

"*Pleasepleasepleaseplease*"

She turned him over, searching for any hint of life, of breathing—

His mouth moved. Just slightly.

Bryce sobbed, pulling his head into her lap. "Help!" she called. No answer beyond an unearthly baying in the fire-licked darkness. "Help!" she yelled again, but her voice was so hoarse it barely carried across the square. Randall had told her about the terrible power of the Asterian Guard's brimstone missiles. How the spells woven into the condensed angelic magic slowed healing in Vanir long enough for them to bleed out. To die.

Blood coated so much of Hunt's face that she could barely see the skin beneath. Only the faint flutter of his throat told her he still lived.

And the wounds that should have been healing . . . they leaked and gushed blood. Arteries had been severed. Vital arteries—

"*HELP!*" she screamed.

But no one answered.

The brimstone's blasts had downed the helicopter.

Only Fury's skill kept them alive, though they'd still crashed, flipping twice, before landing somewhere in Moonwood.

Tharion bled from his head, Fury had a gash in her leg, Flynn and Amelie both bore broken bones, and Ruhn . . . He didn't bother to think about his own wounds. Not as the smoke-filled, burning night became laced with approaching snarls. But the brimstone had halted—at least they had that. He prayed the Asterian Guard would need a good while before they could muster the power to form more of them.

Ruhn forced himself into movement by sheer will.

Two of the duffels of weapons had come free of their bindings and been lost in the crash. Flynn and Fury began divvying out the remaining guns and knives, working quickly while Ruhn assessed the state of the one intact machine gun he'd ripped from the chopper's floor.

Hypaxia's voice cracked over the miraculously undamaged radio, "We have eyes on the Old Square Gate," she said. Ruhn paused, waiting for the news. Not daring to hope.

The last Ruhn had seen of Athalar was the angel plunging toward Bryce while the Asterian Guard fired those glowing golden missiles over the walls like some sick fireworks show. Then the citywide explosions had sundered the world.

"Athalar is down," Declan announced gravely. "Bryce lives." Ruhn offered up a silent prayer of thanks to Cthona for her mercy. Another pause. "Correction, Athalar made it, but barely. His injuries are . . . Shit." His swallow was audible. "I don't think there's any chance of survival."

Tharion cocked a rifle to his shoulder, peering through the scope into the darkness. "We've got about a dozen demons sizing us up from that brick building over there."

"Six more over here," Fury said, also using the scope on her rifle. Amelie Ravenscroft limped badly as she shifted into wolf form with a flash of light and bared her teeth at the darkness.

If they didn't shut the portals in the other Gates, only two options existed: retreat or death.

"They're getting curious," Flynn murmured without taking his eye from the scope of his gun. "Do we have a plan?"

"The river's at our backs," Tharion said. "If we're lucky, my people might come to our aid." The Blue Court lay far enough below the surface to have avoided the brimstone's wrath. They could rally.

But Bryce and Hunt remained in the Old Square. Ruhn said, "We're thirty blocks from the Heart Gate. We go down the riverwalk, then cut inland at Main." He added, "That's where I'm headed, at least." They all nodded, grim-faced.

Tell Ruhn I forgive him—for all of it.

The words echoed through Ruhn's blood. They had to keep going, even if the demons picked them off one by one. He just hoped they'd reach his sister in time to find something to save.

Bryce knelt over Hunt, his life spilling out all around her. And in the smoldering, acrid quiet, she began whispering.

"I believe it happened for a reason. I believe it all happened for a reason." She stroked his bloody hair, her voice shaking. "I believe it wasn't for nothing."

She looked toward the Gate. Gently set Hunt down amid the rubble. She whispered again, rising to her feet, "I believe it happened for a reason. I believe it all happened for a reason. I believe it wasn't for nothing."

She walked from Hunt's body as he bled behind her. Wended her way through the debris and rubble. The fence around the Gate had been warped, peeled away. But the quartz archway still stood, its bronze plaque and the dial pad's gems intact as she halted before them.

Bryce whispered again, "I believe it wasn't for nothing."

She laid her palm on the dial pad's bronze disk.

The metal was warm against Bryce's fingers, as it had been

when she'd touched it that final day with Danika. Its power zinged through her, sucking the fee for the usage: a drop of her magic.

The Gates had been used as communication devices in the past—but the only reason words could pass between them was the power that connected them. They all sat atop linked ley lines. A veritable matrix of energy.

The Gate wasn't just a prism. It was a conduit. And she had the Horn in her very skin. Had proved it could close a portal to Hel.

Bryce whispered into the little intercom in the center of the pad's arc of gems, "Hello?"

No one answered. She said, "If you can hear me, come to the Gate. Any Gate."

Still nothing. She said, "My name is Bryce Quinlan. I'm in the Old Square. And . . . and I think I've figured out how we can stop this. How we can fix this."

Silence. None of the other gems lit up to indicate the presence or voice of another person in another district, touching the disk on their end.

"I know it's bad right now," she tried again. "I know it's so, so bad, and dark, and . . . I know it feels impossible. But if you can make it to another Gate, just . . . please. Please come."

She took a shuddering breath.

"You don't need to do anything," she said. "All you need to do is just put your hand on the disk. That's all I need—just another person on the line." Her hand shook, and she pressed it harder to the metal. "The Gate is a conduit of power—a lightning rod that feeds into every other Gate throughout the city. And I need someone on the other end, linked to me through that vein." She swallowed. "I need someone to Anchor me. So I can make the Drop."

The words whispered out into the world.

Bryce's rasping voice overrode the sounds of the demons rallying again around her. "The firstlight I'll generate by making the Drop will spread from this Gate to the others. It'll light up *everything*, send those demons racing away. It'll heal everything it touches. Every*one* it touches. And I—" She took a deep breath. "I am

Starborn Fae, and I bear Luna's Horn in my body. With the power of the firstlight I generate, I can shut the portals to Hel. I did it here—I can do it everywhere else. But I need a link—and the power from my Drop to do it."

Still no one answered. No life stirred, beyond the beasts in the deepest shadows.

"Please," Bryce begged, her voice breaking.

Silently, she prayed for any one of those six other gems to light up, to show that just one person, in any district, would answer her plea.

But there was only the crackling nothingness.

She was alone. And Hunt was dying.

Bryce waited five seconds. Ten seconds. No one answered. No one came.

Swallowing another sob, she took a shuddering breath and let go of the disk.

Hunt's breaths had grown few and far between. She crawled back to him, hands shaking. But her voice was calm as she again slid his head into her lap. Stroked his blood-soaked face. "It's going to be all right," she said. "Help is coming, Hunt. The medwitches are on their way." She shut her eyes against her tears. "We're going to be all right," she lied. "We're going to go home, where Syrinx is waiting for us. We're going to go home. You and me. Together. We'll have that afterward, like you promised. But only if you hold on, Hunt."

His breathing rattled in his chest. A death rattle. She bent over him, inhaling his scent, the strength in him. And then she said it—the three words that meant more than anything. She whispered them into his ear, sending them with all she had left in her.

The final truth, the one she needed him to hear.

Hunt's breathing spread and thinned. Not much longer.

Bryce couldn't stop her tears as they dropped onto Hunt's cheeks, cleaning away the blood in clear tracks.

Light it up, Danika whispered to her. Into her heart.

"I tried," she whispered back. "Danika, I tried."

Light it up.

Bryce wept. "It didn't work."

Light it up. Urgency sharpened the words. As if . . . As if . . .

Bryce lifted her head. Looked toward the Gate. To the plaque and its gems.

She waited. Counted her breaths. *One. Two. Three.*

The gems remained dark. *Four. Five. Six.*

Nothing at all. Bryce swallowed hard and turned back to Hunt. One last time. He'd go, and then she'd follow, once more brimstone fell or the demons worked up the courage to attack her.

She took another breath. *Seven.*

"Light it up." The words filled the Old Square. Filled every square in the city.

Bryce whipped her head around to look at the Gate as Danika's voice sounded again. "Light it up, Bryce."

The onyx stone of the Bone Quarter glowed like a dark star.

92

Bryce's face crumpled as she lurched to her feet, sprinting to the Gate.

She didn't care how it was possible as Danika said again, "*Light it up.*"

Then Bryce was laughing and sobbing as she screamed, "*LIGHT IT UP, DANIKA! LIGHT IT UP, LIGHT IT UP, LIGHT IT UP*!"

Bryce slammed her palm onto the bronze disk of the Gate.

And soul to soul with the friend whom she had not forgotten, the friend who had not forgotten her, even in death, Bryce made the Drop.

Stunned silence filled the conference room as Bryce plunged into her power.

Declan Emmet didn't look up from the feeds he monitored, his heart thundering.

"It's not possible," the Autumn King said. Declan was inclined to agree.

Sabine Fendyr murmured, "Danika had a small kernel of energy left, the Under-King said. A bit of self that remained."

"Can a dead soul even serve as an Anchor?" Queen Hypaxia asked.

"No," Jesiba replied, with all the finality of the Under-King's emissary. "No, it can't."

Silence rippled through the room as they realized what they were witnessing. An untethered, solo Drop. Utter free fall. Bryce might as well have leapt from a cliff and hoped to land safely.

Declan drew his eyes from the video feed and scanned the graph on one of his three computers—the one charting Bryce's Drop, courtesy of the Eleusian system. "She's approaching her power level." Barely a blip past zero on the scale.

Hypaxia peered over his shoulder to study the graph. "She's not slowing, though."

Declan squinted at the screen. "She's gaining speed." He shook his head. "But—but she's classified as a low-level." Near-negligible, if he felt like being a dick about it.

Hypaxia said quietly, "But the Gate is not."

Sabine demanded, "What do you mean?"

Hypaxia whispered, "I don't think it's a memorial plaque. On the Gate." The witch pointed to the sign mounted on the glowing quartz, the bronze stark against the incandescent stone. "*The power shall always belong to those who give their lives to the city.*"

Bryce dropped further into power. Past the normal, respectable levels.

Queen Hypaxia said, "The plaque is a blessing."

Declan's breathing was uneven as he murmured, "The power of the Gates—the power given over by every soul who has ever touched it . . . every soul who has handed over a drop of their magic."

He tried and failed to calculate just how many people, over how many centuries, had touched the Gates in the city. Had handed over a drop of their power, like a coin tossed in a fountain. Made a wish on that drop of yielded power.

People of every House. Every race. Millions and millions of drops of power fueled this solo Drop.

Bryce passed level after level. The Autumn King's face went pale.

Hypaxia said, "Look at the Gates."

The quartz Gates across the city began to glow. Red, then orange, then gold, then white.

Firstlight erupted from them. Lines of it speared out in every direction.

The lights flowed down the ley lines between the Gates, connecting them along the main avenues. It formed a perfect, six-pointed star.

The lines of light began to spread. Curving around the city walls. Cutting off the demons now aiming for the lands beyond.

Light met light met light met light.

Until the city was ringed with it. Until every street was glowing.

And Bryce was still making the Drop.

It was joy and life and death and pain and song and silence.

Bryce tumbled into power, and power tumbled into her, and she didn't care, didn't care, didn't care, because it was Danika falling with her, Danika laughing with her as their souls twined.

She was here, she was here, she was here—

Bryce plunged into the golden light and song at the heart of the universe.

Danika let out a howl of joy, and Bryce echoed it.

Danika was here. It was enough.

"She's passing Ruhn's level," Declan breathed, not believing it. That his friend's party-girl sister had surpassed the prince himself. Surpassed Ruhn fucking Danaan.

Declan's king was still as death as Bryce smashed past Ruhn's ranking. This could change their very order. A powerful half-human princess with a star's light in her veins . . . Fucking Hel.

Bryce began slowing at last. Nearing the Autumn King's level. Declan swallowed.

The city was awash with her light. Demons fled from it, racing back through the voids, opting to brave the glowing Gates rather than be trapped in Midgard.

Light shot up from the Gates, seven bolts becoming one in the heart of the city—above the Old Square Gate. A highway of power. Of Bryce's will.

The voids between Midgard and Hel began to shrink. As if the light itself was abhorrent. As if that pure, unrestrained firstlight could heal the world.

And it did. Buildings shattered by brimstone slid back into place. Rubble gathered into walls and streets and fountains. Wounded people became whole again.

Bryce slowed further.

Declan ground his teeth. The voids within the Gates became smaller and smaller.

Demons rushed back to Hel through the shrinking doorways. More and more of the city healed as the Horn closed the portals. As *Bryce* sealed the portals, the Horn's power flowing through her, amplified by the firstlight she was generating.

"Holy gods," someone was whispering.

The voids between worlds became slivers. Then nothing at all.

The Gates stood empty. The portals gone.

Bryce stopped at last. Declan studied the precise number of her power, just a decimal point above that of the Autumn King.

Declan let out a soft laugh, wishing Ruhn were here to see the male's shocked expression.

The Autumn King's face tightened and he growled at Declan, "I would not be so smug, boy."

Declan tensed. "Why?"

The Autumn King hissed, "Because that girl may have used the Gates' power to Drop to unforeseen levels, but she will not be able to make the Ascent."

Declan's fingers stilled on the keys of his laptop.

The Autumn King laughed mirthlessly. Not from malice, Declan realized—but something like pain. He'd never known the prick could feel such a thing.

Bryce slumped to the stones beside the Gate. Declan didn't need medical monitors to know her heart had flatlined.

Her mortal body had died.

A clock on the computer showing the Eleusian system began counting down from a six-minute marker. The indicator of how long she had to make the Search and the Ascent, to let her mortal, aging body die, to face what lay within her soul, and race back up to life, into her full power. And emerge an immortal.

If she made the Ascent, the Eleusian system would register it, track it.

The Autumn King said hoarsely, "She made the Drop alone. Danika Fendyr is dead—she is not a true Anchor. Bryce has no way back to life."

93

This was the cradle of all life, this place.

There was a physical ground beneath her, and she had the sense of an entire world above her, full of distant, twinkling lights. But this was the bottom of the sea. The dark trench that cut through the skin of the earth.

It didn't matter. Nothing mattered at all. Not with Danika standing before her. Holding her.

Bryce peeled away far enough to look at her beautiful, angular face. The corn-silk hair. It was the same, right down to the amethyst, sapphire, and rose streaks. She'd somehow forgotten the exact features of Danika's face, but . . . there they were.

Bryce said, "You came."

Danika's smile was soft. "You asked for help."

"Are you . . . are you alive? Over there, I mean."

"No." Danika shook her head. "No, Bryce. This, what you see . . ." She gestured to herself. The familiar jeans and old band T-shirt. "This is just the spark that's left. What was resting over there."

"But it's you. This is *you*."

"Yes." Danika peered at the churning darkness above them, the entire ocean above. "And you don't have much time to make the Ascent, Bryce."

Bryce snorted. "I'm not making the Ascent."

Danika blinked. "What do you mean?"

Bryce stepped back. "I'm not making it." Because this was where her homeless soul would stay, if she failed. Her body would die in the world above, and her soul that she'd traded away to the Under-King would be left to wander this place. With Danika.

Danika crossed her arms. "Why?"

Bryce blinked furiously. "Because it got too hard. Without you. It *is* too hard without you."

"That's bullshit," Danika snarled. "So you'll just give up on everything? Bryce, I am *dead*. I am *gone*. And you'll trade your entire life for this tiny piece of me that's left?" Disappointment shuttered her caramel eyes. "The friend I knew wouldn't have done that."

Bryce's voice broke as she said, "We were supposed to do this together. We were supposed to live out our lives together."

Danika's face softened. "I know, B." She took her hand. "But that's not how it turned out."

Bryce bowed her head, thinking she'd crack apart. "I miss you. Every moment of every day."

"I know," Danika said again, and put a hand over her heart. "And I've felt it. I've seen it."

"Why did you lie—about the Horn?"

"I didn't lie," Danika said simply. "I just didn't tell you."

"You lied about the tattoo," Bryce countered.

"To keep you safe," Danika said. "To keep the Horn safe, yeah, but mostly to keep you safe in case the worst happened to me."

"Well, the worst did happen to you," Bryce said, instantly regretting it when Danika flinched.

But then Danika said, "You traded your place in the Bone Quarter for me."

Bryce began crying. "It was the least I could do."

Tears formed in Danika's eyes. "You didn't think I'd make it?" She threw her a sharp, pained grin. "Asshole."

But Bryce shook with the force of her weeping. "I couldn't . . . I couldn't take that risk."

Danika brushed back a piece of Bryce's hair.

Bryce sniffled and said, "I killed Micah for what he did. To you. To Lehabah." Her heart strained. "Is—is she over in the Bone Quarter?"

"I don't know. And yeah—I saw what happened in the gallery." Danika didn't explain more about the particulars. "We all saw."

That word snagged. *We*.

Bryce's lips trembled. "Is Connor with you?"

"He is. And the rest of the pack. They bought me time with the Reapers. To get to the Gate. They're holding them off, but not for long, Bryce. I can't stay here with you." She shook her head. "Connor would have wanted more for you than this." She stroked the back of Bryce's hand with her thumb. "He wouldn't have wanted you to stop fighting."

Bryce wiped at her face again. "I didn't. Not until now. But now I'm . . . It's all just *fucked*. And I'm so *tired* of it feeling that way. I'm done."

Danika asked softly, "What about the angel?"

Bryce's head snapped up. "What about him?"

Danika gave her a knowing smile. "If you want to ignore the fact that you've got your family who loves you no matter what, fine—but the angel remains."

Bryce withdrew her hand from Danika's. "You're really trying to convince me to make the Ascent for a guy?"

"Is Hunt Athalar really just some guy to you?" Danika's smile turned gentle. "And why is it somehow a mark against your strength to admit that there is someone, who happens to be male, worth returning to? Someone who I know made you feel like things are *far* from fucked."

Bryce crossed her arms. "So what."

"He's healed, Bryce," Danika said. "You healed him with the firstlight."

Bryce's breath shuddered out of her. She'd done all of this for that wild hope.

She swallowed, looking at the ground that was not earth, but the very base of Self, of the world. She whispered, "I'm scared."

Danika grabbed her hand again. "That's the point of it, Bryce.

Of *life*. To live, to love, knowing that it might all vanish tomorrow. It makes everything that much more precious." She took Bryce's face in her hands and pressed their brows together.

Bryce closed her eyes and inhaled Danika's scent, somehow still present even in this form. "I don't think I can make it. Back up."

Danika pulled away, peering at the impossible distance overhead. Then at the road that stretched before them. The runway. Its end was a free fall into eternal darkness. Into nothingness. But she said, "Just try, Bryce. One try. I'll be with you every step of the way. Even if you can't see me. I will *always* be with you."

Bryce didn't look at that too-short runway. The endless ocean above them, separating her from life. She just memorized the lines of Danika's face, as she had not had the chance to do before. "I love you, Danika," she whispered.

Danika's throat bobbed. She cocked her head, the movement purely lupine. As if listening to something. "Bryce, you have to hurry." She grabbed her hand, squeezing. "You have to decide now."

The timer on Bryce's life showed two minutes left.

Her dead body lay sprawled on the stones beside the faintly glowing Gate.

Declan ran a hand over his chest. He didn't dare contact Ruhn. Not yet. Couldn't bear to.

"There's no way to help her?" Hypaxia whispered to the silent room. "No way at all?"

No. Declan had used the past four minutes to run a search of every public and private database in Midgard for a miracle. He'd found nothing.

"Beyond being without an Anchor," the Autumn King said, "she used an artificial power source to bring her to that level. Her body is not biologically equipped to make the Ascent. Even with a true Anchor, she wouldn't be able to gain enough momentum for that first jump upward."

Jesiba gravely nodded her confirmation, but the sorceress said nothing.

Declan's memories of his Drop and Ascent were murky, frightening. He'd gone farther than anticipated, but had at least stayed within his own range. Even with Flynn Anchoring him, he'd been petrified he wouldn't make it back.

Despite registering on the system as a blip of energy beside Bryce, Danika Fendyr was not a tether to life, not a true Anchor. She had no life of her own. Danika was merely the thing that had given Bryce enough courage to attempt the Drop alone.

The Autumn King went on, "I've looked. I've spent centuries looking. Thousands of people throughout the ages have attempted to go past their own intended levels through artificial means. None of them ever made it back to life."

One minute remained, the seconds flying off the countdown clock.

Bryce had still not Ascended. Was still making the Search, facing whatever lay within her. The timer would have halted if she had begun her attempt at the Ascent, marking her entrance into the Between—the liminal place between death and life. But the timer kept going. Winding down.

It didn't matter, though. Bryce would die whether she attempted it or not.

Thirty seconds left. The remaining dignitaries in the room bowed their heads.

Ten seconds. The Autumn King rubbed at his face, then watched the clock count down. The remainder of Bryce's life.

Five. Four. Three. Two.

One. The milliseconds raced toward zero. True death.

The clock stopped at 0.003.

A red line shot across the bottom of the Eleusian system's graph, along the runway toward oblivion.

Declan whispered, "She's running."

"Faster, Bryce!" Danika raced at her heels.

Step after step after step, Bryce barreled down that mental runway. Toward the ever-nearing end of it.

"*Faster!*" Danika roared.

One shot. She had one shot at this.

Bryce ran. Ran and ran and ran, arms pumping, gritting her teeth.

The odds were impossible, the likelihood slim.

But she tried. With Danika beside her, this last time, she could try.

She had made the Drop solo, but she was not alone.

She had never been alone. She never would be.

Not with Danika in her heart, and not with Hunt beside her.

The end of the runway neared. She had to get airborne. Had to start the Ascent, or she'd fall into nothingness. Forever.

"*Don't stop!*" Danika screamed.

So Bryce didn't.

She charged onward. Toward that very final, deadly end point.

She used every foot of the runway. Every last inch.

And then blasted upward.

Declan couldn't believe what he was seeing as the Autumn King fell to his knees. As Bryce rose, lifted on a surge of power.

She cleared the deepest levels.

"It's not . . . ," the Autumn King breathed. "It's not *possible*. She is *alone*."

Tears streamed down Sabine's harsh face as she whispered, "No, she isn't."

The force that was Danika Fendyr, the force that had given Bryce that boost upward, faded away into nothing.

Declan knew it would never return, in this world or on a mist-veiled isle.

It might still have been too long for Bryce's brain to be without oxygen, even if she could make it the entire way back to life. But his princess fought for every bit of progress upward, her power shifting, traces of everyone who'd given it to her coming through: mer, shifter, draki, human, angel, sprite, Fae . . .

"How," the Autumn King asked no one in particular. "*How?*"

It was the ancient Prime of the wolves who answered, his

withered voice rising above the pinging of the graph. "With the strength of the most powerful force in the world. The most powerful force in any realm." He pointed to the screen. "What brings loyalty beyond death, undimming despite the years. What remains unwavering in the face of hopelessness."

The Autumn King twisted toward the ancient Prime, shaking his head. Still not understanding.

Bryce was at the level of ordinary witches now. But still too far from life.

Motion caught Declan's eye, and he whirled toward the feed of the Old Square.

Wreathed in lightning, healed and whole, Hunt Athalar was kneeling over Bryce's dead body. Pumping her torso with his hands—chest compressions.

Hunt hissed to Bryce through his gritted teeth, thunder cracking above him, "I heard what you said." *Pump, pump, pump* went his powerful arms. "What you waited to admit until I was almost *dead*, you fucking coward." His lightning surged into her, sending her body arcing off the ground as he tried to jump-start her heart. He snarled in her ear, "*Now come say it to my face*."

Sabine whispered a sentence to the room, to the Autumn King, and Declan's heart rose, hearing it.

It was the answer to the ancient Prime's words. To the Autumn King's question of how, against every statistic blaring on Declan's computer, they were even witnessing Hunt Athalar fight like Hel to keep Bryce Quinlan's heart beating.

Through love, all is possible.

94

She was sea and sky and stone and blood and wings and earth and stars and darkness and light and bone and flame.

Danika was gone. She had given over what remained of her soul, her power, to get Bryce off the runway, and for that initial rocketing Ascent.

Danika had whispered, "*I love you*," before fading into nothing, her hand sliding from Bryce's.

And it had not destroyed Bryce, to make that final goodbye.

The roar she had emitted was not one of pain. But of challenge.

Bryce barreled higher. She could feel the surface nearby. The thin veil between this place and life. Her power shifted, dancing between forms and gifts. She thrust upward with a push of a mighty tail. Twisted and rose with a sweep of vast wings. She was all things—and yet herself.

And then she heard it. His voice. His answering challenge to her call.

He was there. Waiting for her.

Fighting to keep her heart going. She was close enough to the veil to see it now.

Even before she had come to lie dead before him, he'd fought to keep her heart going.

Bryce smiled, in this place between, and at last careened toward Hunt.

"*Come on,*" Hunt grunted, continuing the chest compressions, counting Bryce's breaths until he could shock her again with his lighting.

He didn't know how long she had been down, but she'd been dead when he'd awoken, healed and whole, to a repaired city. As if no magic bombs, no demons, had ever harmed it.

He saw the glowing Gate, the blazing light—the *firstlight*—and knew only someone making the Drop could generate that kind of power. And when he'd seen her lifeless body before the Gate, he'd known she'd somehow found a way to make the Drop, to unleash that healing firstlight, to use the Horn to seal the portals to Hel at the other Gates.

So he'd acted on instinct. Did the only thing he could think of.

He'd saved her and she'd saved him, and he—

His power felt it coming a moment later. Recognized her, like seeing itself in a mirror.

How she was bringing up this much power, how she was making the Ascent alone . . . he didn't care about that. He had Fallen, he had survived, he had gone through every trial and torture and horror—all for this moment. So he could be here.

It had all been for her. For Bryce.

Closer and closer, her power neared. Hunt braced himself, and sent another shock of lightning into her heart. She arced off the ground once more, body lifeless.

"Come on," he repeated, pumping her chest again with his hands. "I'm waiting for you."

He'd been waiting for her from the moment he'd been born.

And as if she'd heard him, Bryce exploded into life.

She was warm, and she was safe, and she was home.

There was light—around her, from her, in her heart.

Bryce realized she was breathing. And her heart was beating.

Both were secondary. Would always be secondary around Hunt.

She dimly registered that they were kneeling in the Old Square. His gray wings glowed like embers as they curved around them both, holding her tightly to him. And inside the wall of velvet-soft wings, like a sun contained inside a flower bud, Bryce shone.

She slowly lifted her head, pulling away only far enough to look at his face.

Hunt already stared down at her, his wings unfurling like petals at dawn. No tattoo marked his brow. The halo was gone.

She ran her shaking fingers over the smooth skin. Hunt silently brushed away her tears.

She smiled at him. Smiled at him with the lightness in her heart, her soul. Hunt slid his hand along her jaw, cupping her face. The tenderness in his eyes wiped away any lingering doubts.

She laid her palm over his thundering heart. "Did you just call me a fucking coward?"

Hunt tipped his head to the stars and laughed. "So what if I did?"

She angled her face closer to his. "Too bad all that healing firstlight didn't turn you into a decent person."

"Where would the fun be in that, Quinlan?"

Her toes curled at the way he said her name. "I suppose I'll just have to—"

A door opened down the street. Then another and another. And stumbling, weeping with relief or silent in shock, the people of Crescent City emerged. Gaped at what they beheld. At Bryce and Hunt.

She let go of him and rose. Her power was a strange, vast well beneath her. Belonging not only to her—but to all of them.

She peered up at Hunt, who was now gazing at her as if he couldn't quite believe his eyes. She took his hand. Interlaced their fingers.

And together, they stepped forward to greet the world.

95

Syrinx was sitting in her apartment's open front doorway, whining with worry, as Bryce and Hunt stepped off the elevator.

Bryce scanned the empty hall, the chimera. "I left that door shut . . ." she began, earning a knowing chuckle from Hunt, but Syrinx was already sprinting for her.

"I'll explain his *gifts* later," Hunt murmured as Bryce herded a hysterical Syrinx into the apartment and knelt before the beast, flinging her arms around him.

She and Hunt had stayed in the Old Square for all of two minutes before the wailing began—from the people who stumbled from the shelters to discover that it had been too late for their loved ones.

The Horn inked into her back had done its job well. Not one void remained in the Gates. And her firstlight—through those Gates—had been able to heal everything: people, buildings, the world itself.

Yet it could not do the impossible. It could not bring back the dead.

And there were many, many bodies in the streets. Most only in pieces.

Bryce tightened her arms around Sryinx. "It's okay," she whispered, letting him lick her face.

But it wasn't okay. Not even close. What had happened, what she'd done and revealed, the Horn in her body, all those people dead, Lehabah dead, and seeing Danika, Danika, Danika—

Her breathless words turned into pants, and then shuddering sobs. Hunt, standing behind her as if he'd been waiting for this, just scooped her and Syrinx into his arms.

Hunt brought her to her bedroom, sitting down on the edge of the mattress, keeping his arms around her and Syrinx, who pried his way free from Bryce's arms to lick Hunt's face, too.

His hand slipped into her hair, fingers twining through it, and Bryce leaned into him, soaking up that strength, that familiar scent, marveling that they had even gotten here, had somehow made it—

She glanced at his wrist. No sign of the halo on his brow, yet the slave tattoo remained.

Hunt noticed the shift in her attention. He said quietly, "I killed Sandriel."

His eyes were so calm—clear. Fixed wholly on hers.

"I killed Micah," she whispered.

"I know." The corner of his mouth curled upward. "Remind me to never get on your bad side."

"It's not funny."

"Oh, I know it's not." His fingers drifted through her hair, casually and gently. "I could barely stand to watch."

She could barely stand to remember it. "How did you manage to kill her? To get rid of the tattoo?"

"It's a long story," he said. "I'd rather you fill in the details of yours."

"You first."

"Not a chance. I want to hear how you hid the fact that you've got a star inside you."

He looked down at her chest then, as if he'd glimpse it shimmering beneath her skin. But when his eyebrows flicked upward, Bryce followed his line of sight.

"Well," she said with a sigh, "that's new." Indeed, just visible down the V-neck of her T-shirt, a white splotch—an eight-pointed star—now scarred the place between her breasts.

Hunt chuckled. "I like it."

Some small part of her did, too. But she said, "You know it's just the Starborn light—not true power."

"Yeah, except now you've got that, too." He pinched her side. "A good amount from what I can sense. And the fucking Horn—" He ran his hand down her spine for emphasis.

She rolled her eyes. "Whatever."

But his face grew grave. "You're going to have to learn to control it."

"We save the city, and you're already telling me I need to get back to work?"

He chuckled. "Old habits, Bryce."

Their eyes met again, and she glanced at his mouth, so close to hers, so perfectly formed. At his eyes, now staring so intently into her own.

It had all happened for a reason. She believed that. For this—for him.

And though the path she'd been thrust onto was royally fucked, and had led her through the lightless halls of grief and despair . . . Here, here before her, was light. True light. What she'd raced toward during the Ascent.

And she wanted to be kissed by that light. Now.

Wanted to kiss him back, and tell Syrinx to go wait in his crate for a while.

Hunt's dark eyes turned near-feral. As if he could read those thoughts on her face, in her scent. "We have some unfinished business, Quinlan," he said, voice roughening. He threw Syrinx a Look, and the chimera leapt from the bed and trotted out into the hall, lion's tail waggling as if to say, *It's about time*.

When Bryce looked back at Hunt, she found his focus on her lips. And became hyperaware of the fact that she was sitting across his lap. On her bed. From the hardness starting to poke into her backside, she knew he'd realized it, too.

Still they said nothing as they stared at each other.

So Bryce wriggled slightly against his erection, drawing a hiss from him. She huffed a laugh. "I throw one smoldering look at you and you're already—what was it you said to me a few weeks ago? Hot and bothered?"

One of his hands traced down her spine again, intent in every inch of it. "I've been hot and bothered for you for a long time now." His hand halted on her waist, his thumb beginning a gentle, torturous stroking along her rib cage. With each sweep, the building ache between her legs ratcheted.

Hunt smiled slowly, as if well aware of that. Then he leaned in, pressing a kiss to the underside of her jaw. He said against her flushed skin, "You ready to do this?"

"Gods, yes," she breathed. And when he kissed just beneath her ear, making her back arch slightly, she said, "I recall you promising to fuck me until I couldn't remember my own name."

He shifted his hips, grinding his cock into her, searing her even with the clothing still between them. "If that's what you want, sweetheart, that's what I'll give you."

Oh gods. She couldn't get a solid breath down. Couldn't think around his roving mouth on her neck and his hands and that massive, beautiful cock digging into her. She had to get him inside her. Right now. She needed to feel him, needed to have his heat and strength around her. In her.

Bryce shifted to straddle his lap, lining herself up with all of him. She met all of him, satisfied to find his breathing as ragged as her own. His hands bracketed her waist, thumbs stroking, stroking, stroking, as if he were an engine waiting to roar into movement upon her command.

Bryce leaned in, brushing her mouth over his. Once. Twice.

Hunt began shaking with the force of his restraint as he let her explore his mouth.

But she pulled back, meeting his hazy, burning gaze. The words she wanted to say clogged in her throat, so she hoped he understood them as she pressed a kiss to his now-clear brow. Sketched a line of soft, glancing kisses over every inch where the tattoo had been.

Hunt slid a shaking hand from her waist and laid it over her thundering heart.

She swallowed thickly, surprised to find her eyes stinging. Surprised to see silver lining his eyes as well. They had made it; they were here. Together.

Hunt leaned in, slanting his mouth over hers. She met him halfway, arms snaking around his neck, fingers burying themselves in his thick, silken hair.

A shrill ringing filled the apartment.

She could ignore it, ignore the world—

Call from . . . Home.

Bryce pulled back, panting hard.

"You gonna get that?" Hunt's voice was guttural.

Yes. No. Maybe.

Call from . . . Home.

"She'll just keep calling until I pick up," Bryce murmured.

Her limbs were stiff as she peeled herself from Hunt's lap, his fingers trailing over her back as she stood. She tried not to think about the promise in that touch, as if he was as reluctant to let go of her as she was of him.

She ran to the great room and picked up the phone before it went to audiomail.

"Bryce?" Her mom was crying. It was enough to douse a bucket of ice water over any lingering arousal. "Bryce?"

She blew out a breath, returned to the bedroom, and threw Hunt an apologetic look that he waved off before he slumped back on the bed, wings rustling. "Hi, Mom."

Her mom's sobbing threatened to make her start again, so she kept moving, aiming for her bathroom. She was filthy—her pink sneakers were near-black, her pants torn and bloody, her shirt almost in ruins. Apparently, the firstlight had only gone so far in fixing everything.

"Are you all right? Are you safe?"

"I'm fine," Bryce said, turning on the shower. Leaving it on cold. She peeled off her clothes. "I'm doing fine."

"What's that water?"

"My shower."

"You save a city and make the Drop and can't even give me your full attention?"

Bryce chuckled and put the phone on speaker before setting it on the sink. "How much do you know?" She hissed at the icy blast as she stepped into the spray. But it shocked away any lingering heat between her legs and the heady desire clouding her mind.

"Your biological father had Declan Emmet call to fill me in on everything. I guess the bastard finally realized he owed me that much, at least."

Bryce turned up the heat at last as she shampooed her hair. "How pissed is he?"

"Furious, I'm sure." She added, "The news also just broke a story about—about who your father is." Bryce could practically hear her mother grinding her teeth. "They know the exact amount of power you got. As much as he has, Bryce. *More* than him. That's a big deal."

Bryce tried not to reel at it—where her power had landed her. She tucked away that factoid for later. She rinsed the shampoo from her hair, reaching for the conditioner. "I know."

"What are you going to do with it?"

"Open a chain of beach-themed restaurants."

"It was too much to hope that achieving that much power would give you a sense of dignity."

Bryce stuck out her tongue even though her mom couldn't see it, and plopped conditioner into her palm. "Look, can we shelve the whole *mighty power, mighty burdens* discussion until tomorrow?"

"Yes, except *tomorrow* in your vocabulary means *never*." Her mother sighed. "You closed those portals, Bryce. And I can't even talk about what Danika did for you without . . ." Her voice broke. "We can talk about that *tomorrow*, too."

Bryce rinsed out the conditioner. And realized that her mother didn't know—about Micah. What she'd done to him. Or what Micah had done to Danika.

Ember kept talking, and Bryce kept listening, while dread grew like ivy inside her, creeping through her veins, wrapping around her bones and squeezing tight.

Hunt took a swift, icy shower of his own and changed into different clothes, smiling slightly to himself as Bryce's shower shut off and she kept talking to her mother.

"Yeah, Hunt's here." Her words floated down the hall, through the great room, and into his own room. "No, I didn't, Mom. And no, he didn't, either." A drawer slammed. "*That* is none of your business, and please never ask me anything like that again."

Hunt had a good idea of what Ember had asked her daughter. And wouldn't you know, he'd been about to do just that with Bryce when she'd called.

He hadn't cared that an entire city was looking on: he'd wanted to kiss her when the light of her power had faded, when Hunt had lowered his wings to find her in his arms, looking up at him like he was worth something. Like he was all she needed. End of story.

No one had ever looked at him like that.

And when they'd come back here, and he'd had her on his lap on her bed and seen the way her cheeks became pink as she looked at his mouth, he'd been ready to cross that final bridge with her. To spend all day and night doing so.

Considering how her firstlight had healed him, he'd most definitely say he was cleared for sex. Aching for it—for her.

Bryce groaned. "You're a pervert, Mom. You know that?" She growled. "Well, if you're so fucking invested in it, why did you *call me*? Didn't you think I might be *busy*?"

Hunt smiled, going half-hard again at the sass in her tone. He could listen to her snark all fucking day. He wondered how much of it would make an appearance when he got her naked again. Got her moaning.

The first time, she'd come on his hand. This time . . . This time, he had *plans* for all the other ways he'd get her to make that beautiful, breathless sound as she'd orgasmed.

Leaving Bryce to deal with her mother, willing his cock to calm the fuck down, Hunt grabbed a burner phone from his underwear drawer and dialed Isaiah, one of the few numbers he'd memorized.

"Thank the fucking gods," Isaiah said when he heard Hunt's voice.

Hunt smiled at the male's uncharacteristic relief. "What's happening on your end?"

"My end?" Isaiah barked a laugh. "What the fuck is happening on *your* end?"

Too much to say. "Are you at the Comitium?"

"Yeah, and it's a gods-damned madhouse. I just realized *I'm* in charge now."

With Micah a bunch of ashes in a vacuum and Sandriel not much better, Isaiah, as Micah's Commander of the 33rd, was indeed in charge.

"Congrats on the promotion, man."

"Promotion my ass. I'm not an Archangel. And these assholes know it." Isaiah snapped at someone in the background, "*Then call fucking maintenance to clean it up.*" He sighed.

Hunt asked, "What happened to the Asterian fuckheads who sent their brimstone over the walls?" He had half a mind to fly out there and start unleashing his lightning on those tanks.

"Gone. Already moved off." Isaiah's dark tone told Hunt he'd be down for some good old-fashioned retribution, too.

Hunt asked, bracing himself, "Naomi?"

"Alive." Hunt uttered a silent prayer of thanks to Cthona for that mercy. Then Isaiah said, "Look, I know you're exhausted, but can you get over here? I could use your help to sort this shit out. All these pissing contests will end pretty damn fast if they see us both in charge."

Hunt tried not to bristle. Bryce and him getting naked, it seemed, would have to wait.

Because the slave tattoo on his wrist meant he still had to obey the Republic, still belonged to someone other than himself. The list of possibilities wasn't good. He'd be lucky if he got to stay in

Lunathion as the possession of whoever took Micah's spot, and maybe see Bryce in stolen moments. If he was even allowed outside the Comitium.

Fuck, if they even allowed him to *live* after what he'd done to Sandriel.

Hunt's hands began to shake. Any trace of arousal vanished.

But he shrugged a shirt over his head. He'd find some way to survive—some way back to this life with Quinlan he'd barely begun to savor. Unable to help himself, he glanced at his wrist.

He blinked once. Twice.

Bryce was just saying goodbye to her deviant mother when the phone beeped with another call. It was from an unknown number, which meant it was probably Jesiba, so Bryce promised Ember they'd talk tomorrow and switched over. "Hey."

A young, male voice asked, "Is that how you greet all your callers, Bryce Quinlan?"

She knew that voice. Knew the lanky teenage body it belonged to, a shell to house an ancient behemoth. To house an Asteri. She'd seen and heard it on TV so many times she'd lost count.

"Hello, Your Brilliance," she whispered.

96

Rigelus, the Bright Hand of the Asteri, had called her house. Bryce's hands shook so badly she could barely keep the phone to her ear.

"We beheld your actions today and wished to extend our gratitude," the lilting voice said.

She swallowed, wondering if the mightiest of the Asteri somehow knew she was standing in a towel, hair dripping onto the carpet. "You're . . . welcome?"

Rigelus laughed softly. "You have had quite a day, Miss Quinlan."

"Yes, Your Brilliance."

"It was a day full of many surprises, for all of us."

We know what you are, what you did.

Bryce forced her legs to move, to head to the great room. To where Hunt was standing in the doorway of his bedroom, his face pale. His arms slack at his sides.

"To show you how deep our gratitude goes, we would like to grant you a favor."

She wondered if the brimstone had been a *favor*, too. But she said, "That's not necessary—"

"It is already done. We trust you will find it satisfactory."

She knew Hunt could hear the voice on the line as he walked over.

But he just held out his wrist. His tattooed wrist, with a *C* stamped over the slave's mark.

Freed.

"I . . ." Bryce gripped Hunt's wrist, then scanned his face. But it was not joy she saw there—not as he heard the voice on the line and understood who had gifted him his freedom.

"We also trust that this favor will serve as a reminder for you and Hunt Athalar. It is our deepest wish that you remain in the city, and live out your days in peace and contentment. That you use your ancestors' gift to bring yourself joy. And refrain from using the other gift inked upon you."

Use your starlight as a party trick and never, ever use the Horn.

It made her the biggest idiot in Midgard, but she said, "What about Micah and Sandriel?"

"Governor Micah went rogue and threatened to destroy innocent citizens of this empire with his high-handed approach to the rebel conflict. Governor Sandriel got what she deserved in being so lax with her control over her slaves."

Fear gleamed in Hunt's eyes. In her own, too, Bryce was sure. Nothing was ever this easy—this simple. There had to be a catch.

"These are, of course, sensitive issues, Miss Quinlan. Ones that, were they publicly announced, would result in a great deal of trouble for all involved."

For you. We will destroy you.

"All the witnesses to both events have been notified of the potential fallout."

"Okay," Bryce whispered.

"And as for the unfortunate destruction of Lunathion, we do accept full responsibility. We were informed by Sandriel that the city had been evacuated, and sent the Asterian Guard to wipe away the demon infestation. The brimstone missiles were a last resort, intended to save us all. It was incredibly fortunate that you found a solution."

Liar. Ancient, awful liar. He'd picked the perfect scapegoat: a dead one. The rage that flickered over Hunt's face told her he shared her opinion.

"I was truly lucky," Bryce managed to say.

"Yes, perhaps because of the power in your veins. Such a gift can have tremendous consequences, if not handled wisely." A pause, as if he were smiling. "I trust you shall learn to wield both your unexpected strength and the light within you with . . . discretion."

Stay in your lane.

"I will," Bryce murmured.

"Good," Rigelus said. "And do you believe it necessary that I contact your mother, Ember Quinlan, to ask for her discretion, too?" The threat gleamed, sharp as a knife. One step out of line, and they knew where to strike first. Hunt's hands curled into fists.

"No," Bryce said. "She doesn't know about the Governors."

"And she never will. No one else will ever know, Bryce Quinlan."

Bryce swallowed again. "Yes."

A soft laugh. "Then you and Hunt Athalar have our blessing."

The line went dead. Bryce stared at the phone like it was going to sprout wings and fly around the room.

Hunt slumped on the couch, rubbing his face. "Live quietly and normally, keep your mouths shut, never use the Horn, and we won't fucking kill you and everyone you love."

Bryce sat on the rolled arm of the couch. "Slay a few enemies, gain twice as many in return." Hunt grunted. She angled her head. "Why are your boots on?"

"Isaiah needs me at the Comitium. He's up to his neck in angels wanting to challenge his authority and needs backup." He arched a brow. "Want to come play Scary Asshole with me?"

Despite everything, despite the Asteri watching and all that had occurred, Bryce smiled. "I have just the outfit."

Bryce and Hunt made it two steps onto the roof before she caught the familiar scent. Peered over the edge and saw who ran down the street below. A glance at Hunt, and he swept her into his arms, flying her down to the sidewalk. She might have snuck a deep inhale of him, her nose grazing the strong column of his neck.

Hunt's caress down her spine a moment before he set her down told her he'd caught that little sniff. But then Bryce was standing before Ruhn. Before Fury and Tristan Flynn.

Fury barely gave her a moment before she leapt upon Bryce, hugging her so tightly her bones groaned. "You are one lucky idiot," Fury said, laughing softly. "And one smart bitch."

Bryce smiled, her laugh caught in her throat as Fury pulled away. But a thought struck her, and Bryce reached for her phone—no, it was left somewhere in this city. "Juniper—"

"She's safe. I'm going to check on her now." Fury squeezed her hand and then nodded to Hunt. "Well done, angel." And then her friend was sprinting off, blending into the night itself.

Bryce turned back to Ruhn and Flynn. The latter just gaped at her. But Bryce looked to her brother, wholly still and silent. His clothes torn enough to tell her that before the firstlight had healed everything, he'd been in bad shape. Had probably fought his way through this city.

Then Ruhn began babbling. "Tharion went off to help get the evacuees out of the Blue Court, and Amelie ran to the Den to make sure the pups were okay, but we were nearly . . . we were half a mile away when I heard the Moonwood Gate. Heard you talking through it, I mean. There were so many demons I couldn't get there, but then I heard Danika, and all that light erupted and . . ." He halted, swallowing hard. His blue eyes gleamed in the streetlights, dawn still far off. A breeze off the Istros ruffled his black hair. And it was the tears that filled his eyes, the wonder in them, that had Bryce launching forward. Had her throwing her arms around her brother and holding him tightly.

Ruhn didn't hesitate before his arms came around her. He shook so badly that she knew he was crying.

A scuff of steps told her Flynn was giving them privacy; a cedar-scented breeze flitting past suggested that Hunt had gone airborne to wait for her.

"I thought you were dead," Ruhn said, his voice shaking as much as his body. "Like ten fucking times, I thought you were dead."

She chuckled. "I'm glad to disappoint you."

"Shut up, Bryce." He scanned her face, his cheeks wet. "Are you . . . are you all right?"

"I don't know," she admitted. Concern flared in his face, but she didn't dare give any specifics, not after Rigelus's phone call. Not with all the cameras around. Ruhn gave her a knowing grimace. Yes, they'd talk about that strange, ancient starlight within her veins later. What it meant for both of them. "Thank you for coming for me."

"You're my sister." Ruhn didn't bother to keep his voice down. No, there was pride in his voice. And damn if that didn't hit her in the heart. "Of course I'd come to save your ass."

She punched his arm, but Ruhn's smile turned tentative. "Did you mean what you said to Athalar? About me?" *Tell Ruhn I forgive him.*

"Yes," she said without a moment of hesitation. "I meant all of it."

"Bryce." His face grew grave. "You really thought that I would care more about the Starborn shit than about *you*? You honestly think I care which one of us it is?"

"It's both of us," she said. "Those books you read said such things once happened."

"I don't give a shit," he said, smiling slightly. "I don't care if I'm called Prince or Starborn or the Chosen One or any of that." He grabbed her hand. "The only thing I want to be called right now is your brother." He added softly, "If you'll have me."

She winked, even as her heart tightened unbearably. "I'll think about it."

Ruhn grinned before his face turned grave once more. "You know the Autumn King will want to meet with you. Be ready."

"Doesn't getting a bunch of fancy-ass power mean I don't have to obey anyone? And just because I forgive you doesn't mean I forgive him." She would never do that.

"I know." Ruhn's eyes gleamed. "But you need to be on your guard."

She arched a brow, tucking away the warning, and said, "Hunt told me about the mind-reading." He'd mentioned it briefly—along with a recap of the Summit and everything that had gone down—on the walk up to the roof.

Ruhn glared at the adjacent rooftop where Hunt stood. "Athalar has a big fucking mouth."

One she'd like to put to good use on various parts of her body, she didn't say. She didn't need Ruhn puking on her clean clothes.

Ruhn went on, "And it's not mind-reading. Just . . . mind-talking. Telepathy."

"Does dear old Dad know?"

"No." And then her brother said into her head, *And I'd like to keep it that way.*

She started. *Creepy. Kindly stay the fuck out of my head, brother.*

Gladly. His phone rang, and he glanced at the screen before wincing. "I gotta take this."

Right, because they all had work to do to get this city to rights—starting with tending to the dead. The sheer number of Sailings would be . . . she didn't want to think about it.

Ruhn let the phone ring again. "Can I come over tomorrow?"

"Yes," she said, smirking. "I'll get your name added to the guest list."

"Yeah, yeah, you're a fucking hotshot." He rolled his eyes and answered the call. "Hey, Dec." He strode down the street to where Flynn waited, throwing Bryce a parting grin.

Bryce looked to the rooftop across the street. Where the angel still waited for her, a shadow against the night.

But no longer the Shadow of Death.

97

Hunt stayed at the Comitium barracks that night. Bryce had lost track of the hours they'd worked, first through the night, then into the cloudless day, and finally at sunset she'd been dragging so much that he'd ordered Naomi to fly her home. And presumably ordered her to stand watch, since a dark-winged figure still stood on the adjacent rooftop in the gray light before dawn, and a peek into Hunt's room revealed that his bed remained made.

But Bryce didn't dwell on all the work they'd done yesterday, or all that lay ahead. Reorganizing the city's leadership, Sailings for the dead, and waiting for the big announcement: which Archangel would be tapped by the Asteri to rule over Valbara.

Odds of them being decent were slim to none, but Bryce didn't dwell on that, either, as she slipped into the still-dim streets, Syrinx tugging on his leash as she tucked her new phone into her pocket. She'd defied the odds yesterday, so maybe the gods would throw them another bone and convince the Asteri to send someone who wasn't a psychopath.

At the very least, there would be no more death bargains for Hunt. Nothing more to *atone* for. No, he would be a free and true member of the triarii, if he wished. He had yet to decide.

Bryce waved to Naomi, and the angel waved back. She'd been too tired yesterday to object to having a guard, since Hunt didn't trust the Asteri, her father, or any other power brokers to stay the Hel away. After letting Syrinx do his business, she shook her head when the chimera made to turn back toward the apartment. "No breakfast yet, buddy," she said, aiming for the river.

Syrinx yowled with displeasure, but trotted along, sniffing at everything in his path until the broad band of the Istros appeared, its riverside walkway empty at this early hour. Tharion had called her yesterday, promising the River Queen's full support for any resources she needed.

Bryce hadn't the nerve to ask whether that support was due to her being the bastard daughter of the Autumn King, a Starborn Fae, or the bearer of Luna's Horn. Perhaps all of them.

Bryce settled onto one of the wooden benches along the quay, the Bone Quarter a swirling, misty wall across the water. The mer had come—had helped so many escape. Even the otters had grabbed the smallest of the city's residents and carried them down to the Blue Court. The House of Many Waters had risen to the occasion. The shifters had risen to it.

But the Fae . . . FiRo had sustained the least damage. The Fae had suffered the fewest casualties. It was no surprise, when their shields had been the first to go up. And had not opened to allow anyone inside.

Bryce blocked out the thought as Syrinx leapt onto the bench beside her, nails clicking on the wood, and plopped his furry butt next to hers. Bryce slid her phone from her pocket and wrote to Juniper, *Tell Madame Kyrah I'll be at her next dance class.*

June wrote back almost immediately. *The city was attacked and this is what you're thinking about?* A few seconds later she added, *But I will.*

Bryce smiled. For long minutes, she and Syrinx sat in silence, watching the light bleed to gray, then to the palest blue. And then a golden thread of light appeared along the Istros's calm surface.

Bryce unlocked her phone. And read Danika's final, happy messages one last time.

The light built on the river, gilding its surface.

Bryce's eyes stung as she smiled softly, then read through Connor's last words to her.

Message me when you're home safe.

Bryce began typing. The answer it had taken her two years, nearly to the day, to write.

I'm home.

She sent the message into the ether, willed it to find its way across the gilded river and to the misty isle beyond.

And then she deleted the thread. Deleted Danika's messages, too. Each swipe of her finger had her heart lightening, lifting with the rising sun.

When they were gone, when she had set them free, she stood, Syrinx leaping to the pavement beside her. She made to turn home, but a glimmer of light across the river caught her eye.

For a heartbeat, just one, the dawn parted the mists of the Bone Quarter. Revealing a grassy shore. Rolling, serene hills beyond. Not a land of stone and gloom, but of light and green. And standing on that lovely shore, smiling at her . . .

A gift from the Under-King for saving the city.

Tears began rolling down her face as she beheld the near-invisible figures. All six of them—the seventh gone forever, having yielded her eternity. But the tallest of them, standing in the middle with his hand lifted in greeting . . .

Bryce brought her hand to her mouth, blowing a gentle kiss.

As swiftly as they parted, the mists closed. But Bryce kept smiling, all the way back to the apartment. Her phone buzzed, and Hunt's message popped up. *I'm home. Where are you?*

She could barely type as Syrinx tugged her along. *Walking Syrinx. I'll be there in a minute.*

Good. I'm making breakfast.

Bryce's grin nearly split her face in two as she hurried her steps, Syrinx launching into a flat-out sprint. As if he, too, knew what awaited them. *Who* awaited them.

There was an angel in her apartment. Which meant it must be any gods-damned day of the week. Which meant she had joy in her heart, and her eyes set on the wide-open road ahead.

EPILOGUE

The white cat with eyes like blue opals sat on a bench in the Oracle's Park and licked his front paw.

"You know you're not a true cat, don't you?" Jesiba Roga clicked her tongue. "You don't need to lick yourself."

Aidas, Prince of the Chasm, lifted his head. "Who says I don't enjoy licking myself?"

Amusement tugged on Jesiba's thin mouth, but she shifted her stare to the quiet park, the towering cypresses still gleaming with dew. "Why didn't you tell me about Bryce?"

He flexed his claws. "I didn't trust anyone. Even you."

"I thought Theia's light was forever extinguished."

"So did I. I thought they'd made sure she and her power died on that last battlefield under Prince Pelias's blade." His eyes glowed with ancient rage. "But Bryce Quinlan bears her light."

"You can tell the difference between Bryce's starlight and her brother's?"

"I shall never forget the exact shine and hue of Theia's light. It is still a song in my blood."

Jesiba studied him for a long moment, then frowned. "And Hunt Athalar?"

Aidas fell silent as a petitioner stumbled past, hoping to beat the crowds that had filled the Oracle's Park and Luna's Temple since portals to his world had opened within the quartz Gates and the beasts of the Pit had taken full advantage of it. Any who had managed to return were currently being punished by one of Aidas's brothers. He would soon return to join them in it.

Aidas said at last, "I think Athalar's father would have been proud."

"Sentimental of you."

Aidas shrugged as best his feline body would allow. "Feel free to disagree, of course," he said, leaping off the bench. "You knew the male best." His whiskers twitched as he angled his head. "What of the library?"

"It has already been moved."

He knew better than to ask where she had hidden it. So he merely said, "Good."

Jesiba didn't speak again until the fifth Prince of Hel had stalked a few feet away. "Don't fuck us over this time, Aidas."

"I do not plan to," he said, fading into the space between realms, Hel a dark song beckoning him home. "Not when things are about to get so interesting."

ACKNOWLEDGMENTS

This book has been such a tremendous labor of love from the very start, and because of that, I have far too many people to thank than can possibly fit within these few pages, but I shall do my best! My endless gratitude and love to:

Noa Wheeler, editor extraordinaire. Noa, how can I even begin to thank you? You transformed this book into something I'm proud of, challenged me to be a better writer, and worked your ass off at every single stage. You are brilliant and just a joy to work with, and I'm so honored to call you my editor.

Tamar Rydzinski: Thank you for having my back through each step of this (long, long) journey. You are a badass *queen*.

To the entire team at Bloombury: Laura Keefe, Nicole Jarvis, Valentina Rice, Emily Fisher, Lucy Mackay-Sim, Rebecca McNally, Kathleen Farrar, Amanda Shipp, Emma Hopkin, Nicola Hill, Ros Ellis, Nigel Newton, Cindy Loh, Alona Fryman, Donna Gauthier, Erica Barmash, Faye Bi, Beth Eller, Jenny Collins, Phoebe Dyer, Lily Yengle, Frank Bumbalo, Donna Mark, John Candell, Yelena Safronova, Melissa Kavonic, Oona Patrick, Nick Sweeney, Diane Aronson, Kerry Johnson, Christine Ma, Bridget McCusker, Nicholas Church, Claire Henry, Elise Burns, Andrea Kearney, Maia Fjord, Laura Main Ellen, Sian Robertson, Emily Moran, Ian Lamb,

Emma Bradshaw, Fabia Ma, Grace Whooley, Alice Grigg, Joanna Everard, Jacqueline Sells, Tram-Anh Doan, Beatrice Cross, Jade Westwood, Cesca Hopwood, Jet Purdie, Saskia Dunn, Sonia Palmisano, Catriona Feeney, Hermione Davis, Hannah Temby, Grainne Reidy, Kate Sederstrom, Jennifer Gonzalez, Veronica Gonzalez, Elizabeth Tzetzo. It is a privilege to be published by you. Thank you for all of your support, and thank you especially to Kamilla Benko and Grace McNamee for their hard work on this book!

To my foreign publishers: Record, Egmont Bulgaria, Albatros, DTV, Konyvmolykepzo, Mondadori, De Boekerij, Foksal, Azbooka Atticus, Slovart, Alfaguara, and Dogan Egmont. Thank you so much for bringing my books to your countries and to your amazing readers!

A giant hug and round of applause for Elizabeth Evans, the audiobook narrator who so faithfully and lovingly brings my characters to life. It's a delight and privilege to work with you!

Thank you to the incredibly talented Carlos Quevedo for the cover artwork that so perfectly captured the spirit of this book, and to Virginia Allyn, for her fantastic map of the city!

I literally would not have gotten through writing this book without my friends and family.

So thank you from the bottom of my heart to J. R. Ward, for sharing your wisdom when I needed it most, for your unbelievable kindness, and for being an inspiration to me (and not minding that we both have a Ruhn!).

To Lynette Noni: You are the actual best. The BEST. Your clever feedback, your generosity, your general awesomeness—girl, I love you something fierce.

Jenn Kelly, I don't know what I would do without you. You have become a part of my family, and I am grateful for you every day! To Steph Brown, my dear friend, fellow hockey fan, and the person who never fails to make me laugh—I adore you.

Thank you to Julie Eshbaugh, Elle Kennedy, Alice Fanchiang, Louisse Ang, Laura Ashforth, and Jennifer Armentrout, for being true rays of light in my life. As always: thank you, Cassie Homer, for everything! A massive hug and thank-you to Jillian Stein, for all your help. A heartfelt thank-you to the immensely talented and cool Qusai Akoud, for your kickass vision and unparalleled website-building skills. And a *huge* thank-you to Danielle Jensen for reading and providing such vital feedback!

Endless gratitude to my family (both by birth and through marriage!) for their support and unwavering love. (And to Linda, who prefers chocolate croissants on her birthday.)

To my brilliant, lovely, and marvelous readers: How can I begin to thank you? You guys are the reason I do this, the reason I get out of bed each morning excited to write. I will never stop being grateful for each and every one of you.

To Annie, who sat by my side/at my feet/in my lap while I worked on this book for years, and served as the inspiration for Syrinx in so many ways. I love you forever and ever, babypup.

To Josh: I don't think I can convey everything I feel for you even if I had another 800 pages to write it out. You are my best friend, my soul mate, and the reason I can write about true love. You held me together this past year, walking alongside me through some of the hardest moments I've ever encountered, and I have no words for what that means to me. The luckiest day of my life was the one when I met you, and I am so blessed to have you as my husband—and as such a wonderful father to our son.

And lastly, to Taran: You truly are the brightest star in my sky. When things were hard, when things were dark, it was you I'd think about—your smile, your laugh, your beautiful face—and it carried me through. You probably won't read this for a long, long while, but know that you give me purpose, and motivation, and joy—so much joy that my heart is full to bursting every single day. I love you, I love you, I love you, and I will always be so proud to be your mom.

THE CRESCENT CITY SERIES CONTINUES IN *HOUSE OF SKY AND BREATH*!

Sofie had survived in the Kavalla death camp for two weeks.

Two weeks, and still the guards—dreadwolves, all of them—had not sniffed her out. Everything had gone according to plan. The reek of the days crammed into the cattle car had covered the telltale scent in her blood. It had also veiled her when they'd marched her and the others between the brick buildings of the camp, this new Hel that was only a small model of what the Asteri planned to do if the war continued.

Two weeks here, and that reek had become etched into her very skin, blinding even the wolves' keen noses. She'd stood mere feet from a guard in the breakfast line this morning and he hadn't so much as sniffed in her direction.

A small victory. One she'd gladly take these days.

Half of the Ophion rebel bases had fallen. More would soon. But only two places existed for her now: here, and the port of Servast, her destination tonight. Alone, even on foot, she could have easily made it. A rare benefit of being able to switch between human and Vanir identities—and of being a rare human who'd made the Drop.

It technically made her Vanir. Granted her a long life span and all the benefits that came from it that her human family did not and would never have. She might not have bothered to make the Drop had her parents not encouraged it—with the healing abilities she would gain, it provided extra armor in a world designed to kill her kind. So she'd done it under the radar, in a back-alley, highly illegal Drop center, where a leering satyr had been her Anchor, and handing over her firstlight had been the cost of the ritual. She'd spent the years since then learning to wear her humanity like a cloak, inside and out. She might have all the traits of the Vanir, but she'd never *be* Vanir. Not in her heart, her soul.

Yet tonight . . . tonight, Sofie did not mind letting a little of the monster loose.

It would not be an easy journey, thanks to the dozen small forms crouched behind her in the mud before the barbed-wire fence.

Five boys and six girls gathered by her thirteen-year-old brother, who now stood watch over them like a shepherd with his flock. Emile had gotten all of them out of the bunks, aided by a gentle human sun-priest, who was currently serving as lookout at the shed ten yards away.

The children were gray-skinned, gaunt. Eyes too big, too hopeless.

Sofie didn't need to know their stories. They were likely the same as hers: rebel human parents who'd either been caught or sold out. Hers had been the latter.

Pure dumb luck had kept Sofie out of the dreadwolves' clutches, too—at least until now. Three years ago, she'd been studying late at the university library with her friends. Arriving home after midnight, she'd spied the broken windows and shattered front door, the spray paint on the siding of their ordinary suburban house—*REBEL SHITS*—and begun running. She could only credit Urd for the fact that the dreadwolf guard posted at the front door hadn't seen her.

Later, she'd managed to confirm that her parents were dead. Tortured until the brutal end by the Hind or her elite squadron of dreadwolf interrogators. The report Sofie spent months working her way up through Ophion to attain had also revealed that her grandparents had been herded off upon reaching the Bracchus camp in the north, and shot in a lineup of other elders, their bodies left to crumple into a mass grave.

And her brother . . . Sofie hadn't been able to find anything on

Emile until now. For years, she'd been working with the Ophion rebels in exchange for any snippet of information about him, about her family. She didn't let herself think about what she'd done in return for that information. The spying, the people she'd killed to collect whatever intel Ophion wanted—these things weighed on her soul like a leaden cloak.

But she'd finally done enough for Ophion that they'd informed her Emile had been sent here, and survived against all odds. At last, she had a location for him. Convincing Command to let her come here . . . that had been another labyrinth to navigate.

In the end, it had required Pippa's support. Command listened to Pippa, their faithful and fervent soldier, leader of the elite Lightfall unit. Especially now that Ophion's numbers had taken such steep hits. Sort-of-human Sofie, on the other hand . . . She knew she was an asset, but with the Vanir blood in her veins, they'd never fully trust her. So she occasionally needed Pippa. Just as much as Pippa's Lightfall missions had needed Sofie's powers.

Pippa's help hadn't been due to friendship. Sofie was fairly certain that friends didn't exist within the Ophion rebel network. But Pippa was an opportunist—and she knew what she stood to gain should this op go smoothly, the doors that would further open to her within Command if Sofie returned triumphant.

A week after Command had approved the plan, over three years after her family had been snatched from their home, Sofie walked into Kavalla.

She'd waited until a local dreadwolf patrol was marching by and stumbled into their path, a mere mile from here. They immediately found the fake rebel documents she'd planted in her coat. They had no idea that Sofie also carried with her, hidden in her head, information that could very well be the final piece of this war against the Asteri.

The blow that could end it.

Ophion had found out too late that before she'd gone into Kavalla, she'd finally accomplished the mission she'd spent years preparing for. She'd made sure before she was picked up that Pippa and Ophion knew she'd acquired that intel. Now they wouldn't back out of their promises to retrieve her and Emile. She knew there would be Hel to pay for it—that she'd gone in secret to gather the information, and was now using it as collateral.

But that would come later.

The dreadwolf patrol interrogated her for two days. Two days, and then they'd thrown her into the cattle car with the others, convinced she was a foolish human girl who'd been given the documents by a lover who'd used her.

She'd never thought her minor in theater would come in handy. That she'd hear her favorite professor's voice critiquing her performance while someone was ripping out her fingernails. That she'd feign a confession with all the sincerity she'd once brought to the stage.

She wondered if Command knew she'd used those acting abilities on them, too.

That wasn't her concern, either. At least, not until tomorrow. Tonight, all that mattered was the desperate plan that would now come to fruition. If she had not been betrayed, if Command had not realized the truth, then a boat waited twenty miles away to ferry them out of Pangera. She looked down at the children around her and prayed the boat had room for more than the three passengers she'd claimed would be arriving.

She'd spent her first week and a half in Kavalla waiting for a glimpse of her brother—a hint of where he might be in the sprawling camp. And then, a few days ago, she'd spotted him in the food line. She'd faked a stumble to cover her shock and joy and sorrow.

He'd gotten so tall. As tall as their father. He was all gangly limbs and bones, a far cry from the healthy thirteen-year-old he should have been, but his face . . . it was the face she'd grown up with. But beginning to show the first hints of manhood on the horizon.

Tonight, she'd seized her chance to sneak into his bunk. And despite the three years and the countless miseries they'd endured, he knew her in an instant, too. Sofie would have spirited him away that moment had he not begged her to bring the others.

Now twelve children crouched behind her.

The alarms would be blaring soon. They had different sirens

for everything here, she'd learned. To signal their wake-ups, their meals, random inspections.

A mournful bird's call fluttered through the low-hanging mist. *All clear.*

With a silent prayer of thanks to the sun-priest and the god he served, Sofie lifted her mangled hand to the electrified fence. She did not glance at her missing fingernails, or the welts, or even feel how numb and stiff her hands were, not as the fence's power crackled through her.

Through her, into her, *becoming* her. Becoming hers to use as she wished.

A thought, and the fence's power turned outward again, her fingertips sparking where they curled against the metal. The metal turned orange, then red beneath her hand.

She sliced her palm down, skin so blisteringly hot it cleaved metal and wire. Emile whispered to the others to keep them from crying out, but she heard one of the boys murmur, "*Witch.*"

A typical human's fear of those with Vanir gifts—of the females who held such tremendous power. She did not turn to tell him that it was not a witch's power that flowed through her. It was something far more rare.

The cold earth met her hand as she rent the last of the fence and peeled the two flaps apart, barely wide enough for her to fit through. The children edged forward, but she signaled for them to halt, scanning the open dirt beyond. The road separating the camp from the ferns and towering pines lay empty.

But the threat would come from behind. She pivoted toward the watchtowers at the corners of the camp, which housed guards with sniper rifles forever trained on the road.

Sofie took a breath, and the power she'd sucked from the fence again shuddered through her. Across the camp, the spotlights ruptured in a shower of sparks that had the guards whirling toward it, shouting.

Sofie peeled the fence apart wider, arms straining, metal biting into her palms, grunting at the children to *run, run, run*—

Little shadows, their light gray uniforms tattered and stained and too bright in the near-full moon, hurried through the fence and across the muddy road to the dense ferns and steep gully beyond. Emile went last, his taller, bony body still a shock to her system, as brutal as any power she could wield.

Sofie did not let herself think of it. She raced after him, weak from the lack of food, the grueling labor, the soul-draining misery of this place. Mud and rocks cut into her bare feet, but the pain was distant as she took in the dozen pale faces peering from the ferns. "*Hurry, hurry, hurry,*" she whispered.

The van would wait only so long.

One of the girls swayed as she got to her feet, aiming for the slope beyond, but Sofie gripped her beneath a bony shoulder, keeping her upright as they staggered along, ferns brushing their legs, roots tangling their feet. Faster. They had to be *faster*—

A siren wailed.

This one, Sofie had not heard before. But she knew its blaring screech for what it was: *Escape*.

Flashlight beams shot through the trees as Sofie and the children crested the lip of a hill, half falling into the fern-laden gully. The dreadwolves were in their humanoid forms, then. Good—their eyes weren't as sharp in the dark this way. Bad, because it meant they carried guns.

Sofie's breathing hitched, but she focused, and sent her power slicing behind her. The flashlights went dark. Even firstlight could not stand against her power. Shouting rose—male, vicious.

Sofie hurried to the front of the group and Emile fell to the back to make sure none were forgotten. Pride swelled in her chest, even as it mingled with terror.

She knew they'd never make it back to the camp alive if they were caught.

Thighs burning, Sofie sprinted up the steep side of the gully. She didn't want to think what the children were enduring, not when their knobbly-kneed legs looked barely able to hold them up. They reached the top of the hill just as the dreadwolves howled, an inhuman sound breaking from humanoid throats. A summons to the hunt.

She pushed the children faster. Mist and ferns and trees and stones—

When one of the boys collapsed, Sofie carried him, focusing on the too-delicate hands gripping the front of her shift.

Hurry, hurry, hurry—

And then there was the road, and the van. Agent Silverbow had waited.

She didn't know his real name. Had refused to let him tell her, though she had a good idea of what—who—he was. But he'd always be Silver to her. And he had waited.

He'd said he wouldn't. Had said Ophion would kill him for abandoning his current mission. *Pippa* would kill him. Or order one of her Lightfall soldiers to do it.

But he'd come with Sofie, had hidden out these two weeks, until Sofie had sent forth the ripple of firstlight last night—the one signal she'd dared make with the Vanir prowling the death camp—to tell him to be here in twenty-four hours.

She'd told him not to use his powers. Even if it would've made this far safer and easier, it would have drained him too much for the escape. And she needed him at full strength now.

In the moonlight, Silver's face was pale above the imperial uniform he'd stolen, his hair slicked back like any preening officer. He grimaced at Emile, then at the eleven other kids—clearly calculating how many could fit into the nondescript white van.

"All," Sofie said as she hurtled for the vehicle, her voice raw. "All, Silver."

He understood. He'd always understood her.

He leapt out of the car with preternatural grace and opened the rear doors. A minute later, squeezed against Silver in the front of the van, his warmth heating her through her threadbare clothes, Sofie could hardly draw breath fast enough as he floored the gas pedal. His thumb brushed over her shoulder, again and again, as if reassuring himself that she was there, that she'd made it.

None of the children spoke. None of them cried.

As the van barreled into the night, Sofie found herself wondering if they still could.

It took them thirty minutes to reach the port city of Servast.

Sofie leaned on Silver, who saw to it, even while racing down the bumpy, winding country road, that the children found the food in the bags he'd stashed in the back. Only enough for three, but the children knew how to stretch a scant spread. He made sure Sofie ate, too. Two weeks in that camp had nearly wrecked her. She didn't understand how these children had survived months. Years. Her brother had survived *three years*.

Silver said quietly as they rounded a sharp curve, "The Hind is close by. I received a report this morning that she was in Alcene." A small city not two hours away—one of the vital depots along the Spine, the north-south network of train tracks that provided ammo and supplies to the imperial troops. "Our spies indicated she was headed this way."

Sofie's stomach tightened, but she focused on donning the clothes and shoes Silver had brought for her to change into. "Then let's hope we make it to the coast before she does."

His throat bobbed. She dared ask, "Pippa?"

A muscle ticked in his jaw. He and Pippa had been jockeying for a promotion into Command's inner ranks for years now. *A crazed fanatic*, Silver had called Pippa on more than one occasion, usually after her Lightfall squadron had led a brutal attack that left no survivors. But Sofie understood Pippa's devotion—she herself had grown up passing as fully human, after all. Had learned exactly how they were treated—how Pippa had likely been treated by the Vanir her entire life. Some things, some experiences, Silver could never understand.

Silver said, "No word yet. She'd better be where she promised to be." Disapproval and distrust laced every word.

Sofie said nothing else as they drove. She wouldn't tell him the details of the intelligence she'd gathered, for all that he had done and meant to her, despite the silent hours spent together, bodies and souls merging. She wouldn't tell anyone—not until Command came through on their promises.

The Asteri had probably realized what she'd discovered. They'd no doubt sent the Hind after her to stop her from telling anyone else.

But the more immediate threat came from the dreadwolves closing in with every mile they hurried toward Servast, hounds on a scent. Silver's frequent glances in the rearview mirror told her that he knew it, too.

The two of them could take on perhaps a handful of wolf shifters—they'd done so before. But there would be more than a handful for an escape from Kavalla. Far more than they could face and live.

She'd prepared for that eventuality. Had already handed over her comm-crystal to Command before entering Kavalla. That precious, sole line of communication to their most valued spy. She knew they'd keep the small chunk of quartz safe. Just as Silver would keep Emile safe. He'd given her his word.

When they emerged from the van, mist wreathed the narrow docks of Servast, writhing over the chill, night-dark waters of the Haldren Sea. It wended around the ancient stone houses of the port town, the firstlight in the few lampposts above the cobblestone streets flickering. No lights shone behind the shuttered windows; not one car or pedestrian moved in the deep shadows and fog.

It was as if the streets of Servast had been emptied in advance of their arrival. As if its citizens—mostly poor fisher-folk, both human and Vanir allied with the House of Many Waters—had hunkered down, some instinct bleating that the fog was not to be braved. Not this night.

Not with dreadwolves on the prowl.

Silver led the way, hair peeking from beneath the cap he'd donned, his attention darting this way and that, his gun within easy reach at his side. She'd seen him kill efficiently with his power, but sometimes a gun was easier.

Emile kept close to Sofie as they crept down the age-worn

streets, through the empty markets. She could feel eyes on her from behind the closed shutters. But no one opened a door to offer help.

Sofie didn't care. As long as that boat waited where she'd been told it would be, the world could go to Hel.

Mercifully, the *Bodegraven* was idling at the end of a long wooden dock three blocks ahead, silver letters bright against her black hull. A few firstlights glowed in the small steamer's portholes, but the decks remained quiet. Emile gasped, as if it were a vision from Luna.

Sofie prayed the other Ophion boats would be waiting beyond the harbor to provide backup, exactly as Command had promised in return for the valuable asset she'd gone into the camp to retrieve. They hadn't cared that the valuable asset was her brother. Only what she told them he could do.

She scanned the streets, the docks, the skies.

The power in her veins thrummed in time to her heart. A counter-beat. A bone-drum, a death knell. A warning.

They had to go *now*.

She started, but Silver's broad hand clamped on her shoulder.

"They're here," he said in his northern accent. With his sharp senses, he could detect the wolves better than she could.

Sofie surveyed the sloping rooftops, the cobblestones, the fog. "How close?"

Dread filled Silver's handsome face. "Everywhere. They're fucking everywhere."

Only three blocks separated them from salvation. Shouts echoed off the stones a block away. "*There! There!*"

One heartbeat to decide. One heartbeat—Emile halted, fear bright in his dark eyes.

No more fear. No more pain.

Sofie hissed at Silver, "*Run*." Silver reached for his gun, but she shoved his hand down, getting in his face. "Get the kids to the boat and go. I'll hold the wolves off and meet you there."

Some of the children were already bolting for the dock. Emile waited. "Run!" she told Silver again. He touched her cheek—the softest of caresses—and sprinted after the children, roaring for the captain to rev the engines. None of them would survive if they didn't depart now.

She whirled to Emile. "Get on that boat."

His eyes—their mother's eyes—widened. "But how will you—"

"I promise I will find you again, Emile. Remember all I told you. *Go.*"

When she embraced his lanky, bony body, she let herself inhale one breath of his scent, the one that lay beneath the acrid layers of dirt and waste from the camp. Then Emile staggered away, half tripping over himself as he marked the lingering power building at her fingertips.

But her brother said softly, "*Make them pay.*"

She closed her eyes, readying herself. Gathering her power. Lights went out on the block around her. When she opened her eyes to the newfound darkness, Emile had reached the dock. Silver waited at the ramp, beckoning beneath the one streetlight that remained lit. Her stare met Silver's.

She nodded once—hoping it conveyed all that was within her heart—and aimed for the dreadwolves' howls.

Sofie sprinted right into the golden beams of the headlights of four cars emblazoned with the Asteri's symbol: *SPQM* and its wreath of seven stars. All crammed full of dreadwolves in imperial uniforms, guns out.

Sofie instantly spied the golden-haired female lounging in the front of the military convertible. A silver torque glimmered against her neck.

The Hind.

The deer shifter had two snipers poised beside her in the open-air car, rifles trained on Sofie. Even in the darkness, Lidia Cervos's hair shimmered, her beautiful face passive and cold. Amber eyes fixed on Sofie, lit with smug amusement. Triumph.

Sofie whipped around a corner before their shots cracked like thunder. The snarl of the Hind's dreadwolves rumbled in the mist behind her as she charged into Servast proper, away from the harbor. From that ship and the children. From Emile.

Silver couldn't use his power to get her. He had no idea where she was.

Sofie's breath sawed out of her chest as she sprinted down the empty, murky streets. A blast from the boat's horn blared through the misty night, as if pleading with her to hurry.

In answer, half a dozen unearthly howls rose up behind her. All closing in.

Some had taken their wolf form, then.

Claws thundered against the pavement nearby, and Sofie gritted her teeth, cutting down another alley, heading for the one place all the maps she'd studied suggested she might stand a chance. The ship's horn blasted again, a final warning that it would leave.

If she could only make it a bit deeper into the city—a bit deeper—

Fangs gnashed behind her.

Keep moving. Not only away from the Vanir on her tail, but from the snipers on the ground, waiting for the open shot. From the Hind, who must know what information Sofie bore. Sofie supposed she should be flattered the Hind herself had come to oversee this.

The small market square appeared ahead, and Sofie barreled for the fountain in its center, punching a line of her power straight for it, shearing through rock and metal until water sprayed, a geyser coating the market square. Wolves splashed into the water as they surged from the surrounding streets, shifting as they cornered her.

In the center of the flooded square, Sofie paused.

The wolves in human forms wore imperial uniforms. Tiny silver darts glimmered along their collars. A dart for every rebel spy broken. Her stomach flipped. Only one type of dreadwolf had those silver darts. The Hind's private guard. The most elite of the shifters.

A throaty whistle sounded through the port. A warning and a farewell.

So Sofie leapt onto the lip of the fountain and smiled at the wolves closing in. They wouldn't kill her. Not when the Hind was waiting to interrogate her. Too bad they didn't know what Sofie truly was. Not a human, nor a witch.

She let the power she'd gathered by the docks unspool.

Crackling energy curled at her fingertips and amid the strands of her short brown hair. One of the dreadwolves understood then—matched what he was seeing with the myths Vanir whispered to their children.

"*She's a fucking thunderbird!*" the wolf roared—just as Sofie unleashed the power she'd gathered on the water flooding the square. On the dreadwolves standing ankle-deep in it.

They didn't stand a chance.

Sofie pivoted toward the docks as the electricity finished slithering over the stones, hardly sparing a glance for the smoking, half-submerged carcasses. The silver darts along their collars glowed molten-hot.

Another whistle. She could still make it.

Sofie splashed through the flooded square, breath ragged in her throat.

The dreadwolf had been only half-right. She was part thunderbird—her great-grandmother had mated with a human long ago, before being executed. The gift, more legend than truth these days, had resurfaced in Sofie.

It was why the rebels had wanted her so badly, why they'd sent her out on such dangerous missions. Why Pippa had come to value her. Sofie smelled like and could pass for a human, but in her veins lurked an ability that could kill in an instant. The Asteri had long ago hunted most thunderbirds to extinction. She'd never learned how her great-grandmother had survived, but the descendants had kept the bloodline secret. *She* had kept it secret.

Until that day three years ago when her family had been killed and taken. When she'd found the nearest Ophion base and showed them exactly what she could do. When she told them what she wanted them to do for her in exchange.

She hated them. Almost as much as she hated the Asteri and the world they'd built. For three years, Ophion had dangled Emile's whereabouts above her, promising to find him, to help her free him, if she could do *one more mission*. Pippa and Silver might believe in the cause, though they differed in their methods of how to fight for it, but Emile had always been Sofie's cause. A free world would be wonderful. But what did it matter if she had no family to share it with?

So many times, for those rebels, she had drawn up power from the grid, from lights and machines, and killed and killed, until her soul lay in tatters. She'd often debated going rogue and finding her brother herself, but she was no spy. She had no network. So she'd stayed, and covertly built up her own bait to dangle before Ophion. Made sure they knew the importance of what she'd gleaned before she entered Kavalla.

Faster, faster she pushed herself toward the dock. If she didn't make it, maybe there would be a smaller boat that she could take to the steamer. Maybe she'd just swim until she was close enough for Silver to spot her, and easily reach her with his power.

Half-crumbling houses and uneven streets passed; fog drifted in veils.

The stretch of wooden dock between Sofie and the steamer pulling away lay clear. She raced for it.

She could make out Silver on the *Bodegraven*'s deck, monitoring her approach. But why didn't he use his power to reach her? Another few feet closer, and she spied the hand pressed to his bleeding shoulder.

Cthona have mercy on him. Silver didn't appear badly hurt, but she had a feeling she knew what kind of bullet he'd been hit with. A bullet with a core of gorsian stone—one that would stifle magic.

His power was useless. But if a sniper had hit Silver on the ship . . . Sofie drew up short.

The convertible sat in the shadows of the building across from the docks. The Hind still lounged like a queen, a sniper beside her with his rifle trained on Sofie. Where the second had gone, she didn't know. Only this one mattered. This one, and his rifle.

It was likely chock-full of gorsian bullets. They'd bring her down in seconds.

The Hind's golden eyes glowed like coals in the dimness. Sofie gauged the distance to the end of the dock, the rope Silver had thrown down, trailing with every inch the *Bodegraven* chugged toward the open water.

The Hind inclined her head in challenge. A deceptively calm voice slid from between her red lips. "Are you faster than a bullet, thunderbird?"

Sofie didn't wait to banter. As swift as a wind through the fjords of her native land, she hurtled down the dock. She knew the sniper's rifle tracked her.

The end of the dock, the dark harbor beyond, loomed.

The rifle cracked.

Silver's roar cleaved the night before Sofie hit the wood planks, splinters cutting into her face, the impact ricocheting through one eye. Pain burst through her right thigh, leaving a wake of shredded flesh and shattered bone, so violent it robbed even the scream from her lungs.

Silver's bellow stopped abruptly—and then he yelled to the captain, "*Go, go, go, go!*"

Facedown on the dock, Sofie knew it was bad. She lifted her head, swallowing her shriek of pain, blood leaking from her nose. The droning hum of an Omega-boat's energy rocked through her even before she spied the approaching lights beneath the harbor's surface.

Four imperial submersible warships converged like sharks on the *Bodegraven*.

DISCOVER MORE OF THE WORLD OF SARAH J. MAAS!

CRESCENT CITY

THRONE OF GLASS

A COURT OF THORNS AND ROSES